Book XV in the Vampire Queen Series

A life she didn't plan...

From the author who "defies all cliches of the genre", comes a new standalone book in the Vampire Queen series...

It's 1941, and Nina signs up to serve with the Australian Army Nursing Service in Singapore. What happens to her when the city falls to the Japanese will shatter Nina all the way to the soul. But fate seems determined to give her more than she can bear. When her twin sister dies in a car crash, Nina is informed that she must take her place as an InhServ, an Inherited Servant, groomed from childhood to serve a vampire master.

Even as she rages against her fate, she is baffled at Lord Alistair's insistence on having her as his servant. But that's not the most confusing thing about her new Master. The ways in which he commands her surrender to him lead her to a terrifyingly different understanding of her will and her dreams. By binding herself to him, can she become whole again, but in a way she never expected?

VAMPIRE'S EMBRACE

A Vampire Queen Series Novel

JOEY W. HILL

Vampire's Embrace

A Vampire Queen Series Novel - Book #15

Copyright © 2018-2019 Joey W. Hill

Cover design by W. Scott Hill

SWP Digital & Print Edition publication November 2018 by Story Witch Press, 452 Mattamushkeet Dr., Little River, South Carolina 29566, USA

The following material contains graphic sexual content meant for mature readers. Reader discretion is advised.

Digital ISBN: 978-1-942122-79-1

Print ISBN: 978-1-942122-80-7

ACKNOWLEDGMENTS

As always, my editing team deserves huge thanks for the story improvements their input provided. Thank you, Judy, Lauren, Debi, Sheri and Angela, for helping Alistair and Nina put their best foot forward. Also a fervent thank you to Kristen, who reminded me to trust my instincts.

A special thanks to my Aussie beta reader, Kath, who ensured I didn't make too many gaffes on language, geography or, worst of all, Australian Rules Football. Alistair would have never forgiven me for that.

To my "Nurse Team;" Fran, Karen, Jarylynn, Judy, Kelly S, Kelly L, Trish, Stephanie, and Lee. The generous and resolute nature of those in this profession was entirely evident in your feedback, ensuring Nina didn't commit errors in her patient care she would never make. While reading through Nina's experiences, many of you shared your own perspectives and emotions as nurses, which meant an unexpected gift of your critiques was a better understanding of the kind of person Nina would be, so I could add even more life to this fabulous heroine.

To my readers. Thanks for continuing to join me on my journeys with my characters. However many we have ahead of us, I am grateful for all of them, and every one of you.

To my husband, who handles the highs and lows, and still loves me, even when I'm at my most unlovable.

NOTE: I have some mentions about the history in this book, but to avoid spoilers, I'll save them for my end Author's Note. However, one important note. Yes, there *were* hand-held vibrator devices and sex toys in the 1940s. I checked. :>

CHAPTER ONE

The battlefield was so close they could hear the sharp staccato gun reports and constant rushing booms from heavier artillery. Nina knew she wasn't the only one who felt the vibrations in the pit of her stomach. Ambulances and lorries with casualties had been arriving throughout the night, Japanese snipers making it too dangerous for the wounded to be transported in daylight. Her tin hat had to be with her at all times, a bloody nuisance, but fortunately she only had to don it when the air raid sirens wailed. The hospital was north of Singapore, which was getting the heaviest concentration of the bombing.

The beds set up in the school's concert hall were full, the overflow patients installed under the marquees set up at the tennis courts. The hospital had arrived here less than forty-eight hours ago, but all of them—nurses, orderlies, doctors and support staff—had transformed the commandeered school into a serviceable facility. They'd had to move repeatedly in the past few weeks, so they'd all become quite practiced at breaking down and setting up in record time.

Before the first set of ambulances had arrived, Nina had prepared intravenous lines, positioning the IV poles and hanging bags to be ready to run vital fluid into the incoming critical care patients. She laid out extra linens and pajamas on the cots. Under the marquees, she'd set out trays with bandages, scissors, and other supplies necessary for the arriving casualties.

1

They were a general hospital. Normally, a soldier needing further care than the dressing station near the front lines was sent back to a casualty clearing station, where emergency surgery or other stabilizing measures could be taken. After that, he might be moved to the advanced care available at the general hospital. However, the front was so close now, their hospital had become the casualty clearance area as well.

The tension permeating the staff and patients had built with every relocation, because they all knew the enemy was closing the distance between them. But Matron stayed upbeat, firm. *Tend to your duties, girls. Follow orders. Care for our boys.* Just prior to the heavy Japanese attacks on the Australian lines, she'd even invited each woman to have tea with her in her quarters. A reassuring, one-on-one, "how are you holding up" that helped them keep their wits about them as things became progressively more unstable.

As the casualties arrived, a card pinned to each man's shirt informed the nurses and orderlies who was in the worst shape, but that could change en route, so Nina double checked in case a man with a white card needed to be upgraded to the higher priority red. Some men bore the faint imprint of an "M" on their foreheads, written there in indelible pencil. It told the staff they'd already been dosed with morphine for pain.

Even as she moved swiftly to handle other tasks, Nina's gaze was always moving over the men on cots or stretchers she passed, making sure no one's needs in her assigned area were being overlooked.

It was hard to believe that mere weeks ago, the war had barely intruded into their lives at all. She and her mates in the Australian Army Nursing Service had seen very little action compared to their counterparts in the Middle East and Europe. Articles written a few months before had even resulted in some scathing backlash toward the personnel posted here, who were depicted as having ample opportunities to enjoy the picture shows, restaurants and shopping Singapore had to offer. In truth, she'd felt no different from any young woman given the chance to indulge in an overseas adventure to see the world.

But Matrons Drummond and Paschke had not overlooked their training even a single day, drilling them over and over to ensure they were as prepared as possible, able to carry out their duties under the most stringent conditions. When the war had finally arrived, they'd been ready. Most of her fellow nurses wrote home once a week. Nina suspected many were grateful not to have much time to do so now, for how could one describe it? To anyone who wasn't in it, there was no way to do it. No movie, no book, could depict the reality, the unimaginable brutality, that mankind could wreak upon itself.

She had no idea when she'd last eaten, slept. When she wasn't assisting with the arriving soldiers or the nurses attending the doctors in the operating theater, she patrolled her rows of injured in the recovery ward. At times, she spoke gently, touched a hand, took a too-brief moment to offer comfort.

As bad as many things were, that affected her the most. Those flashes of stark eyes in the semi-darkness, a man hungry for a single gesture of reassurance. An ounce of hope that he'd be okay. That he'd see his mother or girlfriend again. Be able to fall asleep on the veranda on a sunny day, his dog draped over his feet. Be able not to remember this, not to have his every waking thought and sleeping nightmare invaded by screams of wounded and dying friends, gunfire, the blast of exploding shells.

The nighttime was worst for the men, as anxieties were exacerbated by the mandatory blackouts, and the near constant sound of battle nearby. There'd been terrible rumors about what the Japanese had done when they overran the hospitals farther north. Sister Marjorie said it was just propaganda to fire up the men. The generals routinely sneered about the Japanese soldiers, asserting they had genetically hampered fighting abilities.

Nina had a hospital of men who'd seen firsthand evidence to the contrary. Many obviously feared what would happen if the men who'd inflicted their wounds reached the hospital.

A conversation between two men thankfully pulled her out of that dark track. "The whole damn team," one of them said. "He got everyone out, except Mort and Pete, and he went back for them after putting me in the bus. Last I saw him."

"I saw him before that. Against that patrol of Japs..."

One of the men was sitting up on his bed, his arm in a sling. The bandage around his head was stained with blood. Nina leaned in behind him to check the wound. He glanced back at her, nodding his gratitude, though his mate, stretched out on the other bed, didn't seem to notice her. His eyes were on something inside his head.

"He wasn't... No one could have done what he did. Moved like that." His Adam's apple bobbed. "He tore them apart, Rigby. With his bare hands. Like an angel of death..."

"You've gone wobbly. It was Alistair, Charlie," his friend said, crisp and sharp. His shoulder twitched under Nina's hand. "Just Alistair. The one you called a useless shit. Said he bought his way out of a uniform."

"He still wasn't wearing one. But he was there. How was he there? We last saw him in Brisbane, drinking cognac and smoking a cigar like an arrogant prat. A ghost. He moved like..." The male shuddered. "It was like he wasn't human."

Nina cleaned her hands and moved from Rigby to Charlie. He'd lost a leg above the knee yesterday, so Rigby was likely right about Charlie's disoriented state of mind. Plus, men saw all sorts of things in the horror of battle. Some of it they turned into unlikely stories that would help them better manage the meaning of the images. Though admittedly this seemed like just the opposite, something the man didn't want to believe he'd seen but couldn't deny. His gaze was haunted, more than she usually saw, which was a lot.

Touching his cheek, she knew his perspiration was fever-induced, not the relentless tropical heat. One of the reasons they kept the recovery ward so dark was so they could meet blackout restrictions yet keep the curtains pulled back from the windows to allow some air flow. Even with their aversion to the battle noises, the most trauma-tized man preferred that to being shut up in a hot box. She'd get a cool cloth on him, ask the orderly to stop by and change it out as often as possible.

"Better stop your ranting, Pug," Rigby advised, sending her a wink, though his face remained tight, unsmiling. He had a long, bony face with an assortment of freckles, marred here and there by crimson-colored nicks. "The pretty nurse won't let you take her dancing."

"I have so many offers, I'll be dancing until I'm a grandmother," she said. "But I'm sure I can fit in another."

She had learned to smile even when it was the last thing she felt like doing. They needed a woman's smile sometimes more than they needed medical care.

4

Charlie's gaze turned to her and cleared somewhat. He had a squarish face dominated by large dark eyes, a combination that did remind her a bit of a pug. Aussies loved their nicknames. Probably half of her mates in the service were known more for that than their actual names, herself included. Doe, they called her. For her blondish-brown hair and brown eyes, long legs and height.

"You need to put us one-legged blokes at the head of the line, Sister," Charlie said, with an attempt at a smile. "We'll do ten times better what the others need two to do."

Her heart tightened. These men were the best in the world, and she didn't care if anyone thought she was biased. Yes, a good many of them had a hard time of it at night, their trauma making them suscep-tible to anxiety, but the nurses knew that because they were trained to recognize it, not because of any excessive whinging. Most of them carried on with one another like this and flirted outrageously with the nurses, even in their worst moments, and would act dismissive if anyone got too clucky over them.

"I've no doubt," she said lightly. "Is there anything I can get you lads? The orderly will be by to change that dressing soon," she added to Rigby. If Gray was overwhelmed, she'd do it.

She wasn't surprised when they said they were fine and asked her about two other men, apparently the others they'd mentioned. It took her a few questions to narrow down which ones they wanted to know about. When she did, she answered them without hesitation, though her voice was sympathetic. Most the lads preferred the information to come straight out, no cushioning it.

"Jonathan died while the doctors were working on him. We're monitoring Horace for complications from his wounds, but we're hoping he'll be fine. If he stabilizes enough to be in recovery, I'll try to make sure he's put as close to you two as possible. You serve in the same unit, then?"

"Yeah, but we were a team before." Rigby's gaze had met Char-lie's at the news of Jonathan's loss. His jaw tightened, but when he spoke, his voice was even. "We all played footy together. Enlisted together."

"Mates. That's good." One of the staff nurses bending over an unconscious Gurkha rifleman caught her eye and Nina swiftly moved away, with a look of regret. "I'll check back with you later. Try to get

5

some rest. Hold on there, Temple," she called, catching the young nurse's attention.

A woman had to be at least twenty-five to be in the AANS, but she had a sneaking suspicion Temple—like herself—had lied about her age. But Nina had entered the hospital nursing school in Sydney at sixteen—again lying, saying she was twenty—so she'd had almost five years out of school as a staff nurse and was promoted to Sister before she came here.

Whereas Temple had barely obtained her certification and minimum amount of experience before coming to Singapore. While she would be an excellent nurse once she had more time, she hadn't yet learned how to shuffle efficiently the million bits of information a nurse in these conditions needed to manage.

"Don't remove his knife," she told the girl. "It was left belted on him on purpose. He has to be conscious and give his permission for its removal. It's part of their code of honor."

"Oh, of course." The young woman, whose real name was Greta, scrubbed a hand over her face, rumpling her pulled-back curls. They were coiled as tight as Shirley Temple's in this humidity, so they'd nicknamed her accordingly. "So sorry, Sister Nina. I knew that from the morning lectures."

"Carry on. You're doing fine. It's a lot tonight."

They'd gone from treating a scattering of tropical diseases, sports injuries and the occasional Australian battle casualty, to caring for hundreds coming through their doors every night, including those from the British and Indian Army units. Nina wasn't sure how the girl was remembering her own name, let alone anything else.

"Ready for a break, Doe?" Sister Helen waved her down as Nina pressed a reassuring hand to Greta's shoulder and headed up the corridor. "Though shifts might mean little tonight, Matron says everyone takes a dinner break. It's an order. Can't have us getting muddled and giving some poor chap the wrong thing."

"I'll say. I'm pretty sure you meant to put beer in this IV, Sister." One of the men, Tom Caldwell, bumped it with his shoulder. He had compound fractures in both legs and broken ribs, the result of being hurled through the air, colliding with a couple trees and then bouncing off the top of a lorry, according to his mates. He was pale with the pain but had refused the additional morphine Nina had offered. He was worried supplies could run short and he didn't want to be the one who'd made another man go without, no matter how they reassured him over it.

"Are you still here, Tom?" Helen arched a brow. Though Nina was tall for a woman, Helen was one of the shorter women in their service, the top of her head barely reaching Nina's shoulder. She had a raspy voice like a stern frog, and the flaxen hair of a fairy tale princess. "I could have sworn I saw orders to send you back up to the front with a crutch."

"Well, give me a brew and a stick, and I'll be out of your hair." He winked at them.

"If I find a brew, I'll be drinking it myself." Helen shook her head at him, and looked at Nina. "I've got this lot. Tell me what I need to know."

Nina sent the shorter woman a grateful look and proceeded to fill her in on anyone who needed extra looking after, like the feverish and possibly hallucinating Charlie. Then she grabbed a bully beef sandwich and a drink, and headed out one of the side doors. They'd used some of the adjacent abandoned buildings as temporary sleeping quarters, so she might lie herself down for a quick nap to get her through the rest of the evening.

As she stepped outside, she drew in a breath, but it was to steady herself, not because anyone would willingly draw the air into their lungs. When she'd first arrived in Malacca, the stench had been overwhelming, the land of "stinks and drinks," as many of the expatriates here called it. The jungle and pervasive mangroves had their own aroma, as did the villages, where the people cooked with spices and fruits unfamiliar to her at home. That would have been tolerable, but when those scents mixed with the constant smell of stagnant water, populated by waste and sewage, it could kill the appetite. The standing water was a result of the drains dug everywhere there was human habitation, to avoid flooding during the rains.

She'd lost nearly ten pounds her first couple months here. The relentless tropical heat added to that. It was even worse for the nurses and doctors in the operating theater, where the bright lights increased the temperature to the point they drenched their own clothes with sweat.

Over time, though, one got used to all of it. And learned to breathe shallowly.

She'd chosen the exit door on the side of the building more likely to get air movement, since another nearby cluster of buildings formed a funnel down a slope of lawn to some smaller outbuildings. A light rain was falling. The diesel fumes of the latest ambulances still lingered in the scent mix. Someone was burning something. She suspected the smoke was coming from the same places the next wave of wounded would be.

She closed her eyes, put the modestly cold bottle to her forehead. Was there any more horrible thing than people who started a war? How could they think that what they gained by making others fight for their lives, their homes, as well as the cost the armies of the instigators would pay themselves, would ever be worth it? The humid air, the fumes, the undercurrent of tropical decay, blood and male sweat, was a combination she'd ever after associate with this dense eye in the storm of violence.

Yet it was in this moment of calm when nothing else was, that he appeared.

He emerged from the gloom, cutting across the lawn and moving more swiftly than she'd ever seen a man move, yet in a rigid way, a soldier trying to run dead-out in an odd, arms-straight-down manner. Then she realized he was dragging a travois, weighted with another man.

The man transporting the wounded one briefly lifted his head, as if he was trying to find the entrance to the hospital. She broke into a trot toward him, calling out. "You there! This way."

His head swiveled toward her, registered with a curt nod that she was pointing him to the closest marquee. She could have simply made sure he reached the orderlies, but it was rare men weren't brought by vehicle. She was curious to see what the situation was.

As she converged on the marquee with the arriving man, Nina saw he wasn't wearing a uniform. Brown daks, a torn and bloodstained grey shirt, nondescript utilitarian wear. Heavy boots. His face was streaked with soot or black paint like a soldier with camouflage, though, and his bearing seemed to suggest military training. His first words proved he had familiarity with casualty setups, and that he was solidly Australian, not a Brit. He had a strong, forward way of speaking that suggested he was used to being obeyed.

"I'll take him inside. He needs surgery. Doctors. Now."

Several nights ago, they'd processed nearly two thousand casualties in a twenty-four-hour period. At one point, Nina had despaired at how many "nows," were needed to ensure as many as possible had "laters." But despair was the type of emotion that could cause unnecessary haste, which was when fatal mistakes happened. She was well-trained enough that she'd pushed it aside. It made her grateful for how hard the Matrons had drilled them so that panic couldn't get the upper hand. But the word "now" could still trigger that despondent feeling, no matter how well she controlled it.

"Here first," she said firmly.

"He's already been tagged," the male said brusquely, trying to maneuver around her.

Nina was no stranger to having to pull a man out of a battlefield mindset. Stepping directly into his path, she slapped a hand to his chest and dug in her heels, because it was like stopping an advancing brick wall. His gaze snapped down to her. In the near darkness, it was impossible to tell eye color, but they were piercing, as determined as the most high-ranking officer she'd met to date. Maybe more so. She felt an odd compulsion to give in to his will, and shoved it away, too. But it took enough effort she practically bared her teeth at him, which caused a flicker of surprise on his intent face.

"Let us take a look and move him to a stretcher. The orderlies can carry him into the critical care area, where the surgery is," she explained. "You can't go there. The sooner you let us do what we need to do, the sooner we can get him help. Are you wounded yourself?"

"No, damn it." The man muttered an additional curse, but accepted Tim's assistance to ease his burden to the ground and let the two of them take a look. She maneuvered around the men to do just that and had to suppress a curse herself. She tacked a prayer onto it.

God have mercy on him.

The wounded man had a serious stomach wound, his abdomen dressing bulging, probably that and a few emergency stitches the only thing holding his intestines and organs where they should be. In the field, they wouldn't fully seal a wound because the transport conditions in the stifling heat badly affected a wound deprived of oxygen. Sewing it up too securely encouraged infection faster than leaving it completely open. But the bandage was wet with blood.

"Leave him tied to the travois," she decided, instructing Tim. "It's putting pressure on the wounds we don't want released until he's with the surgical team. Get him inside and put him at the front of the line."

Though it would likely only confirm the inevitable. She'd seen wounds like that, and so had Tim. The way his green eyes met hers briefly, the tightening of his chapped mouth, told her he knew the likely outcome. He gestured to another of his mates to help him carry the stretcher and nodded to the man who'd brought him in. "They'll do all they can," he said, not unkindly. "They've got the best surgeons here."

The best that were available. It was a standing joke among the doctors themselves, a self-deprecation that made her appreciate them even more. They gave their all to every patient, as hardworking as any of them, such that she fully agreed with Tim.

The man didn't seem to hear him. He had his gaze pinned on the face of the wounded man, and he'd clasped his hand. Nina was shocked when the injured soldier's eyes opened. Given the severity of his wound, she wasn't surprised his morphine had worn off, but she was surprised he was coherent enough to speak through the unimaginable agony he must be feeling. Three words.

"Thanks, mate. Sorry."

"Bollocks to that," his transportation said bluntly. "See you soon, Mort."

Nina touched his wrist, letting him know they had to move away, but the standing man didn't let go. It was the other man's hand who fell away, and Tim tucked it next to him. They headed off toward the hospital, while Nina stayed behind. From the other man's expression, she realized she might need to run interference to keep him from following Mort and getting underfoot.

She put her hand on his arm to break his focus on the departing stretcher and its precious contents. "Are you sure you're not hurt? I'm going to check, all right?"

The amount of blood on the back of his shirt was astonishing, almost obliterating the original color, and it still looked damp, though that was likely perspiration. But she would check, because often they didn't register their own injuries while trying to protect a mate.

He was still staring over his shoulder. The man who'd moments before had stormed out of the jungle and insisted on seeing a surgeon seemed at loose ends now. Also not an unusual thing. He had thick black hair that was a little longish over his brow, but cut short and sharp on his neck.

"Sir?" She wasn't sure why she switched tactics and spoke so formally to him, except he did have the air of an officer about him, or at least someone who would be called "sir" in some capacity. She was right, because that brought his gaze to her. He looked in his thirties. Though there was a weariness about him, it didn't affect how he stood, straight and tall.

She drew him under the flaps of the marquee where the dim lantern light could be turned up for examinations without violating blackout restrictions. Once there, she got a better look at his eyes. They might be blue, but when he turned his head, they were touched by grey, an almost silver glimmer. Almost too iridescent to be human.

Right, Nina. She chided herself. It wasn't just soldiers from the front lines who could get fanciful. She must really be tired. More than usual. She needed that sandwich.

"I'm not hurt," he said at last. "It's all his. The blood on me."

"If you don't mind, I'll check. I've had men with sucking chest wounds who didn't realize they had them. Let's get this shirt off you. We might even be able to find a clean one around here somewhere."

His gaze had returned to the hospital entrance. With a brief hesitation, she moved closer and began to slip the buttons of his shirt. He was a few inches taller than her, something she noticed since she wasn't a short woman. When his head turned, she felt the stir of his breath on her brow as he dipped his chin to watch what she was doing.

His passivity about it increased her concern about his state of mind. Usually a soldier would courteously brush her hands aside to prove he could do it himself.

But his body stiffened as her fingertips brushed him. A shy one, maybe, not sure about a woman touching him. Not that most of these blokes had an aversion to that, but sometimes after coming out of the thick of things they were twitchy, the way Rigby had been when she touched his shoulder. She kept her movements steady, brisk.

"Why didn't you wait for an ambulance to bring him from the dressing station?" she asked by way of a distraction.

"I was told the next one coming would take too long."

She glanced up. From the way the man adjusted his gaze, not meeting her eyes when he said it, she suspected what they'd told him was the man wasn't going to make it at all.

He wouldn't have listened. If she hadn't intercepted him, he'd likely have taken himself, Mort, and that determined hard jut to his jaw straight to the operating theater. She could well imagine him putting his precious cargo on a table, even if he had to sweep off whoever was on it.

She noted his pallor had lost another full shade. If he'd run all the way here through the jungle, adrenaline alone may have carried him here, but that would be draining away rapidly now that he'd found help for Mort.

"Easy there. Sit down." She pushed him into a chair since the nearest cot was occupied, and finished opening his shirt. "I *am* going to check you," she said firmly as she moved around him, tugging the shirt from his shoulders. "So be a good lad and be still for me for a moment. You've been brilliant getting your mate here, but let's be sure you're all right. John, bring me water, will you? What's your name?"

"Alistair," he said shortly.

Strewth, he had broad shoulders, and an upper torso that would make an artist reach for a brush. The strong curve of spine and taper to the waist were beautifully formed. It was a practical observation. She saw a lot of male bodies, and noted the ones that had been blessed with beauty.

He clasped her wrist before she could listen to his heart, take his pulse. The firm steadiness of the grip drew her attention.

"I'm all right," he said, the syllables precise and clipped. "Go make sure Mort is fine."

Mort... With the repeat of his mate's name, recent memory stirred. The conversation between Rigby and Charlie came back to her then, the bits of information they'd revealed.

An aristocrat, they'd said. One who didn't wear a uniform. Maybe he was an expatriate living in this area, with a beach home in Brisbane. His focused expression was that of a man of means, used to everyone around him being a subordinate. But his tone wasn't impatient or rude. Just flat, as if laid out beneath many other things. She knew how that weight felt.

"Careful, mate," John said, putting the water she'd requested on the table. "The sisters give the orders around here, or there's hell to pay." He shot her a wink, but it was also a quick unspoken question she answered with a nod. She had this one in hand. He could go back to what he was doing.

Alistair's face twisted with impatience, and she spoke quickly, evenly. "You brought Charlie, Jonathan, Horace and Rigby to the dressing station."

That unusual gaze snapped to her, roved over her in a blink, taking her in, perhaps for the first time. "Did they make it?" he asked in that same heavy tone.

"Jonathan didn't," she said quietly. "But we hope Horace will. Two are in recovery now. Rigby and Charlie."

He digested that, his expression tightening briefly. "And they're doing well?"

"Well enough to be giving you a hard time in your absence. As men do, when they care very much about one another. I understand you're a 'damn fine footy player, and a total larrikin.'"

She'd heard them say that right after she moved away to correct Greta. She expected it had been Rigby's attempt to lighten the moment and ease Charlie away from visions of an angel of death.

Alistair's lips twitched, and eyes warmed slightly, but his tone remained brusque. "I need to get back. Tell them you saw me and I'm fine, if they're of a mind to worry about me."

He began to rise, but she tightened her grip on his shoulders. His skin was firm and not clammy, which was good, but she worried about dehydration since he wasn't perspiring, and everyone sweated here. Clothes dark at the armpits and lower back were a Singapore fashion statement, Helen liked to say. Thigh sweat was an unmentionable yet constant aggravation.

"Just give me a quick moment to do this," she said. "Here, drink this water. Where are you going, anyway?"

He paid no attention to the water. "There's another one out there. I have to go get him."

Sensing her time was limited in direct proportion to his tolerance for delay, she started her exam as he was speaking. He winced as she probed his skull. The wetness of his dark hair had suggested she start there to ensure none of the dampness was blood. Some of it had been. He'd suffered a close graze with some kind of projectile, enough to have taken out a furrow of flesh that had exposed bone.

"Bloody hell," she murmured, and signaled subtly to John in case she did need help keeping this one pinned down. "You need stitches here, at least."

"No, I don't."

But she'd already adjusted to press him forward on the stool so she could see his back down to the waistband of his daks. She drew in a breath.

It had to have been shrapnel that tore into his flesh so deeply, right above the kidneys. The gaping hole should have poured most of his blood out. And completely incapacitated him. Which was why instead of shouting for a gurney, she was frowning and probing the coagulated, fist-sized hole. It was already trying to close, clusters of skin cells crisscrossing it like a web.

John had approached, and Alistair stiffened once more, though this time his posture and the glance he shot the orderly's way was even more aggressive. At her slight head shake, John didn't retreat, but he didn't advance either, waiting on her. They were all aware that the men could be hypervigilant and combative. They could do damage without meaning to do so. Fortunately, Alistair seemed to relax as John stood down. At least toward the orderly.

Her wrist was clasped in that hard grip again as he twisted around. Even with him sitting, their faces weren't far apart. Those blue eyes glittered, dark brows drawing down to add to the tension highlighting the strong bones of his face.

"I'll be fine," he said, his voice strained. "I need to go...now."

It was then she noticed his gaze had latched onto a particular part of her. Not her face. And not her breasts. Many of the chaps got caught up in those. As long as they weren't cads about it, a nurse could hardly get in a blue over it, when they were bent over the poor fellows so often, their brassieres practically in their faces. But Alistair wasn't looking at that, either.

He was looking at her throat. More specifically, she thought he'd latched onto the jump of her pulse, because what was flickering in his eyes seemed to match that vibration.

Even adrenaline wouldn't have kept a man on his feet with his kind of injuries. They definitely would not have permitted him the strength to pull another full-grown man through the jungle to their hospital. Even the hold he had on her wrist was far steadier than it should have been.

If he was mortal.

As if he sensed the direction of her thoughts, his eyes now lifted to her face. She saw open hunger in his gaze, not pain.

Alistair. It wasn't an uncommon name, but all the other things...it should have added up. Shock coursed through her.

She knew what he was. What's more, she knew *who* he was.

A small, handheld portrait wasn't always the best likeness of a person, especially when the man in question was in far rougher circumstances than the groomed and suited person in the picture. However, when she took a closer look, she knew she was right.

Her heart thumped into her throat, and a surge of impossible-to-separate emotions flooded her. Charlie hadn't been hallucinating. The man who'd carried near half a dozen men to safety was no man at all.

He was a vampire.

CHAPTER TWO

*T*here were families with ancient, secret ties to the vampire world, having loyalties and obligations to them for a variety of reasons. If required, the first born of every generation was promised for training as an Inherited Servant, or InhServ, as they called it.

The first time Nina had heard it described, she'd had another word for it. Slavery. A vampire's property. Bound to him or her for three hundred bloody years.

Sher had come out of the womb minutes before Nina. Her at-home training to be an InhServ had started at the age of six, preparing her for "assignment to an elite member of the vampire world."

Whereas Nina's raising had been that of a mostly normal child, like that of her two younger siblings, Jim and Manny, Sher's treatment had been far different. At least she'd been able to live under the same roof with Nina. Until she turned sixteen. On that day, Sher underwent a formal ceremony at which she received official notice of who her assigned vampire would be, which included a small portrait of him. Sher had kept it on her person like her most precious memento, studying it as if she expected the image to start issuing her commands. His desires, she called them.

On that day, Nina had told herself her sister was happy, which should be all that mattered. But Nina couldn't wrap her mind around it. Perhaps because she didn't want to understand, any empathy overshadowed by dread. The same day of that ceremony would be the last night she and Nina would share a room, because the next morning Sher would be transported to the InhServ training facility, where she'd live until she began active service for her assigned vampire. Nina's chances to see her might be few and far between going forward—if any. And entirely dependent on her vampire "Master."

It was one of the reasons Nina had lied about her age on her nursing application, so she could start school at the hospital the very next week.

But on that night, she'd sat with her sister in their shared bedroom, listening to her talk. Nursing her hurt and fears for her sister in silence while Sher gushed on excitedly about the life that had been mandated for her since birth.

Brainwashing, Nina thought. But her sister didn't act brainwashed, not exactly. Sher insisted her devotion to a male she'd never met wasn't a romanticized delusion, but a deep, true feeling.

"It's part of the training, Nina," Sher explained. "But it's also who I am. They evaluate us every year to be sure of it."

"How do you train someone not to have any dreams of their own?" Nina retorted.

Sher was lying on her side on their bed, her fall of brown hair across the spread so shiny it was absurdly like silk. Nina sat cross-legged, her arms hugged tight against her until Sher tugged one hand free and squeezed it. "This *is* my dream, Nina," she said earnestly. "I don't know why it's so hard for you to understand. It's bred into our family, after all. They told me. Even you have it. A limitless desire toward service. It's why you want to be a nurse."

"Service to those who need help. Not to a spoiled blue blood with a spoon up his arse."

"I don't know if he's a blue blood, not that way. He's a made vampire, and it's really unusual for a made vampire to receive the honor of an InhServ." Sher's hand tightened on Nina's. "But think of it, Nina. I'm considered an honor to him. Apparently a very high-ranking vampire turned him, a queen. She's not on the Council, but has a great deal of influence upon them. Thanks to her, and to his own capabilities, he's risen in their ranks and is in line to be a Region Master, watching over and protecting other vampires."

"Anyone is lucky to have you," Nina said staunchly. "If he doesn't realize that, I'll come put my foot up his arse. I don't care what he is. Just that he's good to you. Oh, Sher...what am I going to do without you?"

Sher's face softened, her own eyes glinting with tears. While it was petty, it did gratify Nina to see her sister wasn't entirely reconciled with leaving her.

Sher wrapped her arms around her, the two of them holding one another like when they'd been children. Nina felt like one; resentful, helpless, angry, sad and tearful. "Silly goose," Sher whispered.

"I don't want to lose you. Sometimes it felt like I lost you when you were six."

"You're not losing me," Sher said firmly, stroking her hair. "We're twins. We'll always be connected. Always. I'll bet he'll give me permission to come see you sometimes. You'll see." Her voice broke a little, though. "It will be okay. We have time, Nina. Don't worry, love."

Fast-forward, and Sher and she were twenty-one. Sher was still living at the InhServ training facility, but was allowed two trips home a year, one on their shared birthday. With each visit, she demonstrated she was becoming more cosmopolitan and educated than the most well-traveled university graduate Nina knew, male or female. It made it hard to argue that being an InhServ was keeping Sher from experiencing life to the fullest.

But all of her experiences were for the service of another. Not for herself. And some of the sexual things she was learning...they made Nina uncomfortable. Not because she was a prude about naked bodies. She'd graduated and was a nurse now, working at the Sydney hospital where she'd trained. No, it was how she reacted to the appalling and provocative things Sher told her. How much she thought about them.

For a vampire and servant, sex was...different. The things Sher described would come back to Nina in the dark of the night, stirring odd feelings, making her fingers fist in the covers and her body throb as she imagined herself...doing the things Sher said she was learning. It appalled her, but it didn't stop the imaginings that couldn't be characterized as anything but fantasies.

She usually covered her reactions to Sher's tidbits about the sexual side of things with mock gagging and by putting her fingers in her ears. But this time, on their twenty-first birthday visit, when the subject came up, admittedly because she asked about it, Nina couldn't be as flippant. Maybe because she knew this was probably Sher's last visit home for the foreseeable future, since twenty-one was when most InhServs started their service.

"So how is having to do for him, however, whenever he wants, not unpaid prostitution?" she asked in a sullen tone.

"It's not like that at all," Sher said sharply. Her reproachful gaze told Nina she'd been unkind, creating a flood of regret. But it just went along with the other disagreeable feelings she was having.

"Nina." Sher's voice softened, and when Nina wouldn't let her hold her hand, Sher moved her foot so it linked over Nina's ankle. They were on the back veranda bench together.

"It's...service. It's a way of giving yourself completely to him. It's something that, when I think about it, I want to... You'll laugh at me, and I don't think I could bear that."

Sher actually flushed a little, her articulate sister stumbling over the explanation like a flustered, lovesick girl. It pulled Nina out of her own darkness, somewhat, enough to realize being a shrew was not how she wanted to spend their time together.

"No. No, I won't." Nina might be privately horrified, but she wouldn't show it. She told herself that, fiercely.

Sher sighed and looked straight at her. "It makes me want to call him Master. For him to be all that means to me. And I can't describe what that is. I just know it's everything that matters." She took a breath. "Which is why I'll be remaining in InhServ training for another seven years."

"What?" Nina straightened so quickly the bench creaked.

She gave herself credit for looking past her own sudden flood of elation to see the somber set to Sher's face. Sher had looked forward to reaching twenty-one so very much. No matter how Nina might feel about that personally, she knew how much going into her vampire's service meant to her twin.

"What do you mean? You were so excited to be going to him this year."

"I was. And I admit, it was a hard blow." A shadow passed through

Sher's brown eyes, the hint of tears she swallowed back, though Nina realized it was the aftermath of the flood. She'd probably had her hardest cries with her fellow InhServs who, unlike her twin, would understand how disappointing it was to wait longer. Nina hated falling short on that, and made an effort to do better, at least in the here and now. She slid closer to her sister, turning on her hip so she could put an arm over her shoulder, stroke her hair back.

Sher gave her a grateful look and took a breath. "But it's what he wants, and that's all that matters. A vampire has the right to extend his or her InhServ's training so they go through the full training curriculum before they come into their vampire's service. It means I'll be given the maximum amount of time to learn the skills with which to serve him. Language, dance, social demands, mechanical aptitude, fighting, weaponry..." She cleared her throat. "And the sex. I mean, Nina, really, it's a good thing. I will have training that even most InhServs don't."

Nina digested that. "Well, that's good then. Maybe it will go faster than you expect. And once it's all said and done, you get to live three centuries. So seven more years is like one in normal people years."

"Normal people years?"

"Exactly."

A little smile teased Sher's mouth. "Daftie. He sent me a letter."

"He did?" Nina elbowed her. "Were you going to share it?"

"No," Sher said soberly. "Not at first. But I will, if you promise me something, Nina. Don't say anything negative when you read it. Okay? This letter is very important to me."

"All right. I won't. I promise." She touched her sister's hand. The sun was moving to mellow afternoon, the bugs making hot weather sawing sounds. They were barefoot, the two of them, their feet stretched out side by side. Their hips touched. Twins down to the soul. It was what they'd always told one another.

That said, Nina wondered what else the InhServ school could have left to teach her sister. Every time Sher came home, not only was she more well-educated and well-traveled, she looked more and more beautiful. She gave Nina and their mother makeup, hair and clothing tips. It was like she'd entered the same world that Hollywood movie stars frequented.

They were twins, but physically they were so different. Sher had always had a fresh glamor, even before InhServ training, while Nina had a practical, serious look, the gift of a mature face that allowed her to pass as a few years older. She kept her hair cut to her shoulders, wispy lengths more likely to fly about like feathers, rather than ripple along her shoulder blades like Sher's thick curtain of locks.

But Sher wasn't just a pretty face. She was equally capable of debating politics and economics with Nina's father, and when Jim, a fair boxer, had goaded her to share her "fighting skills," she'd left them slack-jawed when she put him in the dirt in less than ten seconds, her knee on his throat. For a moment, the level stillness in her gaze had been something almost chilling, then she'd helped Jim to his feet, dusted him off and laughed, becoming their sister once more.

Sher removed the letter from her skirt pocket. The page was a heavy cream stationary with a black script on it. Not even or elegant, but bold. Decisive. Nina laid her head on her sister's shoulder and read it while her sister held it and waited silently for her to finish.

Dear Sher,

The Mistress at the InhServ training school has been instructed to provide you the full curriculum available to InhServ initiates. It is my desire to have you exceed all standards of an InhServ for the benefit of my household.

Being an InhServ is a lifelong and challenging commitment. As such, it is also my desire for you to have the maximum amount of time to enjoy your family and experience your human life to the fullest, before you come into my service.

Lord Alistair

Though Nina didn't share the thought, the words seemed so carefully chosen. It made her wonder if the magnanimous explanation was his real reason for holding off.

"See how considerate he is?" Sher pointed out.

"This bloke can do no wrong," Nina said dryly. "Sure he doesn't have a unicorn up his arse?"

"Nina," Sher said reprovingly, but her eyes twinkled and she squeezed her sister's hands, telling Nina she hadn't mucked things up too badly.

If nothing else, she had her sister for another seven years. She liked Lord Alistair a little better just for that. The total bastard.

Then the war had happened.

~

So now she was in Singapore. Nina rarely wrote to her mother and father. Her weekly letter went to Sher. Sher's letters came far more infrequently. When they did, they were more guarded than war correspondence, because no uninitiated human could know the vampire world existed.

But she still wrote of Alistair with genuine devotion, despite not having met him face to face, even now. She shared every scrap she learned secondhand about him with Nina, framing those scraps so he seemed the best of men.

Nina had doubted it all. However, seeing him here, in the middle of a human conflict, trying to save his friends' lives? She had to admit that helped balance the more negative, poisonous thoughts she'd had about him over the years.

Those had been the thoughts of a lonely girl who missed her sister. She was a woman now, a woman who'd seen horrible things she couldn't control or fix. She could only help the next man in front of her. At the moment, that was him. He needed blood.

As the door to the hospital opened and closed, even at their considerable distance from the tennis courts, she saw his nostrils flare and the hunger in his expression increase. Too much, and he obviously recognized it. "I need to go," he said, short to the point of rudeness, and pushed out of the tent. Waving John away despite his perplexed look, she followed the male.

"The one you're going to go get," she called after him. "Is he as bad off as Mort? Will the dressing station be able to help?"

He stopped, glanced back. Something gripped his features, and when he spoke, his voice was rough. "No. He's already gone. He's where no one who cares is likely to find him, and I need to make sure he gets home."

"Oh."

As he turned, began to walk away, her blood started to pound in her ears, a sure sign she was about to do something impetuous and unwise. They were on the slope of lawn, out of earshot of the men in the tent.

"I've been told… a vampire drinks from a servant because it steadies him. Centers him. Protects others from his blood hungers while bringing him comfort. Calm seas."

She might have challenged her sister's choice at every turn, but she remembered verbatim every word Sher had shared about that choice. Maybe because they were twins, or maybe because she'd run her sister's words through her head so much, trying to make sense of them. Or maybe for other reasons. That inexplicable fascination.

A girl's fascination, she reminded herself. Though when he pivoted, his gaze sharpening on her like scalpel blades, the unanswered questions she'd carried for so long were even more unsettling.

"My family is bound to your kind," she said. "That's how I know what you are."

"I see." He studied her. "Small world."

It was such an unexpectedly courteous and mundane comment to make about such a remarkable thing, she couldn't help a bubble of laughter. His eyes warmed again, his lips doing that appealing reserved twitch. Then that expression disappeared and became something more discomfiting.

"What are you offering, Sister…?"

"Nina."

He took two steps toward her and stopped. There was still a good few feet between them, but he seemed much closer. What had she intended? She was mad. She took a breath.

"I suspect…you're thinking of getting nourishment from an enemy. I don't think you'll get strength or calm from their blood, will you? And you really need it if you're going to do what needs to be done for your friend."

"I'm not taking any of the blood that the other chaps can use, but I thank you for offering." He bowed to her, an oddly formal gesture, and pivoted again. He began to retrace the way he'd come, which would take him up the opposite slope and the shadows would reclaim him again.

For a lot of years, she'd thought of her family's obligation as something that rested wholly on Sher's shoulders. But her parents had sat all of them down as soon as they were old enough to understand, and declared that keeping the secret of the vampire world, realizing they were tied to that world, was something that bound all of them, for the overall welfare of the family. To think otherwise was very...unwise.

The idea of her family being pushed around by some kind of blackmail had infuriated her, as much as the rest. But Nina thought of how Sher looked at Alistair's portrait. She might not understand it, but she loved her sister.

Perhaps none of that would have been enough, but this male was trying to take care of the soldiers, same as her. Strangely enough, in a world made so complex by chaos, some things became simple.

Then there was one more reason to do the crazy thing she was thinking about doing. She might understand a little better how Sher felt. When all this was over, she could possibly make a better peace with it. Even if she couldn't ever imagine feeling better about her sister being beyond her reach.

"No," she said. "Alistair...wait."

She retrieved the drink and sandwich she'd left just inside the tent flap and headed down the hill. She noticed he'd left his bloody shirt. He'd likely snag another from somewhere else, one less likely to attract attention.

He seemed very relaxed as he was, in only the boots and trousers. She hadn't seen a single mosquito bite on him. Was that also a vampire thing? Did they possess a natural bug repellent? She'd always focused on the big questions with Sher, the why, not the details about his kind.

He'd stopped when she'd called to him. There was a faint impatience on his face, that underlying urgency which she expected was partly the need to assuage the bloodlust, and partly the urge to get it done, the sad task of retrieving his friend's body.

She'd broken into a quick step to catch up to him. The lawn was slippery with the rain, so she skidded the last several feet and bumped into him. He steadied her as she flushed and pushed her hair out of her face with her free hand, the other resting on his forearm with the sandwich and bottle of tea clutched in it.

"If you'd like, you can drink from me. I have what you need, and I'll give it willingly."

Surprise flitted across his features and then they reflected something else, something which made her hesitate and repeat herself. "I mean, if you like."

His expression was somewhat like the one he'd possessed when he was going to bull around her into the hospital. When she'd felt almost overcome by that will, wanting to do as he demanded simply...because he demanded it.

She saw bodies all the livelong day, and yet she was suddenly quite aware of how close the bare expanse of chest was to her, filling up her field of vision, the curve of biceps under her palms. His long, strong fingers, half curled upon her hips.

Being a nurse, she was also caught up for a blink or two in clinical absorption, seeing a member of a different race close up, so human-looking, and yet surviving on the life essence of her own kind. Well, human-looking in a rather intense way.

It was those eyes, she told herself, staring up into them. The absolute attention he could center upon someone with them. She expected when he cleaned up, he was quite devastating to female senses. To break that feeling, she gestured to one of the smaller buildings. "That one isn't occupied. We think it might have been used by a school caretaker who lived on the property. It's mostly clean and has a couple items of furniture in it, if you'd prefer some privacy."

He seemed to be thinking it over. Yet his reserve wavered, and she saw him swallow. The hand on her hip twitched. When his glance shifted, there was a reddish tint in his eyes. That might have made her anxious, but he'd also gotten paler, and the twitch became an outright tremor in his hands.

He was going back out there to make sure one of their boys made it home to his mother. So she could bury him. Mort likely wasn't going to survive, but Alistair had given him and Jonathan the same gift. He'd likely saved Charlie and Rigby's lives. Maybe Horace's, if he pulled through.

Sher had told Nina a good bit about certain things. Vampires were invincible, so when they showed signs they weren't, it wasn't good. A moment of inattention, being too slow, and he could get blown up. Which killed everything, maybe even vampires.

She didn't know how far he had to go tonight to reach shelter before dawn, but the answer to every question she had led back to his need for sustenance. Which she could provide.

She adjusted their grips so their fingers were interlaced. Slowly, keeping her eyes on his, she tugged on him. After a weighted second, he followed her. She led him past the converted building for the nurse's quarters, to the caretaker's cottage. The door was unlocked.

There was an easy chair with green floral upholstery, and a rumpled floor rug full of dust. No electricity, not that they'd be turning on any lights, but it meant they had plenty of shadows. Nothing inside could be seen through the windows. They'd have their privacy.

As Nina drew him to the chair, she recalled the places Sher had said vampires liked to feed. Throat, most often. Nina was startled by the surge of heat through her as she envisioned him biting her there.

Daft idiot, she told herself. For one thing, he was now sitting and she was standing. He'd have to tip his head back. She didn't want him doing that, because it would increase blood pressure against that healing part of his skull. Vampire restorative powers aside, it didn't need extra aggravation until fully restored.

She thought of a better option, though it gave her pause. Until she reminded herself it was a method of treatment, that was all. The man needed replenishment.

Bracing herself on the arm of the chair, she sank down to the carpet on her knees, adjusting herself between his spread ones. She lifted her wrist toward him. "Will this work? Do you need me to cut it first?" She kept a pen knife in her pocket.

When he said nothing right away, she wondered if the throat might be best after all, somehow providing him a richer source of blood that he needed in his current state. There were ways to accomplish that, but the idea seemed extraordinarily intimate, especially when he was staring down at her like this. It gave a strange significance beyond function to her being on her knees. Her breath caught in her throat, her heart speeding up.

Sher had talked about wanting to be on her knees to him. Letting him feed from her wrist, just as Nina had presented it to him. She'd talked about the way she imagined him looking at her.

Just like this.

His eyes seemed capable of holding her in this position as long as he desired. She'd only seen concentration like that with a predator. Cats, stalking mice. Dingoes after rabbits. A tiger in the zoo, captured and yet never subjugated, always knowing that what lay outside the bars was weaker, slower. His to take, if given the opportunity.

Did meeting their gaze cause such disturbing thoughts? Even so, such thoughts felt improper. While her sister would be his servant, not his wife or girlfriend, Nina thought if she was bound to a male like this, she wouldn't want to see his lips on another female. She'd honor her sister's devotion to him, sight unseen though it was.

She lowered her gaze. Another decision that seemed to have two meanings, and caused another leap in her lower belly when he made a hard-to-define noise in his throat. A growl, if she was still indulging her oddly fanciful mood, but whatever it was spread warmth through her lower regions.

"Drink, sir," she said, low. "I don't want to offend, but I've only a short dinner break and many patients to tend. You don't have to hesitate. I don't fear pain. I know you have places to be as well."

"You're right, sweet nurse. But some meals it's a crime to rush."

He reached out, cupped her wrist in his palm. Her arm was quivering, and it wasn't all nerves. She knew what it was, but was surprised he recognized it as well. He nodded to the sandwich.

"Eat that first. Drink."

"I—"

"You will eat first." He picked up the sandwich, unwrapped it, handed it to her.

He was right. It was sensible. But taking the food from his hand, putting it in her mouth under his regard, following his unmistakable order, brought more of the same peculiar rush of feelings. She ate quickly, and he said nothing. His gaze shifted to the windows, watching whatever was going on outside. She stole glances at his chiseled features, the set mouth. When she looked down again, her gaze slid over the bare chest, the way his belt clasped his waist, the length of his thigh against the fabric of his trousers.

As she finished the last bite with a hard swallow, he touched her shoulder. She lifted her head, realized he was holding out his hand again. As she laid her wrist back into it, she realized she was anticipating the strength of his grip, the heat of it.

"Better?" he murmured. "Steadier?"

She wouldn't say that. Whatever he saw in her face seemed to satisfy him that she was ready, though. Perhaps it was other things, her uncertainty about the proper answer to the question, that made his eyes gleam in the darkness. Then the shadows cloaked his face as he bent his head.

Her fingers convulsed on the cool bottle of tea as his nose brushed her skin. He took his time, as if he were inhaling her, then his lips were upon her wrist, tasting her pulse, making things flutter within her. Her own lips parted, her fingers curled, and she gasped as he bit. She'd known what he was, but seeing the momentary flash of sharp fangs through those shadows, feeling the fiery burn as he sank them into her flesh, was unexpected.

His mouth moved upon her as he drank, and she started to feel heated and strange. She had to resist the urge, not to pull away, but to rise on her knees and press closer. The bottle was left on the floor, her nerveless fingers slipping away from it.

Then she was following that urge, not even realizing she was until it was happening. Or maybe he'd pulled her up, for his hand was at her waist and then lower, gripping her buttocks as a wanton moan broke from her lips at the pressure of his strong grip. What was the matter with her? Things were spiraling up between her legs, tightening the tips of her breasts, making her whole body dance and shudder in his clasp.

His fangs were far larger than the largest bore needle they had, but the excruciating pain was gone. He had his head turned and bent over her captive wrist as he continued to drink, and she wanted to move her hand from his shoulder to his hair. She didn't, though her fingers curled hard into his flesh.

His hand slid from her backside around to the front, under her skirt. He was caressing her core, finding his way under her knickers. When he touched her, her sex was wet, so his fingers slipped just inside the labia, stroking, playing, and moving up, to the clitoral hood above.

As a strong paroxysm swept her, her fingers convulsed upon his shoulder, biting into bone. "Oh..." She was rocking against his touch, mercy, riding it.

He made that approving growl again, as he continued to drink and stroke, drink and stroke. She wrapped her other arm around his back, pressing her face into his chest. She couldn't think about stopping, didn't wish to do so. Control was lost.

He hitched her up against him, adjusting his touch to push his forearm between her legs and spread his hand full over her arse. She continued to work and rub herself against him as he kneaded her buttocks, traced his fingers over the seam, sending tendrils of sensation dancing down into that forbidden crevice. His hand was still beneath the cotton, flesh against heated flesh. For the first time since she'd come to this humid jungle, she welcomed the heat.

She was coming down. So, so slowly. She'd think she was regaining control of her faculties, and then another little spasm would shake her, arch her against him with a soft cry. He'd hold her tighter, work her some more against him.

"Little wanton," he murmured, his voice throaty and rough. "All that passion. So innocent."

He nudged her jaw with his nose, a tender playfulness, before he eased her back to her feet, adjusting his grip to hold her hip. He'd retracted his fangs, licked the puncture wounds, which normally she'd consider a very unsanitary treatment idea, until she realized the blood coagulated under the stroke of his tongue, the healing neat and clean. Remarkable.

"You look shocked, sweet nurse," he said. "You've never had a man bring you to climax, have you?"

She shook her head. Mortification would arrive soon, she was sure, but for a moment, amid death and despair, she'd felt so brilliantly alive.

"It does that," he said, and she realized she'd whispered it. "No shame on having a measure of that, in the midst of all this. It's my fault anyway. I released something in your blood to ease the pain of the bite, a strong aphrodisiac injected through my fangs."

"Oh." She wasn't sure how she felt about that, stiffened a little when he squeezed her hip.

"It enhances whatever is already there. You'll be a very passionate and uninhibited woman with the man who deserves the gift." His smile was tired, though she could still feel the heat of his eyes on her. "But since I had control of this moment, and I wanted to thank you for your generosity, there is no guilt and no regrets, little beauty. If you're pure, consider yourself that way still."

He paused, his head cocking. Her mind still whirling, she wasn't sure what he was hearing until she heard it, through a broken pane of the window. Pure sweet notes, poignant and playful by turns, were drifting through the night air, a woman's voice raised in song.

"It's Lainie. One of our nurses," She cleared her thick throat, thought about easing back to stand away from him, in front of the chair, but he still had an arm looped around her hips, her own curved around his shoulder as she half sat on his lap. It wasn't unpleasant, and her heart rate was still slowing. Plus, at this proximity, she could verify his color was looking much healthier, and she no longer felt a tremor in the grip at her waist.

"She sings at times to help calm the men, quiet their fears about the things that have happened to them." Could happen to them.

"'The Last Time I Saw Paris.' A good choice." Alistair laid his head back against the chair's cushion and gazed at her. She wasn't entirely sure what he was thinking, but he seemed content, pleased. He was studying her so thoroughly. He kept her in place, stroking her waist and gripping her waistband, tugging lightly. As his gaze shifted toward the window again, toward that music, his expression became more serious.

"Are you afraid of what could happen here, sweet nurse? If the Japanese come?"

She made a noncommittal noise. The Matrons set such a good example, she rarely allowed herself the luxury of fear except for brief frissons of anxiety. "I think most of the stories we've heard are simply to scare us away from our duty. But the soldiers…I worry what would be done to them."

"Hmm." Unexpectedly, he switched topics. "You said your family is pledged to the vampire world. Is a member of your family a servant?"

"She will be. My sister. She's training to be an InhServ." For some reason, she couldn't bring herself to volunteer that Alistair was her intended Master. Maybe because Nina was still remembering his arm between her legs, his hand kneading her bum, making her practical army knickers feel like far scantier, silkier lingerie.

The thought and his question reminded her it was time to return to reality. Her dinner break was surely close to done. When she pushed off his lap and stood, he allowed it, after a lingering moment when he didn't, his eyes measuring her as he held her still. Then there was space between them. She needed to go. The shadows cloaked him, still sitting, but she caught the sudden bleakness that entered his expression, rooting her feet to the floor.

"He's going to die, too, isn't he?" he asked quietly. "Mort."

"I'm not a doctor." But she was experienced enough to know. Whatever Alistair sought from her, it wasn't false hope. She found she couldn't lie to him.

"Yes, most likely. I'm sorry. But they'll ease his pain as much as possible. It's good you brought him here."

"He was in agony for most of it. He'd pass out, only to have the pain rouse him again. He wouldn't scream because the enemy was too close. Bloody bastard. Fucking hero." He leaned forward, linking his hands, and stared at the floor.

"You were mates."

"Yeah. Much as I can be with a human. He told me to take the others first. Should have ignored him. Maybe, if I'd gotten him here earlier..."

"You honored his wishes," she said, and had her hands on his shoulders, had closed the distance between them again. This time to feed a different need. He lifted his head to stare up at her.

"Wishes don't seem to have much place here, do they?" he said.

"No," she said honestly. "But maybe that's all the more reason to have them. Candle in the dark, and all that."

He nodded, sighed. Looked down. She didn't know if he moved first or she cupped the back of his head, bringing it to her breast, but suddenly that was where they were, his arms wrapped tightly around her hips, his head on her bosom, mouth warm against her as he drew in soft, painful breaths, his shoulders quivering.

A powerful man, but not broken. When he at last lifted his head again, he stood. His face was unmarked by tears, but his eyes were raw, reaching into her. She stepped back to let him rise, but he retained one of her hands, holding that connection between them.

"I hope we both see a day where wishes are more than candlelight, sweet nurse. I'd like them to be a fucking bonfire in the night, and dance in the flames with you. Thank you."

He squeezed her hand and moved away, sliding out the door of the cottage. As she stood there, she realized she'd likely never see him again. At least, not like this.

She leaped for the door, yanked it wider and brought herself up short when she found him standing there. He was looking up the slope, toward the hospital.

"Please," she said.

He tilted his head, looked at her. It was a curiously formal gesture, suggesting that distance was back between them, vampire and human, but she still found the courage to say what she needed to say to him.

"My twin sister. You're her intended Master."

He lifted a brow. "Your twin?"

"Yes." She folded her hands together, nervous but determined. "Please... Please treat her with care. Take care of her, I mean. I love her dearly, and she's very special. I mean no offense."

"None taken." He didn't show much reaction to the astonishing coincidence, but with what else was going on around them, nothing seemed too outlandish, did it? "Fraternal or identical?" he asked at last.

"Fraternal. Lucky for you. She's far prettier."

"I find that hard to believe."

She chuckled dryly. "Any woman amid this sea of men looks like a beauty queen."

"No. It's not that." His jaw tightened, and he reached out, ran a knuckle down her cheek. "Things are going badly for us out there, Nina. They should evacuate you and the other medical staff sooner rather than later."

Her heart sank at the news, combining with a tiny flutter of fear at the look in his eyes, but she shook her head. There was no way any of them would leave their patients. It would have to be a direct order, and she couldn't imagine either Matron giving it. "I'll go when all you lads have had enough and decide it's time to get back to your footy."

"That was yesterday. Tomorrow. Any day that's not today." His jaw kept that firm set, though. "I mean it. Don't endanger yourself. It would make me very unhappy to hear that something bad happened to you."

He used that direct look again, the one that shot right to her core and made her knees do a funny weakening. As if he had the right to tell her what to do. Maybe he did. She'd never covered much of that with Sher, the restrictions relating to the rest of her family's bond to the vampire world.

Regardless, rather than annoyance, she felt that odd flutter in her belly from it. So she covered it with a neutral smile.

"I've already had to deal with a bossy vampire today who didn't have enough sense to eat properly. How much worse can it get?"

The skin around his eyes crinkled. "A fair point. Good-bye, sweet nurse. Thank you for taking care of my friends. And me."

It was on the tip of her tongue to say something else sassy, since he seemed to enjoy that, as all the lads seemed to, but before she could say anything else, poof, he was gone.

Her grip on the door constricted and she started back, a foolish reaction. But it had startled her. Sher had never said they could dematerialize, yet she had said they could move incredibly fast. Faster than the human eye could follow.

So her blood had helped, then. That was something. Nina realized when she'd cupped his skull, she'd barely noticed the wound that had been there. If humans had those kind of healing abilities...

She shook her head before the thought could impale her heart. She needed sleep. And not to think too much about what he'd done to her body, how her knickers were wet between her legs, and little shudders were still going through her at odd moments.

He's my sister's, she reminded herself, though she knew even Sher would consider that inaccurate. Sher belonged to him, not the other way around. Out of all of it, that was what Nina had the hardest time understanding. To enter into a lifelong commitment to another, where you couldn't consider the bloke as much yours as you were his? That wasn't love to her, and love should be the bloody bottom line for a relationship that could span three hundred years.

Long after Nina herself was dust, Sher would be with him. When she was ten, she'd plotted a rescue for her sister, if it turned out her vampire was an ogre. Three hundred years with a brutal Master. Did Sher really know what she was getting into? It had kept Nina up nights, even more than it did her parents, which had baffled her. Everyone seemed to accept this except her. Even her younger brothers.

He'd made no promises about taking care of Sher. Though Nina knew she certainly had no way of extracting them, it would have been nice to hear him say something to that effect. But this momentary meeting, seeing that Alistair was the type of male who would help his mates on the front lines, made her feel a little better. A little more reassured.

He wasn't what she'd expected, but maybe, just maybe, she could comprehend something of what Sher found so appealing about belonging to their world. The portrait didn't do justice to the sheer force of his presence.

She also felt a small hope that maybe he *would* be kind enough to let her visit, see how her sister was doing with him.

That would be the only reason she would anticipate seeing him again.

She had to say it twice to believe it.

CHAPTER THREE

*A*listair had been right. The enemy's advance had the hospital personnel relocating and retreating once more, eventually setting up at facilities close to the heart of the city. Soon thereafter, evacuation of Singapore was mandated. According to reports, the city was almost completely surrounded by the enemy now.

The nurses unanimously refused to go, until the doctor in charge left them no choice, making it an order. Matron Paschke asked for volunteers for the first boat, the Empire Star. No one volunteered, so she chose the fifty-nine women.

Nina was relieved not to be one of those, but she knew it was a temporary reprieve. Matron Paschke indicated the remaining sixty-five would be departing on their heels. Matron Drummond stood tight-lipped during the announcement. They all knew she believed they should give the nurses the choice to risk court martial and stay with the wounded, but Matron Paschke's calm insistence that they follow orders and serve as soldiers should had prevailed.

At breakfast only two days later, Matron Paschke announced the remaining nurses would be departing that day. She instructed the women to collect their belongings, anything that could fit into one small kit bag with a tin of beef and beans.

It had been emotional enough to witness the leaving of the first fifty-nine women, and not just because friends were split up in such an uncertain time. Their mission was to care for the wounded, and they had been ordered to abandon their patients. Most of the women had cried as they boarded the vehicles and were driven away. The day Nina and her remaining fellow nurses left was no different.

As they assembled at the rendezvous point, soldiers came with letters to take home for them. Keeping a brave face was one of the hardest things she'd ever done. And when they at last boarded the ambulances to head for the wharfs, her heart broke when she saw that the orderlies, officers and ambulatory patients had lined the drive to salute them. She pressed against Helen's side, furiously waving her handkerchief, just like many of the others, a handkerchief she had to use on her own face to mop away the tears.

"Bloody stupid," Helen said, anguish in her voice. "Just the doctors and orderlies to take care of our boys. I've never wanted to be a man more."

Nina fervently agreed. The face of every man she was leaving behind felt as if it was being branded upon her soul.

It wasn't a long drive to the wharf, but she would never forget it. It was the backdrop of nightmares. Smoke blanketed the city, and fires were burning everywhere, fueled by the stores of oil and rubber on the dock. More than once, the Matrons barked at the drivers, making them stop so the nurses could help wounded along the road sides. The smell grew progressively worse, and it wasn't just the usual sewage smell. There were bodies, in the buildings, the streets, vehicles, no personnel left to remove them. The living, mostly civilian families, swarmed toward the water, everyone looking for a way out.

"This is what hell must look like," Helen said, her raspy voice weighted with horror. "And it feels worse than it looks."

Nina gripped her hand. "Hold steady," she said softly. "We'll get through."

The drive to the docks was interminable, though. When they reached them and assembled on the one where they were told to wait, they were a somber group.

Then, as if the Devil thought things weren't decorated enough to his liking, another air raid began.

Bloody, fucking hell. Nina had never been caught out in a bombing before, always having the illusion of a building to protect her. Not only were they out in the open, people packed the docks as well. Children, families.

"Take cover, take cover."

"Don't trample each other."

"Calmly now, calm as you can. Get whatever shelter you can."

The nurses, veterans at keeping their wits about them during the indescribable, terrible noise, did what they could, shouting and directing those in the crowds to whatever shelter was available, pulling the wounded into those alcoves, ducking and covering themselves as the projectiles screamed down from the roaring planes.

As Nina snatched up a child and ran with his mother, carrying another baby at her breast, she stepped into a burst open suitcase and saw a blue dress, a string of pearls. Then it was gone as they ducked into the overhang of a storefront.

The mother was crying, wailing something in what might have been Dutch, but Nina shoved her into a crouch around her baby, sandwiched the other child against her back and put herself over as much of them as she could. She felt something strike her back, a handful of somethings, and her heart skittered, but a second later she collected herself enough to realize it was merely mud and gravel from the road, kicked up by the plane gunfire that had missed them by a few feet.

It didn't last long, thank God. While the crowd had panicked at their exposure, air raids had been happening in Singapore for some time. Almost as soon as the planes departed, they were scrambling for the dock edges and jockeying for the few spots that could possibly be had on the boats with renewed desperation. No one wanted to be standing here when the planes came back.

Because they would be back.

The mother fled into that riotous group, clutching her older child's hand tightly. Nina paused only long enough to verify, as much as she could, that none of the three had been hurt before she ran back to the other nurses. They were triaging with whatever small amounts of supplies they had. When the call came for them to leave, Nina wasn't the only one who wanted to wish the offending bellower to bloody hell for shouting at them to get it moving, insistently pointing them to the boats that would take them out to their ship.

"Come, ladies," Matron Paschke said at last, though her eyes were suspiciously wet. "We must go."

"This is total bollocks," Temple said, tears streaming freely. "Matron, we can't leave them. Please..."

"We must follow orders. We will do no good to the wounded men being transported home if we do not survive to help them." But the Matron tempered the stern words with a touch on Temple's plump arm, her cheek. "Come," she said again. "We have done what we can. Now we do what we must."

Her glance at Nina and Helen said she expected their help to get the younger woman moving, but the tightness of her face said the Matron felt no differently from the rest of them.

Nina shepherded Temple onto a dinghy. She saw other, more experienced sisters doing the same until they were all loaded onto small craft, which took them out to the ship. Once there, The Matron told them to find a spot until the boat was underway. She also reminded them to keep on their Red Cross armbands. Nina suspected they were little to no deterrent to the Japanese, but on the slim chance they were, they would stay on. If for no other reason than they'd been ordered to do so. Absurd as it might seem, having structure, orders and duties kept awareness of the total insanity around them at bay, such that odds of survival could be heightened.

But nothing could close out the piteous pleas of those paddling on small craft near the Vyner Brooke, begging for passage. She found a spot in one of the trussed life rafts and sat down there with Helen and Temple, the three of them watching the fires of the city and the sun slowly sink toward the horizon. Somewhere, a few of the nurses tried to sing, as they often did to raise spirits, but the music died away not long after it started. Today was a day for grieving.

When she closed her eyes, the past few months flashed through her mind. To get through this unbearable moment, she purposefully focused on one memory, no matter how guilty she felt about it.

She thought of Alistair.

She'd written a letter to her sister about their unexpected meeting, keeping it high level, but it had not felt honest. Realizing just how judgmental she'd been about her sister's feelings, without firsthand knowledge of what serving a vampire was like, she'd started over and written a more detailed account. Leaving a few personal things out.

Her small taste of it did not put her anywhere close to where Sher was on it, but it was enough that Nina considered the rewritten version an apology of sorts, as well as a reassurance. Sher would have a fuller measure of her support and loyalty, and perhaps a more open mind than before.

Anything she shouldn't have left out of the letter would be ferreted out of her, regardless. When Sher learned she'd met Alistair, Nina would be interrogated until Sher had every single detail, including Nina's unexpected reaction to him. She expected Sher would be smug and teasing, but in a way that Nina didn't dread. Such normalcy as a sister's teasing would be indescribably welcome.

She thought of the days ahead. Once all were aboard, the Matrons would set them up with a routine, an order of things to do which would help occupy their minds and keep them mindful of their duty. There would be civilians on the boat, a far-too-small handful.

Bloody hell, she just wanted to draw in a breath not filled with this stench. A smell she knew now included far too many corpses. It was unconscionable what could become familiar. The norm. Madness.

She centered herself once more, pulled it together. Thought of Alistair's penetrating blue eyes. Strewth, Sher had said vampires were fair to look upon, and she hadn't exaggerated. Dirty, bloody, tired, pale, he should have looked like a corpse himself. Instead, she remembered the set of his mouth, the grace of his strong hands. How his hair, though dirty and damp, had been thick and dark, like silk against her knuckles.

But mainly she remembered his voice, all the nuances of emotions he'd given her. Weariness, sadness. Surprising touches of humor. Almost a smile once. And desire. A man's desire, which reminded her of his comment about dancing around bonfires together.

We'll get through. She'd said that to Helen, and she said it to her and Temple now, threading her arms through theirs to hold tightly. She was a Sister with the Australian Army Nursing Service. Upon the return to Australia, she'd be assigned to one of the mainland hospitals, helping in the recovery and rehabilitation of men so severely wounded they'd been sent home. She needed to turn her attention to that, because her time near a battle zone was likely done for now.

She couldn't have been more wrong.

～

Two days later, Nina leaned on the rail, sharing a cigarette with Helen.

Tensions were high on board, since earlier in the muggy day, a lone Japanese plane had discovered them, and peppered one side of the deck with gunfire. While it had soon departed, it was very possible that it would return with others. They'd all gone over their instructions for battle stations with the Matrons and were as prepared as they could be.

She was keeping a close eye on Nate, one of her patients from the hospital. He had a bad chest wound and one amputated leg, but he became extremely agitated inside the boat cabin area, enough to jeopardize his life by aggravating the wound. So the decision had been made to let him stay out, despite the risk, under a metal overhang near one of the entrances to the enclosed part of the vessel.

Once settled aboard, they'd discovered they had the care of a small handful of critically injured soldiers, including Nate. Someone had smuggled them out to the boat. Who had made that happen, she didn't know, but it had provided a small balm to them all, to give them soldiers to care for. While the men were unhappy about leaving mates behind, they'd been too injured to prevent their own evacuation.

She found a tired half-smile inside herself as Nate tipped his face up to the wind, half closing his eyes against the morning light. He hadn't cried when he'd woken up without a leg. But she'd tell no one that she'd dried his tears when he spoke of Sherman, the mate who was still in Singapore. Who was now at the mercy of an advancing Japanese army.

His eyes snapped open, sought the skies. A blink later, she heard it, too. The drone was like a distant bee hive. As the sound grew stronger, a ball of fear spiked in her lower belly. The Matrons' and crew's prediction had been correct. The Japanese pilot was bringing back reinforcements.

She was already in motion as the wounded men instinctively reached for guns that weren't there.

The handful of soldiers assigned to protect the boat raced to the mounted guns while others prepared their rifles, in case the planes swooped low enough to be in their range.

Civilians were clogging the doorways to the cabins and lower decks, so Nina went to Nate and drew him further against the closest cabin wall, tugging the stretcher bodily. "We need to get you inside," she said firmly. "Just as soon as the way is clear."

He shook his head, his eyes tracking the pilot, his expression taut. "Going to be on us by then. Go below, Sister. I'll be fine."

"And let you enjoy all this fresh sea air by yourself? Not likely."

Nina crouched next to him, figuring the best way to protect him from what might happen. She had to put a restraining palm to his chest above the wound to prevent him from shoving himself up on his elbows, though she could well understand his desire not to feel like a helpless turtle.

"Easy," she said sharply, and drew his attention. "Let's just look together, all right?"

"Like a couple of lovers under the fireworks," he managed, but there was no flirtatious glibness to it. His expression remained just as tight as they looked toward the skies again. At the escalating shouts of the soldiers, the sharp cries of the women, it was impossible not to do so.

The planes dropped out of the clouds, the metal sides glistening with the morning light. Dread gathered in her chest, dried up the saliva in her mouth. Initially looking like the random flight of birds, the planes centered themselves, heading toward them with unmistakable malevolent intent.

They were caught in the crosshairs of the enemy with nowhere to run.

As she stared up at that plane, there was an odd, still moment where her gaze flitted quickly over everyone around her, as if capturing a picture of the souls she knew would soon be lost forever. Including herself.

Then she snapped herself out of it and did the only thing there was time left to do. Curled herself over Nate, protecting his head and chest with her body.

She felt his arms curl clumsily around her, as he tried to protect her, too. Wouldn't want his mates teasing him that he let a girl do all the work, would he? But she knew it was more than that. He would try to protect her because that was his nature. Alistair flashed through her mind again, his expression when he told her he would be unhappy if something befell her.

Hopefully not for too long. If he smiled without the weight of war upon him, she was sure girls would swoon. She would have liked to see that.

41

She lifted her gaze enough to see the first flash from the lead plane, a blossom of fire, and then she ducked her head down and prayed.

Strafe bombing. She'd heard the term from her patients' lips, but knowing a term was not knowing what it truly meant. Much as she hadn't known what being a vampire's servant meant, and still didn't, but now had a far more vivid idea than she'd held before.

She'd much prefer another taste of that experience than this one. Nurses taught themselves to compartmentalize fear, any emotion that didn't serve the men they were caring for and, in this case, trying to protect. She thought she knew what being truly helpless meant, nothing within her control, but in war, there were always deeper, more horrible ways to learn that lesson.

She knew the ordered chaos of a wartime field hospital, dealing with men torn apart by gunfire and bombshells. This was pure chaos, nowhere to go. Fires started, and flames flashed against the water. The smell of salt, blood, burning. Screaming. The noise was relentless, overpowering, like standing where thunder was born. Terror was a contagious disease impossible to avoid.

It seemed to go on forever. The noise, the explosions, the flying debris. She was cut and hit, but not knocked from her post, and Nate held onto her grimly as the boat shuddered. Then her ears reverberated painfully at an explosion so loud it obliterated everything. Sound, smell, taste. Only touch survived...the loss of it. She was thrown into the water, Nate torn from her arms.

Even as she cried out his name, she had to duck under, protect her face as burning pieces of the boat fell against her, around her. Then she was driven under, a terrifying feeling. Too dazed to try to swim, her brain screamed that she must, or she would die.

She was floating up, natural buoyancy, her arms somehow thrashing, helping, taking her back to air. She seized a piece of the boat, little more than a large stick, but she saw nothing bigger.

"Nate!" She screamed his name again. She saw others floundering as she was, each in their own private, desperate struggle for survival.

Eerily and just like that, things got quieter, the roar turning to a drone once more as the planes headed away, their grisly task done. The noise of their destruction was replaced by the sound of people calling out, the splash of bodies in the water.

"Nina." Her name was being shouted and she saw Helen, her head bleeding, holding onto a slightly larger piece of debris. Nina made her way to her and they combined their two rafts, holding onto each other amid a world of water and fire, and despairing cries drifting on the breeze.

"God help us," Sister Helen said. "Temple's head was blown apart in my lap."

～

What did God think of the things men did to one another? And at what point did He decide to help them? It crossed her mind, vaguely, a few times during the hours they were in the water, trying to work their way toward the shore they saw far in the distance. They had no idea if it was land that belonged to friend or foe, but it was the only hope of aid.

They had little control over direction, and attempts to stay close to one another, the little knots of people who'd put together life rafts, were only marginally successful. When groups of nurses were swept away from one another, there was no way of telling if they would find one another again.

Nina was in a numb trance when she suddenly realized her feet had bumped something solid. Land. They'd reached land. "Helen," she said urgently. She'd helped Helen keep her head up out of the water as much as possible, the only way they could attempt to keep the head laceration dry and safer from infection. It had been the best tending they could do and Nina was glad to see it looked no worse. Her friend looked at her blearily.

"We made it, mate," Nina said, her maternal instincts kicking in with the endearment. Though the other woman was older, Nina was stronger and more awake at this point, and Helen looked vulnerable. Which helped reassure her, truth be known. It was always easier to keep her wits about her if she could focus on someone else's needs.

They had to pry their fingers off the boards, and kind of laughed over it, a harsh, sobbing sound. They helped one another to shore, staggering, and collapsed there, just beyond the surf. With it being night time, the light house was strobing, allowing Nina to see some other shapes on the beach, but she wasn't sure yet if they were other survivors or not. Unless someone had been able to grab onto Nate, he was lost. He'd have had no ability to swim with any strength, to keep himself afloat for long.

It was a hard pain under her ribs, a nurse's failure to care for her patient. To save him. But there were plenty of things to worry about now. If Nate was on the other side, she could just imagine him chiding her not to waste time on him when there was plenty left to do to save her own arse and, more importantly, care for the others on this beach.

But for just these few moments, she had to rest. She could barely move, but she managed to help herself and Helen further up the beach, so they were out of the wet and could hopefully start to dry out some. For once she was grateful for the perpetual warmth just below the equator, else the lot of them would have been lost to hypothermia.

Her few minutes of rest turned into full unconsciousness, where she dreamed of bombs, Nate sinking down to the bottom of a deep sea, staring up at her, his hands reaching for her. Her hands were outstretched, mouth open on a silent scream as the futility of trying to help anyone in this madness gripped her. Then Nate was gone, and her hands were gripped by strong, familiar ones. Alistair. Pulling her out of the water, pulling her out of this world and into his own.

She opened her eyes with a start. Her mouth was dry, gritty, her clothes stuck to her. But the ceaseless rock of the sea gripped her no more. She pushed herself to her elbows and looked around. Helen still slept next to her, and Nina immediately came awake enough to check on her. Helen's repose was normal sleep.

Nina struggled to her feet and looked down the beach. Her heart leaped, seeing they weren't alone. Perhaps a dozen or so survivors here, trying to rouse themselves like her. Maybe others had landed further up the beach. They'd see. As the sun climbed in the sky, maybe their hopes could, too.

In the end, about ninety souls found their way to that shore. Some soldiers, some wounded and some not, a little over two dozen nurses, other passengers. The nurses who were able put themselves to work to tend where tending was needed. The soldiers and others foraged for fresh water and something to eat for them all. Finding things sparse, it was agreed a delegation would try to find a nearby village and see what aid could be secured.

There was no doubt they were somewhere that the enemy was too, so there was fear of what leaving the beach to find help might mean. However, there seemed little recourse if they were going to get fresh water and food, and medical help for the more severely wounded. They'd survived the destruction of their boat, after all. That was some cause for optimism.

Later, Nina would believe Nate and the others who'd perished in the boat attack were the lucky ones. Because they didn't have to experience what happened next.

She'd just adjusted a tourniquet on one lad's leg. A strip of cloth donated from someone's clothing was doused in the sea water and wrung out, so she could return to his side and bathe the sweat from his forehead. Sharp male voices barked out commands in Japanese. Her patient's head jerked up on the same string as her own and they looked toward the forest, where their delegation seeking a village was emerging. At the muzzle end of a group of armed Japanese soldiers.

She would remember the brief press of the soldier's hand on hers, where it rested on his shoulder, even as his brown eyes stayed trained on the advancing men, the uncertain looks on the faces of the small group who'd gone out in the hopes of finding some kind of help.

"'S okay," he murmured. "You'll be all right, nurse. You're women."

She'd learned weapons of war didn't discriminate. And that often included the men who wielded them. He knew that as well as she did, but he was offering the comfort he could. Even knowing his own terrible fate was far more certain. A sudden surge of anger filled her. Anger at the advancing men with guns who had so little regard for their distress and fear, for the honor and nobility of these young men, most of them boys. She also felt a terrible, terrible fear. A knowledge in her gut she couldn't define, couldn't face, but knew would come to pass no matter what. She tightened her fingers on his, and then the soldiers were close, shouting orders, waving the guns, forcing them all to their feet, separating them all out. Nurses in one group, the soldiers in the other.

She found herself pressed between Helen and Sister Charlotte, who had a twisted ankle and so was leaning on a stick they'd found her. Her black hair was pulled back in a ragged knot, exposing the bird-shaped birth mark on her neck.

There was a lot of milling, a lot of sharp, rapid speech between the Japanese soldiers. Some were passing among their boys, kicking those who were wounded to make them get to their feet. If they couldn't, they made other soldiers lift them.

Sister Madeleine stepped forward, lifting her hand. "Please, they shouldn't be walking—"

The other nurses cried out as one of the Japanese soldiers guarding them bellowed, stabbing at her with the sharp end of his bayonet. Her sisters pulled her back into their ranks, holding her, and they all stared at the enemy, then toward their own soldiers. They were being corralled. Herded. Moved up the beach, toward the spit of land that curved behind the lighthouse and disappeared.

"No," Sister Charlotte whispered. "God have mercy on them."

Nina had her eyes trained on her boy with the tourniquet. One of his mates was helping him, and another joined them. With their arms around each other's shoulders, for a surreal moment she imagined them at a footy match in that same pose, congratulating one another and laughing after a try was scored. She thought of Alistair's mates, the one teasing him about being of not much account on the field, which probably meant he was an excellent player. Men cared for one another that way.

Her gaze slid back to their captors. They weren't much older, and some were younger. She wanted to see such humanity in them, but that ability escaped her. She hated their dark, expressionless eyes, the inscrutability of their faces, the cruel set of their mouths, the lack of any mercy. Helen had said this was what hell must look like. Nina thought this *was* hell, firmly, squarely planted on this beach, and the flames were closing in.

The Japanese soldiers were snarling at them again. Wanting them to sit, to face the waves, to turn their faces away so they couldn't see the soldiers being marched off. When a few nurses couldn't tear their eyes away, they were struck. Nina stared out at the waves, but she watched in her peripheral vision. Watched until the boys were out of sight.

Seabirds dove and called to one another. The water rushed on shore. She'd always thought the sound of the ocean a peaceful thing. Now it was a ticking clock. Forward, recede, forward, recede.

Gunfire. Pop, pop, pop...a scream, snatched away on the wind.

The women jumped at the sound, held one another's hands. She saw tears, but sobs were muffled, faces stone masks. Becoming hysterical over it did nothing. They couldn't help if they broke down. A nurse helped. Served. Made things better, even when a lad was at death's door and about to step through it. That was what gave her value, purpose. A reason to push on.

The soldiers were returning. She heard one of the sisters mutter, "God punish and rot every one of the heathens, starting with his privates," and Nina couldn't argue with it. She wished she had a gun. She would stand up, start shooting, and she wouldn't stop until they cut her down. Until this was all over and she was far beyond it.

More discussion, more harsh talking back and forth. Then suddenly, the Japanese soldiers were prodding at them, shouting, forcing the nurses onto their feet. But not to walk them up the beach, take them to a prison camp.

They were forcing them to walk toward the water.

CHAPTER FOUR

*A*ll those hours she'd been in the water, salt on her chapped lips. Now, she licked them, tasting that bitter taste, as the Japanese soldiers barked, gestured at them fiercely to keep walking. Helen was next to her and grabbed her hand, holding tight.

Many of them joined hands, knowing what was coming. A chain of connected souls, and somehow that made the unbearable bearable, seeing the machine gun being set up and readied on the beach. She looked back to the water, not at the soulless eyes of the men behind the weapon. If that was the last thing she saw, she would be lost forever, unable to find Heaven because she wouldn't believe in it anymore.

God help us.

Nina lifted her gaze to the sky. More seabirds, diving and weaving. And then, with little pause, no fanfare, the machine gun erupted, and the birds scattered.

Screams. Was it seconds or hours that it took? Probably seconds. Maybe she blacked out, the trauma too much to handle. But suddenly Helen's body was bumping hers, and Nina got a glimpse of staring eyes, of the skin leaching of color as death set in. Was Nina dead? Her heart was pounding like a hammer in her throat, her lungs straining. No, she wasn't dead.

The gunfire was still peppering the water around her. There was no escaping it. If she wasn't yet dead, she was going to be. So she thought.

Then the gunfire stopped, and she was still alive. Surrounded by bodies.

She'd been trained to keep her wits about her in trauma situations. It was the only thing that saved her now, though this was far more than she'd ever faced before.

She'd fallen, been knocked forward, and a fortunate bit of surf had pulled her out somewhat. The next period of time was impossible to quantify, both the longest and shortest moments of her life, as she tried to use subtle twitches of her body to take her in deeper, where her body floated free of the ground.

Fire in her side told her she'd been hit. The Japanese were splashing into the water, guns fixed with bayonets, checking. Stabbing. There was a part of her that wanted to be dead, that didn't want to survive something this horrible, continue living in a world where people did such monstrous things to one another.

Instead, she drifted out further, and when the soldiers went by, she was deeper than they wanted to come. But she suspected they would stand and watch, scan the shore for any signs of life. A couple times she had to hold her breath so long she thought she might drown.

She had hazy impressions as she pretended to be a corpse. Floating, floating, using slight movements of her arms to bring her back up in an aimless, bobbing way when the water pulled her under. The way she imagined a dead person would act, at the total mercy of the elements.

They stood there a long time. Or at least it seemed that way. She couldn't really see that well, since she couldn't risk lifting her head, so everything was peripheral impressions, stray bits of noise. Some still squatted down on their heels on the beach, watching, while others were occupied with other things. A few left.

Even if they all left, she knew going back to shore here would mean death. Going out to sea meant death. Other bodies had been picked up by the surf, moving around her, with the currents, and that provided her some cover. Those close enough to shore were being dragged up, piled together. She didn't want to see that. She made her decision.

Slowly, she sank below the cover of those other bodies and started to stroke outward, past the surf, away from shore. She was a strong swimmer. She could do this, no matter the pain in her side, no matter what manner of creatures her blood was likely to attract.

She kept going until she was well past the breaker line, then she turned over and floated once more, trying to keep just her face above the surface. She didn't dare look toward shore again. She wouldn't want to know what was happening there anyway. Would the bodies be left like drift wood, treated as nothing? Or would they burn them?

She needed to just float, keep moving her arms. Every time the surf grew stronger, suggesting she was being pulled in, she worked her way out, but shock gave way to exhaustion far too quickly. Still, she kept floating. She didn't know how long, but she knew when night closed in, and then she couldn't see. But they couldn't see her, either.

It didn't really matter. She'd gone out much further than she expected. A somewhat hysterical laugh bubbled out of her. *Yes, I escaped being bombed by the Japanese, their massacre of the survivors, but like a total ninny, I swam out too far and drowned.*

Her side was numb. She couldn't tell if the bullet had gone into her, or had merely taken a healthy chunk out of her flesh, but since her exhaustion seemed normal, not because of organ damage, she would assume the former. And hope the blood wasn't calling every shark within a ten- mile radius to her.

Plenty enough blood closer to shore, she realized, and remembered the tang of it in her mouth. Horror gripped her anew. She was too tired to make it to another beach, but perhaps too stubborn to die. She wouldn't give the bastards the satisfaction. Someone needed to survive this, to tell others what had been done here. Oh, God, what if she were the only survivor of their ship?

Telling what had happened, that would be a purpose. But beyond that, to spend the rest of her days haunted by those faces... She'd do better to let herself drown.

No. She thought of Sher. Sher wouldn't want her to give up. She had Sher. Nina had a reason to live.

She thought of the intent gaze of the vampire. Alistair. Okay, it was daft, but she'd assume he was a good reason to live, too.

Something clamped down on her, and she discovered she could still feel full blown terror. Her scream was lost in a choking swallow of seawater. A shark had her in his jaws, and adrenaline was keeping her from feeling its deadly bite. One small mercy.

Then she realized hands were holding her. Strong, relentless hands.

Her mind couldn't process it. Had someone else made it out, swum like she had? It seemed impossible, but she was being pulled further out, unmistakably. Was that wise? They were already so far out...

Her rescuer kept her on her back now, shifting his arm across her chest in a swimmer's rescue position, as he stroked with the other arm. She knew the person was male. The press of his chest against her, his size, were all evidence of a masculine presence. And he was a bloody strong swimmer.

"Can you shift onto my back and hold on?" he said, his voice rough and urgent. "I need to get you to a boat."

A boat. That was why he was pulling her out further. Not a soldier from the beach. Not a soldier at all. Not technically. She knew that voice. Knew him. Had she conjured him?

The world was orienting itself, and suddenly she remembered the moment behind the tent, only a few days before. Alistair. It was Alistair.

In answer, she turned over clumsily in the water. She was so cold, even though logically she knew the water was likely not much colder than a swimming pool. He dipped below her, helping, and she had her arms around his chest, her body resting against the back of his, so he could breast stroke more swiftly. He was warm, and he briefly clasped her hands, giving her more of that warmth. The moment of compassion, an acknowledgement that he was here with her, and she was not alone, meant enough to her that tears leaked from her eyes, joining the ocean.

She had enough of her wits about her to note that, while his strokes were powerful, there was a curious lack of buoyancy to him. He moved more like a boat under power than a person bobbing up and down with the movement of the waves. His body kept an even cut through the water.

"Told you...to...leave. Hate swimming."

She blinked and had no response to that. Her mind couldn't form an answer to anything. He didn't seem to require that, however, since he continued to grumble to himself even as he made admirable progress.

Perhaps because of shock, she simply drifted as she had been doing, flotsam carried along by his will. But when she managed a glance toward the parallel shore, she saw the red-tipped lighthouse that had guided the survivors was much more distant. The soldiers were no longer visible, though even with the lighthouse, the beach was too dark to see much.

Could anyone else have been in the water like her, in need of the boat to which he was taking her? She couldn't admonish him for not checking. Really, what choice had there been? But it gave her a sick feeling, to think they might have left someone alive behind.

It took quite a time, but then she realized he'd reached the boat, a small craft. "Climb me like a ladder and get in," he said. "Can you do that? You won't tip it. Don't worry."

She tried, and she was just too cold, her limbs not listening to her. "I'm sorry," she rasped. Though the real problem was she couldn't let go of him. It was mortifying, in some distant world where embarrassment mattered.

He paused, turned his head where the side of his face brushed hers, another welcome contact. "It's all right, love. Hang on tight, then."

His shoulders tensed, and she remembered that *poof* moment where it seemed like he'd disappeared, but he'd simply moved that fast. There was wind on her face, like from a roller coaster's descent, and she was in the bottom of the boat, him over her.

He didn't let her go, though, shifting his hold to bring her in between his spread knees where he sat on a seat. "Are you hurt?" His hands roved over her, probing, and she flinched as he found her side. Her hands followed his there.

"No," she said through stiff lips. "Graze, I think. I could swim well enough."

"Not bleeding," he said, and reached over her to a knapsack, if the shape of it were any indication. He pulled something out and she felt a blanket brush her. "We'll have to see about all that when we're somewhere safer, then. Can you get your clothes off? Need to get you wrapped up in this, get you warm. The water's not that cold, so it's the shock making you shiver."

She knew that. Warmth would pull her out of the grip of it, make her less logy. She'd be no good to him so debilitated, unable to help him in whatever ways were needed to keep them both safe. Her coat and shoes had been lost in the sea. Her blouse had been in tatters under her lifejacket when she reached the beach, but an ambulatory soldier had brought her a T-shirt, likely taken off one of his mates who no longer needed it, or maybe he'd held onto his duffel. She remembered his politeness, the way he did his best not to look at how her bra had been visible beneath her torn shirt.

So she'd been wearing that T-shirt over her skirt. The latter had at least held up well, a sturdy uniform fabric like her regrettably lost coat. When the soldiers had come onto the beach, she'd had her shoes sitting tidily to the side, drying out. She'd walked into the surf barefoot.

It was full dark, and modesty was not something she would dwell upon, regardless, so she stripped off the shirt, unhooked her bra and slid it down her arms with practical efficiency. Wriggling out of the skirt and knickers in a rocking boat took a little more flexibility, but she felt the heat of his hand on her back, below her shoulder blades, steadying her as she did it. His thumb brushed her, stroking the bumps of her spine, a reassurance. She reached for the blanket, her fingers shaking but her mind steadying with the occupation of doing something that made sense, had purpose.

He helped, wrapping the blanket around her. When he touched her chin, she looked up at him. His face was shrouded in darkness, but she saw a brief flash of his eyes, caught by the distant strobe of the lighthouse lamp. His jaw was firm as he studied her.

"Going to have to be quiet and move fast. Have to have you well on your way back home before daybreak."

"How did you..."

"I would have been here sooner except for the damn daylight," he said brusquely. "Heard that they'd evacuated you and that you'd come under fire. Came as soon as I could. When I bit you, I gave you the first mark. It's a locater. Don't know why I did that, but now I'm bloody glad I did. I need you to sit down here between my knees in the center of the boat and be quiet for a bit. Let me focus on our surroundings while I haul our arses to one of the few spots on shore we might not get ourselves shot."

She could be quiet. She settled back down in the bottom of the boat and laid her hand on his inner thigh, her hands curling around it behind the knee. His clothes were all dark, and damp. In some other alternate world, she'd be aware that she was leaning intimately against his groin, but right now he was warmth, safety, and none of that unsettled her. He started rowing, and crikey, he was fast. She expected he wasn't using the motor so as not to alert any soldiers still on the beach or who might be doing boat patrols around the island.

She drifted, following the rhythm of the craft, the shift and flex of thigh and calf muscle against her. She inhaled the ocean-bathed scent of his flesh. She'd coiled her hair into a knot on her neck, so the curve of her throat was against the tough fabric of his daks. He didn't noticeably breathe, except when he was speaking, when air had to be pushed across the vocal cords to make sound. So he must have lungs, even if he didn't need to breathe to live. Curious questions and foolish thoughts.

"Why do you hate swimming?" she asked, forgetting she wasn't supposed to talk. But he answered her.

"Vampires don't swim. We pull ourselves through water like anchors, using strength alone to stay above the surface. No buoyancy. Hush now, sweet nurse."

She processed that for a while. He swam very well for an anchor, she thought, but couldn't find the sad giggle that should go with such a silly thought.

The boat thumped to shore, jarring her out of her torpor. He didn't pause, adjusting her so he could stand, then reaching down to swing her up in his arms. He did it effortlessly. Since she was a taller-than-average woman, she'd never been carried by another person, and definitely not like this. He had the strength to carry her curled up like he was cradling her in his grip. He'd stripped off his own wet shirt at some point, so she laid her head against his bare chest, listening to the hard pounding of his heart.

He had the rope to the boat tied to his waist and pulled it along with him with seeming ease until they were in the cover of the forest. Then he put her down against the base of a tree and left her to erase the track of the vessel. Her eyes followed his silhouette.

Well, clung to it. She refused to panic that he'd left her for these few moments, but it was a near thing. A lot of things were settling in that she'd been able to keep at bay. She needed to be somewhere quiet and alone, where she could fix herself a spot of tea and get her wits about her. Not go all weepy and female.

He was back and had lifted her again. Despite her thoughts, she curled her arms around his naked shoulders and neck and held tight. He wasn't even sweating. Just solid heat and muscle. He pressed his face briefly against the side of hers. "Hold fast, love," he said gruffly. "I've got you."

Striding through the woods, not very far, he took her into a wide, long clearing. After he sat her down again, she watched him move back inside the perimeter of the forest. Her eyes had acclimated enough to the night she realized he was pulling something off a large thing, and her mind filled in the gaps her sight could not. He'd removed the camouflage cloth off a small airplane, a two-seater.

"Pilot," she said as he came back to her. She didn't seem capable of full sentences yet.

"Pilot," he confirmed. He must have had another pack in the plane, because he'd donned a dry shirt and was carrying another one, much like the T-shirt she'd taken off, but this one was dry. Dropping to one knee, he guided the shirt over her head, helped her find the sleeves. She might have been embarrassed to need help dressing like a child, but he kept talking, in a calm, matter-of-fact voice, as if it were of no account.

"Been flying since airplanes became a thing, so I'll get you out of here. With it being nighttime, and the air patrols not too heavy among the islands here after dark, we have a decent shot at getting you where help can be found. We'll have to island hop at least once, since this one doesn't carry much fuel."

"The others..."

"Don't think about them right now."

He sat back on his heels before her. She could make out more of the outline of his face, the fall of his hair over his brow. He touched her face, his fingers so blissfully warm she wanted to weep from that simple blessing. Yes, she needed to squash her emotions. Hard.

"Say your name to me again, sweet nurse."

"Nina. And you're Alistair."

She thought a faint smile touched his face, though his voice remained serious. "I like the way that sounds when you say it. You've got the courage to rival a lioness. Still want to blister your arse for not leaving when I told you to do it." His tone became thoughtful. "Actually, I'd blister your arse just for the pleasure of it. A nice thought to hold onto in the middle of this hell."

She blinked. He really was an odd one. She couldn't comprehend him any more than she knew how to process her reaction to his words. If it was possible for a person to be cut down the middle by circumstances, she was evidence of it. There was a cannonball lodged hard under her heart. She wanted to cry, to scream out her horror. She also wanted to kiss him, absurdly enough. She realized with a harsh dose of honesty how often she'd thought about the curve of his mouth, the strength of his body, his insane beauty, in just the few days since she'd seen him last. It had seemed a harmless and logical enough fantasy amid the ugliness of war. Sher would forgive her, because it meant nothing.

But this, this didn't mean nothing. This sudden urgent need to lose herself in something real and normal and amazing before her horrible reality set in and she was encased in ice forever. Because it was going to happen. Soon as he got her somewhere safe, she would come face to face with what could never be unseen or forgotten, and the world would never again be as hopeful or beautiful to her as it had once had the chance to be.

She reached up and traced his mouth with her fingertips. Though she couldn't really see them in the dark, she knew those blue eyes had steadied upon her. Locked.

"I want..." she whispered.

His hand dropped to her shoulder, then the side of her throat. When his grip tightened, it sent a shocking bolt of need right through her center. She wanted him to spread out his large hand, hold her throat fully, hold her fast. She wouldn't be able to surge toward him as she wished, but him controlling her movements, that would provide her the still point she needed for the chaos within her.

"What do you want, Nina?" he said, just as low and quiet. "You have to ask, and I have to tell you that you can have it. But you know that, don't you?"

Did he mean she knew the protocols between vampires and servants? Or did he mean something different? She remembered what Sher had said.

You understand it, Nina. It's in you, too.

She swallowed, those butterflies startling up and then settling again. "I want to kiss you. Need to. Please. It doesn't have to mean anything."

"A kiss always means something," he said. "And I'm going to kiss you instead."

She parted her lips to say however he wanted to manage it, she was fine with it, but then his mouth was on hers, and he was pulling her close, deep into the shelter of his body. God, she would have climbed inside him if she could. Her hands were on his shoulders, clawing into them. Not like a woman experiencing controlled passion, but as if she was literally trying to dig into his flesh so she could crawl inside him. She drew blood.

Life in this second was a denial of death, a defiance to all the evil in the world. She was wrapped around him, and he was on his feet, carrying her again, with her still being kissed as he put her back against a tree. When she locked her legs around his hips, a strangled groan vibrated through her throat, for his thick and quite noticeable cock pressed against her core, causing another starburst of sensation through her lower body.

He didn't remove the clothes between them. Just fisted his hand in her wet hair, pulling the knot free. He controlled the direction and pace of the kiss. Controlled her, helping her to savor this with an intensity that was savage. Helping her to forget.

Lord in Heaven, what was she doing? She managed to pull her mouth away, which didn't make things better, since his moved along her cheek, her jaw...to her throat. Her sex contracted, and that sound she'd thought was a growl was an unmistakable one now as his fangs scraped her.

He lifted his head without biting her, and stared into her eyes, as if trying to work something out about her. When he shifted his hand so it replaced his mouth at her throat, his fingers formed a firm collar over it. As he constricted her airway, just as she'd imagined, his thumb pressed against her rapid pulse. It made them both more aware of the strength of her life force, how he held it in his even more powerful grip. Her breath grew shorter, but not as a physical reaction. What was he doing to her? She couldn't move; could only stay within the lock of his eyes, his grasp, and think wild thoughts of being bound to him.

"You have what is irresistible to a vampire, Nina," he said. "Perhaps they chose the wrong sister."

It was better than a cold slap of water in the face, returning things to reality. She drew back, pressed the heels of her hands against his chest, rather than flattening her palms and spreading her fingers over that muscular terrain as she wished.

"No. I'm sorry, Alistair. My sister is devoted to you. It's wrong of me to have done this."

He cocked his head. His voice was still throaty, animal like, even as he spoke with mild, implacable logic. "Your sister will be my Inherited Servant, Nina. Not my wife. She'll serve me in many ways, but she does not expect, nor would she ever demand, that my attentions belong only to her."

"So even if she loves you with all of her heart, you'll feel no obligation to return that loyalty?" Though she was weak, she squirmed enough to get him to lower her back to her feet. He held her an additional moment, however, making sure she was steady.

"It can't be framed in the context of what you know in your world," Alistair said, not unkindly.

Sher had told her much the same thing. *"You don't know, Nina,"* her sister had said once. *"You have to be willing to understand it."*

Alistair squeezed her arm, a truce, and left her propped against the tree, returning to his preparations with the plane. Nina moved forward, because the distance from the tree to the plane seemed too far. The distance from the tree to him. Her legs were wobbly, so she sank to her knees, watching him. He glanced back at her. Stopping what he was doing, he strode several feet away and picked a dark shape off the ground, the blanket that had fallen unnoticed from her during their embrace.

As he moved toward her, she wished it was daylight, so she could better see how he moved, the expressions on his face. But if it was daylight, he wouldn't be here at all. When he reached her, he folded the blanket into a thick square and put it on the ground next to her. Dropping to his heels, he gripped her elbows, helped her shift onto it.

"That'll be more comfortable," he said shortly, and then rose, turning toward the plane again.

They had more important things to worry about. She should leave it alone, move on. Pretend that crazy moment had never happened.

"You were of this world," she said to his back. "A made vampire. You were human. Didn't you want a wife and children someday? Someone to fall in love with, pledge your loyalty and care to them, until death do you part?"

She was trying to distract herself, she knew. Distract herself from that screaming black hole in her mind. Distract herself from the guilt that wasn't enough to keep her from hoping he would kiss her again, hold her body so hard and tight, so demanding, against his. Guilt couldn't touch the need to do something that would allow her not to think of anything, take away her fear of falling into that hole.

He paused. She saw the tilt of his head, his chin toward his shoulder as he considered it, then shrugged.

"A servant is mine even deeper than that," he said. "Her soul is bound to mine, throughout eternity."

He closed a side hatch of the plane and turned to her. "Let's get moving, sweet nurse. We've got a lot of ground to cover."

Because it was her first experience in a two-seater airplane, she didn't expect she'd sleep. But that was exactly what she did, the rhythmic roar of the engine like being in the warm belly of a dragon. Before they got in, Alistair offered her socks to warm her feet, and she found her skirt and underwear were almost dry at this point, so she could be mostly clothed, except for the absence of shoes. He wrapped her in the blanket anew when he settled her in the seat before him.

She twisted around enough to see him after he had the plane in the air and leveled out. He had his attention on his controls and the world around them, but at her regard, he'd met her gaze, nodded. She simply stared at him a while, until her head began to droop. She sank back into the seat, and soon into the grip of oblivion.

Extreme trauma exhausted the body, put a person in a stupor. A full orchestra playing "God Save the King" might not rouse them. That stupor came when there was no strength left for fear or vigilance...or when they were safe. Sleep was the subconscious acknowledgment that they were where no further harm could reach them.

His gaze held that surety, when she would have sworn she'd never feel safe again. He gave that back to her, if only for the short time they were together.

When she surfaced, it was because he woke her. They were on the ground. She was astonished to find he'd made a stop for fuel and taken off again, all without waking her. It was still night time, though perhaps not far from dawn.

"We're in Timor, sweet nurse," Alistair said. "Things are getting worse fast here, but they tell me they're still squeezing some supply transports in and out. You'll be going out on the next one. Don't worry; these are good lads. You can trust them."

He was unbuckling her seat belt as he spoke. She watched his deft fingers move over her body, and then they were touching her chin, her cheek, a light caress that drew her eyes back to his face. The jewel-like quality of his eyes seemed less human. She wondered if that happened closer to dawn.

She thought about getting on a boat where she'd once again be at the mercy of Japanese air attacks. His gaze dropped, and she realized she'd clutched his shirt, her fingers digging into the man beneath. Flushing a little, she let him go and struggled to find some dignity. Her nap hadn't refilled her reserve of backbone entirely, but she found enough to straighten it.

"I understand. I'm grateful to you, in so many ways. Thank you, Alistair." Her voice only broke once. She considered that a victory.

He cupped her face, stroking his thumb along her lips. What might have been intended as a casual reassurance became more on the second pass, when he slowed the track, teasing her mouth so her lips parted. As he traced the upper and lower, he applied enough pressure she felt the moisture of her mouth ease the slide, encourage him to keep doing it. Her nerve endings responded to his touch like feathers to the wind, lifting toward the caress of it.

His other fingers stretched along the side of her throat, so they both registered her increased pulse rate. When she lifted her chin, giving him greater access, his eyes darkened. His lips moved in a silent oath. "I'd stay with you all the way if I could," he said. "But sunrise isn't so far off, and my situation might be a bit tricky to explain."

"They'd just sigh and say, 'Not another bloody vampire. We've had three of them through here in the past week.'" She attempted a smile. The effort caused her eyes to fill, several tears tumbling forth.

When he stroked them off her cheeks, she shook her head. "All I need is a proper tea. With a full dozen biscuits."

"That would fix anything," he said gravely. She firmed her lips, tried to get a lock on everything quivering inside her.

"How old are you?"

He considered it, as if calculating in his head. "Somewhere around three centuries, I think. I was sired when I was barely in my twenties."

"Do made vampires count their age from birth or from when they become a vampire?"

"Depends on the vampire. I expect the female ones leave that off. You sheilas don't like admitting your age after a certain point. 'Oh, darling, I'm only two hundred and fifty-eight, you know.'"

She shook her head at him. A loud report made her startle, start to scramble down into the plane's cockpit, but he held her fast. "Just the chaps loading up a truck. Tailgate slammed."

She closed her eyes, tried to loosen her fists. "Of course. You need to go. I'm sorry for holding you. Just tell me where I need to wait for the transport and I'll be fine."

"I appear to be the one holding you," he said mildly. "And I'm not sorry at all. Come on. I'll show you where you're supposed to be. I've got a little time. I can wait with you for a while."

She wasn't sure if that was true, but she wasn't going to argue with him. She saw what he meant, when he helped her from the plane. The airfield was a hive of activity, but the organized chaos and number of soldiers were familiar and reassuring.

He took her to a tent where a handful of men were typing up reports, counting things in large metal boxes, and shooting comments at one another. A radio barked with frequent communications, answered by a thin young man with red hair sitting next to it. He barely filled out his uniform.

Alistair offered them all a brief nod before he directed Nina to the far side of the tent, which had a cot sequestered behind a wall of those boxes. She deduced it was a place for the men to take turns catching cat naps during long shifts.

She was used to the affable ogling of diggers, their outrageous yet harmless flirting. They did none of that. Their glances were curious but not unkind.

"Did you tell them..." She wasn't sure how to finish that, but Alistair understood. He eased her to a seated position on the canvas and pulled up a chair beside her.

"No. I had to fill in the blanks for the chap who'll be transporting you, so he could justify you to his commander, but they have so much else going on, his main concern was confirming you weren't Japanese. Most of them know that look."

He nodded toward a mirror hung on the side of the metal boxes, directly across from her. When she looked, she nearly started back again. It took several moments to realize the pale woman in a man's oversized shirt, with bedraggled hair and haunted eyes, was her.

"I look like I dug myself out of my own grave." Her voice startled her with its hollowness.

"That you did, sweet nurse."

"Ma'am?" One of the men was standing at the opening formed by the boxes. He was a tall, broader bloke with friendly blue eyes, but deeper lines around his mouth and forehead than a young man should have. "I'm Yates. We've got some tea. It tastes like pee, but it's hot and we've got some sugar and a little milk. Would you like some?"

She stared at him. *Yes, of course.* But suddenly, such a normal question had her throat tightening as if there was a screw there. The compulsion to laugh hysterically was so strong she felt a wave of panic.

"Yes, she would," Alistair said firmly. Yates nodded and disappeared.

She started to shake. Alistair moved next to her on the narrow cot, pulling her against him, cocooning her in heat. When she burrowed into him, he shifted, stretching out on his side and sandwiching her between him and the wall. He hooked a leg over her hip, pulling her in closer, almost beneath the shelter of his body. It could have been so there'd be enough room for them both on the cot, but it worked fine.

"It's okay, Nina," he said. "You will not believe it. Not today or for a long time, but life goes on. Life endures all the bollocksed-up shit we can think to do to it, and to one another. A good heart like yours will shine again, brighter than the sun."

"Not strong enough," she said to his chest, to the comforting darkness he'd just given her.

"Bugger that," he said. "You're strong enough. If you think you're not, I'll beat your arse until you realize you are."

She snuffled. His chin had a rock hardness against the crown of her head. "You sound like one of our Matrons," she said. "Only they'd threaten to put a foot up our arse."

"There are other, better things I'd like to put up your sweet arse."

He said that in a whisper against her ear. It surprised her enough that she would have drawn back, but he was holding her too closely, her face pressed to his throat and chest, her arms curled over his sides, her fingers hooked in the waistband of his trousers.

Though she was a virgin, she knew how sex was done. She had never contemplated other methods than the usual way of doing it, though. She had overheard some of the soldiers talk about such things in their adventures with paid women. She just hadn't thought of it as something...

She tilted her head up, and narrowed her eyes. "That was a vulgar distraction."

"Well, you were about to get weepy and female, and I knew you'd never get over the embarrassment of that. But it doesn't make the statement any less true." His smile didn't reach his eyes as he threaded his fingers through her tangled hair, stroked, smoothed. "You make it difficult to remember that you're in distress and I'm not a total bastard. Sex is a wondrous balm on the evils of the world."

She thought of that sudden odd surge of lust that had taken her over when they reached the beach, and she knew what he meant. But though his regard kindled things in her lower belly, made her long for that distraction he was offering, she wasn't so far gone that she'd lose her virtue in a tent where a handful of men were within earshot.

However, as his gaze steadied on hers, the things she might do to put him off disappeared, particularly when he dipped his head and spoke in her ear so only she could hear.

"You think you could refuse me, Nina, if I decided to take you here. But you would not. And you wouldn't regret my claim on your body, heart and soul. You'd embrace it."

His speech had become more formal, increasing the power of the words. He'd said he was three hundred years old. Did that cadence, the authority, come from an earlier part of his life?

A consideration for another time, far distant, because he brought her sharply into the present when he dipped his head below her ear, set his fangs to her throat. Her hands moved, curled over his biceps, tightened and dug in as he penetrated her flesh, the flash of pain intense enough to strangle a gasp from her, but she embraced that, too, bringing her body more tightly against his. She pressed the bridge of her nose against his shoulder, trying not to make further incriminating noises.

His hand dropped, cupped her buttock. His long fingers would have nestled between the cheeks if the fabric hadn't been so detestably sturdy. As it was, he pressed firmly enough there the nerve endings in that valley tingled. She bit back a moan as he rubbed a steel erection against her mound in the front, teasing a shudder through her as he swallowed a brief taste of her blood before he slowly withdrew from her throat, a nuzzling lick helping to close the punctures.

"When you get back home, the demons from that beach may chase you there," he said in quiet voice. "If they do, I'm going to give you something to help protect you in my absence."

He gripped her wrist and pulled her arm behind her. With the other hand he had wrapped around her, he freed the fastener on the skirt, so it loosened. He pushed her hand inside it, over the curve of her backside in the practical knickers, then lower. He was insistent about his destination, which arched her back, made her feel as if her arms were bound behind her. She bit her lip as he cupped her fingers over the lips of her sex, the heel of her hand pressed between that and the opening to her backside he'd threatened in such an unexpected way. Further surprise, it sent shards of arousal shooting through her lower belly and chest. Her buttocks clenched over the sensation it sent between them.

Alistair's eyes glowed with approval when she tipped her head back, stared into them. "Put your other hand on your throat," he growled.

She somehow got her hand between them. "Do it as I would do it," he ordered. "Grip yourself as if it's the hand of the man who claims you as his."

She wet her lips. A lot of things were going through her mind right now, but none were louder or more compelling than his command, the piercing hold of his gaze.

"If those demons come, you will touch yourself like this. You will remember you belong to me and they have no right to you. You will put your fingers between your legs, stroke your cunt, make yourself wet, and wetter, until you are shuddering with the need to release. Then you will imagine me commanding you to climax. But only when you are past the point you think you can bear any more. I want you begging me to let you release. Nothing in your mind but your need for that permission. If you get too close, you tighten your grip here as a reminder of whose will you serve."

He dipped his head, nipped at her hand on her throat. "You'll know when I would speak the words. Because you know what I am, and you know I can be ruthless. I'm far scarier than anything you saw on that beach."

More ruthless, yes. But not more heartless or soulless. She had to believe that, because she was mesmerized. If she thought of this moment later, she might scoff that any man could own her, could command her in such a way without her laughing in his face. But right now...it wasn't laughter she felt when she stared into his.

"If I heard the words 'Yes, Master' from your lips, I could die with no other needs in the world," he observed in that same dangerous, husky tone. "But it's only in this you belong to me. So say 'Yes, Alistair,' and I'll know I have your obedience, at least on this."

"Yes, Alistair," she said, and his mouth was on hers. He still had her wrist in that grip resting on her arse, his fingers tightening, drawing her tauter so her breasts pressed into his chest, her hips rocking forward. Her heart thudded as his erection stroked her sex, making crazy swirls of sensation, spreading upward and outward.

"Would I let you release now?" he said, breaking the kiss to whisper in her ear again. She shook her head, his hair brushing her temple, his mouth grazing her throat.

"Why?"

"You want me to beg."

Her breath caught as he nipped her throat again, more sharply. She didn't think anything would stop him if she did beg. He wouldn't care that the men would hear. She'd already guessed that about him. What startled her was knowing she might not either. Not enough to do anything to stop him, that is.

Later, she would say it was the circumstances, the trauma. But right now the truth was impossible to deny.

She was pulled out of her head by the sudden loss of his body against hers. He sat on the chair, leaning forward, holding her hand in tight fingers. Footsteps were approaching their secluded nook. She drew her legs up, her other arm folded across her upper abdomen, her gaze locked in his, as Yates returned.

"We managed to hunt up a couple biscuits the others hadn't eaten yet, as close a thing to a miracle as we get around here. They're likely stale, but at least they make for a proper tea."

She nodded, perhaps formed the words "thank you," but she didn't think any sound came out. With a squeeze of her hand, Alistair rose. He took the tea and brought it to the crate that served as a bedside table.

Kneeling beside her, Alistair helped her to a sitting position, his grip firm and strong. Yates remained leaning on the stack of crates, studying her.

"It's closer to dawn," she said to Alistair.

"I know."

Bemused, she watched him pick up the tea, blow on it, take a sip, nod. "Pee is a good description. But hot takes the edge off it, makes it damn near comforting."

Yates chuckled. "Yeah."

Alistair wrapped her hands around the sturdy black mug and those inexplicable tears almost rose anew at the familiar feel of a hot cup of tea between her palms. As she raised it to her mouth, it began to shake alarmingly.

Alistair cupped his broader palms over her knuckles, steadied her grip, so she made it. She took a small sip, and the faint burning on her tongue and lips was welcome. She closed her eyes.

"Does she need a doc, mate? We've got one here who could look her over."

"If there's time, that would be good."

"No, I'm fine," Nina said, but Alistair helped her lower the tea and set it aside before he framed her face and gave her that look which inspired such odd flutterings in her stomach.

"If there's time, that would be good," he repeated. "She was shot. She says it was a graze, but she hasn't done a thorough accounting of her injuries. Bastard transporting her was keeping her on the move. Gave her no time for it."

"Inconsiderate of him," Yates said dryly.

Alistair straightened. "Drink the tea and let someone take care of you for a change," he told her. "You remember what I said about those demons."

Nina felt her cheeks warm and didn't dare look toward the other man. "Thank you, Alistair," she repeated. The feeling in her stomach became far less pleasant as she realized he was leaving her. But he needed to do so. Dawn was coming, and his task was done. He'd gotten her to safety.

One more squeeze of her hand, and he let her go. As he moved out of the space, he stopped next to Yates. "You'll take right good care of her."

"Count on it." The soldier met Alistair's intent blue eyes with a direct look from his own. If he felt unsettled by the razor sharpness of Alistair's regard, he didn't show it. "Next transport leaves in two hours. She'll be on it, and headed back home. Would stow myself away with her so I could look forward to my mum's roast, but these bastards can't wipe their arses without me."

She registered a volley of responses to that from the other side of the crates, which produced a tight smile from her tea-bringer. His gaze touched her again, briefly, then returned to Alistair, a harder look in it as he reinforced his words with more forceful intent.

"We'll get her home safe, mate."

Alistair nodded, then glanced back at her once more. One more lingering moment.

And then he was gone.

CHAPTER FIVE

Three years later

*S*alt water. Helen holding her hand. The soldier on the beach, also gripping her hand, before he was shuffled off to his death. Gunfire. Staring, dead eyes.

God help us.

Nina came out of sleep with a scream on her lips, but it happened so often, her subconscious managed to stifle it before she woke everyone in the boarding house.

That scream escaped, though cut short, as the screen door downstairs clapped closed. It was the wind, she told herself. It was the middle of the night. The wind would lift the door and release it suddenly. Happened all the time.

She settled back into her pillows, clutching one to her breast, bringing her knees up beneath it. She'd sweated through her nightgown again, damn it. She'd have to wash up in the sink in the morning to be clean enough for work.

Such thoughts didn't stop her shaking or soothe the spiked ball in her throat that wanted to become a choked sob. Though she despised her weakness, she thought of another set of hands to steady herself.

The memory of *his* hands, reaching out to her in the water. Holding onto her, bringing her onto the boat. Carrying her out of the ocean, pressing her against a tree. Clasping her throat. Alistair's hands. His eyes and mouth.

She shut her eyes and gripped the pillow tighter. A few hours from now, when she rose from her bed to go to work at the hospital, she'd look at things with clear pragmatism. She'd finish up the nightmare ritual the way she always did. By reminding herself she was a sexual innocent who, until her encounter with Alistair, had done nothing with a man. Letting a boy equally as inexperienced as herself paw beneath her blouse and give her kisses during a summer romance hardly qualified. A three-centuries-old, sexually experienced vampire could easily brand himself on her brain like the be-all, end-all of romantic lovers.

But since the memories often helped her get back to sleep, she wouldn't reject the gift.

The war was finally over. It didn't seem to matter to her subconscious, though it didn't take a genius to know why she couldn't seem to get past it.

Yates and the others had gotten her home safe. But there were times she wished she'd never set foot on her homeland again. She'd been checked out by a doctor, who confirmed the bullet had been a graze. He'd indicated she was bruised, a little dehydrated, and had experienced a fairly severe bout of shock, but otherwise was no worse for wear. Which somehow seemed obscene when she thought of Helen floating in the water, her staring eyes.

She jumped at loud noises, disappeared into her own head, losing time. For the first few days back at her parents, she'd barely been able to get herself out of the bed. But then she remembered she could tell someone. She could make sure that someone knew that her friends had not "merely" been sunk on a boat attacked by Japanese planes.

"You can't do that, love," her mother had said.

The matter-of-fact calmness had brought Nina up short. She'd just finished telling her parents what had happened, which had been far harder than she'd expected. Her father had leaned against the wall, listening, while her mother sat on the edge of her bed. Nina knew they were worried. Her mother had come in to coax her out of bed, offering her a chance to join them for a late breakfast in the kitchen. Instead, the whole horrible tale of what had happened, the sinking of the boat, the massacre on the beach, had spilled out of Nina. She'd also told them how Alistair had rescued her, after meeting her some-time before that at her hospital in Singapore. She hadn't included any of the stuff that she wouldn't be explaining to anyone, though she wondered if she needed to confess it to Sher.

Yes, she knew what Alistair had said, but what people said and what they felt were often very different things, and she wanted Sher to know...what? What reassurance could she offer? That it didn't mean anything? Because at the time, it had meant everything. It had kept Nina from losing hope, from letting herself sink to the bottom of the sea and drown with everyone else. And every day she got further from it, she felt she was being drawn back to the sea and into those depths. She was drowning again now.

"What do you mean?" Nina asked slowly.

Her mother looked toward her father, drawing Nina's gaze there.

"Because of our connection to Alistair, we can't do anything to incur public attention," he said quietly. "Your story would make national news. Don't worry. Someone else will report it. I'm sure there's another survivor. Or maybe not all the soldiers were executed." Her father tightened his jaw over the terrible words. "Perhaps some were taken to prison camps and will tell the story after the war is over."

"I'm not going to tell them about Alistair. I'll say I drifted up to shore and a kind stranger brought me to the base in Timor. But I have a responsibility..."

"Your first responsibility is to your family, isn't it?" Her mother's voice had that note that baffled and hurt Nina at once. Implacable. Devoid of understanding. Sharp. "If you draw attention to yourself, you draw attention to your family. To Sher. If she draws public atten-tion, it will draw attention to the vampire world. I'm sorry, Nina."

"I'm sure someone else will report it," her father repeated. "But you cannot be the one to do so. Do you understand, Nina?"

They weren't loud or angry about it. They'd never raised their voices about anything, so controlled and disciplined about everything.

She argued, she cried. They stroked her, patted her. Destroyed her. Eventually, worn down, she'd told them she understood. Yet when they hugged her and left her to finish her tea in bed, she felt like they'd simply put it out of their mind. If their daughter didn't talk about it, it hadn't happened.

70

~

Back in the present, Nina left the bed, padded to the window. Stared down into the empty street. There was a bank of trees and a pond on the property across from the boarding house, and she watched a child's sailboat float aimlessly across it, likely left on the bank's edge by its owner when called to dinner the night before. The wind had decided to take it for a sail.

A few weeks ago, with the rest of Australia, she'd learned about the nurses on other life rafts. The ones who'd washed up at different places onshore and been taken prisoner. They'd spent the last three years in internment camps. She also learned there had been one other nurse who'd been with Nina's group and survived the beach. Vivian. Bull, they'd called her, for she was a tall, strong woman, even taller than Nina.

Her story was printed in the papers. Another survivor, one of the soldiers, had indicated that he'd returned to the beach to find bodies of soldiers and nurses, some in the water, some not. Which gave Nina a permanent vision of the faces of those she'd known, bobbing in the water like corks, or strewn up on the beach like rotting fish.

The full details of the nurses in the internment camps hadn't been made public yet, but from contacts Nina had kept in the AANS, she'd learned that many of them had starved to death or succumbed to disease during those years. The survivors were emaciated to a shocking degree. They were currently feeding them up and providing them care at an undisclosed location before bringing them home, for fear of what public reaction would be to their appearance.

Three years ago, when she'd returned to Australia, she'd been reported as one of those who'd made it back to the Australian mainland "without incident." Those two words, combined with all the rest, could plunge her into a quagmire of guilt and regret. If she'd been able to tell her story then, would it have made a difference to those in the camps? There'd been rumors of nurses surviving, but nothing confirmable. She couldn't have confirmed it either, but knowing that other life rafts hadn't made it to her shore, that they might have made it to land elsewhere, might have galvanized efforts to find them sooner. Help them.

Had Vivian been where she and Alistair could have found her? She thought of the faces of the nurses who might have survived, women she'd known. She imagined them wasting away from hunger and the diseases that came with malnutrition, their staring eyes joining the ones she dreamed of nightly in the water.

It flooded her with a despondent sense of futility. The silence of her rented room was as stifling as a coffin.

She returned to her bed, drew her knees up, put the heels of her hands against her eyes. She rocked, and began to hum, a desperate measure she'd developed for staying out of that sucking mud of her subconscious. Sometimes it worked. Especially if she added in the drone of a two-seater airplane, a lullaby laced with images of Alistair, and her trip to safety.

She'd found work at one of the hospitals overflowing with soldiers enduring rehabilitation. It had been far enough away she no longer had to live under her parents' roof. She eagerly embraced the long hours and volunteered for more when the matrons there would let her.

She loved her family, but it was clear that they saw her as out of step with them, the family member who didn't quite get it. Whereas she felt she was the only one who saw things clearly.

Or she had. Of late, everything was far less certain. Only work made sense. Helping the boys put their bodies back together she could do. Her heart ached at their struggle to put everything else together, but she understood that in a way she might not have before. One of the matrons had praised her recently. Told her that out of all the nurses, she had the best rapport with the soldiers. "You connect to them, help bring them back from the edge, Nina," she'd said. "They feel like you understand."

Yes. She did. She was just as lost as they were. When the war had ended, in the initial flush of relief, the whole country, the whole world, had celebrated. They'd all heard the news while she was at work. She'd looked at the faces in her ward. Many of the boys had been cheering. But she'd seen others caught in the shadows of their minds, a prison wall they were trapped behind that kept that feeling of victory out of reach.

But for most it was a blissful if temporary respite. The relief and celebration would eventually be re-infused with the more sobering reflection of the great cost.

She did celebrate, was genuinely glad there was an end in sight for the stream of broken men brought in from the battlefronts. But she also went to the supply closet and cried and shook, a fist stuffed against her mouth to muffle her sobs.

For the first time in her life, she was glad that the demands of Sher's training had cut her twin's visits home to only upon approved request. According to reports to their parents, Sher was one of their stars, and glowing even more brightly with every passing day. During the war her letters had dropped to once every few months. From what she said— and didn't say—in them, Nina realized her parents hadn't told Sher what had happened to her. She thought Nina had simply been evacuated from Singapore and come home before any real significant fighting had occurred there. That she'd been discharged and was working at the hospital.

Were you able to bring home that charming necklace you found in that Singapore clothing shop? Did you meet any handsome officers before they had to spirit you back to our poor old boring Oz?

Nina could have told her differently in her letters, but she didn't. But it was worse than that. During her first year back, Nina had learned from her parents that Sher was going to be able to come home for their birthday. The first chance she'd had to see her twin since before she'd left for the war.

Nina had expressed her excitement and pleasure. Then called back two days later to tell her mother, regrettably, she wouldn't be able to make it. Work schedule conflicts.

Sher was the person she loved most in the world. Her twin, the person closest to her soul, no matter their differences. Nina just couldn't bear being that open to anyone. Couldn't bear to look into her sister's face, tarnish the brightness of her life and purpose with the darkness and listlessness that had taken over Nina's own. She didn't have the energy for it. Just for the work. She convinced herself Sher was better off not seeing her.

She had tried countless times to write to Sher about it. She'd started with Alistair's role in it all, because that was the easiest part. She could confirm his heroism, bravery and kindness to her. She'd written a dozen different versions of it and everything else, and couldn't find the will. Just wasted her money on the lost paper.

As far as the more intimate things that had happened between her and Alistair, she wouldn't put that in a letter anyway. She'd told herself she'd share that with Sher when she saw her again. Maybe. If Sher would understand, just as Alistair had said, that helped Nina rationalize her silence. If it didn't matter to anyone but her, she'd rather keep it to herself, not tarnish it with the indifference of others. Or make it less significant by having to pretend it wasn't.

Nina curled back up on her side, hugging the pillow, and stared out the window once more. Weariness was gripping her, pulling her back down. She didn't know if it was physical or emotional, but either way, she was headed for blessed oblivion. If she did the one thing that usually ensured it.

She didn't know why she resisted it so strongly every time, because it always worked. If she'd do it before the nightmare, maybe it would eradicate them completely, at least on the occasional night. But she always started the night determined to deal with it herself. Or maybe it was that she felt like she deserved the punishment of those nightmares. And she resisted the path she took afterward because the respite it brought felt like an undeserved reward.

Or maybe because, as a nurse, the fight to keep control over the uncontrollable was endless, and she had to resist until the final moment, until she had to admit his will was stronger than hers, and she could commit herself to his care.

A fantasy, but it came down to that. When she was so exhausted she couldn't fight with herself over it anymore, or try to solve the puzzle of why it helped so much, she would give in to it. To the temporary relief it brought.

She closed her eyes, brought back his face, his voice. She'd kept the shirt he'd given her and, insane as it was, even washed repeatedly, she thought she could still detect his scent. She slipped off her nightgown and put it on, lay there in it and her knickers, the covers off because it was easier to imagine his body pressed down on her that way. She slid one hand under her arse, giving her that impression of her hands bound behind her back, lifting her body up to him.

The other hand went to her throat as if pulled there by a rope tied around her wrist, as sure and strong a grip as his hand had been. A couple times, she'd looped her robe sash around it, the other part around her throat to hold it there, to increase that sensation. She didn't tie it when she did that, merely kept the slack looped over her hand, but one time, she'd started gathering it up, tightening the hold on her wrist and throat, and kept doing it until her vision started to blacken. The way her heart had speeded up, the eagerness she'd felt to keep doing it, had frightened her. She wouldn't let herself use the sash anymore, though her gaze would often turn to her robe, hanging on the door peg, as she did this, and she'd imagine it. Crave it.

It would have been easier to put her hand upon herself from the front. Doing it from the back put a strain on her arm over time, but she did it as he'd ordered her to do it, and somehow that effort, complying with the discomfort, imagining the set of his mouth, the intensity of his eyes as she struggled to do his bidding, helped her put the other things away, lose herself in this.

She'd tried to masturbate just for herself, imagining one of those handsome officers Sher had teased her about, and her body was so unresponsive she worried that she'd lost the desire for intimate physical contact altogether. But the moment she followed Alistair's directions, put her hands upon herself at his imagined command, she came alive, the nerves between her legs pulsing madly, her body moving restlessly, hips pushing into her touch, hungry for it. She didn't touch them, because it had not been part of his direction, but her nipples became firm, aching points, and behind her closed lids she imagined his mouth on them as he held her fast with the grip on her throat, his other fingers stroking through the slick heat of her cunt.

That was what he'd called her sex, and it had been erotic in a way she never would have imagined the word to be. Her breath quickened, a whisper of breath in her silent room. Corpses didn't moan like this in their coffins. She was alive. Connected to this life, even if only by her work and this thread that got her through the night.

Beg for it…

She waited until her forearm was aching fiercely, her back was arched to the point where to go further would snap the spine, and the waves of arousal were crashing against a wall of self-restraint. No, not self-restraint. It wasn't her will holding that release at bay.

"Please...please let me."

And because it was just her and him here in the graveyard hours of night, she did the one thing he hadn't commanded, but which she needed to go over that edge, to find release and a few hours of uninterrupted sleep.

"Please...Master."

~

She was wrong. She did have another nightmare, but this time, it was something different. Or rather, a mix of things. The salt water, the shore, only she wasn't in the water or standing on the beach. She was driving along it, and there was a steep drop to the beach below. She could see the pounding waves, and she felt excited, exhilarated, because they had the top of the car down. A glance at the mirror showed her she wasn't her. She was Sher, with her gorgeous long hair whipping back behind her head scarf, her smile flashing to the other two women in the car, at the man driving.

She'd done it. The final test passed. When she went home this time, for her birthday, it would be the last time she would do so as a student of the Inherited Servant program. She would go straight from home to Lord Alistair's household.

But she was headed for Sydney first. Her sister had said she couldn't come home because of her work schedule. Sher wanted to see her one more time before she became Alistair's servant. Her mother would only speak generally of Nina's life over the past couple years. She'd moved out, she was working in Sydney, she seemed content. Nina's letters, though fewer than before, had been cheerful enough.

She was her twin, though. Sher knew something was wrong. For years her training had underscored in myriad ways that an InhServ must let family conflicts be resolved without her direct input. Her first priority was always serving her Master.

After assignment, she would be even more aggressively discouraged from family contact, weaning herself and her family completely from that connection. For two reasons. First, she would outlive all of them, by decades. When Nina was a very old woman, hopefully with great-grandchildren at her knee, Sher would still look in her twenties, and have a couple centuries of life left to her. Second? Serving her

Master's will would determine every moment of her daily life. Any distractions drew her away from that prime directive.

But remembering how often her sister had looked so desolate when she left her, Sher wanted to give Nina this one more moment. She wanted to put her arms around Nina, tell her she loved her. She hoped that one day her sister would understand how much Sher truly wished for her to find happiness and the family she wanted. And how very much Sher cherished the bond between them, even if she could give nothing to it that Nina desired.

She might not be able to be part of Nina's life, but Sher would never forget her. She wanted her sister to be sure of that.

The strength of her resolve to see Nina one more time made her feel a little discomfited. To reassure herself and center her mind, she recalled her core training.

My Master's will determines my life's path.

I surrender to that.

Confirming it, Sher called his name to mind with deep reverence. "Alistair."

In sleep, Nina's lips moved, saying it. She moved restlessly again as she imagined strong hands on her, stroking her. Lifting her arms, pinning them above her on the bed as his head dipped, fangs flashed. Her body would rouse to his if he had the slightest need of it.

She imagined herself kneeling, meeting him for the first time, presenting herself as his in the formal ritual. His gaze slid over her naked body, studying, assessing. She straightened her back, hands clasped behind it, even as she kept her eyes lowered. She would be an asset. Would make him proud to have her in his service. She would do anything he needed. Be his. It was what she'd been born, bred and trained to do. She would do it well, love her vampire master with everything she was.

The car wobbled on the blind curve, and suddenly it was facing a squadron of Japanese soldiers. They'd set up a machine gun right on the center line. They were gesturing fiercely, speaking in angry voices, pointing over the ledge, toward the water below.

"No!" Nina's scream in the dream was loud. In the quiet darkness of the boarding house, it came out a strangled gasp, a whimper, her hands tearing at the covers then letting go, to reach out and grasp nothing.

The car spun, the loose wheel rolling away as the vehicle skidded, flipped as if tossed carelessly by a giant. It somersaulted over the edge of the drop, plummeting toward the water. Gunfire followed it, and Nina was holding Helen's hand and Nate's, only they were dragging her down into the water. She glimpsed Alistair on his boat, but he had the engine running, churning the water, and he was moving away swiftly. He didn't hear her, see her, because she wasn't there. She didn't exist. She was below the water's surface, dropping deeper and deeper, her dreams of being an InhServ lost forever.

More gunfire, harsh language, rapid syllables. The taste of blood, the rush of water over bobbing bodies. There were no hands to pull her out this time, only the sheer will to survive helping her claw her way out of the dream.

Nina gasped for air in the suffocating stillness of her room. Despair gripped her. This was never going to get better. It felt like her life was ending.

Had ended, in the water.

~

An hour later, when the phone rang, waking the landlady and sending her to Nina's door, she realized it had. But the life she'd felt ending in her dream wasn't hers.

It was Sher's.

Then she learned it was both.

CHAPTER SIX

*N*o. No, no, no.

It was the most useless word in the English language, capable of stopping nothing, except the helpless human compulsion to fire it off in the subconscious like a machine gun toward an undefeatable foe.

Having her twin ripped from her consciousness was bad enough. Waking to that shrill middle-of-the-night message from her brother to learn Sher had died in a car accident had merely confirmed what Nina already knew.

Numb from that, from all of it, she wouldn't have expected anything else to cut as deeply, or shatter her heart further. She was wrong. When she'd come home, her father had waited exactly one day to tell her.

We are still required to comply with the InhServ requirement, Nina. We must provide our next oldest child, which would be you.

The two days that followed had vacillated between screaming fights, aching silences. Her brothers lived elsewhere now, but had come home for the funeral. They'd wisely fled to the homes of friends. Nina had made countless turns around the neighborhood, walking miles in circles. She slept under a tree in a park, was brought home by a police officer and treated like some poor wobbly mental patient by her parents, who'd ushered her up to her room. Her mother had offered the policeman tea. Offered Nina tea.

Because tea would solve all the world's problems, wouldn't it?

Her whole future had been turned upside down and been put on a one-way track where she had no choice to get off the train. She was told she would be "allowed" to attend her sister's funeral, bloody fucking, buggering hell.

Her father had said her language had become far too rough. He had no idea how much Nina restrained herself.

Later that night, she was sitting on her bed, staring at a wall she couldn't see, when her mother came into the room. She was carrying a suitcase, and began speaking quickly as she entered, not meeting Nina's gaze.

"I decided it's best to go ahead and pack your things." She gestured with a piece of paper as Nina stared at her blankly. "I...uh, didn't realize I'd kept this, from when Sher went off to the program when she was sixteen. The Mistress told me to use it to help you pack, and gave me some additional notes. It says what things you can take with you. You'll be taken to the InhServ training school first, to get you oriented."

Her mother spoke too fast, and then rattled off the list as she bustled around the room. No items that were too personal. No pictures, no childhood stuffed toy for comfort.

Nina rose, picked up the picture of Sher that was by her bedside and put it in the suitcase. Her mother watched her, biting her lip. When Nina sat back down, her mother approached and put trembling fingers on the photo. Looking up, she met Nina's eyes for the first time. "I'm so sorry, love," she said softly, and tears shone in her eyes. "This would be one of those things."

Davinia. Her mother's name was Davinia. It was easier to think of her that way than as her Mum as she took the picture out of the suitcase. Nina noted how gently she set the picture on the shelf, before she wiped her eyes.

"Are those tears for me?" Nina asked coldly. "Or because she's dead?"

Davinia's attention snapped to her, her mouth tightening. "It's for all of it," she said shortly.

"Do you have any idea how cruel this is?" Nina demanded. "Do you even care?"

"The purpose is not cruelty," Davinia corrected. She was back to that steady, logical voice that Nina hated so much. She wondered if the woman who bore her was really human, or a robot that had been created in some laboratory to raise her and Sher. "It's to help you fully embrace the InhServ life. Facilitate your rebirth as a member of the vampire world."

"As a slave of the vampire world," Nina picked up the picture, put it back in the suitcase again. "I'll pack my own things. After the funeral, I'm returning to the hospital. I won't do this. I'm not Sher."

She sounded rational, firm. She'd detach herself, treat her parents the way she'd treat a patient who couldn't make sense of things, who was suffering. Though those two qualities might just as easily describe herself, Nina wasn't oblivious to the fact her mother was suffering.

"You can't go back to the hospital, Nina. If you try, they will go to collect you."

"I'll go to the constables."

"Then you will get people killed."

Nina collapsed into a chair, staring at her. "Why am I worth so little to you? And what they give you worth so much?"

Her mother flinched, but when she spoke again, her voice was lower, as if she was holding onto strong emotions with both hands. "Serving the vampire world is a great honor to this family, Nina."

"For generations, I know. You've told—"

"You will listen to me," her mother snapped. "For once, will you just...*listen*."

Nina started at the tone. Her mother closed her eyes. When she spoke again, she was calmer, but Nina could still hear the frayed edges. "This family has been bound to their world for over two hundred years. If a promised InhServ candidate refuses, the family's loyalty to the vampire world must be questioned, as to whether the existence of vampires is a secret that will be safe with them anymore. If the Council deems it is not..."

Nina swallowed. "So they've blackmailed you, threatened you for decades. Fear. That's why—"

"No," her mother said decisively. She laid a hand over Nina's, gripped. "It never happens, Nina, because those bonds are deep. They are formed and based on many exchanges, precious favors owed and given. There has never been a situation where a family was sacrificed because of an InhServ candidate betrayal, because it simply never occurs to any of us to desire the ending of that link. I know you don't understand. This is so unfortunate, all of it. I wish more time could be given to help you see..."

"Yeah. It's so unfortunate that Sher died."

Her mother's hands clenched. For a moment, Nina thought she might slap her face as she'd done when she was little and wasn't minding.

"I can't talk to her about this. Sher was better at it."

Her mother's voice cracked, and she started folding up a shirt as if her life depended on it. Looking up, Nina saw her father in the doorway.

He also was grieving; she could see it in the deep lines of brow and around the mouth. But there was a distance that she couldn't bridge, that made her grief for Sher seem unshared.

"Please, Nina," her father said, and there was a harshness to his tone, suggesting he was holding onto control of his emotions by a thread. "Please, for once, try to understand. Don't tear this family apart. Don't dishonor us. We wouldn't do this if we knew it wasn't for the best. You've always trusted us before in that."

"No," she said slowly. "I didn't. I never did. Sher did. I never understood, and I never will. I don't even know who you are."

There'd always been a chasm in the path of love she bore for them, one growing ever wider by the moment. She was losing everything.

Her mother raised her dark brown gaze to her father. "Call The Mistress. Tell her Nina needs to be brought to them now."

"Before the funeral?" Nina demanded, surging off the bed. "You'd deny me the right to say goodbye to my sister?"

"If I think giving you that chance will provide you time to put together a futile escape plan, yes." Her mother nodded her head, her jaw set like brittle granite. "Which is what you are thinking."

Nina stared at her. "I should have died on that beach. I wish I had."

But she didn't, she knew she didn't, and that made this all worse. She swayed suddenly, and when her mother started to rise, she shook her head, backing away. "Don't," she said in a terrible voice. "You have their eyes. Don't come near me."

Her parents didn't ask who she meant, and perhaps that was just as well. They wouldn't want to hear that she was remembering the soulless eyes of the Japanese soldiers before they fired the machine gun. Before they shot down a row of women walking with clasped hands into the water.

The memory swamped her, as it sometimes did, taking over all her senses. She broke out in a cold sweat, and when her parents came toward her anyway, she started screaming and crumpled, her room and their presence swallowed.

It was poor but undeniable evidence of their love for her that, when she surfaced, she was on her bed, her head being bathed by a wet cloth, her mother's scent close. She stroked Nina's hair, her shoulder. Her voice was soft as she sang a soothing lullaby she'd sung when they were young.

Davinia's mother had sung it to her, Nina remembered her once saying. "The Night Nursery." The song was achingly appropriate. Though instead of the sleeping children being visited by a dead mother, she could well imagine who her mother was thinking about.

> For when the sun has gone to sleep
> and all the world's in bed,
> then someone comes to see us here,
> whom Nursey says is dead...

Her mother faltered over the next stanza, tears choking her voice, and then she managed to rally enough to make the next two more coherent. Nina kept her eyes shut, allowing herself this moment with her mother's touch on her brow, her hand clasped in hers. She needed to believe in this small evidence of her love, even as she knew she'd never understand the shape of it.

> She comes in thru the skylight
> for the door is not allowed
> Her eyes are bright as little stars
> Her dress is like a cloud.
>
> She holds me very kind and tight

and talks about her land,
where all the flowers are boys and girls
with mothers close at hand...

Nina opened her eyes. She and Sher had their mother's brown eyes, the shape of her face, but they'd gotten their height from their father, because their mother was barely five feet and he was just under six. She looked even smaller today.

They said nothing, just held gazes. Eventually, her mother took her touch from Nina's face, but clasped Nina's hand. When Nina finally turned her head, she saw the suitcase had been packed and was by the door. Her mother quelled her abrupt panic with a squeezing of her fingers and quiet words.

"You will attend the funeral, Nina. I did put Sher's picture in the suitcase. The Mistress permitted it, for the time being, given the special circumstances. But..."

She swallowed, the hesitation drawing Nina's gaze back to her. She realized her father stood in the doorway, watching them, a faceless silhouette. It was dark, the only light from the hallway.

"You'll be picked up from the graveside," he said, when Davinia didn't say anything. "No sense in drawing it out. We know this is hard, Nina."

You don't know anything, she wanted to say. They'd never seemed bothered by the requirement that Sher be turned over to the vampire world, trained for it like a monkey since birth. The surge of anger was too easy to fuel, though, and she was too weary to go there again. At least right now.

She made herself focus on her mother's face. Remembering how she herself had dealt with what had happened to her in Singapore, shutting down, living life behind a pleasant mask, Nina wondered what emotions lived behind her mother's facade.

She didn't want to know, she realized. She simply couldn't deal with finding out if what she wished was there was genuinely absent.

"We hope that, once you're there, at the InhServ campus, you'll understand more and find it in your heart to forgive us," Davinia said at last. "If you write, I will answer. I promise, Nina. Until they don't let me anymore."

When Nina said nothing, Davinia looked toward Willem.

Thinking of him by his name was easier, too. She remembered Sher had been required to call them by their names after age six. No more Mum or Da.

"Let's let her rest," he said quietly.

Davinia nodded. She rose, her hand slipping away from Nina's. When she moved to the door, the two of them paused there, looking at her. She turned away, faced the wall, and closed her eyes. She heard the door close, the light reduced to a mere sliver along the white wall.

Numbness set in. This was it. Her future supposedly no longer her own to determine. The only way to get away was to come up with an amazing, daring escape, and she had no resources for that. Ironically, the only one who came to mind with those talents was the male to whom she was being given like some feudal tithe.

And yet... Was that the solution she was overlooking? She couldn't dissuade her parents, and appealing to the Vampire Council was like being a sacrificial sheep petitioning the Old Testament God for mercy. So that left one person who might hear her appeal.

The one who now owned her.

No diplomatic language, no prettying it up, because in the InhServ world, it was an honor to be a vampire's property. For up to three hundred years, the natural lifespan of a third marked servant.

She didn't know exactly how that worked, but she wasn't marked yet. Maybe. The words she hadn't really thought much about came back in bold relief in her brain.

When I bit you, I gave you the first mark. It's a locater. Don't know why I did that, but now I'm bloody glad I did.

She clenched her hands into fists. Alistair was three hundred years old. It was unlikely that a couple days of shared memories had helped ease any of his nightmares about what they'd seen, the way they had for her. But the things he'd said, those two nights she'd known him, told her he had to feel some kind of connection to her. If she couldn't find a way out of this through her family, maybe she could find it through him.

We'll get through. Her words to Helen mocked her, but where they hadn't helped Helen, they might succor Nina now. Patience, waiting to see what happened as variables changed, might present her options this seemingly hopeless moment did not.

~

Basic needs, hunger and thirst, finally drove her from her room the next morning. She donned slacks and a blouse, sturdy shoes. Did her hair and makeup. Though she could care less about how she looked, she recognized them as a physical and emotional armor she would need. When she came downstairs, she discovered she was too right about that.

Her mother had granted Nina the dubious kindness of attending her twin's funeral. She hadn't trusted her not to attempt escape. A guard detail had been posted on their house.

Davinia introduced him as a family friend, though she didn't explain how they knew him. Nina refused to play the game and ask for details, force her mother to come up with more lies. The bodyguard was aptly named Steele. No indication of whether it was a first or last name, and it was the only name offered. A tall, formidable-looking bloke with military short hair and cool grey eyes, Steele said little or nothing. Except for her mother asking periodically if he needed tea or a sandwich, the rest of the family moved around him as if he was a necessary but somewhat hazardous piece of furniture. He had only one purpose, and nothing distracted him from it. The way his eyes tracked Nina told her what it was.

In comparison, Davinia studiously avoided direct eye contact with her daughter. "Nina, I let you sleep in late," she said with forced cheerfulness. "Knew you could use it. Your breakfast is on the covered plate on the stove if you want it."

Nina crossed to the kitchen, poured herself a glass of juice. Ignoring the table where her father was sitting, finishing his own meal, she retrieved the plate and moved into the living room, no matter her mother's rule about eating only in the kitchen. Bollocks to that. She sat down in the chair that faced Steele, and pinned him with a baleful glare.

"Is this close enough to keep you from getting a crick in your neck?" she asked. "Will you need to go into the loo with me?"

Steele's expression didn't alter. "The windows have been nailed shut in there," he said. His voice was deep and enthralling, like a stage player cast to fill the role of a Shakespearean king. "If you like, we could open the door and you could try running. I can show you how quickly I could catch you." He took a sip of his tea, handling the cup with startling delicacy, for his hands were large.

She eyed him. "What if I'm screaming and kicking as you're dragging me back?"

"Your father and mother will reassure the neighbors you're having a hysterical episode, due to your sister's loss and your lingering wartime trauma. I'm the doctor handling your treatment and medication." He lifted one of the biscuits. "Your mother is an excellent baker."

His matter-of-fact, non-empathetic answers and behavior were oddly more appealing to her right now than her parents' incomprehensible mix of professed parental love and cruel resolve. She considered that as she buttered her toast. Belying her outward calm, she fumbled the utensil and smeared the upholstery with an oily streak. The knife tumbled into the crack between the cushions. As she retrieved it, it left more stains. Maybe they'd leave a permanent reminder for her parents of the daughter they'd forced into indentured servitude.

Steady. Her hand had clenched the knife, making it quiver. She saw Steele's gaze on it as she eased her grip, set the toast aside. She was hungry, but had no energy for eating.

"So it bothers you not at all that you're taking a woman against her will into a life she doesn't want, didn't ask to have?" she asked politely.

"We can't always choose the path our life takes. We can only determine how to live within those boundaries. Correct?"

She stared at him. He met her attention with a frank expression that said the things she'd experienced, endured, were things he could match with his own experiences. He offered a glimpse of that with his next words.

"I'm a hundred and sixty-seven years old. I became my Mistress's fully marked servant at twenty-five years old, when I was part of a pirate crew. Ship got caught in a storm, dashed to pieces on the rocks."

"A pirate? That's something the boys would love to hear about," her father said. "They'll be here for dinner."

Steele's eyes flicked toward him. "This conversation is between your daughter and me."

While his tone was cordial, the coolness in his gaze was unmistakable. Her father cleared his throat. "Of course. My apologies. Sir."

"It's not sir. Just Steele." He returned his focus to Nina. "I washed up, half drowned, on the shore of the island where my Mistress lived. She brought me into her household, took a liking to me, made me hers. I consented. It was the last choice I had the right to make without her leave. Regrettable but necessary, it's one you're not being given. Not exactly."

Steele set aside his tea. In a move too swift for her to follow, he drew a knife from his coat. Wickedly sharp, the curved blade reflected her mother's curio cabinet behind her.

Nina sensed her parents freezing in the kitchen, but Steele ignored them. She might have been the only other person in the house with him. He placed the blade between them.

"You can kill yourself," he said. "Finish the job you're doing on that chair with blood as well as butter. It's the only way out. The only answer the InhServ program respects and honors, for it removes the question of your family's loyalty."

He wasn't goading her. He was serious. Chillingly so, because she realized it was one of the options she was legitimately contemplating.

"I expect they could kill me themselves to do that. What percentage takes either course?" she asked, her voice absurdly steady.

"Because most are raised from the age of six to be offered to the vampire world, we rarely have an initiate that chooses that route," he said. "They already understand the nuances, the honor, the never-ending wonder of being part of the vampire world. Of serving creatures who are of the fantastic dimension, like our imaginings of unicorns or dragons, but far darker, more demanding."

She would have scoffed at the romanticizing, but his tone was flat, as if he'd simply told her flowers died in winter.

He leaned forward, his gaze clasping Nina's. His breath smelled like tea and the vanilla and brown sugar from the biscuits. The man himself had an appealing aftershave scent, interspersed with another aroma she would later realize was the scent left by a woman's frequent touch upon him.

"You will discover things about yourself, about what you want and need. Who you are, at the most primitive levels of your stripped, exposed soul. A clarity you will never find in their world." He tipped his head toward her parents, her brother. "You think they are pushing you out of their world. But in truth, from here forward, they have no place in yours."

She swallowed. Her hands had closed on the chair arms. Steele cocked his head. "As far as having your family take your life, I expect you wouldn't put that on them. You seem the type who shoulders what must be done and gets on with it."

He extended his palm. "Your right hand," he said, in that same courteous but not-to-be-denied tone.

When she lifted hers and placed it in his grasp, he picked up his napkin in his other hand and wiped her palm, lightly holding her wrist to keep her steady. His grip was heated, smooth, and though she sensed it wasn't his intention, there was a caressing feel to his fingertips, as if he was used to every incidental touch with a woman being a sensual exchange. "The butter," he said.

She almost smiled, but the pain of it was too much. Fortunately, he kept talking.

"It's a clarity that admittedly, most do not desire. But you're different. Lord Alistair met you, didn't he?"

It was an unexpected question, one that took her off guard. "Yes." *Lord* Alistair? That certainly fit.

Steele grunted. "I expect that's what he saw, and why he still wants you, despite how little training you will have. But even your intended Master cannot interfere with this choice."

Another move, smooth and unseen, like a flit of air across her face. Now the knife was against her throat, angled over her carotid. She heard her mother's gasp, her father's noise as if quieting her, though it had an uncertainty to it, as if he'd wanted to protest as well. But then they were silent.

Steele brought her other hand up, molded it over his on the knife handle. His touch was warm, strong, reminding her too much of Alistair. It was an intimate pose, their two faces inches apart. "If you tighten your grasp and start to pull, hard enough to prove your commitment to it, I'll make sure it's done quick and painlessly."

He would do it. He wasn't trying to scare her into good behavior. In their mad, mad world, suicide was an honorable and acceptable way of resolving such a conflict.

"Will my brother Jim have to become an InhServ if I do it?" Her voice vibrated against the blade. She felt no fear. She felt...nothing.

He shook his head. "Informed suicide breaks the contract with your family for all time. Your sacrifice assures the Council that they can be trusted with the secrets of the vampire world. That, and their history of service, permits them to live without the binding upon them any longer, as long as they do not reveal it to future generations."

"No. Nina." Now her father did speak, urgent. "It is something we gladly embraced. We have no desire to be free of it. Do not do this for us."

"I know that," she said, leaving her gaze on Steele. His grey eyes flickered. "The decision is mine. For me and me alone."

"On the threshold of the training is the only time the choice is allowed," Steele added. "An InhServ trainee who kills her or himself once the training is begun dishonors the family irrevocably. Everything is taken from them, and all debts must be repaid. In some cases, depending on the circumstances, their lives can be forfeit."

She tightened her jaw. Human nature was to cling to and fight for life, as long as it was possible to draw breath. But she'd had more than one man in her ward with his body so broken as to be useless. Facing a lifetime of being cared for like an infant, with not even enough motor control to take his own life. During the long hours of a graveyard shift, one had begged her softly to do it. The man in the bed next to his mate had heard it, but when she looked toward him, she saw no protest in him, just a fixed, steady understanding. There was some of that in Steele's gaze now.

Was she at that point? Did she really consider her fate as bad as a man who had no feeling below the neck?

It would make me very unhappy to hear that something bad happened to you...

It had been wartime, where emotions ran as deep as they were fast, most not surviving in a world not bathed in blood. She would not make the decision based on what Alistair might or might not feel for her. He would own her, she reminded herself. He would not be her husband, nor her lover. Not in the way she imagined.

Your sister will be my Inherited Servant, Nina. Not my wife. She'll serve me in many ways, but she does not expect, nor would she ever demand, that my attentions belong only to her.

But he might give her a way out that no one else could, she reminded herself. It was a slim hope, but surely a slim hope was better than a decision that couldn't be undone.

"Did you ever regret your choice?" she asked. Her voice was thick.

Steele's gaze softened a few degrees. "Quite a few times. But not anymore. I'd rather be at The Mistress's side...*my* Mistress's side, than anywhere else. Even at the helm of my ship, plowing through the waves on a fair day, a bright sun on my face. Take your chances, lass," he said quietly. "Death is the only certainty in life, and it leaves you no choices at all."

Nina thought of the pose they were in. Steele leaned over her, his knee pressed into the side of the chair, one hand holding the knife, the other on the side of her neck and shoulder, steadying her. Their faces inches apart. Yet they spoke as if they were sitting at the table, having tea.

"I can never marry or have children like a normal human," she said. What he'd said, about her parents having no place in her world, it made sense in this moment. She wasn't even aware of them. Only him. "No home and family. And if I can't be a nurse, I can't be who I am."

"We never stop being who we are," he said. "We just discover a far different scope to the definition."

Her fingers tightened over his, and she felt the edge of the blade. He was right; it was very sharp. When he drew it across her artery, she'd barely feel the cut. Just a sting, and her blood rushing from her. She thought of her blood, how it had fed Alistair.

In the days when the Japanese were closing in, more than one soldier had steadfastly asserted he would do the nurses the kindness of shooting them before letting the Japanese take them. For the most part, the women's response had been, "Thanks, but if it's the same to you, I'll take my chances, see how it all turns out."

Would those who suffered three years in the internment camps, died there, feel that way if they could do the choice over? Or those who'd walked into the water with her at Bangka?

That was the rub, wasn't it? You had to take your chances and never give up on life, the thought that it might go better, in unexpected ways. If not now, or even in the next year or two, maybe a few years in the future. She'd have three hundred years to find out.

The alternative was it could be three hundred years of sheer hell, worse than anything she'd faced. And she'd thought nothing could be worse than that.

Her eyes shut tight. The motion made her fingers constrict even more, but she'd moved them to his wrist, was holding it. After a long moment, he lowered the blade, bringing their tangled hands down to her lap. He extricated the weapon and himself from her and returned to his chair. After he reclaimed his tea, she lifted her head. He lifted the cup in a silent salute.

She'd made her decision.

～

The funeral was held just past sunset, an odd time for it, unless one knew the deceased was honoring the vampire world to which she'd been bound. It didn't matter. Alistair didn't come. Though no one had told her he intended to be there, she'd expected it to the point Nina hadn't thought to ask.

His absence offended her, deeply. Her sister had given so much to be everything he wanted her to be. She was equally angry at herself, for wanting him there for her own reasons, to see if the male who'd cared for and supported her in a war zone could ease any of her terrible loneliness in this most desolate moment.

When it started to rain, she didn't move to stand closer to her family, though her father and brother opened umbrellas to shelter their mother. Nina shifted away, stood apart.

Only later did she realize she wasn't drenched because Steele had moved close enough to shelter her with a large umbrella he'd brought with him. He didn't touch her, but his big body was close enough to give her heat.

When the service was over, she moved forward and put her hand on Sher's coffin, her forehead to it. She almost broke then, but when her mother's hand touched her back, she snapped up straight, moved away. Walked toward the car Steele had brought, which had her one suitcase in the back.

She asked him in a wooden voice to retrieve it, let her open it.

When he did, she fished out the picture of Sher. As she walked back to the grave, she wouldn't look at it. Couldn't. She laid the picture on the top of Sher's coffin, below the spray of white and yellow flowers. She hated thinking of her sister's body in that box. She would forever remember her in those moments before the crash, the wind streaming through her beautiful hair. All her hope and joy for the life she'd embraced to the fullest.

Nina lifted her gaze to the sky, as if she might see her there, dancing and twisting through the clouds.

> She comes in thru the skylight
> for the door is not allowed
> Her eyes are bright as little stars
> Her dress is like a cloud.

"I don't know what to do, Sher," she whispered. "Help me."

But she was too practical to believe in that hollow thought. Sher couldn't help her now. No one could. She had always relied on herself to find the solutions to her problems. The only one she could trust now was the person she couldn't bear to look at in a mirror.

Pivoting, she returned to the car, let Steele shut her in away from the rain and her family, and drive her away.

CHAPTER SEVEN

*I*t took a few hours to reach the school, and Nina stared out the window blindly through most of it, not caring to know where it was. Based on the things Sher had said, Nina had initially been surprised that a school for elite vampire servants was based in Australia. But apparently that was the point. To train them in a more isolated setting, far from the distractions that the European vampires could pose.

She thought it was more than that, but Sher hadn't known or asked. Until now, it wouldn't have mattered to Nina, either. She supposed she should be grateful she wasn't being taken out of the country, but it might as well be the Antarctic, really. She couldn't even bring herself to ask how long she would be at the school, or when she'd be given to Alistair. All she could see was the rain falling on Sher's coffin, the drops pattering and rolling away, becoming part of the earth again.

She broke out of her self-imposed trance when they were passing through a gate. Steele decelerated on the winding road flanked by thick forest. When it opened up, she was looking at an estate with a circular drive around a terracotta fountain. Old trees canopied and framed the drive and doorway. It looked like what it was, essentially. An exclusive private school.

Steele took her down thickly carpeted hallways with elegant light fixtures, pictures and woodwork, until he reached the dormitories, twelve rooms on a grid of three hallways. Her room was a suite that held four, and three of the beds were occupied by other young women.

Nina ignored them. She folded herself onto her bed, turning to the wall, too exhausted by it all to engage or even undress. She didn't tune into Steele's murmurings to them, but whatever he said had them leaving her blissfully alone.

Maybe they'd leave her alone forever.

She fell into a fitful, anxious slumber that was nevertheless deep, dragging her down like a current into a cold, cruel ocean. When the nightmare woke her, she was thankfully alone, no one to witness her distress or hear her suppressed cries. It was mid-morning, but no one had come to wake her. Shrugging that off as irrelevant, she fell back asleep again.

When she next woke, it was late afternoon. She couldn't remember the last time she'd slept so long, and yet she just wanted to keep sleeping. She was still alone, though someone had left her a light breakfast on her nightstand and a note that Steele would deliver her to The Mistress at sunset. A blanket had been spread over her. She vaguely remembered one of her roommates doing it. With her mind less fogged, she remembered the girl, a buxom redhead who'd introduced herself as Melanie, looked barely out of school. Nina wasn't much older, not really, but a chasm of experience put decades between them.

In Singapore, she'd learned it was the familiar rituals that could help her keep her sanity, her control, in the face of the uncontrollable insanity of wartime. So she forced herself to rise, washed up, combed her hair, brushed her teeth. Found a neat outfit of skirt and blouse, tidy canvas shoes. She perched on the edge of her bed and stared into space, and that was how Steele found her.

Whatever he saw in her face caused a flicker of something between surprise and concern on his own, but he nodded. "Good evening, Nina. The Mistress will meet with you now. Follow me."

She could be quite mad at this point, but she found herself appreciating the man's manner more and more. He didn't ask her pointless, absurd questions like "How are you going?" and "Did you sleep well?"

She followed him through wide hallways, registering more details this time. Cherry-colored wood, gleaming glass and gold metal from the fixtures. An aroma like vanilla candle wax touched her nose and she realized the wall sconces were candlelit, while the elaborate chandeliers above were electric. The carpet was dark blue bordered with gold.

Apparently, the dorms were quiet because all their occupants were here. Everyone seemed busy, young men and women coming or going from tasks happening behind the array of ornate wooden doors. A comfortable chatter was happening behind most, some quick snippets of laughter. Except for the presence of the men, it reminded her somewhat of nursing school, but she refused the trap of false comfort.

Ages ranged from mid-teens to early twenties, though she occasionally saw a younger student. The first time Sher had been away from home for InhServ training was a weekend thing when she was twelve. Through one open door, Nina saw a girl about that age sink to her knees, touch her forehead to the floor and then straighten, waiting for critique. She had glossy dark hair that reminded Nina of Sher, but when she lifted her chin and gazed forward, her eyes were green and long-lashed.

An older girl circled her with a critical eye. Placing an elegant, well-manicured hand on the younger one's back, she guided her to straighten her spine further.

"Now bend," she advised. "Don't curl the spine. And remember, you keep your eyes lowered unless ordered to raise them."

The young girl bent forward again, this time the spine remaining level as a plank. As she put her forehead to the floor, her hips lifted off her heels. She held there, without an obvious quiver of effort, before the older girl nodded her approval and ordered her to sit back, lift her gaze. The younger girl beamed at the senior one's smile of approval. Subservient and yet radiating pride, confidence, in that service. Again, it reminded Nina of Sher.

Gymnastics and dance had been requirements of Sher's training. Nina could see how flexibility would come in handy for that bowing maneuver. Top physical condition was required by InhServ protocols... and the sexual demands of the role.

The thought sent a hard shudder through Nina from gut to knees. Only stubbornness kept her from stumbling under the curious glances she saw directed her way. She probably looked like someone's granny in this fresh-faced group.

If protocol demanded she kneel and bow like that, she was already going to be a disappointment. But maybe that wasn't a bad thing. Maybe if she failed so miserably this month it was obvious she couldn't be servant material, she'd become the exception they'd let off the hook, without requiring either ritual suicide or another member of her family to take her place.

Slim hope, she was sure. But slim was all she had, to the point it almost counted as none.

Steele stopped before a double pair of doors with polished gold latches. As he opened one, he gestured her forward and spoke in his deep smooth voice. "Do not speak until you are given permission."

Nina remembered the way the little girl had lifted her chin. She lifted her own and stepped inside, off of the blue carpet onto polished wood. She'd tended boys in so much pain they gave over and screamed. She'd given comfort to those on death's bleak door who cried for their mothers. All nurses knew it was the refuge most often sought by the despairing. Thoughts of mother and home. The safety of the womb, of unconditional love, protection from life's horrors.

She viciously blocked the image of her own mother, but bolstered herself with the thought that nothing she faced in this room would be worse than what those boys had endured. Nothing.

The room had heavy gold curtains, an elegant tea service on the center table, and a scattered arrangement of embroidered love seats and chairs. Several of them were grouped before a fireplace with a wrought iron screen that looked like metal lace.

The Mistress stood beside the fireplace. Nina had envisioned a formidable drill sergeant, a sturdy, block-bodied nurse matron. But The Mistress was a vampire, so Nina should have known she would be stunningly beautiful.

Not in that delicate way that encouraged a man's protective instincts. At least if he kept his wits about him enough to take a second look, and Nina expected that number was few. The Mistress had caramel-colored hair that gleamed in the firelight, the strands swept up in a loose style. Her eyes were dark amber with a striking dark ring around the irises. She possessed movie star classic cheekbones and figure, as well as a bow mouth. But the set of that lush mouth, as well as the intensity of her gaze, warned of a ruthless nature.

But that ruthlessness was part of the charisma that captured Nina's attention, a sexual energy impossible to ignore. Though it had nothing to do with her clothing, that enhanced it. The Mistress wore tight black riding pants, shiny boots and a white corset that lifted generous breasts and highlighted a tiny waist, the flare of her hips. A necklace of black glittering stones with an opal pendant graced her cleavage.

A poignant opera piece was playing, the woman's voice a wordless appeal to the heart, to lost dreams and disappointments. Nina immediately wanted it turned off, because it made her throat tighten and warned her just how precarious her control was.

Steele had left her side to go to his Mistress's. He bowed his head before he stepped close to her, facing the fireplace so the two of them were shoulder to shoulder, The Mistress looking at Nina as he dipped his head and spoke in her ear.

Steele brushed his lips against her temple. A slight smile crossed The Mistress's mouth, a fleeting thing, gone in a blink as she stepped forward, dismissing him. Steele moved to a corner and took up sentry duty there, motionless, watching.

As the female circled her slowly, Nina had never felt so thoroughly appraised—and found wanting. Her back stiffened, her jaw tightening.

The Mistress stopped her circling, as if noting it. Nina's gaze flicked to her, an automatic response, and the amber eyes glittered. "Eyes down, girl. You never meet a vampire's gaze unless given leave to do so. Your first lesson. Your second is that you will only be told something once. The first time you forget, you are punished. Typically that punishment escalates with every repeat infraction, but we have no time to initiate you slowly."

Her voice was the sensual purr that Nina would expect, but it had a terrifyingly cold quality, too.

"It is unfortunate we have only been given a month to prepare you for Lord Alistair." Nina detected an odd relishing of the title. "But we will do everything possible and more."

A month. A month to endure this before she could even hope to speak to Alistair, appeal to him for her freedom. She swallowed over the bitter pill of it, as The Mistress continued.

"Much will depend on your intelligence, strength and courage. You've been a nurse on the front line, so you have ample amounts of

all of those, and don't insult me or waste your own energy by
pretending otherwise. You will sleep and eat when you are told to do
so, to ensure you are at full strength and alertness to absorb your
lessons."

"I can't be what Sher was. I can't be what I'm not."

"And you do not speak unless you are given permission to do so."
The Mistress tilted her head, the firelight sending a reflected shard of
light along the lock of hair nearest her high, flat cheekbone. "Did you
tell her that, Steele?"

"As we entered the room, Mistress."

"I don't want to waste anyone's time," Nina said. "I can't—"

Crack!

Her mother's slaps had been quick, painless discipline for childhood infractions. She'd been hit in the face by a struggling soldier,
nothing intentional, the poor lad thrashing from fever. The force and
sting of this was targeted and deliberate, so strong that the impact
jerked her head down, pressed her cheek to her shoulder.

"Don't put your hand to your face," The Mistress snapped, keeping
Nina's hand at her side with the vehemence of the command. "If a
vampire has punished you, you do nothing to comfort or protect yourself. You stay in the position you're in until he commands you otherwise. Now lift your head, but keep your eyes down."

Nina managed to comply, blinking back hated tears she hadn't
summoned. She hated this woman. Hated Steele. Hated all of them.

"You will not have to be what you're not," The Mistress said,
surprising her by answering Nina's declaration. "Whether you have
embraced it or not, it's in your family's blood. InhServ families are
chosen very carefully, and more than the first born is watched, in case
a situation exactly like this one happens. You were a nurse because
you have a deep need to serve, to anticipate, to fix and care. With
your new Master, those skills will repurpose themselves. You will
begin to anticipate his needs more quickly than you realize.

"But for now, you are ruled by one directive alone. Whatever he
tells you, whatever he expects from you, that is what you do. Until you
are in his service, I and any of the staff here, represents him. We are
your practice ground, and we will train you, drill you, until that natural
part of you manifests fully."

Nina's face was throbbing. She had never been hit that way by anyone. Treated this way. The Mistress was apathetic to her feelings. The same way her parents had been, only The Mistress had no emotions to confuse Nina the way her parents had. But The Mistress's blow had brought it all to the surface. Nina wanted The Mistress to hit her again. The pain was a detonator, and she was fast moving to an explosive point she was savagely eager to embrace.

"You only have one question to answer every day, every moment of your service." The Mistress was reiterating the point. "'What will please him?'"

What will please him. *Because nothing about my life matters anymore.* Fucking, bloody nothing.

A hundred things leaped into her head, punctuated by internal screams of denial, angry invective. But then an icy calm stole through her. Keeping her eyes down, she sank to her knees. Not as gracefully as the girl in the hall, but Nina was strong enough to manage it without faltering. She stared at the carpet and spoke in a flat voice. If a dead woman could speak, she expected she would sound just as Nina did now.

"I don't give a shit what pleases him," she said. "I will learn what the fuck you want me to do, for my family, a family who betrayed and abandoned me. I will do it for the honor of my sister. You can beat me for talking out of turn, for bloody well meeting your eyes, for acting like an intelligent adult with my own will, but you cannot change what's in my head or heart. So let's get on with what kind of puppet act you need me to learn and I'll become the marionette you wish. But every time you strike me, I will fight back. I refuse to be beaten, by you or anyone, without a fight. Even if it means you kill me. And if not for the sake of my family, and my value of my own life, I would consider death preferable to this. So sod off, every fucking one of you."

There was a grandfather clock in the room. The prolonged silence that followed her proclamation was abruptly punctuated by the achingly familiar Westminster chimes, followed by the sonorous gong as it counted out the hour. It finished on the eight, dying away, leaving the room vibrating with tension.

She didn't look up. She was proving her point. She'd do as she was told. While she would feel whatever the hell she wanted to feel.

"Take off your clothes. Fold them up and place them on that chair, there."

She lifted her gaze enough to see that The Mistress was pointing to it. Not with her finger. With a slender, flexible cane made out of a pale wood. She must have pulled it from one of her boots. Perhaps it had been on the mantle. Or Steele had pulled it out of his arse. Nina's pulse accelerated. The Mistress was going to test her futile threat. Determine if it was a bluff.

Nina had led with her emotions. She had no idea herself if she truly meant to the soul what she said, no matter how true it felt, but she expected they were both about to find out.

She'd had to undress in a lot of circumstances more public than most women preferred, but wartime allowed little room for modesty. Though this was different, she treated it as the same. She unbuttoned her blouse, shrugged it off. Unzipped her skirt, rose to step out of it and her shoes. Folded the garments and set them in the chair, the shoes neatly aligned beneath it.

"I said undress, Nina. All of it. Gods, that is the ugliest set of underwear I've ever seen."

Nina reached back, jerky movements, and unhooked the service-able cotton bra, took it off her arms. Slid off the waist-high panties. Folded those and tucked them into the already folded outerwear.

"Bend over the chair and place your hands on the arms. Spread your feet out to shoulder width."

No. Absolutely no. When she didn't move, The Mistress's hand clamped on the back of her neck. Nina spun and shoved at her, hands curling into fists to strike. She didn't fight like a girl. Soldiers had shown her how to deliver an uppercut, a sock to the gut, a knee to the balls. Sher had taught her some of the hand-to-hand maneuvers she had learned. But those were tactics that worked against a human, not a vampire.

The Mistress seized her wrist, twisted her arm behind her back and shoved her over the chair arms with enough force to educate Nina about the chasm between human and vampire strengths. One chair arm pressed painfully into Nina's sternum, the other biting into her hips. The shove's force had tipped Nina forward so her feet left the floor.

The Mistress was between her knees. Struggling shot fire through

Nina's shoulder as The Mistress hiked the arm up her back, bending it at an angle sure to break bone if she kept it up. It put a hard stop on Nina's movements.

"Your resolve is noted," the female said. "But you were making assumptions. Another rule broken. You assume nothing with your vampire, except in anticipation of his desires and needs. You thought I was intending to beat you, so you had to deliver on your threat. I will beat you for that, but I will enjoy my examination of you first."

Nina was decisively pinned. A protest escaped her lips as the woman used her free hand to run her fingertips along the small of Nina's back, over her buttock. Then between her open legs.

Nina snarled. The Mistress only laughed, that sultry sound. Her touch glided over Nina's sex, the petals and that bud of nerves above them. So lightly, lightly, like a feather stroking. A very unwelcome tendril of response unfurled, a feeling that oddly increased as Nina tried to struggle again.

Steele must have brought his Mistress restraints, because she bound Nina's arms, forearms folded over one another in the middle of her back. Then she lifted Nina like a child to place her knees on the chair seat and her upper body facing the back of the chair. When she grasped Nina's hair, twisted a rope around it and attached it to the boxed part of her arms, it arched her so the front point of her rib cage was pressed against the chair back. Nina was staring at the ceiling, effectively prevented from seeing what The Mistress was doing.

She roped Nina's knees to the chair arms, which spread them wide. She didn't rush. She seemed to relish the process of binding Nina, caressing her flesh, gripping a curve, teasing and probing between her legs, playing against an upwardly jutting nipple with her knuckles.

Nina's breath sobbed in her throat, her body quivering. She wanted all her movements to convey protest, but what terrified her was that her loss of control was more than physical. The Mistress was doing something that was confusing her mind as well as her body. The rage was still there, glorious and strong, but a terrifying helplessness was intertwined with it, as The Mistress did exactly what she'd threatened. Making Nina's body react with desire and pulling her mind and will into it.

"Steele."

The man moved from the corner. Bracing his hands on either side of Nina's displayed breasts, he held the chair steady to prevent Nina or his Mistress from overbalancing it. He was close enough Nina's chin brushed his chest, and she was looking up into his face. When he glanced down at her, his gaze was inscrutable as always. She had a mad thought that The Mistress had conjured him from a statue. Something that stood in the shadows of a garden overgrown with nightshade and tangled vines, a being covered in grey stone until she touched him and the façade cracked, bringing his body to life while the still implacability of a statue remained his core, his soul. But his knuckles, pressed against her shoulders, were infused with heat.

"No." Nina's protest was ignored as The Mistress covered her eyes. She was in darkness, but it wasn't merely a blindfold. It was a hood that covered her head, laced on the sides so it molded to her face like a second skin. A breathable fabric at least, but she couldn't see, and her mouth was covered.

"It is not Steele before you. It is your Master. It is Lord Alistair, watching your training, taking pleasure in your submission."

Would the man who rescued her from a beach of death take pleasure in seeing her robbed of all her choices, her will subjugated to a world and a future she hadn't chosen?

I want you begging me to let you release. Nothing in your mind but your need for that permission. If you get too close, you tighten your grip here as a reminder of whose will you serve... You know what I am, and you know I can be ruthless. I'm far scarier than anything you saw on that beach.

Some part of her knew he would take some pleasure in this. But that wasn't as horrible to her as feeling the contraction between her legs that responded to the thought. How could she convince them this wasn't what she wanted, if The Mistress's words, the images she was spinning in Nina's brain like a deft spider, had her tongue-tied and confused? Aroused, and not just physically. That was the worst of it.

She didn't want this. She didn't. But with her sight taken, and Steele's strong hands on her shoulders, his body close enough to her face she could inhale male heat, she thought of Alistair on the beach. In the caretaker's cottage.

Her on her knees between his spread ones, his hand on her throat as he drank, his fingers caressing her rabbiting pulse.

"You think you can hide in your head," The Mistress said. "You can't, Nina. There is no room for pretense. Your Master will give you three marks to bind you to him. When he does, he will have access to every room of your mind, your heart and your soul. There will be nothing you can hide from him."

Fear clutched her anew, trying to deposit her in the hands of panic. Her lips moved against the fabric, a soundless *what*, but The Mistress must have read her body language.

"You have been told of it by your sister, perhaps, but didn't believe it? Assumed it meant something figurative, that it would be 'like' he could read her mind. No, Nina. Lord Alistair gave you the first mark, the geographic locater. The second mark gives him access to your mind. He can read your every thought, and speak to you in your head. You can communicate with him without words as well."

A quick stroke of her temple, her quivering jaw. Her neck was beginning to ache, a lot, and the repetitive swallowing of her stretched throat was a strain. "It is a comfort, a reassurance. And a way to learn his needs even more quickly."

The Mistress paused, her thumb caressing Nina's lips. Nina remembered how Alistair had done that, the firmness of the touch. The Mistress knew about Alistair giving her the first mark. Had he told her how he'd touched her during their brief time together, to help The Mistress conjure him this way?

"Open your mouth. Be very still so I won't cut you."

Nina froze, but parted her lips. The quick hint of a slim blade, and The Mistress had slit the fabric of the laced mask over Nina's mouth. She adjusted it around Nina's lips so she could feel the female's touch on her mouth more directly. She realized The Mistress had taken Steele's place and stood directly over her, probably looking down into her tipped up face as she spoke.

"Then there is the third and final mark. The one that binds you to him for all eternity. This life, and every life thereafter. Whereas the second mark gives your Master access to your mind, the third leaves no room closed to him, as I said. Your heart and soul are his to explore, to dig deep into everything you are, and bring you to a depth of connection you cannot envision until you have experienced it."

Ludicrous. Impossible. No one knew what happened in the after-life. But if the other was true...never to have a thought that was truly private again, to have no part of herself she could hold only for herself, in a world she was being forced to accept...

No. She would fight and fight and fight until they knew they couldn't have that. She loved her brothers, her family, but surely they didn't understand what was being demanded of her. No one had the right to demand another's soul.

Breath harsh in her throat, she abandoned thought, rationality and led with pure passion. Hawking up as much phlegm as she could, she spat into The Mistress's face.

From the sound, she achieved a direct hit. Since her head was tipped back, she got baptized in the spray, but she didn't care. "Kill me," she demanded. "Kill me now, or I do it myself. I will never accept that, never agree to that."

She would have expected a fist in her face, or the business end of that switch at the least. She heard nothing. The Mistress had withdrawn, and Steele was back, his hands on the chair again. Had he given his Mistress a kerchief, helped to wipe her face?

"One knee, Steele," his Mistress said. She was behind Nina again.

Her next order must have been pantomimed, or, if she wasn't lying about that second mark ability, The Mistress had spoken in his mind. Steele's capable hands closed over Nina's breasts. In the next blink, his mouth was on her nipple, heated breath teasing it, tongue coming out to play. She jerked, but had nowhere to retreat. Nowhere to lessen the intensity as he traced around it with the tip of his tongue, touched it in little maddening caresses, then a full, wet circle. His mouth closed over it and he started to suckle, a pull that grew stronger as heated liquid swirled in her lower belly, her thighs. He squeezed her other breast with his opposite hand and, after a leisurely suckling of the one nipple, moved to the other.

Back and forth. Back and forth. It was the only way she was being touched, and yet as he continued doing it, Nina's whole body was being affected. She tried to hold herself apart, keep her reactions compartmentalized to sheer physical response, like eating a sandwich to assuage hunger, or drinking water to appease thirst. But then The Mistress made it worse.

"It is not Steele doing this, Nina. Is it? In your mind, it is your Master. Lord Alistair has bound you for his pleasure, and is enjoying a thorough tasting of your gorgeous breasts. Your nipples are getting hard and aching under the pull of his mouth. Your cunt is dripping. You have to swallow back the desire to beg. Not for anything specific. You simply want him to hear the pleading in your voice, because your helpless need pleases him like nothing else. His treasure. His servant."

He'd told her he wanted her to beg before she came. How many nights had she done that in the quiet of her room to get through, to get some sleep? The Mistress pushed her into that mindset with little more than a handful of words, because Nina had been bloody well practicing compliance to the idea already.

Zzzzt! A whistling through the air, and Nina bit back a shriek as the switch hit her directly between the legs. She had no way to close them, to guard herself, though her thighs pulled harder than she'd ever imagined they could, trying to do so.

"Spit in my face, will you?" The Mistress said pleasantly. "I'm going to do that once again. You will ask me for the strike, as your apology for your rudeness. If you do not, I will do it again. And again, until you deliver a proper apology. With the proper deference."

She sounded not the least bit angry, not even annoyed. Which increased Nina's terror. "I don't care if I make your tender skin bleed, Nina. Flesh heals. After your Master marks you, he could tear the flesh from your back at dinner, and you would be completely healed by dawn, so he could take you rough as he pleased. You don't have that resilience yet, but I have been doing this long enough to know just how much I can hurt you and ensure your training progresses with no delays. That will still be far more pain than you wish to bear, I promise you. So, ask."

Nina set her jaw, even though it trembled, hard. The Mistress chuckled. "A tester. Such a pleasure."

The next blow was worse. Nina's scream broke through her attempt at restraint. This time The Mistress didn't give her a pause to think about it. "Ask."

Nina shook her head, as much as her binding would allow. And screamed again. It hurt so damn much. Steele hadn't stopped what he was doing. His mouth was firm and warm on her nipples, his tongue a wet heat that helped him suck and lave, his strong teeth making tiny little nips. Despite her torment, Nina wasn't unaffected by what he was doing. The Mistress confirmed it.

"Your clitoris is so full and plump. It makes it all the more ripe for a switching. Feel that."

The Mistress's fingertips slid between her labia. When she rubbed, Nina was ashamed to realize she was collecting moisture. The female vampire held her hand close to her face, so Nina could smell her own arousal. "You see? Now, ask."

Another refusal, but Nina thought it might be the hardest thing she'd ever do, because her body was howling for her to surrender. On the heels of that scream, another sound broke from her lips, a deep groan as Steele did something different with his suckling that speared sensation straight to her core.

"He's very accomplished, isn't he? His mouth is a gift from the gods. I've kept him between my legs, servicing me for hours, and his jaw never tires."

The Mistress's tone changed, became brisk. "You cannot change your future, Nina. You can change how you feel about it. I will help you do that. Your evaluation is telling me how hard I will need to push you."

This was an evaluation? Not even the real training? Nina had a mad vision of The Mistress setting aside her switch to make some notes in a grade book. But before Nina could hope that she would get a momentary respite, that this part of things might be over, The Mistress continued.

"It appears extreme measures are needed. From this moment forward, while you are here, you will wear no clothes. You will not be allowed a blanket, nor even a napkin at meal times. Another student will wipe your mouth when needed. When you need a bathroom, you will be accompanied. You will be given no privacy, no place to hide. During daylight, our sleeping time, you will be tied to your bed, your legs and arms spread. Your roommates will be tasked with bringing you to climax through a manner other than penetration, while the other two watch."

She had to be joking. She must be. But she wasn't. Nina knew it. She shook her head, and tears clogged her throat, spilled out of her eyes, no matter how hard she tried to hold them back. She didn't know why she was trying, since she wore the hood and no one could see. Unless the tears became profuse enough to stain the fabric.

"Stop this. Please."

The Mistress stroked her head. "There it is. The side of you that will be so irresistible. Such fire, such need. You think I'm cruel, that all this is so terrible. But did your Matrons not have to push you hard at times, be seemingly cruel, to ensure you learned your lessons well enough not to endanger the lives of your patients?"

It was an unexpected comparison that put a hitch in the whirl of thoughts and denials in Nina's head. The Mistress leaned close, whispered to her again. "The life I am helping save with my cruelty is your own. And I am giving you the chance at a different life. Pain and grief, fear...if roused for the right reasons, they're all ways to cross thresholds, open your eyes to a far wider world, one that a place deep in your soul knows."

Her fingers danced over Nina's body and Nina gasped again. "Still wet, as if Steele's mouth had been between your legs all along. The body will respond to physical stimulation, Nina. But you respond to sexual dominance, even the merest suggestion of it, which means your heart and soul are involved. It is the foot in the door that will take you to the rest. You will release for me here before Steele takes you back to your room to begin your training. What's more, by the end of this month, your body will ready itself with little more than a command from my lips. If you allow yourself the gift, your fire and need will be channeled into a passion for your Master that he will learn to treasure. Though I will not have time to get you all the way there, I will get you as close as anyone can."

Nina was shaking her head, couldn't seem to stop. All of her was shaking, but The Mistress held her fast with the one hand, with the strength of her voice. Though she was blindfolded, it was as if Nina could feel the powerful lock of the woman's gaze upon her.

"My promise to prepare you in every possible way for the life of an InhServ is not just a promise to Lord Alistair or the Vampire Council. It is a promise to you as well. I will not break your mind, unless such things can break it. But I will show you what you refuse to believe is possible. That you are not *acting* as a vampire's servant. You will not be a puppet. You will *be* an InhServ, from now until the end of your life. You will honor your family, just as they wished."

I don't care. I don't understand them. They're like strangers. I want to hate them. I don't want to love them. But it seemed like she had no choice in that, either.

"Let's change this up, show you something else marvelous."

Nina tensed, anticipating another blow between her legs, but this time the switch landed against the broadest part of her arse. The strike was followed by a punishing crack with the palm of The Mistress's hand. She hit Nina's buttock in a way that made it wobble. And sent more sensation flooding between her legs. The Mistress said nothing more for a little while, merely alternating the spanking with the switch as Nina made little cries and sobs, and Steele suckled her nipples with all the leisure of a man enjoying the taste of his evening cocktail.

Her body was singing with pain, with pleasure, with arousal, with shattering emotions, and Nina couldn't command a single thought. The stimulation was cataclysmic.

Then The Mistress's voice was against her ear, her body against Nina's, so she felt the rough lacing of the corset, the pillowing of the woman's breasts against her back. The Mistress's knee was on the seat, and Steele adjusted so his weight countered them on the other side.

"I will beat you often while you are here, Nina. Whenever I desire. For that is your Master's right as well. But as you have found here tonight, with just this little taste, we can teach you to enjoy it. Pain and punishment are not always about violence and cruelty."

When The Mistress's knee pressed between Nina's open legs, she strangled on another cry. "Ride me, little rebellious one," The Mistress murmured. She flexed her leg, the muscles providing friction against Nina, and Nina couldn't stop herself from trying to move with it, to establish a rhythm. Her knees were bound, but her hips were not. As The Mistress ground against her, demanded a response Nina couldn't refuse, Nina's arse lifted and rose. Her wet cunt rubbed against the slick stuff of The Mistress's tight pants.

"Oh...oh..." Her aching neck craned back like a long-throated bird's, and The Mistress helped, tangling her fingers in the bound tail of her hair and hiking back on it further, her mouth moving to Nina's nape. Nina felt the prick of fangs.

"Such a temptation you are. Your little cunt so needy. Give me everything. It is what your Master will demand. What Alistair will be greedy to call forth from you, again and again. Say his name."

Alistair. She formed the word without sound, not willing to give The Mistress that, but it was a small victory.

She'd had little climaxes, tentative things, thanks to Alistair's direction to her. Following his command to keep the nightmares at bay.

Following his command.

Oh God, she was lost.

The screams that tore from her throat as she climaxed were more than it could bear, the rawness hurting the vocal cords. She wouldn't be able to talk tomorrow. But that might keep her out of the kind of trouble her mouth could make for her.

Or not. She had a despairing feeling that, whether she defied The Mistress or not, Nina was going to be taken down a road that would shatter every shield, remove every illusion she had that her life would ever be her own again.

They both already knew she was too strong to kill herself. She'd seen men with useless bodies who found the will to live. She couldn't justify sacrificing her life merely for pride. Even for freedom. Damn it all to bloody hell.

Steele escorted the new initiate back to her room. He supervised the other three girls as they tied Nina to the bed, made sure the far-too-quiet woman didn't try to hit them or struggle. Fortunately, she didn't. She was mentally exhausted, which helped, but there was a wooden-ness to her features that made him advise the three to keep a very close eye on her. He gave them his Mistress's interim instructions, commanded Chele to give Nina's back, neck and shoulders a thorough massage, and then returned to the drawing room.

He knew Nina had been given her first taste of The Mistress's implacability. She was soon going to learn what every initiate did. The most ruthless thing about The Mistress wasn't that the female knew exactly what buttons to push. It was that she had no compunction about stabbing them repeatedly, and with the joyous abandon of a manic toddler. Except she did it for carefully calculated reasons and purposes that would eventually make sense, and prepare them in ways they'd never imagined were vitally necessary.

It was a tougher journey for some than others. It was going to be particularly rough for Nina, and he had mixed feelings about that.

When he returned to his lady, she was sitting by the fire. She'd changed out of what she called her training uniform, and now wore slacks and a blouse. Her hair was down, but she'd pulled it back into a loose tail to do paperwork at her desk. Her head lifted as he entered. He'd shown her Nina's state in his mind, but added to it now.

"She'll sleep. Until they wake her and continue her training regimen."

"Tell them to spread the word to the rest," The Mistress said. "Everyone is going to help with and reinforce her training. Keep her room warm so that she is not cold."

"Mistress?"

"It was one of the three stipulations Lord Alistair had. First, that we not take her virginity, an entirely unwise decision on his part, but his right to require." She shrugged. "Second, that no male brings her to climax. The third was that she not be cold."

"Mmm." Steele took off his coat. Removed the two knives, one stake and pistol he carried beneath and within it. Then he unbuttoned his shirt and shrugged out of it, unfastening the cuffs with the shirt gathered at his elbows, his shoulders and upper body bare. She paused to watch, her gaze becoming molten like the flames dancing in the fireplace. Heat licked over his flesh wherever she looked, as if he could already feel the taste of her mouth, the prick of her fangs.

When he was only in his slacks, his feet bare, he knelt at her side. She absently ran her fingers through his dark hair, returning her attention to what was on her desk. He glanced at the paperwork, showed her the error in his head. A light smile touched her face and she made the correction.

"I have no idea why I do this and don't let you handle all the books. I hate maths."

"Because you refuse to let anything defeat you, my lady. Even if the fight is already lost."

That drew her attention. As she rotated her chair toward him, he sat back on his heels. She propped her foot against his shoulder. She wore short heels now, but they were the toothpick kind that could dig into a man's shoulder joint, command his attention, if she went that route. Right now, though, she didn't. They regarded one another silently.

"I advised Alistair that her brother would have been a better choice," she said at last. "He need only make the request to Council. The circumstances would not reflect poorly on him, at least in this instance. He refused. He wants the nurse."

Steele nodded. "She's not a suicide risk."

"No. She's not. She's a fighter. He needs a fighter." The Mistress tapped her pen on the ledger. "Lord Alistair is the first made vampire to ascend to Region Master. We will do whatever is necessary to ensure his servant does not appear like a defective graduate, assigned to him as an insult by the Council members who oppose his ascension."

It was important to her, he knew. She was a made vampire and knew well the political obstacles in their world, where born vampires had held all the power for centuries. It wasn't entirely unmerited. Made vampires were often plagued by impulse control problems. Most didn't come close to matching the talents and strengths that born vampires could achieve at the same ages.

But some did. Like the woman sitting before him. Yet she had been passed over for the overlordship in her own territory. It had been given to a born vampire who didn't have half her intelligence. That vampire, recognizing her as his greatest rival, had maneuvered her into this position. The training of InhServs required vampire oversight, and the Council had awarded her the appointment.

The overlord had intended it to be a not-so-underhanded insult to her. Instead, she'd approached it the way she'd approached everything for the past couple centuries. Taken the challenge and excelled at it, such that she had the Council's esteem and support.

Yet, ironically, now she might never be considered for an overlordship, because she was so damn good at this. Though he knew how she felt about many things, Steele didn't know how she felt about that.

What he did know was vampires were patient.

She was following his thoughts, for her eyes glittered with a hard amusement, then her mouth softened in a curve as she leaned forward, cupped his jaw. He turned his face toward her palm, and she dropped her forehead to his, a brief affection, before she straightened and leaned back in her chair once more.

"She must learn," she said. "Or whatever she experiences at our hands will seem kind in comparison. Lord Alistair will be tested by those in the born vampire world who think he has overstepped himself, which means his servant will be tested. She must be able to bear much. It's a fine line for us to walk in her training, between being too harsh and too unclear. She must understand. Be able to use her mind for him, not against him. Compliant but not broken."

"She's close to breaking now."

"No." His Mistress opened her mind to him, replayed the image of Nina grabbing her wrist, right before she'd put the girl on her knees. He saw the rage in Nina's eyes, the set of her mouth. The twist of it when she spat in The Mistress's face. "As I said, she's a fighter. She has seen how horrible the world is, and has been hit close to home, with the loss of her sister. Yet she responds not with tears or pleas, but with a fighting rage. That is not a spirit that breaks."

She sobered. "But we will have to take her perilously close to destruction to help her understand. She has channeled her natural submission into professional service, and has not recognized it has a deeper, far more complicated side. During their brief meeting, Lord Alistair indicated she showed great promise, in terms of unlocking that potential. So, we will help with that process."

"Did he discuss the details of that meeting? The circumstances that brought them together?"

"He said it was during the war, when he was in Singapore. He was unwilling to tell me more. He said it wasn't necessary for me to have that information." The Mistress lifted a shoulder, a brief sign of irritation that translated to sarcasm. "Because obviously, of the two of us, he would have a far better grasp of what is relevant to her training."

"Good to see he's already cultivating a Region Master's sense of superiority. That's half the job description, at least."

He made her chuckle, as he'd hoped. She rocked her foot against his shoulder, digging in the heel enough to have him bracing against her, his gaze lifting to her in glittering challenge. Her lips curved.

"He doesn't need a title for that. A vampire male, born or made, bleeds pure arrogance. Yet truthfully, he spoke with great seriousness. I believe he would have given me anything he thought would have helped with her training. It is regrettable that we only have a month, but it was the only extension the Council would grant for her delivery to him, since he prolonged bringing her sister into his household for so long. So we proceed with what we have.

"But now, it's getting close to dawn. Time to put away the work for another day." She lowered her foot and rose, stepping away from her desk. As she did, she beckoned to him to rise. He had difficulty not closing the distance between them, but he stepped around the desk and waited on her. She liked tormenting him, unbuttoning her blouse, a mirror of how he'd taken off his own shirt, letting the silk fall from her shoulders as she undid the cuffs. She let it flutter to the floor and pivoted, her back to him as she untied her hair so it tumbled against bare flesh, the slim straps of her bra. She shot him a teasing look over her shoulder as she pivoted toward him slowly, straightening her arms out to her sides.

"It is much easier for me," she said, "because I have no weapons to discard."

"Your weapons are not the kind you remove, Mistress. They're far more lethal than anything I could ever carry."

She said nothing to that, but he felt how she responded to his sincerity, to the need rising fast in him for her. The emotions woven into the bond between them had grown over the decades, ever since a nearly-drowned pirate had washed up on an island on a moonlit night and looked up to see a bare-footed woman standing over him. One with a gaze that pierced him to the soul to this day, and made him willing to do anything for her.

She closed the distance between them at last, sliding her hands up his arms, his chest, over his shoulders to curve her fingertips at his nape, scrape his flesh. She lifted onto her toes, slow, so slow. He knew what she demanded and stayed still, his heart thundering and cock getting even harder as she leaned into him, denied him the right to touch her, to initiate the kiss, even as her lips hovered so close to his. He stared into her eyes. She wouldn't let him detach. During those first few decades she'd taught him that distraction wasn't permitted. He must steep himself in her, let himself think of everything he wanted to do to her, and yet stay so still. Every atom of his being responded to her, even as he was forbidden to be responsive.

Her "casual" attire had only made it worse. He loved her corsets and provocative clothes, but when she wore her blouses and slacks, things any woman of taste might wear in her home, or when she went out into the world to do mundane things, he desired her even more.

Both faces were hers. But this was the one that was more likely to accept the gift of his heart he always freely offered, in open hands and in his willing surrender to her ownership.

He bit back a groan as she palmed him through his slacks, her lips parting. Wet. "My servant loves watching me play with the girls. You're still hard. And even more impressive than usual."

The Mistress finally brought their mouths together, her hand tightening on his nape and his cock. He restrained his own passion as she'd trained him to do, but she'd know just how powerfully the beast inside him was straining against its leash. With one word, he would have her down on her back, and would rut between her legs like the untamed stallion he could be...at her command.

The power of it was always intoxicating, especially when she felt his impatience, and gave him a reward anyway. "Put your hands on my hips."

He did, sliding over the curves, fingers constricting on soft flesh, thumbs pressed into her hip bones.

"Our little morsel has given me an overwhelming need," she murmured. "I will ride you hard until dawn, Steele. Show you no mercy. You will need to live up to your name."

"I would never do less for you, my lady."

"I know. And it makes my dreams all the sweeter, with every sunrise."

CHAPTER EIGHT

*T*he past month had been the most intense non-wartime experience of Nina's life. Which alternately dismayed and terrified her. Because all of her roommates had been in InhServ training for at least a decade. Sher had been in it for just over twenty. Which meant that Nina's month didn't even qualify as the basics.

She was as prepared to be an InhServ as a six-year-old was to be a nurse, merely because she pretended to be one with her dolls. Not that Nina was supposed to care about being prepared.

Throughout the past few weeks, she'd fought, she'd pleaded. She'd made logical arguments, over and over. Her lack of suitability would not be pleasing to her vampire "master." She'd made herself say the words without invective, mostly.

It wasn't enough, as one of her three roommates told her. "When you say 'Master,' it's said with a capital M," Melanie said. "You don't say it that way."

How the bloody fucking hell did you "say" something in capital letters? Though Nina knew what she meant. Melanie gave her a look that said she knew she knew it too, then proceeded on with another lesson full of things Nina didn't want to know, things she didn't want to hear.

Bloody fucking hell.

She'd had one blessing. No nightmares. For one thing, she was too exhausted. For another, about the time she'd fall into the type of sleep that would bring the shadows, she'd instead have a dream about Alistair, his mouth between her legs, his strong hands curling around her wrists. She would wake to find it was the mouth of one of her roommates, or another trainee.

They left no part of her unexplored with tongue, fingers, objects that plugged into the wall and vibrated against her body, making her climax with shameless abandon. Multiple times during the daylight hours.

After those first couple days, the actual restraints were replaced by slim, decorative things she was capable of breaking, but if she did, the punishments, the torments that could be inflicted through pleasure, taught her obedience.

If the Master tied you up with a piece of thread, no matter what he did to you, you would not break the restraint, because it is his pleasure to bind you, his will alone that releases you.

But her roommates didn't rely only on physical tactics. As they caressed, stroked and teased Nina, they looked at her adoringly, whispered praises as Nina became more and more aroused. In short, they never let it be only about the sex. That was the worst thing of all.

The trainees who brought her to climax were always female. Which left her hungering all the more for the contrasting male touch of the vampire she fantasized about.

At dusk, she would be unbound, taken to the shower and cleaned thoroughly for the upcoming night of training. That training sometimes left her bruised, her skin cut and throbbing, and not just for the reasons The Mistress had threatened. Or promised. The two ideas sometimes became interchangeable in Nina's brain.

She was surprised she was taught how to fight. How to use a gun, a knife, her fists and feet. Any handy blunt object in the room. One of the highlights of this whole miserable thing was at least once a day she combat trained directly with The Mistress. When she did, she was encouraged to unleash all her rage, her helpless frustration. Getting a chance to land one blow on that dispassionate, perfect visage had become Nina's number one wish in this hateful world.

She never did, but after those sessions, she'd expended enough emotional as well as physical energy that she could indulge the delusion, at least for a few minutes, that she'd regain enough personal control to handle the rest of the evening detached, unaffected by any of this. Then The Mistress would show her another thing she'd threatened. That there was no fortification Nina could build in her mind that she couldn't tear down.

And she wasn't even technically inside Nina's head the way Alistair would be.

The breaking down of her sexual inhibitions was part of the process. Her body was tuned like a piano when it came to desire. The whisper of fingers along any expanse of skin produced a response. It seemed her nipples were always hard, her sex wet, her knees trembling.

Her body was taught to rouse instantly. She had been schooled extensively in how to take a man in her mouth, but not by direct experience. She'd been shown it by other students. Some male and female pairings, but also two men, something that startled her at first. She knew men who preferred men existed, but she'd never had a front row seat to how they would handle one another. One particularly eye-opening classroom session had been three men, one buggering the arse of the man in the middle, while the third man knelt and took the buggered one's cock in his mouth to the hilt.

Under the skilled hands of too many sexual experts to count, with all sorts of enthusiastic visual stimuli like that, her body was completely out of her control. Which she supposed was part of the whole lesson being hammered in, again and again.

Everything is controlled by him.

Your Master.

You are his property.

Your will belongs to him.

Your cunt, your breasts, your arse, every inch of your skin, your heart, soul and mind. It is all his. Say it.

She would never say it. But she'd learned to be silent, because snarling defiance meant that they would prove the lesson to her in yet another creative way, some of them so humiliating she couldn't bear to even think about them.

Because the damn thoughts would arouse her again.

When tears were running down her face, not because of the injustice of it, but because she refused to say the words, instead wanting to scream it was all a sham, brainwashing, not real, they didn't push it past that point. Didn't make her say the words.

Too many other lessons to learn, she supposed, but it niggled at her, because it was the only battleground where they allowed her victory. And since they easily laid siege and conquered her everywhere else, it left her doubting whether it was a victory at all. More like one of those situations where someone sat in the middle of a ring of fire in a dry wheat field and insisted they weren't going to get burned.

On the more laughable side of things, The Mistress had been appalled to find out she didn't know how to set a table service for twelve, do her makeup properly, or keep the seams of her stockings straight. She learned a lot about underwear. Flimsy little garters, barely-there bras and knickers. She was given a whole new wardrobe, and not a piece of it picked out herself. Even though it allowed her to wear clothes for a few seconds, all of it made her look like some kind of exotic, sexual creature she knew she wasn't.

No matter how often they made her feel like she was.

It was too much, every day interminable, and yet, it was over far too soon. Tomorrow, she would be bundled into another car, taken to Alistair. To a terrifying and uncertain future where, no matter how they prettied it up, she would be a sex slave, a person who had lost control of not just her destiny, not merely her body, heart and soul. Her mind, too, the one thing that had always been hers to control and own, would belong to another.

She was at the end of her tether when it came to logic, or strategy or even self-preservation. She was an animal in a trap, and the madness could no longer be kept at bay.

During the day-to-day regimen, they'd been able to channel it, keep it tamped down, but the anxiety of it all coming to a head overwhelmed everything, making her feel she was about to explode. She almost feared for the safety of her young roommates.

For nearly thirty days, she'd seen The Mistress demonstrate an uncanny awareness of everything going on in the halls of her domain. Tonight was no exception. For just as Nina was on the cusp of that breaking point, a summons came. Not to The Mistress's study.

To The Mistress's private rooms.

◇

The carved stone marble fireplace, a pale golden color, provided the only light. The white area rug before it looked deep and thick as a snowfall. The random scattering of furniture created amorphous shadows beyond the fire's reach. For once, the woman wasn't armored in her corsets and tight skirts or like-a-second-skin pants. She'd recently taken a shower, for her hair was damp and she wore a soft robe that clung to her curves. She looked almost...human. Except for those amber eyes, which held all the power of the earth in them.

"Kneel, Nina."

Her knees gave automatically. They'd taught her to assume a subjugated posture upon command. Elbows, knees and forehead on the floor, knees spread shoulder width, arse in the air. Naked, as always. She'd learned to find an odd, cocooned comfort to the position, a little dark world all her own, down on the floor, no matter what else was happening above or around her.

She couldn't hide there. Couldn't hide anywhere. So she couldn't explain why the position felt reassuring, a fortress in a way nothing else was. She expected The Mistress could help her understand. If she'd just ask.

Nina didn't.

And her reaction, her instinctive obedience, brought more despair, and that squeezing anxiety and panic. She shut her eyes tight, fighting it. She could hear The Mistress moving around, brushing her hair. Smell the scent of her bath soap, her shampoo.

Then the rustle of clothing, a silence that had her lifting her head, just enough to see The Mistress's crossed legs, the robe falling away from her knees. She'd sat down in a love seat near her. Then Nina saw the graceful hand drop below the knee, open, palm up.

"Come to me, little one."

She came to her on hands and knees, expecting nothing. Just more punishment, more loss of control.

Instead, The Mistress bent and gathered her up, lifting her to sit her on her lap. She held her upper body in her arms, Nina's legs tangled in a limp sprawl across the cushions, her head on The Mistress's shoulder, sheltered by a thick curtain of the damp hair. Her fragrance should have been called Ghost, because the aroma was haunting, calling forth a jumble of memories. Home and first love, an exhilarating ride on a motorbike under a moonlit sky. She wondered if

The Mistress and Steele had ever done that. Steele driving, The Mistress's arms wound around his body from behind.

"All right, then," the woman said quietly. "Let it out."

Nina shook her head, even as she squeezed her eyes shut and a couple stingy tears found their way free. "I can't," she said brokenly. "If I do...I'll never put it back together. I won't be strong enough to do this."

An acknowledgement that she *was* strong enough to do it. Insane, what a human spirit would do to survive. Even when it shouldn't. For all she'd lost of herself, they could have everything but her grief. There was no one she could give that to now, except a woman who was dead.

In her darker more despairing moments, like this one, she doubted she could have given even Sher all of it. How could she understand what Nina had seen, felt? Or what it was like to lose the other half of herself, the other spirit within their mother's womb...

The Mistress could have pushed it. Could have cracked that part of Nina against her will. The vampire female had proven it, time and again. But tonight, she didn't. She held Nina, rocked her, as Nina brought her erratic breaths under control. She was gripping the woman's forearm, she realized. But The Mistress didn't make her stop.

The Mistress rose to her feet, lifting Nina. She cradled Nina in her arms like Alistair would have, with that same ease and comfort. Nina remembered him carrying her toward the plane. Though it was against The Mistress's bosom her cheek rested, Nina remembered the thud of his heart, the hardness of his chest.

The Mistress took her to the white rug, letting Nina stand on her own feet a few steps away from it. Then The Mistress moved onto the rug and dropped the robe off her shoulders onto a chair. As the silk slid away, it left her bare body highlighted by the flames. It was no surprise that she was as perfect beneath her clothes as she appeared in them, a firm arse, slim back, generous breasts and long legs. But a pretty flower was a pretty flower. The Mistress was more. She was moonlight, absorbed in every breath and upon every inch of skin, coaxing a woman to dance and reach for her, even if the closest touch was to trail one's fingers through silver-lit air.

Nina had moved three steps forward, unconsciously, proving the point. This woman had beaten her, spent the month teaching her how little power she had. Yet she'd given Nina that one chance, every day, to best her in a fight.

No. The chance to fight. To let out the anger so she didn't feel so pinned down, so suffocated. Tonight it hadn't been enough. But tonight The Mistress offered another way.

The female tilted her head, her chin to her shoulder, so Nina saw her in profile. "Come stand with me."

Nina did. The Mistress retrieved the robe from the chair. She threaded Nina's arms through it, slid it up on her shoulders, belted it.

It was the first time in nearly a month that she'd been allowed any clothes, other than the brief exercises in how to wear lingerie and other appropriate InhServ garb. The Mistress wrapped the sash in her hands, holding Nina fast, the silk over her knuckles. Without her heels, she was the same height as Nina, so they were eye to eye.

The Mistress dropped to one knee, startling Nina, making her tremble as she parted the robe, put her lips on Nina's thigh. Nina swayed, her body readying itself, but The Mistress's hands went back to her hips, holding her as she tipped back her head.

"Come down and play."

"I'm not...I don't prefer women." Nina's cheeks colored at the woman's laughter, not unkind, thankfully.

"If there is one thing I expect you've learned while you were with us, it's that the body doesn't care about gender. Pleasure is pleasure. But more than that," the woman's eyes sharpened, "You have felt desire because you moved past all that. You saw the shape of Chele's mouth, the softness of Melanie's eyes, savored the gasps that came from Edith when she rubbed her cunt against yours. You wanted to give her more. If your hands had been freed, you would have run your palms along her face, over her breasts. By the end of this, you wanted to offer them as much or more than they did you. You like Melanie's laugh. You gave advice to Edith about talking to her family."

She'd given up on taking out her ire on them. It wasn't their fault and truth, they were too damn much like Sher at those ages.

"They're girls," she said defensively. "Just like my nurse mates. That's all."

"But having carnal knowledge of them, that's pleasant, isn't it? Another dimension to the relationship."

The Mistress changed positions, going back onto her arse with astounding grace. Slowly, she lay down before the fire, the flickering light making love to her amazing body. The woman stretched her arms over her head, her knees slightly parted. "What would you do to this body, Nina, if I allowed you anything you wished tonight? Would you whip it? Cut it? Caress it with your mouth or hands? Would you rub your cunt over mine to make us both climax?"

"I could never hurt anyone."

"No? Didn't you try to hit me that first night? Haven't you tried to best me every day in our sparring?"

"Being in a blue is different. And there is bloody well little I could do to cause you actual harm, and we both know it. I could never plan to hurt someone. Premeditated like that."

"Even if it aroused them? What about your Master?"

Nina's brow creased. The Mistress blinked, a mysterious, exotic creature. "A servant draws strength from her Master's blood. He might offer it to her when she has been wounded. Or simply for the pleasure of giving her nourishment, of seeing her take what he offers. But perhaps he hands you a knife, offers his arm to you. He is a well-formed man, Lord Alistair. You have seen him shirtless?"

It took very little for her to remember him on the beach, the shirt stripped off. Particularly now, when her body seemed on a low sexual hum not only during every waking moment, but even in her dreams. "Yes."

The Mistress made an approving purr. "Nice biceps. He holds you close in one arm, his hand on your hip. He raises that arm, bends it, so those muscles curve, and he tells you to take the little knife he's given you, make a cut. You are perhaps shy at first, but then you do it. And though you jump a little when you cut him, and the blood comes forth, you notice the breath he draws in, the spark in his eye, is arousal. And then you put your mouth there, taste him..."

She was a nurse. The idea of tasting blood revolted her. Should have revolted her now. But the picture The Mistress painted left her with only confusion.

"You've mixed up my mind," Nina said shortly, taking a step back. "It's all brain washing."

"Did you consider your nurse schooling brain washing?"

"Of course not." Nina looked around. She wouldn't lie down by The Mistress, but sitting in a chair felt wrong. This was absurdly like a polite debate, a conversation over tea. "It was a skill to be learned," she added. "This is different."

"It's not different, Nina." The Mistress propped her head on her hand, her other hand resting on her hip, fingers trailing over her thigh. Biblical stories of Lilith came to mind. But then The Mistress's practical next words dissipated that visual, replacing it in Nina's mind with one of the Matron, a highly disturbing switch.

"Different jobs require different skill sets," the woman said. "To be adequate at them requires training. To excel at them requires more than that. How often did your intuition tell you what a suffering man needed, or had you stopping at the bed of a man who appeared as if he were fine, but you knew he needed to be checked upon, for something was amiss?" The Mistress considered her. "Based on what I have observed about you, I expect you were a nurse who exceeded expectations."

"Something I'll never get to be again." The bitterness twisted in her, had her taking another step back.

"Perhaps. But your healing talents might be employed a different way. We may think we know our future, Nina, but Fate opens some interesting paths for us. Come down here."

Nina set her jaw. "I thought I got to say what I do or don't do to you."

The Mistress's lips quirked. "Then what is it you want, little one?"

Nina's gaze slid down over the woman's mouth, her throat, her magnificent breasts. All the soft, inviting flesh. The woman had no hair between her legs, so the lips of her sex were silky-looking. They reminded Nina of the frangipani flowers her mother grew. Her sister had brought them to her when she'd taken a trip to Hawaii, and their scent always tempted Nina to bury her nose in them, take a deeper inhale.

"You haven't pleasured a woman between her legs yet, Nina." The Mistress had followed the direction of her eyes, and her long thighs widened, her fingertips sliding over one to stroke her labia, show her a hint of gathering, glistening moisture, dew on those petals. "Though many of our students have had the sweet taste of your cunt. Do you wonder what it's like? Think of how their mouths made you lose control, get lost in desire. Would you like to control me that way?"

Nina's gaze snapped up to her face. "No," the woman decided, studying her. "You wouldn't think of it as control. Your submission, your need for service, is a deep, wide river inside you. Would you like to pleasure me so thoroughly I can let go of everything, entrust myself to your care?"

Trust myself to your care. It was what her patients did, believing she could help, even if it was only with her presence, telling them they weren't alone.

"What's your name?" Nina asked. She knew The Mistress wouldn't give her that, so she continued without pause, the question only part of the explanation. "It's what I would ask my patients first," she said. "So I could connect to them when they were hurting, help take their mind off what unpleasant things the doctor was doing."

"There is no unpleasantness here, thankfully," The Mistress said. "Tonight, at least. Set aside your worries and anger, Nina. Enjoy what's being offered."

"Anything I wish?"

"Anything," The Mistress said, her eyes glowing in the firelight. "Until dawn, when I must sleep."

She lifted her arms over her head again, which lengthened her incomparable body, made the toned, smooth muscle shift, her breasts quiver. The Mistress closed her eyes, turning her face toward the heat of the fire, so the flames praised her flawless features. Nina had noticed a hint of an accent in her words at times, though not enough she'd been able to place it. Her skin wasn't British milk and cream. It reminded Nina of the cream-beige of fine beach sand, up beyond the tide line, near the dunes. Only far smoother. It complimented her satin fall of dark hair and rich-earth brown eyes.

Dropping to her heels, Nina laid a tentative hand on the female's ankle. She knew The Mistress meant what she said. For all the things that had happened while she was here, Nina had never been told a lie. Sometimes she wished they'd told her a basketful, so she didn't have to be sick with worry about what would come.

Three things in particular had topped her worry list.

Lesson One. There were no sexual barriers in the vampire-servant world. None except those set by a Master or Mistress...or a vampire more powerful than them. *If a Master or Mistress more highly ranked than your own wishes you to perform for their pleasure, your Master will accord them that honor. Proper etiquette would suggest your Master should be present, though it is not required.*

So she could just be handed off to whomever, whenever.

Scary Lesson Number Two. While everyone made a lot over the whole pleasure part of things, they hadn't given her the illusion that it would always be that way. *"Your pleasure is your Master's. Even when his pleasure brings you only pain."*

Steele had been chosen to inflict that lesson. He was quite the sadist when he chose to be. Nina had been bound on a wheel, her arms and legs pulled out to the maximum level of muscle strain. Then he'd taken up his Mistress's switch and gone after Nina's arms, legs, torso, sex. When she'd screamed and cried, he'd ruthlessly had her gagged with a rubber plug shaped like a very thick male organ, wrapped in cloth so her cries were suppressed.

He'd been wearing only a pair of pants that were like no pants she'd ever seen, so tight his sex was clearly visible. The more she struggled, the harder and thicker he became, showing her that her distress was exciting him.

When at last he set the switch aside, she was almost faint with relief. He sat down on a chair before her, reached into the pants and took out his impressive organ. He leisurely pulled on it, massaging himself to climax, all while his eyes devoured her spread and tortured body.

After he finished, he tucked himself back in, rose and came to her. Turning the wheel so her head was down at his knees, he put his mouth between her legs. Though her body shook with the stress of the whipping, and she had blood drying on her from places where the switch had cut through, she nearly came to a hard, terrible climax from the manipulation of his mouth, the rough tweaking of her nipples from his strong fingertips. But as always, a female trainee stepped in at the last moment to push her over the edge, while Steele watched.

It wasn't close to her definition of pleasure. Yet her body had still responded. Because she'd given her Master what he wanted. Her foundation and fear had crumbled somewhere during the process, leaving her with a fierce determination to live up to everything he wanted from her.

Everything. *His pleasure is your pleasure, even if he gives you intolerable pain.* She'd thought that meant that, even if she derived nothing from the moment except agony, she was supposed to be happy she'd pleased him. Instead, Steele had shown her the horrifying truth that serving him had become the most important, satisfying thing to her.

"What scares you the most, Nina?"

She wondered if The Mistress had some avenue into her mind like that second mark she'd described, because the female was too damn good at picking up on her thoughts.

"You know," Nina said, bitterness giving way to weariness. She shifted to her knees, and stroked a fingertip over the woman's delicate ankle, just one questing touch. She didn't look at her face. Instead, Nina's chin dropped to her chest, her other arm hugging her body.

Lesson Three. "That I understand this without understanding it. Even as I hate it, and I want to go home. I want to go back to my life. But I fear you've broken my mind and soul, which were none too solid to begin with. You've made me addicted to the things that you can make my body do. It's a drug, is all. As hopeless and pointless as all addictions are. A waste of life."

The Mistress slid her foot closer to her, touched Nina's curled toes as Nina's hand remained on her ankle, slid listlessly up her calf. "It's not an addiction, but a craving that was always there. We simply opened a road to it, to all the possibilities that can come with it."

"But this isn't what I wanted to do with my life." The tears were there, but they were as useless as saying what she'd already said too many times before, so she pushed them back.

"I know. Come kiss me, little one. Let the disappointment go, for one night."

Nina didn't kiss The Mistress yet. Instead, she adjusted and slid her hand across The Mistress's throat, from shoulder to shoulder, tracing the collarbone, the tender pocket between. Then, at length, she followed the sternum between the woman's breasts. Back up, back down. Over the top of one, then the other. Fingertips trailing.

The first night, her three roommates had done that. Just fingertips, all over, until she was shuddering and crying out as if in climax before they ever got her there. The first lesson they'd taught her was that any part of the skin could conduct arousal.

When The Mistress shifted, Nina's gaze went to her face. The female's lips had parted, her fang tips showing. She was lifting to Nina's touch as Nina herself might do. She was arousing The Mistress.

It was startling, though she told herself there was no reason it should be. Hadn't they proved to her, over and over, that skilled touch could do that to anyone? No emotions necessary. But she didn't deny it fascinated her, watching the vampire lift and fall at her stimulation. That The Mistress was allowing her desire to show, she had no doubt. But the desire was genuine.

Nina grazed the full curve beneath her knuckles, spread her fingers out over the round expanse, and slowly brought the knuckles together to squeeze one taut nipple.

The female arched, the tip of her tongue touching her full lip. Nina squeezed harder, and won a moan. As well as an increase in the moisture between her own legs. She'd shifted close enough that The Mistress could reach that, and the female vampire's hand slid beneath and between Nina's folded thighs. She cupped her sex, her thumb rubbing through Nina's wet folds.

Nina hovered over the pinched nipple, and slowly, slowly, licked it. She stifled her own moan as The Mistress pushed the tips of three fingers inside her, holding her there. Nina did it again, then swirled her tongue around the nipple, moving her fingers out of the way to allow her to suckle.

The Mistress gripped her hip, her other hand sliding free so she could shift Nina. It allowed Nina to rest on her side, draped over The Mistress, her head dipped over her breast, her hand kneading the other one.

"There you are, you sweet, wonderful girl. So lovely." The Mistress's words were breathy and yet still very much in control, in a way that inspired a different kind of tears. Nina had stopped trying to identify what all the emotions meant that they summoned from her. She'd shed a hundred kinds of tears here, for a hundred reasons, known and unknown. She just suckled and savored, held The Mistress to her, and experienced the throb of her own aroused body as she brought pleasure to another, an odd stasis of aroused tranquility.

In time, she moved to the other breast, gave it equal attention. She shifted so her body lay between The Mistress's legs, and The Mistress locked them over Nina's arse, pressing her to her core in an unmistakable rhythm. It pushed Nina's mound into the carpet, a distracting friction that had her pulling harder on the firm points, and then The Mistress was pushing her down even further.

She took a circuitous route there, not because she wasn't eager to sample the honey between the female vampire's legs, but because she didn't want to overlook tasting any part of The Mistress's skin. Her flat stomach, the navel that winked with a jeweled bead pierced through the thin skin on the rim. Nina gripped it with her teeth, pulled, and discovered another erogenous zone as she won another quick breath from The Mistress, a pull on her hair.

Then on to the tops of her thighs, the smooth skin over her mound. Nina inhaled deep and found the scent of tropical flowers and sex.

"Does Steele rub cream into you here?" she asked, lifting her head. It was an amazing view, from The Mistress's smooth sex, up the slope of her torso, between her breasts. To the swanlike throat and intent, heartbreakingly beautiful visage of the female vampire.

"He does. He has the most adept fingers." The Mistress dropped her head back, obviously relishing the thought of Steele's skills as much as Nina's ministrations. "And tongue. It's difficult to choose between the two, so I usually just avail myself of both. Why have a servant if you are going to deny yourself anything and everything he can provide?"

"He knows how to be a sadist."

"He is a sadist, at times. Steele has a very interesting past."

Nina rested her chin lightly on The Mistress's upper thighs, studying her. "Do you love him?"

The Mistress angled her head, so she was gazing down her body at Nina. "No. Not like you mean, Nina. What is between a vampire and a servant—"

"Has no frame of reference in the human world. We've had slavery. Still do in some places. Indentured servitude."

"Careful," The Mistress warned. "I am giving you room here, Nina. But it does not permit you to interrupt me and be disrespectful. Your training still applies to this situation, even if the reins are loosened somewhat."

Bugger. Nina knew what was required when that tone and admonishment were used. Her body was practically doing it before her mind instructed it. She sat back on her heels, adjusted so she could put her palms on the floor, forehead in between. "My apologies, Mistress."

Now it was up to The Mistress to choose to punish, dismiss, or order her to proceed. Nina realized she found the dismissal idea the least favorable. Even if she was punished, The Mistress might still allow her to ask more questions afterward. And do other things.

What she'd said in bitterness and The Mistress had framed a different way was simple truth. Gender didn't matter when it came to pleasure.

She wanted to put her mouth back on The Mistress. If The Mistress put her head on Nina's lap, let Nina stroke her hair as The Mistress touched her how she wished, Nina suspected she would find that same zone of stillness she found while kneeling in a submissive posture.

She didn't ask herself why anymore. A month was a very long time here. A whole lifetime, and still too short, especially when she was once again thinking of tomorrow and leaving the school.

She had to be hopeful, optimistic. Going to him could be a good thing. Nothing to dread. Alistair might help her, she reminded herself. Though getting her hopes up might merely be setting herself up for a very sharp, painful fall.

"Does this truly seem like slavery to you?" The Mistress asked, after letting her rest on her hands and knees for a few unnerving moments.

"Some parts of it," Nina said honestly, speaking to the floor. "Because I have no choices that don't belong to my Master."

"Hmm. If I ask you that question in several months, you may be surprised to find you have a different answer."

"Will you be surprised if it's not?"

The Mistress touched her bowed head. Nina had to force herself to be still, because the caress was so disturbingly welcome, tender and yet firm, in control. Reassuring, though it shouldn't be. Brainwashing, she told herself. Or she was lying to herself. Either way, it still felt good.

"You have a clever tongue, Nina. It will help you, or it may get you into endless amounts of trouble. Learn the difference. I will allow you one more question, and then you will employ your tongue in different ways."

So, no punishment, and no dismissal. Anticipation tightened her thighs.

"I thought you said I could do as I wish."

"I did. I never said I would not do as I wish as well."

"Has Steele ever...do you order him to use his sadistic side on you?"

"You are learning," The Mistress purred approvingly. "You were going to ask if he has ever dominated me, and that is something a human never does to a vampire. If any vampire would allow it, he or she would forfeit both their lives, for that human would have been given a stature in our world that is not permitted. But I have on occasion allowed him to mark my flesh."

That purr became a near growl. "On the condition that, whatever he does to mine, I get to do three times as intensely to his. In the same session. Some of the scars he bears come from me. I marked them with my blood, so they become permanent."

The words gave Nina images of Steele put through some of the same rigors she'd had inflicted upon herself. "He wears them with pride," The Mistress continued, "but he is only allowed to touch them, beyond functional cleaning, when I command. So when I allow him to stroke them, he gets hard, remembering the many ways I have marked him."

Nina thought about that. The only vampire-servant relationship she'd witnessed firsthand so far was The Mistress and Steele. At the beginning, so much of this had dismayed and frightened her. Some of it still did, but familiarity, repetition, helped dull that edge, gave her space to think about it. If she asked Steele if he loved his Mistress, Nina wondered what he would say.

She was certain he would say he did and, though he likely *wouldn't* say it, she suspected he believed The Mistress loved him, and in certain ways that did have a human world context. Because Nina felt it between them. It was not a truth found with words.

"It is time to put that mouth to better use, Nina. Show me the devotion you will show to your Master's care."

Nina lifted her head. Not enough to meet The Mistress's gaze, but enough to focus on her destination. She scattered kisses once again over her thighs, savoring, caressing, taking her time so that the female could get the maximum response from the stroked nerve endings, awakening sensation from knees to hips.

As The Mistress had pointed out, Nina hadn't brought a woman pleasure this way. However, the conversation over, she found she did want to do so. She wanted to feel The Mistress writhe beneath her touch, from the thrust of her tongue, the way she had for Chele, Edith, Melanie...hell, they'd all had a go. Good thing communicable disease wasn't a worry for vampires or their servants. She'd been told Alistair's geographical mark alone would make her immune to that.

"Oh, Gods and Goddesses..." The Mistress sighed as Nina found her, began to kiss, lick, explore. "That's it, lovely servant."

The Mistress was right. Nina was dedicated to service. It could make her despair, even as it made her hope that her willingness to serve would lead to an avenue where she could embrace something of what she'd been. Even if the other servants had exchanged glances when she'd said such a thing aloud. Glances full of pity, but she refused to think of that right now.

She gripped The Mistress's hips, really settled into the business of driving her wild. She didn't have to think about it. She just keyed into the woman's movements, her cries, and moved along on that tide with her. Intuition, just as The Mistress had said.

Nina turned her head to The Mistress's thigh, bit her, hard. The female vampire strangled on a moan and a half chuckle, and her fingers tightened in Nina's hair. Nina bit her harder, then started biting her along the inside of the thighs, sharp, hard snaps that left red marks, then she was back into her cunt, suckling, playing, swirling. The female vampire was bucking beneath Nina's mouth. Nina wanted to see her come, feel her muscles contract on Nina's tongue, taste the heated flood of her juices as she climaxed.

But The Mistress had another plan. She pulled on Nina, gripped her, turned her with those strong vampire hands and arms so Nina was straddling The Mistress's shoulders, and then The Mistress let her go back to pleasuring her orally. As she did, The Mistress put her mouth between Nina's legs.

Nina cried out against the female vampire's moist flesh. The Mistress reached down, tangled her fingers in Nina's hair and jerked back roughly, breaking the contact between Nina's mouth and her sex.

"Stay like that." The Mistress eased her grip, but her order was clear. "I'll let you go back to eating pussy soon. Maybe. Look down at what will be yours again if I say so."

The Mistress was sliding slippery fingers between Nina's arse cheeks, stroking as she put her mouth on Nina again. Nina realized she was collecting the honey from Nina's cunt to allow her to push on that rear opening, put just the tips of her fingers in, parting the cheeks with other digits to increase the sense of invasion.

She'd had more than one tongue play in that area, mortifying her initially, and then taking her even deeper into that mortification when the sensations that spiraled through her had her making odd, keening noises and clawing the bedding.

"Lord Alistair is quite fond of arse-fucking," The Mistress said against her. "It's why he enjoys men as well as women. I would love to be a voyeur the first time he bends you over and thrusts his substantial cock into your tight arse. Put your mouth on my cunt again, sweet Nina. If you work hard enough, I might just give you my climax. What's the lesson, my little dove?"

Nina's voice came out breathless. "No matter what freedoms he gives you, he never stops being your Master. Never. His will always comes first."

It came to her without thought. Though she still fought it, resented it, they'd forced her to internalize it to levels of her subconscious she wouldn't have thought possible at the beginning of her time here.

When a vampire gave a servant freedom, it was the freedom given a pet. Never did the servant step out of the boundaries of the Master's control.

Torn between despair and violent arousal, Nina dipped her head back to The Mistress's body. She pushed the darker things away and immersed herself in teasing, sampling. Being awed by the countless reactions the simple contact of her mouth on those sensitive tissues could bring. And groaned, undulated, experienced those reactions herself, as The Mistress used her own mouth and fingers to drive Nina to the edge of sanity.

Her words made Nina think of Alistair pushing into her arse. She'd been told when she opened to him fully, relaxed, trusted him completely, she would be able to take him there, all the way. If she trusted enough, it could be a sudden, deep slide, filling her.

"Beautiful. You are imagining him, I can tell."

The Mistress raised Nina up enough to put her mouth fully back on her pussy. She tightened an arm over Nina's hips as Nina tried her best to keep up, licking, nipping, suckling, thrusting. The Mistress lifted and locked her legs over Nina's head and shoulders, holding her against her sex, grinding her face in it, as she worked her with her mouth.

Slick, heated skin and musk on the inside, soft, sweet-smelling silk and flowers on the outside. The strength of The Mistress's arms and legs were like the bars of a cage wrapped around her, holding Nina in place to service her, and that bondage took away further thought. There was only now, and this.

"Not until I come," The Mistress said. "Or no matter what your Master ordered, I'll let every bloke in these halls take your arse during the daylight hours." She laughed against Nina's flesh. "You tightened on my tongue there, little one. I think you like the idea. Lord Alistair is getting a gem. A fucking gem."

"I...I can't..." Nina fought as hard as she could not to come, but The Mistress didn't give her any respite, working her with her mouth. Nina tried as best as she could to make The Mistress come first. She failed, but only by a matter of seconds.

Nina screamed out her climax as The Mistress moaned hers, their bodies locked in a sensual combat, rocking, writhing, honey spilling forth on the tongue.

The flames leaped, spiraled, and the heat in the room increased, or so it seemed to Nina as things took on a haze, so powerful and uncontrolled. She was hoarse when she stopped, though she kept making little bleats as The Mistress teased over-sensitized tissues with her mouth. She had her own mouth pressed to The Mistress's sex and thigh, her temple resting there. Slick heat and rigid muscles gave way to dampness and languid limbs, caressing touches.

At length, The Mistress let her shift and brought her up to cuddle, pressing Nina's head down on her breast. Nina, in an idle drift, closed her mouth on the softened nipple, squeezed, played her tongue over it. The Mistress stroked her head, her shoulder. Nina felt too heavy to even lift her body.

She was just...done. She had no fight left for it. There was no point to it, anyway. Not here. The Mistress had done all she'd said she'd do to Nina. Tomorrow night, her part was done. Nina would be on her way to Alistair's home.

At least in a post-climactic fog, she wasn't as anxious about that. With no more than a poignant twinge in her heart, Nina could even give up on hope, as an unnecessary expenditure of energy.

For now.

"One final lesson, little one." The Mistress spoke against her brow. "One you're smart enough to learn for yourself. The heart can be dominated, broken down. Owned. But it can never be forced."

Her fingers tightened with bruising force, as if sensing Nina's surprise was going to make her lift her head, and The Mistress wanted the pain to remind her of the boundaries that such words didn't remove. Not exactly.

"Even an InhServ has that choice. It matters not the cage you think yourself in. The ability to love, to serve because that is what you genuinely wish to do, is the treasure every vampire of worth desires from his servant. You think you have been stripped of all control. But no matter how out of your depth you feel, I have given you the tools and the paths to be a true InhServ. The core of it was already inside you. And that is not merely the submission you embrace so readily. You have a connection to Lord Alistair. Do not deny yourself the strength it can bring you."

Nina squeezed her eyes tight. She knew that, only her view of it was far different from The Mistress's. It was that connection to Alistair that made all of this so confusing, that could rip her mind to shreds.

She was tired of all of this. She'd just stay here. She'd rather stay here than face one more dreadful challenge, laden with uncertainty.

The Mistress stroked her hair. "You wondered why we didn't make you say it. Calling Lord Alistair your Master. It is because that is *his* lesson to teach, to enforce however he wishes. My hope for you is that you realize sooner than later your devotion and willingness to embrace his ownership is the key to everything you truly want."

Her voice dropped to a whisper, and her teeth scored Nina's ear, savage and playful. "Even if you're saying bollocks to me right now, I know it to be true. So did Lord Alistair."

She raised her eyes to The Mistress's face, another disobedience, but The Mistress allowed it this time. She looked at Nina with her usual impenetrable mask. But then she leaned in, brushed her lips against Nina's mouth, her cheek. Her voice was a murmur against her flesh.

"Killara is my name. My father was Maori, my mother European. Do not be so focused on what you have lost as to ignore what treasures may lie ahead. Good luck, Nina. Help him, and you will help yourself."

CHAPTER NINE

*I*t had ended as it had begun, in The Mistress's drawing room study. Now Nina sat in the backseat of a shiny Hudson, being driven to her new Master's home as she stared down at the still throbbing mark on the inside of her wrist.

She'd been brought to Killara's presence, been told to kneel. The Mistress had blindfolded her, then that caressing, strong hand had cradled her arm. Nina's brow creased as something wet was brushed onto the inside of her wrist. The smell was familiar, and yet not, as if it should have been a disagreeable odor but wasn't. It was something that made her want to touch it...taste it.

Then she heard a clank of metal, smelled a whiff of fire and smoke. Steele's large hand clasped her forearm, close to the elbow, his other gripping her shoulder, holding her fast.

"Be still," The Mistress said, and then pain exploded in Nina's arm.

She'd cried out, the agony making it impossible to be silent, and she gagged at the smell of her own flesh burning. A smell she knew all too well. She fought Steele's hold, but he was far stronger than her, and she couldn't get her arm free. Not until it was done.

The brand was taken away, and The Mistress's hand was on her head, stroking her hair. "You did well," she said. "You have been given the InhServ mark, over your Master's blood, so when you get his third mark, it will remain for some time. When it must be refreshed, after you are third marked, it will be permanent."

Oblivious to the scenery passing outside the car window, Nina stared at the symbol. In the center of the circle of reddened flesh was the brand that had been marked by Alistair's blood. A fleur-de-lis.

"The mark of the InhServ, a symbol that you belong to another, forever."

Her gaze passed from her arm to the rest of her. She was dressed in a white silky blouse and a snug dark skirt that stopped just above her knees. Shoes with pencil thin heels that made her glad she'd been given instruction in how to walk in them. It felt odd to be wearing clothes.

Her driver, Mr. Coleman, was part of Alistair's staff. He was a stocky man in a black suit. He had no hair, and his face was shaped very much like a block of wood. It was also equally as expressionless. Was that a requirement for working for a vampire? He had a scar running from his ear to his jaw and some pocking on the opposite cheek she knew were burn scars. His eyes were a clear color, reminding her of shallow water over a bed of ashes.

Alistair had not come. The Mistress hadn't said he would. But of course a Master wouldn't come and get his servant. She would be brought to him. She cleared her thick throat.

"Did you get the scars in the war, Mr. Coleman?"

The driver glanced at her briefly in the rearview mirror. "No, miss."

"There's a poultice that we used in the hospital in Sydney to help the skin feel less tight and uncomfortable. It was a concoction one of the nurses created from her herb garden and can be put on the face at bedtime. I will send away for some, if you like."

The driver made a noncommittal grunt and returned his attention to the road. That had been the pattern of their conversations for the past hour. He would answer a direct question, but wouldn't elaborate. If she was looking for some casual conversation to help her feel less nervous about what was ahead, he wasn't in the mood to oblige.

So she decided to make it worse. The Mistress had given her a sealed envelope, to be opened upon her arrival. Mr. Coleman had one, too, sitting next to him on the seat. Rationalizing that now or later didn't make much difference, Nina opened her letter and let her gaze fall on The Mistress's flowing script.

The communication started out innocuously enough. Mr. Coleman would deliver his letter, which would formally present her to

Alistair, certify her credentials. She wondered what kind of creative wording The Mistress had used to make those sound like more than they were. But she really wouldn't have to dress it up for Alistair. He already knew Nina didn't know what the hell she was doing.

Then you will kneel before him as you have been taught, bow your head. You will say, "It is my honor to serve you, my lord. How may I attend you first, or would you prefer me to familiarize myself with your household until you have direct need of me?"

An unexpectedly simple ritual. After that, what was the maxim?

What will please him?

What will please him?

What will please him?

Pretty much all vampires who deserved the privilege of an InhServ already had household staff, who could fill in the blanks on the minutiae, like where she would sleep, what the daily schedule was. Normal, straightforward things. If she wasn't so worried about the wide range of unlikely things he could demand from her, she could pretend she was entering his home as a new housekeeper. Sadly, she was even less prepared to be his household help than she was to be his InhServ.

Yet in the vampire world, the third marked servant was unquestionably in charge of the household, no matter what other staff worked it. Her word could be overruled only by that of her vampire master.

One of the training mistresses had explained the ranking system among a vampire's human staff. *"You are considered the elite. Because you embrace a level of servitude that shames a nun or priest. Unquestioning, anticipating everything your Master or Mistress needs. Never with an ounce of pride, always grateful to be of service to your vampire."*

She wondered what the current housekeeping staff would think of her being placed in charge of them. She barely knew how to boil an egg.

Whereas, from the first day of her nurse training, Nina had known that was what she was meant to do, what she wanted to do.

Don't do this to yourself. Not now. She tightened her hands on one another, realized how cold her fingers were, and loosened them. But with every mile the car put between her and the InhServ training school, she was returning to the real world in her head. The absurdity of what she was being mandated to do, the fantastic nature of her role.

Yeah, girls, can't help our boys anymore. Have to go be some vampire's property for the next three hundred years.

The Mistress would have known a month's worth of training, no matter how immersive, couldn't stem the flood of a lifetime of other wants and beliefs indefinitely. The dam could break in the time it took to drive to Alistair's home.

Maybe she'd thought that last little intimate share the night before would help her keep things together. Which meant maybe it had been a straight manipulation, and that wasn't her name at all. But Nina thought it might be.

She dropped her attention to the last part of the letter, and her fingers shook on the paper.

You will leave the clothes you are wearing in the car and they will be returned to me. You cross your Master's threshold with nothing but what belongs wholly to him. If he is not home or ready to inspect you, you will kneel inside that threshold in submissive posture until he is ready to do so.

"Bugger that," she muttered. The Mistress wasn't here. She wasn't doing it. She glanced up at the mirror and met the driver's gaze. It was steady, cool. Unsmiling.

It reminded her of Steele's implacability. If she tried to escape, Mr. Coleman was prepared to stop her. She was sure of it. She had no idea what the consequences for trying to run would be. To her, or to her family. But she could guess.

Was the driver prepared to tear the clothes off her body if she didn't present herself the way it was expected? Dump her unceremoniously in the entranceway? Was that what was in his letter?

She was clutching her hands again. Taking a deep breath, she turned her mind to other things in an attempt to quiet the surge of panic, the renewed sense of being shut up in a coffin before she was dead. Oh God, why had she had that thought? It was far too close to the truth.

Everything closing in. Salt water. Always the salt water. Followed by those eyes. Dead eyes, apathetic eyes...the staccato firing of the gun. The screams.

It was too difficult to breathe. She kept going under. No, she wasn't in the water. She was in a car. She was here. In the present.

140

It was a very near thing, but she pulled herself out of it, even though she surfaced shaking and sweating. For the next few moments, she focused on breathing.

Steady, old girl. Steady. She imagined the hospital in Singapore, those times when there'd been a mob of lads brought in all at once and it seemed so overwhelming. She'd focused on putting one foot in front of the other. Getting through.

But she'd been saving lives, making a difference. Helping. Not being an unpaid whore some man could treat however he wished. Sher, her roommates...they thought it was some great honor. Maybe they were just like the boys who thought it was such a romantic, amazing thing, running off to war, until they faced the godawful reality.

You think you have been stripped of all control.

She didn't think it at all. She bloody well knew it.

But Steele had the reality of being a third marked servant, and seemed to embrace it. He and The Mistress seemed very reserved toward one another, but that was to someone who wasn't paying attention. The connection between them was as strong and constant as the ocean tide. Everyone involved in this insanity seemed to buy into it, except her.

Everyone involved in this insanity had trained for years for it. Or, like Steele, had come to it willingly.

When would Alistair mark her? When would she reach the point of no return? Immediately? She'd been told that some vampires made a big ritual of it, offering the marks over a period of weeks, as an InhServ proved themselves. Others did it within the first twenty-four hours.

"If you're hungry or thirsty," Coleman said, bringing her back to the present, "there are some things in the cooler."

For lack of anything better to do, she opened it. Her brow lifted. Soda, water. Cheese and fresh bread. And a couple bottles of wine. Perhaps to settle her nerves? She'd take it. Another basket produced cups, a bottle opener, napkins. Traveling in style, she was.

One pampered and turped sex slave, coming right up.

Maybe a little more than turped. In her cups, really, but that was what happened when you drank a whole bottle of wine yourself and ate only a couple pieces of cheese. When the driver turned into the entrance to Alistair's place and drove along another half mile, her first sight of the house was enough to bring the worries surging up again, a heaving sea in her lower belly.

Bloody hell. It was a bloody estate. It was also beautiful.

She'd been told he kept a place in Brisbane as an office of sorts for more formal Region Master duties. But this was his primary residence, outside Brisbane, in a quieter, exclusive section of the beaches making up the Gold Coast.

His home rested in a spot of grand isolation, a jewel that overlooked the shore. It was a sprawling Victorian with iron lace framing the triple layer of terraces that wrapped completely around the structure. A whimsical array of parapets broke up the lines. His landscaper was worth his weight, because there were enchanting layers of flowers and plants that folded in toward the pathway to the door and followed the drive around to a garage.

Was this place a perk of being Region Master, like a governor's mansion of sorts? Or was it his? If so, what had he done to earn the money to have it built? He'd said he was three hundred years old. She expected that was plenty of time to earn the quid. Since Australia wasn't colonized until the 1700s, she expected that meant he started life in some other part of the world, no matter that his accent and mannerisms were solidly Australian.

She remembered Charlie and Rigby discussing him as if he were some type of aristocrat. The way he'd acted had only reinforced it. So yeah, he'd had money a while. Even if he'd been born dirt poor, a couple centuries were enough to refine a man's manners, and money could teach him to put on airs.

He really hadn't put on airs with her, but that sense of command... he was used to being in charge.

A gilded cage, but still a prison. The size of it, the power and money it represented, only reiterated how locked into all of this she was. She felt sick.

Oh, bollocks, she really did. As Coleman brought the car to a halt on the circular drive, she scooted across the seat and shoved open the door. She made it two steps before baptizing an arrangement of ornamental grasses and nodding purple flowers with regurgitated wine and undigested cheese. Since she'd gotten lots of practice with target vomiting when she worked at the hospital, she felt a mild sense of accomplishment at keeping it all off the driveway. Until she looked down and bit back another curse. Crimson drops were sprinkled over the front of her ivory-colored blouse, quickly setting in to stain.

But that wasn't the worst of it. She wasn't alone.

She'd vomited on the far side of the car, not in direct view of the front door. That had mattered not at all, for when she lifted her gaze, she met the appalled expression of a man dressed in a black suit. Even the tie and shirt were black. He was tall, rangy, like a colonel she'd seen visit their hospital a few times.

He had remarkably steady eyes in a craggy face with bushy eyebrows. One had a slight cock to it that made him look perpetually caught between austerity and disapproval. He had big ears, and a receding hairline compensated with lots of fine silver hair along the sides. His blade of a nose made his piercing eyes look as if they were sighting down the bore of a weapon.

His age might have been anywhere from forties to mid-fifties. She saw no evidence of arthritis in his big hands, but they were somewhat gnarled, like an older person or manual laborer. Yet the nails were manicured, and his impeccable appearance suggested a gentleman's gentleman.

He'd obviously come down from the front veranda to open the door for her. She could have claimed car sickness, but first off, the strong odor of the wine would eradicate any sympathy for that, and second, one had to care to make excuses. He could just sod off, couldn't he, with his disapproving looks and his monochromatic dress theme.

"Believe me, with the month I've had, it's a miracle I didn't arrive in worse bloody shape," she said crisply and straightened. "Nina. I assume I'm expected, though you'd be my hero if you said he'd changed his mind and wants me to go home."

"Nero, miss."

"Seriously? Nero the hero." She stifled a giggle. The wine was definitely not out of her system. She was going to bollocks this up beyond recognition. What had The Mistress said about not shaming her? Well, that train had left the station.

Nina dove back into the car on hands and knees, crawling across the cushion to find the little toiletry kit that had also been helpfully provided. She leaned over the seat, pressing against Coleman's boulder-sized shoulder for balance and because being straight upright was too much effort. She used his mirror to tidy her hair and touch up her makeup, just as she'd been shown. Light touches, to highlight her "natural beauty." Right-o. Though she wished she had a bright red lipstick, because she'd lay it on thick, make her lips look macabrely blood-kissed. A vampire should appreciate that.

Why the hell hadn't The Mistress accompanied her? She'd been told, *There is no need. You are his now.* But that was the normal process for someone like her roommates, who'd done this for so long it was practically the only life they knew.

Was Nina really wishing for someone to babysit her through this? "Pull it together," she muttered.

She backed out. The skirt rode up, leaving her frowning as she put her teetering heel on the gravel drive. She wiggled, tugging down the hem before she faced Nero. His expression brought to mind her father, when she was eight and had turned up at the church social in her knickers. She'd been covered with mud and toting a basket of frogs to show him. She couldn't remember why it had been so important to show those to him, then and there. She'd explained she was in her knickers so she wouldn't get her church clothes dirty, but she'd left those by the creek.

Though he'd initially had a very disapproving look, she remembered seeing some twitching around his mouth when she delivered her solemn explanation. A little twinkling to his eye.

She'd made him laugh, she was sure of it. She'd seen love in his eyes. But it hadn't been enough. She'd never been enough. She wouldn't be now. Nero's expression, devoid of any amused twitches, said it as clearly as a shout in her face.

She collapsed onto the car seat and put her head in her hands, her feet on the drive. "Bloody hell, I've a headache," she said, her voice suspiciously thick.

She lifted her head at the silence, and found Nero was no longer there. She looked over her shoulder. "He went back inside," Coleman said.

"Course he did. Probably telling the rest of the staff that they sent a reject."

"They are expecting that."

She sent him a sharper look, despite the pain that increased in her temples. "What does that mean?"

Coleman rubbed at his smudge of a nose and lifted a shoulder, as if he was already saying too much. Nina lifted the other bottle of wine. "Tell me, and I give you this and cop to drinking both bottles. It's good stuff."

Coleman eyed her and sighed. "Bribery isn't necessary, or appropriate to your position, miss. Lord Alistair is the first Region Master appointment who's a made vampire. Not a born one. Many vampires oppose made vampires ascending to positions of power in the vampire ranks. So, when Lady Lyssa said he should be accorded the honor of an InhServ, a privilege reserved for vampires of power and influence, but always born vampires of power and influence, there was speculation that they would send the bottom of the barrel."

Coleman served Alistair. She might have questioned why he was being so forthcoming, but it was obvious. He was letting her know up front they were prepared for her to completely cack this up.

She didn't care. She didn't want to care. For once in her life, she wanted to be like so many others and not strive to exceed expectations in every way, as if it were mandated in her blood and bone.

She tuned into her surroundings to find Nero standing before her again.

"Miss." He offered a new blouse, to her surprise, and a bottle of mouthwash. "I brought them from your room."

"Nero, you may be a hero after all." She jerked open the buttons of her shirt, shrugged out of it and tossed it into the back seat before putting the new one on, tucking it into her straightened skirt. She swigged some of the mouthwash and spat it into the abused flowers. Only when she was done with that and had handed Nero the mouthwash back did she register his faintly horrified look. Coleman looked like he'd choked on a bark of surprised laughter.

"What? It's not like you won't be seeing me bare-arsed eventually, especially when his friends come over to play." She was proud that her voice didn't break on the words, but that was just because she didn't think about them too hard.

"Lord Alistair has two staff members who are unaware of his nature," Nero said. "And his relationship with you. Discretion needs to be observed."

That brought her up short. Why would Alistair not have a fully indoctrinated household, with vampire-faithful humans and second marks? She'd been told that was the norm for most Region Masters. Christ, she'd just stripped in the driveway like...well, like she shouldn't have. Bugger it.

"Fine, then. Let's get this done. Where is Lord Alistair?"

"He is in Brisbane, miss. He should return later in the evening, unless affairs keep him later than expected. Once you attend to your InhServ requirements, I can introduce you to the rest of the regular staff. There are five of us. A housekeeper, maid, cook, groundskeeper and myself. Help is often brought in for official gatherings at his home, but they are temporary. The maid and the cook are the two uninitiated. They are relatively new hires."

After worrying so much about it, finding Alistair wasn't even here left her bogged down in a confusing mess of reaction. Irritation that she couldn't go ahead and grab the bull by the horns topped the list, but she supposed it might be good to have some time to get the drink out of her system. In the face of Nero's unflappable and shrewd personality, she was managing her heaving cauldron of emotions better. She reminded herself Alistair wasn't likely to help her if she acted like a madwoman.

"That sounds fine, Nero," she said, straightening and smoothing her hands over her hair, her clothes. "Take me to everyone so I can introduce myself. I expect you keep everyone in line here."

"I am the butler, miss," he confirmed. "Though you would now provide my supervision."

He delivered that in a flat voice, no indication of how that made him feel, but she could put it together well enough. "I expect you require precious little of it," she said. "Here's the truth of it, Nero. Over the past few weeks, my life has been turned upside down. I don't want to take it out on any of you, but I'm going to have my rough moments. I'm not what anyone expected to be coming here. However, I've helped run a hospital, and what I know from that is that if everyone does their job, then we work together to make everything run properly, nobody wasting time on rank. I'm not a fool or a doormat, but if you keep him happy as you always have, then you and your lot will have little interference from me. Plus, help when you need it and I can provide it. Okay?"

Nero listened without a change in expression. She wondered if he and Steele had gone to the same blacksmith to get that cast-in-iron poker face. However, Coleman grunted, a sound that might have reflected a mild surprise at the bluntness. Nero's gaze flickered to him, then he inclined his head to Nina.

"Very well, miss. I will show you to the front hallway and leave you there until the Master arrives, as is appropriate."

She blinked at him, puzzled, and then his other words sank in. *"Your InhServ requirements."*

Hell, The Mistress had apprised the butler of what would be required of her. Naked, kneeling at the doorway until Alistair returned and she could say her little speech.

"If he's not returning for a while, I'll meet the staff and get myself acclimated first."

"The school director said—"

"I know what she said," she snapped. "And I'm bloody well not squatting in his foyer in my altogether for hours. I'll do it when he's coming up the drive. Not before."

Reaching back into the limo, she retrieved her letter and tore it into pieces. She tossed it into the air between them, the wind spinning the fragments in all directions. "They're just words. Words mean nothing. I can promise you that."

Efficiency. Authority. Calm. What had the Matrons taught them? *Those three things help reassure the boys and yourself. No matter how chaotic things get, if you can project that, it helps keep your head on straight. The men and the doctors listen to you better.*

Taking a breath, she grabbed the thought with both hands, and spoke calmly, meeting Nero's gaze with a steely one of her own. "What I am or am not to the Master, how I fail or please him, is between him and me. None of you. Please take me to meet the staff."

Nero exchanged a glance with Coleman. The driver shrugged, apparently his most common form of communication. It eased the sudden worry that he or Nero might be authorized to force the issue, physically if needed.

Maybe I have more choices than you know, Mistress Killara. I certainly have more than Helen, don't I?

Bolstering herself with that thought, she followed Nero up the stairs to the house.

During the next two hours, Nina discovered she had two rooms. One was in the upper levels of the house, and was a typical bedroom, with feminine appointments and a lovely view of the ocean. She'd looked away from that quickly, knowing she'd draw the curtains as soon as she was alone. She wouldn't be leaving the window open as Nero suggested, to let the night air sound of the surf lull her to sleep.

The housekeeping staff had been polite, reserved, watchful. Except for Winifred, one of the two staff members who didn't know their employer was a vampire. The night maid's barely veiled scorn when Nina was introduced, her mean eyes, said without words what she thought Nina's role was here.

In Nina's normal element, the woman's behavior wouldn't have flustered her in the least. Here, it had the power to make Nina feel smaller, less certain. Reminding her that none of this was her. None of it felt natural.

With effort, she imagined herself as a nurse supervisor and conducted herself as such, asking reasonably intelligent questions about their duties, their backgrounds. She told them she would integrate herself into the daily routine as the Master required and looked forward to working with each of them to care for him.

When the proper words spilled from her lips, Nina was surprised to find them there, ready to be called. The Mistress's intense lessons, the endless repetition, had apparently stuck in some ways. The problem was she didn't feel any of it.

She remembered when she'd learned her multiplication tables. Seven times seven equals forty-nine. But the teacher had never explained what it meant. Sher didn't care, simply learning what she was taught, and passed the test.

Nina's mother had unfastened a bag of dry beans and counted out forty-nine on the kitchen table. She'd directed Nina to separate them into seven piles of seven so she could understand what multiplication meant.

"Always needing to understand why and how," her mother had said fondly. "Never just accepting something at face value."

Her mother had been amused by it, then. Almost proud. She hadn't been surprised Nina wanted to be a nurse, learning about medical procedures and anatomy.

Her other room was on a level below ground, an engineering feat this close to the shore. It was a basement like no basement she knew, since every effort had been made to make it feel like the aboveground parts of the house.

Though it had no windows, the five bedrooms, three baths, study and sitting room below had plenty of pictures, hung curtains and tapestries, and airy beach-style furniture. Her room there was much smaller, an antechamber to the Master's room. She would use it when he wished her to attend him during his daylight sleep, Nero explained.

"If that is all for now, Miss Nina, I'll return to my duties." Evidently feeling he'd spent enough time with her, Nero politely—if somewhat abruptly—indicated that was the end of the guided tour.

"Thank you. Just let me know when you think he's on his way."

"Yes, miss." He headed back up the stairs, his shoes making no sound on the carpet runner. Nina watched him go, fighting the return of the panic. She wanted him to stay, to keep talking, to give her something to focus upon.

But that would help nothing. She turned to face the lower level accommodations again. Her bed in the antechamber had a pretty sea-colored coverlet with wheat-colored embroidery that looked like scatterings of beach grass. The picture over the bed was of a tide line, sunlight reflected off sand and shells. A shadow of a person was in the picture, posed as if gazing down at the life beneath their wet feet.

Her gaze strayed to the side table, to a glass sphere sitting upon it. A decorative paperweight, she thought, until she came closer, and saw it was a snow globe. She picked up the lead glass and, another surprise, discovered it was a music box. After she wound it up, she turned it over, watching the pieces of sparkling glitter slowly start to swirl and float. It was a beach scene, the ceramic ocean painted in various blues, washing up on a sandy textured shore. There was a tree line.

Suspended inside the globe and slowly circling was a plane, the propellers oscillating with the movement of the liquid. As she watched it, the music began to play "You Are My Sunshine." A funny choice for a vampire.

Alistair's house could have been featured in one of the fancy decorating magazines. The back terrace on the upper level of the home had that breathtaking view of the shore, and more beautifully landscaped plants and trees. Anyone could imagine themselves enjoying a sit-down in one of the rockers, watching the waves roll in and out. Well, anyone who felt a meditative peacefulness at the rushing sound of the surf, rather than an inexplicable terror from it.

She pushed that away to stick to her point. Everything in the house looked chosen by an efficient decorator, employed because the owner was too busy or apathetic to select the contents, as long as they reflected what was necessary about him or his station. But this...

Her fingers curved around the globe and she sank down on the mattress, watching the pieces slowly, slowly settle, and hearing the music wind down. This piece was personal. A welcome message of sorts, for her?

Thinking, she rose. There was one room that she hadn't seen yet. Alistair's. Nero had merely gestured at it, not entering it himself. As she opened the connecting door between her room and that of the master of the house, she stood in the frame, looking at the interior.

Him. It smelled like him. She closed her eyes and took a few more steps, slowly pivoting on her toe as she inhaled that scent of ocean-touched male. She had her arms wrapped hard around her middle as she remembered his quick, weary smile before he left the hospital, the feel of his hands pulling her from the water. The heat of his mouth.

When she opened her eyes, she was gazing at his bed, standing at the foot of it. It was one of the largest she'd ever seen, enough for five or six people it seemed, with a frame that looked like an elaborate box. The cherry-colored wood posts were carved with leaves and roses as big as her hand. The blanket was a pale yellow comforter that lightened up the room.

There was a cushioned bench at the foot to allow for sitting and putting on shoes. He had a desk in one corner, a reading chair. Seascapes hung upon the walls.

She moved to his walk-in wardrobe. She told herself it was appropriate, that she didn't have to be shy. A third marked servant was in charge of all domestic requirements her vampire had, like ensuring his clothes were cleaned and pressed properly, or doing it herself if there was no house staff. No worries for her there. She expected the housekeeper, Mrs. W as they called her, would be horrified if Nina asked to do the ironing. Which she should be, because Nina doubted she knew how to appropriately operate the contraption for something as complicated as men's shirts.

Opening the door, she was surprised that he didn't have as many as she'd expect for such a well-heeled male. Maybe a couple dozen. A decent selection of suits and casual clothes.

She frowned and gazed back out at the room again. The desk had an assortment of pens, a blotter. A bookshelf had a few carefully chosen volumes. Classics, travel memoirs. The classics were in handsome bindings.

Not much in the way of personal items, especially for a male who'd lived as long as he had. But it matched the upstairs. If one had never met him, they would assume the fellow who lived here was seaside gentry, but little else could be concluded about him, though many stereotypical assumptions might be made. Things that would keep the reality of the man well-masked.

She moved deeper into the dressing room. At the very back, on the floor, in the shadows behind the suits, she found a chest. Tugging it out far enough to lift the lid unencumbered, she found what she sought.

Something that reminded her of the man she remembered.

Folded footy gear. Pressed and put away. Based on the location, it didn't appear to have been disturbed in some time. A football was tucked in another corner of the chest. She drew it out, turning it in her hands. It had been quite scuffed, well-used at one time.

She also found vintage firearms which she expected hadn't been vintage when he used them. Old, washed-out pictures of young men that appeared to date back to before the turn of the century were carefully arranged in a pocket of the chest. Then she found a more current one. She clasped it for a long minute, recognizing the men in the picture. The ones that Alistair had made sure reached the hospital that night.

The one on the right, closest to Alistair on that side, was the first one who'd died. Jonathan. He had a careless grin, his elbow propped on Rigby's shoulder while Charlie, far less haunted-looking in this picture, was in the middle of saying something to the other two men, Horace and Mort, who were kneeling before them, like an informal team snapshot. Another man draped his folded arm on Alistair's left shoulder, his chin propped on it as Alistair gave him a fond look. She guessed that was Pete, the one whose body Alistair had gone back to collect, make sure it got home.

They still mattered to him. She found herself clutching the picture too tightly, and pressed it against her breast instead, bowing her head over it. She sank down on the floor by the chest, holding the picture, her other hand resting on the footy shirt.

She wasn't given to acts of foolish sentiment, but she still brought the shirt to her face. Clean laundry smell, not much of him, but a trace of it there. She held it to her cheek, the picture to her heart.

Maybe she was grasping at loose straws, but the biggest enemy she had in all of this was the utter loneliness. Ever since Bangka, she'd struggled with it, always feeling out of step with a world that didn't seem to realize darkness was breathing down their necks. That they were all barely a moment away from it opening its maw and swallowing them all whole.

Then Sher had died, and that surety had increased to a nigh-unbearable level. Ironically, The Mistress had employed Nina's mind and body with so many shocking things, it had backed off some of the despair. During the car ride here and the driver's unhelpfully laconic conversation, it had started to rise again. She'd dulled it with alcohol, a temporary and destructive route, she knew, but it had been the tool at hand.

Left down here to her own devices, it could strangle her anew, but a sliver of hope kept some slack in the rope. Whenever she'd needed not to feel so alone, her thoughts had turned to Alistair. She was holding proof of why. Someone in this house had been where she'd been. Which meant she maybe wasn't as desolately alone as she felt.

Sher's death, the training center, The Mistress, her parents...they'd all made her forget who Alistair had been on the beach. The picture reminded her.

They could sort this mess out together, and he would help her get back to the life she wanted to live.

"I'm not alone." She said it aloud. But when she looked up at all the other things in here, their lack of personality, the words were tagged with uneasy feeling.

"Miss?" Nero startled her out of her contemplation. She managed, barely, not to jump guiltily when he put his head in the room. Nero's gaze swept her, kneeling on the floor with her hand in the chest and the photograph against her bosom, but his voice remained the same as he spoke.

"The Master is due back in a few moments. He rang to let me know he was on his way and that he has one of his territory members with him, such that I should have additional tea prepared. I expect he anticipates your presentation." A subtle warning, though Nero added, "Winifred and Mrs. Clyde have been sent out on errands with Mr. Coleman. They shouldn't return for another half hour."

So the ones currently unaware that Alistair was a vampire wouldn't witness how she was supposed to present herself to him. She met Nero's gaze.

Look at each person for who they are. Not who they are to you, and then you will see them. See how to connect to them. Sister Helen had told her that. Nina wondered how long it would be before the first image that sprang to mind when she thought of her friend would be something like her reserved smile when she imparted that kind of wisdom, or her exaggerated trot to keep pace with Nina's longer legs. Rather than her dead body floating in the water.

"Miss."

She cut off a short yelp as a hand touched her shoulder. She grabbed at it. He would pull her out of the water, he was here, he was...

Nero had frozen. She had a death grip on his wrist, her nails digging in. His gaze was on it, then it moved to her face. Nina stared at him, her eyes feeling too big, the emotions in her chest churning. He was only inches from her face, because he'd bent forward.

"I'm so sorry," She forced her voice not to shake. "I'll be up in a few moments."

"Very well," he said after a significant pause. He didn't move, though, until she recalled she was still holding his arm. She made herself let it go. When she did, he straightened and began to back out of the dressing room, but he wasn't quick about it, and she could feel his intent gaze on her face, studying her. She didn't know his thoughts, but they were loud in that small space.

Closing the top of the chest, she eased it back in place, but then realized she'd kept the shirt. She didn't put it back. Instead, she held onto it as she left the room and headed up the stairs. She went to her upper level room. Just as she'd known she would, the first thing she did was close the curtains. She did it with only a quick look at the ocean, so it was as if she glanced at a painting of the sea, not the reality of it.

It was a senseless aversion, she knew it, but one that had grown progressively worse. She wasn't afraid of the ocean, but of the emotions it triggered, how it could pull her down into darkness so quickly.

She hadn't allowed herself to explore her wardrobe, and even now was only vaguely aware there was an assortment of clothes there. Taking off the ones she was wearing, she hung them up. Then she slipped off her bra and knickers, and stood there naked in the coolness. A shudder went through her, and she jerked into motion, leaving the wardrobe to go to the vanity.

Letting her hair down, she brushed it vigorously, too vigorously, her naked body quivering, making her all the more aware of how exposed she was. She pinned her hair up again, her heart back to its thudding, her jaw set so hard it might crack. But when she went to the bedroom door she'd closed and put her hand on the doorknob, she could go no further.

I really can't do this. I'm not Sher. This doesn't feel right to me. She thought of Nero's eyes on her. The staff's. Alistair would have a vampire from his territory with him. Would her virginity be given to two men at once? Terror gripped her, even as she admonished herself. She was a grown woman. She knew what sex was, and it was no more terrifying than learning to ride a bike. It didn't mean anything anymore, because she was never going to be married, was she? It wasn't a gift she was going to be able to give the man she loved.

Her hand had tightened on the doorknob, her forehead pressed to the panel. *Damn it, move your arse.*

She couldn't. But she could breathe. And she could kneel. Slowly, she sank down to the floor. She couldn't believe she was seeking

InhServ training for strength, but the voice of one of the InhServ training school Masters came to her as if he stood over her now.

"The submissive posture is an attitude of prayer for a reason. It is the position a servant takes to find calm. If you are feeling nervous or upset, it will bring you back to center, your focus on your Master, and not on your own self."

While at that time she'd had the mental kneejerk reaction, "Of course, it's always about him, isn't it?" the message wasn't unfamiliar to her. Though the context was certainly different, she'd learned almost the same thing from a nursing school teacher. Old Knotwood was what the students called her, affectionately. Martha Nottingwood had worked as a nurse in World War I. She'd known firsthand what young women like Nina would face when they started signing up for the AANS duty.

Perhaps you can only afford a heartbeat's worth of time, but with practice, you'll find that's enough. Take a breath, find a still space inside where you can step back, look at what's happening, and determine the best way to help, to handle things. Calm is everything. Panic and rush will kill your patient as fast as a bullet.

Nina raised her chin and looked at the bed. She'd left his shirt there. She thought of The Mistress's instruction, the introduction protocol, then thought of Alistair and her on a beach. She rose and put the footy shirt on. He had broad shoulders and chest, so she had room in it, and it fell to mid-thigh. In submissive posture, it would still ride up her spine, expose her arse and nether parts. But that was all right. When the fabric enveloped her, she found that still space.

At least for this moment, it would be enough.

She stepped out into the hallway. It was cool, and she shivered, but she quelled that and padded to the end of the hall, which was a round-shaped space, being one of the upper level parapets. The ceiling beams were carved like his bed was, and in the spaces in between were paintings of owls. Dipping, gliding. One had a dead mouse in its claws. She didn't care overly much for that one, but the others were pleasant to gaze upon. She lowered her attention to the bank of windows. Darkness turned most everything to silhouettes, except the lit driveway. As she watched, a black shiny Nash convertible with wide white bands on the tires was pulling up.

She needed to be at the door, kneeling the way she should. Much as she wanted to ignore The Mistress's instructions, defy any evidence she was accepting this as her fate, she couldn't forget the driver's words. She wanted freedom, not to shame Alistair. And while she had no idea if her hope for his sympathy was misplaced or not, she was certain that appearing like a half-trained incompetent—no matter how horrifyingly true that probably was—would not help her case.

In short, while she didn't want to do any of this, if the vampire world wanted to see Alistair diminished by her behavior, she wasn't going to oblige. Not until she found out if her savior had become a right bastard.

But she lingered an additional heartbeat. She wanted to see him, because with her forehead to the floor, she wouldn't get the first glimpse of him she desired.

He exited the car from the driver's side. No surprise there. A male who preferred to pilot his own plane wouldn't care to be chauffeured. As he straightened, she remembered his height, his shoulders blocking the moonlight as he leaned over her.

He was quite cleaned up. At this distance, she might not have even recognized him, except she remembered the patrician set of the head, the dip of the chin. He wore slacks and a well-fitted suit coat. Tie and shiny shoes. But he looked like no stodgy businessman she'd ever seen. She thought of Rudolph Valentino, particularly when Alistair turned his head, the standing white collar highlighting the line of his throat, the curve of the ear, the dark hair feathered over his brow.

He'd cocked his head toward his companion, a handsome, slim man in a jaunty hat getting out the other side. He was talking and gesturing at Alistair with what appeared to be a bottle of brew. Then Alistair lifted his chin, and he was looking directly at her window.

Standing in darkness, she thought he couldn't see her, but then she remembered vampires could see in darkness. He started toward the door with those long, ground-eating strides.

"Bollocks," she muttered, and dashed for the stairs.

She should have eaten something, but her stomach hadn't been up for it after expelling the wine. Crikey, had he smelled that when he got out of the car? Vampires had extra keen senses. She should have drawn a pitcher of water from the kitchen, watered those flowers copiously. He'd parked the car near there. Maybe the housekeeper or Nero had thought of it, or maybe they didn't care what impressions she made.

Regardless, she had bigger issues, because halfway down, she tripped over her own feet. Fortunately, she caught herself on the smooth banister, but she stumbled into the balustrades and the carved edges cut her knee. Swearing a streak, she recovered and flew down the remaining steps, skidding to a halt, ten feet inside the door. She'd intended to thump down into the proper posture with all the grace of a dropped elephant, but she was peripherally aware of Mrs. W peeping at her through the kitchen pass-through.

Be Sher. Be Sher. She slowed her final few steps, lifted her head, gazed straight ahead as if she had all the time in the world, and sank so gracefully to her knees even The Mistress would have been impressed.

Or maybe not. If Killara had been at God's side during the creation of the world, she would have said to Him what Nina had heard her demand of every initiate, even her star pupils, at least once a day.

"Can you do better than that?"

Back straight, knees spread, forehead to floor. She was glad Winifred wasn't here. She couldn't have borne hearing her snicker.

Sher. Think of Sher.

The door opened. The men were talking, muffled voices suddenly clear and sharp.

"If that's what Ruskin thinks, he'll be thinking it a long time," Alistair said. "We'll open the map in my office and take a look. I'm sure he's wrong, but hopefully the borderlines will prove it, so we don't have to bloody well deal with a tantrum that has to involve the Europeans. Not that the Council would be any help."

She remembered his voice as rough, urgent. Low, able to stroke her like a physical touch. Maybe she'd embellished it in her memory, keeping the other remembrances at bay. Because the voice she was hearing now was polished, urbane. A little too much studied interest and a lot of formality, as if he were going through the proper motions, and yet not all that invested in the outcome of the conversation. Most people didn't really listen to others, except as intel gathering to contextualize their own opinions, but in her job, paying close attention was critical. Hearing that cynical yet detached edge increased her uncertainty. The words she had to say to him felt like lead bullets in her gut.

It is my honor to serve you, my lord. How may I attend you first, or would you prefer me to familiarize myself with your household until you have direct need of me?

Then he laughed at something his companion said. Still measured, but in that more uninhibited reaction, she heard *Alistair*.

Maybe he'd see her on the floor and help her up, tell her not to worry about all that Master nonsense. He'd assure her that he'd help her get her life back, that this was all vampire bollocks and they'd work around it.

"Bloody hell, this is the way to live, mate," the other male said. "Coming home to find choice quim with its arse lifted, waiting to be buggered."

Everything in her froze. Humiliation swamped her, and it was all she could do to hold the position and not cringe or bolt. She dug her fingers into the wood floor and tried hard not to think about how she looked through her own eyes, through the eyes of those who'd known her in the world before she'd been thrown into this one.

If he's going to help you, you have to control your reactions. It was the only hope she had, and it gave her the strength to hold fast. As did his reaction, thankfully different from his vulgar companion's.

"She is a gift from Council, Stanley," Alistair said mildly. "Try to act like you weren't sired by a horny female vampire who paid more attention to your tight arse than your brains."

"She paid well for this tight arse. Kept me in posh style for a decade before she tired of me. Best mark I ever had."

"Mmm." Alistair grunted. "Shut up a moment, Stan."

He'd dropped to his haunches before her, for she felt the passage of cool air over her flaming cheeks. He was looking her over, she expected. A lump was in her throat, and she thought of the photograph in his dressing room.

His forearm brushed her temple, her hair, and he curled a finger in the hem of the shirt, which had slid down, gathered between her waist and shoulder blades. As he traced her spine, a shiver went through her. Then he stilled.

"You're bleeding, Nina."

She had to do the greeting first, didn't she? But he'd said something to her. Was it a question or not? Oh, bugger it. She wasn't going to let her brain be pummeled to paralysis by nonsense.

"I tripped on the stairs. My lord." She'd been reminded of that constantly. *Always use his title when speaking to him, unless he instructs you otherwise.*

Stanley laughed, a raucous noise like crows. "Oh, aye, 'my lord.' They sent you the cream of the crop."

Alistair sighed. "Nina, this foul-mouthed arse is Mr. Stanley Welch, a relatively new vampire in my territory. I don't expect him to live long, because he's an idiot. Say hello."

Though there were few things she wanted to do less, she obeyed, lifting her head briefly in his guest's direction, without making eye contact. "G'day, Mr. Welch."

"She's not as glammed up as some I've seen," Stanley observed. "Pretty and fresh, though. Well done."

"It's my honor to serve you, my lord." The words stuck in her throat, but she got them out, since it seemed the appropriate time, with Alistair's attention still upon her. Never mind that they sounded as erratic as what had come from her throat when she vomited a bottle of wine in his garden.

She kept her eyes on the floor during the pregnant pause, rather than see what reaction her less-than-stellar delivery had elicited. But Stan took care of that.

"An honor," Stan echoed. "Translates to 'I'm here to suck you off whenever you want it, you lucky blighter.' What a waste. To be handed pussy when you prefer cock. The Council likes to fuck with you, mate."

"Second warning, Stan." Alistair's tone changed only subtly, but Nina heard the sharpness of a hidden knife blade there. "There won't be a third. Go find a drink in my study. I'll be along shortly to teach you some manners. You're being a jealous bitch and a bore."

Stan grumbled, but Alistair's tone seemed to quell his vulgarity. His retreating footsteps told Nina he was leaving them in the foyer together. But his impact lingered.

She was used to men being crude. Most of the men at the hospital hadn't used such crudity toward her, though, no matter how much they flirted. If one of their number stepped over the line, it was his fellows with better sense who knocked him back over it. They knew she was a nurse, not a loose woman.

But how would they act if she was displayed before them like this? She'd always been a good girl. Not this. She wasn't this. Suddenly the pose was exactly as it had been the first time she'd been knocked to her knees and forced into it. Obscene, distasteful. Vulgar. A woman on her knees with legs spread, waiting to be fucked by a man who was in so many ways a total stranger to her. She was going to bolt.

Then Alistair spoke. The words were still formal, a bit distant, but there was a tag to the syllables, a hint of the warmth she remembered.

"He was a boy whore when he was turned, which wasn't so very long ago, in vampire terms. Ten years under his sire's care, and his wild, rough ways amused her, so she taught him no better. Now he's loose on the world and it's a wonder someone hasn't staked him. Pay no attention to him, Nina. Stand for me."

Alistair put a hand beneath her elbow. They hadn't prepared her for assistance, so the way she was supposed to rise wasn't as smooth as her descent. The firm touch of his fingers on her elbow was another shockingly strong memory brought back to life. She wanted to look at him, but she didn't, too, so she kept her gaze down. Since he remained on one knee, his hand at her hip, she found herself gazing at him anyway.

He was studying her knee. He passed his thumb over the cut. She quelled the urge to put a hand on his hair, stroke her fingers through it. It had been dirty, bloody, wet. Now it was thick and lustrous, well-groomed at his nape.

She could see that because he leaned forward and put his mouth on the wound. Nina started, and he tightened his grip on her hip. He teased the blood away with his tongue, making a noise that said the taste met his approval. Then he tilted his head enough to nuzzle her thigh just below the hem of the shirt.

Her body readied itself instantly. The Mistress's training was good for that, and yet she didn't want it to react so non-specifically. She was like the music box in her room, playing for anyone who knew how to operate it. He'd barely said hello and had his mouth within inches of her sex. Well, his mate Stan had said that was what she was here for, right?

She'd stiffened before she could stop herself, and Alistair stilled. Drew back. Now she had her gaze purposefully glued to the floor, even though the slightest shift would have brought their eyes into a lock.

After a long moment, he spoke in a dry tone. "As to your assertion that serving me is an honor, I'm sure that's less than true, but I am honored by Lady Lyssa's efforts on my behalf. I should have used her name in Stan's presence, because that's usually enough to stifle his vulgar ebullience. Too busy trying not to piss himself to be a smart aleck. Be more careful on the stairs, Nina."

Nothing else. No "How have you been," no recollections of their shared past. Brief it had been, but not insignificant. At least to her. She swallowed, an ache in her chest. "Yes, my lord."

He rose, stood before her. His shirt was white and crisp. He'd loosened his tie, opened the button at the throat, so she was staring at the corded strength of that column, the set of his jaw. She lowered her eyes again and spoke the rest of the leaden words she was required to say.

"How may I attend you, my lord, or would you prefer me to familiarize myself with your household until you have direct need of me?"

"If you can tell Nero that we are prepared to have tea, that's all for now."

When he moved, she lifted her gaze, watching him stride away from her. Briskly, as if the intimate moment of his mouth on her knee had never happened. He still moved with purpose, a fluid and powerful grace. When he reached the entrance to the study, he turned back. She hadn't expected it, so their eyes met.

Once in that lock, she couldn't find it in herself to look down. A million emotions rushed back into her chest, a thousand useless pleas to her lips. She felt strangled by everything she was holding back.

He seemed oblivious to it, for a slight smile touched his mouth, and heat slid into his gaze, only adding to her body's lingering reaction to his touch.

"It's good to see you again, sweet nurse. You look far better in that shirt than I ever did."

CHAPTER TEN

or practical purposes she changed back into a blouse and skirt. For the next hour or so, she spent time with Nero, learning more about the household schedule and duties. The day staff would come on at seven, and Nero and the rest would return late afternoon. Alistair's staff worked twelve-hour shifts. Nero's group were considered the senior staff, holding authority over the day shift. He and Mrs. W worked later hours when needed, more involved in the nighttime demands the master of the house's waking hours created. But Alistair was a generous boss, allowing rotations, such that his people only worked a four-day week, with three days off for family.

Whereas an InhServ didn't get any days off. Her leisure time was entirely dependent on her Master's whim.

After she was done with Nero, she wandered the house. As she passed the study where Alistair was behind closed doors with Stan, she took a closer look at the room next to it. It was a small, cozy place with a comfortable, female-sized chair, a book case, a side table with a tea set and a window out to the garden. Winifred was just leaving it, duster and polish in hand.

"Winifred, what's this room?"

"Old-fashioned notion. The retiring room for the lady of the house. She could keep tabs on her husband through the connecting door. Know when he was finishing up with them and they needed more tea and such." She tossed Nina a derisive look. "Expect that would be useful for you, since you're supposed to keep track of all the things he needs. Things women like me, Mrs. W and C don't provide."

"And what would that be, Winifred?" Nina asked it pleasantly, but with an unmistakable injection of steel to her tone.

Whatever Winifred saw in Nina's expression had her eyes widening a bit, then narrowing like an alley cat's. "I don't know who —" she started, but Nina shook her head and cut across her words.

"I've worked in a general hospital near the front, Winifred," she said evenly. "Because I've dealt with things so beyond your limited, small view of the world, I won't fetch you the slap against your ear you so richly deserve. I'm not much of a slapping kind of girl anyway. I'll just punch you in your sullen mouth, or break that nose I'll bet you're quite proud of. I might even be able to set it for you, but I won't be gentle about it. I know a lot about pain. Don't push me. And I won't push you. We understand one another?"

One bated moment passed while the maid took her measure. Nina wasn't worried. On top of everything else, she wasn't going to endure one discontented maid's spitefulness. She had her footing for this. She'd worked among women for nearly ten years of her life.

"Yes, marm," Winifred said at last.

Nina shook her head. "Just Nina. I don't need you to act the hypocrite. Keep your mouth shut and expressions polite when you're around me if you have nothing useful to impart, and we'll get on just fine. Go on with you now."

As Winifred fled, Nina moved into the retiring room, ran her fingertips over the pretty doily on the side table. An old-fashioned notion for certain, but the room was a welcoming nook. Something that could be hers. She liked to read and, during a time like this, she could curl up in the chair and expand her mind. Vampires expected their InhServs to be highly educated, intelligent and cultured. Alistair seemed to have a good library, and Nina had been told books, additional training and the like were entirely appropriate for an InhServ to request. It expanded their abilities to serve their vampire. But she could expand her mind and skills for herself, too.

She was used to paying her own way, though. It rankled, being entirely dependent on his funds, but perhaps she should think of it as her salary, her InhServ status a form of employment.

Or perhaps she was just playing games with her mind. Slaves

weren't given a wage. And if she was paid...well there was a whole other word for that profession, wasn't there?

Stop it. Not helping.

Brow furrowing, she drew closer to the door between this room and that one. At eye level, there was a small square cut into the wood. One with a bronze knob. When she plucked at it, it swung open noiselessly, and she had a postage-stamp-sized peep hole into the room. Which answered the question of how the woman of the house could check on her husband without disrupting him.

She was about to close it, not knowing if Alistair wanted her to avail herself of that avenue or not, but then she saw him. He was sitting in a chair, legs crossed, smoking a cigarette with easy elegance. However, his eyes were sharp as lightning.

Shifting so both his feet were on the floor, he stubbed out the cigarette and leaned forward, his profile intent. "Why are you fucking looking at me?" he said with quiet menace.

Her heart jumped in her chest before she realized he wasn't talking to her. Shifting her view, she saw Stanley was in the opposite chair. The other man's dark eyes heated, but not with anger. He looked down, though he did it by deliberately letting his gaze course down Alistair's body, inch by inch. Alistair's lip curled and his gaze flashed. "So it's going to be like that."

She bit back a gasp when Alistair left the chair, almost faster than she could follow. He had Stanley out of his and shoved down to hands and knees before he could counter, though he made an admirable attempt. Alistair was just that much faster. And stronger.

Alistair held Stanley by the back of the neck, straddling his hips. He shoved his pelvis against the curve of his visitor's back as he leaned over him, nuzzled his hair, took a deep inhale. His fangs lengthened with an ivory flash. Nina drew in another breath. Having felt them was not the same as seeing them like this. Sharp, curved, they looked capable of sinking into flesh and never letting go. Or tearing open someone's body. He grazed the male's neck with them.

"Who's in charge here?" Alistair said, in the same quiet voice.

"You're having delusions of grandeur, mate." But a shudder ran through Stanley, his fists clenched, and he didn't fight Alistair's hold. Alistair must have tightened his grip, because Stanley made a pained noise and then strangled it out. "You. You're in charge."

"Correct. You were very rude to my InhServ gift. You know how to behave like a gentleman. If she wasn't human and a servant, I would force you to apologize. Maybe I will anyway. Until you can act like a better, you likely don't deserve to be treated as one, do you?"

Nina blinked at that. She knew vampires viewed humans as an inferior species, but hearing the implication come out of Alistair's mouth so matter-of-factly was...dismaying.

Alistair straightened, but as he began to step back, Stanley wrapped his arms around one leg, put his mouth on Alistair's inner thigh. His fangs unsheathed but didn't puncture. He simply rubbed them against Alistair's slacks.

The expression Stanley had on his face was far different from the sardonic aggression he'd shown Nina, or even the challenge he'd possessed before Alistair put him on the floor. There was aggression, yes, but purely sexual. Beneath that, so close to the surface it made the aggression a fragile veneer, was a desperation of sorts.

While her mind couldn't classify it, her body could. She'd been startled to feel that desperation over and over, when her roommates and the other members of the training center had roused her body and held it so close to the edge of release, forcing her to face the emotions goaded by such deprivation. Parts of her soul she hadn't wanted to believe existed had been torn open.

Any port in a storm, she'd told herself. Even a prisoner would bond with a brutal jailer, to have some form of emotional connection. But Stanley was a vampire. He was free to come and go. Yet when he looked up at Alistair with that expression, she felt an answering chord inside herself.

The desire to serve. To belong to someone.

To call someone Master.

God, it was all bollocks. She told herself that, viciously. They'd planted all this manure in her head, brainwashed her with it. None of it was the truth.

If Alistair had wanted to remind her right off the vampire-servant relationship was nothing like a husband and wife, he'd done it with ruthless promptness. So she shouldn't be surprised at all that, her first night here, the male she was supposed to consider her Master might bugger a man in the next room before even giving her so much as a proper greeting.

It's good to see you again, sweet nurse. You look far better in that shirt than I ever did.

Okay, mostly not a proper greeting.

Alistair freed himself from Stanley's grip on his leg. She noticed he was firm about it, but not brutal. He pushed the man back to the floor and Stanley stayed there, on all fours, staring at the wood beneath his flattened palms. Alistair stroked his hair, a brief caress. "You know how to prepare yourself for me," he said shortly. "I'll be back when I'm good and ready. None of my brandy better be missing when I return, or I'll shove the bottle up your arse and break it off. You can pray I'll do it in that order."

He strode from the room, closing the study door after him. She heard his footsteps as he went down the hall. Protocol suggested she should seek him out, see if he needed anything now that he'd emerged, but she found herself lingering at that view port, curious about Stanley's reaction. And Alistair had said he'd summon her if needed.

Stanley dropped his forehead to the carpet, staying that way for a long moment that had Nina's brow furrowing. When he lifted his face, she saw a bleakness in his expression, a sort of hopelessness that twisted her heart, despite her earlier revulsion toward his behavior.

At length, the male rose to his feet and stripped off his waistcoat, followed by his shirt.

He was bony but muscular. Nina's attention went to a horrific scar that ran from his left hip bone to his right shoulder. The scar had the shape of a meandering river, plenty of curves. As if someone had carved upon him, rather than laying him open with one sweep of the blade. No one could lie still during the entirety of that cut, unless they were bound.

He'd been tortured with the intent to kill.

Since scars inflicted on a vampire healed and vanished, it had happened when he was human. She had no idea how a human would have survived such a wound, unless there was a surgical team in immediate attendance. His transition might have lightened the scar's appearance, which made the implication of what had been done to him even more harrowing.

Nina bit her lip. An indecipherable mix of emotions were suddenly churning in her chest and stomach.

"So you like to watch, sweet nurse?"

Alistair's voice was at her ear, his heat behind her.

Vampires could move noiselessly. She knew that. She just hadn't expected him to employ the skill to creep up on her. But she knew he hadn't been there long, because his proximity was as tangible to her as a rush of heat from a fire.

Would it be easier or harder to handle all this if she didn't react to him so strongly? Three years, and his voice, his touch, could still affect her. She could rationalize it, say it was the circumstances that had brought them together that made his presence in an unbearable situation bearable, but she wasn't sure. After her time with The Mistress, she wasn't sure of much anymore. Except she needed to escape all this before she lost herself entirely. It was the only thought that consistently made sense, so she clung to it, returned to it as often as the moment allowed it.

This was not going to be one of those moments.

Alistair closed his hands on her shoulders. His lips found her throat, teased there. Her heart accelerated, and he acknowledged it, his grip tightening further.

After he nudged the peephole closed, he turned her toward him. A step forward put her back against the door. As he had in the hall, he dropped to a knee, laying his hands on her thighs. He slid his touch beneath the hem of the skirt, raising it to study the state of her sore knee.

"You cleaned and tended it. Good." He gave the wound a chaste kiss, bemusing her. Rising to his feet, he clasped her hand. "Come with me. We can leave Stanley to his own devices for a while."

"He looks unhappy."

"Well, he should have behaved better." He drew her out of the study, led her down the hallway toward the lower level stairwell. "But he's got a nasty, bottomless need to be punished. It will keep."

She had no idea what Alistair had planned, but his bedroom was downstairs. The ball of tension in her belly coiled tighter. She didn't think she could bear the loss of her virginity in a slap-dash fashion. She was even less mentally prepared for the second and third marks that would irrevocably bind her to him.

"I don't mind waiting on..." She colored and chose a different path. "I don't want to interfere with your time with your guest."

Alistair came to a halt. He did it so abruptly she had to place a hand on his chest to avoid stumbling into him. He tipped up her chin, holding her face in a firm hand.

"How polite of you. To be willing to wait while I bugger that poor sod. Will you wash my dick when I'm done? Dry it with your hair? Have they trained you so well in a month?"

The vindictiveness took her aback. Her eyes snapped up and this time she didn't lower them as she was supposed to do. He'd raked his hands through his hair somewhere between leaving the study and arriving behind her. He hadn't aged, wouldn't have, but there was something older about his eyes, the set of his mouth, that she didn't particularly like at this moment. It reminded her of the house, she realized. Empty of personality, though all the right polish to make it pretty.

Her thoughts of finding an ally in him faltered once more, her hopes taking another hard hit. But The Mistress had devoted considerable effort into driving in the harsh truth, hadn't she? She'd considered making Nina face that reality a gift, and now Nina understood why. At the gateway to Hell, one last glass of ice water wasn't a kindness. It merely increased the craving for what one would never have again. The true gift was the ability to endure constant thirst.

She let her expression go flat. "If my Master wishes me to clean him that way, he merely needs to command it," she said. "My hair isn't long, but shoulder-length is amply sufficient to dry the desired area. More than needed, I suspect."

Alistair stared at her, then blinked once. His lips curved, a dangerous smile. "There she is. The woman I remembered was a submissive, but not timid in the least. Goading me, sweet nurse?"

He moved in closer, and she took a step back, her shoulders meeting the wall. His eyes bored into hers, pinning her body in place. "Why are you looking at me?" he said, with that sensual menace she'd heard with Stanley.

A quiver ran through her. He was telling her she was supposed to look down. But she had to speak the truth.

"I can't look away."

His expression didn't change, but the energy between them did. Maybe a minute passed, maybe ten. She wasn't sure. He leaned in, bracing a hand by her shoulder, the other grasping her by the throat, squeezing just enough to make her lift her chin. Her hands opened and closed at her sides as her body tightened. A shot of need and fear, anticipation and dread, hit her vitals. They weren't on the beach anymore, but the feelings he could rouse in her were all there, only the circumstances were so different. Far more terrifying. Because he wasn't her savior here, but the lynch pin of her prison.

"I gave you the first mark three years ago." The brandy he'd sampled was sweet on his breath. "It's brought me comfort, knowing where you are. But I've thought so often about what you were thinking. Wanting to know what was going through your head."

"Please...don't..." She couldn't help whispering it. She wasn't ready. If marking her was just one more thing on his to-do list, surely it could be put off another day or two.

His thumb swept her pulse, a distracting caress. "Can you deny me, Nina?"

Was he asking her to remember the rules of being an InhServ, or about her ability to think straight when he was this close? Did vampires have a chemical effect on a human?

Sher had been this besotted with him before even meeting him, and yet had seemed so certain she'd stay that way after being in his service.

Where her own will failed her, Sher's memory didn't. It was a cold-water reminder that he hadn't come to her funeral. He'd also told Stanley he didn't have to apologize to Nina because she was human. And a servant.

If she had longer hair, she could knot it around his bloody cock and cut off the blood flow to it.

Nina lowered her gaze, though she couldn't stop the tightening of her jaw. "No, my lord. I submit to your will as you desire."

"But it's your desire that intrigues me." He dropped to his knees again, laid his hands on her thighs. As he looked up at her, she thought of Stanley. How Alistair had stroked a hand through his hair. But whereas Stanley's expression had fit with his desire to be on his knees, there was no relinquishment of power when Alistair knelt. His touch was strong, holding her in place, his gaze alone commanding her stillness. He pressed her legs open so she was flatter against the walls as he slid his touch up under the skirt, his wrists pushing up the fabric.

"You're angry with me," he said.

"I'm angry with the whole fucked-up world."

His gaze flickered. "Words I'm sure the InhServ school didn't teach you to use with your Master."

She didn't know what to say to that, but since he didn't seem to need a reply, and he was sliding her skirt to her waist, she didn't have to summon one. She closed her eyes, willing herself to relax, but she couldn't. She couldn't...

His mouth touched her inner thigh as he caressed her legs, her hips. When his fingertips slid under the elastic of the knickers, she trembled. He drew back enough to study the columns of her thighs, the point of her sex clad in the gauzy silk. He made a soothing noise in his throat, even as she saw by the flash in his blue eyes that her reluctant and uncertain submission fueled his own arousal. His reaction increased her own, which made her hate herself a little.

"So sweet," he muttered, as he brought his mouth back to her flesh. She drew in a breath as he found her sex, flicked his tongue over the mesh covering it. It created a friction that had her hips rising to meet his mouth. A little sighing breath escaped her.

That breath became a gasp as he tore the knickers away with one jerk.

The force and suddenness startled her. In a blink, his grace and confidence had been replaced with animal need. Her hands landed on his shoulders, then moved to his hair as he buried his face in her core. "Oh..." The guttural moan tore from her throat.

She'd expected the stimulation to be too much, too soon, even with her training, but her sex was eager to let him sate his hunger upon her. The wet noises between his heated tongue and lips and her cunt provoked an even more intense arousal. Her legs widened, quivered. She needed him to be deeper. To force his way inside, to fill the emptiness.

"No..." It was a poignant plea, a cry from her heart, but one that her body heeded even less than he did.

Fear gave her the will to twist, to fight. He was far stronger, but instead of inhibiting her movements, he simply matched her contortions, a writhing dance. His tongue was too clever. The swirls and thrusts, the nips from his teeth, had her crying out for different reasons.

He was playing with her, even as he was ruthless, driving her up and up, but he held the peak out of reach, easing back, countering and angling as her body bucked. She cursed him, and he merely chuckled, a growling response. When her legs gave out, he lifted her, gripping her thighs and guiding them over his shoulders, so her back and hips were braced against the wall and her legs were curved over his broad back, heels digging into the valley above his tight arse. He widened her with the pressure of his hands, and she screamed as he worked his way deeper, then slid out and under her clit hood, teasing those hyper-sensitive nerve endings.

He only gave her relief from that when he turned his head to her inner thigh and bit. The pain shot through her, but it was so tangled with the pleasure, it perversely intensified it. Then she remembered how he'd used that sensual stimulant in his fangs, as he'd done for the first mark.

"No..." But it was too late. The erotic surge of response clamped down on every muscle, awoke every nerve she'd thought was already wide awake. She was distantly aware of a fiery burn through her leg that spread out through her lower belly, her chest. It ran through every limb and sent a direct charge to her brain, overwhelming it with colors and feelings, a twisted rainbow ribbon cut loose by a lashing storm.

Though she was already experiencing an intensity of feeling that surpassed that of the innumerable climaxes she'd had this month, remarkably he was still holding her back from release. She hovered on a knife's edge, moaning, hips tattooing the wall, grinding her sex against him as he sealed his mouth over the bite, his fangs retracting.

When he put his fingers on her, stroked flesh on flesh, she came apart. In the violence of her reaction, she threw her head back without restraint. She should have seen stars from the impact against the wall.

Instead, with that vampire swiftness, he was standing, pressed against her, his palm cupping her skull before it came to harm. He pinned her to the wall with his body even as his other hand remained between them, stroking and squeezing her sex, her clitoris, in all the right ways, so that sensation kept battering her.

When her eyes fluttered open, she was staring into his. The intensity of the blue was indescribable. It was like no color she knew, infused with an otherworldly power no human could understand.

He was devouring her response, her hoarse screams. The steel heat of him pressed against her core, but he didn't act upon that. Merely watched her go over and shudder through wave after wave of her climax, until she was limp in his arms, her head resting in his palm like an infant's.

Can you deny me, Nina?

She wasn't remembering the question. She was hearing it repeated in his voice, inside her head, as clear as if he'd spoken aloud.

The second mark was done. Her mind was no longer hers alone. Tears clogged her throat as she gave him the simple, heartbreaking truth.

No.

～

He saw her tears, but he didn't say anything about them. Not with words. Instead, he lifted her. She slid her arms around his shoulders, her legs around his hips, her face buried in his neck. She could fight him, but she knew this battle of her war was lost. She'd take what comfort she could, even if technically she was in the arms of the enemy.

Enemy, hmm?

He paused halfway down the stairs to the lower level. After a weighted pause, he reversed course. He took her back up the stairs to the first floor. Then the second. And the third.

The only enemy you have here is Stanley. After hearing your lovely cries, he will be so envious he would cheerfully tear out your heart. If I'd allow it, which I never would. Your heart belongs to me, like the rest of you, sweet nurse.

She wished he wouldn't say things that were supposed to mean something but didn't. He'd been what she needed in Singapore and Bangka. He knew how to say the right things now, to her and to Stanley. But what did any of it really mean to him? She'd stared into his eyes and seen emptiness.

If he was listening to her thoughts, he had no response to that. When he stepped outside, she was curious enough to lift her head. Letting her feet slide down to the wooden platform of the widow's walk, he directed her to turn toward the polished gold railing. During daylight, this elevated view provided a marvelous panorama of the ocean, miles along the horizon.

Fortunately, right now, the breathtaking view was a brilliant tapestry of stars in the sky, an occasional cloud scudding over them. The surf was a distant white milky line reflecting the moonlight. The noise of it mixed with and was muted by the breeze that lifted her hair and fluttered strands across her lips.

They stood in silence for a few moments. The wind fluttered up under her skirt, teasing her damp folds. She realized her awareness of the connection between their minds was like an open radio channel, only she assumed he was blocking on his end, since she didn't hear any of his thoughts.

Her Master could listen to any of her thoughts at any time, whereas his mind would only open to her when he permitted it.

"It seems invasive at first, but after a while, not so much. Saves a lot of time. You don't have to find a phone if you can't remember what I wanted you to pick up at the market," he pointed out. "You just ask. Also, no reason to pick or choose words, be diplomatic, when all the emotions are right there. That's probably the hardest part for a made vampire to handle at first."

She blinked. "Why would it be hard for the vampire?"

He glanced down at her. They were standing close, shoulder to shoulder, but not touching. "Kind of takes you by surprise, doesn't it? That any of this servant thing could be problematic for the one with the upper hand?"

"I've not yet heard why you think it's difficult," she said dryly. "And you've never been on the other end of it."

"Yes and no. Lady Lyssa is my sire, which means she has access to my thoughts however, whenever she wants. Sometimes a vampire can learn to block the sire a bit, control the flow, depending on how accomplished he gets. She's a thousand years old. My chances of ever getting the upper hand with her are right there alongside the lamb with the lion."

He grimaced wryly. "At first, the novelty of having a marked servant has you listening in all day long. Over time, it becomes more of a functional thing. Or something to intensify the sexual moments. I don't tune in to every thought. But it depends on the vampire, really."

"You've had a servant before," she realized.

He nodded. "Twice."

He'd said he was around three hundred. A vampire didn't release a third mark from service, so if he had no third marked servant, it meant they were both dead. He'd lost both of them before their full life span.

Since he didn't volunteer further information about the two servants, and she wasn't sure if it would be an easy topic for either of them, she stuck with the point. "So why is it a problem, hearing the servant's thoughts? Trouble blocking at first?"

He shook his head. "People alter their thoughts considerably when they turn them into words. So when you hear something straight from someone's head, you have to learn not to react so much to the emotional component."

At her curious look, he expanded, propping his elbows on the railing and tossing her a grimly amused expression. "How many times have you had a situation where one of your patients, one in pretty bad shape, needed you back to his bedside a dozen times? With a hundred other things needing your attention, there's going to be at least once you think, 'oh, bugger, there the whiny bastard goes again, needing something' Even if he's not whiny in the least."

"But that's not his fault."

"Not at all. You don't mean it, and you don't resent him for it, not really, but your emotions are your emotions. For that moment, you feel despair, resentment, a little annoyance because you're frazzled, having to work him into twenty other things. A vampire hears all that. We learn to separate what's the true, enduring emotion amid the noise, if that makes sense. And we do," he added. "Which is why you don't have to be self-conscious about any of it. We pick up what you really feel, really mean."

She stiffened. "Or do you just hear what you want to hear, and interpret it according to your own needs?"

The surrounding night made his eyes dark, hard to read, despite his deceptively pleasant tone. "I expect you'll determine the answer to that in time. You asked me, that day so long ago, had I ever had dreams of a family. A forever love. I expect you did. Right?"

The truth was there in her mind for him to see. When he gave her the third mark, he wouldn't even need the cracks in her broken heart to see them. He would see them from the inside.

She turned away, stared out over the rail. It really was a marvelous view, a stunning home. But if she had been in a five-by-five cell with no windows and only a concrete floor upon which to sleep, she wouldn't have felt any more trapped. Suffocated. Helpless.

She hadn't really thought it through. All the explanations and logical arguments she'd imagined having with him about why he should help her get free of this? There was no need for those conversations. He could see it all, respond to it as he liked. Or ignore it entirely.

He was behind her, the heat of his body able to penetrate her clothes without even touching her. If she leaned back, she would be against him. Supported by him. Which would be a lie. She stayed standing straight and tall. Holding herself up, no matter that the weight of the world made her want to crumple to the floor, curl up in a ball and never rise again.

He touched her lower back, so that she looked up at him. When he'd carried Mort to the triage station, when he'd rescued her from the surf, his hair had been disheveled, a tangle over his brow. Now, though the wind was playing with a few strands, it was mostly smoothed back, a gentleman's sharp style. It emphasized the razor cut of his cheekbones and brow. Perhaps it was that which gave his lips a crueler cast than she remembered, as well as that jaded look in his eyes.

When he spoke, she occasionally heard the same notes of kindness and patience she remembered from before. She also vividly recalled his male awareness of her, but now there was another note to it. A knowledge that he could have anything he wished from her, at any time.

The thought brought a shiver, and she turned from him. He shifted, rested his hands on her upper arms, let his palms glide up and down her biceps. She stepped forward, away, her back still to him.

He didn't follow her, but his quiet words constricted the chains she felt weighing her down. "You're here because you chose to honor your family's commitment, Nina. Have you changed your mind about that?"

So it really didn't matter to him. Or human free will was so outside the realm of a three-hundred-year-old vampire's thinking, even one who'd once been human, that he didn't feel it necessary to bring it up. She closed her eyes, tears stinging them. The lump in her throat was going to choke her.

She truly was alone in this.

She had stood hip deep in dying men, survived a massacre on a beach. Survived her twin's death. Maybe. She wasn't really sure she'd survived that one. Some days she felt numb as a corpse, an empty place inside her where Sher's presence had been.

But though Sher's loss couldn't be altered, other variables could. Change was the inevitable result of moving forward. It was the only thought that could give her the courage she needed. She didn't have enough to turn to face him, but she found enough to take one step back, within his reach. And waited, her head bowed. She felt the weight of his gaze on her nape, her shoulders. Though she wore clothes, it didn't seem that way. She'd never felt so vulnerable.

After a long pause, his hands returned to her arms, but this time he closed the distance between them, his chest against her shoulder blades. Nudging her hair to the side, he put his lips on her throat.

Her head tipped and her pulse sped up. His grip tightened, slowly, and when he eased back, he drew her arms with him, keeping his hold on them, so her spine was arched, her breasts tilted up. Her head dropped back on his shoulder fully as he suckled her neck, grazed her with his fangs, used his tongue along her carotid.

He'd done things like this moments ago, and yet her body was already responding to his again. Like a drug. Her breath escaped in a harsh sob, making his hold on her tighten.

"I remember how to touch you, Nina. You know I know how to do it. To give you the pleasure you seek from a Master. Have you found that from a man's touch yet?"

At the InhServ training facility, men had handled her, taught her, but only women had been in charge of her release, her orgasms. "No."

"You're still a virgin."

"Not sure if you can call it that, except for the technical definition."

He moved his grip to her jaw, and she was pierced by his gaze, her pulse thudding against his hold. "Are you a virgin?" he repeated, with more emphasis.

He could read it from her mind, but he wanted it from her mouth. That felt significant to her, though she wasn't sure why. "Yes."

"All of it?" His thumb swept her lips. "Your mouth, your cunt, your arse. None of it has been stretched by a man's cock?"

It would have sounded crude, like Stanley, but for the way he said it, low and husky. She shook her head, though she was aware her cheeks were flaming. "No. None of it."

She remembered asking her roommates about it, because clearly the other InhServs were being sexually initiated before leaving the school.

"We were told your Master-to-be ordered you to be delivered to him intact," Edith had told her. *"A virgin in all ways. You'll get your first full sexual experience at his hands."*

At the time, Nina had bit back a harsh laugh. Edith had a different definition of full sexual experience, because a month at the school had been a thorough initiation into all sorts of debauchery she'd never even imagined.

But now, she realized the significance of it. Alistair would be her first. She might not have a choice, but he'd ensured that it would at least be with him. Had he done that out of kindness? Or as a gift he was bestowing on himself? She wasn't sure how she felt about either explanation.

"Good." He'd straightened, his demeanor casual again now that she'd given him the honest answer. "You have a pretty blush. So they jammed the rest into a month of training?"

"All twenty years of it." When he turned her to face him, she pressed her lips together, stared at his chest. "They should really consider having a policy manual. Something they can send off with the new InhServ for quick reference. Particularly those of us who get the crash course."

When she found enough strength to look up into his face, she saw some humor there. It might not count for anything of substance, but she found the reserves in herself to pick up their conversation where it had left off.

"You know my thoughts on it. I don't know yours. About whether you wanted a family or not. Before you were turned."

He drew her by the hand to a wooden chair with sturdy broad arms that likely served as a place to put a drink or snack plate. As he sat down, he settled her arse on one of them, her feet on the chair seat between his knees, his hand resting with intimate familiarity on her hip.

He didn't respond right away. Instead, he propped his head on the chair, closed his eyes. They sat that way for a while. Her hand's natural resting place was his shoulder, and her fingers wanted to make small patterns on his neck, slide through the strands of hair brushing her knuckles. She made herself stay still, though.

"I did think about it," he said at last, surprising her. "Home and family. But then... Do you remember how you were before the war? Even before becoming a nurse?"

A younger version of herself flashed through her mind. Laughing, biking with friends, dreaming of handsome men and wedding dresses. Writing in a diary that had flowers drawn on the front.

A poignant smile touched his lips. "It's like a dream, isn't it? Another person entirely. You had long legs. Knobby knees."

"My brothers nicknamed me Colt. For a while, I could outrun all of them. Then they caught up, became taller than me."

She turned her gaze to him, and emotion surged hard into her chest. "Alistair, can't we talk—"

"I thought becoming a vampire wouldn't change my humanity," he said, cutting across her. "I ignored the inescapable fact that I was being changed into another humanoid species entirely. With far different moral imperatives and motivations. What I want as a vampire isn't the same as what I wanted as a human. I possess you because I want you, Nina. Because you are mine."

His look told her he knew what she wanted to say. He stood inside her mind like a circus ringmaster, driving back the unspoken pleas with words disturbing as the snap of a whip. All the more so because he spoke them in an even, quiet tone.

When she would have averted her face, he cupped it, brought it back to him with a firm hold. "When I mark you three times, you'll change, too. And understand better. I also don't think it will be as alien to you as you fear."

"You would take that which is not given to you willingly?" she said, trying to hold back the anger, but it wasn't like she could hide it from him. Her spine had become ramrod stiff, even as his hand glided up the rigid track and down again.

"You made a choice to be here," he pointed out.

"Because the choice is be here, or my family suffers. To a person of conscience, that is not a choice."

"To a person of courage," he corrected. "But your family isn't unwillingly bound to our world. They have a long and distinguished history of devotion and service to it."

"I'm so pleased for them. Unfortunately, it all happened centuries ago, so I wasn't present for the family discussion about it."

Why did no one else see how unfair this all was? To bind her to a promise that she'd had no say about?

"You can tear yourself apart over it, or accept that it is what it is. But know this, Nina." He touched her face again, one fingertip tracing the line of her jaw with slow purpose as his blue eyes bored into hers. "What I take, I promise—you will give it willingly."

Before she could process that, his manner changed. He rose, lifting her to stand by his side again. As he looked out into the night, he curled his hands over the rail.

"But I know what it is to feel helpless. To need to be in control of something, even if it's a temporary respite from the chaos of knowing you have none."

He glanced down at her. "Stanley hurt your feelings. I'd whip him until he bled just for that, but the poor sod's messed up in the head."

She struggled to tamp down her emotions, keep up with where he was going. "What happened to him? I saw his scar."

"And here I was, thinking you were ogling his manly bits."

"He hadn't removed his pants yet. You arrived and shut the peep-hole before then."

Alistair's gaze glinted as she blinked at him. "You have a clever tongue. Sharp and sweet. I expect that will give me some excellent reasons to punish you." He sobered. "Stanley was a boy whore, as I said. Some blokes who found man-love unnatural jumped him and a customer in an alley. Disemboweled the customer, made short work of him. Left him there with his cock stuffed in his mouth and 'sodomite' written across his chest, to ensure the police didn't expend much effort on an investigation.

"But Stanley was too pretty. Probably made them have thoughts they didn't want to have about a man. Took him into an abandoned building and spent more time on him. Carved him up good before they pulled out his guts and left him there. As luck would have it—I won't say whether it was good or bad—a female vampire happened on the scene. She tucked it all back in, turned him, which she's not supposed to do without Council approval, but they allowed it. She batted her eyes, explained he was too grievously wounded and too close to death's door for him to survive the servant marking process."

"So it was an act of compassion."

"No." Alistair said. "She just presented it that way. A true act of compassion would have been to kill him humanely, end his suffering. But Gellana is not on the warm and fuzzy side of the sociopath spectrum. The Council was none-too-pleased, since Stanley is quite obviously not vampire material, but since done was done, and our rules say that a fledgling is not punished for the crimes of the sire, they decided the best territory for him would be mine. Primarily because they want me to fail as Region Master here. Giving me a bloke who has as much business being a vampire as a half-wit does being a brain surgeon, offers me another excellent opportunity to cack this up."

He took them back to the subject of Stanley. "She did stay with him the proper amount of time a sire is supposed to do, but her mentoring was sloppy at best. She didn't value the gift that lies within him. Now no one will, because he's a vampire, and we're not allowed to submit, except to vampires stronger than us, and only within the boundaries of protocol. What happens between him and me here isn't exactly protocol, but that's no one business but his and mine...and maybe yours, if you're game."

He looked down at her, capturing her in that close, assessing way of his that could be flattering or unsettling, depending. "I don't understand," she said.

"He needs a woman's touch. I could ram my dick into him all day, and he'd get off, because his cock is only slightly less simple minded than the rest of him, but what he really wants is a woman pounding some manners in him. Want to hold the upper hand over this blighter who treated you so shabbily? Want to help me with his schooling?"

She blinked. "They didn't... I don't know..."

"They didn't let you have that, did they?" His gaze swept her. "While I could say it was a training thing, part of it was reading you down to the core. You're not a Mistress. But that doesn't mean you don't have topping abilities. You were a nurse, after all, having to keep unruly boys in line."

"You don't believe much in pleasantries, do you?" she managed. "Tea first, catch up on the past three years. That kind of thing."

"When was the last time you were able to sit and have tea with someone, and not have your mind wander off into fields of blood? Paths to oblivion are far better than stagnant rituals we both know mean fucking nothing," he said.

The words had more than a jagged edge. Warmth, polite emptiness, cynicism; that mix was gone in a blink. Now all she saw in his gaze was an abyss, where Alistair, if he was there, was down deep in the well. No charm evident, not even frosty politeness. It was empty. Desolate.

He'd turned to her when he spoke, put his hands on her biceps. Gripped her to the point of bruising. Now his attention snapped to the painful hold. As quickly as it had happened, he let her go and stepped back, the empty, dispassionate look on his face again. "Never mind. I'll handle Stanley. You should return to your duties."

She wasn't sure what was going on with him, but the decision for the immediate moment was simple. The alternative was wandering through the house aimlessly with little to do until she had enough of an understanding of his needs to occupy herself. He kept her on her toes enough she wasn't getting lost in her own head, a boon for sure. Seeing the mercurial changes in his mood, she wondered if she might be serving a similar purpose. Her ability to read a patient had been augmented by InhServ training. That radar said Alistair didn't want to handle Stanley on his own.

"I have no duties other than serving you. My lord. Allow me to help you with your guest."

The formal words came from the lessons she learned. The dry tone was all her own, one she'd used in the past to goad a doctor into better humor, particularly one with an overblown god-complex who had difficulty accepting not everything revolved around him—or was in his control. It was why other nurses at the Sydney hospital had often maneuvered her into working with the more difficult physicians.

"You have this way about you," she recalled Misty Brown saying. *"You're so helpful, he can't get cranky with you. If he does, you turn a mirror on*

him, so he realizes he's being a bit of a bastard and steps back. Even feels a bit remorseful, something they school out of most of them."

She didn't think Alistair was feeling remorse, but the expression on his face was no longer empty. The corner of his mouth turned up, a dangerously sexy expression that made her heart skip a beat.

He blinked once, slow. "Think you can manage me, Nina? Keep *this* unruly lad in line?"

Before she could think of a response, he'd closed the distance between them, holding her once more. Not bruising this time, but in a way that made it clear she couldn't get away. Then he dipped his head, laid his mouth on hers, and she couldn't even think of escape. She kept her eyes open, looking into his, but they fell shut when he spoke in her mind.

I have an order for you, Nina. You won't call me Master until I say you can. No matter how much you wish to do so.

She wanted to be outraged, annoyed. She didn't want to call any man Master. He deepened the kiss and she swayed into his body, her own arching into his grip as it tightened on her upper arms, pulling her onto her toes. It was a physical response. They'd taught her physical response, hammered it into her, so her body could respond, even if her mind wasn't on board.

She knew that wasn't entirely true. Yes, InhServ training turned sexual arousal into a muscle memory response, like riding a bike. But it had also tapped into a longing inside her that connected to what she'd imagined wanting from the man with whom she'd share her life. She hadn't been able to define it. But Alistair seemed to know what it was.

A blatant desire to serve... You have it in you, Nina...

God, what she would give to get out of her own fucking head for ten minutes.

He eased her back to her heels, but his face stayed close, his eyes heated. "Wish granted. Would you like a taste of The Mistress's power?" he asked, low. "I'll help you."

"Managing an unruly boy?" She managed it, narrowing her gaze at him. "Turning him over my knee?"

The flash of a smile was devastating, as much because the heat in his eyes was something far from humor.

"Watch yourself, sweet nurse," he said. "Else you'll be the one over my knee before this night is over."

Her traitorous mind could have conjured an immediate and very provocative image to go with that, but she discovered Alistair could inject a detailed and graphic one that made hers pale in comparison.

Him, in his bedroom near dawn. Wearing his slacks, unhooked at the waist, no shoes and no shirt. Sitting propped up on his pillows, with her draped over his lap. He'd ordered her there, after he made her undress, except for black lace knickers. He'd had her come to him on all fours, across the mattress. Once she got there, he stopped her, loosened her hair so it tumbled over her shoulders. He scraped his fingers through it, tugging, bringing her forehead down to his thigh as he ran his other broad palm over the curve of her back.

Put yourself over my lap. Elbows on the mattress. Legs spread and arse lifted.

She raised her head, and didn't recognize her face, the fire in her eyes, the hunger in the parted, moist lips. Her hair was a sultry curtain around her taut, aroused features.

The image disappeared, and she started. She'd forgotten she was a member of the audience, not on the stage itself. Alistair was still so close, his heat and energy. He was gripping her hand. The saltiness of the night air was on her lips, the sea breeze cooling her heated cheeks but not what was going on inside her body.

"Keep that memory in mind," he said, low, "because it might be what you'll be doing right before I go to sleep at dawn. And you should recognize that face in my mind." He touched her mouth with a light finger of the other hand, and she realized her lips were parted. "It's the expression you have right now."

CHAPTER ELEVEN

*A*listair's grip on her hand was strong, his fingers insinuating between hers to hold them in a firm lock, as if they were about to leap into something together that might require a tight hold to keep from being separated. He kept them connected that way as they returned to the first floor.

She'd noted a curious lack of servants on their way back to the study, and wondered if he had certain prearranged signals for Nero to keep them out of the way. Maybe they were on a dinner break. She hadn't really thought about food, and realized she should be hungry. Maybe the second mark had taken her appetite.

It usually increases it, temporarily. But perhaps that's just with men.

Did that mean his two earlier servants had been men? So why had he wanted her, then? Uneasily, she remembered Stanley's implication. Obviously, he could enjoy women when the moment required it, but if in his relationships, Alistair preferred men...

Why should that give her a sinking feeling? It could provide her more freedom if he did.

He could be listening to all this. He didn't seem as if he were, though. Or if he was, he was choosing not to comment. Maybe that was what he'd meant about a made vampire learning how to filter over the decades. It would give a servant a semblance of privacy in her own thoughts. Until he spoke and reminded her it was only a semblance, not the actual thing.

They'd reached the study door. She suffered a moment of uncertainty, realizing she might have volunteered herself for something she knew nothing about. He had an answer for that, though.

Follow my lead. Until you find your own path with it. I want you to do that.

He put a finger to his lips, telling her to stay silent, and opened the door, drawing her into the room with him.

She'd seen a lot of shocking things at InhServ school, so what was before her wasn't unfamiliar. But she'd viewed the training center like a carnival, where outlandish things were expected. Seeing Stanley presented as he was now took some mental adjustment.

The younger vampire was standing in the center of the room. What looked like a metal wagon wheel, turned on its side, had been lowered from the ceiling. Chains dropped down from that wheel were attached to manacles, and Stanley had put them on his wrists, the chains slack enough to allow him to do both arms. His head was dropped into a resting state, because lifting it to look around the room would have been a useless occupation. He wore a laced eye mask, bound tight to ensure he couldn't see anything.

He was also gagged. Beneath the eye mask, a thick piece of leather was strapped over his mouth, fully concealing it. From the set of his jaw, the working of his throat, she knew there was something attached to that piece that was filling his mouth, holding down his tongue. They'd had gags like that at the training center. She'd had one put in her mouth when she couldn't hold her tongue. The depression piece had been like a man's shaft, only much thicker, stretching her lips and working her jaw muscles.

Stanley had removed all his clothes, and now she could see the manly bits she'd tartly teased Alistair about. That insidiously meandering scar had come perilously close to taking off his male organ, and she wondered that the brutal sadists who'd attacked him had left it.

Maybe they had preferred to taunt him with the possibility of it being removed. Or maybe his vampire sire had interrupted them before they could do it.

Stanley was erect and, despite Alistair's prolonged absence, she understood that. Alistair's last words to him had been, "Prepare yourself for me." The Mistress and all the InhServs had showed Nina the mind could become the most potent of erotic weapons, keeping arousal endlessly on high alert. Especially when it had nothing to do but occupy itself with thoughts of what was to come.

Nina saw no resistance in Stanley's posture. He needed, wanted, what was happening in this room.

Alistair shrugged out of his coat, draped it on a rack. The casual movement only emphasized his command of the situation. Before he went to Stanley, he moved to switches on the wall. An electronic hum, and the chains retracted up toward the wagon wheel with a clink, clink, clink of noise, a slight rocking of the wheel. As Stanley's arms were lifted, his body was stretched. Alistair kept the chains going until Stanley's heels left the floor. He stopped him when he was balanced on his toes. It defined all the fine, lean muscle, from Stanley's working jaw and throat, to his quivering abdomen and thighs.

As Stanley tipped back his head, even with so much of his face covered, she could see what Alistair meant. The jaunty hat had shadowed his face, downplaying what she could see now, an androgynous loveliness to his jaw and sharp line of cheekbone, full lips. His body, so lean and angular, was nevertheless an artistic play of muscle and sinew that moved with a dancer's grace against his bonds, the muscles of his taut arse and thighs tempting a person to stroke. Touch.

She glanced at Alistair and saw he was admiring the same terrain that she was examining. *Beautiful, isn't he? He's all ours, Nina. Think of that. What it means. What it feels like.*

Leaving her with that remarkable thought, he moved across the room to Stanley. Standing close, Alistair touched his captive, gliding his knuckles down Stanley's side, to his hip.

Stanley's body swayed, and his body strained for that touch. Alistair took it away, circling him. He pulled the area rug out from beneath Stanley, folded and shoved it to the wall with one foot.

"Won't have you making a mess on my carpet."

The removal served another purpose. Now as Alistair circled him, his hard-soled shoes made precise, crisp noises against the wood, telegraphing to Stanley what he was doing. Studying. Evaluating. Enjoying what was his to enjoy, however and at the pace he liked.

Women enjoyed flesh, too, but there were other things equally engaging to them. As provocative as it was to see a finely made naked male on display, Nina watched Alistair. How he walked. The turn of his head, the sharp focus as he studied something he wanted. The firm set of his lips. How his clothes molded to his strong body. The flex of his fingers as they stroked Stanley's side in a deceptively casual way.

Then casual disappeared as Alistair shifted so he was pressed against Stanley's back. His hand curved over his hip, fingers curling around Stanley's cock. When he squeezed, hard, the bound vampire made a noise against the gag and dropped his head back to Alistair's shoulder. Alistair was having none of it. He seized Stanley's thick, unruly hair and wrenched his head to the side.

His fangs shot forth, fully visible to Nina's gaze for a blink before he sank them into Stanley's shoulder. The view through the peephole hadn't done them justice. Those monstrous things had been in her neck. The pain had been followed by that rush of sensual pleasure, which had eased the discomfort.

Alistair wasn't using the stimulant on Stanley. She was sure of it. Yet he rocked against Alistair's hold, a moan escaping around the gag. It made her wonder what it would have felt like when Alistair had fed from her, if he hadn't used that aphrodisiac in his fangs.

Alistair made a quelling, fierce noise at his captive. "You want to be fucked, but you'll get what I give you and thank me. Come into my house and act like a little shit. Say you're sorry."

Stanley said something against the gag. There was contrition in it, but also a challenge. He tilted his head away, toward Nina, showing he was aware of her presence.

"Yes, she's here. When we're done with you, when she's done with you, that apology will be sincere. She has no training with my toys, so she can practice on you until she sorts out how to use them. It doesn't take too long to learn a stockman's whip, does it? Only a few months, maybe a year of practice, before she won't cut flesh when she wields it."

Nina blanched. She'd been intrigued by Alistair's offer to help with Stanley, but she hadn't imagined he would pull her into the sadistic side of things. She didn't want to cause true harm to someone. Not like that.

Don't worry, sweet nurse. Part of the art of this is playing with his mind. If he gets worried enough about what might happen, a smack with a riding crop will feel like a barbed cat o' nine to him. Though I have used that on him. When I sipped from the blood of his cuts, he came all over himself like a school-

boy. He needs the pain. Enjoys it. I don't give him more than does him good, though. I won't let him cross that threshold.

Opening a tall armoire made of glossy dark wood, Alistair gestured her over to it with a tilt of his head. She drew closer, uncertain but curious. Some things she didn't recognize, but their erotic potential could captivate the mind. He had plenty of tools she did recognize. Whips, floggers, paddles, canes. Her backside throbbed at the memories they evoked.

Other parts of her throbbed at the image Alistair placed in her mind. *I've got a barbed cushion with a center vibrating piece, a phallus with a clitoral stimulator. Put you down on it, you'll come even as you're going mad with the feeling of those tiny needles pricking your arse. As you come, you writhe, no help for it, and it all becomes one impossible tangle of reaction. I'll stroke myself to release, just from watching you endure it. But for now...*

Had she said he kept her from getting lost in her head? That wasn't exactly correct. He kept her from getting lost in her head by herself, with thoughts she didn't want to have.

"She's the exact right weapon to teach you a lesson, Stanley," Alistair said. His tone was hard, but the heat in his gaze, the way he looked at her, showed his pleasure with her distraction.

I'll have to think about whether I want to use that cushion on you after your spanking. That could be intriguing. But let's handle Stanley first.

He lifted an item off a backboard in the armoire. Taking the mix of rubber and straps to an occasional chair, he sat down, his knees spread, before gesturing Nina to him.

As she complied, she recognized what he had. It had never been used on her, but she'd been instructed in its existence and function. The female teachers had made good use of them with both male and female trainees.

It was a strap-on, outfitted with a rubber cock shape equal to Stanley's own aroused size. Alistair didn't unhook her skirt. Instead, he pulled a folding knife from his pocket, one so sharp that when he ran the blade down the center line of the skirt in front, the fabric parted as if he'd used sewing shears.

She was still without knickers. Working beneath the now slit skirt, Alistair put the straps over her hips and sex, fastening the harness and adjusting the straps efficiently. When he tightened it, the pressure had her lips parting. As did his fingers, brushing her inner thighs, her hips and buttocks. The rubber shaft jutted out from the slit in the skirt, and he gave the look an approving nod, caressing her upper thighs as she swayed into his touch. Her sex throbbed in the compression of straps that ran between her thighs and up between her arse cheeks.

"You should see her, Stanley. Her sweet little body in a short skirt and a thin blouse that shows off the lace of her bra. Her nipples are tight with excitement."

She bit her lip as Alistair brushed his knuckles over one. His gaze held hers, registering her reaction, even as he continued to speak. "All of her feminine and dainty, except for that thick, punishing dick she'll drive into your insolent arse to teach you manners."

His tone changed, became deceptively casual. "Should we have mercy on him and use lubricant, or would you prefer to ram into him dry? Hmm...dry it is. I don't blame you a bit. He was a horse's arse to you. Well, have at it then, whenever you're ready."

Stanley made a noise that could have been outrage or cheek. Alistair slanted her a devilish smile, producing a tube of unscented lubricant he uncapped silently. After dipping his fingers into it, he liberally coated the dildo. The oil would get on her clothing, but based on his treatment of her skirt, she expected he wasn't worried about the cost of replacing them.

He'd left her clothed, and armed her, in a manner of speaking. Against Stanley at least.

Sitting where he was, her breasts were at eye level, outlined in the blouse as he'd described. Alistair reached out, traced the curve of one with one long finger. Slow, meditative. Her breathing hitched again.

I love how responsive you are, Nina. The Mistress knows her business, but she has to have the raw material.

He slipped one button, two, so the blouse was open below the bra. He dipped his fingers into her cleavage, let a fingertip follow her breast inside the cup of the bra, so close to the nipple it tightened further.

Nina watched him. Felt the heat of his breath against her skin. He lifted his gaze back to her face, logging her reactions. Inside and out, she expected, since he was in her head.

He left her blouse like that and rose. Drawing her over to Stanley, he picked up a step stool on the way, one tucked behind the more comfortable furnishings. It was adjustable, and Alistair was obviously practiced in its use, because after he adjusted the height and handed her onto the top platform, she saw it put her at the right level to push that dildo right between Stanley's tense, tight buttocks.

She didn't know if she could do this. She wasn't even sure how to do it, but Alistair moved behind her and put his hands to her hips, his thumbs pressing into her buttocks, against the thin skirt.

Trust me to lead, Nina. Get out of your head and into the moment.

"He's all yours, Nina," Alistair said aloud. "He's one of the naughty boys in your ward, the one who tries to grab your arse every time you come by and looks down your blouse. Who makes crude comments about fucking you when he thinks you're not around, but actually knows you are, because he wants you to hear. He's begging for your punishment, needing you to teach him better manners. He needs your firm hand, Nina."

For every moment you've felt out of control of your destiny, sweet nurse, take it back now. Take it out on his fine, fine arse, and I promise you he will be nothing but grateful. He will burst with gratitude.

And you? What will you be?

The thought had no ready answer. Entertained? Intrigued? Sexually satisfied and nothing more, like pushing away from a table after a good meal.

He'd said get out of her head, but she wasn't sure she could do that. He hadn't answered her unspoken question, leaving her nothing but what was before her. He had his hands on her hips, ready to guide her, but he wasn't pushing her to go right to buggering the bound male. Which left her time to consider her options.

Except for the night with The Mistress, she'd had a month of no options, only the mandate that she do what she was ordered to do. Now she'd been given only two restrictions. Get out of her head, and find her own path.

She settled tentative fingers on Stanley's shoulder blade, followed the elegant line of it, the straining muscles. Down to the lower back. Turning her hand, she trailed her knuckles over his rib cage, the same track Alistair had covered. Stanley quivered in his chains, said something obviously uncomplimentary against the gag.

Alistair's hand left her side. Fortunately, he wasn't moving at vampire speed, so she intercepted the smart slap he'd intended to land against the side of Stanley's head. She gripped his wrist, her slim fingers overlapping his forearm.

What did he say? She asked in his head. How peculiar to be able to do that, and have an immediate response, all of it done right here with Stanley, but him able to hear none of it. *And how can you understand him?*

He said, 'Get on with it, stupid human bitch.' I've imposed the blood link of a sire, so I can be in his head. He can try to block me, but to be even marginally successful at it takes focus and practice. Maturity and strength of will. He's as disciplined as a fawn cavorting through a field of flowers, the blighter.

She nodded. And thought about what else Alistair had said about Stanley.

A nasty, bottomless need to be punished.

She remembered a soldier brought into the hospital. He'd panicked, hadn't been able to pull it together and be there for his mates. Instead, he'd ended up curled in a fox hole, screaming for an end to the noise of the guns. When he was brought to the hospital for evaluation, he'd laid open his arms with the cut glass from a cup of juice one of the nurses had left with him. Not an attempt to cut his wrists. He hated himself so much he wouldn't give himself that out. Just kept slicing his flesh, until she and the other nurse had to wrestle his arms down, restrain him. The two of them had been painted with blood when it was done.

As she'd bent over his wrist, using strips of gauze to tie him to the bed rails, he'd swiped his fingertips over her cheek. Since his hands were still bloody, it had left a stripe there like war paint. The man's fevered eyes had rested on her as he spoke in a harsh voice.

"Braver soldier than I am."

Perhaps Stanley did have a nasty, bottomless need to be punished. But if he did, it connected to another need. A need to be loved. To be forgiven. To find a peace inside himself that eluded him when he wasn't like this.

She could understand that. They all three could. She thought of that abyss in Alistair's eyes. She leaned in, propping a hand on Stanley's shoulder as she spoke in his ear, brushing her cheek against the straps of the gag and eye mask, reminding him of their presence.

"This stupid human bitch is in control of you right now, Stanley. I'll do as I wish with you, and you can do nothing, can you, mate?"

She gripped the shaft of the dildo, pressed the tip of it between his buttocks, finding his opening. Sex this way might not be familiar to her, but the angle of a man's arse certainly was, and how those internal muscles released to allow objects to penetrate.

He was tight, holding himself against her. She would have eased her way in, but her Master had a different idea of how to handle the situation. Snaking a hand around her and Stanley to hold the three of them flush against one another, Alistair pressed his torso against her arse. Using that and the hold around Stanley's waist, he thrust her past the two sets of muscles with brutal force.

Even with lubricant, she knew it hurt, for Stanley stiffened and made a noise between a cry and a moan.

"Don't think you heard her clearly, mate," Alistair advised. "She's going to bugger your arse good. She can make it enjoyable, or I can make it utter hell. Up to you."

Stanley snarled something against the dildo, and Alistair chuckled darkly. "Hell it is."

I'd rather go a different way. If you meant it, about this being up to me.

She looked back at Alistair. He'd wrapped his fingers around hers to ensure he'd chosen the right angle for his forceful penetration, but at her silent entreaty, he released his grip there, returned his hands to her hips.

I did. What do you have in mind, sweet nurse?

Actions made more sense than deeds right now. Slowly, slowly, she drew the phallus almost all the way out of Stanley's arse. Then she slowly pushed back in, the lubricant greasing her way. He was still tight, but now she thought that was physical, the narrowness of the channel, not active resistance.

He's got a tight little arse, that's for sure, Alistair confirmed it.

Stanley had braced for a pounding, his shoulders quivering, but she drew out slow again. She returned at the same pace, but going as deep as she could, with an extra push that earned an uncertain grunt from him. Alistair picked up the rhythm easily and helped with that extra push.

As she kept going, she turned her attention to the hand she had resting on Stan's shoulder. As she pushed in this time, she began to dig her nails into his flesh. Harder, deeper. Her nails had the ability to cut, or make him feel as if he were cut. More of the mind play Alistair had suggested.

She could feel his attention on everything she was doing. His thumbs were lightly caressing her buttocks, a sensual encouragement as her hips pressed forward and came back. He tightened his fingers on them, a reminder of his closeness and presence. She hadn't needed much instruction, but she needed his touch to do this right. She wondered if he'd expected that, because she hadn't.

Leaning in, she wrapped her arm around Stanley's bare chest, her hand on his heart, over the top edge of the scar there. And dug her nails into it.

He dropped his head back, much as he had with Alistair. He strangled on a groan. Whatever he said now still had belligerence, but there was a note of desperation to it, too. An improvement.

What did he say?

Harder, faster. Stop teasing me with your little girl thrusts. They're not doing shite for me.

She tsked. "Still haven't learned, Stanley. It's about what I want. And you're a liar. She dropped her hand, wrapped it around his cock. "A big, fat liar."

She played, caressing the ridged head, rubbing her thumb in his wet slit, using that lubrication to stroke the taut vein running along the bottom of his shaft. She put pressure on it, right beneath the head, and held that grip as she pushed in again, drew out. Pushed in, drew out.

Stanley was getting more agitated. Emotionally. His fingers clawed at the chains, gripped. He tried to lift his lower body, she supposed in an attempt to kick out, away from her.

Alistair was able to reach the armoire without taking a steadying hand from her, and withdrew another handful of cords from it. As Stanley protested against the gag, Alistair moved from her to wrap the cords beneath his knees and worked a rig that drew them up. It was as if Stanley was sitting on a chair, only his bent legs were in the air, where they provided him no leverage against Nina. The new position changed the angle, and while Nina enjoyed Stanley's deepening groans as she pressed in deeper, the nurse side of her was concerned.

His shoulders...

He's a vampire, Nina. He can handle the strain without permanent injury. And he won't be hanging for much longer.

When Alistair came to stand behind her again, he lifted her blouse in the back. As he began to kiss a line up her spine, another swirl of sensations bloomed throughout her and across her flesh. He rubbed his face against her skin, breathed against it, and she closed her eyes at the intimacy, struggling with the feelings that rose within her.

Fortunately, Stanley provided a distraction. He was getting closer to a point of decision. Wrapping her arms around him, she ground her hips against his arse, digging deep with the rubber phallus.

She whispered what came to mind. The message she'd given to so many souls, stranded on a sea of cots.

"We're here, Stanley. I'm here. Sshhh...I'm here...be still. Inside and out. Be still. Let it go. Quiet. We're in a womb. No need for anything to be done or said. It's all here."

Alistair's mouth lifted from her skin. She felt his gaze upon her, but she kept her focus on Stanley. As she repeated different versions of the same words, she felt it. That connection she'd worried she'd never get the opportunity to feel again. That moment when she found the right note of emotional reassurance the patient needed, to help with their physical healing. To help them get through the pain, to go just a little further. To believe they could survive a world full of unimaginable horrors.

The younger vampire made another noise, and there was no mistaking the word he said this time, though she liked hearing it from Alistair's mind.

He said please. *The bugger can be taught.*

Please what?

Just please. It covers everything, doesn't it?

It did, sometimes. She made a humming noise against Stanley's shoulder, pushed her hips a little harder against his arse, became more demanding as she issued the next directive.

"Next time you come into Lord Alistair's home, you will be courteous and polite," she said in her most no-nonsense Matron-like voice. "To him, to me. If you cannot behave, you will not be allowed to come. In any way you wish to interpret that."

Stanley choked on a half chuckle. It made her smile.

Once, a smile had been something easy. Casual, sometimes

genuine, other times just polite, or a reflex. Now, the smiles she remembered were those that had happened in extraordinary situations, where a smile was something just short of a miracle. But those were the smiles that took one by surprise, made the unbearable bearable. They had ten times the value and weight of gold. How many times had a soft smile crossed her face, remembering Alistair in the caretaker's cottage?

"If my dainty little InhServ makes you come, Stanley, I'll give you the hardest, most painful arse-fucking in your life. So learn a little self-control, mate."

Make him come, Nina. I want to see him unable to resist your touch. Wrap those lovely fingers around him and don't take no for an answer.

When she hesitated, he answered her unspoken worry. *I won't be hurting him more than he desires, sweet nurse. Do it.*

Alistair had his steel organ pressed firmly against the base of her buttocks, taut from standing on the stool. When he rubbed against her, her body quivered. She lowered her hand to Stanley's groin again, circling the base of his shaft and tightening her grip, earning another groan. As she began to work him in her palm, her fingers twitched and played along him, circling, stroking, squeezing. She began that slow withdraw and thrust again.

Alistair moved his hands to her arse, cupping her buttocks beneath the skirt, adding more force to her movements. His thumbs played along the seam between her arse cheeks. Her breath quickened and body dampened further. Her pulse rate accelerated as each push against Stanley pressed the strap-on against her clit.

You better not come, either, my lovely servant. That climax belongs to me. You'll scream out your pleasure when I take your virginity, and all of it will be your gift to me. Your Master, even if you're not yet permitted to call me that.

Won't call you that, she managed. *Not unless you order me to do it.*

"Be careful of lines you draw in quicksand," Alistair murmured against her flesh before he scored her with his fangs. She gasped, thrust harder, and Stanley let out a futile snarl against his gag. His cock jumped in her hand, and his seed started to pump out, his body rocking hard against her.

A full-grown man was stronger than her, but she knew how to counter his thrashing. A vampire was a different matter. She might have been flung from her perch if Alistair hadn't banded his arms around her, flattening his palms on Stanley's abdomen to hold him steady as his hips jerked and thighs quivered.

"Ah, Stanley," Alistair said, a grave note to his voice. "She's made my dream come true."

~

As Stanley finished, Nina was so aroused she couldn't orient herself to know what to do next. Alistair guided her, helping her withdraw from Stanley. He ran his palms up and down her arms, steadying her, and pressed a kiss to the back of her neck.

"Well done," he murmured. "You're breathtaking to watch when you top a male, Nina. The Mistress deprived herself of a pleasure, but I expect she didn't have time to plumb a tenth of the potential that's in you for this."

Over a month ago, she'd known how to do none of this. Even longer ago, she'd had normal dreams of white dresses, giving her virginity as a gift to her husband. Not being in the center of a three-some, buggering a male stranger...and getting swept away in it.

Lust-driven euphoria ebbed away. She didn't want Stanley here. She didn't want to be wearing this thing. She wanted to be back in that boat, kneeling between Alistair's feet, her head on his inner thigh. Cold and afraid, she'd still somehow been in a better place. A more comprehensible one.

But she couldn't deny she still felt that connection to him here, though it was touch and go. Was that why she'd been able to get immersed in this? Because she could find that connection to him, no matter the circumstances? She had to face what that meant, but she wouldn't, not right now.

Alistair unbuckled the strap-on while she still had her back to him. He set it aside and drew her back against him. Sliding his hands along her thighs, he massaged where the straps had dug in. From there he moved up her sides, over her rib cage, to the outside of her breasts, her shoulders and throat, to tunnel his fingers through her hair. He did that several times, making her lie back against him in response as he stroked. Cosseted.

He didn't touch her sex or her breasts, but came so close, his fingers so knowledgeable, that it awoke nerves there anyway, turning her whole body into a compass gravitated toward him.

"There," he murmured. "I have no boat handy, but that helps. Doesn't it?"

She didn't know how to respond to that. Her throat was tight, incapable of allowing words to pass through. He spoke, his lips against her temple. "Return to the retiring room now and sit in the chair. Leave the door open. I want your gorgeous legs spread, draped over the chair arms. You'll put your fingers on your cunt, stroke and play. You don't get to come, but I want you close. So close you'll beg me for the privilege of coming."

How often did you do as I ordered you to do, to keep the nightmares at bay? How often did you beg?

He didn't push for the answer, but instead eased her to stand on her own again, giving her a gentle push toward the retiring room. She drifted that way, her mind a confused mess, such that the easiest thing was to do as he'd asked. For now.

A qualification. She heard the chuckle in her head, dark and dangerous. *I doubt I'll be able to beat that out of you. Though I think we'll both get a lot of pleasure from me trying.*

She found her way to the chair. As she sank down on the cushion, she was suddenly self-conscious, but she needn't have been. Alistair's attention had swung to Stanley like a gun finding its target.

The energy in the room shifted to pure male testosterone, so dense she felt its heat. Alistair untied the ropes so Stanley could straighten his legs, then brought the chains down, so Stanley was still manacled, but he had enough slack to drop his arms to his sides. The younger vampire had his head down, and his shoulders were tense. Suggesting she wasn't the only one dealing with a confusing mix of emotions.

Alistair took off the gag, but left the blindfold. Stanley's head lifted, his mouth set. "You let her do that to humiliate me," he accused in a tight voice.

"Did I now?" As Alistair tossed the gag aside, he massaged Stanley's shoulders, a quick, functional thing. Despite his sullen words, Stanley swayed into the touch, yearning for it. Alistair took it away almost immediately, leaving the bound male obviously at loose ends, even a little bereft. It twisted Nina's heart. Why not give the poor lad what he needed?

"No worries about that," Alistair responded out loud. He turned his head, pinned her with his gaze. "Aren't you supposed to have your legs draped over the chair arms? I want to see you wet."

There was a big difference in doing what she'd done with Stanley, and being out here in a big wide space by herself, on display and touching herself.

She started to look down, and Alistair arrested her with a sharp one-word command that made her start. But the silky words that followed riveted her attention upon him.

No. You look at me as you obey.

Her cheeks flushed. Slowly, she raised her gaze to him once more. Though a quiver ran through the muscles, she lifted one leg, adjusted it so her knee was bent over the arm of the chair. Then the other, spreading her thighs wide. In the short, split skirt, the position bared them to the hips, and his gaze zeroed in on what was between them, making her sex react in a way that caused a soft sound to escape her lips.

"So responsive," Alistair said, his voice low and rough. "I could make you come without allowing you to touch yourself at all, Nina. But today I won't deprive myself of watching your hand upon yourself."

"Why don't you go bugger her instead of me, since you're all up in her cunt rather than my arse tonight?"

"Still haven't learned any manners." Alistair sighed. He reached up, unshackled one of Stanley's wrists and loosened the blindfold, jerking it down so it draped around Stanley's neck. The male blinked at him with eyes dominated by dark pupil. "Try your luck, Stanley. Let's see if you've improved any since your last visit."

Nina had started to touch herself. Tentative, though her sex responded as if she'd given it a much more effective and decisive stroke. Her body arched, hips lifting, but in the next moment, she froze, as Stanley responded to Alistair's challenge.

He spun, whipping the chains around as if he'd strike or tangle Alistair with them. Her vampire ducked the tactic, but Stanley missed him by a hair. No more sardonic looks on Stanley's face now. He looked mean and intent, sending a spike of fear through Nina. A jab from his fist caught Alistair dead in the mouth, knocking him back. Blood bloomed on his lip, and Nina was out of the chair and halfway toward the two males. Alistair was already back in the fray, shoving the male, lifting him full body around the middle to throw him down to the floor. All while avoiding swaying, twisting chains.

Nina gripped the doorframe. Stanley squirmed free, kicked. Alistair blocked and returned the jab, only she was pretty sure he pulled his punch, something Stanley hadn't done. Stanley spun and kicked again, Alistair narrowly avoiding the contact to his middle. He swept Stanley's leg, sending him to the floor hard enough to shake this level of the house.

In the midst of this, a calm message interjected itself into her brain. *You are in harm's way this close. Go back to the chair and do as I ordered.*

Stanley wrapped the chain around Alistair's foot, so fast she didn't see the movement, and yanked. It set Alistair off balance and brought him crashing down halfway over Stanley. The two men grappled on the floor, wrestling moves that were distracting since one man was completely naked and Alistair, in his well-fitted slacks and white shirt open at the throat, moved with the twisting, sleek moves of a powerful cat. Then Stanley laid his hands on the shirt and tore it all the way open, managing to sink his fangs into Alistair's chest just above the pectoral.

Alistair's speed increased exponentially, confirming he'd been holding back. Stanley didn't have a chance to enjoy any of Alistair's blood, for Alistair freed himself and was gone. When Nina's vision could follow him again, Stanley grunted as Alistair flipped him to his stomach and brought him to knees and elbows. Alistair had the slack of one of the chains wrapped around Stanley's neck, the manacled wrist to which it was attached held against Stanley's throat.

Nina's heart was rabbiting, but the calm mind message had told her Alistair was in control. Her reaction to the tautness of muscle in Alistair's body as he held the other man beneath him, the formidable show of restraint that had allowed him to put him down but not cause him true harm, wasn't trepidation. She was experiencing that perverse female but undeniable full-blown response to a show of alpha male strength.

It didn't help that Alistair chose that moment to look up at her, his eyes glittering, mouth set. His gaze coursed over her body, the open blouse that displayed her breasts in the lace bra, the slit skirt that revealed her bare sex. He was like a conqueror, examining his spoils of victory. *What shall we do with our bad boy, Nina? Want to see me take his arse, show him who's boss?*

She did. She didn't have time to censor the thought, examine why the hell she had that reaction; it was just there. Yes. She wanted to see Alistair dominate the male, prove he was in control. Even felt a little stirring of primal satisfaction that her Master...

She cut that thought off fast, but he gave her a look of satisfaction that sent shivers through her body.

He turned his attention back to Stanley. "Not bad," mate," he said in a different voice, milder. "Serious improvement in your fighting skills. We'll go over some corrections later. But since you made my dick hard, you have to deal with that. Ask me nicely, or you get nothing."

Stanley put his head down to the floor. Nina could feel his struggle. He wanted what Alistair was offering, but he fought. That was what he did. After very little time with him, she understood that about him, and obviously so did Alistair. But there was a certain line past which the mind had no control over what the rest of a person wanted.

"Yes. Please." Stanley's voice broke, and he pressed his forehead hard to the ground, tipping it against the hand pinned close to his face.

Alistair stroked a hand down Stanley's spine, a comparatively gentle touch, and Stanley shuddered. "There's my boy," Alistair murmured. "Stay like that. Inside and out. No more fighting today."

Now at last, he released Stanley's other hand. Unbuckling his belt, Alistair stripped it out of his slacks. Unhooked them. As he paused, his head tilted, obviously capturing Nina in his peripheral vision.

Alistair turned in her direction. As he walked toward her, he shrugged out of the torn shirt with a ripple of muscle. The pants rode low on his hips, and the belt swung loosely from his hand, making her stomach knot uncertainly. As he reached her, he kept coming, and she started backing up, toward the chair. The intensity of his gaze increased, telling her she was doing exactly what he'd intended his body language to compel her to do.

When she reached the chair, she sank into it. He slid his hands under her knees, opened her, spreading her thighs so they were draped over the arms of the chair again. As he leaned over her, he traced a finger over her lace-cradled breast, down her belly. She stared up at him, her mouth dry.

She was gripping the top of the chair. He made a loop of the belt, dropped it over her wrists, cinched it to bind them together. When her lips parted in reaction, his eyes sparked. Wrapping his fist in the tail, he drew her hands down, placed them over her sex.

Cupping his free hand over them, he began to manipulate her fingers like a piano, sending notes of sensation deep into her core. His gaze held hers and she couldn't look away, even as her tongue touched her lips in response to all the sensations.

He left her hand there, moving on herself, and tucked the loose belt strap beneath her arse. "You stop again," he said, "I will use that belt in a way you will not like at all. While I will enjoy the hell out of turning your arse red."

Keep those fingers on the outside. Don't want them having the pleasure of your cunt before I do.

With that, he pivoted and sauntered back to Stanley. After that series of arrogant statements, she should have been glaring daggers at his back. Instead, she was equally distracted by the view in this direction. The man had a fine, tight arse, even with the pants loose.

Had Stanley ever done to Alistair...what she'd just done to Stanley?

Alistair stopped, looked back at her. Though his gaze stayed on her face, she could feel his attention to her obedience in a way that kept her fingers moving over herself, her hips twitching in reaction.

In his dreams, sweet nurse. If those were the kind of dreams he has. In Stanley's fantasies, he's always on his knees. Serving a Mistress who will love his poor broken soul and let him cherish her as he wishes he could, if he weren't so fucked in the head over it all. But we all get in our own way worse than anyone else, don't we?

On that unexpected note, he turned back to Stanley. He knelt behind the male, stroked his back again. "Shall I make it hurt, then?" he asked.

Stanley closed his eyes, nodded, with a little sigh. Alistair's expression became less stern.

"You need it to hurt, Stanley. But you don't want it to. Someday you'll learn why that's important."

Alistair drew his cock out of his slacks, and Nina's fingers spasmed as he stretched out the thick organ, rigid with arousal. Alistair gripped himself, added more lubricant, and then angled himself. He took Stanley with one powerful thrust, wresting a high cry from his throat.

"There you are, you little bastard," Alistair growled. "When are you going to learn, hmm? Every tangle with me ends up with you on your knees, taking my dick. I'll have that apology now. A sincere one. And I do... mean... fucking... now."

He punctuated each syllable with more thrusts, so strong the man's knees and elbows scraped against the floor.

"I'm sorry...Alistair."

A particularly punishing thrust resulted in a cry. And a correction. "My lord. Lord Alistair."

Alistair didn't respond, at least not in words. One of the chains dragging the ground was close enough that he snagged it, pulled it over. Jerking Stanley's upper body up by his unruly hair, he wrapped the chain around his throat, tightly enough that Stanley choked.

Nina knew vampires didn't need to breathe, but understood what Alistair was doing when he eased his hold, then tightened it again. Increasing the endorphin rush, the euphoria of it for Stanley. She'd learned of it from the InhServ training. An incredibly dangerous practice for a mortal, but for vampires, it was lumped into their chaotic menu of sexual play choices. But she suspected it had a more serious note for Alistair's intent.

As his thrusts continued to be brutal, he reached before Stanley and captured his cock in a hard grip. Stanley let out a yelp.

"I can pinch it in half. I don't think that apology was sincere enough."

"I'm so sorry. My lord, please..."

Alistair grunted, held the grip, Stanley's face screwed up in agonized reaction as Alistair continued to pound into him. Nina was horrified, fascinated and...aroused. Her hand was working on herself furiously, she realized, and her body was tightening, lifting. Oh God, she was going to...

Not without your Master's permission.

That didn't come from Alistair. It came from her own mind. She was lost. So bloody lost.

As Alistair began to release, he let go of the chain and gripped Stanley's hip instead. His own hips pumped, back and shoulders flexed, his head thrown back as he groaned out his pleasure. The thick strands of his dark hair caught the room light, his eyes glittering as they went to slits.

He was beautiful, she realized with despair, and she couldn't look away. Which meant she saw the aftermath, when he dropped his forehead to the center of Stanley's back and stayed there a long moment. If he were human, he would have been breathing hard. As it was, his shoulders were lifting and falling more rapidly. When he lifted his face, he was staring at the wall, but she could still see his profile.

She recognized the stark loneliness in that expression. It was what she'd seen in her own face, every time she had to look in a mirror. Ever since he'd gotten her onto a boat taking her back to Australia, to face a life she wasn't sure she understood anymore.

Only he had no reflection to stare back at him. Maybe that was another blessing to being a vampire. Or a curse, if one already felt unbearably alone in his own head.

Maybe she wasn't as alone as she'd feared.

Abruptly, Alistair shoved himself to his feet, withdrawing from Stanley. He gave his hip a hard squeeze before he left the male where he was.

Striding over to Nina, Alistair gripped her bound wrists and pulled them above her head, the strap of the belt slipping from beneath her. The decisive gesture, the set of his face, made it clear that was where he wanted her to keep her hands as he dropped to his knees before her spread thighs and plunged. It was the only word that fit. He scooped under her thighs with strong hands and drove his mouth between her legs. He didn't play or tease, burying his lips and nose into her cunt, going after her with single-minded purpose, devouring her.

It was like he'd been in the hallway, only even more insistent and sensually ruthless, something she hadn't thought possible at the time.

Her body bowed up into his as she grabbed at the back of the chair, clawing at the cushion, at the strap wrapped around her wrist. No time to think, to resist. He was demanding her climax, now. All the stimulation of the past hour came together and detonated in her lower extremities. Her body quaked and then shattered, her lips parting on a cry that became a prolonged scream as the orgasm ripped through her. Her head tilted back so far she was gazing at the ceiling, while every part of her was focused on the grip of his hands on her, the demands of his mouth. Her fists cramped with the force of her hold on the thick cushion.

It went on far longer than she expected, her body bucking up, dropping, bucking up again. She writhed and pleaded. Begged for mercy and was ignored. He took a climax past pleasure and into a dark world where she thought she might be pulled apart, nothing making any sense. Except what he wanted. What she could give him.

She'd become so used to women bringing her to climax, the relentless force of a male energy was like plunging into a whole new world, one full of power and heat and demands that couldn't be denied.

Or maybe that was simply the effect Alistair had upon her.

By the time the climax started to ebb, it seemed the universe had been through a few rotations. She released the cushion, her restrained hands dropping to his shoulder. She dug in, pushed, everything so sensitive, too sensitive.

He reached up, gripped the belt, wrapping the strap around his hand, his fingers tightening over hers and holding her there. But he didn't stop.

I will taste my fill until I wish to stop, sweet nurse.

The right of a Master.

She continued to dig into his shoulder, but now it was to help her bear it, ride those crazy sensations. He'd used the strength of his hands to hold her open when she resisted him, but in time he let them slide to her hips, her waist, and she kept her legs open wide, the rest of her still and shuddering until he finished. Lesson learned. And there was an additional reward for learning it.

He pushed up, bringing his mouth to hers. Oh God. For all the things he could do to her body, this intimacy drove away so much, let in other things she needed. She tasted herself on his mouth, which roused the same primal satisfaction she'd felt when he'd overpowered Stanley.

He sucked on her lips, nipped, and at last drew back to stare into her eyes. Then he sat on his heels, putting distance between them.

He'd allowed her to access a carousel of emotions from him in the bare few hours she'd been here, but now there was a mix she couldn't decipher. It held her still, her heart thudding in her throat, as he kept looking at her. Until he spoke, his voice a rasp yet oddly formal. Responding at last to her formal greeting.

"That's all I require from you now, Nina. You'll sleep upstairs tonight. I'll seek you out when I need you. Until then, you can devote your time to figuring out how you fit into the household."

CHAPTER TWELVE

*H*e'd confused her. Maybe hurt her. Alistair wanted to feel something about that. How fucked was wanting to feel something? Seemed contradictory, since wanting was a feeling, wasn't it?

He should have scooped her up, taken her to his bedroom and enjoyed giving her the third and final mark, taking her virginity. His cock became rigid as a hammer at the mere thought of being the first to break through the barrier, bury himself to the hilt in her wet heat. He'd go easy, arouse her until she was pleading for release in her throaty voice, so the pain would be fleeting. Like sinking his fangs into her neck, another penetration.

But after spending himself in Stanley's arse, his mood had changed. She'd seen what he hadn't wanted anyone to see. And she thought he was beautiful. It had unlocked that door in him that closed others off.

He wasn't going to leave her hurting for it, though, so he'd taken care of that. Lost himself for a few blissful moments in the wet heat of her pussy, steeping himself in her scent, her cries. The bite of her nails into his shoulder was a savage pleasure. He'd regretted the healing power of vampires that made the little crescent marks disappear too soon. She'd drawn blood, a little tiger, and he'd rubbed his fingers over it, tasted himself.

When she'd lost herself to him, he'd felt the fierce drug of having that impact on someone, on getting them to let go of control and feel something real. Something not fleeting, something that didn't disappear only moments after it happened, as if it was illusion. A mind trick on oneself. Living on pretense.

His cock wasn't happy with him in the slightest. Vampires were like cats, in that ninety percent of their day could easily be spent doing one thing. But it sure as hell wasn't napping.

Christ. Why had he insisted on her? He needed a fully trained InhServ, one who would perform as expected, be a credit to his household. He'd made a mistake. He'd made enough of them in his life, he knew what one felt like. He never should have done this, to either one of them.

During the months following Singapore, Alistair had reached a couple epiphanies. He was no longer human. Hadn't been, for nearly three centuries, but apparently he was one of those blokes who took a lot longer than others to get the hint. His place was no longer elbow-to-elbow with humans. On the battle field, or the footy field. He'd turned his attention to being a vampire. With a single-minded ferocity that he knew was an escape from other things, but bugger it. Self-reflection wasn't his thing.

His sire, Lady Lyssa, hadn't bothered to conceal her relief with his change of course. He imagined she'd done a whole series of cartwheels, at least in her head. He couldn't see the formidable female doing them in real life, but if she ever did, the shock would probably shatter the rigid foundation of the vampire world.

He'd been an overlord for some time. Years ago, she'd prodded him into it, telling him he had a penchant for leadership, and the vampire world needed that, particularly from its made vampires. He'd have sworn she was blowing smoke up his arse, except she was less likely to do that than she was to do cartwheels. He suspected the real reason she'd pushed him to do it was to try and break some of those human ties that concerned her so much.

Initially that plan hadn't worked out too well. Being an overlord in Queensland hadn't required too much of him. Australia didn't have a lot of vampires, but he watched over the few in his territory, did what needed to be done, and divided his time between those responsibilities and what he considered far more interesting things in the human world.

The Region Master over him, Luigi, wasn't a bad sort, but he was a lazy Italian pretty boy. The Council had thought sending the born vampire to rule a strategically unimportant Region in Australia was the best way to placate his Italian Region Master mother, who probably knew he was worthless and didn't disagree overly much with the choice.

That had suited Alistair fine for a good long time. He preferred a place where no one was telling him what to do. However, the problem was the overlords in Queensland had no competent oversight. Problems with that started to mount, particularly because of one megalomaniac, consummate prick, Queensland overlord.

Donovan.

That change came along with more aggressive moves outside their Region. Ruskin, the Region Master of the Northwest Territory, covered Northern and Western Australia, a geographically larger area, but less vampire-populated. The ruthless bastard felt Australia should be run by one Region Master. By astonishing coincidence, he considered himself the man for the job.

Then there was the South Australia Region Master, who kept suggesting to anyone on the Council who would listen that Queensland would make more sense as an overlordship under her auspices. Which would be fine if Catalina was interested in truly managing Queensland. Her main interest was having Alistair—and his considerable amassed wealth—under her thumb.

His fortune wasn't Alistair's main concern about those strategic movements, however. Over the decades, Queensland had become the dumping ground for vampires like Stanley, misfits who could cause enough problems to get themselves executed by Council decree, or just as bad, easily become the prey of stronger vampires.

Born vampires didn't seem to care much about that. Survival of the fittest was their guiding philosophy. But Alistair had discovered he was still human enough for it to matter. His response to bullies hadn't changed in three hundred years. Not from the first time he'd taken up a weapon to defend a village from a half dozen raiders. He'd been thirteen years old, out riding his parents' lands. He'd shamed the men of the small hamlet into halting their headlong fleeing into the woods and joining him in repelling the attack.

He'd never forgotten the way that felt, protecting their homes, sending bad men to hell, or running away with such fear in their hearts they'd never think to come back. But war was a lot more complicated than that. Just like its despicable bedfellow, politics.

When the problems started to develop with Donovan, and the other Region Masters, Alistair had found himself putting in his two cents on the situations. Once. Twice. He got more embedded with Luigi, helping the bloke keep Ruskin and Catalina at bay. Somewhere along the way, he realized Luigi wouldn't be up for the increased responsibilities that were coming with those threats from North and Southwest.

He wasn't a bad bloke; Alistair and he became mates of a sort. Luigi just didn't really want to do anything but drink and play and be the center of some doting female's world. A momma's boy to the end.

The overlord in Mackay, Lady Bertrice, liked pretty boys. Being Italian, Luigi fit the bill. Alistair engineered a few key meets between them. Before long, Luigi was spending far more time in her territory, at her side. He also liked the milder temperatures north of Brisbane. With Luigi's blessing, Alistair became the acting Region Master during his increasingly prolonged absences.

Lady Lyssa had suggested to the Council that, once some of the European unrest was over, a propitious time for transition, Alistair should take over the Region Master role. Luigi had formally endorsed Alistair as his successor and was willing to abdicate the role. He'd share overlordship with Lady Bertrice as long as she wanted his "assistance."

The Council's lack of attention to Australia could be as helpful as it was sometimes not. No one objected. Except maybe Alistair, but even he realized it was time to shit or get off the pot. If he didn't like the way things were going, he needed to step up.

It was probably the least volatile change of leadership a Region had ever experienced. Which could be considered good, except it likely confirmed to Council that Australia and its vampire population had the political importance of a flock of ducks.

He himself had honestly never thought it would happen. Made vampires didn't ascend to Region Master. But then he had his epiphanies. Three years ago, overcome with the need to escape things he didn't want to remember, he'd suddenly turned himself into the most ambitious vampire in all of Australia. As he saw signs of the war's conclusion, he worked even closer with Luigi, sorted the things he was supposed to be doing, was actually doing, and what needed to be changed.

In hindsight, Lyssa's patience with him had been remarkable, since she'd been pushing him in this direction for years. But to a woman over a thousand years old, a few decades wasn't more than a few months to the rest of them.

Then the war ended, and he received the official notice. He was Region Master. It was done.

Luigi had broken open a bottle of his finest champagne and he and Lady Bertrice toasted his success. Afterwards, they left him nursing his drink by their opulent fireplace while they went to enjoy one another and their servants. Alistair was warmly invited to be part of the dogpile, but he abstained.

As he stared into the fire, he kept his mind on the things he needed to do, to handle. His might not be an important Region politically, but it would be the best run of any Region there was. No vampire in it would worry that they'd be treated unfairly. He would start by visiting every one of the hundred and two vampires in the Region, he decided. He'd sit down with them, go over any concerns with his overlords. He'd already submitted and had approved the vampire he'd recommended to take his overlordship, so that one's loyalty was assured. Truth, he wasn't really concerned about the others, with the exception of Donovan. He'd have to stay on his toes with him.

It might be easier to go ahead and kill the bastard.

He took a swallow of his drink. At his elbow was a satchel of files he'd made. His gaze fell on the folder in the middle, the bold dark ink highlighted by a strategic fall of the flickering firelight. *InhServ Reports.*

He pulled it out, balanced it on his knee as he opened it, flipped through the pages of the official reports. Lyssa had earmarked an InhServ for him long before even he'd decided on this path. The female was uncanny. And had the influence of the Devil, since he had no idea how she'd managed to get an InhServ committed to him long before the Council had grudgingly acknowledged they would back him in the Region Master position.

What's more, she'd made sure it was a woman. He'd questioned that, saying if he was going to have an InhServ, a male would make more sense.

"No," she'd said. "Men are too easy for you, Alistair. A woman is better for your temperament."

God help the man who thought he could argue with the damn female. Lyssa had known he didn't want another servant. Not for another century or more, if ever again. He'd had two, and he routinely pushed their faces out of his mind because they were lumped in with the other faces he didn't want to think about, see in his head.

He'd dealt with it by not dealing with it. Over the years, when he received periodic communications about "his" InhServ, he mostly ignored the communications or passed them off to Nero to handle responses. A few years back, he'd even told Nero to request the extended training, to give the InhServ a double helping of her supposedly awesome skillset. Lyssa had called him an idiot at the time, since she was sure the InhServ would get him to a Region Master title sooner, but he'd stubbornly held out.

He'd thought a lot more about having a fully marked servant again since meeting Nina, though. If her sister was his InhServ, he could be magnanimous, let her invite Nina for visits. Yeah, that had had some interesting and provocative possibilities.

Except Nina wasn't an InhServ. Despite her practical nature and amazing generosity, her submissive nature, which was as obvious as her soft breast nestled in his palm, so too was her innocence, her traditional view of the world. His sweet nurse was destined for a husband and children, a mortal life.

She wasn't for him.

He would be getting someone who had some of her qualities, he reminded himself. He'd focus on that, no matter that something felt strained about it. He was still resisting having a full servant. That was all.

Lyssa was right. He was being an idiot. As he flipped through the latest report on the woman assigned to him, he made the effort to read the details. Of course her skills and marks were top notch.

Then he lifted her picture from the file, studying it. Nina was right, in a sense. Her twin was the more physically stunning sister.

But she'd been groomed for it, the preparation of skin, hair and body all part of the same program. She hadn't trained to be a nurse since she was sixteen years old, done her three years of required hands-on learning in the hospital before she was twenty. Yeah, he'd looked into Nina's history after he returned to Brisbane, then shut the information in a drawer. A temptation he couldn't afford, but something he could draw out now and again, to remember. Like he needed the help.

Nina's face had possessed a compelling mix of exhaustion and resilience. What was in her eyes had reflected the steady calm and broken heart of a woman working in a war zone. Her hair had been scraped up and held by pins. She'd had a scratch on her arm, her nails broken and a few smears of blood and other more unappealing things on her apron.

Yet when she'd knelt between his legs and brought her wrist to his mouth, her gaze sliding up to touch his briefly, his reaction to her was the same as if she'd knelt before him in transparent lace, surrounded by a haunting, feminine bedroom fragrance of perfume and arousal.

Oddly, though, he found the memory of her in blood and darkness more real, more appealing, than the fantasy of her in lace and flowers.

Her sister was exceptional, and she was Nina's twin. He was on the rise in the vampire world. He needed someone who understood how important that achievement was.

No matter that another part of him hungered for at least one person in his life who knew how really unimportant it was. Before he forgot it himself. Before he forgot himself entirely.

Returning to the present, he remembered when he'd been notified of his assigned InhServ's death. He'd been given the choice of a new, fully trained InhServ.

He was aware enough of how the InhServ program worked to ask how the death would impact the girl's family. The Mistress had confirmed they would be required to present the next oldest child for the training program. She would be given a few years of accelerated training, followed by another vampire assignment.

"She will not be as polished as some InhServs, but with several years, we can do much, as long as her age doesn't make her too unmalleable."

"Do I have the option of choosing her?"

She paused. "Your butler informed me you had an interest in this. Which is why I called to discuss this directly, to ensure you understand the situation. You already extended the training on your assigned InhServ. You are at the maximum allowed time you can delay before accepting the InhServ honor. If you wish to wait upon her training, it would have to be put to a Council vote for reconfirmation in three years."

Which meant he'd be trusting her fate to what mood the Council was in that day. "Can I have her now?"

The Mistress's silent shock was practically palpable through the phone connection. "My lord," she said carefully. "She would be coming to you with little more preparation than a Random, a servant a vampire chooses for him or herself from the general human population."

"I'm aware of what a Random is. I've had two of them. I asked if it was allowed."

"It is allowed," The Mistress said coolly. "But if you hope for your InhServ to be a credit to you politically, that outcome will not be assured. Allow me to send you information on the other options we have available. You have several days to consider. You can choose."

The idea of the spirited nurse, who'd been through so much, in the hands of a born vampire like Donovan? Just no.

"I want her. I want the second oldest daughter."

There was no reason to pretend, at least to himself, that his motives had been so selfless. He'd hungered for a connection, to feel, hadn't he? The last time he'd really felt something, it had been with her. Pathetic, how his memory had latched onto that and wouldn't let it go.

So, with almost no training to prepare her for being ripped out of her life, Nina had been delivered to his door. He thought of that first moment he'd gotten her alone, how he'd gone after her like an animal, something overwhelming him that he hadn't expected.

She'd teased him with that poignant sadness about no small talk, no 'how've you been.' Yet the reason for that was simple. From the moment he saw her, it was as if he'd never been away from her. Or had been away from her for too damn long.

She'd held her own, and responded to him, which only maddened him further. But fortunately, his own reaction had startled him enough he'd been able to rein himself back. Eventually.

He didn't even know if she understood his role or its importance. Bringing Stanley here might have helped some things, but had mucked others up. No one but himself to blame for that.

"Another drink?"

Lifting himself out of the well of his own thoughts, he nodded. After Stanley had gotten dressed and Alistair had Nero bring him a new shirt, the two of them had sat out on the back veranda, sharing cigars and drinks, just shooting bull. Sports, vampires, Stanley's business. The bloke was a decent tailor, so Alistair had helped him set up a shop, and he was starting to acquire a customer base. He'd be repairing Alistair's shirt for free, or providing him a new one, the blighter.

Though Stanley necessarily promoted himself as a tailor, the ladies were learning word to mouth that he was an accomplished seamstress. Hemming men's pants were the least of his talents. The fellow could create a whole party dress, complete with flounces and tucks and whatever the hell pretty dresses had, so his clientele was mixed gender, not the usual thing.

Stan hadn't run into any human backlash on that. Yet. Under normal circumstances, Alistair wouldn't worry about a vampire's ability to deflect human curiosity or societal censure. However, Stan had an unsettling way of freezing, forgetting he was a vampire, when confronted by a mob who might be after him about being a ponce. It was unfortunate, but not difficult to understand why. Even for a vampire, some memories could overcome the present-day knowledge of who one was.

Nina had picked right up on it, hadn't she? She was a nurse, but more than that, she was a healer. Drawn to wounded souls.

Alistair grimaced, threw back the rest of his drink, which did very little to dull his senses, more's the pity. Vampires only had a couple of outlets to get out of their own heads. Violence and sex, and the lines between them were pretty fucking slim.

She didn't need to be near that part of him. Not right now. Which was why he'd sent her away, with no intention of visiting her again before dawn. He'd made sure of it, ordering her to be in the upstairs bedroom. He knew having her in the room next to his underground would have blown his resolve straight to hell.

Yeah, he'd hurt her, left her alone, and she was way too damn alone right now. But they had to take this at the pace that would work.

Soon as he determined what that pace was. The most important thing was that she was here. He had her. For the first time in way too long, some small part of his discontented spirit felt at peace.

Nina dozed fitfully throughout the night, expecting every sound to be Alistair. It wasn't until the sun was up and streaming through the crack in her curtains that she realized he wasn't coming to her. She told herself to be relieved by that, but she wasn't. For the first hour or so, with dazed wonder, she'd relived every passionate moment. But as he stayed away, gradually the picture in her mind changed, and she saw herself as just a body, one he'd enjoyed thoroughly. A pleasant diversion for his cock before he'd moved on to other more important things. As she'd occupied herself, she'd smelled the cigar smoke, heard the male conversation and laughter from the veranda.

In the hours alone in her bed, pleasure and possibility had been slowly, poisonously replaced by shame. She'd behaved exactly as trained, hadn't she? Bravo to The Mistress and her intense schooling techniques.

May she and all of them rot in Hell.

Nina curled around her pillow, held it tightly, and stared at the wall until it was daylight. She'd thought about pretending she'd misunderstood his order, and taking the bedroom next to his, even if only to hear him when he came back to bed.

But she had her pride. Not to mention her resolve to stay as emotionally uninvolved as possible, resist this role in whatever way she could. Yeah, that had been a complete failure, her first night here.

But she'd been vulnerable, uncertain. Tired from the overindulgence of wine.

She might need a nap later in the day to be awake for his waking hours, but for now she was too restless to stay in bed. Rising, she showered, dressed, and left her room with the intent to find Nero, see what she could do to keep her from going out of her mind with boredom.

But she wasn't the type to avoid things, and she didn't like spending extra moments worrying over matters that could be resolved with a good conversation. She needed to talk to Alistair.

She'd approach him tonight. Just the two of them, no vampire sex games. Even if they had to handle her virginity and third marking first. And she congratulated herself for having *that* thought with only a mild rash of frogs bouncing off the inside of her stomach and chest.

Just in case she could hasten things along, she went down to the lower level, to Alistair's bedroom. But the connecting door between their rooms was closed. It was daylight; of course he'd be asleep. She didn't intend to disturb him, but she couldn't stop herself from trying the knob.

Locked. Sunlight was dangerous to him. Though it was dark enough and protected down here, there were plenty of reasons he had for locking his door. It didn't have to mean he'd specifically locked her out.

Was he wrapped around Stanley in there?

Stepping into the hall, she realized something she hadn't the first time she'd come down. There was no door to his room in the hallway. Anyone who wished to access him in his room had to come through his servant's quarters.

A servant was intimately connected to her vampire master. Should an enemy try to get to him during daylight, the servant could sound the alarm, give the vampire that much longer to prepare for the attack.

"Servants safeguard their vampires during daylight," Edith had told her solemnly. "There are vampire hunters out there, though most of the stories about them come from Europe and America."

"But sometimes a rival vampire will send a human to try and catch the vampire off guard," Melanie added. "Though that's considered very cowardly on the part of the vampire."

The thought of being the one who watched over Alistair's sleep gave Nina odd feelings, which mixed with her frustration and confusion. Returning to the main level, she learned from Nero that Stanley had gone home well before dawn. She was annoyed that she felt some relief about that.

She spent the rest of the day pitching in wherever she could manage, to convince the staff to let her do something without making them feel she was interfering with their duties. When that short list was exhausted, she walked the grounds, tagging along behind the groundskeeper, JD, and his couple of assistants, offering to help pull weeds. While at first he seemed appalled at the idea of her getting dirty, she suspected he had other reasons for sending her away at his earliest opportunity. Her best guess was it had to do with the far-too-attentive way the two men hired as his temporary help watched her. She admitted they made her a little uncomfortable, too, so she wasn't sorry. Except it left her at loose ends again.

She eventually ended up on the front veranda, staring sightlessly at one of Alistair's books. Her fitful night at last caught up with her and she fell asleep in a rocking chair. When the book fell from her hand, it didn't wake her. Not exactly. She had a hazy memory of someone grasping it, setting it on the table beside her. A male hand brushed her cheek, a warm mouth pressing against her temple.

"Let her sleep until she wakes. She doesn't sleep well."

The deep voice soothed, lulled her back into dreams. Good dreams, no nightmares.

She woke an hour after sundown. Resolutely, she grabbed a cup of coffee from the kitchen and headed down to Alistair's room. Their door was standing open, the room empty. Mrs. W was making the bed and glanced at her.

"Gone already. Said he wouldn't be back for a couple days. Has to make the rounds with some of the people he watches over."

His InhServ was supposed to be at his side to visit vampires in his territory. Both as his assistant and, since she was supposed to be an InhServ, a visible mark of prestige that added to his authority. Since everyone probably knew her circumstances, was there no perceived advantage to him in that?

Shouldn't she be glad that he really didn't want much from her? No. Because she'd never appreciated feeling useless.

~

For the next two days, she discovered that nothing fed anxiety and irritability like boredom. She continued to help where she was allowed, but the staff had most things covered and viewed her desire to assist with suspicion. She took walks along the roads of their wide-spread neighborhood, planted flowers with JD on a day when he had no other help. Finding cans of bright orange paint in one of the outbuildings, she seriously considered painting Alistair's room the lively shade.

On the third morning, when she could take it no longer, she decided to go into town with Mrs. C, as the cook had announced she needed to visit the market. Nero had frowned, but when Nina questioned him, he reluctantly admitted Alistair had left no direction on that. Though he added the stern admonition, "It could be that he didn't anticipate you would have a need to leave the grounds."

"I don't. But I've no reason not to be helpful. Mrs. C is going to the market. I'm going to join her."

Nero's jaw set, as if he thought he should object on general principle, but Nina gave him a warning look. "I'm not trying to run away. I just need to get out. I'm bloody useless here right now. Mr. Coleman is driving us. It's Brisbane, not the Outback. Give me a list of things you need for yourself and I can take care of your own market shopping for this week."

She'd deduced from snippets of staff conversation that he didn't have a wife. Nero gave her a narrow look. But before she departed with Mrs. C, he did give her a short list of things. A very specific one. A bag of rainbow-colored hard lollies dusted with sugar. A pretty scarf, but only in blue. And a loaf of fresh bread from a particular baker.

"He might not have a wife," Nina murmured to herself. "But I think he has a sweetheart somewhere." Intriguing.

The bustling activity of Brisbane was a startling contrast after the quiet serenity of Alistair's Victorian home on the sea. The streets lined with brick buildings were filled with noisy traffic and people on the footpaths. Men strode purposefully on matters of business, while women took care of their market shopping or enjoyed a cup of tea at one of the restaurants.

She trailed Mrs. C in and out of the stores, learning where things were in case she could help her with the market shopping in the future. She also asked questions about cooking techniques. Since her lack of skill in food preparation had horrified The Mistress, Killara had admonished Nina to spend some time learning, if the opportunity presented itself.

Unfortunately, Mrs. C didn't bother concealing her suspicion and impatience with Nina's questions. She became increasingly more baleful in her responses. Nina was getting close to the end of her own patience, but she tried once more, asking the woman about the use of a particular spice she'd put in her basket.

"Why do you care?" the woman said, shooting her a glare that swept over Nina's modest but obviously expensive clothes. "Himself has more money than the Almighty. I'm his cook, not you. I tend to his stomach, and you tend to lower areas, as you're kept in style to do."

Nina's grip on the spice tightened in startled reflex. Mrs. C's sharp-voiced accusation attracted the attention of several curious patrons. Nina was sure her face went red to her ears.

Until now, she'd assumed Winifred's crass hostility was the worst of it. But away from Nero, Mrs. C had dropped the veneer, her matching scorn now obvious. Which was bad enough, but it made Nina realize why the stares of JD's two assistants had made her uncomfortable. They'd likely been told by Winifred or Mrs. C that she was a woman with loose morals, and had been speculating on their chances of taking advantage, if they could get her off by herself. The implication made her skin crawl.

With none of them being aware of the vampire world, there was really only one explanation for Alistair, a wealthy, single male, to have her set up in his house, wasn't there?

But did knowing about the vampire world really make a difference? Though not blatantly unfriendly like this, Mrs. W was reserved with her.

Alistair was fairly new to his Region Master role, and she'd learned from Nero he'd only recently acquired and moved into the Victorian home. He paid the staff's wages, so earned the respect and fear that entailed, but her...she had no obvious standing in the house.

When he'd sent her to bed alone, he'd sent a message that said her influence was even less than they'd imagined. The gloves had come off all the more easily as a result, and they didn't mind punching her directly in the face with their thoughts, rather than making any effort to conceal them. They had no way of knowing the difference between an InhServ and a woman being kept as a mistress.

She knew the difference. A man made some effort to keep a mistress happy.

"Very well." While it took effort, she made sure she met the woman's hostile gaze with a steady one of her own. "I'll go for a walk."

"We were supposed to stay together," Mrs. C said, though she didn't look as if she minded Nina's idea.

"I doubt that will matter, as long as we both come home. How long will you be?"

"About an hour."

"If I'm not back then, please ask Mr. Coleman to take you home and return for me. Thank you."

Mrs. C's expression flickered with something like uncertainty or regret, then hardened. "I expect you'll tell the master I didn't guard my tongue with you."

"I can't change your opinion, since it's based on nothing you actually know about me. Getting you sacked won't change that, will it?"

Nina didn't wait for a reply. She turned and walked away. She thought her pace was casual, a woman strolling along the storefronts, but before long, she realized she was eating up ground as if she was one rapid heartbeat away from breaking into a run.

She'd worn sunglasses and was thankful for it, because though she refused to let tears fall, she probably had that distressed, glassy look women could get before they succumbed to such a pointless waste of emotion.

The blare of a horn startled her into a full stop. A man's hand on her arm, his "Watch yourself now, miss," brought her back to the present. She'd nearly stepped into traffic at a busy intersection.

She nodded, embarrassed, and he gave her a searching look before he stepped out, the intersection now clear, and left her standing there. Watching him and others walk by, some glancing at her curiously, Nina realized she needed to get hold of herself. She drew a breath, then another. Closed her eyes, tried to calm down. "She's a stupid cow, is all," she said to herself. "It's about everything else, not that."

As she oriented herself, she blanched as she realized how much ground she'd covered. She also realized where she'd been headed, though it was much too far to reach on foot. Her heart tightened in on itself, and her fists clenched.

"It's all right." She couldn't tell herself she was okay, but she could tell herself it was all right. Because she was breathing, the sun was shining...

And the ground was shaking.

Her eyes popped open.

People were shouting, some pointing. Pivoting to see what they were all looking at, she noticed smoke and dust clouds billowing out from the front of a building she'd passed two blocks back. A building under renovation, she remembered, with scaffolding and workers crawling over it like an ant hill.

It was a shocking indication of how deeply she'd been trapped in her own head, because the ground shaking was a resonant echo of the aftermath, not the event itself.

She saw several men stumbling free of the smoke. One fell. He was holding his face, unmistakable blood oozing between his knuckles.

She was in motion before she had to tell herself to do it. She'd fortunately worn sensible walking shoes, so covered the distance fast. This time she stepped into traffic fully cognizant that she was doing it, throwing up a hand to stop vehicles, ignoring squealing tires as she ran for where she was needed.

By the time she reached the accident site, some of the dust had cleared, but what it revealed choked her with a different kind of worry. So much building was happening in the wake of the war, as if everyone was determined to prove the world could recreate itself, make itself shiny and new again. Structures were going up so fast, the proper precautions weren't always being taken. At the hospital she'd worked at in Sydney, they'd dealt with more than one construction accident.

The scaffolding had collapsed, and the cause wasn't structural. Fire licking out the windows and chunks of concrete scattered across the street told her something within the building had exploded. A burst water pipe spewed, forming a hole in the smoke and dust. She'd covered her mouth with the hem of her shirt so she could breathe through the choking mix, but she dropped it when she reached the man who'd fallen to his knees. She grasped his arm and brought his hands down from his face.

"I'm a nurse," she said, repeating it several times with the authority and volume necessary to penetrate shock. "Sit down, sir. Sit here."

The blow to the temple had created a furrow along the side of his head. Like most scalp wounds, it was bleeding profusely. However, after stripping off her light coat to wipe and clear the field of blood, she probed the wound and determined that a skull fracture wasn't likely. He'd need stitches and watching, but he should be fine.

"Stay down, sir. Please." She grabbed the arm of a spectator, one who looked like he had his wits about him and no obvious injuries, despite the dust coating him saying he'd been close to the blast. Seeing he carried a pocket kerchief in his jacket, she snatched it and pressed it to the other man's wound, then clasped the wrist of her spectator and brought his hand up to cover it.

"Keep pressure on his head wound, and stay right here with him until an ambulance comes," she ordered him. "I know there's a lot of blood, but if you can do that, he'll most likely be okay. He's stable but disoriented. You stay right here with him. If he tries to wander off, you get someone else to help you keep him here or stick with him until an ambulance arrives. Tell me you understand." She barked that last as a command, and the young man nodded, paling.

Nina spun and waded into the fray. There were men carrying out other men, other passersby getting involved. However, no one other than her had any apparent medical knowledge. She ran from injured to injured, falling into her experience with triage as if she'd never left Singapore.

It was terrible, awful. And yet, she couldn't deny the feeling that swelled into her breast, that made her almost shamefully giddy. For the first time since Sher's death, she felt exactly as she should. Nursing was the only thing that had made sense since Singapore, and having it taken away from her so abruptly... She almost cried from the familiarity of it. A fierce rage rose in her, one that said she was goddamned unwilling to be anything less than what she was meant to be, no matter how she had to accomplish it.

If she'd been looking for a sign of that, she couldn't have asked for a more appropriate one. Though she immediately prayed an apology, in case that sounded like she'd wished for a sign this extreme.

About fifteen wounded men had been extracted from the building. One had been killed by a falling beam right off. Two others had been carried out in ways they shouldn't have been, which she feared were going to have serious repercussions for the spinal injuries they obviously had, but what was done was done.

By the time the first ambulance arrived, she had everyone evaluated enough to provide the drivers guidance. Several more ambulances pulled in, and she quickly had a circle of men waiting for her direction.

"Good on you, love," one said as they were loading the last man on. "Jump on and come with us, all right, so you can tell the docs what's what. Can't keep track of all of it, and you seem to have it ordered in your head like your market list."

She'd loved to hear Mrs. C's reaction to that. She shook her head. "Can't cook worth a zack," she told him. "This is easier than putting together a recipe."

He chuckled, though his gaze was hard, strained, as he took in the mass casualty work he and his fellow drivers were managing around them. "That's okay. A girl that can keep her wits about her in something like this is worth ten times a good cook, to my way of thinking."

"Not to me," his partner said cheerfully, handing her into the ambulance and patting his more ample girth. "I need my Velma's mutton to be a happy man."

She settled next to the male who'd been critically injured as the ambulance shot off. Velma's husband was the driver, and he worked his way skillfully through the congested traffic toward the hospital. As the other responder monitored the patient, she put her hand on the unconscious man's arm. "It's all right," she murmured. "If you have a Velma out there, or even one in your future, you need to hang on for her. Hold on, man."

When they came screaming up to the hospital, she was braced to be turned away as soon as she delivered her report. However, the first person she saw was a familiar face.

Tracy Miller, one of her classmates from her hospital schooling days, was at the open door, ready to help with the stretcher. Surprise crossed her broad face, followed by quick pleasure in her shrewd grey eyes. "Good timing, mate," she said, with the blissful practicality Nina remembered with heart wrenching fondness. "Let's catch up after we get these fellows settled in. Give me what you know."

Nina nodded and launched into reporting on the man's condition. From there, she followed Tracy in. She didn't even think about the fact she wasn't supposed to be a nurse anymore.

She was always going to be a nurse.

CHAPTER THIRTEEN

*F*or the next three hours, Nina worked side by side with the other nurses and doctors, treating the casualties, helping with pre-operating and recovery, standing fast in blood and responding instantly to fired orders, anticipating many before they were hurled in her direction.

"Is she new?" she heard one doctor say.

"No, she doesn't work here," Tracy responded brusquely. "Trained down in Sydney with me, worked with the AANS in Singapore. Visiting in the area I expect."

"If she's looking for work, lock her in before she can get away."

Tracy flashed her a grin. "Run, mate," she advised. "If Dr. Worst here wants you, you'd do better to make a deal with the devil."

That struck a little too close to home, but she summoned a smile at the teasing nickname they'd given Dr. Worchester.

When she at last stepped out of the hospital, she was startled by the late afternoon sunset. Nero stood by the shiny car that had brought her and Mrs. C here earlier in the day. As always, he dressed in black, except for the pristine white shirt beneath his vest.

She'd washed her hands, arms and face repeatedly over the past few hours, but had thrown a spare gown over her clothes, a temporary hospital garb she'd discarded in the laundry before emerging. As his impassive gaze slid over her, suddenly she was very aware of what a wreck her hair and street clothes must appear. Even as she felt more put together inside her own head than she had in some time. She sighed and gave him a "what of it" look.

"How did you find me?" she asked, as she approached the car.

"You are a nurse," he said in his studied way. "When I came to find you, everyone in town was talking about the building accident. It seemed straightforward enough. I entered the hospital a couple hours ago, located you, and then came out here to wait."

"Oh. I'm sorry. I could have taken a cab home."

"Hmm." He gestured to the backseat. "When I determined you would be some time, I went home and retrieved some items I thought you might need when you emerged. Mrs. C prepared you a sandwich and some lemonade."

"Oh. Well, that was nice of her."

"Indeed." Nero lifted a brow. "She said she was unkind to you, and you did not respond as she expected."

"Like a catty whore, using my command of the master's cock to lord it over the rest of the household staff?" She winced at his expression. "Sorry, Nero. I'm used to being around soldiers, doctors and nurses in the thick of things. Language gets pretty rough."

"Indeed," he repeated. Then he extended a courteous hand to help her onto the step into the back seat of the vehicle. His gnarled hand was surprisingly strong.

"Do you mind if I ride up in the front with you?" she asked.

"No, Miss Nina."

"Just Nina's fine. Unless it breaks a rule of some sort. I can't keep them all straight."

He shook his head, putting a hand out to stop her when she reached for the front door handle. He opened it for her once again. Then he reached in the back and moved the small basket of food and drink up by her feet where she could more easily reach it.

As he circled around to the other side to get in behind the driver's wheel, she opened the lemonade and drank from it. When she stopped, she'd drunk half, her body informing her she'd fallen out of the habit of watching her hydration and nourishment, a critical thing for a nurse, especially during a high casualty event.

She thought of the two chaps who'd driven her to the hospital, in particular the one with the pretty blue eyes and lots of thick, sandy hair. His flirtatious teasing hadn't detracted a bit from his skill and serious focus on his charges. The firm set of mouth and chin had said he'd do his best to give all the wounded he transported to the hospital a fighting chance to survive.

His eyes weren't as blue as Alistair's, but the connection between her and him over something they both understood had warmed that cold ball in her chest. At the hospital where she'd worked before all this had happened, there was a good chance a man like him would have asked her out to dinner. It had happened there, more than once, with the other doctors or male staff.

But she'd always politely declined. When they asked her, she'd thought of Alistair. His touch, his expression. It wasn't that she'd been holding herself for him. Just so many things hadn't been quite right for her since she'd come back. While flirting for a few minutes in an ambulance had a reassuring familiarity to it, the idea of a dinner or dancing, where she had to act happy and vivacious for a prolonged period, had been too daunting.

Nero was watching her. "Perhaps eat some of the sandwich, too," he said, his voice a little growly. "You look a little pale."

Only a few days ago he'd watched her throw up in the bushes without comment or succor. But he'd also brought her a fresh blouse.

"Are you nice to me because you're supposed to be, Nero? The others I can kind of work out. Either indifferent, jealous, or disapproving. But you seem on the fence. Undecided."

"I tend to let the actions of others determine my opinion of them, not my preconceived notions," he said stiffly.

"Do they teach you to talk like that in butler school?" She opened the sandwich and sank her teeth into the bliss of meat, cheese and a sauce that was the perfect complement to both. Mrs. C might not be the nicest person, but she knew her trade.

A slight smile touched Nero's mouth, relieving the sternness of his expression. "Lord Alistair says my education far surpasses his. I am a third-generation butler. My grandfather worked in the Duke of York's home until he was wrongly accused of stealing and shipped to Australia as a convict. He taught my father his trade, who in turn taught me."

She'd stopped chewing. "The Duke of York?"

"Yes. I'd say I have some grand stories of that, but true to the honor of our profession, my grandfather revealed none of what he ever saw, to my father or to me." He slanted her a glance. "The Inquisition, if it had still existed, could not have pried anything from us."

"Sounds like you'd make a far better InhServ than me."

"I did apply, but Lord Alistair said I wasn't pretty enough."

She chuckled at that, especially when she saw that light smile touch his lips again. He wasn't insinuating anything dirty, the way Mrs. C had.

"Oh, I almost forgot. I'm so sorry. I didn't get a chance to pick out the bread or scarf because of everything that happened, but I'd found these before." She fished the bag of rainbow-colored lollies out of the small purse she'd carried with her to the market. "I do admit, three or four are missing. One of the wounded was a little girl who'd been on an errand for her mother. Only some superficial cuts, but while we were waiting on the mother, I gave her a handful to help her feel better."

"They went for a good purpose, then." He took one hand from the wheel to accept the bag and considered the colorful lollies, before handing them back to her to hold. "You are very kind, Nina," he said quietly, returning his gaze to the road.

She studied him. "You still haven't answered the question. Or did you? Is that why you're nice to me? You understand the box I'm in?"

"Yes, and no." The sun had now set so she saw his pensive expression in silhouette. But she caught the flash of pain, too real to be mistaken.

"You don't have to tell me." It was the most natural thing in the world for her to inject reassurance into her tone. "I don't want to pry."

He tilted his head, an acknowledgement. Another mile or two passed in silence before he spoke again.

"My daughter was a nurse in the Great War," he said.

"Oh. *Oh.*" The verb tense registered, and she reached out, touched his prominent knuckles. "I'm so sorry, Nero."

His attention stayed on the road, his expression quiet. "Your sympathy is appreciated, but she is not dead. Not technically. She was captured. Treated badly. She returned home...broken."

"Oh, Nero."

"The doctors suggested we put her in a sanitarium," he said at length. His jaw tightened, and the flash in his eye revealed a far more dangerous side than she suspected most butlers possessed. "I visited one of those horrible places. The only people who deserve that are the monsters who did this to her. I keep her at home. A home nurse stays with her while I work, for the care she requires is constant. Lord Alistair's salary allowed me to hire one to help. But if my daughter sees any tools of your trade, she...becomes very unmanageable. The doctor must dress like a visitor, and examine her without examining her, so to speak. Same with the nurse. She wears my wife's clothes. The scent helps her. My daughter thinks she is her mother. She..."

He stopped, and his gaze slid over her. "You have blood on your clothes, the scent of smoke in your hair. Yet you look happier than I've seen you in three days. It's truly a capricious world, isn't it?"

She bit her lip. "Ah, Nero. It's a bloody messed up one."

He grunted. She paused, mulled whether to ask. "Your wife...when did she pass away?"

"About ten years after she left us." His lips tightened and his voice became flatter, but Nina could hear the swells of emotion that he so ruthlessly pushed down. "May, that was her name...she couldn't bear the pain of what happened to our only child. She left in the middle of the night a few months after I decided we would be caring for Dorothy at home. I never saw her again. The hospital where she died contacted me."

"Oh, Nero." She repeated it, sympathy overwhelming everything else, all the more powerful because of how evenly he delivered the news, without any indication he desired sympathy. But she could well imagine the days, hours and minutes of pain he'd endured as his daughter's mind was lost and his wife abandoned him to manage that loss alone.

She saw his throat work as he swallowed, though his face remained quiet. "I received postcards from her at first, but after several years, not so much. I pledged my service to Alistair, to the vampire world, because he helped care for my daughter. At first, I thought that was his condition of service, that I must be in his household according to his terms in order to continue to receive the financial help that is so desperately needed for her care, for the nurse who must be with her. But he showed me that was not the case.

"One morning, she was having a terrible day, but because of my fear of losing his support, I came to work, though I was sick with worry. He picked up on it, asked me about it. I tried to act the butler about it, telling him it was a home issue and all was fine, but he pried it out of me." He smiled faintly. "A butler is inscrutable, Miss Nina. If we show an emotion, it is fully intended and planned for its impact."

She thought of the day at the car, her throwing up, and his expression betraying nothing of his thoughts despite the extraordinary moment. "You're very good at it."

"That is so. But did I have ten times the skill at it, I can tell you our lord is that much more intuitive. When he determined the truth of the matter, he told me that I should be at home with my daughter. And that any day she had need of me like that, I would not be required to attend him. "There are things that matter, Nero," he said. "And things that matter."

Our lord? And then she realized. "Crikey, you're marked."

"Third marked." He nodded, unperturbed. "I was in my early fifties when Lord Alistair did that. But our relationship...he made it clear I was not a 'third mark' in the traditional sense of his world. I would continue to serve in the capacity of a second mark household staff member."

As she digested that, he added, "Lord Alistair proposed it as a way to increase the chances I could outlive my daughter, care for her until her death. But we have an agreement. My wife, despite her inability to be with us, has never stopped being the love of my life. When my daughter passes...Lord Alistair has agreed he will end my life for me, so I can be with them. I've no interest in a world without both of them."

"So you don't think it will ever...get easier to bear?"

He glanced at her, a searching look, and his expression became granite, as if he knew he should tell her something that wasn't true. But in the end, he didn't, and she was grateful for it.

"Not if the ones who hold my heart are where I can't be with them. It leaves the whole world tombstone grey. Wherever they went, that's life to me. As Lord Alistair well knows. As I think you know, too."

She did, but it surprised her to hear him mention Alistair. Then she recalled the starkness she'd seen in Alistair's face when he leaned against Stanley's back.

They drove in companionable silence for a while. She offered him some of the sandwich and he declined, but she split one of the biscuits Mrs. C had sent. An oatmeal raisin with nuts that was a meal itself.

Nero had opened up to her because of their shared circumstances. She suspected no one but her, Alistair and possibly Mrs. W knew about Nero's circumstances. She was also sure the lollies and scarf were for his daughter. Nero dealt with the pain by doing. The same way she'd immersed herself in her work for the past three years. By continuing to move, one didn't have to stop and think.

Lives were going on around her, with their own worries and challenges. She wasn't alone in that.

She revisited the moments before the scaffold collapse and explosion. She'd wanted to keep walking, not be back in an hour. Not be back at all, and she'd fleetingly considered some improbably optimistic outcomes if she'd followed through on that desire. In an ideal world, she could still see Alistair, have something of him in her life. But it wasn't an ideal world.

She recalled how she'd come to a halt when she realized where she was going. While she hadn't consciously intended a destination, she'd been headed toward the hospital.

She'd stood on the footpath, people moving around her, sunlight on her head, cars moving. Everyone in the world moving but her. Then the ground had shaken, people had started shouting, and the world started moving again. The world was always moving.

As he turned into the drive, she touched Nero's arm once more. "Thank you, Nero. If ever you need a nurse on a day when yours is off, I can come over pretending to be an acquaintance and help you out." *If Alistair permits it.*

Her fists curled into balls in her lap, and she looked down at them. When she glanced up, she saw Nero studying her in his peripheral vision. Maybe he said nothing because he knew she didn't have the flexibility, the right, to offer her time to anyone. If she did, no matter how sincerely meant, it was an empty promise.

"I think you have one of the most stoic expressions I've ever seen," she told him abruptly. "Alistair says I have a transparent face. I'll need you to give me some tips."

Nero's attention sharpened on the view ahead, and she followed his look. Alistair stood in the driveway. Mrs. W had implied he'd be gone a couple days, but perhaps his plans had changed. He must have been somewhere close enough to drive home after sundown. Or maybe vampires had underground tunnels running all over Australia.

For a moment, she was excited to see him. Wanted to tell him what had happened, about the men she'd helped, who they were, how they were doing. As he moved toward the car, her hand was already on the door. But when Nero brought the car to a halt, Alistair opened it. The words caught in her throat as he studied her up and down, taking in the dirt, lingering on the blood. He wore slacks and a white shirt even more immaculate than Nero's, but open at the throat rather than graced by a tie. His hair was brushed back from his broad forehead, the silken strands falling with that artful carelessness that drew the eye to the deep blue eyes, the sensual mouth, the strong jaw and cheekbones.

A male so striking in appearance he would make any woman take a second look, but his foreboding expression would discourage a third. Her heart, which had oddly accelerated at the sight of him waiting for her there, went cold.

"I was assisting at the hospital," she said carefully. "There was an accident, and I was nearby."

The explanation was clearly unnecessary. She was second marked, so he could read her thoughts. He already knew where she'd been, what she'd been doing. There was no surprise or curiosity on his face, just a set look almost as hard to read as Nero's. Instead of offering her a hand out of the car, Alistair gripped her wrist and drew her out, as if he expected her to resist. She didn't. When she looked up into his face, trying to understand, his grip tightened.

"I didn't give you permission to work at the hospital," he said.

"There was an accident," she repeated. "I wasn't intending to work there without asking you, but since you brought it up, I did want to get that permission. They have need of help. If I—"

He spoke as if she wasn't in mid-sentence. "What if I'd intended to bring guests home tonight, where my InhServ is expected to be in attendance?"

"You didn't communicate that to me," she said stiffly. "Else I wouldn't have gone with Mrs. C to the market."

"I don't need to communicate that to you, since attendance to my needs is supposed to be your primary focus."

"I'm sorry if triaging some poor blokes who nearly got themselves squashed by a building interfered with your dinner plans," she said tartly.

She could have bitten the words back, should have, but really? He knew what she'd been doing was important. Necessary.

His cold expression became arctic. Appropriate, since she felt as if there were a wall of solid ice between them.

"Your place is here, in this house," he said. "Unless I give you leave to do otherwise."

"There's not much to occupy myself with here during the daylight hours," she pointed out, in what she hoped was a reasonable voice, not an accusing one.

"It's not my job to entertain you. But I'll be sure to leave you enough to do in the future. The Mistress gave me instructions on how to reinforce your training." He jerked his head toward the house. "Go to the foyer. Take off your clothes and kneel in the required position until I decide how to deal with you."

She stared at him, her heart thudding up into her ears. "What?"

Her first few hours in Alistair's house, circumstances had allowed her to hold onto her indoctrination, the idea that someone could order her to do what he just had, without a blink. Spending the afternoon at the hospital had changed things, dismantled her mindset like that ruined scaffolding. He might as well have told her to strip and walk down a city street.

"I'm not clean," she stammered, her face flooding with heat. She couldn't bear to look at Nero, no matter that he knew how things were between vampires and servants. "I need a shower."

"Did I bloody well ask you to take a shower?"

The snap of temper had her own back stiffening. But it wasn't just anger that flooded into her. Everything did. Mrs. C's earlier scorn. Winifred's rudeness. Being unable to offer Nero a simple kindness to ease his pain. Facing the utter boredom of being in this house with nothing of any consequence to do. The idea that her life for the next three hundred years might be nothing but this, waiting on his whims, entertaining his guests in a variety of ways, all of them humiliating. Like the humiliation of what he was asking of her now.

"No," she said, low. Then stronger. When their gazes locked, and his body tensed, she threw up her chin in challenge. "You can force me to do your will, if that's what you've become. How would you like it if someone had jerked me away from your injured mates, saying I needed to help with some bloody dinner party, rather than saving their lives? Or do you even think about them anymore?"

She gestured around her, at the opulent house, the shiny car. "Does all this help you forget?"

A rage flashed through his eyes, there and then gone like the slamming of a steel door. She could feel it reverberate inside her chest, press against her heart. He shifted a step toward her, and menace was in the gesture.

"Do not presume to know what I think about."

On another day, she'd realize just how terrifying a vampire in a temper could be. But she was riding on a pretty high wave of emotions herself. She matched him, step for step. Bumped toes with him.

"Well, that's bloody true. Unlike you, I have no way of forcing someone's mind open to know everything they're thinking. I have to do it the old-fashioned way and ask you politely"—she showed her teeth on the three-syllabled word—"to pull the stick out of your arse and tell me straight out what you're thinking. My lord."

She heard a tiny gasp and looked toward the door to see Mrs. W standing in it, her eyes wide as saucers. Nero stood by the car, and even he looked a little tense. Nina brought her attention back to Alistair in a blink. "Forgive my breach of manners in front of the rest of the help. Allow me to tell you exactly what I'm thinking, without even opening my mouth."

She wasn't going to tolerate sitting around for hours with her thumb up her arse, waiting for him to need something he could likely bloody well do for himself. And she wasn't kneeling in the bloody fucking hallway. At least until she got a damn shower.

She was shaking, her body showing more sense than her mouth. The most intimidating Matron she'd ever met looked like a simpering novice next to him.

He shifted much closer. "You are relying far too much on my self-control," he growled. "You do not know what kind of day I've had."

She saw sparks of crimson in his eyes. She also felt a full blast of what he was holding back, strong enough to send a hard quiver through her. She wasn't a shrinking violet, but animal instinct had her heart triple-hammering.

Fury. He was holding back fury. But about what? This was more than just her defiance.

As the seconds ticked by, really only two or three, she still had time to shift her gaze to the open throat of his shirt. She remembered sliding her fingers there, putting her mouth against his pulse. How cruel were the gods, that they made physical intimacy so powerful a magic it could convince a woman that a man had a heart and soul worth wanting?

"Do you even remember her name?" she asked quietly.

Her gaze flicked up as she asked it. If she hadn't done that, she wouldn't have seen it. Could have left it as a rhetorical question, another jab at him where she hoped or believed the answer wasn't as bad as all that.

However, at his momentary blank look, something crumbled inside her, crumbled and squeezed the pieces. "Oh my God, you don't. You really don't."

She backed away from him. "How could you not..."

"Nina." Alistair's gaze flickered with something that might have been real regret, but regret was nothing more than a straw house before the tidal wave of what crashed through her.

"Her name was Sherry Evelyn Smithfield," she said. She didn't realize she'd shouted it until the echoes bouncing off the side of the house hit her like gunshots.

Suddenly she couldn't even see Alistair, because of everything else that surged forth in her. He was a dark silhouette behind her memories. Ironic, because that was how much form and detail Sher had possessed for him.

"She was my twin. When we were little, she would kiss my scrapes and then mark up her own knees so we could match. I called her Sher." She was hoarse with the tears clogging her throat. "She was connected to my heart, my blood. When I breathed, I knew somewhere she was breathing in the world. She dedicated her life to being ready to serve someone like you. To serving you. You couldn't even be bothered to come to her funeral.

"She kept a picture of you pinned inside her clothes, against her heart. She talked about you as if you were going to be the sun, the moon, and all the stars in between. Thank God she never learned differently. Or maybe the InhServ training is all about blinding someone to the disappointing truth about your lot."

She bolted for the stairs. He caught her, pulling her back against him, wrapping his arms around her, containing her. She twisted around, shoved against his chest with both palms. He didn't move. His expression was rock hard, yet still he did nothing. Except make her lower belly quiver at his unrelenting expression, even as her heart was breaking just above it. Again. She hated herself for ever letting him affect her in any way. How many times could the heart break before it would stop trying to put itself back together?

"React," she snarled. "Hit me. Punish me. Lock me into a cage. But what's the use of that? I'm already there, aren't I? Have you become such a bloody bastard you don't feel anything anymore?"

One hand shot up, gripping her throat, bringing her to her toes. She bared her teeth at him, even as she felt that weird jump in her stomach. It was as if they were on a battlefield in truth, standing on ground soaked by the blood of the fallen. A matching feral response had reared its head within her, eager for the purge of combat.

"Sir." Nero had shifted away from the car, dispassion replaced by something else, a sharp urgency to his tone.

"Stand down, Nero," Alistair said, his eyes never leaving her. "Go into the house. Stay there with Mrs. W."

"With respect, sir, not while I'm uncertain of your temperament toward her. I can't stand by and let you do something you won't forgive yourself for."

The tips of Alistair's fangs showed, that energy swirling around them getting even denser.

"You forget yourself, Nero."

"Again, with respect, sir, I think I'm not the only one."

Nina registered Alistair wasn't hurting her, just holding her. There was a quiver in his arm, like there was something fighting inside him. Probably fighting the urge to clout her. But that was okay, because she had so much pain welling up out of her, she'd barely feel it if he crushed her larynx.

"I'm fine, Nero," she said, despite the quaver in her voice. "It's between him and me. Please...listen to him."

Despite her body's quivering response, she was somehow certain Alistair wouldn't truly hurt her. But she wasn't sure about Nero. The energy pumping off Alistair was pure male wild animal, who wouldn't brook another male's interference in this. It reminded her of the primal reaction he'd had to John when the orderly came too close to them, during Nina's examination of Alistair's wounds.

After a long pause, Nero's feet crunched away on the gravel, though she could almost feel his reluctant disapproval, and fully expected he might be keeping an eye on them through the front windows.

That quiver in Alistair's arm increased. Or maybe it was her shaking that was making them both vibrate, two electrical currents in danger of setting fire to their immediate surroundings. He'd stayed motionless, holding her rigid, his eyes upon her. He was hearing every word, even as his expression remained storm-cloud dark. Impenetrable.

Christ, he had the bluest eyes. He had to be something created by the devil, to be that soulless and so beautiful at once. "Losing her broke something inside me," she said, low. "You all tell me I have it in me, to serve, to submit. Maybe that's all true. But that's missing the real point, isn't it? What the bloody hell have *you* done to deserve that kind of devotion?"

With that, she broke loose, shoved at him. When he merely caught her by the shoulders, she snarled at him. Why wouldn't he say anything? Why did he keep holding onto her like he'd never let go?

A full moment passed, her shaking like a leaf, staring at his chest, him with his hands gripping her upper arms, their bodies close together. She fought the strangest notion to put her forehead down on his chest and cry forever. It was okay. He was as immovable a column as the wood ones holding up the front veranda. Like them, he wouldn't give her anything else back except physical support.

His breath was on her face. It smelled of a fragrant tea, some sugar, a familiarly comforting odor that felt out of place in this horrible moment. Her nose could betray her, because it smelled him and remembered safety. Warmth. A mockery.

"You'll calm down now," he said quietly. His voice was so steady she could feel the effort behind it, to keep it that way. "You have a right to your feelings, Nina. But not to defy me."

Unexpectedly, he lifted her, carried her stiff body up the stairs to the veranda. Once there, he put her down on her knees, held her there, standing over her. She pushed against his hold, but she knew that wouldn't get her anywhere. And truth, this position was too close to the fetal ball she wanted to curl into to cry. Without conscious thought, she sank into the prescribed InhServ kneeling position, putting her forehead to the deck and wrapping her arms over her head. His hand rested on the base of her neck as he knelt over her.

She felt the sheltering heat of him, his bent thigh pressed to her side. She didn't want his shelter, the false haven it offered, the confusing mess it made of her emotions.

"I understand you were not expecting to take on this role," he said. "But you'll settle into it."

A harsh chuckle ripped from her throat. "Know that for certain, do you? I wasn't aware you'd had a lot of experience with being yanked out of your life and sentenced to three hundred years of mindless slavery as some stranger's whore. I need to sit up. Please."

The words were jagged, painful, but she'd given him as much respect as she could summon. Perhaps knowing that, he withdrew, let her sit up. She stared a hole in his chest.

"I've put up with all this bloody nonsense in a futile attempt to honor her," she said tonelessly. "To give to you what she wanted to give so much, but I failed her, worse than you did. I loved her, but I can't be what she was. This is what you get. So get rid of me, kill me, whatever. But I'm taking a fucking shower first."

She struggled to get up, turning away from him to grasp a veranda balustrade to manage it. But he rose with her and took her hand, lifting her to her feet. She was numb and didn't resist. But a part of her deep inside was surprised when he opened the door, strong fingers spreading out like a taut spider to push against the panel, open it for her. His hand grazed her lower back as she stepped past him, into the foyer.

"Go take your shower, Nina." His voice was neutral, but there was something brittle in it, like a wall that had sustained an internal detonation of daunting incendiary proportions, but had held firm. Barely. "But tomorrow evening, we will discuss this."

She told herself she didn't care about that. That she wouldn't cater to the despicable part of her that yearned toward the steady power and unrelenting authority in his tone, as if he could make the truth better.

He hadn't known Sher's name. There was no making that truth better.

"Please...please don't take it out on Nero," she said. "He was just trying to protect me. It was my fault."

Alistair's hand whispered across her shoulder. "You don't decide your crimes, Nina. I do."

His fingertips dwelled there, stroking along the delicate point, the curve of neck to shoulder. He was close again, his heat right behind her, and she closed her eyes. *I want to stop feeling anything for him.* If she was given one wish in the world at this exact moment, with no time to think of anything else, it would have been that.

She was in a world populated by ghosts of things she wanted, and the real things were obstacles to manage, put aside, placate so she could retreat inside to the place where things didn't hurt quite as much. The list of things she'd mucked up, fallen short on, couldn't understand or control, was getting unbearably long.

"You don't need to fix or control anything, Nina. And you've failed no one. Go take your shower."

With no real plan left for anything else, she nodded, and left him.

She took her shower. When she came down from it, Nero—who appeared no worse for wear—indicated "the Master" had said she should retire to her room for the evening.

So he wanted her out of his sight. Nero didn't say that last part, but Nina deduced that was the message. Hang him. Instead, she played cards with Nero and Mrs. W for a while in the kitchen. Mrs. C put a good dinner at her elbow. She'd missed the fireworks, obliviously working in the kitchen during it, but she expected Mrs. W had warned her things had gotten heated between the master of the house and...whatever Mrs. C considered her. She wasn't mean to Nina, however. Not like at the market. Nina supposed Mrs. C had eased off because Nina looked like she'd been kicked enough for one day.

Nina picked at the food, told her it was very good, but she didn't have much of an appetite. The woman nodded. "I'll leave it wrapped up in the warmer if you want it later. Do you want a cup of tea?"

Nina shook her head. "I'm headed to bed."

She rose. They said their good nights. Nero and Mrs. W had kept the conversation quiet, about neutral things, though the looks they'd exchanged said that she was likely to be the topic of conversation once she departed the room.

"Miss Nina."

She turned on the stairs. Nero stood at the bottom, studying the polished banister as if evaluating its cleanliness. "May I speak of something to you, something about your sister? I do not want to upset you, but I think you will find my point interesting."

With a sigh, she nodded, turned toward him. He continued to stare at that post. Since he was the type of male who met someone's eyes, it drew her enough out of her head to be curious where he was going with this.

"When I told Lord Alistair of your sister's loss, he was not indifferent. He told me to set up an ongoing scholarship for girls to go to university who might not otherwise have the opportunity."

She blinked. It pricked at the numbness, even if it didn't completely dissolve it. The words that came to her lips were grudging, but honest.

"I didn't know that."

"Yes. He is a good man, but I can tell you, that is what he would expect of himself. No more, no less. He did not get very involved in decisions related to the InhServ program. He left most of that to me, to pen responses in his name. A cursory nod or an offhand, 'Whatever you think is best' was his usual response if I asked for his input. But when I told him I was going to inform The Mistress he would, of course, take the next most experienced InhServ, rather than the untrained sister of his assigned one, his answer was not offhand in the least."

His gaze lifted to Nina's, locked. "'No. I want her.' That is what he told me. When I began to offer some sensible logic against that, thinking he hadn't understood, Lord Alistair cut right across me, sharp as a general. 'I don't need to repeat myself on this one, Nero. I want the sister. I don't care how untrained she is.'"

Nero's expression flickered. "For the past three years, it's the only thing I've seen him behave passionately about. Or act as his kind do when they know what they want, and God help whatever stands in their way."

Nina recalled the letter sent to Sher, her first communication from Alistair. Now she knew why it had seemed so formal. It had been Nero. That broke her heart a little more, but she couldn't block out Nero's words, his intent look up the stairs at her.

"You are dissatisfied because you want to frame it in the terms of the world you feel was taken from you. Yet here it is. The sun still shines, the flowers bloom, the moon waxes and wanes. Your patients who lost limbs or abilities they had before their injuries? Their lives didn't end. They changed. That's worth thinking about, Miss Nina."

She stared at him as he nodded, almost to himself, and ran an appraising finger over the banister once more. Then he pivoted, returned to the kitchen. She stood there a few minutes. The words had struck a wall inside her. They were lying next to it, there to be gathered if she ever had the interest.

Right now, she didn't.

Once back up in her room, she laid on the bed and listlessly looked at the ceiling. A couple times she sensed Mrs. W or Nero checking in on her, and it felt like concern, care. She would have appreciated it if she'd let herself feel anything, but she wouldn't. She was as tightly locked down as a bound chest in the hold of a ship, sailing for a distant and unknown shore.

He never came to see her, not that she'd expected him to do so. She wasn't even sure if Alistair was in the house. She hadn't asked Nero. Hadn't wanted to know.

An hour after sunrise, Nina rose, collected a small bag of travel items, put on her walking shoes with a trim traveling outfit, skirt, blouse, light coat. She walked down the steps and out the front door. She would catch a ride on the main road below the house's long driveway.

She wasn't coming back. Not unless he dragged her lifeless body there.

I'm sorry, Sher. I can't make this work.

CHAPTER FOURTEEN

*E*arlier in the day, right before Nina would have her unpleasant encounter with Mrs. C in the market, Alistair had been drifting toward that deeper sleep vampires enjoyed as the sun climbed toward noon. Yet today, he couldn't get past the drifting point, and circled back around to consciousness. Since a vampire had little energy to do much more than lie there when experiencing an inexplicable bout of insomnia, he reached out to the mind of his new servant to see what she was doing, thinking.

He had a front-row seat to Mrs. C's dose of contempt for her. The self-righteous old wowser. His surge of anger only intensified when he registered Nina's hurt. From her thoughts, he learned that Winifred had subjected her to more of the same. Even Mrs. W wasn't rolling out much of a welcome mat to their new arrival. Then Nina thought of JD's two hired laborers, and his blood ran hot.

Nero had recommended a cook and maid who'd already been in a vampire's household, but they were Luigi's second marks, and Alistair didn't want anyone with a direct line to another vampire. Nero had delicately pointed out that, by necessity, every staff member in a vampire's household usually became a second mark, unless the vampire could keep all the questionably non-human activities behind closed doors. What man wanted to be that guarded in his own home?

But he'd decided to try. He'd had uninitiated human staff in the past and it had worked out well enough. Plus, Mrs. C had come with an impressive resume. Knowing how vampires were about the quality of the small amounts of food they could eat, he thought she'd make a good impression when he had to offer vampire dinners at his home. Winifred was her niece, so it had seemed a good package deal. Human staff members who could make the transition to trusted second marks, aware of the vampire world, often became obvious as time went on.

That was obviously not going to be the case with these two.

He winced as Nina's further imaginings showed him how she thought her wounded soldiers would have treated her if she'd been paraded before them naked, or was brought in with the clear duties of a bought woman. It was an uncomfortable reminder of how often the respective cultures of the vampire and human worlds were not a good fit.

He'd distanced himself from the human world for the past three years, so hadn't recalled such mores as Mrs. W displayed. Plus, men ran into far less of that shit than women did.

He would fix it. He would discuss it with Nero and have him make it clear to the female staff members that any of them who treated Nina like a woman of ill repute, adversely reminding her of the expectations of a world she no longer inhabited, would be looking for work. And would not be getting a recommendation from their most recent employer.

As for JD, Alistair would be handling that conversation himself, making it abundantly clear how any male would conduct himself around his InhServ, if he wanted to keep breathing.

The Mistress's report had been usefully frank, and he should have paid closer attention to it.

A month's worth of InhServ training has prepared Nina to step over the threshold of our world. She hasn't the slightest conscious grasp of how to live there. To make it her home, she will need her Master to show her the rooms inside herself that are already there. Her success as an InhServ will be directly proportionate to your ability to be her Master. There are many different types of strength.

He mulled over those words. The Mistress had been trying to say something to him, likely something useful and unexpected. It would have been helpful if she'd just said it straight out, the bloody female.

She is angry, grieving, willful, and a mature woman. Her mind can be overcome through her blissfully strong submissive triggers, but sexual manipulation is a drug, a temporary method only to open doors. The aftermath of such sessions, if she is not properly succored, will result in severe emotional crashes.

The challenge she presents is much to ask of a new Region Master with many other responsibilities, who must act squarely in the public eye of our society with his servant by his side. As such, I've classified her first thirty days in your home as a trial period. The Council has approved this, such that during that time, she can be returned to my house to exchange for a properly vetted InhServ.

Because Council is aware of the uncertain nature of the girl involved, there will be no mark against you for this. I have a very suitable male InhServ. He has been placed on a thirty-day assignment hold in the event you make that decision.

He'd told her he didn't want that option, and the wily female had left the door open for him anyway. But despite the presumption, he couldn't fault her intelligence.

While I am certain you are aware of this, consider any additional marking decisions carefully during these thirty days. If you do return her to me, any mark of yours she carries cannot be reversed. In several years, when she is properly trained and assigned a new Master, a stronger vampire than yourself would have access to you through her mind if you've given her the second or third marks.

You specifically requested this woman as your InhServ, despite my recommendations against it. In fairness, I have seen things in Nina which help me understand what motivated your insistence. But with all due respect, Lord Alistair, do not deny yourself the resources you need to meet your ambitions.

In the meantime, I have enclosed some training exercises that will help refocus her when needed. Though some appear harsh, they had good effect on her when utilized at the training house and will reinforce what you sensed in her from the beginning. It is something she cannot deny when faced with it, and puts her off balance in positive ways, if the previous mentioned points are kept in mind. They are a method to opening her mind, but I reiterate, once opened, other paths must be found to seal the bond with her.

The Mistress was right. And yet he'd given Nina the second mark within twenty-four hours.

He couldn't regret it, though. Not as he lay here, touching her mind as she walked along the store fronts. He wanted to know what she was thinking, even knowing it likely wasn't complimentary in any way toward him and his kind.

She was angry because Mrs. C had hurt her feelings. She was walking. Walking so fast. She had beautiful breasts that he suspected moved the right way when she strode in such a determined fashion. If she looked down he could verify that, but she didn't accommodate him. That was all right, since he had a good imagination. Hips swaying. Trim calves. He frowned, thinking of her on the crowded street, other men seeing that, and chided himself for being an idiot.

Awareness of other things exploded in her mind. She spun, and he jacked up out of bed as he sensed danger, fear. She was running. Running right for it.

Where the hell was Coleman? Alistair couldn't be there, couldn't protect her. He was about to shout in her mind, tell her to stop, retreat from wherever she was going, and then she was kneeling over a wounded man. As her gaze coursed over him, her thoughts, assessing his injuries, both visible and possible, were almost too quick for his mind to follow. She barked at a bystander, commanding him to watch over the injured person, and she was on to the next.

Her eyes swept the area, gathering intel on the big picture, the materials that would exacerbate the conditions of the wounded, like the billowing dust or the splintered debris that could have embedded small pieces in their flesh. At the same time, she was cataloging things she might use for tourniquets or splints, pressure bandages.

Her unhappiness had been a continuous state since she'd crossed his threshold. Even when he'd aroused her, the discontent had flavored the physical reaction with a strangled desperation. She believed her body was betraying her, taking her further into a prison she'd never be able to escape. The second mark had articulated those feelings in rather off-putting ways. He'd told himself she'd get past it. He'd help her with it. Yet even her sleep had been fitful.

Which was why he'd let her keep sleeping on the veranda when he had to depart. He'd reached into her mind, steadied those turbulent waters that were only just then beginning to get choppy.

He'd noted the closed curtains in her room, her aversion to the beach side view of the house that most visitors and his own staff found so appealing. Even before he'd given her the second mark, it wasn't difficult to determine what was happening there. That was something else he wanted to address, to help her be happier here.

But when the scaffolding collapsed, and she skidded into the accident scene, all of that bumpy emotional terrain suddenly vanished as if it had never been. In an instant, his servant transformed from an angry, unhappy woman, unbalanced by her emotional turmoil and sexual responses to him, into a force of nature, practiced calm in the eye of a storm.

He wasn't the only one caught up in it. The people at the accident site quickly gravitated to her, recognizing her skill in her unassailable confidence. Yet he viewed it from a depth inside her they couldn't access. The second mark didn't give him the full depth of her heart and soul the third mark would, but he could push enough past her thoughts to feel the nerves on active alert beneath them. It was as if he were walking through a field of them, and he imagined stretching out his hands, calming the ripples with his palms, giving her reinforcement.

You're all right. You know what you are doing. You'll help them.

She didn't recognize the voice as his. She was too bogged down in a hundred things, but she steadied from it, and that was enough to make him feel better. Being in Nina's mind now, he rediscovered the woman he'd met three years ago, her energy so strong that his heart leaped in his chest, absurdly like a school boy's. This was the woman who'd remained prominent in his memories during some desolate times since, a connection that could steady him. But the contrast between who she was in the middle of an industrial accident, versus kneeling on the expensive carpet of his foyer, surrounded by luxury, was impossible to ignore.

He'd hoped to rediscover that connection with her. How pathetic was that? It wasn't simply that she couldn't be who she'd intended to be within the more restrictive boundaries of the vampire-servant relationship. He couldn't be who he'd been to her during those couple life-altering days.

This was a world she knew nothing about except as bedtime stories from her sister. She'd never intended or wanted to inhabit it. He didn't have to third mark her to know that for certain. Hell, he hadn't even had to second mark her. She was happy to tell him her feelings about it, with every action and word she'd offered since she'd arrived.

The ambulances came. She directed the responders, based on the status and priority of the wounded, and brought them up to date. He saw what was happening through her eyes and, though others might see a scene of total chaos, he could see the pieces of the puzzle she'd organized into a coherent system to get the injured the help they needed.

Her competence and compassion, combined with the tempting evidence of her submissive nature, were what had stuck with him so strongly. The whole package, not just part of it.

Then his attention snapped back fully to her immediate surroundings as she put her hand in the clasp of a male one. The ambulance driver helped her in, teasing her, but Alistair could see his eyes. He liked what he saw and, like any man, he'd push the advantage if she seemed receptive to him.

She did respond to his flirtations. Not inappropriately. But Alistair could easily see how a man like this one, who said she was the kind of girl he'd marry, would indeed be the type of man she'd want. Be willing to build a family with him.

You asked me, that day so long ago, had I ever had dreams of a family. A forever love. I expect you did.

All of that made logical sense. But as the male spoke to her, touched her, it didn't stop his fangs from lengthening, his bloodlust rising. Evidence of Alistair's need to mark, reclaim what was his.

She saw him as her jailer, the end of her future. She was nursing forlorn hopes that she'd be able to talk him into letting her go, or at least giving her freedom in ways that would minimize her contact with him and his world. Ironically, that would be easier if he wasn't a Region Master, with Nina expected to present herself as an InhServ at his side.

If he told her that she was locked into being an InhServ no matter what, whether she was with him or not, would that help? Better the devil she knew? It stuck in his craw, having to use that information as an advantage.

He thought he'd anticipated the obstacles, and so had tapped into her deeper longings on that first night, the ones he'd found and remembered so vividly three years ago. The sexual avenues had made the most sense to him, and even The Mistress had encouraged him to use that direction.

But being a Master was about a hell of a lot more than sex. It was about holding the reins, providing structure, guidance. Helping a servant understand the realities of her world, but also the endless opportunities of it, that lay in the matching desires within her to serve, and the Master's desire to possess.

He had three centuries to know certain things about himself. And one of them was quite clear. He knew when a servant was meant to be his. The challenge was helping her see that without breaking her spirit. And he'd brought a broken spirit under his wing.

His lips twisted grimly, thinking of Stanley. Well, that was his specialty, wasn't it?

~

In the aftermath of their terrible argument on the driveway, a great deal of his evening was spent thinking about how to solve the problem.

He wouldn't let her go. He couldn't make himself believe she'd be better off in the InhServ program, going to another Master. So, a new strategy. That was the past. This was the future.

His initial reaction to her defiance had been that he had to force her to face her reality in the ways The Mistress had recommended. But he hadn't followed her, made her kneel on the foyer naked, used physical force to bend her to his will, or even seduction. Because he'd been about to employ those tools for all the wrong reasons. Anger, jealousy, helpless rage that she couldn't give him back that connection he wanted with her, even though none of it was her fault.

He hadn't anticipated her ability to twist a knife in some raw wounds he carried, and Nero, damn the man's interference, had nevertheless helped him maintain the control so vital to the vampire-servant relationship.

So instead, he'd stood out there for long minutes in the dark night, her accusing eyes and words filling his mind.

What the bloody hell have you done to deserve that kind of devotion?

Not a bloody thing. In his world, that didn't matter. Humans served, and vampires took. They took from one another as well, from those weaker than themselves, though he seemed to be gathering quite the menagerie of misfits, like Stanley.

But in their taking, they gave something the humans they chose craved, needed. It was a synergistic relationship, and a vampire knew that. They had the immortality and years to know how to light that path, bring a human through it.

When he finally went into the house, he shut it all off, and tackled the evening's business. He was being overwhelmed by paperwork, phone calls, household matters, things a servant should be doing. He'd intended to stay away longer, travel farther, arrange more meets with his overlords and the vampires beneath them, but he knew the problems of being seen without a servant. It didn't help that word had been passed as swiftly as a conga line of gossiping washer women that he now had an InhServ.

But that wasn't why he'd returned tonight. He'd come back because of what he'd seen in her mind at the hospital. He'd needed to put his hands on her, ensure she was safe, and his.

All of it went together; The Mistress's emphatic advice, Nina's confusion, his reaction and expectations... He had a thirty-day grace period, not to decide whether to return her, like a defective piece of merchandise, but to see if he could sort out how to make this work, for both of them.

Tonight, he would leave her alone, block her thoughts from his mind. There was no point to hearing over and over how much he wasn't what she wanted. Maybe there was some way to let her have a few hours a week at her bloody hospital.

When he finally went to bed at dawn, he was irritable, annoyed and sexually frustrated. He might be able to block her thoughts, but not his awareness that there was a female in the house who was his to do with as he wished. He had the skills to seduce, to make her willing, to crack open that submissive side that was such a treasure trove to a Dominant, and a vampire was the extreme end of that sexual orientation. Denying himself was likely to make him all the more demanding later, and wasn't that an unhelpful thought that only spurred him to greater need?

But since he hadn't become a total bastard, he told himself to start fresh the next dusk. Give them both time to cool down.

Her words followed him into sleep, however. *Deserve... Didn't bother to come to her funeral. Sherry Evelyn Smithfield. Sherry Evelyn Smithfield.* He wanted to think about it, but his mind kept moving over to what he really wanted to think about. *Nina Hopeward Smithfield.* He knew her middle name, had remembered it when he was told the sister... Sherry, had died.

He'd had countless letters from and reports on Sherry over the years, but it was Nina he remembered everything about. Kneeling in the boat and leaning against his leg as he paddled silently through the night toward the beach, his senses straining for any evidence of Japanese patrols. Falling asleep in the plane, head nodding, tendrils of hair dancing wildly along her nape.

He wanted to reach out to her. He could. He could talk to her and encourage her to talk back to him. Mind to mind.

No, not her mind. Her heart. Because in truth, he didn't have to have the third mark to listen to a person's heart. Humans did it all the time.

That was the key, he realized. Use the second mark like a courtship tool of times past, letters, phone calls. It was a way he could perhaps give her more breathing room, rather than being in a proximity where his sexual desires would make him ignore the need to take it slow, hear what her heart—and mind—were truly saying to him.

Fortified by the feeling he was on the right path and hadn't completely mucked this up beyond repair, he was finally able to drop off into a few hours' sleep. But the impetus stayed with him, such that immediately upon waking, he reached out, seeking her, wanting to act on the idea immediately.

And discovered she'd left hours before, with no intention of ever coming back.

If she'd followed her preferences, she would have simply returned to the hospital, told Tracy she'd like a job and asked if there was a flat she could share with someone until her first paycheck, when she could find more permanent accommodations if needed. But if she did something that close, Alistair would find it necessary to come and retrieve her. Whether it was wobbly thinking or not, she hoped if she got on a train and took it much farther away, maybe he'd simply tell The Mistress she'd abandoned her duty to her family.

If a promised InhServ candidate refuses, the family's loyalty to the vampire world must be questioned, as to whether the existence of vampires is a secret that will be safe with them anymore. If the Council deems it is not...

But she'd been delivered as promised. Surely that meant her family would be considered innocent if she'd cut and run...afterward. No fault of theirs. Maybe. Their three centuries of loyalty surely would be taken into consideration. Right? And her brother, like Sher, would be more than willing to step into her place. That would be a balm on it, too.

She'd thought to protect Jim from it, but knowing he understood this in a way she didn't, never would, combined with her desperation, was making her rationalize her need to protect him. Even as she was pretty sure she was wrong and the guilt of that could crush her if she thought of it too much. She just couldn't go back. She couldn't.

You don't decide your crimes, Nina. I do.

The way he'd said that had made her shiver. His compulsion to come find her might not be the only reason she thought it wise to put distance between them.

She refused to think about it more. That day on the beach, she'd survived a machine gun and the worse possible face of humanity she could have ever imagined. Since then, there had been times she'd gone numb so she didn't have to feel anything. She'd gotten better at it than she'd realized. She could shut it all down. It wasn't so hard, really. She'd been the only one in the family who hadn't accepted the situation. Her brother would be fine if he had to serve. Better at accepting it than her, at least.

They wouldn't kill her family. They wouldn't. She refused to believe that.

She was headed for Sydney. It was a good distance from Brisbane and Alistair's beautiful Victorian home outside it. There'd still be a position for her at the hospital there. They'd been sorry to see her go and had assured her she'd always be welcome.

When she'd accompanied Mrs. C to the market, Nero had given Nina an unexpectedly generous amount of money. Not his money for his daughter's gifts, which was a separate handful of folded bills. Money from Alistair for items Nina might want or need. That generous allowance was probably part of what had inspired Mrs. C's unpleasant comments. And he'd never asked for it back. She would mail it back when she was able to repay it.

Hours passed on the train, yet she was barely aware of the passage of time. She dozed, she watched the scenery pass by. She paid for her meals and beverages, sat alone in the dining car. Discouraged any conversation, though at one time she'd been the type of cheerful person who'd be interested in her travel companions. Now she wouldn't have been able to remember any of their faces if her life depended on it.

You're all right. You know what you are doing.

She frowned as she thought that. It was familiar. Too familiar. Not her voice. As she searched her memory, she returned to the construction site, the dust, the cries of the men. Her triage. The momentary panic when she realized the enormity of it, that she had no support staff on scene, that it was all on her, and she would likely not be fast enough or have the resources to prevent more lives being lost. Her nerves had quaked, her stomach had heaved, and then that quiet reassurance had filled her, steadied her.

It had been a male voice. A male energy. Alistair. It had been him. The same male who'd ordered her to kneel in the foyer...naked. Like everything that had just happened hadn't mattered. Like she didn't matter, except as an orifice for his lust.

It did matter, and so do you. I didn't handle that situation well, Nina.

She started, her fingers clutching her travel bag. Though she knew he was far away, reflexes still had her looking around her. She saw only the people with whom she'd shared coach accommodations these last many hours. It was dark now, lamps providing some illumination. Most passengers were asleep, nodding in their seats.

You had enough to pay for a private berth.

Not if I want to make the money last. Get myself set up in Sydney. No use not saying it straight out. He could read it from her mind. But he proceeded as if she hadn't said anything about striking out on her own.

I didn't handle it well, because I brought you into my household thinking we'd simply connect the way we did three years ago. That those memories would help us over the hurdle of both having to be something entirely different.

She blinked. *That was entirely daft thinking.*

A sense of a chuckle, far too sensuous, drifted through her. Warmed her. *Yeah, it was. But I've since had another thought. Maybe a better one.*

Hard to imagine a worse one.

You underestimate my ability to bollocks-up a situation to previously unimaginable depths, my sweet nurse.

Her lips twitched despite herself. She rubbed her forehead. "Oh, Alistair," she murmured.

A sudden stillness. *Do that again. Say my name like that.*

She shook her head, but her cheeks flushed. *What was your thought? I'm thinking we sort it out. Slow it down. Away from watching eyes. Just you and me. The way it began.*

The train was slowing for the next stop. For those who were awake, there'd be the chance to step out into the fresh air, stretch their legs a few moments. She doubted any women traveling alone would be doing that at a dimly lit though seemingly clean outpost. But she would be one of them.

Because Alistair stood in the circle of the thrown light of one of the station lamps. His hands were tucked in the pockets of his overcoat, the collar turned up against the nighttime chill, so his dark hair brushed against the fabric. Those intense eyes passed over the cars, as purposed in direction as water in a current, and locked onto not only her car, but her very window. He didn't lift a hand in greeting, but he dipped his head.

Come to me, Nina.

He didn't sound angry or frustrated, as he had during their fight. Nor conciliatory or apologetic, at least not in an ingratiating way. He had the upper hand here, and yet he didn't sound smug or patronizing, either. Like most things about him, he was coming from a perspective she didn't necessarily fathom. But despite everything else, when it was just the two of them, he could draw her to him with a simple command. It confused her, miserably.

I'd like for it to confuse you a less miserable way. Do I need to repeat myself?

A little jump in her lower extremities was the answer to that, another annoyingly involuntary reaction she had when he used that tone. But she shouldered her bag and made her way to the car's exit door. By the time she reached it, he was there. As the porter opened the door for her, Alistair reached up. She put her hand into his sure

253

grip, and he drew her down to the bottom step, where they were closer to eye level to one another.

"The lady will not be continuing with this train," Alistair told the porter.

"She's your wife, then?" The porter said, seemingly talking to Alistair, but really to her. Making sure this was what she wanted. That Alistair was telling the truth. He was a good chap, protecting his female passengers traveling alone.

Alistair looked at her, his fingers tightening. "She's mine," he said quietly. "I'm a fortunate man."

The porter chuckled. "That's the right way of it for any man who gets himself a good woman." He tipped his hat to Nina. "Marm."

She managed a nod, and Alistair slipped an arm around her waist, bringing her down to the ground. She could have stepped down, but he'd done it so smoothly, she'd no time to assert herself about it. And he let her slide down him intimately.

You can fog my head with your seduction, my lord. It changes little.

You mistake why I want to touch you, Nina. I woke up to find you gone, and have traveled far and fast to get to you here.

Can vampires fly like bats, then?

"I can fly, yes." The skin around his eyes crinkled far too attractively. "But with no wings of my own, I use my plane's. Pilot. Remember?"

He'd drawn them away from the train, under the shelter of one of the wooden buildings. It was just the two of them. She heard frogs warbling and bugs chirping. He had her hands in his. He smelled good, like his soap and clean linen. His hair had been raked back with his fingers, so it was tousled, maybe from agitation, or tidying it after taking off the helmet he would have worn while flying.

"Just the two of us," he said quietly, repeating her thoughts. "For the next little bit, that's all there is. All right? Let's leave the rest, for now." Dropping his hold on her, he took a step back, and extended a hand. "If Stanley hadn't been there, this is what I would have said. Welcome to my home, Nina. You're very welcome here. I'm glad to see you again, more than I can say. I've thought a lot about you, these past three years. Have you thought about me?"

She was going to say, *you can tell, you can read it from my mind,* but gazing up at him, she couldn't find the tartness to summon the words.

Slowly, she put her hand in his. "I have, Alistair. Every day. Some days it was the only thought I had that made me feel less alone in the world."

Which is why I honestly can't bear you becoming one of the things that make me feel even more lonely.

His fingers tightened on hers, his expression registering both the words and the thought. He drew her closer, his other hand coming up to cradle her jaw, tip her chin, so when he bent, his mouth found hers. The kiss wasn't hard and demanding, but it commanded her all the same, her heart fluttering up into her throat, her fingers closing on his wrist.

Yes. This was what she'd remembered. She wasn't a fanciful girl, unable to separate the illusion of physical response with true emotion, but with him, it was one and the same. If it had been the memory alone that maintained the connection between them, this spark wouldn't burn so fierce still. This kiss would be a pleasant nostalgia, not this. Not something that flooded three years' worth of need and thoughts into the gesture.

Her nails dug into his wrist as things spiraled up from the soles of her feet, through her thighs and into her lower body, getting tighter, more concentrated. His lips moved on hers, her mouth opening to him so his tongue swept in, teasing and tangling. She made a little moan in the back of her throat, which he answered with a quiet noise of his own, part soothing note, part male growl of approval.

When he broke the kiss, he tucked her hand into the crook of his elbow, his other arm sliding around her waist, keeping her securely in the shelter of his body. "I want to show you something you'll like. It's only a short distance."

"Alistair..."

"There it is again." He stopped her, dropped to one knee, startling her, especially when his hands dug into her hips with hard purpose, his eyes piercing, demanding. "Say my name again, Nina. Look down at me and say it."

She swallowed. She understood now. Staring into his eyes, his hands upon her, her own resting on his shoulders, the word was a connection that couldn't be denied, because she couldn't keep her emotions out of it. Couldn't deny what even she heard in it when she said it aloud. She wanted to say no, knew she needed to resist that dark magic, but then he made it impossible to deny him.

"Please."

"Didn't know vampires knew that word." She gave a desperate half-laugh, her hands clutching him in a jerk of reaction.

"Nina. Sweet nurse." His voice dropped low. "Say it."

"Alistair," she said. "Alistair."

Something tense left his expression, replaced by something no less significant. He dropped his head, resting his forehead on her midriff, against her breasts, his breath on her lower abdomen. She slid her arms around his shoulders, fingers through his thick hair, tightening.

The way you say my name. It's the first time in a very long time that I've felt something like...what I feel when you say it.

It was a bit of nonsense that didn't clarify anything, and yet she understood it. With despair, she realized she might be able to fight the whole bloody vampire world, and even her own world, but she couldn't fight her own self. At least not tonight. If he was giving her tonight, just the two of them, she would deny herself nothing.

She would deny him nothing. Until dawn.

CHAPTER FIFTEEN

*T*he train from Brisbane to Sydney wasn't far from the coastline at most points, so she could smell the sea air through the open windows of their car. She didn't know where Alistair had obtained the vehicle, but with it being so late at night, it could have been borrowed from an unsuspecting owner's garage for all she knew. But it was clean, prepared. Having seen the size of his home, she thought he might have vehicles available to him anywhere he needed them. Whenever he had a wayward servant to retrieve.

As he drove, he clasped her hand, their tangled fingers on his thigh. He used the other hand to change gears, letting go of the wheel briefly to do it. Until she put her free hand on the gear shift, an unspoken willingness to help. A tacit agreement that she didn't want to let go of his hand, either.

Anticipating the gear shifting was effortless with him in her mind, able to tell her right when it was needed. His thigh shifted under their combined grip, and she was aware of the muscles there. His gaze slid to her often, but they said little after leaving the train station. Yet they weren't silent. There were things in the air between them that made it a living, breathing conversation, without any words being said.

He pulled onto a sandy road, lined with vegetation, and in short order came to a little sea cottage. It had a stone foundation, and the wooden siding was weathered. A blue wooden sign proclaimed it Hal's Port. Beside the house was an old boat and a pair of rusted bicycles with vines twined through them, closed-up purple blooms showing between spokes and frame. A garden of spiky bayonet grass grew in the dirt-filled boat.

"Wait there." Alistair exited the car, came around and opened the door for her, offering her his hand. It was something she'd expect from any male escort with manners, but she realized she'd needed his gentle reminder. The Mistress had done her job well enough that she hadn't expected it from a vampire. A servant's job was to serve him, not the other way around.

"Maybe it's like anything else. You learn the rules, and then determine which ones apply to the situation."

"And which ones can be broken?"

"And which ones can't," he said, but he squeezed her hand and drew her away from both the car and that troublesome topic. The stairs, though also weathered, looked sturdy enough. Alistair paused at the base of them.

"This cottage, at least the stone foundation and cellar area, is quite old. Built in the seventeen-hundreds by an ancestor of the last owner. Each son has had to do his fair share of repairs and replacement as the weather took its toll. Most of the original wooden structure is gone, but there's a shelf inside that holds a few pieces of it. What wasn't washed away by the temperamental next-door neighbor." He cocked his head. "Hear it?"

She could. The roll of the ocean on a nearby shore. Giving her a half-smile, Alistair took her sure-footedly away from the cottage and through the darkness, broken only by the whiteness of the sand. He was guiding her along a path laced with sea grasses, which she knew would lead to the open beach. Her feet started to drag, her heart to pound.

Then she could see the froth of the surf. The moon was behind clouds, but there was enough light for it to glitter off the curves of the rushing breakers. A few lights dotted the shoreline, but not many. The air was full of clean night time salty ocean smell.

She balked. "Here is fine. Please."

"Nina." He turned toward her, blocking her view, and regarded her with knowing eyes. "It's all right."

"I know it. Don't you think I know it, how silly it is? Just please... can we go back to the cottage?"

"In a minute. Stay right here with me." He closed his arms around her, holding her in the cocoon of his body so she wouldn't see it, so the sound was muffled, especially when he spoke against her ear.

"It's not silly. I'll take you back into it sometime. Help you feel better about it."

"But you said vampires don't swim."

"We're champion waders. I like the water, just not the swimming part. Maybe you can swim around me like a mermaid while I slog."

That gave her a tiny smile. She wasn't sure she wanted to smile yet. "Why does it matter? Why does it matter to you, how I feel about the ocean?"

About anything, she wanted to say, but she couldn't be that cruel. But when she looked up at him, he didn't look angry with her or her thoughts, though he was somber. He stroked a hand along her face.

"Because you used to love the sea. Since I'm part of what you feel has taken so many things away from you, I wouldn't mind being the source of giving some back."

She realized nothing was as dangerous to her sanity and the fragile state of her heart than his kindness. As if he knew how close she was to flying apart again, he spoke again, distracting her with less serious things. "There are a few scattered cottages here, but as you saw on our drive, this isn't a hugely populated area. Mostly fishermen escaping from it all for a weekend."

He turned her to face the cottage, his hands at her waist, and she let herself lean back against him. He crossed his arms over her, and she curved her fingers over them. He had strong forearms. A strong body, firm and resilient behind her.

"A vampire's strength has a lot of uses," he murmured. "I could stand here and hold you upon me, take you while standing, so there'd be no sand getting into unmentionable places, but you could feel the sea air on your bare skin, hold onto my shoulders and bury your face into my neck as I took you to climax."

She trembled. "I've never done it, you know."

"I know."

Of course. She remembered how he'd asked her. Demanded to know if she was still untouched, that way. "Why did you require that?"

"I was selfish and wanted that gift for myself, Nina."

He nudged her temple with his jaw, making her look up at him. "It

259

was also more than that," he said seriously. "This wasn't the life you wanted for yourself. You imagined yourself giving your virginity to your husband, after a beautiful wedding. Nothing fancy, just every part of it well thought out. Flowers, a little church, a few friends. A party afterward with champagne toasts."

He eased his grip to turn her, hold her at arm's length, but to look her up and down, not to let go of her hands. "You'd have a neat little travel outfit and the two of you would drive away to a cottage on the coast. Something more female-oriented than this fishing shack, but still. Similar. You'd go into the bathroom, bathe, brush your hair, put on a lovely nightgown with lots of lace and sheer cloth. When you stepped out in it, he'd be momentarily overcome, thinking if he lived to be a hundred, he'd never forget the way you looked, a gift for him."

The ache in her throat had grown to the size of a sharp-edged whelk. Alistair drew her back to him, turning her once more so his arms were crossed over her. "Do you think a vampire's memory is any less sharp with the passage of years, Nina?" He murmured it against her ear. "We don't forget what matters. None of us do. Even if it gets buried down where we think we have."

He shifted, dipped, and her breath caught in her throat as he lifted her off her feet and headed back toward the cottage. He strode up the stairs without hesitation. When he reached the door, it was unlocked. He pushed it open, carrying her over the threshold.

Based on his description, she'd expected a very male abode, with the lingering aroma of beer and fish. Instead she smelled a clean, fresh home, populated with the scent of flowers. As he let her down, she saw the fresh bouquet on the table. Purple and white flowers, a spot of orange here and there. The furniture was rustic but comfortable, a wood-framed living room set of sofa and two chairs, all with wide arms and deep cushions, a blue-green plaid pattern. The kitchen table could seat six, the kitchenette possessed of modern appliances that gleamed. The ocean-facing side was mostly windows, with sliding doors to the deck. On the walls were seascapes.

She saw them when Alistair lit lamps on the tables, ignoring the electric switches. She liked the ambient lighting, which let her see details but not any harsh realities.

Her knees quivered as Alistair drew closer, running his hands up her arms and back down again. Clasping her wrists, he brought her

hands up to his mouth, kissed the knuckles, a palm. He made his way
to one wrist, her other hand falling to his chest as he teased the artery,
scored it with a fang, which had her drawing in a breath. His grip
tightened on her wrist as he did it. It made her keep holding that
breath, heartrate accelerating again. "Go into the bedroom, Nina. See
what I left you there. Decide what you want to do with it. I'll know
when to come to you."

He stepped back from her, but didn't turn away, holding her gaze.
Her hand was still on his chest. As she moved back, it slipped away,
and she was aware of every inch of him she covered before that
contact was lost.

The door to the bedroom was behind her. Over that threshold, she
discovered a man-sized bed, taking up most of the space. Another
bank of windows included a door to the deck. During daylight, she
expected a person would wake to the sight of the shore. Alistair would
never have had that pleasure, since he'd been a vampire for over three
hundred years, and this cottage had been built later. Had he ever had
the pleasure of seeing an ocean at dawn before he was turned?

So many of the questions she'd thought about asking him since
she'd arrived had revolved around her situation, the answers
containing information she might or might not welcome. The idea of
asking him something simply to get to know him better was startling...and not unpleasant.

The bedspread was a masculine blue, similar to the color in the
plaid living room set. The pillows were white and blue, with a print of
a seagull above the bed, giving the room an airy beach feel. But then
her gaze was caught by what lay upon the bed, and the rest of the
details of the room disappeared.

Spread out on the bed was a peignoir set, in a butter-colored sheer
fabric, edged with lace. A spray of fresh yellow flowers tied with a
white ribbon lay next to them. And a card.

She drew closer. The bedside lamp threw its light on the words.
I'm glad you are mine.

If he'd been her husband, it might have said, "I'm glad you *chose* to
be mine." But she was here, wasn't she? She'd as much as admitted
she'd thought of him for three years. If she hadn't been forced to bind
to him because of circumstances, would she have chosen him anyway?
Could she deny that for certain?

Of course not. There were too many unknowns, too much of her life derailed and destroyed, for her to predict a track that was no longer available to her.

She touched the fabric. So silken soft, it coaxed her to stroke it. Her gaze lifted to the dresser and her throat tightened. A brush and comb set had been placed on a mirrored tray. They were silver, with an intricate raised pattern of roses on both the backing of the brush and along the spine of the comb. The mirror tray, too, was edged with the roses. Another white ribbon was tied around the brush handle and trailed down the front of the dresser. The dresser itself was a scarred wood, but it had been draped with a blue cloth so it wasn't that noticeable. A mounted mirror above it would give her a view of herself to the waist.

Music drifted in. He'd started up a record player. The Ink Spots, "I Don't Want to Set the World on Fire." The male voices rose and fell gently as they declared they just wanted to ignite a flame in their chosen woman's heart. It was a song that suggested the woman in question was the center of their attention. The gift Alistair was giving her tonight, if she was willing to go along with it.

She knew what tomorrow would bring. Why not clasp what was being offered now?

She closed her eyes, thought of Alistair's hands upon her. Putting her hands to her blouse, she slipped the buttons. Slow, not thinking, she did it like in a dream. The blouse slid to the floor.

She tilted her head enough to see the door in her peripheral vision. He was standing there, though as she glanced toward the mirror she couldn't see him. Vampire. No reflection.

He didn't move, didn't say anything, but that feeling from the car returned, so much compressing the air between them, giving it weight and heat.

Lifting her head so she was gazing at the mirror again, she unhooked the skirt, let it fall. Reaching behind her, she unhooked the strap of the lacy bra, let it slide down her arms. Then she released the garters to the stockings, which she bent to roll down, her hair tumbling over her shoulders.

Still no words from him, but something electric sparked through her mind, so strong she paused, her head down, her mind hyperaware of the picture she must be creating, naked from the waist up, back curved and hips tilted, one toe leaving the floor so she could remove the stocking. Then she straightened enough to do the other.

After unfastening the garter belt, she was standing only in the underwear. She hooked her thumbs into the sides, slid them off. As she'd removed her clothes, she'd done each piece slower and slower. At times her eyes had closed, for it felt like the fabric were his hands, his mouth, gliding along her too-tight skin. Were those his imaginings, or all her own?

When she dropped the underwear, she saw the blot of dampness that proved what she already knew, that her body was aroused. It didn't feel practiced this time, not an automatic response to what The Mistress had trained into her. It was a direct reaction to his closeness. His palpable awareness. The male standing silently in the doorway, watching her undress. For him.

On unsteady legs, she moved to the bathroom. There was a shower, no bath. She turned her head in time to see him leave, cracking the door, giving her privacy. Time to bathe if she wanted to do so.

She did. She saw there was an unopened shampoo, verbena soap and razor, all the things a woman would desire. She had hair pins in her travel bag. But her travel bag was in the car.

Had been. Alistair entered again, the bag in his hand. He put it on the bed, looked at her a long moment, eyes sweeping over her bare body. She felt like a statue in a garden, no need for self-consciousness, though her fingers, resting lightly on the bathroom doorknob, tightened. He registered it, a muscle flexing in his strong jaw. Those cobalt eyes held her in place with the male hunger in their depths.

"Take the time you need, sweet nurse," he said quietly. "But don't take too long."

Pivoting, he left her again, pulling the door to the jamb, but not closed. She could see a sliver of him, moving around in the living room. With her second mark, she picked up the light scent of a whisky, heard the clink of a glass. She might need one of those herself in a bit.

With a wry smile that twisted her confused and battered heart, she retrieved the pins from her travel bag and went back into the bathroom to pin up her hair. Running the water until it reached the temperature she wanted, she then stepped in and washed away the hours of travel.

She could have framed the things that went through her mind, tried to order and make sense of them, but that would have led to things she didn't want to think about. It was as if he was giving her a wedding night, though he could give her nothing else, and even that wasn't exactly as she'd envisioned. But something else had happened at Bangka Island, and maybe even before then, when she'd seen so many other people's dreams lost. A person could hold onto the wrong things when it came to a dream, and miss the most important part, which was usually something very simple, the heart of it, really. Nothing could muck up a person's happiness like their own head.

Hadn't Alistair said something like that? So maybe vampires did it, too.

She stepped out of the shower, dried off with a thick, fluffy blue towel that smelled like lavender and sage. The bathroom door had been closed, the yellow nightgown hanging on the back. No peignoir to go over it. She suppressed a smile. "Decided against that, did you, cheeky fellow?" she murmured.

She'd dried herself, but her skin still felt damp. Soft to the touch. The nightgown flowed over her skin like water. The lace-edged, diamond-shaped satin piece at the waist was a gathering point for the tiny, shimmering folds of sheer fabric that molded to her breasts. The sleeveless straps bared most of her shoulders and her back to the waist. The skirt was translucent, too, with scalloped lace points at the hem, which fell to her calves. There was nothing to go under it, so what was beneath was as visible as fingertips reaching through a mist. He would be able to see the shadow of her sex, the cleft between her buttocks.

Her body was tight again. Needing. She'd washed off any makeup. She'd come to him as she was. As Nina. Her brush and comb were still out on the dresser, so she assumed that meant he wanted to watch her do that part when she emerged.

She gazed at herself in the round mirror over the sink. It only provided a view of herself to just below her breasts. She could see the dark color of her nipples, their press against the fabric, the valley between her breasts, and their generously rounded shapes.

Her hair was damp at the nape. She liked the smell of verbena that wafted to her from her skin. Choosing not to think, only to act, she stepped out of the bathroom.

Alistair was stretched out on his hip on the bed. He wore his slacks, but had taken off shoes, socks, coat and shirt. He still wore the cotton singlet he'd had on beneath the dress shirt, which allowed her eyes to feast upon the curves of his biceps and chest, the latter molded by thin stretched cotton. He had the whisky in one hand, his elbow propped against the mattress.

She reminded herself to breathe again, holding his gaze. It was difficult to keep doing it, though, and eventually she looked away, down. When he didn't move, she knew he was taking his time, looking at her, what was his, as long as he liked. The thought made her tremble harder.

"Brush your hair for me."

She realized she wouldn't have moved until he gave her leave. The uneasiness tried to push back through, but she wouldn't allow it. She might not have a will against him at times, but against herself and her own thoughts, trying to take this night from her, yes, she would fight that tooth and nail.

You might only get this moment, she reminded herself for the last time. *Make the best of it, damn it all.*

Moving to the dresser, she removed the pins she'd used to keep her hair from getting wet. Picking up the brush, she began to stroke it through her golden-brown locks.

She believed in presenting herself well, but she'd never been the type of girl who primped and preened and thought about being the prettiest. Silly as it sounded, Sher had always been so astonishingly beautiful, Nina felt that need was covered in the family. A pleasant presentation helped her patients, made her more approachable to them, which was enough. Truth, beyond that, she didn't give a lot of thought to her appearance most days.

Today was the exception.

Her hair might be more feathery than Sher's thick locks, but it shone and had a lovely color under the light, one even Sher had said made her envious, because it made her think of sea sand, the sun, the sparkle of gold, all in one.

As Nina brushed and brushed, she did it the way she'd undressed. Getting slower, more deliberate in her motions, and then she stopped entirely, because he was right behind her, even though she couldn't see him in the mirror. His hand came before her, took the brush and set it down. Then he coiled that hand in her hair, gathering it all together to twist it, tilt her head away from him, toward that grip. She turned her face to it, her lips inadvertently resting on his knuckles. She closed her eyes as he spoke.

"You are the most beautiful thing I've ever seen in my life, Nina."

He'd set the whisky down on the dresser and slid his hand down her other arm, to her wrist. Slowly turned it, with an intriguing pressure, slightly uncomfortable, as he pulled her hand behind her back to her buttocks. Her palm met a rigid heat beneath his slacks, a weight and size that filled her hand and considerably more. "This is what you do to me, just looking at you. Turn around."

She obeyed as he released her and pivoted, her shoulder brushing his chest, he stood so close. He let her hair fall free through his fingers, the strands caressing her mostly bare shoulders. Rising on her toes, she slid her arms around his neck, putting her face against his throat, his shoulder, burying herself there as his arms tightened around her back and beneath her hips. He lifted her, hitching her up his body so she was looking down at him when she lifted her head.

His lips had a warm curve that matched his blue eyes. His expression was intent, his gaze so deep, the brows and lashes so dark. He had such a strong face, a firm chin and cheekbones. He was movie star hero handsome, and yet here he was, in a quiet room just with her. When he laid her down on the bed and leaned over her, his hair tumbling over his brow, she was trembling even more. Yet she reached up and captured a strand of his hair between her knuckles, letting it slide through.

"Do you fear me, love?" he said, his eyes darkening.

She shook her head. Nodded. Her hand dropped to his biceps, gripping. He studied her face a long moment, then lowered his own to kiss her. Like at the train station, only this time as it deepened, he went to his elbows, bringing the weight of his body onto her. Her legs opened at the unspoken insistence, cradling him, her hips lifting to the pressure of his. A little moan escaped her lips, and he answered with more teasing penetrations of his tongue. His hands slid over her face, her throat, her shoulders.

When at last he broke the kiss, he pushed himself up, but he cupped a breast through the soft folds of the nightgown, finding the nipple to tease it to a sharper point. Her hips jerked. His eyes got even darker, his mouth more set. She saw the flicker in his gaze. Her Master, liking her desperate need. She responded to that, wanting to show him just how desperate she could get. She wanted to please him, God help her.

"You do that merely by breathing. Don't distress yourself. Stay here with me. This cottage is our world. Our only world tonight."

He bent, put his mouth to her throat. Nina thought he might feed on her, wanted him to do so, but he denied her for now. Instead, he suckled on her flesh, nipped and played, moving down, his hands cupping both her breasts. She arched, crying out as he closed his mouth over one aching nipple through the thin fabric, his thumb flicking over the other, refusing to leave either one unattended. She writhed beneath him, shocked at how responsive her body was to him, so quickly. Again, not the training. This need stemmed from three years of imaginings, fantasizing.

Fantasizing, hmm? You'll have to share some of those imaginings with me, sweet nurse. So I can spend time making them reality for you. His other hand dipped to stroke her knee, up her thigh.

"Whisky and cream is one of my favorite combinations," he murmured, and he slid his fingers between her legs, teasing, spreading her wetness over the lips, moving with her convulsions. He worked her into a rhythm against his hands like she was performing a sensual dance. She moaned and whimpered with every new shot of sensation his clever fingers sent through her. Every sound made his eyes spark and his expression become more intense, capturing her, making her even more willing to surrender, to keep that look on his face. Pleasing him.

He didn't merely focus on those parts of her that men wanted. It was as if he wanted every single inch of her flesh and what lay beneath it, and he took his time, exploring, caressing, kissing, making noises of approval that had her losing every part of herself to him. Willingly. Gladly.

"Sweet nurse. Beautiful girl. Lovely woman. A treasure. Do you know why you stayed in my mind, Nina? Why this tears you apart so?"

She had no spare brain cells to consider the complexity of the first question and didn't want to shred her heart further by examining the second. But he didn't require her to answer either.

"You remember how I told you to handle the demons of the past? Did you do that?"

Heat filled her cheeks, but he framed her face with his hand when she would have averted her gaze. "You didn't answer me last time I asked. You'll answer me now, Nina."

"I did."

"How often?" The husky demand made her shiver.

He might as well have asked her how often she thought of him, for the demons came more often than not, every night. She'd chased them away with thoughts of him, her hand slipping between her legs as she imagined him there instead.

"That must be why I woke hard and aching for you so much. Even without the second mark, I could feel your need for me. But I'm here now. Real and alive. That night, I implied that you didn't belong to me. Do you remember?"

She remembered everything about that night. About him. Over time, she'd suspected she'd exaggerated some details to give her fantasies even more power. But with him upon her, so close, his heat and scent and sheer energy surrounding her, she knew she'd actually fallen short.

Undeniable male satisfaction surged at her thoughts, but there was no smugness. Just more fierce approval.

"Minutes after I left your side, I knew what I said was total bollocks." He spoke against her lips, even as his hips pressed harder against her core, wresting another whimper from her. "You do belong to me, and I am your Master. The InhServ bullshit, it doesn't mean anything. This is you and me. The way you look at me, how you say my name, tells me that you know it."

She shook her head, wanted to deny it, but couldn't get anything to come to her lips as he looked back at her. Her heart tried to pound out of her chest.

She remembered that moment in the boarding house when she'd thought about giving into his will, because he'd proven it was stronger than hers. That she could commit herself to his care and it would be all right. That she could trust him with her deepest worries, the questions whose answers she feared.

I want to belong to you, but I want to belong to me, too. Do I have to lose me to have you?

A muscle flexed in his jaw. Rather than answering, he lowered his head again. She sucked in a breath, her eyes closing as he pushed aside the fabric, framed her now bared breasts with it, a contrast of silk and heated male skin as his mouth began to torment and worship, stroke and bite, driving thought and worry away. Her legs lifted, clamped over his hips, her body rising and lifting in an instinctive way that rubbed her damp center against his slacks, against his ready cock straining beneath it.

He wouldn't be rushed, though. He spent so much time on her breasts she was afraid she was about to release, her body struggling against his, the friction taking her so very close. But when her body was vibrating on that very cusp, he moved down, his mouth on her sternum, then lower, to put a lingering kiss on her navel through the sheer garment.

He stood up on his knees, unbuckled his belt, pulled it free and set it aside, then unfastened his slacks. He slid off the end of the bed to rid himself of the rest. She was glad for it, wanting to see all of him. He stripped off the cotton singlet with a careless flex of rippling muscles and broad shoulders. Then he pushed off the trousers and the boxers under them.

Her gaze dwelled upon the lean flanks and smoothly muscled thighs, the hint of tight arse and the high, thick cock. The tip was glistening with fluid as he put his knee on the bed and leaned over her. His gaze coursed over her, from parted lips and feverish eyes to taut-peaked breasts and trembling limbs. Her legs were open for him and, under the demand of his gaze, she couldn't even think of modesty or denying him the view he so obviously demanded.

"I give you permission to call me by the name we both want to hear," he said. "No matter your doubts and worries of where it will take you. I want it from your lips. Need it. It will rip something inside me to hear you say it. Something I want destroyed."

His voice was rough, and those crimson sparks in his eyes, the slight lengthening of his fangs, let her see him as the otherworldly creature he was, crouched over her, waiting, vibrating with power, all muscles taut and defined along his shoulders and sides.

It would rip something apart in her to say it, too, but he was leaving her no choice. She had to face it. Accept that one truth in order to go any further. Wherever it took them.

Master.

"Aloud," he demanded, and it came to her lips, along with tears in the corners of her eyes.

"Master."

He slid the sheer fabric of the night gown up to her waist and lowered himself to his elbows. Her inner thighs pressed intimately against his bare hips, and his cock rested against her lower abdomen. The smooth, heated weight of his testicles rubbed the lips of her sex, making her quiver harder.

Her kissed her again, gentle, soothing, taking away the tears. He kissed her the way a lover would, making her hold onto his shoulders, press her face to his neck again. "Love me, Alistair," she whispered. "Please love me..."

He stilled against her. She couldn't take it back. Couldn't hide her deepest wish from him, could she? It was what it was, but if he withdrew from her now, she would shatter.

She let out a shuddering breath as he let his lips drift across her cheek, things resuming once more. His fingers were between them, stroking her sex, opening her, finding the slippery evidence of her arousal before he guided the head of his cock there.

Hold onto me, sweet love.

Clasping his shoulders, she pressed her mouth to his collarbone. At the same time, he gripped her hair, holding her head tilted away from him again, telling her what he intended. Whenever he tightened his hand in her hair like that, things stilled, inside and out, her mind a whirling point. It took away any trepidation.

Then he pressed forward, sliding into her in one smooth, strong motion. As that barrier broke, he sank his fangs into her throat.

The pain was there, a sharp stab between her legs that made her suck in her breath, but the arousal was still there too, fighting with the pain, and it was stronger. Getting stronger by the second. She embraced the pain, tightened her legs around him, arousal thickening her tissues and making her body strain up to him, take him impossibly deeper.

She remembered the night behind the tent, when he said he could inject something into her bloodstream that would lessen the pain of the bite by increasing the arousal. It was a spike that felt like being catapulted up a hill, the stomach bobbing and the whole body tightening in anticipation.

She had the odd thought that she really didn't want him to make a habit of doing that, of changing the experience with something chemical, but she had to admit her gratitude in this instance so the pain of losing her virginity couldn't override other feelings and sensations he was giving her.

I might permit you the full experience for future feedings or punishments, but tonight, I will not allow you to feel any pain I can prevent. And there's more to it tonight...

It was a feeling like being in a whirlpool, a slow, dizzying spin that got tighter and tighter. She constricted her arms around his back. He had such broad shoulders, such smooth firm skin and musculature. And he was a furnace, heating her within and out. Filling her. Her mind was whirling in that same spin, and she registered it was different, something more. As if beneath that whirlpool was a deep cave, and she was sinking, sinking, even as she tightened her grip on him, ensuring that he was with her, holding her fast. He was. In her mind, her heart and soul. And it wasn't merely romantic imaginings.

As she tried to grasp what was happening, he withdrew slightly, then pushed back in, a slow glide that had her sore channel recuperating, contracting on him. She let that breath out, a shaky thing, and he caught it when he put his mouth over hers again, tangling with her tongue, nipping at her lips, delving deep. He cupped her skull, fingers tightening. He could crush bone, which made his gentleness even more compelling. She felt held, protected.

Loved. There it was again, that word that had to be an illusion, but if her reality was going to be devoid of any dreams of her own, she would take the illusions and make what she could of them. Whatever he'd done made her vulnerable, open beyond anything she'd ever felt, but he was doing things to shelter her, keep her from panicking.

He was beginning to be more insistent in that rhythm, more aggressive, and she embraced his aggression. Her nails dug into his shoulders as the response between her legs built to her lower abdomen and chest, making everything urgent. God, he filled her so deeply, stretched her, and she wanted that, wanted him.

"You like my cock inside you, hmm? The feeling is fucking mutual, sweet nurse. I don't want to ever let you up. I may keep you tied to this bed, legs spread, so I can do this to you whenever I wish, as long as we're here. Your pleasure is mine to command, and I plan to be a very demanding Master."

She shuddered at his words, uttered in that deep, husky voice. She was the center of his attention, an incredible, terrifying, exhilarating place to be, for she felt his need, and it was endless. As the climax started to take her, he gripped her wrists and pulled them up above her head with one powerful hand, the other settling on her throat, tipping up her chin so she was captured by the look in his eyes. "Not until I say so, Nina," he said. "You release when I give you permission. Fight it for me. Make it build to please your Master."

His voice was hoarse. From the ripple through his shoulders and jerk of his body between her legs, she knew he wasn't far from his own release. But somewhere in her dazed state, she understood commanding her at the edge of his own completion made it more intense, for them both. Things quivered deep inside her, things breaking, changing, as she gave in to his will and denied her own. For them both.

He pushed in further, withdrew, stroked in a maddening way, his expression becoming savage as hers became more desperate, her lips parting, body quivering violently, fingers clutching over his grip on her wrists.

"Alistair...please."

"Just a moment more. Love the feel of your cunt squeezing me, holding me. So tight."

She strained against him, her arms, her body, and reveled in his strength, how he compensated, the male animal in him rousing even more as he registered she was actively fighting him to distract herself, hold back on her release.

He released her wrists, caressed her face, a quick movement before he brought his own wrist to his mouth and pierced it, drawing blood to the surface. Then he was cupping her cheek, bringing the wrist to her lips.

At the hospital, she'd dulled her senses to the smell of blood, the detachment necessary. Another layer of horror buried where it couldn't interfere with her duties. If she'd ever been told then she'd find the smell of blood appetizing, she would have told the person they'd turned the corner. Let all the kangaroos loose in their top paddock.

Yet his blood had the compelling sweetness of the best wine, the comfort of hot cider in winter or refreshing restoration of lemonade in summer. Her lips parted, tasted, and then she was feeding at his wrist, suckling, her body bucking with the need to let go even as her throat worked, swallowing him down.

My sweet nurse. My beautiful strong girl.

She'd lowered her gaze as she drank, but now her eyes widened, snapping back up to him. The whirling sensation became a full roller coaster spin. Her body bowed up, every muscle tensing, and she clutched his shoulders once more, holding on. That sinking feeling became a free fall, everything spinning even as his hands remained sure and hard upon her. His cock, buried inside her, was an anchor point that assured her she wasn't alone in whatever was happening.

Deep, deeper. He sank deep inside her, deep as he was in her body and more, through the shadows and nightmares, hopes and dreams, and he saw them all.

He'd given her the third mark. She realized it at the same moment he started to move inside her again, insisting, his eyes so close, mouth so taut. Her own lips parted, her breath on his lips. "Please..."

She didn't know what her plea was for this time, but he gave her an answer. "Come for me, sweet nurse. Be mine and come for me."

She wasn't sure what to do, but her body was. The climax seized her, threw her off the edge, even as her heart and soul fell even further, right into his waiting palms.

CHAPTER SIXTEEN

*Q*uiet. She was still beneath him, but curled, her head dipped so her forehead was against the base of his throat. He cupped her skull again, as her hands fisted against his chest between them, her breath shallow. Managing the third mark connection was different from the second mark. One was a voice, and a sharing of some feelings, some thoughts without words. This was an awareness that whatever feeling, stray thought or even unconscious compulsion she had was within his grasp to realize and examine. A full invasion of self, no privacy of her own, ever again. Nowhere to retreat, to shield herself.

"Perhaps no need to do so, either."

"That's your perspective. You're not the one pried open like a helpless clam on the beach," she said against his skin. She realized she was still clutching him as if she thought she might fall off a precipice if she let go, so she made herself do so, push against his chest. "Please. I need some space."

He didn't have to listen to her, didn't have to do anything she asked. It choked her, but before another wave of panic could take her, he'd shifted off her, withdrawing from her body, which protested the loss. Ignoring it, she scrambled off the bed, stumbled. She had no idea where she was going, but she just had to move. To go.

Maybe he wasn't as keyed into her mind as much as she'd thought, because when she bolted from the room, she heard a startled and muttered curse. She ran blindly, through the kitchen, out the back door, and down the path toward the beach. The ocean was there, the waves, the enormity of it perhaps enough to swallow her, make her feel insignificant again, unnoticed, rather than accessible to the mind of the male who'd made her feel ways none other ever had. And that was even before she'd found out she was bound to him for eternal servitude.

Master. She'd called him Master and meant it. She needed to go. Before it was too late, before she could acknowledge it already was.

Nina. His voice was a thunder in her head, her rapidly beating heart. She was headed for the ocean, and she vaguely registered she wasn't wearing a stitch. But it was also the dead of night. Who would see her, except a vampire who could see in the dark?

Or another third marked servant, since she vaguely realized her own night vision seemed to have improved exponentially. All the better, then. She plunged into the surf, and kept going.

It wasn't until she was past several breakers that she realized how badly she'd panicked. She hadn't been in the ocean for three years, had actively avoided it, and every cell of her being suddenly came to full screaming life, infused with the memory of why, drowning her even before she stumbled and went under.

Helen's hand, tight on hers. The choking salt spray as she tried not to give away she was still alive by coughing, floundering. The pain of the bullet wound, making her fear she was bleeding out.

She was back off the shore of Bangka. The water churned, pulled her down, and she needed to let it take her down, so she wouldn't be visible. But she couldn't breathe. She was gasping, dying, every conception she'd had about the line past which humanity would go destroyed. Their brutality was unstoppable, limitless, so far beyond the realm where hope could live.

She should sink. She'd known it then, that she should just give up, let the sea take her, never surface and face the aftermath of something so horrible. But she'd fought, and then Alistair had reached down, drawn her up, held her. Got her through.

He should have let her die. Better for them both, really.

So this time, when he gripped her, she fought him. Fought him with everything she had, using teeth and nails and kicks and punches, everything she'd ever learned. She screamed and begged. Begged him to let her die.

This was so much more than what had happened in the past few moments. It was a culmination of three years of lost confusion, of detachment from the world, from her family. His third marking had been a trigger, the wall coming down on all that had gone before. She could never go that way again, all of it lost. Everything she was or had ever thought she'd be.

She wouldn't have been surprised or even really blamed him if he'd gotten rough with her to subdue her. But he didn't. He held her fast, took her abuse, brought them both to shore. There was a blanket there, one he must have pulled from the bed, and he immediately wrapped her in it, an effective cocoon and restraint when he pulled it around her snugly. He sat her in his lap on the sand, letting her cry and struggle, scream at him. There really was no one else on the beach, because he didn't seem concerned about that, his attention on her alone. He tucked her head under his chin, wrapped both his arms around her, and rocked her.

He'd pulled on his slacks to chase her, but she was pressed against his bare chest. It took her a while to realize he was talking to her, both in her head and echoing the words aloud in his deep voice. Rough with emotion she didn't expect.

It's all right, sweet nurse. I know. I know.

But he didn't know. Even if he was in her mind, heart and soul now, he didn't know, because she refused to believe he could understand the depth of her helplessness and rage and not be willing to let her go. She knew the world was impossibly cruel, but she couldn't believe he was.

Which maybe said more about her than him.

Yet what he was giving her was comfort, no matter how meager, and the heart responded to that even if the mind wanted to reject it, wanted to close off and be cold, unforgiving.

She was weeping now. She thought of Sher's grave. There'd been flowers from a few people, the typical and expected types of arrangements. But there'd been a lovely New Zealand tea tree, the deep pinkish crimson blooms displayed in a clay pot with a cream and golden glaze, a gorgeous piece of work to complement the plant.

Nina had stared at those blooms throughout the service, because the New Zealand tea tree blooms had been Sher's favorite flower. Though always under its supervision, the InhServ program had encouraged her to gain experiences, travel, and she and other initiates had traveled to New Zealand in her teens. She'd liked the flower so much she'd pressed one in her diary. Had her mother kept that?

Had her InhServ friends sent the plant? Everything else at the funeral had been from family friends who really didn't know much about Sher. They'd just been there to support her parents.

"Nero kept track of your sister's progress in the program," Alistair said quietly. "He read the reports, the letters she sent, when she was approved to send me communications. A one-way correspondence, to give me the opportunity to get to know her better. He has them, if you'd like to read them."

"Did you ever read them?" From what Nero had said, she was sure the answer was no, so she didn't know why she was torturing herself, but she wanted to hear his answer. He gave her honesty. She gave him credit for that. And at least it was a qualified *no*.

"Not until recently, when someone pointed out I didn't even remember her name." He shifted, adjusting her so she sat on the sand between his spread thighs, one crooked around her hip, one bent before her so she could shift her head to his knee to gaze at him. He braced himself on one hand, the other arm still circling her loosely.

"I read through a few of them," he admitted. "I didn't get much of an impression of her...uniqueness, because most of them were similar, expressing her devotion, her willingness to serve. The emotions that the InhServ program targets and sculpts."

Before she could stiffen at what sounded like a criticism, he continued, and she noticed his expression became thoughtful. "But she wrote to me about going to New Zealand, and how she loved the little tea tree flowers. She said she imagined creating a chain of them and putting them around my neck."

Nina blinked at him through her still-wet lashes. "You sent the tree?"

"I wish I could tell you so," he said, meeting her gaze. "But it was Nero. I asked him to read through the letters and decide what would be appropriate, so thanks go to him."

She looked down at his chest, her fingers worrying the blanket from the inside, where it was so securely wrapped over her hands.

"Why didn't you go to her funeral?" she asked in a small voice. "I suppose I can guess, but you meant so much to her. Please don't say it was the idea of you that meant so much to her. She spent her whole life trying to convince me otherwise. I don't want us ganging up on her when she can't defend herself."

Plus, after spending time with vampires, she understood Sher's point of view enough to question her own doubts.

"It was not appropriate for me to be there." He sighed, touched her face, fingertip sliding over her cheek. She supposed she could have resisted the touch, but what was the point of it anymore? It was easier simply to enjoy the comfort the contact could bring.

A muscle twitched in his jaw, but he answered her question. At least she detected genuine regret in his voice, even if it was probably more for her than Sher. "Her letters were charming and lovely, and yet she was a stranger to me, Nina. A great deal of that is my fault. Many vampires, when awarded an InhServ, will spend much time reading through those letters, anticipating the InhServ's arrival like a favorite Christmas present, because their reputation is without compare. A true gift. Some of my kind will even write back. We have that option. We can even arrange for some visits to the InhServ school. But I did not."

What would have happened if he had? Would their meeting have been different? Would Sher's opinions have changed? Some terrible part of Nina wondered if he would have gravitated toward her as much, connected to her so strongly, if he'd made that connection with her sister first. She really hoped Alistair didn't pick up on that thought, because it shamed her enough to have to hear it herself.

"She was a political choice pressed upon me," Alistair said. He gripped her shoulder, as if anticipating her drawing away from him, but Nina merely stayed still, numb, listening. "I intended to accept her into my home and treat her the way I view Nero and the rest of the staff. Perhaps when I met her face to face, and saw the depths to which an InhServ trains, I would have had a far deeper appreciation of her loyalty and value. But I can only give you the truth."

She nodded. They sat silently for a few minutes, only the movement of the surf and the response of the wind creating any conversation on the beach.

"You told me I didn't believe in small talk," he said after a while.

"Like 'how have you been these past three years?' 'What have you been up to?'" His lips curved, but there was no humor in his gaze. There was that straightforward relentlessness, but she also detected a strain of the bleakness she'd seen in him before. "Most of the first year after you and I saw one another was a blur. I came back to Brisbane, did nothing useful, unless independent tests to determine if a vampire can get alcohol poisoning or fuck himself to death in an endless line of tight arses is possible. Neither one, apparently. I can't even get tipsy. It's God's cruel joke, one of many."

"On the flip side, imagine the damage you could do if you *could* get drunk," she said, snuffling. "Perhaps it's just evidence of God's practicality."

He paused, gave her an odd look, then half-chuckled. "Yes, that's true."

"My nose itches. I need my hands free."

"Here?" He carefully rubbed her nose with one finger, the tip and around the nostrils, up to the bridge. She stared up at him. Despite herself, a painful smile touched her lips. She'd done that once, for a soldier who had casts on both arms and hands.

Seeing her smile, Alistair's own expression eased, but the tightness around his mouth lingered, as did the tension in his body. It had been a rough few moments, and perhaps not just for her.

"I won't tolerate you telling me you want to die," he said.

"I don't think I want to," she said. "But sometimes, it becomes so painful, it's like being trapped with nowhere to run. It's the only avenue out of it."

"Well, we've just established God is either imminently practical or a right bastard. I expect there are consequences to that avenue that likely land you right back on the same point on the path until you sort out a different way. You're an efficient woman, Nina. You don't want to have to go round the track another time to get right back to where you started."

She dropped her head back to his knee. He had loosened his hold on the blanket and she was able to free her hands. He took one, lacing their fingers.

"What happened to your previous servants?" she asked.

"They both killed themselves. Told me anything was better than putting up with my bullshit."

Her head jerked up, but she registered the twitch around his mouth.

"You arse," she said, without rancor, and he chuckled again, though it was a hollow sound. She expected they both felt that way. Hollowed out, tired of it all. But there was a peace to that, sitting here together on the beach. And she was all right. She was pretty close to the shore and not being pulled back into those bad memories. She just smelled the sea and Alistair, wound so close around her. "Will you tell me, really?"

"I lost both my servants during wartime, Nina. Two separate conflicts. Being blown into too many pieces to be put back together will kill a human servant even more efficiently than a metal stake through the heart. So will being decapitated by a flying piece of shrapnel."

She swallowed as he looked away, at the darkened beach.

"How long were you with them?" she asked quietly.

"I had Nick for thirty-nine years. Hal...eighty-six. Haven't had one since him. He threw himself on that grenade to protect me. Because being blown to bits is pretty much fatal to a vampire as well, and I was right with him. We were both charging the line. He decided he'd absorb enough of it I'd survive. It was the last thought he had, and turns out the daft bastard was right."

Despite his even tone, she had dealt with too many men holding their feelings inside. Her hand slipped from the blanket and covered his.

"I'm sorry. You cared for them." Of course he would. Vampires might be ruthless in getting their way, but certainly they bonded with others. In fact...

With an odd tilt inside her stomach, she realized that maybe a human servant was the closest bond they had. From everything Sher had said, their relationships with other vampires were like navigating mine fields.

He was studying her with that penetrating look. She didn't want to go there, give him that avenue, so she quickly changed the subject. Not that it would help if he really wanted to pursue it, but maybe he'd give her some space, since she was still trying to wrap her head around the third mark thing.

"Can you…" She frowned, thinking it through. "What happens when you cut off a vampire's limb?"

He pursed his lips, reaching down to fold back a piece of the blanket, clasp her thigh. Run his thumb along it, an idle caress. "Not sure, really. Can't remember ever seeing one without all his arms and legs, fingers and toes, but I know we don't re-generate like lizard tails. Maybe." He slanted her a glance and then dropped it to his hand, resting against her skin. "Maybe we'll chop off one of my fingers sometime for a lark and see."

"We will not," she said staunchly.

"You say that now, but what about next time you're in a blue at me? You may pick up the nearest butcher knife and start happily hacking."

She sniffed. Her hand had fallen upon his when he'd suggested cutting it with a knife and now they both looked down at their hands, the fingers loosely intertwined. As he turned her hand over, playing with it, his brow furrowed. Supporting her forearm with one hand, he released her fingers and lifted it. She followed his gaze. She thought he was looking at her InhServ mark and realized he was, only he was looking at more, too.

There was now an additional mark there. What looked like a swirling, stylized Y, the upper arms of the letter flanking the InhServ fleur-de-lis. But something told her that it meant more than the letter Y.

"Were you told about the third mark, Nina? The physical manifestation of it?"

She shook her head. His fingers passed over it, his eyes on the symbol and its new addition. "When a servant is third marked, a new mark shows up on her body. It usually means something, but it's nothing that we control. It's some other magic that makes that decision."

She wasn't sure she believed that, but there was no doubt the symbol had not been there before the third marking. She wasn't sure what it meant and, from the intent way Alistair was studying it, she suspected he wasn't, either. But it was additional proof of the new bond between them.

He paused, then spoke carefully, returning to their earlier, more difficult topic. "I was given a choice, Nina. To take a fully prepared InhServ. To release my claim on you, allow you to be inducted into their official training program. As an adult, you would have spent several more years with them, where you would have been far better prepared to be an InhServ. The Mistress has given me thirty more days to be sure."

Her heart sank, even as her stomach jumped. "They wouldn't have let me out of it if...you hadn't wanted me," she ventured carefully.

Darker emotions passed behind his gaze, but when he spoke, his tone remained mild. "No," he said. "Your family is bound to the obligation. They could take the next in line if you're a complete washout, but they'll go to considerable lengths, a year or more, to determine if you're not suitable. And your family would suffer for your recalcitrance. For submitting a candidate unsuited to the role, no matter that it was due to circumstances beyond anyone's control. Born vampires are rigid and unsympathetic about certain things, because they reason if a justified exception occurs, it will lead to attempts at less justified ones. A straight line is always the shortest distance to the goal.

"The biggest problem...well, not a problem." He amended it as her gaze sharpened on him, and his tone gentled. "The challenge is that your sister was exceptional, even for an InhServ. You're her twin. They would want to make very sure. And truth, Nina, you do have a submissive's nature. If you try to resist that test, you will fail it, again and again, because it's at the core of who you are. Just as it was for her."

As she felt a wave of misery try to take her, he wouldn't allow that. He touched her face. "I want to show you something."

He rose then, shifting her so she remained sitting on the sand as he stood, stepped back several paces from her. As she lifted her head to look at him, she found his attention had sharpened on her in that way that could hold her motionless, even if he wasn't touching her.

"Release the blanket," he said.

She loosened her grip on it, let it pool around her. When he shifted a step closer, she pressed her lips together, swallowed. He studied her, from her face, to her neck and lower, his gaze coursing over the tilt of her breasts, curve of hips, sex and thighs, all the way to her feet and back.

"Come and kneel at my feet. Facing me."

She obeyed, shifting forward. He watched her, so closely it felt like his hands were upon her, guiding her.

"Now down further." His voice was low, caressing. "Put your hands flat on the ground, your cheek against my calf."

Hesitantly, she complied, placing her palms in the soft sand on either side of his foot, and then...

He stepped back half a stride. "Continue. Leave your knees where they are."

She had to stretch out further to reach him, and when she did, it sloped her body downward. Her cheek and jaw were against his calf, clad in his slacks, but she could feel the muscle and heat of him beneath. His foot was bare, her thumb brushing the outside of it.

"Good. Beautiful." He bent enough to slide his fingertips along her spine, starting between her shoulder blades and then trailing upward toward her canted hips. "Be still and quiet. Quiet your mind. Feel my touch. What I feel, having you this way."

She wasn't sure what he meant, and he had to admonish her a couple times to quiet her thoughts, still the cascade of emotions going through her mind. His fingers continued to glide up and down her back. He dropped to one knee, curved over her.

The tide rushed in, rushed out. The seabirds cried, and the air slid over her bare body like his touch. Natural, easy, something that made sense. His heat, his scent, enveloped her with those things. She was weary, but there was more to this than that.

A feeling unfolded within her. She wasn't sure when it happened, but at a certain point she didn't have her cheek pressed to his calf because he'd commanded it. It was there because she wanted to put it there. She turned her head, brushed her lips against it, wishing the slacks weren't a barrier. The mindless act of devotion startled her, but that reaction occurred in some hazy part of her mind that didn't disrupt it.

He murmured in approval, but kept stroking her. Then he adjusted that hand to the back of her neck, adding pressure to hold her there, emphasizing the difference in their positions. Her breath shortened, her heart thumped an extra beat, and her thighs trembled. Her body eased and tightened as the desire to give herself fully to his attentions, to his utter attention on her, grew. His other hand slid up the slope of her back again, his palm cupping her buttock, fingers drifting over the lips of her sex, which were damp, responsive.

"Does this feel good?" he asked, a rough note to his voice.

"Yes," she answered. Though she might not be able to say why, exactly.

He paused. A long pause. It wasn't so much that he was waiting, expecting the correction, as he was giving her an opportunity to find the path herself.

"Yes, sir. Master." The word set off countless other things inside her, so that her voice hitched over it. She curled her fingers into the sand as he rewarded her, stroking her some more. Between her legs, her upper thighs, up her spine again. She made a sound suspiciously like a yearning plea when his other hand tightened on the back of her neck.

She rubbed her face against him again, pressed harder. What made the reaction terrifying and confusing was it wasn't merely sexual. The sexual response was a manifestation. Heat from a fire, light coming off of a star that burned brightly because it existed. It was.

It made her think of that new mark on her wrist, that had appeared itself independently of either of their desires. Or had it?

"What does this give you?" she asked, a breathless whisper. It aroused him, she knew, but there was a deeper component to it for him, just as there was for her.

Another long pause, then he spoke in her mind.

Peace.

She nodded against his leg, stayed quiet and still as he continued to stroke. There was peace in passion, in need and yearning. In pleasing and desiring him at the same moment.

He seemed to be mulling something over, something causing him to be in his head. She tried to be patient, wait him out. Brushing her mouth against him again, she closed her eyes. She could feel his attention on her bowed head. It wasn't an uncomfortable pose for either of them, no matter how unsettling the thought was.

"Tell me what you want to say to me," he said at last. "I want to hear the words."

This was a different side to him, but she also felt closer to the man she remembered. She needed to remember both sides, just as he was acknowledging both sides of her. Even the side that she wasn't as uncomfortable acknowledging, for either of them. But it didn't make it less true.

Master and submissive.

She heard his approving growl and her stomach leaped a little, emphasizing the truth of it. "You can sit up," he said quietly. "Speak while looking at me."

She complied, but found it too hard to look in his face quite yet. "I believe you're trying to deal fairly with me," she said slowly. "As fairly as your world allows. I truly...if I am going to have to have a vampire master, then you're..."

"The devil you know?"

Her lips curved, a little sad, but truth was truth. She left that sensitive topic alone and forged toward another one. "Is there any room to have something for myself?"

"The nursing."

She nodded, and continued, despite the slight tension in his jaw she saw as she finally found the courage to look at his face. "It's what I always wanted to do with my life, Alistair. It's who I am. I understand that I must be what you, as a Region Master, need from an InhServ. But if there is even a little room in that, for me to spend a few hours of daylight being a nurse, helping at the hospital, it would go a long way to helping me accept who I need to be for you."

He sighed, rubbed a hand over his face, and then gazed at her, frowning. Reaching out, he extended his hand. She put hers into it. "I know how much it means to you, Nina. It's part of why I've been reluctant. I'm not sure either role is something to which you can only give half of yourself. Sometimes it's worse to have a taste of what you can never have your fill of, than to not have the temptation at all."

His fingers tightened on hers. "Which is why there've been times I've thought about taking you back to The Mistress before those thirty days are up," he said, low.

She wasn't entirely sure of his meaning, but his expression made her feel that surge of unstable emotions again, so many things warring within her. What she wanted, needed. Hoped. What she could have.

"Can we at least try?" she persisted, pushing those feelings away.

He studied her a long moment. "Perhaps. I will think on it. Can you trust me enough to believe I will?"

"Yes." She let out a breath, and a light smile touched his grim mouth. But even as she let out the relieved sigh, it felt somewhat as if he'd stepped further away from her. Or she had, away from him. There was a reserve to him again, but it wasn't unfriendly.

He stood, holding out a hand. "Come back to the cottage with me, Nina."

She hesitated, looking up at him. She was on her knees at his feet, her hand resting lightly on his knee, and the position, the expression on his face as he gazed down at her, made her swallow. She didn't want that distance between them.

"When I came off the boat in Singapore," she said slowly, "I thought I knew how to be a nurse. When the war reached us and suddenly we had so many casualties, that first day I must have thrown up three times. I bandaged lads while swiping the tears out of my eyes, and I felt so overwhelmed I wanted to scream at everything and everyone to stop. I was like a spinning top, with everyone bumping me and shoving me this way and that, keeping me out of the way or pushing me where I needed to be. I thought, I'm not ready for this. I'm not. I keep trying to see this in that way, thinking I'll work it out."

He reached down to trail his fingertips along her face again, brush through the wisps of hair dancing along the curve of her cheek. "I know you will. You're the most capable woman I've ever met. Except for a certain vampire queen I know, and she has about a thousand years of experience on you."

"She would have been a good one to have around during those history quizzes I was so bad at," she said.

He smiled then, and the gesture made her feel better, too. She put her hand in his grasp.

When he brought her to her feet, they were close. He held her, tipping up her chin. He kept the two of them there, silent, motionless. There were things in his expression that she didn't understand, but some part of her knew they needed her attention. Maybe needed her. Familiar, in a way she couldn't pinpoint, and then it was lost as he broke that contact, stepped back, though he retained her hand.

"Though it's very inadvisable, we'll stay here until dusk tomorrow."

He didn't explain that, but instead bent and lifted her, letting her clutch the blanket to bring it with them, and carried her back to the cottage. Up the stairs, into the house, with strength and the surefootedness of a night creature. He closed the door behind them with a push of his foot. The lamp light threw shadows on the wall as he navigated through the kitchen. He'd opened a couple of the windows earlier so the breeze rippled the curtains like whispering angels as they passed.

He carried her to the bedroom, laid her down. He leaned over her a long moment, gazing down at her. She didn't feel a need to say anything. When her fingers grazed his mouth, he kissed them, squeezed her wrist lightly.

Then he straightened and removed his slacks. She watched him as he had her, and he stood by the side of the bed where she could reach out, trail her fingers down his thigh. Giving her a tenderly reproving look, he climbed into the bed and slid in behind her, nudging her to her side to bring her hips into the cradle of his. She shuddered as he pressed an erection against her lower back that told her he would have her again. Now. Her body's trembling response welcomed the idea.

He placed his palm low on her abdomen, an anchor point, as he guided himself carefully into her channel at that angle. The third mark's healing ability had erased the soreness of losing her virginity. He sank deep, rocking against her, his fingertips playing over her clit as she made little noises, biting the pillow as the response built and he kept teasing her, higher, higher.

"Squeeze down on me, love. Fuck, like that. Just like that." He cupped her breast, moving his hand from her clit, toying with her nipples and stroking.

This time, it wasn't the poetic dance it was before, but she felt his need, his desire to claim, and it was a different kind of magic. Rougher. Faster. Yet when he came inside her, she was already close to begging for her own climax.

Actual begging works. As he slowed, he planted himself deeply in her, holding her tight against him. Her lips parted on a rasping breath.

"Please...Master."

"What do you want, Nina?"

"I need...I need to climax. I want...I want to please you."

"You think that will please me?"

She nodded desperately.

"Why?" he asked conversationally, though she could still hear the hoarseness in his voice from the power of his own release.

"Because my pleasure serves yours...it's for you, Master."

"And that," he murmured, his hand falling to stroke between her legs again, "Is something that can't be taught. Come for me, Nina."

She screamed her way through it, his clever fingers knowing how to take her up and up, her arse pressing hard into the cradle of his pelvis. Unbelievably, he hadn't softened. She couldn't imagine how many more times he would do this before dawn came. Even if her body tired, she expected he had the power to bring it back to life to meet his demands.

Not my power, Nina. Yours. Your endless desire to submit and meet my demands. I will take all you have to offer and treasure the gift, even as I demand more.

～

He did. Several more times. When dawn came and she was drifting in a haze, he finally bade her rest, pressing a kiss to her neck. He left his mouth there, his nose burrowed in her hair.

"I'm not sure I could let you go back into the InhServ program," he said. "I don't think I could bear seeing you give that gift to another. I'd rather maintain the pathetic illusion it's a response to me alone."

He spoke the rest in her mind, rough, demanding, with a touch of darker feelings to it. *I am impossibly cruel. And selfish. I can't let you go, because when I'm with you, I feel...*

He didn't finish it. But then, as sleep pulled her down, she realized he had.

When I'm with you...I feel.

CHAPTER SEVENTEEN

I *feel less alone.*
  I feel real.
I feel hope isn't an illusion.

He hadn't articulated those things, but Alistair suspected they were blanks that she could fill in, if turning that same mirror on herself. Maybe that was what made their relationship so very fraught with peril. They made one another feel those things, even as he had the power to shred her, on so many levels.

Ennui was an indifference malaise that attacked many vampires as they closed in on five hundred, apparently the far more dangerous equivalent of the mid-life crisis. But it could happen much younger, on occasion. It hadn't been lost on him that his intensity toward becoming Region Master smacked of trying to make something out of nothing. Each step he'd achieved had been met, not with celebration or reflection, but feverish planning for the next step.

Maybe that was why he was taking more seriously her request to work at the hospital. Humans could despair as well, when they felt their lives had no value. But he wondered if his hesitation had to do with him, rather than a bending of the rules. Her passion for being a nurse made him feel a little lonely, which he knew was pathetically stupid. Faith, he was no better than Luigi, a momma's boy, needing a female to put him at the center of her world.

He stood at the entrance to the cottage bedroom. During daylight, he'd gone to ground in the cellar that Hal had enlarged for him. A little damp and in need of some repair now, but it had served the purpose. He'd let Nina enjoy her day above ground, and had seen her walk along the dune line, testing her ability to see the ocean beyond as she'd seen it once before, instead of as a trigger for her nightmares. He'd stayed with her in her mind during the walk, and she'd done well, but he'd told her not to test it when the sun grew higher in the sky and he had to sleep more deeply.

So she'd passed her day reading some of the books in the cottage, and taken a walk along the beach road to a bakery. She'd brought back some pastries for them to enjoy when he woke. And fallen asleep in the bed, her nose pressed to the pillow where he'd laid his head the night before.

Now another night had come, and it was past time for them to be on their way. But she was still sleeping deeply. She had nightmares a lot. He already knew that. He also found out when he slept curled protectively around her, she didn't.

Most vampires slept separately from their servants. For one thing, the third marks handled a variety of tasks during the day while their vampires slept. But when he could rest with her, he would. He had a whole houseful of staff to do for him. She could align her sleep schedule with his. Except when she worked at the hospital.

He realized he'd been standing there for some time, watching her. And while he'd been doing that, his mind hadn't drifted toward the dark corners where bloody, broken bodies waited. He'd done standing what she was doing sleeping. Taken a break. He sighed. Time to wake her.

Sweet nurse. Come back to me.

His lips twitched as she murmured something and burrowed deeper, a frown crossing her brow. Cranky. He contemplated a few ways of waking her, and decided to start with her pretty feet, working his way up her ankles and calves with his mouth. As he did so, his intent became far less playful, and he eased her thighs apart, stretching over her, gazing up at the changes in expression, her dawning awareness as his demands penetrated her sleep.

She shifted restlessly, opened to him, her hand falling upon his head, fingers tangling in his hair. He rubbed his nose in her cunt, undeniable satisfaction surging through him at the scent of himself there, and began to tease her with tongue and lips. *Mine. All fucking mine.*

She sighed, a whisper of sound. A name. "Rick…"

Alistair's head jerked up. Whatever she saw in his face caused her aroused eyes to widen, but not before he caught the sparkle in their brown depths, the arrested twitch of her lips.

She was teasing him. Astonishingly. Unwisely.

"Casablanca. Humphrey Bogart's character. You did say you wanted me to share my fantasies," she reminded him, albeit breathlessly. "You just assumed they were about you. And it's your own fault. You have a Buick Phaeton in your garage at home, just like he drove. It planted the thought."

When he didn't say anything right away, her smile became more tentative, uncertain of his response. He was still trying to manage it himself. But one imperative wouldn't be denied. Lifting her out of the bed, he put her against the bedroom wall, himself against her. Her eyes widened anew at the size of his reaction, and then her lips parted as he sheathed himself in wetness.

"That better be all for me," he growled. Her flush spread along her lovely jaw. When she parted her lips to speak, he captured her mouth and thrust even deeper, holding her pinned against the wall. His body pressed her thighs wide so he was hitting her clit with a repetitive impact that would drive up her arousal but give her no relief.

He'd gone from seduction to taking, and it had all happened so fast, he saw it had unbalanced her. Strewth, the fierceness startled him, too. Genuine savagery had taken over, near bloodlust, when she spoke another man's name while Alistair had his mouth between her legs.

"Tell me," he said against her cheek as he drove into her, wresting groans from her throat. "Who are you wet for?"

"You…"

"Who am I? No thought. Just say it."

"My Master," she said on another shaky breath. When he turned her face to him, he saw it in the desperate glitter of her brown eyes, her parted, hungry lips. He'd have his cock there before they went on their way this evening. He wanted to feel that clever mouth on him. Yes, he was acting like a caveman, but she'd started it. Teasing or not.

She wanted to have a chance to be a nurse; he might be able to give her that. But she would be reminded that she was his. Often and thoroughly. And maybe that would make it not matter that she hadn't chosen him. Or a life with him.

He thought again of that leap he'd felt in her heart when, for just a second, she thought he had the ability to free her from the InhServ responsibility, rather than simply take her back to the school. He pushed it aside, viciously.

Instead, he laid her down on the bed, put himself upon her, driving into her again, relishing the bite of her nails, her cries. He could give her this, right enough. Make her mindless with need. He drove her up, watching her every expression, feeling every touch.

Then, on the cusp of having the pleasure of her release around his aching cock, something far less pleasant intruded.

"God damn it," he snarled and pulled out of her, so fast she let out a sound of protest and surprise. When he lunged to his feet and reached for his pants, her expression became wary. He had his hand on her thigh, though, and the way he tightened it had her lust-dazed expression clearing, filling with further alarm at the look on his.

"We have company," he grated, trying not to sound like he wanted to rip someone's head off. "Another vampire and servant. Get dressed, Nina. Meet me outside. Follow my lead exactly."

As he shrugged into his shirt, he locked everything else down but what was needed in this moment. Which included giving her a hard look, one that brooked no discussion or disobedience. "Do you understand?"

She nodded, but still didn't move.

"This is like a casualty event. Move your arse."

That she understood. She scrambled for the edge of the bed, a distracting picture. It only made him more irritable. And not all of the frustration was lust, though that had been powerful as a summer sun and as unrelenting. Even now, his cock was still throbbing.

One brief respite from the world, to help her feel better about things. To give him a few moments where he didn't have to think about being a Region Master. But that had apparently been too much to ask.

He used vampire speed to put himself together in a matter of seconds, raking his hands through his hair, belting his slacks, tucking in the shirt. As he left the room, he stopped at the wet bar, poured a drink and tossed it back, giving himself one more blink to calm himself.

He was good at shifting roles, even though tonight, given what he'd anticipated doing, it felt a lot like ripping off one set of skin to don another. Still, as he stepped out on the front veranda with a drink in hand, he knew he looked as relaxed as if he'd been sitting out back, gazing out at the water. Vampires could smell recent sex on one another easily enough, and that would only help the façade.

Lady Anahera was exiting her silver-grey Pontiac Streamliner. Normally the car itself, with all its polished chrome, gleaming white-wall tires and sharp lines, would command attention, but vampires being vampires, Lady Anahera eclipsed it. She did it more than most, being part Maori. The cream and olive skin and dark waving hair added to the curvy, long-legged body. She had a direct, piercing look, despite her thickly lashed, almond-shaped eyes.

Somewhat of an absurd description, my lord. All human eyes are almond-shaped.

He imagined Nina saying that in her practical voice, and it helped ease something in his stomach. He'd wanted time alone with her, but he'd known he was taking a risk. Damn it, it would have taken five minutes to make a phone call. He'd just been so intent on getting to Nina.

The man holding the door for his Mistress always earned a second look, even if he was "only" her servant. Alistair had often wondered if she chose her servant specifically because of how well he comple-mented her show-stopping looks.

Tane meant "man" in Maori, among other things. Alistair suspected that amused Anahera, since Tane would be considered the epitome of such by men or women alike. Tall, broad and muscular, with dark long hair he had queued back over his shoulders right now. He wore a custom suit, because nothing off the rack was fitting over those shoulders and falling to the nip of waist and hips correctly.

Last time Alistair had seen Tane without a shirt, he'd had his whole right arm and half of his chest covered with dark ink. It hadn't been an actual tattoo, since that wouldn't take without his Mistress's blood, and Anahera didn't want him to bear anything that permanent. She was an artist, and loved to leave what designs she preferred on him, though she returned to that same location and design style time and again. Covering all his heart fore and aft, perhaps a message unto itself.

"Alistair," the female vampire said. Her gaze was steady and cool as she approached him. He noted that Tane was watchful, of him and their surroundings. No matter how well vampires knew one another—or perhaps because they did—they anticipated danger from one another. Particularly when they were not where they were supposed to be.

"Anahera." He executed a bow that seemed to ease that coolness a degree. "To what do I owe the pleasure?" Though he fully knew why, it gave him time to review options in his mind, ways to explain his presence here that would fit an etiquette exception.

"I am aware this cottage belonged to your former servant, and you have chosen not to sell the property, something I approved. But you are still required to make me aware when you are in my Region, even if you are a Region Master yourself. Formalities must be observed."

She was older than he was, and she had combat experience. She'd been around long enough to be part of the Maori's far more warlike times. A breach of etiquette required a pacifying gesture of the offended party's choosing. There were certain boundaries within which it had to fall. A first infraction was taken seriously enough that a geographical marker blood sampling was permitted, so that the offended party could be aware if the vampire entered the Region without leave again.

Unfortunately, he'd committed the first infraction when he'd come to Hal's cottage to settle his effects, some years ago. Which was how she'd known he was here, he was sure. It required active monitoring, though, so he was surprised she paid attention that closely. But then Anahera had fought to have the New South Wales Region, and it was rumored that the political machinations to keep some of her more ambitious vampires at bay rivaled Machiavellian times.

A second infraction allowed a much wider scope of possibilities. The use of his body however she wished. If she could take him down. Which was why he was measuring her battle skills.

"Forgive me, my lord."

He'd been caught in his thoughts, so Nina was kneeling at his feet before he could detect her presence. He'd bade her to follow his lead, and she was deliberately disobeying him. She'd obviously picked up on the gist of the conversation and had learned just enough from The Mistress's teachings to land herself squarely in hot water.

"It was my oversight, my lord," she said, her head bowed in apparent shame. "You told me to contact Lady Anahera's servant and gain approval for our visit here. I was distracted by our other travel preparations and forgot."

Anahera's brow rose. "Was it not for the look of surprise on your face, Lord Alistair, I might have thought you put her up to it. I had heard your InhServ has not received the same level of training as is the norm."

"Circumstances brought her to me more quickly than anticipated," Alistair said smoothly, though in his mind there was a chaotic mix of emotions. *Oh, Nina.* Christ, what was he going to do about this? She'd stepped in it and didn't even know it.

"If she cannot remember something as simple as Region and territory protocol, you may want to get your money back, so to speak."

But as the band of tension tightened in Alistair's gut, Anahera tossed a fond look at the vigilant Tane, who'd yet to show a flicker of emotion on his chiseled face. "In truth though," she mused, "I find the value of a servant to be less about their knowledge of etiquette and more about pleasing me in other ways. Do you agree?"

"Wholeheartedly." He shrugged with studied indifference. "While my servant has taken the burden of guilt, you know I'm not overly conscientious of these things."

"That's to be expected. Made vampires don't have the same respect for tradition, and are often influenced by the more undisciplined human world."

Alistair met her gaze. Yeah, she was pissed, for a couple different reasons. He should have been far more cautious. How difficult would it have been to make a fucking phone call? He could have had Nero do it, so Alistair calling personally wouldn't have elicited curiosity. But most of the time, such things took several days to approve, an exercise in respect toward the approving vampire. He hadn't had that kind of time. With two marks on her, and an InhServ tattoo on her wrist to boot, if Nina had caught the attention of any of the vampires in the New South Wales Region, with him not anywhere nearby to represent why she was there...

He also hadn't thought about the general climate toward him right now. Luigi and Lady Bertrice were ambivalent toward him, even apathetic, but Ruskin, Anahera, and Catalina were likely nursing some serious irritation about a made vampire being handed the Region with the second highest number of vampires in it, no matter how politically unimportant the European lot viewed it.

Anahera had, to Alistair's way of thinking, been on the fence about him. She had the most vampire-populated Region in Australia, most of them in Sydney—another reason he'd been determined to get to Nina before she arrived there—and was the most senior of all the Region Masters in Australia. Unlike Ruskin, who considered Australia a place of exile until he could maneuver himself to a "real" Region post in Europe, Anahera had been raised in New South Wales by a vampire father who was one of the earliest European arrivals, and a human Maori servant mother.

Their last meeting hadn't gone badly, even with the geographical marker issue, and it had seemed she believed his intent not to give offense had been sincere. But him doing it twice would suggest that, having been given an InhServ, he thought he was now important enough to be carelessly discourteous.

Nina had patched it, somewhat, but vampires had a tendency not to let something go that easily. Especially if they detected even a whiff that their power and strength was being questioned.

Alistair had a good bit of that himself, and he wasn't going to be pushed around. This could get very ugly, very fast, if he didn't handle it correctly. He just wasn't sure if Nina could handle what was about to happen. That worried him most of all. A worry he couldn't show. Because he couldn't cater to it. Not visibly.

Placing a hand on Tane's chest, Anahera used him as a prop as she lifted her foot, slid off a high heel, and tapped it lightly against him to dislodge a bit of gravel that had gotten into it from the drive. Tane put his hand to her waist to steady her as she put it back on and faced Alistair again.

"You've advanced far more quickly than most," she continued. "Which is why I expect you've managed to secure the Queensland Region Master post, despite the displeasure of other born vampires who felt it should be theirs."

"Like you, my lady?" Alistair arched a brow, injecting a teasing note in his voice. Trying to keep it charming. "Are you seeking to expand, like Napoleon?"

She laughed outright and swept her hair back off one shoulder with that natural sensuality that all extraordinarily beautiful women seemed to possess. "While power is always appealing to a vampire's primal nature," she said, "I have the good sense to enjoy the pleasures of controlling my own corner of the world and not borrow more trouble. We all know Queensland is the dumping ground for misfits and weaklings. You have my pity, Lord Alistair. I have no ambition for a Region you'd probably happily turn over to me if something better was offered to you. Which, given the way Lady Lyssa is ensuring your star is rising, is probably sometime in your near future. I can clean house then, and fight Ruskin for the pleasure of managing it."

That was a fight he'd be interested in seeing, though it worried him some on Anahera's behalf. Ruskin was a duplicitous sort, and bloody strong. Alistair threaded his fingers through Nina's hair, pinching her nape lightly as she knelt at his feet, her head down.

"Lady Anahera, I think you would be surprised at the strengths and talents of those who are deemed marginal to our society," he said. It was time to turn conversation to a relaxed downriver flow, taking them away from the troublesome areas, instead of a creating a whirlpool that kept them right in the middle of them. "But our politics are always a bore. May I invite you in for tea? Since this is technically your property," he showed his teeth in a smile, "no invitation is necessary, but you are truly welcome here. My servant can serve us."

"Yes, she certainly can." Anahera turned her gaze to Nina. Though to outward appearances his servant was motionless as a statue, her training sufficient enough to maintain an InhServ's stillness, Alistair could feel the threads of tension running through Nina, quivering beneath the exterior.

Hold steady, sweet nurse.

He managed to make it reassuring, though in truth he wanted to shake her. Most of the time, she chucked her InhServ responsibilities and training to the wind, and the one time he needed her to do so, she stepped right up to...

Try to fix things. Protect him. Anahera's words had told her that Alistair was here illegally. His nurse would shoulder that responsibility, since he'd come to find her. Though he could also imagine her thinking if he'd just let her go, there'd have been no problem at all.

"Since she is due a punishment," Anahera noted, "I say we share tea while it is administered. As it is my territory, it is my right to determine what that punishment will be. Punishing an InhServ is so stimulating, and it's rare any of us get the opportunity, since they are usually assigned to the most powerful of us."

She laced the veiled insult with a laugh as distracting as silk sliding along skin. "Their endurance is legendary. But since she is barely trained, she is more like a fledgling servant. Initiating one of them has its own pleasures. I always enjoy a display of a servant's loyalty under duress."

He didn't want Nina to suffer a punishment. Yes, he enjoyed punishing her, but he knew how to do it, to give her pleasure. She felt safe with him. But if he offered to accept the punishment for his unsanctioned appearance in a territory to spare his servant, that had far worse repercussions. A vampire couldn't protect the servant in any way that was construed as caring more for the servant than was appropriate.

In short, a male vampire's chivalrous instincts could make things far worse. Plus, a well-trained InhServ genuinely embraced anything her Master or Mistress demanded. Wholeheartedly, with enthusiasm.

Fuck, why hadn't he taken her home last night?

Because he'd wanted to give her this. Because he'd wanted it, too. A night to be what they'd been behind that hospital. It was beyond bollocks that, amid all that death and suffering, he'd returned to that moment again and again, as a sanctuary from everything. Just being with her, just the two of them.

It was still just the two of them, he realized, with a sharp jolt of understanding. He just had to help her understand that, too.

As if he needed another imperious, sharp-tongued female voice in his head, he recalled that perplexing statement in The Mistress's letter. *Her success as an InhServ will be directly proportionate to your ability to be her Master. There are many different types of strength.*

Now he got it. The crux of the message? The same thing he'd made clear on the beach to Nina, that would get her through anything, if he made it clear to her on every level.

He was her Master.

Anahera had fixed Alistair with a steady, waiting gaze. Her dark eyes glittered, her full mouth in a soft pout. She really was quite stunning, even for a vampire. Which didn't cause him an ounce of wishful distraction right now.

He touched Nina's shoulder. "Nina, prepare tea for Lady Anahera and myself. Quickly."

"She will not need her dress for that. Is she wearing something pretty beneath it? I recall you have a penchant for lovely lingerie."

Wordlessly, Alistair brought Nina to her feet with a hand under her elbow, but then he released her, nodded to her with a brusque look. "Remove the dress."

∾

Nina couldn't pick up all the details of what was happening, but the tension between the two vampires felt dangerous, no matter that Alistair's expression remained unconcerned. Drawing on the InhServ training which was feeling far too sparse to handle whatever this was, she didn't hesitate. Almost as soon as he gave the order, she removed the dress. She had put the underwear back on beneath it, so her breasts sat up high, barely cradled in lace, and the satiny knickers were so low her hipbones showed in front and the dimples on either side of the crease between her buttocks in back.

Alistair took the dress from her. "Go prepare tea."

She pivoted and hurried inside, trying to make it look like she hurried because of the command, not because she felt exposed in front of the other three fully dressed members of this party. Tane's blue-grey eyes, deep set and intense, had coursed over her from head to toe. If he'd licked his lips, he would have looked like an extraordinarily large dingo preparing for the hunt. And kill.

She desperately wanted Alistair to say something, anything, in her head. But she felt him there, felt that connection, and touched it in her mind, closing mental fingers on it like a rope. He was here. He wouldn't let anything bad happen to her.

Or would he? As she reviewed all the things that had happened at the InhServ school, as well as the things she'd been told by her roommates would happen in the company of other vampires, she realized she was being naïve. Had it taken so little time for her to forget?

Alistair and she weren't building a relationship with the expectations of a human man and woman. He was her Master, she was his servant. His property. His earlier possessiveness had warmed her, because her mind had treated it as evidence of his desire for her to be his exclusively. In the vampire-servant world, it didn't mean that at all. That realization brought back the cold ball of fear that was always ready to take up every bit of space in her lower belly. And grow spikes.

Before Bangka, she hadn't feared the unknown and unexpected. That was because she hadn't experienced the full, crushing weight of what those two elements could bring. She hadn't understood enough to fear them.

But wasn't that the definition of courage? Not the absence of fear, but the ability to face one's fears, make the best of it. Persevere. Thrive. Find her own way, on her own ground, even if she had the narrowest of spaces to call hers.

Locking her fear down, she went to prepare tea. Thank goodness, things were well-stocked in the kitchen. After she started the kettle boiling, she tried not to focus on the fact she was preparing tea almost naked. She didn't know if it helped or disrupted that effort, Anahera and Alistair entering the house with Tane at their heels, the two vampires engaged in casual conversation. To all appearances, they were ignoring her the way the help often was, as long as they were doing as told.

As Anahera took a seat on the couch, Tane moved to the wall at his Mistress's back and stood there, his hands folded. Nina had been taught the protocol, but hadn't really believed it until she saw it. If Anahera spent the next eight hours on that couch, Tane would stay right there, barely moving, ready to attend whatever she needed.

It was then Nina realized she'd set out a service with three teacups. Alistair had said to prepare tea for him and Anahera. Not Tane. He wasn't a guest.

Yet Nina felt the touch of his gaze, frequently. Did Alistair not notice? Not care that the male was examining her in a blatantly sexual manner? But then, so was his Mistress. As Anahera spoke to Alistair, her eyes went to Nina often, and lingered. When Nina brought the tray to the table between them and bent, the female's gaze slid over the quiver of her breasts. She reached out, her fingertips brushing Nina's sternum.

"Stay bent over, girl," she ordered as Nina started to straighten. "Hold onto the tray. Keep it an inch above the table and remain in that position."

Nina's gaze flitted to Alistair. He lifted a brow. "Your gaze should be lowered, Nina."

"There's another way to teach that," Anahera said as Nina instantly complied. "Take off your jacket and shirt, Tane. Then come braid her hair. The way I like."

Nina heard the rustle of clothing as Tane shrugged out of his jacket. In her peripheral vision, she saw the white flash of his shirt as he pulled it free of his trousers, unbuttoned and removed it, revealing tan skin. Tan marked skin. She had a brief impression of a complicated black ink design marked over a great deal of muscle. When he moved from the wall, the china on the tray rattled, the quiver in Nina's arms translating to the delicate glassware. Anahera's full lips curved, a gesture Nina caught before she jerked her gaze back down, but Anahera had seen her infraction.

"She definitely needs reinforcement of her training, Alistair. While you could fault them for sending you one that's not as prepared as she should be, the insult comes with the secret delight of being able to do it yourself."

Tane's thigh pressed intimately against Nina's side as he grasped the tail of hair Nina had clasped with a barrette at her nape. Now Tane unfastened the barrette, and threaded noticeably powerful fingers through her hair, once, twice, again. With each pass, he pulled harder, dug in deeper, until she felt the tension against her cheek bones and jaw, her brow. At length, he began to braid the hair, swift and deft.

He made the braid tight, leaving the impression that he'd restrained her hair the way Alistair might have done with her arms and legs. Her body responded accordingly, her folds dampening, nipples growing tight, her breath more shallow, but she took no pleasure in the involuntary response.

"You may put the tray on the table, Nina," Anahera said. "Remain motionless, however."

That sick feeling in her stomach was growing. How long did it take someone to learn how to accept something so contrary to what she'd ever known? Her gaze flitted up again, trying to find Alistair.

Even with that tether in her mind, it wasn't enough. She needed to see his face.

Anahera reached out, seized the braided rope of her hair and yanked it forward, straight over her brow and down. It jerked Nina's chin toward her chest. A thunk, and Nina gasped, startled, as Tane drove a knife into the table through the braid. Now her head was held down next to the tea tray, so close to the table her forehead almost brushed the wood surface.

She couldn't see anything but the tray of sugar cubes and pitcher of milk right in her peripheral vision. Unless she twisted her head around with enough effort that disobedience would be an intended infraction. The heat of the tea pot was close enough to condense moisture against her cheek.

She then became aware of other presences. Tane was gone and the leg pressed against Nina's hip and thigh was Alistair's. Anahera was standing on the other side of her, the soft whisper of her clothes against Nina's flesh.

"You can let go of my wrist, Lord Alistair," Anahera said mildly. "I intended her no harm."

"One cannot be sure, Lady Anahera. You looked rather vicious. I'd rather not have to tell the Council I've already damaged this InhServ irreparably."

Alistair's voice was cordial, but flat. As if a lot of compressed emotions were behind it. Nina didn't know if that was something only she intuited, or if it was equally apparent to Anahera. From the woman's casual response, perhaps not.

"You have third marked her. She is quite sturdy, I'm sure. Fragile only in experience, not in body. Nina, I want my tea with two sugars and milk, please."

She wanted her to pour it from this position? Obviously so. But that wasn't all.

"Tane, could you please start the punishment?" Anahera settled back on the couch. Alistair moved back to his chair as well, though Nina missed the contact far too intensely. She wrapped her mind around that connection again, the lifeline, though she dearly wished he'd say something, anything, in her mind.

"I assume Nina will not spill any of my tea," Anahera said. "For if she does, the punishment will have to continue until she does it right."

"You missed your calling," Alistair said lightly. "Perhaps you should have joined The Mistress."

"I have spent some time at Taonga. Did you realize that's what she calls it, informally? She honors the Maori, since she is part Maori herself. Though I think she gave it the name merely because she likes the meaning. Treasure is the simplest interpretation. But there are older definitions. Property obtained and held through aggression or rather, 'by the spear.'"

Moving as carefully as possible, Nina poured Anahera's cup of tea. Dipped the small spoon into the sugar. Anahera tsked as a few grains slipped off the spoon, the result of Nina orienting her movements to her awkward position. Her breasts rubbed against the table and her stomach muscles clenched at the effort of performing the task.

"She should have named it *whakamaurutanga*, though that is far more of a mouthful." Anahera chuckled. "Sanctuary. The Mistress welcomes Region Masters and overlords there when they feel a need to get away from cares. It's one of the few attractions we have for the upper echelon outside Australia."

There was a cynical edge to the comment, but then it was gone, Anahera's tone casual again. "It gives her initiates real vampires to serve, practice their skills. The Mistress herself is an added benefit. She is not as old as I am, and a made vampire on top of that. I have forced her capitulation to me before, but we both found it a good fight, as well as a good outcome. She is a pleasure. Her and her Steele man. You could take Nina back there for a couple weeks of continued training while enjoying the restorative qualities of the place. When there is less to occupy you in Queensland."

"Like that's ever likely to happen," Alistair observed dryly, and won another feminine chuckle.

Hearing The Mistress had been made to capitulate to the demands of another was an eye opener. Was that part of why Killara had tried to show her the power that came unexpectedly with submission? The Mistress had learned from it, learned how to give and take, ebb and flow. Could Nina do the same?

Maybe. But now all she wanted was to rewind a few hours and

wish Alistair had decided to leave earlier, no matter what she would have missed with him during that time.

But would that time have any meaning when this was done? Any true intimacy between them seemed perpetually disrupted by a reminder that she was his property, no rights but what he gave her. Even those rights could be overridden by the politics that governed his life.

A clinking of a belt had her hands tightening on the tray. Tane was removing it from his slacks. Opening them, from the sounds of it. Her stomach did a somersault.

His large hand appeared in her field of vision. She'd prepared some toast for the vampires, since they enjoyed a few mouthfuls of food with their tea. Tane picked up the butter knife, cut a pat and put it on a plate. Then he ran his fingers through the softened substance. Oiling them up.

They hadn't put fingers inside her at the InhServ school, because Alistair was determined to take her virginity. He had, and now it didn't matter who did it, apparently. The prize won and taken. Taonga. The clattering of the cups was increasing.

"She is so green, Lord Alistair. Now I'm not surprised to hear you haven't been bringing her out in public. I'd want to keep her all to myself, enjoying her every exercise in experience first."

The ache in Nina's throat told her she was getting perilously close to tears, but she shoved them down viciously. She would not give this lot that satisfaction. She had given them to Alistair, and he'd wiped them away on his fingers. It was as if she was bound to a man with more faces than she could track, and—

Tane eased her knickers to her knees, and his fingers probed her. She managed to hold still with tremendous effort. She was shamefully wet, but that was how she'd been trained, hadn't she?

Then he set his hands to her hips and started to drive a cock the size of a mallet into her.

A shockwave of ice-cold rage and revulsion exploded inside her. She twisted away, hitting the tray so it spun off the table. The teapot crashed to the floor, but by the time it did, she'd reached over her head, seized the knife, yanked it free of her braid and spun.

She'd been given precious little combat training. Not enough for it to be second nature—or so she'd thought. She'd cut her hand finding the knife handle, but it didn't slow her down. Glass shards and a spray of hot liquid stung her calves. The blade flashed in a vicious arc as she swiped it at her attacker, driving him back. The fleeting shock in Tane's eyes was so gratifying it almost made her snarl in triumph.

The only thing that kept her from laying him open like a fish was his own defensive skills and the two vampires who could move far quicker than her.

Her arm was seized in a bruising grip intended to crush bone. Before that could happen, she was yanked free, her shoulder wrenched so brutally and fast the joint was dislocated and then wrenched back in place, a snap of agonizing reflex. Screaming, she cursed them all. She had no friends in this room.

She was pummeled, kicked, her body giving way before savage blows. But she felt no pain from them. At first, she thought it was because of the adrenaline. Then she realized she wasn't being hit at all.

Alistair was.

She was jammed into a corner of the living room, down in a crouch, with his body a shield above her. He and Anahera were engaged in close quarters combat, ugly, brutal fighting. Nina heard fists hitting flesh with incredible force. There was kicking, pulling, shoving, as the two vampires struck at each other.

No. She was wrong about that, too. From Alistair's grunts and shifts, his movements over her, she realized it wasn't his fists hitting flesh. He was blocking, shoving the other vampire back. The grunts came from the blows he was absorbing.

Oh God. He wasn't actively fighting the other vampire; he was putting his energy into protecting Nina.

Nina cried out as the ferocity of the attack increased. Did Anahera have the knife? Nina had dropped it when the female vampire had seized her arm. She knew it had been her because of the four deep gouges the female's nails had made in Nina's arm.

Surely, he had to fight back. She wanted to help. Wanted to...but she was helpless to do anything but huddle there under the arc of their struggling bodies. The violent energy, the smell of blood and rage, was too much. She wanted to escape it, black it all out, go somewhere quiet and still, but Alistair was here, taking this for her.

Stop, please stop stop stop...

She was shrieking it. So caught in a maelstrom, she didn't realize that the combat had stopped until she felt Alistair's hand on her shoulder, heard his mind-voice penetrating her pleas.

It's over, Nina. Be still.

Anahera had at last recognized Alistair's passiveness and backed off. Or something else. She felt the female vampire's eyes on her and wondered if it was her hoarse pleas that had disrupted the fight. Then her words confirmed it.

"What is wrong with her, Alistair? Is her mind broken?"

Nina had her head down, but her eyes open, so she saw the woman's bare feet retreat several steps, brace. She must have kicked off her expensive heels when chaos erupted.

"She is not broken," Alistair responded sharply, his voice a warning growl. "She went through things during the war."

Tane was off toward the left. He hadn't been involved in the fight, apparently, but Nina could sense the tension in him, see one clenched fist at his thigh. She suspected he hadn't been happy for his Mistress to be fighting the male vampire without his help. Perhaps registering Alistair's defensive strategy had helped rein him back, or his Mistress had that much control over him.

Unlike Alistair's over her, woefully apparent. But Nina couldn't have reacted any other way. She couldn't have. Yet now, in the aftermath, she was realizing with a sinking heart just how bad this was. It wasn't merely an infraction. She'd actively, violently refused to comply with a vampire's command, a command that had been supported by her own Master. Or at least not opposed by him, she corrected herself, though it made her heart ache like it had been poisoned to think it.

"I see." Anahera's voice was flat, now hard to read. She paused a curiously long moment, and Nina felt her eyes on her again. When she spoke next, her tone was different, directed fully toward Alistair. "You are unwise to hesitate to fight a female vampire, Lord Alistair. You only encourage more of my ire. Your own sire is a woman, and powerful enough to take most of us down."

"I mean no disrespect to your strength, Lady Anahera," Alistair said. His voice was strained, but remarkably cordial. As if they'd merely had a slight disagreement, rather than a full bloody altercation. Even though it was a relative thing to vampires, Nina wanted to know how badly he was hurt.

"My InhServ's reaction was due to her inexperience and the trauma I mentioned," he continued. "I would not have her spirit broken by a stumble along her learning curve. No more than I could strike out at you when you are the insulted party, albeit truly unintended."

She had her hands curled around his calf, Nina realized, and she was shaking hard against the wall. *Alistair, I'm sorry. Are you okay? I just couldn't...*

Be silent. His command was so stern, she jerked at the sound of it in her head. Pulling her hands back against herself, she huddled against the wall. She wanted to stand, be straight and proud, look Tane and Anahera in the eye and tell them to bugger off. Her legs were trembling badly, though, and she needed to do nothing that undermined Alistair's authority further on this. That much, she'd worked out. The sinking feeling in her stomach told her she'd put him in a sticky situation on several different levels.

It's not your job to worry about such things, Nina.

That wasn't true. Not if her InhServ training had clued her into things right, but maybe that was just his way of saying he didn't expect her to be capable of acting like an InhServ. That he didn't expect that from her.

Then she thought of Tane's hands, his...oh God, his cock, shoving into her body.

Bloody well right he can't expect that of me. Let a stranger fuck me as part of bloody tea and expect I'll just go along with it. The rest is bad enough.

He had a choice to take her back before thirty days. If she mucked this up enough, he probably would. But she couldn't change, couldn't suppress the plaintive thought that rose to the top, wanted to come spilling from her lips in a harsh whisper.

If I had to be yours, I wanted to be yours alone. She wouldn't have thought she had any such girlhood dreams left, but apparently some things stuck.

"If you'll give me a moment, my lady," Alistair said formally.

He must have received an acknowledgement from Anahera, for the woman moved back toward the couch, Tane retreating with her. Alistair dropped to his heels, laid his hand on Nina's hair. He presented his back to the other vampire, a decision that made Nina worry, but was obviously intentional, an act of trust. *Look at me, Nina.*

She'd had her gaze on the floor, on his shoes. Lifting it to his steady blue eyes was so difficult she almost didn't manage it, but he helped, putting a hand under her chin.

His expression hardened. *I'm your Master. When there's a choice to be made about you, about your well-being, it's up to me to make the decision that's best for you.*

I don't want to go back. I don't. She wanted to grip his arm, but she kept her hands tucked against herself, staring up at him with the plea in her face. But she didn't want to be here, either. She was miserably aware that it was all a mess in her head.

Did you hear me say that I am taking you anywhere? Lower your gaze.

She did. He didn't say anything for a moment or two, simply ran his firm touch along her bare shoulder, her upper arm, in that way he had. He lifted her hand away from her body to inspect the knife cut there, and licked away the blood, nuzzling her briefly, making her relax the clenched state of both her hands.

Let's focus on what you do want. He brushed his knuckles against the side of her face. *Put the rest of it aside. You wanted to be mine and mine alone. Yes? Look at me and tell me.*

She lifted her gaze and stared into his eyes, the depths of them. So deep, so many things to know and share about one another. *If the world was an entirely different place. I did, yes.*

There it was. An outright acknowledgement of what she'd probably known when he'd stayed in her thoughts all those months after their chance meeting. And from how she'd used his memory to keep herself together after Bangka.

She hadn't fallen in love with him. That was a process that took time. But she'd been bound to this man from the beginning, and that bond was still just as strong, no matter all this other nonsense that she couldn't understand.

I thought I could handle all this if...if I was yours. It was simple, romantic. Foolish.

A muscle twitched in his jaw. *No, it wasn't. You are mine and mine alone, Nina. If you have the strength to continue what we've started here, I will prove it to you. You're a servant, Nina. Not a sex slave. One encompasses the other, but also surpasses it, in countless ways.*

His knuckles slid along her face again, more tenderly, and she saw a glimpse of the same emotion in his eyes.

Am I a liability to you?

No, Nina. You are not. Not in any way. Three simple sentences. No elaboration, but that helped, to hear the unvarnished sincerity in his mind-voice. *What is your decision? The last one I will give you tonight.*

She closed her eyes, pressed her cheek to the wall. It was more than a decision about going back or not going back. It was a decision about trusting him, when he'd just allowed something unspeakable to happen to her. Something accepted in his world. But when she'd rejected it, he'd fought for her. Protected her.

Sometimes a decision was made with nothing but hope. This was one of them. She nodded, once.

CHAPTER EIGHTEEN

"*L*ady Anahera," Alistair said aloud, his eyes remaining on Nina, "I understand there is the matter of punishment. But if we can table that for the moment, I would request your assistance with something I think might be far more satisfying, to all of us."

He rose, turning to face the other vampire. But he shifted as he did, so his calf was pressed against Nina's hip, close enough she could grip it again if needed. Showing he'd been aware of her doing that, and hadn't disapproved of the contact.

If you'd gripped my arm, it might have hampered me protecting my pretty face, so I'm grateful you chose a leg. As it is, it's just my ribs that have been turned into a pile of matchsticks.

The dry humor penetrated and eased, just enough to let her draw a shaky breath. She kept her eyes closed, though. Focusing on his words and thoughts. Trust was easier if she didn't think of what might be ahead.

"Shall we show her why so many servants serve their vampires as your Tane does?" he continued. "How we unleash that compulsion inside them that wants to serve their Masters and Mistresses with such joyous abandon and uninhibited desire?" He dropped a hand to Nina's head again, stroked his fingers through her hair, tugging lightly so she lifted her gaze to his face. In this position, her chin was almost propped on his thigh. He allowed a light smile to play over his face, a very calculated expression, but what was in his eyes was genuine, and for her.

"How would you like to help augment her training in a way she will never forget, and which will earn my sincere gratitude?"

There was a weighted significance to those last words. Nina sensed it in the vampire female's sharpened attention on Alistair. "You offer much for the protection of this servant."

"She's an investment, isn't she?" Alistair lifted a shoulder, caressed the side of Nina's face. "In my standing and reputation. To my way of thinking, if she can embrace her InhServ training properly, she will make the rough diamond of her Master appear somewhat more polished."

"Her Master's silver tongue seems polished enough," Anahera retorted, but there was amusement in her sex-and-honey tone. And curiosity. "What do you have in mind?"

"Let me get us started, and then you can command Tane and participate however seems appropriate. But if you will allow me to direct him somewhat at key moments, it will help, and I promise be satisfying to all of us."

"I am intrigued." Anahera pursed her lips, considering, but then nodded. "Proceed."

Strewth, vampires truly lived in an odd world, where violence and the shedding of blood one moment, and polite conversation the next, were all par for the same course. Anahera seemed almost friendly now.

During their interlude, Tane had apparently been commanded to clean up the mess she'd made. Nina saw no evidence of the tea tray, and the spilled liquid was gone. The male was once again standing along the wall as his Mistress settled back on the couch. She stretched out on a hip, dress hiking up to expose some amazing legs, her ankles delicately crossed, knees bent like a mermaid's tail. She folded her arms over the back of the couch to watch.

Alistair dropped to his heels before Nina once more, and her view was his set face and mouth, his broad shoulders. He touched her cheek, tacit permission to lift her gaze to his again, hold there. Dwell there.

Give your mind to me, Nina. Give it fully. See into mine. See what sanctuary you can find there and come to me.

He wasn't speaking figuratively. She felt an opening inside his mind, one that drew her. As she drifted into it, it closed around her, making a veil fall around everything else. She blinked, even reached out physically, as if to brush against some corporeal manifestation of it, and met air, and then him, his chest. She flattened her palm over his heart and he covered her hand.

Do you remember the night with Stanley?

It would be hard to forget it.

You had the power to touch him, to give him what he needed, and you swept the three of us away. You have that power now, for all of us. This is a world you can learn to navigate and find pleasure in it, I promise. Come along with me, inside me, like this, and see.

She swallowed, moistened her lips, and nodded again. He lifted her to her feet, removed her bra, had her step out of the knickers that had been tangled at her knees. After he set them all aside, he took her hand, led her to the middle of the room, and put a footstool there. She hesitated, then let him help her onto it. He released her, but only to step back, gaze upon her from head to toe, taking his time. She saw Lady Anahera doing the same.

Stand straight, Nina. Chin up. You are beautiful, and mine.

It reminded her of how he'd acted toward her on the beach, that total attention when she'd knelt before him on the sand, while all those feelings had rushed in. She obeyed, though she quivered, her knees shaking a little. A large set of hands came to rest on her hips.

"He's there to steady you. Feel his breath on the small of your back. Tane is caring for you. He meant no harm before. It is the way of vampires and servants, when they are together, to play sexual games. They can be serious, brutal. But the end goal is what I said to Lady Anahera. We want to take your fear, your trepidation, your pain, and transform it. We can. Fight it, don't fight it, there is pleasure in both responses. For all of us, including you."

If you trust me.

She wanted to do so. She truly did.

"Turn to look at him, Nina. You may enjoy and explore."

She pivoted slowly, Tane's hands adjusting upon her. She realized now how gentle he was being, for he truly was a very large male. Alistair was not slight, and Tane's shoulders were at least a hand's breadth wider, chest deep and neck thick and corded. Her gaze fell to the intricate tattoo that covered his shoulder and chest.

"My Mistress paints these designs upon me," Tane said. His voice was calm, the blue-grey eyes watching her. She remembered how he'd tested her to ensure she was wet enough to take him. If he'd meant to brutalize her, he wouldn't have done that. Even if Alistair hadn't said it, she would have known it was truth, for the InhServ training had told her what a servant could expect when vampires got together. But hearing it, learning it, and experiencing it...she hadn't been ready for it.

Alistair was with her. Helping her. She could make it work.

Nina slid her fingertips along the inked area over Tane's pectoral. Tane dipped his head, watching the movement. It allowed her other hand to touch his hair, stroke through the thick lengths of it. He'd untied it so it was loose on the broad shoulders. He had a clean, sea scent.

"Do you spend a lot of time in the ocean?" Nina asked. Her voice was still thin and high, but she wanted to speak. Wanted to ask something normal.

"He swims every day," Lady Anahera said. She'd let her cheek rest on her folded hands and was watching Nina's hands on her servant with an almost dreamy hunger. "Sometimes I clasp my arms around his chest and ride, to feel the way his body moves in the water. He came from the sea. I think he is a siren, and must have its touch to maintain his vitality."

"I need only your touch for that, my lady," he said, his gaze sliding to her before returning to watch Nina. She'd reached the ink on his biceps and they flexed under her touch.

"My servant's breasts are very sensitive, Tane," Alistair said. Nina drew in a breath as he slid his hands onto her hips over Tane's. "Please attend to them."

He moved up close behind her. As a hint of trepidation rippled through her, Alistair cupped her jaw, the heel of his hand pressed against her throat as he tipped up her face to him. On the stool, her eyes were level with his, their mouths close. Her gaze flickered to his lips, and they curved before his grip tightened, drawing her breath in further. She couldn't see what Tane was doing with Alistair restraining her, but he reminded her of her proper thoughts.

I am doing this to you, Nina. By him suckling your nipples, I can dedicate myself to the pleasure of watching your face, the delicious panic as arousal takes over, your wonder at allowing your body to respond as I desire.

He spoke the next words aloud. The gentle seduction dropped from the tone, sending an emphatic message. "I am your Master, and everything you feel under my command is acceptable. There are no limits but what I impose."

Explore that labyrinth in my mind, Nina. Wander that maze, and discover you are not lost. There is a pleasure to a journey without a destination, because the journey never ends, is never limited to just one road.

She let out a little cry as Tane's heated mouth pressed between her breasts, his large hands cupping them, kneading, awakening nerve endings. He took his time with it, and she wondered if Anahera was commanding him to prolong it, for Nina's body started to lift into the stimulation, her nipples aching and tight, wanting...

She could feel Alistair's absorption, his intense, fierce pleasure at watching her get aroused at his command. How much it made his desire for her grow, his need to possess her, take her, filling all those pathways with a licking blue flame.

Tane's lips closed over a nipple and she jerked, made another cry. Alistair continued to hold her throat, his lips cruising over her temple telling her he was gazing down at Tane as he did what he was doing. Tane suckled, easy, slow, then harder, bringing teeth into it. Her lower body began to buck more urgently, her toes gripping for a precarious purchase on the stool.

"Oh..." She had a little plea in her voice, and Alistair made a growling noise against her throat. His fang scraped against her artery. The hint of the dangerous predator who was her Master bumped up her arousal further.

"Is her cunt wet, Tane?" he demanded.

Tane dropped to one knee and Nina bit back a harsher sound, closer to a scream, as his mouth pressed between her legs.

"I want to hear her sing," Alistair said. "Take her to the couch."

He withdrew, but his touch was a lingering caress, a reminder that he was close. Tane banded his arms around Nina's hips and hefted her off the stool. When she automatically braced herself against those wide shoulders, he grinned up at her, his eyes alight with clean lust and pleasure at serving his Mistress and her Master. No malice toward her.

He draped her over the top of the couch, facing up. Alistair circled to the other side and pressed a knee onto the seat behind her. He had to have it against Anahera's mermaid legs, for the woman still had her cheek resting on her stacked hands a couple feet away from where Nina was.

The position put Nina into a straining arch over the back of the couch. As her legs were spread and guided over Tane's shoulders, Anahera adjusted, folding her legs beneath her and sitting up, reaching out to stroke Tane's shoulder. Her dark eyes were lit with arousal, enjoyment, pleasure...and the connection with her servant. That rope that Nina had felt between her and Alistair; she could feel it between them, through the avenue Alistair had given her in his mind. He could detect the bonds between vampire and servant, and so she felt it, too.

Moreover, when Tane put his lips between her thighs, Alistair's mind opened to her, so she knew just how much he was savoring her reaction. Her shudder, her arousal, the movement of Tane's roughened chin against her delicate sex, the clever curling of his tongue and suction of his lips.

You please your Master so fucking much, Nina.

She shuddered harder, her hips lifting.

Do you want to please me?

A nod, an involuntary jerk, no thought to it. It just was.

Then enjoy every single thing he's doing to you. Your nipples are so large and dark. So sweet. I want to suckle them until you're begging for mercy.

The slick slide of Tane's tongue into her folds, his noise of male approval, was a clear answer to Alistair's earlier question, but the male pulled back enough to speak it aloud.

"She's so wet she could take both our cocks together, my lord."

"Except she's got such a sweet, tight little pussy. But it's an intriguing thought." Alistair's tone turned hot, forceful. "Who is my servant pleasing?" He caressed her nipple, then pinched it, twisting with just enough force to send pain spearing through her, tangling with the throbbing arousal.

"God...you, my lord."

"And who am I?"

"My Master. Oh..." The desperation in her tone, the panic, came with shock at the clever skill of Tane's mouth. He was manipulating her clit with his tongue and lips in a way that was pushing her right into orgasm.

"Not yet, my bad girl." Alistair must have given Tane a signal, for the man stopped. Anahera now stood behind the couch. As Tane turned toward her, she caressed him from his sternum down to his straining cock beneath his trousers. When she squeezed hard, he groaned and she nipped at his collarbone. Then clasped the side of his throat and bit hard, drawing deep. He swayed against her, fingers curling against her hips. As she pulled back, she was enjoying the small taste of his blood, her lips moving over the flavor, her deadly looking fangs retracting behind the lush lips.

Alistair scooped Nina off the couch, swinging her over his shoulder. Spreading his hand over her buttocks, he pressed his thumb between, stroking her rim. He crossed the room in two strides, headed for the bedroom. "My lady, would you enjoy the honors?"

"I would indeed."

Anahera slipped into the room ahead of them. As Alistair turned, Nina briefly saw the female vampire sitting on the bed, her back against the pillows. She had removed her own clothes except for what was beneath, a satin and gauze bra and knickers. Not surprisingly, her body beneath the clothes was as stunning as the garments suggested. She also bore ink she'd done on herself, a whole landscape of star-like symbols that scrolled under and around her breasts, framing them. The artistic tendrils dipped down toward her lace-covered sex like roots headed for the deep, heated earth.

Alistair laid Nina face down over Anahera's lap, her knees pressed to the edge of the mattress, her forehead to the other side. He moved around to the side where her face was and knelt, tipping up her chin to look at him.

"You will hold my gaze, Nina, as Lady Anahera punishes you for the insult to her and her servant. Do you deserve the punishment? Be honest."

"I...I wanted to please you, but...I couldn't handle him touching me like that. Without..."

"You are new to this. You are given wings, shown how to dance with them, leap through the air, but then you are flung from a cliff, expected to fly. It is like that."

Surprisingly, that came from Anahera. It didn't cover all of it, but it was close enough for Nina to give a slight nod. Alistair's gaze flickered, hard to read, but Nina didn't detect disapproval or anything that would make her uneasy.

Anahera's smooth palm slid over her buttocks. Because so many of those who'd touched her intimately at the school were female, it didn't discomfit Nina as much, but there was a different power dynamic here. More like The Mistress. She thought of that night by the fire. This was different from that, but she could hold onto some of the sameness of it.

Tane came into the room, and Nina was peripherally aware he was carrying something.

"Thank you, Tane," Anahera said. "This one." She settled her hand on the back of Nina's neck. Alistair adjusted so Nina's cheek was pressed into his palm. But Anahera's touch remained on her nape, holding her. "Spread your knees, girl."

Nina complied. She tensed as Tane wrapped something around her thighs above the knee. A slight shift revealed that there was now a bar between them, keeping her spread. Her breath shortened and her fingers curled into the comforter.

Alistair...

Give yourself to me and this moment, Nina.

"Count my strikes, pretty InhServ," Anahera said. "Understand that you don't jerk back from another servant when a Master or Mistress has ordered you to play together. Tane."

Nina yelped as something snapped over her buttock, stinging like three bees at once. "You make a noise like that again," Anahera said conversationally, her grip on Nina's nape tightening, "And I will gag you. Tane, again. And keep going."

Nina tightened up, wanting to tuck under, but the vampire female reached beneath her, stroking over her belly and down between her legs to capture her clit in fingers as clever as her servant's tongue. She stroked Nina, pressed her thumb between her labia, teasing her channel so Nina's hips lifted.

Crack. Crack, crack, crack!

Nina bit back on the cries, but nearly strangled herself doing so. Anahera continued to play between her legs as Alistair bent down and kissed her cheek, her mouth, put his fingers there so she could suck and bite on them in a frenzy of pain and arousal. All while

Tane struck her with some kind of whip that turned her flesh to fire.

Tears were running down her face. The pain was too much. She had to cry out. She simply had to. Then, after the latest pop where she was terrified she was going to shriek and earn that gag, the whip stopped. Tane's mouth was cruising over the abused area, then he parted her buttocks and his mouth was on her rim.

The same crazy response she'd felt when Alistair played in that area exploded like a deck of cards fluttering in all directions. She'd been able to hold back cries about the whip, but now moans strangled past her lips. She bit into Alistair's palm and his hot breath on her ear preceded his lips on her neck. Anahera's hand shifted from her nape to rest between her shoulder blades. Nina wailed with an overload of sensation as he bit, sinking his fangs in to hold her there and drink at once.

"That's a pretty girl," Anahera crooned. "Now my Tane is going to fuck you, just as he was going to do before. And you will take it, beautiful InhServ. Every magnificent inch of his big cock. Ask for it and thank me."

Your Master wants to hear your pretty pleading, Nina. I want to see him take you. Know you do it to please me. I want to watch him take you to mindless release, knowing I will do the same to you afterward. Hold onto me and do it. Don't think. Just feel. All of this serves me. Serves my desire for you.

Tane's tongue thrust into her, and his thick fingers took the place of his Mistress's, pushing, flicking, twisting her clit lightly to send spears of near-orgasmic sensation through her.

Nina floated in the desire-filled mists of Alistair's mind and discovered she was everything there. He was immersed in all she was feeling...feeding on it, the way he fed on her blood.

He'd intended it to work like a fantasy. Help her immerse herself in a world that would work for this if she didn't allow reality to intrude. If the only reality she held onto was him. But her, her willingness to trust him and let go, was the magic carpet that took them both up beyond everything else, so there was nothing but a deep, endless pleasure. Because she was serving him. Caring for him. Keeping him sane and driving him mad at once, taking him away from anything dark and ugly. She was his shelter.

It was a revelation, and one she wasn't sure if he'd meant for her to see, for her to drift that deeply into him. Regardless, the words trembled from her. Uncertain, but still...she said them. "Yes...please. Please, Lady Anahera."

Anahera tsked. "Such a shameless girl, Alistair. Begging for another male's cock. You'll need to punish her for that."

"I will," Alistair said with dark satisfaction. "I'll remind her who she belongs to."

You think that whip was a challenge? I will bind you to the frame of my canopy bed and take a cane to you. Then have you over and over until dawn, until you can barely stand on your own. You'll finish on your knees, with the comfort of my cock in your mouth, knowing you have served me well. And I will never let you go.

You will stay with me, Nina.

She let out a guttural cry as Tane drove into her, deep and wet. Her pussy contracted on him, her fists opening and closing against the bedding as she tried to hold back the orgasm. Not for him. Only for her Master. Only at his behest.

Fucking right. You would have earned three times the punishment if you'd forgotten that. His blue eyes were fierce upon her face. Another male was inside her, taking her body, but he was right here, filling her vision, tangling images in her head of him inside her, pressing her to this bed, holding her against Anahera's lap as he took his fill of her, relished the way she clawed at the bedding, her cries of pleasure.

"Alistair," Anahera said. Her voice was a throaty purr. "That matter of gratitude? I think I want it now."

A significant pause occurred between the two vampires, and then the tableau began to change. Tane shifted, removing himself from Nina with a tantalizing friction of his substantial cock against her channel and labia. As she was shuddering through that, his hands moved to her knees, and he unstrapped the spreader bar, took it away.

"Come then, beauty," he murmured, leaning over her.

Alistair caressed her face, then took his hand away. As Tane drew her off his Mistress's lap, Nina had to remember to unclench the bedding. The big male turned her in his arms and lifted her. Being face-to face with him like this brought some of her nervousness and panic back, but he spoke in a firm, not unkind voice. It was a voice that matched the man, deep and rolling thunder. "Legs around my hips."

With an impressive flex of his body and adjustment, he slid back into her before she could tense against it in this new, far more unsettlingly intimate pose. His Mistress no longer held her nape, but Tane did, cradling her skull. She kept her eyes down, not wanting to be pulled out of her head or away from Alistair by looking into another man's eyes.

But some of it did translate to her body. She realized Tane was holding her head because she had her palms against his chest, her biceps locked. If he hadn't been supporting her, it would have put an uncomfortable strain on her head and neck.

Then Alistair was at her back, his arm sliding around her waist between her and Tane, tightening, a reminder. Her elbows bent, her upper body melting back into her Master. He stepped close enough to Tane her breasts were against Tane's chest, her shoulder blades against Alistair's.

And Alistair was naked.

His firm abdomen pressed into her back, his erect cock nudging her buttock. He must have moved with vampire speed to divest himself of his clothing, and that was not the only preparation he'd made.

He slid slick fingers into her rim, stretching her, stimulating her, reminding her of Tane's mouth there moments before. *I told you that each orifice you have belongs to me, first and last, did I not?*

Not in those words, but certainly in a variety of ways. A groan slipped from her lips and she caught the flash of arousal in Tane's eyes. He pushed more deeply into her, a growl rumbling through his chest. He released his hold on her skull, and her head dropped back onto Alistair's shoulder, so she was looking up at him. The tension in her body became something else as he re-captured her in his gaze, in his mind.

"She's a beautiful morsel," Anahera purred, outside of Nina's vision. "I think she's rousing the beast in my servant."

Alistair didn't reply. His focus remained upon her, and now his cock nudged against her opening. *I am slick with oil, sweet nurse. Push out against me and relax. Accept me inside you, and you will not regret the journey, though the beginning might be bumpy.*

That could be said for a lot of things beyond this moment. If she thought of the whole of what was happening, she might come unraveled again. But she couldn't deny the responses of her body. Or the demand of her Master.

It wasn't just training. She was beginning to think of him that way.

The flare of heat in his mind, in his eyes, was volcanic.

Alistair crushed his mouth down upon hers, parting her lips, his grip along her throat and jaw, taking possession once again. As his weight pressed her more firmly against Tane, his own body flush against the back of hers, he slowly eased his cock inside her. There was a burning feel, but he eased back and forward, back and forward, as Tane stroked.

Now Anahera's hands came around Alistair and captured Nina's breasts, stroking, teasing the nipples, while Tane's motion rubbed against her inside and out, making her body undulate and soften, relax and strain for more. Alistair pushed through the rings of muscle and he was all the way inside. It burned, but it felt good, too. She let out a long, low plea against his mouth, and he spoke against her lips.

"Yes, sweet one. We're all deep inside you now, but you're the one holding us captive. Your wide eyes and soft lips, your frantic breaths. Hold still for me, and just feel."

She couldn't. She just couldn't. But she did, for the two men held her fast. Her body shuddered in their grasp, impaled, and Alistair's face remained just above hers, mere inches between their eyes. She reached up with trembling fingers to touch his mouth. Something was unraveling, something raw and emotional, the origin point oddly enough where he was sunk deep inside her backside. Feelings unfolded like a field of butterflies with knife-edged wings, taking flight to leave cuts on her heart and soul.

She wanted to plead with him for something nameless. To take her on journeys like this, moments far beyond the pain, that proved there was something more than uncertainty, fear and loneliness. That there would be some fixed point in the universe she could count upon, again and again, no matter what happened in this world she hadn't chosen.

But maybe no one chose this world. They each only made what choices in it they could. People asked so much of life, when so much was already given. If only they noticed.

He kissed her fingers, let her play them upon his lips. *You are my blessing, Nina. The one I didn't expect.*

He kept saying she was his and his alone. In this moment, with those words in his mind, in his eyes...in his heart, they could have been in the middle of the most elaborate orgy the vampire world could devise, and all of it would just be amusement park rides they were enjoying together, just the two of them.

But nothing was ever quite that easy, was it? Anahera was behind Alistair, bringing her body up as close to him as Alistair was to Nina. As the female vampire did that, her arms were lowered, shoulders moving as if adjusting something. Nina didn't understand her intent until Alistair's lips tightened, his body following suit. When he pressed into Nina in a reactionary move, his grunt, the shift of his body, the light in Anahera's eyes, told Nina what was happening.

Anahera had thrust into his arse, much like Nina had done into Stanley. From the tension in Alistair's face, however, Nina suspected Anahera had not spent nearly as much time lubricating the shaft or easing into him.

Anahera had donned a strap-on. She was...taking Alistair. "Gratitude." The meaning of that word, what Alistair had offered, now made sense. Had he taken the brunt of it for her, this debasement by an equal Region Master? There was a victorious light in Anahera's eyes that spoke of triumph over an adversary. A satisfaction that made Nina uneasy.

Master...

Anahera put her mouth to his shoulder, her fangs grazing over it. Nina felt Alistair tense in a different way now, and he shot a glittering gaze at the female vampire. Anahera smiled around her fangs, playful, and didn't bite. She was just enjoying the threat of it.

The etiquette of the vampire world might be beyond Nina's comprehension to understand. But Alistair kept breaking it down for her, bringing it back to one simple basic. The Mistress had taught it to her from the very beginning. Nina had treated it like learning multiplication tables or taking medicine one didn't want to take. But now she knew that most important lesson was as much a gift to the servant as to the vampire.

What will please your Master...

She couldn't do as he could, gain pleasure from watching another woman take him, because it was a power play, something intended to teach him a lesson. She didn't know how to help. But Alistair watched her with avid, obvious satisfaction as her climax built from Tane and his stroking, from the movement of their hands upon her, the whole lust-saturated situation. Anahera looked at her, too. At Tane, at Alistair, enjoying all of them, her lovely face getting more concentrated as she pushed into Alistair, the impact on her own body building.

Alistair cupped the side of Nina's face, thumb tilting her chin up then pressing against her parted lips. She drew in breath, his scent. Those blue, blue eyes.

Do not be distressed on my behalf, Nina. I know what I am doing.

She didn't doubt that. She was starting to believe the man never had an uncalculated moment. Except perhaps...with her. She stroked her fingers over his lips again.

You can use my mind as a haven too, if it makes things easier to bear. I don't mind being your shelter.

When she spoke the words in his mind, it was as if she'd flipped a switch. Every shield dropped out of his mind, revealing a violent tornado of raw emotion. She'd seen hints of it before, but it was impossible not to see this for what it was, an open wound that had not been treated, that was hemorrhaging. Then it was gone, and she felt only his tender appreciation for her kindness. It was such a civilized contrast, she knew it was a façade covering that storm of feelings.

She didn't want him to close that door against her. She wasn't a child. She might have trouble with the rest of it, true, but she could handle whatever was inside him.

A child's desire to help is a selfless act of caring, a rare treasure in a moment like this. Don't discount it. And don't bite off more than you can chew, sweet nurse.

He closed his eyes as Nina moved her fingers up to his brow, back to his lips, and then settled them on the base of his throat, fingers digging in as he pushed deeper into her at the same moment Tane did.

"She's at a lovely angle to attend to her breasts again, Tane."

"Yes, my lord. You read my mind." Tane's eyes glittered and he dipped his head, using one hand to grip Nina's breast and tilt it to his mouth, the squeezing pressure adding to the sensation as he closed his lips over her nipple.

"Oh..." Nina's thoughts fled again as her body spasmed in reaction, arching up into the firm hold of both men's hands.

"Reading his mind is my job," Anahera chuckled, and thrust into Alistair hard enough to earn another grunt from him. As well as Nina, when the movement shoved both men further into her. "Gods, you have such a nice, tight arse, Alistair. As good as my Tane's." Her long-nailed hands ran down his biceps, stroked. "I tie him up when I take his."

"Good luck doing that to me." Alistair kept his gaze on Nina. His face was tighter now, his voice rough.

How did he think through all this? Tane's mouth played over one nipple, then the other, his hands squeezing and tugging. Whereas Alistair started moving in and out more freely in Nina's arse, making that crazy friction feeling grow. Oh...it felt so... Oh God.

Alistair's eyes lit with pleasure, easing that tense expression. "Look at her, Anahera," he murmured. "She didn't realize it would feel like this, to have someone in her arse. She's about to go wild."

He clasped her throat again, put his fangs there and teased, nipped. His tongue and fangs were another erotic stimulation that drove her up into places she didn't expect. Anahera's hand slid under Alistair's arm, over his chest, playing over his nipple before moving to clasp Nina's biceps, hold her pinned back against her Master. Every time the Mistress thrust, she pulled back on Nina, a thumping, strong rhythm that Tane matched and Alistair countered, the friction sending Nina screaming toward a destination she wasn't sure how to manage.

There is no managing. You let go for me. Right now.

She wanted to see him let go. Wanted him to lose control with her, take her over, she realized. Feel his strength, his command, his desire to take everything from her. It made no sense, her wanting to hold onto everything of herself she could, while an equally strong part wanted to simply open and give it all into his keeping. She was torn between the two, and a fearful, dark part of her wanted him to take the choice. What was wrong with her?

Nothing at all. They're all you, Nina. Blessed, fucking treasure. Now. Your Master is commanding you. Let go.

He did just as that odd part of her wanted. He took the choice, forced the issue, pushing her off the edge into the swirling abyss of heat and pleasure. He changed his angle, and gripped her breast beneath Tane's jaw. Alistair pulled upward on the curve to both take it deeper into Tane's mouth and to add strain, a little discomfort but a lot of demand to the gesture.

It was the final straw. She came, gushing around Tane's cock, her arse and cunt tightening on both men. Alistair let out a guttural groan as Anahera pushed him toward that pinnacle as well, with driving strokes, the sweep of her hands over Alistair's body that often included Nina in the caresses, the scrapes of her nails.

Nina was screaming, lost, bucking against all of them, but they moved with her, a turbulent sea. She had no control over the arc of the climax, how long it stayed flying through the clouds. A rushing descent toward ground and a loop, and she was flying again. Screaming, her throat hoarse, her body shuddering and quivering.

She was aware that the others came directly after her, part of what kept driving her up and onward. Tane's release bathed her cervix, and then Alistair jetted into her arse, teasing all those sensitive nerve endings. Anahera came last, crying out her orgasm like a bird cry, pressing against Alistair so that he penetrated Nina more deeply.

There was that settling period, that sense of spiraling back to earth that seemed to be part of having such an earth-shattering climax. As she regained her senses, Nina recognized they were leaned into one another like tent supports. A momentary equality between them. Everyone needed that after an orgasm that intense. But she wasn't surprised that Anahera recovered first.

She eased out of Alistair, and there was a clink as she removed the strap-on, set it aside. At least, that was what Nina supposed she did. Tane eased out next, and her hand clutched convulsively at the side of Alistair's neck, a reaction to the sensation of Anahera's servant sliding along the channel that had been narrowed further by Alistair's presence in her backside. Then Alistair was turning her, laying her down on the bed, his palm braced by her side as he eased himself out of her. He'd taken his time and courtesy getting in, but when things had let loose, he'd let her feel all that demand she craved, and her virgin tissues were feeling it, third mark healing abilities notwithstanding.

"Allow Tane to attend to her while we get a drink," Anahera said. Now in Nina's field of vision, she looked despicably composed. She threaded her fingers through her silken hair, rippling over her shoulders. With a cheeky, lecherous look at Alistair, she tossed him his slacks, but held his shirt on her finger a moment before slipping it on, leaving it open over the undeniably tempting view of her toned body in lace and satin. "Think I'll hold onto the shirt as my trophy. A reminder of the pleasure of having the arse of my neighbor."

"That's custom-tailored. I'll deduct the cost of it from my next tithe for this rental cottage," Alistair said dryly.

Anahera ignored the comment. "Maybe Luigi wasn't the only one who wanted a mama to care for him." Sauntering closer, she trailed her fingers down Alistair's chest. "Maybe you'll come to stay with me on occasion, enjoy what not being in charge feels like."

"Why is it every dominant female I meet thinks all a dominant male needs is to be topped?" Alistair closed his hand over her wrist, lifted her hand to kiss it. "Yet they get in a hellfire blue if anyone suggests the same about them. Ever have any hot, wet dreams about someone taking you over, Lady Anahera? Putting you on your knees to suck his dick?"

Her eyes flashed. "That's a bit crude."

"Maybe. But why don't we just enjoy the moment and leave the yard dog posturing for another time?"

He obviously startled the vampire female when he drew her close enough to brush his lips across her temple, an almost fond gesture. "Can't we just get each other off and leave it at that? I've just had two beautiful women, one in my arse and me balls deep in the other. Life doesn't get better than that."

He sounded composed, unconcerned. Whereas Nina was still trembling, her mind unable to do much more than follow the conversation, and experience a couple primal reactions.

Utter hatred toward Anahera wearing Alistair's shirt, teasing him and being teased in return.

Despair as her Master strolled toward the bedroom door, pulling on his slacks, leaving her to Tane.

Meal consumed, she was the dinner dishes set aside for someone else to clean up. She wanted to curl into a ball. The two vampires could go on their bloody way, because once they were out of the room, she'd care for herself. Tane would touch her again only if he wanted to lose skin.

Alistair stopped in the doorway with Anahera. With a light smile, he ran his hands lightly up and down the female vampire's arms as she leaned into him. "I'll take a moment with my servant. She needs correction on some things happening in her head."

"An investment takes some upfront effort to pay off, hmm?" Anahera said, arching a brow.

Alistair made a noncommittal noise. "There's a good Scotch in the upper pantry. Why don't you have Tane pour you a couple fingers and enjoy the back veranda view of the ocean? I'll join you momentarily."

Anahera studied him, then glanced Nina's way. "She's a beauty," she said, with those sultry tags to her voice. "There's something to be said for innocence. It's her broken side that will get her through the darkness in our world, I think. I'll never forget those first days, teaching Tane how to serve his Mistress."

Her gaze slid to her servant, lingered. "Come, Tane. I need more than a couple fingers after such strenuous activity. And your cock needs a reminder of who it serves. You were somewhat too enthusiastic about plunging it into the body of Alistair's sweet servant."

Tane's brow rose. "I serve my Mistress's wishes. I cannot help that I can only do so with great enthusiasm."

Anahera barked with silvery laughter. "We'll see how enthusiastic you are when I tie your cock up in rope for a week."

They left the room, banter continuing, though Nina was pretty sure the female Region Master would likely do what she said and more.

Tane would draw pleasure from it, because he was serving her. Because he liked that, and the fight, the push-pull between his Mistress's desires and his own male nature to take. Nina had felt the latter unleashed fully as he pounded into her...all while his gaze had stayed locked on Anahera's face, his blue-grey eyes piercing and intent. He'd been fucking her, not Nina. Nina thought of what Alistair had said, and wondered if Anahera had ever given Tane that gift. Allowing him to put his Mistress on her knees, wrapping the miles of long hair around his big fist to push her mouth down on him...

She couldn't imagine it. No more than she could imagine Alistair willingly getting on all fours to be buggered by Nina. Or by anyone, really. He liked men; Stanley was proof of that, but he was pure dominant. He didn't take the bottom. Unless forced to it...or if it was politically expedient.

Alistair had stepped into the bathroom for a moment and she heard running water. Perhaps he was washing himself. She had Tane's stickiness between her thighs, and now, in the aftermath, that made her feel...wrong. She would go in after Alistair emerged, and clean herself. Surely there'd be time to do that.

When he came to the bed, she did curl into a ball, turning away from him. "I can attend to myself, my lord," she said. "You've guests."

"Think you can tell me what to do, Nina?" he murmured. He put his knee on the bed, bent over her. "You've thoughts in your head that don't belong there."

"I don't—" She choked on the word as he brought her to her back and, in one smooth motion, he'd pushed a cock still impressively erect deep inside her cunt.

He framed her face with his hands, his body stretched on her. He filled her vision, all her senses, overpowering her, making her helpless to the sheer demand coming off of him in waves. *Take me, Nina. Your pussy is still vibrating from having him there. I won't tolerate any man's touch remaining on your flesh a moment longer than necessary.*

She'd been told the third mark was relentless, that a servant would be ready for her Master within minutes of the last climax. That had been an understatement. She measured it in seconds. With his skill and stamina, she could stay in a constant state of desperate want.

"I look forward to inflicting a full day of orgasm denial on you sometime. Followed by a day of orgasm torture. Do you know what that means?"

She shook her head, let out a little moan as he pushed into her again. He had his arm around her hips, keeping them canted up. Her arms spread like wings, fingers clutching the covers. "I expect you understand the denial part. A whole day where I bring you to that edge again and again, but counter it with ways to drive it back, so you can never orgasm, just stay on that delicious cusp. By the end of the day, you will be so hot for it I will have to suspend you with your legs spread wide and no ability to move, since the slightest twitch of your hips might set you off. I'd leave you like that, no relief, through the next day."

He pushed, withdrew. Pushed, withdrew. "Alistair..." she whimpered. "Don't do this."

"I will do all of it and more, sweet nurse." His voice became rougher. "You think I like the idea of him tending to you? Enjoy having to take your arse here first, when I'd planned to do it at home, where I could take hours, enjoy your discovery of it, just the two of us? I punished you earlier, but now I know I'm not done. Those two days will be the perfect balance to my feeling about it. And an avenue to opening your soul even further to me. Helping you give everything to me. I don't have to have your full, lasting trust to open your soul, Nina. But it is a treasure I want to have, so I will pursue it relentlessly."

His lips captured a tear as he burrowed deeper, making her hips push restlessly up against him. "Be still," he murmured, and she managed to obey, those swirling feelings from his tone of command helping her.

"You are the sweetest gift," he muttered. "Orgasm torture would start the next dusk. I will finally let you come, which at first will make you thank me for my mercy. But that day, at every strike of the half hour, I will make you come again. And again. Until it seems like torment, until you are begging me, because orgasm torture comes with an excruciating side effect. All the emotions that get bottled to the point of explosion the previous day now detonate with every climax, a wound cut open again and again."

She could sense it, had already sensed it with what they'd done here. "Why would you want something like that from someone else?" she asked, her voice breaking on the syllables as he thrust. But she knew. She knew.

When she looked up into his blue eyes and still face, she remembered that raw look. Maybe for some vampires it was a matter of the power. Some part of it was for him, too. But it was something else.

Something he needed, too.

He scooped her up against his body and brought her up, sitting back on his heels so she straddled him as he thrust into her, harder, his face against her throat as her arms wrapped around him. She was making feminine noises of distress, because it felt good, but it hurt, too. In ways too hard to describe.

He stilled for just a moment, his back rising and falling as if he were breathing deep, and he kept his face against her throat, her chest.

I'm here. I'm here with you. She didn't know what brought the thought to mind, but his response to it was to tighten his arms around her so tightly, she knew he'd forgotten his strength.

"My lord," she gasped, and he eased the hold. When he laid her back down on the bed, himself above her, his expression had eased, but still reflected satisfied male lust at her parted lips, wide eyes, the shudder of her body. "Keep your legs spread far open and knees bent, feet flat on the bed," he said hoarsely.

She did. As the sensations built, so too did her small cries, at every in and out motion. At long last, she was too close to hold out, and he gave her an imperceptible nod.

They came together, his face tightening and eyes flashing, body hardening from shoulders to thighs against hers. She moaned, cried out his name, held onto him, burying her face in his chest as he rocked her to completion.

I don't want her wearing your shirt. I hate that. Hate it.

He held her, made soothing noises. "The moment she took it, it was no longer my shirt. Not in my mind. I have a wardrobe full of shirts and you will wear all of them, so your scent will be upon them."

It made her feel better. Even as the next words broke her open.

"Now *I* will care for my servant, because that is my desire. To clean her up, to put a soothing balm on the places we've treated harshly. To give her something loose to wear and take her out to rejoin our guests. If I'd had to do it, I would have left Tane with the charge, but it was not my wish, Nina." He touched her face.

"I can think of nothing better than the pleasure of caring for you."

He did all that, found her a short robe and wrapped her in it, and then brought her out to the back veranda, his hand wrapped firmly around hers. Anahera was there, curled up on the veranda bench against a sprawling Tane. They were both sucking on lollipops, an unexpectedly whimsical and more-than-a-little unsettling picture. Tane had his fingers threading and twisting through his lady's hair. She wore her skirt but had left on Alistair's shirt, open over the pretty bra. She removed the treat from her mouth at the sight of him and waved it. The scent suggested cherry and vanilla.

"Tane found these in a jar in the kitchen," she said.

"No idea how old they are, so buyer beware," Alistair advised. He took a seat in a spacious wicker chair. He dropped a cushion on the boards between his feet. Nina sank down on it, resting her body against his leg, her head against his knee as his hand settled on it, stroking her hair, her ear and neck with caressing fingers. With a little sigh, she curled her arms around his leg. She didn't look at Anahera in the hated shirt. Fortunately, vampire protocol said she shouldn't look at her without permission anyway. Tane waved at her with the lollipop and lifted the jar, silently offering. She shook her head, but her lips twitched despite herself. He looked as relaxed as a sated hound.

"Vampire constitutions can survive old lollies." Anahera popped the treat back into her mouth in a curiously carefree and youthful manner. Rolling over onto her stomach, her feet in the air over her back, her knees bent and elbows propped against Tane's thigh, she considered Alistair thoughtfully. "You are an odd one, Lord Alistair. To let me take you so baldly and seem so...accepting of it."

"It gave you pleasure, my lady, and settled the matter between us. It was fair. I have no problem with fair."

She gestured with the red-colored sweet again, pointing at him imperiously with it. "You gave me the advantage over you."

"No, I didn't," he said. "I allowed you to fuck me. No more, no less. I suspect on your rise to Region Master, you had moments where you were seemingly on the bottom or losing side of a situation. Even as you endured what must be endured, you were already formulating how, one day, that situation would be reversed. How you would be three times as merciless in inflicting the lesson of power upon the one who inflicted it upon you."

"Was it that horrible?" she said testily.

He smiled faintly. "It wasn't horrible at all. I'm using that example to make a relevant point. Why should I be any different, because I am a male? I didn't get to where I am by wasting my time on pointless pride. Or empty ritual. I know who I am, Lady Anahera, and where I am going."

Nina glanced up at him. His expression was resolute, calm. She expected she wasn't the only one who was getting a better understanding of why Lyssa had thought he'd be a good Region Master. "I have no quarrel with you," he continued in an affable tone. He nodded to Tane. "Throw me one of the purple ones."

Tane obliged and Alistair snagged it neatly from the air. He waved it at Anahera. "It was my way of personally asking your forgiveness for the oversight that put us here without your prior approval. You and I have dealt with one another before. Fairly and honestly. We reached an accord that made common sense between us, not something driven by absurd vampire politics."

As he settled back in the wicker chair, he stretched his arm out along one side, his leg firmly pressed against Nina's side. He didn't open the lolly right away. Instead, lounged back like a king in his palace, he gave Anahera a much cooler look. "But make no mistake about it, Lady Anahera. If I'd chosen to make a fight of it, I would have won."

"Really?" Her expression also became far less casual, her tone far more dangerous. "So you're saying you *let* me win, Lord Alistair?"

Nina felt the thrum of tension. Tane had become watchful again, and Nina's grip on Alistair's leg was a little tighter than she'd intended. She tried to relax it.

"I am saying it served no purpose to make you my enemy here tonight. But do not unwisely think the decisions I made tonight were not fully my choice."

"Indeed." She studied him a few moments, then turned her attention to their surroundings. "This place is cared for."

Nina let out the breath she'd been holding. Tane relaxed slightly. Though his eyes remained alert, Nina expected the danger had passed.

"I allow renters," Alistair said, accepting the subject change with smooth grace. "You get a percentage of it from the quarterly income. Your financial person can verify it."

"Very considerate of you."

"It's vampire law. I try not to break something unnecessarily." Alistair's gaze slid to Nina. "Especially when it's something of great value."

CHAPTER NINETEEN

*U*pon their return, the staff didn't comment on her absence, except for Nero telling her that he hoped she'd had a good trip with Alistair. It suggested her vampire had made them believe she'd simply preceded him to a shared destination, on his orders. They didn't know she'd tried to cut and run.

Once they'd arrived, Alistair had touched her face, given her a warm look. And then promptly been sucked into a pile of phone calls and visits away from the house that had kept him apart from her for the next couple of days.

She might have reverted to some of her earlier insecurities and worries, but this time he kept a line open to her. He talked to her in his mind, reaching out to her several times in the evenings.

There is a full moon here in Mackay tonight. Go onto the rooftop so you can see it.

It's breathtaking, my lord. What are you doing?

Trying to get Luigi to focus on something more than his latest shiny toys.

Don't you have five cars, my lord?

That is a far different matter. Very impertinent of you to draw that connection.

Another night:

Where are you, sweet nurse?

Taking a walk through the neighborhood. The Victors have planted Dutch tulips. They look like a rainbow.

Tell JD to get us some. I want you to walk on the beach tonight for me. Walk barefoot in the tidal pools close to the dunes after high tide and watch the crabs scuttle about. Perhaps we'll even build a sand castle.

And when he was mired in business:

You sound frustrated, my lord. Are they not being overwhelmed by your charm?

Like my impertinent servant, they are far too clever for that. I may have to resort to threats. Though they don't seem to work well on her, either.

Maybe you should simply appeal to their self-interest and tell them the sooner they agree with you, the sooner you can go home and they can be rid of you.

And so it went. Yet while he gave her some details of what he was doing, it was always high level things. Not the things an InhServ was supposed to know and handle. When she'd ask him more serious questions, he would always circle around those areas. Surely, he could see her willingness to help in her mind. He hadn't made a decision on the hospital yet, and she was trying not to push him on that. They had a fragile truce, and she was loath to disrupt it. But she was getting frustrated.

After Anahera and Tane had taken their leave from the cottage, it had been close to dawn. Alistair had taken her to bed, taken her again, thoroughly. When dawn came, and he went to the cellar his former servant had outfitted, she went with him, and he hadn't denied her. She'd remained belowground, held in his arms, and thought about the sun rising above. While it would be there when she finally did get up, this moment might not be there for her again. She curled her arms around his forearm, pressed her cheek to it and had succumbed to sleep as well.

She'd liked sleeping with him. On the first night he went away, she went downstairs and stood in the doorway between their rooms, looking toward his made bed, inhaling his scent.

She thought she'd sleep in her small room down here tonight, since her bedroom upstairs seemed too empty, even though she had begun putting a few things in it that belonged to her. Rocks found on her daily walks. An arrangement of flowers. A book or two borrowed from Alistair's library.

After a while, she ventured into the room, going to his bed. Furtively, as if someone might tell her off for it, she plucked the covers away from where they were neatly tucked over the pillow and slid herself in, disrupting the linens as little as possible. But once in their cocoon, where she imagined him sleeping, she curled there, and thought of him, her hand smoothing over the pillow.

I don't think you have permission to be there.

She smiled, for his tone was reproving, but in a teasing way.

Then perhaps you should be here to scold me.

Had she really just suggested that? She hid her reddened cheeks in the pillows as his sensual chuckle filled her mind.

I'll keep it in mind.

Then that link went silent again. However, she lay there for a while longer, and thought more about the past few days. The fine lines Alistair himself was walking.

She thought of what The Mistress had hinted, the pieces of information she'd collected, however unconsciously, from his actions with Stanley. The lines of protocol he'd broken to come retrieve her. The give and take between him and Anahera. The few times all the control and self-discipline had slipped and she'd seen that despondency at his core. She'd felt it when he'd held her, lost himself in her. He opened up, let light into that dark room. But when it was over, she thought the darkness remained, shut up again.

He held a lot of power, but there were strings attached, and minefields to navigate. Why wouldn't he let her help? She wasn't sure, but intended to talk to him about it when he returned.

❧

He came home on the third night. He summoned her from the enclosed tower portion of the widow's walk, where she was reading a book by lamplight.

I'm home. Come to me in my office, sweet nurse.

She wasn't ashamed to say she ran a great deal of the way, though she hoped he wasn't tuning into her mind to see her girlish foolishness. She took time when she reached the hallway to smooth her hair, get her breath, but when she rounded the corner and found Mrs. W dusting the front foyer, the woman gave her a knowing smile.

"Not the only one happy to find him home, I see."

Nina coughed self-consciously, but nodded, ducking into the study. As she slipped in, she found he was working at his desk, a phone tucked under his ear as he flipped through some paperwork, scribbled on one page. He had his other hand tented on a competing stack of papers, his forefinger tapping in a way that suggested some tension.

"You may feel as you wish about that, Donovan," he said. "As long as you are here for the quarterly meeting. Then you can say to my face what you're willing to say to others. I won't play games with you. Do me the same courtesy. A real man accepts the consequences of his actions."

Alistair paused for the response. His jaw hardened, his eyes becoming flint. The wave of the energy coming off him suggested Donovan was close to reaching the end of his Region Master's patience. She also suspected Donovan didn't know how dangerous that could be. Perhaps if he saw Alistair's face right now, he would.

She'd seen him look frightening and intimidating before. But there was an underlying weariness to his expression that also made her think of Matron Wilma, who'd dealt with much of the Sydney hospital politics when Nina was training there. In a rare frustrated moment, the Matron had declared she was chucking negotiation in favor of a blunt instrument. So she could beat stupidity into submission indiscriminately.

She'd been a clever, strong woman who appreciated others like her.

"You are water, Sister Nina." Wilma had told her that once, when she cornered Nina in the hallway. Thinking she'd done something to be compared to some appalling quality that water possessed, Nina had braced herself for a tongue-lashing.

"You adapt and change for the obstacles in your path," the Matron said. *"You use your agile mind to determine whether they need to be worn down, eased around without disturbing them, or pummeled until they give up their ground. Your judgment of which is necessary is excellent. You bend the rules too often, but often to good purpose."*

The older woman nodded, a crisp movement. *"You have brilliant instincts. Keep following them, but try not to make too much trouble for those of us who have to follow them. Unless it's absolutely necessary."*

With a tight smile, she'd continued down the hallway, her dress creasing demurely over her compact yet generous hips.

Thinking of that moment, and how it had filled her with unreasonable exhilaration, Nina straightened her shoulders and lifted her head. As she watched Alistair, his profile, the crisp lines of his white shirt, the flexing of his long-fingered hand, she went with her instincts.

She crossed the carpet and went around his desk. He'd turned now and had his polished shoe propped on the bottom bracing piece of the window table behind him, his other flat on the floor. His elbow was on the chair arm as he held the phone. He must sometimes get up and move around while talking on the phone, because the cord was long, spiraling down over his thigh.

She knelt at his feet, bowed her head. Laid her hand over the top of his shoe, Just a light touch, but she couldn't resist moving upward, stroking his ankle through his thin dress sock. At a light thump against her cheek, her shoulder, she lifted her head to see he'd wrapped a length of the curled cord around his knuckles and was swinging it lightly against her, a rebuke, but not a serious one. There was a slightly easier light in his eyes.

He lifted his free hand, making the flapping sign of someone talking way too much. Apparently Donovan on the other side. Then he crossed his eyes, a comical face. It startled a smile out of her, and she ducked her head, not sure why, but not wanting to seem too forward. She wouldn't have thought twice about it when they first met, but things were different now.

She felt a wave of something not at all unpleasant from him at the unconsciously submissive gesture. His hand touched her face instead of the cord. Stroking along her jaw, lifting her face. He kept his eyes upon it as he concluded the call brusquely.

"Donovan, you spend so much time thinking you are not Region Master because of some undeserved political advantage I have over you. You're missing the flaws in your character that actually explain the reason. Flaws you are more than capable of correcting. Try conducting yourself in a manner deserving of the post, rather than merely asserting that you are. We'll settle it at our meeting. Don't make me come find you."

He set the phone in the cradle, she suspected less violently than he wanted. Taking a breath and lifting both hands, he scrubbed them over his face before staring down at her. "Sometimes I don't see any reason not to stake the whole lot."

"It might be difficult to be a Region Master in a Region with no vampires in it," she pointed out.

"On the contrary. It would be far easier. You look very pretty today. I like the ribbons in your hair."

As she warmed at the compliment, he turned his attention to the paperwork, frowning, but then set it aside, cleared his throat. "You may work at the hospital, Nina. It's why I called you here this evening. To inform you of the terms of that."

To have what had been niggling in the back of her mind offered in such a straightforward manner startled her. "What?"

"You heard me." He rose, reaching down to lift her to her feet. His hands upon her after three days of not being touched by him at all made her wish that she had the right to put her arms around him, ask to be held. That he would want to hold her without her asking. But he was suddenly acting so formal, she held her tongue.

At least he kept her hand as he guided her to stand before the desk. He positioned himself between it and her, propping his hips against it and stretching out his legs on either side of her.

"You may start tomorrow," he said. "There are several rules. If you break them, I will withdraw the permission. Do you understand?"

"Yes, my lord." Her mind was whirling. He was really going to allow her to work as a nurse. The Mistress and other InhServ novices had insisted he could never allow that, that no InhServ could have an occupation beyond serving her vampire.

"Well, I'm not exactly the usual kind of vampire an InhServ serves, and you're not exactly the usual kind of InhServ. Right?"

She nodded, uncertain at his tone, which wasn't condemning, but still had that distancing politeness to it.

"One: You're home before dark, Nina. No exceptions, and no leniency. The first time you're late, you will not be allowed to return to the hospital for a month. If you do it more than once, I will extend that time by an additional month, each time. Make it clear to those you work for, that it is an inviolate stipulation of your assistance."

She frowned. "But if they're paying me, and patient care extends beyond..."

"They will not be paying you." His expression hardened. "I care for you, Nina. Your services will be all volunteer. That will increase their support of your time restriction."

She couldn't argue with that, but being paid...it was a sign of independence, of accomplishment.

"You are very accomplished, Nina, and they will value your services highly, if they have any sense at all. I am responsible for your care and support," he repeated. "That's the end of it."

She would have expected that attitude from a husband. If she'd married and continued to be a nurse, she fully expected he'd have treated her income as supplemental, not vital, to meet his perceived responsibility as head provider. She'd been raised in an upper middle-class family. Not wealthy, but definitely well-off. While there were families where both adults had to work to take care of children and the home, that was what poor people had to do. Alistair's home, his wealth, made it clear he would not tolerate any other interpretation.

Men.

She suppressed a sigh, but nodded. Though he continued without comment upon her less than gracious thought, his warning glance told her not to push it.

"Two: Nero or another trusted member of the staff, one who knows what I am, will pick you up and drop you off."

She thought of the day Nero had retrieved her from the hospital after the construction accident. How alert and attentive he'd been to their surroundings. Nero, Mr. Coleman and JD, the landscaper, the three men who knew Alistair's true nature, all looked like they could handle themselves more than capably in a fight. He was ensuring her protection, she realized, and wondered what threat Alistair antici- pated toward her specifically.

"Three. You will be available at midnight each night for my meal and to meet any other needs I have."

His attention lingered on her, and her body heated at the implica- tion of what those needs would be, even as her heart tilted uncertainly at his continued formal tone. "And fourth, you will complete any tasks I give you within the time limits I prescribe. I'll let you know when I have any for you."

Before she could respond, or act on that lingering look, he'd straightened and moved back around his desk. "That's all. You're welcome to start at the hospital tomorrow. I don't have further need of you tonight."

"Oh." The spear of disappointment held her in place an extra moment, as well as the follow up dose of confusion. He'd just given her what she wanted. So why did she feel...out of sorts?

"Um...can I help you with any of your work?" she ventured. "So maybe you could get done early and we could walk along the beach? Or whatever you do when you're not working?"

"I'll likely call Stan and get together for a drink with him later, if I wade through this." As he sat back down with his paperwork and picked up a pencil, he didn't look up. "You're going to have a big day tomorrow. It's probably a good idea for you to get some sleep."

"Thank you. That's kind." Though that really wasn't what she was thinking. She was getting a little irritated, but she also knew the irrita- tion was a defensive reflex, to cover the hurt. She thought of the cottage, the lingerie, how he'd intertwined with her mind to help with Anahera. Now, it was as if he was as distant as one person could be from another, and still be in the same room.

"Ah, would you like me to keep sleeping in the room next to you?" He might want her to sleep with him, or feed him. She was willing to be close, was willing to offer him that, freely.

Maybe even eagerly.

"No, you sleeping upstairs is more optimal. For your schedule as well as mine. Thank you for asking. I'll let you know if that changes."

She shouldn't have asked. Should have just kept doing it. But she was trying to confirm...what? She nodded, headed for the door, then came to a stop. "Have I done something to offend you, my lord?" She was proud her voice stayed calm, though it was getting a little higher and thinner. An ache was in her throat.

He glanced at her, gave her a practiced, warm smile she hated. "No, Nina. Not at all. Just busy right now. I'll see you at midnight tomorrow." The smile disappeared, and she saw something hungry in his eyes before he looked down again, but his words stroked up her spine, making her even more confused.

"Don't be late."

~

As she closed the door behind her, Alistair broke the pencil he'd been holding in his hand. "God damn it," he swore softly, and pushed up from the desk.

Have her sleep in the room near him? He certainly would like that. He'd like even more to have her in the same bed, not just to enjoy her body and responsiveness, but to curl his body around hers, shelter and hold it, feel the whisper of her hands along his skin, hear her soft sighs as she slept.

But he needed to keep it compartmentalized like this. For several reasons. As long as she held onto the thoughts that he could become her "rescuer," freeing her from this life, encouraging too much unregimented intimacy between them wouldn't help her.

Neither would letting her work at the hospital, but he'd done that. Even knowing it was unprecedented for an InhServ to have a job beyond being an InhServ. But after seeing the Nina he'd remembered come to full, vibrant life at the accident scene, he'd wanted that picture in his mind again, not three years in the past, but in the present as well. Bugger it.

He would figure it out. But maybe it was time to get a perspective from someone else.

Through the three hundred years since she'd sired him, Lady Lyssa had been someone he could count upon for good advice and direction. Even when it was provided with a tongue so sharp that it made sticking a bayonet up his arse and twisting sound like a jolly good time in comparison.

Like now.

He might have to do it as a telephone call, but if she was within range, he preferred the privacy of the mind-to-mind communication that her being his sire allowed him.

My lady? Are you available to speak?

He waited for a few minutes, rocking on the axis of his chair, clearing his mind, willing himself to relax further. Vampires didn't trust one another readily, even when the blood exchange was willing. Therefore relaxing, making sure one's shields were at ease, so to speak, made the process easier. And he damn well made sure his mind call to Lady Lyssa was akin to a light knock on her front door, not a pounding or an attempt to wrench it open.

To communicate with a human servant was straightforward, but vampires were guarded with one another. Except for a sire, they avoided exchanges of blood that would give another vampire even the most cursory access to their mind. Vampires in a territory were required to give the overlord enough blood they could be tracked and their emotional state be ascertained at a distance, in case they were in distress. But it wasn't enough for full mind reading and probing to deeper levels. Unless they committed an infraction that necessitated it, and then, when forced, it could be a nasty business, making physical rape seem like a walk down lover's lane hand in hand with one's attacker.

This was definitely not that. He even felt some relief and undeniable reassurance at her touch, silken tendrils unfurling inside his mind. It tickled a little, but it showed her power and experience, that it wasn't the least bit uncomfortable to him.

It is also evidence of your willingness to trust me. Which would please me, except I have recently been informed of some nonsense about you I didn't want to believe.

He almost smiled. She didn't believe in preliminaries. "And what would that be, my lady?" He spoke aloud, to increase the clarity of the message, and suspected she was doing the same. He could even imagine the sound of her voice, an intriguing mix of sex and authority. She could rivet and paralyze at once.

He wondered if she was sitting at some elaborate dinner party, with other vampires far more important than him. There'd be some kind of decadent, sexual display happening, involving the servants at the dinner. She would appear to be attentive, even as she remained aloof, sitting back in her chair, a light smile on her lips. Her jade eyes would see everything going on around the table, with every vampire there.

"The evening's festivities are over. I am actually now in the guest room my host furnished me. Thomas is drawing my bath."

Her servant was a monk, a very unlikely choice for a human servant. Through the power of her position, Lady Lyssa had ensured he was exempt from the sexual demands that were part of vampire social protocol. The rumor was not even she availed herself of his body, but they seemed more closely bound than any vampire-servant pairing he knew. Which gave him another reason to make this call. Her relationship with her servant wasn't exactly inside the boundaries of the usual thing.

"What I heard," she continued, "Is that you decided to take on an InhServ who has a month's training, rather than sensibly taking another. I can't believe that anyone I sired—even a male—could be that stupid."

"And greetings to you, too, my lady. I hope life is showering many blessings upon you."

When he was met with frosty silence, he sighed. "Yes. Nina only has a month's training. I met her during the war."

"You met her during the war, and her sister was your chosen InhServ? How did that come about?"

"Entirely by chance. How's that for Fate kicking you in the teeth?" He leaned forward in the chair. "She's a nurse, she's brave as hell, and has a backbone of solid steel. She also has a submissive side that's deeper than a bottomless honey pot. I know she has what it takes to be a vampire's servant."

"So why not give her time to train longer, be more prepared for whoever becomes her master or mistress?"

So Lady Lyssa knew that he would not be an option, if he made that decision for Nina. He shouldn't be surprised. The woman seemed to know everything.

"I do," she confirmed flatly. "I spend an inordinate amount of time holding my tongue, waiting for others to figure out their own foolishness. Which is why I hadn't reached out to you first."

He winced, but he also felt a little surge of his own irritation.

"Why should another benefit from her gifts, when her sister was promised to me? Maybe I prefer to be the one to train her up."

"I'm sure that's true, but it's certainly not all of it." Another moment of silence. "Do you know what I remember about siring you?"

His brow creased at the change of topic. "I'm sure you're going to tell me."

"Don't be disrespectful," she said coolly. "You asked me what being a vampire entailed. When I told you that it involved cutting all ties with the human world, you looked at each mortally wounded man near you on that desolate battlefield, told me about them. This one had a fiancée, this one a living mother and father, the other a deep desire to be a career soldier, a calling. I said nothing, watched you think it through. You realized one-by-one that, to any of them, being a vampire would have been a prison sentence, continuing to live without being able to have those ties or opportunities."

"You've changed the rules somewhat since then. I might have made a different choice. Bob didn't really care all that much for his parents."

She ignored him. "Whereas you were an orphan. Your family was on that battlefield."

Had died on that battlefield.

"It's a pattern you keep repeating," she replied, picking up the subtext. "As if you think the outcome will change. You have a penchant for befriending or shagging human males of military age, and humans start fights with one another quite often."

"Isn't befriending and shagging the same thing?" But he rose from his chair, paced to the window.

"Don't deflect." Her tone sharpened, but then she sighed. "The few times I have sired a vampire, it is most often on the battlefield, where a man's mettle is shown. Sometimes, though, I think he brings guilt with him. Guilt that he didn't have the courage to die with his fellows. Perhaps he even questions his own bravery, thinking his desire to live robbed them of a chance. Makes him a coward."

He felt a surge of his own irritation. "Even if I'd had such a wobbly thought, three hundred years of perspective would have fixed it."

"Indeed. Because it takes a great deal of courage to embrace a new life, in a world you do not know. Babies have to do that, whether they like it or not, so they never give it much thought. For an adult to do it takes a great deal of courage. Imagine being a soul who has to choose to be born."

"Thankfully, God makes those weighty decisions. Unless you've received a promotion I haven't heard about."

"I will get on a plane specifically to come kick your obviously over-inflated testicles up into your throat. Is that why you called me?"

"No." He shook his head, propped his elbow against the window and gazed out into the night. He could see the white line of the surf. A boat was out fishing in the night, far out. He could see the running lights.

Was Nina looking at the same thing? No. A quick check showed she'd just climbed into bed, and had turned away from the window. She was doing better with the ocean, but emotional stress would set her back. She'd closed her curtains, making him grimace and curse himself.

"I'm sorry, my lady. I don't want this to be a mistake. I need this not to be a mistake."

"You need her."

She nailed it, in three words. And hearing it out loud, he knew that did make him a fool. A stupid one.

Lady Lyssa's mind voice softened. "You are not a stupid man, Alistair.

"Even if I sometimes make short-sighted decisions based on 'self-absorbed arrogance and testosterone poisoning.'"

"Bah. I said that ten years ago. You have improved somewhat. And I have learned that following your gut is your way. It's how you've gotten where you are now. Tell me what this is about, Alistair."

With Nina, he could simply reach into her mind, and figure out what was happening, the underlying reasons for her behavior. It was why he'd made the decision he had, to put some distance between them. Well, partly. The Master side of him had made the decision, because the man simply wanted her in his bed. Lyssa could plumb for his reasons the same way, if she wanted to do that mind-rape thing, something she would not do. He'd have to put words to it himself.

"You know what I particularly like about a good footy match?"

"Oh, good God, please do not give me a footy analogy."

He grinned, he couldn't help it. His sire's lack of patience for any sport other than jousting, which she still felt should be in style, was well known. "Sometimes you put together a game with the fellows who are out on the field when you get to the park. You haven't played together before. Some you might have seen play or have brushed elbows with here or there, but you haven't necessarily played as a team. But then, as you get to playing, you find out there's something about this group, how they view the game, how they play it, that just clicks. And in the heat of the match, you're hand-balling and kicking the footy back and forth, and though you're working toward scoring a try, it's not even about that anymore. You're just bloody loving every minute of it, because you're in this zone where you're moving together, understanding one another, all connected. All easy."

He paused, his jaw tightening. "I know you've been alive far longer than me, my lady. And yet, of late…I feel so very old."

He was braced for her scorn. She was over three times his age. But she said nothing. Just waited on him.

"You're right. I've fought in too many human wars. Over a half dozen now, at least. I stopped counting." He wished he could stop counting the mates he'd lost in them. "Humans kill each other. You're right about that, too. Our Territory Wars told me we weren't much better. This last time, I realized I had to back off. Immerse myself in our world, in being an overlord, in doing dinner parties and other glittery things. Find prey with tight arses I could feed upon and make them forget. And lose myself for a while with them. But I don't feel… anything. And some days…some days the sunrise calls to me, my lady."

He swallowed. Had he meant to go there? Before she could say anything else, he pushed on, fast. "I built a wall, which is what someone does when they don't have a place to grieve. Someone to grieve with. She knows. She understands. And she…I feel that connection with her. I felt it, during the war. I feel it now, too, and I know it's within her, even though she's still at the point where all the rest of it is bloody well painful and confusing to her. Christ, I miss Hal. But this…I wanted her, Lyssa. I wanted her, yes, I need her, and I took her. And I'm keeping her, damn them all."

"All right," his sire said, after another of her long pauses. "But can you keep perspective, Alistair? You must be her Master first."

"I know that. And I am." He straightened. On that, he was on sure ground. "I'm not confused about what being a Master is. You know me better than that. I also have a good grasp of what I need from my servant this go round. She has it. I can make it work. I just had to... hear myself talk it out. I shouldn't have bothered you."

"You did have to talk it out. But words spoken into a vacuum have a way of getting lost. Speaking them to someone is better. Passing a ball back and forth at a footy match gets you down the field faster, where you can score a try."

"You've been watching footy, my lady." He smiled, things loosening back up in his chest.

"I've done no such thing. I've merely picked up a few things from your incessant fascination with it. Alistair." The way she spoke his name drew his attention. As if he were in the room with her, he could feel her regard, the touch of her cool, slim hand on his cheek.

There was a magic to her that sometimes seemed even more than vampire. He visualized her compelling jade eyes, and the long, straight dark hair that fell to her waist. When she moved, the strands tumbled over her shoulder and emitted a light, haunting perfume, like one of those flowers whose scent barely touched a person before it moved on, leaving a wish for more.

"Yes, my lady."

"Heal your heart. But don't forget who you are, and what you are. Call me again if you need a reminder. And I will come kick some sense into you."

"Your affection is one of the largest blessings in my life, my lady."

Her disconnection of their minds was as testy as the snick of a disconnecting phone, making him smile. But as silence settled back over the study, he fingered the broken pencil, thinking of the woman two floors above. And what he needed—and wanted—to do.

Lyssa felt his withdrawal. She sat in her chair a few extra moments, tapping her fingers lightly on the arm, considering. His comment about the sunrise had alarmed her no small amount. She had been around long enough to know the warning signs for the Ennui, and had lost her own mother to it. But when he spoke of this Nina, it was clear that lassitude was shoved aside. If it went well, it would help. If it didn't...well, she would talk to him again, and more often, until she was sure all was well.

Alistair was very dear to her, a man of great honor and bravery, who had his greatest difficulties when it came to peacetimes. He was born to be a warrior, but he had the intelligence of a statesman when it came to politics, the playfulness of a boy when it came to his sports, and the heart of a male who needed a servant entirely devoted to him.

"That was an interesting conversation," Thomas commented, coming out of the bathroom. She'd opened her mind to him, let him follow it as he prepared her bath. There was very little she didn't allow Thomas to hear, for it saved her time. He was quiet and unobtrusive, and yet every bit of knowledge she gave him he used to serve her all the better.

"And what would your thoughts on it be?" she asked him.

He gave her his serious smile. Though most servants didn't need glasses, he had always kept his reading glasses, and the wire frames glinted from the fire light now, periodically making his eyes disappear behind the reflection on the lens. She didn't like that, so she reached up, drew them off his straight nose and caressed his jaw, fingertips whispering along his throat. She might not take his body, but she enjoyed it as she wished and let him struggle with his God over the temptation.

His wry look was one that was part of that ritual, one she suspected they both enjoyed though he might deny it. But then he sobered, thinking through his response. "You might not like my response, my lady. Because vampires don't speak of love, when it comes to their servants."

"Yet you are a servant, not a vampire. So speak your peace on it."

He shrugged and dropped to a knee by her chair, taking up one of her feet to begin to remove her shoes. She'd worn heels for this evening's event, and stockings. She'd require him to remove it all, enjoy how carefully he did it, how gently, and without a hint of sensual caress. She enjoyed sexual pleasures, like all vampires, but knew on the day she lost Thomas, a day she didn't like to think about at all, she would dearly miss the way he touched her. With reverence. And yes, love.

"You can speak of love, Thomas," she encouraged him again. "Tell me."

He sighed. "It's a perpetually mysterious thing, ever changing, in what it reveals about us and the world around us. You're right, I think, in how it will help him come to terms with the losses he's sustained. It's complicated, yet has a heartbreaking simplicity. What we expect from it, how we disappoint it, yet we always come back to its breast, for it nourishes us like nothing else. And without it, what is inexplicable, is hopeless."

"My philosopher and scholar." But her amusement was replaced by a frown, a tightening around her heart she knew too well. "He sounded without hope, the first part of the conversation."

"It worried you."

"Yes."

He looked up at her, then bent his head again, sliding up the flowing hem of her sparkling black gown, unhooking the garter from the black stocking and working it down her leg to her pointed toe with a careful touch. "You have lost many these past few decades as well. You don't want him added to the number. But I don't think you will. This woman has captured his attention. Is in his heart. Can help to heal what needs to be healed."

"Or destroy something already wounded." She set her jaw, and what she felt was chilling enough to bank the fire. "If she does that, inadvertent or not, I will make her regret it."

"She is a child," Thomas reminded her. "Struggling to find her way. Alistair is her Master. He will help her. He's a smart man, a strong vampire. He'll help her figure it out."

"Figure what out?" she asked. She knew what he was going to say, was already mulling it, but she liked to hear him speak. He would have been a fine orator, but she liked the low, even murmur of his voice in her chambers like this. They'd had innumerable pre-dawn debates on an endless number of topics. Sometimes esoteric, sometimes about specific issues. Like this one.

Thomas patiently folded and set the stockings beside her. He took her hand, helped her to her feet. She turned, lifting her hair so he could unzip the back of the dress. As it pooled around her ankles, she felt the hitch of his breath, the heat of it caress her nape. And then closed her eyes as he bent and pressed a chaste kiss to her shoulder. Who knew chasteness could have such potency?

"I think we can live and find our way without full understanding,"

Thomas said thoughtfully. "But we can't do that without hope, faith, connection. Those are the things that love provides us, and are its essence and soul. It saves us, makes clear our path, even when nothing else is."

Things she knew a vampire would never say. But a servant could.

Nina slept very little that night. She couldn't determine what was happening, though she also knew the truth might be something she didn't want to face. If a vampire didn't view his servant as a relationship, at least not in the sense of lovers, then Alistair's behavior made more sense. Brief, intense interludes, between which he had his life and she had hers. If she was a true InhServ, she knew she'd be far more involved in the demands upon him as a Region Master, but she had a disturbing feeling that by giving her the hospital work, he'd had to shut down that avenue. Hadn't he told her earlier? Both jobs required a great deal of commitment. They couldn't exist together.

She should be ecstatic that he'd disproven what she'd been told, that vampires put themselves first, and there was no room for an InhServ to be anything but an InhServ. Yet it felt like he'd shut her out of even more than was necessary.

But it did effectively remind her of what their relationship was... and what it was not, and never could be. She shed a few tears that night, but eventually she slept, and then it was time to go to work.

Arranging it with Tracy was relatively easy. Suddenly, for a few hours each day, Nina was "normal" again. Her experience and dedication to the job, as well as her ability to work without pay, made her a welcome asset. While there were initial misgivings about her need to leave exactly on time, she quickly proved it wouldn't lessen the quality of her work while there.

From his tone that night, she knew she couldn't test Alistair on it. His commands were to be obeyed, and not being able to work at the hospital for a month when they were depending on her was far more detrimental to patient care than having to promptly turn her patients over to another shift nurse at her prescribed quitting time.

Nina referred to Alistair as her evening employer, saying she was doing in-home care for a relative of his. The reason she had to leave on time was she had to treat that as her primary position or lose it. Tracy understood and promised to make sure she left on time.

Nina was delighted to discover a third mark needed far less sleep than a normal human. Four or five hours was more than sufficient, so she could maximize her daylight time and be fully available to Alistair by midnight.

So... She was doing what she'd wanted to do with her life. In a more limited way, perhaps, but she was still doing it, still helping. She missed the camaraderie with the other nurses, going out together to eat or share a drink at the end of a shift. Watch them flirt harmlessly with the blokes at the same watering hole. Consider the prospects of a handsome doctor or other available bachelors that came through.

Truth, she had no interest in that part of things anymore. She'd never been much for the husband-hunting side of things. She'd been open to having a husband, liking the idea of falling in love and starting a family as much as any woman. But she'd always felt it would come in its own time. She wasn't desperate for it, because she loved her work.

She still did, but her lack of interest in husband and family was more than that. And it wasn't just that the avenue was firmly closed to her forever.

It was what happened at midnight each night.

His schedule purportedly kept him busy in the evenings, so she usually didn't see much of him until midnight. That bothered her, his insistence that she be there at dusk, even if he didn't need her attendance, but she complied.

After work and dinner, she slept several hours, then rose and showered. She'd don whatever clothes had been hung on the back of her bathroom door, which told her Alistair had been through while she slept. Sometimes there were no clothes at all, just a robe, a nod to preserving her modesty before the staff. That was the case this evening.

He might be in his study, the bedroom. Tonight, though, was different.

Come to me on the rooftop. Leave the robe downstairs.

She left the garment on a hook at the bottom of the spiral stair-

351

case. When she reached the final turn to the top, a strong hand reached down, helping her take the last few steps. She tilted her head up to meet his gaze, her other hand capturing her hair as the breeze found it, rippled it across her lips and cheeks. When they were both on the deck level, they stood in the wild, windy darkness and he took over, sweeping it back, holding it to her nape as he drew her naked body flush against his clothed one. His mouth settled over hers.

She made a soft, surprised noise. He didn't often start the evening so intimately, but her knees weakened and the rest of her melted into him as he took over her senses. She curled her fingers into the hard muscle at his waist through his shirt while she lost herself in the movement of his lips and tongue against hers. The pressure and demand of him was clear, from the hold of his mouth to the brush of his thighs against hers, his sex straining against his trousers.

The breeze eased, became a caressing touch, the stars brilliant above. When he released her and stepped back, he held onto her fingers an extra moment, and she saw that raw thing in his eyes. Then his expression changed to the steady, intent one he maintained most often around her, except when in the throes of passion. Her heart did a little painful turn, but it did no good to wonder why he kept closing himself off to her. He could hear the thought, but he never answered. Just waited for her to do what she knew was required of her.

She sank to her knees and bowed her head. Alistair liked to gaze upon her for a few moments, which always built her anticipation of his needs. Her desire to meet them. As he watched her with that intent, unsmiling expression, she'd press her cheek to his calf until he bade her straighten. Putting her cheek there was her own alteration. But he seemed to like her touching him while on her knees before him.

When she heard his footsteps retreating, the creaking as he settled into a chair, she was already quivering. "Come to me," he said quietly.

She rose and he took her hand again to guide her, bringing her down into his lap, cradling her. He tipped her chin up with his hand clasping her throat. Her eyes closed as his fangs pressed to the artery. She gripped his biceps as the drawing of nourishment from her created a swirl of feelings that made her need the solidity of him to anchor her. Her small gasp compelled a murmur of approval from his throat, something close to a purring growl, a tightening of his arms around her hips.

She wound her arms around him, moistening her lips as his hands wandered over her backside, up her spine. She liked wearing the beautiful things he bought her, but sometimes she liked this most of all, being completely naked, no adornment, while he was fully dressed. She wasn't sure why.

Yes, you are. Say it.

That little leap of anxiety in her stomach. He never let her get away with it, trying to gloss over the things she hadn't wanted to acknowledge about herself. The things she'd at one time claimed were a twisting and warping of her service drive, instead of a symptom of what lay deep inside her. The undeniable thing that he brought to full, vibrant life, such that he could read it from her mind as easily as written words on a page.

"Because you're my Master. I belong to you. And when you stay clothed and command me to remove my clothes...you're making me acknowledge that."

Removing every shield, to stand before him unprotected. Because his command overrode any other hold the world had upon her.

Close, sweet nurse. Make it simpler.

It made her throat ache, telling a truth that had no safety net.

"Because I want you to remind me of that," she whispered, and then bit her lip as the truth was rewarded. His hand moved between her legs, which automatically fell open at his touch. He stroked slow, as if he were savoring every millimeter of the tender flesh, the slickness his fingertips drew forth and painted over her labia. He eased in two digits, rubbed her and sent tendrils of sensation unfurling through her lower abdomen. Her arms tightened around him.

"Master..." she said softly, because she wanted to say it. Because here, in the dark, she could.

Tell me about your day.

Not in general terms, either. He wanted details. It made her both envy and despise his control. He asked questions that showed he was actively listening, even as he moved to caress her breasts, play with and pinch her nipples. He stroked her abdomen, her arms. It felt like he didn't leave an inch of her untouched, unattended.

She was gasping over the words in no time, for he required them to be spoken aloud.

"And Sister Tracy thought he might respond better to...oh God..." He'd changed her position so now she straddled him, and he opened his slacks, freeing himself.

Guide me into you, Nina. You've earned a punishment for interrupting yourself. No climax for you for a while. His eyes glowed in that darkness like blue fire. She wrapped her fingers around him, stroking, squeezing, until he made that warning noise that told her she was overinterpreting his instructions. She couldn't regret it, though, loving the heft and girth of his shaft in her fingertips. She squeezed him, just one more infraction, and he showed her just how strict he could be...when it pleased him to torment her.

He lifted her free and shifted her, startling and yet reminding her of his strength as he bent her knees over his shoulders and draped the rest of her down toward the deck. Her back was arched over the seat edge of the chair, her hands resting on the concrete as her hair swept the ground. His mouth sealed over her cunt and he began to lick and tease her there, her body shuddering and her cries carried on the wind. He brought her to a crazed peak and then rose, collecting her upper body against his so that he could hold her as he moved to the railing.

Then he eased her away from him, making her bend backward over empty space. He kept her going, steadying her, his grip strong and sure, until she was upside down, over the rail, her lower back and hips pressed against it. All while he continued to feast on her cunt, only his arms keeping her from a fall. She twisted in the wind like a whipping flag, her arms free, her stomach muscles tightening in instinctive preservation. She never feared he'd drop her. As the climax tightened within her and she knew he would deny her, she instead focused upon—even gloried in—the soaring feeling of her arms spreading wider and her body twisting like a ribbon.

The ocean was thundering out there, but it matched the rise of her need, obliterating any bad memories.

Master...

Beg, Nina. Beg in my mind.

Don't want to beg...for anything. Only want...to please you...

His arms tightened, and he burrowed his face deeper into her, making her scream into the night. How did he take her so close to orgasm, make it so intense, without her tumbling over? Some of it was training, that he reinforced nightly. He taught her to withhold it all at his command, until she did it unconsciously. Which meant some part of her own will was now beyond her own control. It only obeyed his will. Terrifying, thrilling. Much like this.

Fuck...

The curse told her she'd pleased him, taken his feelings about things to a more intense level. She wanted that too. She wanted him to lose control with her. Wanted to feel his power and danger. Knowing he could take everything from her, even her life. Even while also knowing she was never safer than when she was with him.

Such revelations were so clear in these moments, no matter how fuzzy they were when she was away from him, when doubts could come in. So she focused only on him right now.

He bit her when she had that thought, turning his head to her thigh, sinking his fangs into the femoral. The rush of blood into his mouth was dizzying, and he clotted it within moments, but when he brought her to her feet, she was swaying, staring up at him, seeking his face with eyes, fingertips.

He clasped her wrist in a strong grip before she could make contact, held her there. "Back on your knees, my servant," he said in a rough voice.

She sank down, and licked her lips as he guided himself into her mouth. He cupped her skull, and tonight he wasn't gentle about it. He hit her gag reflex, forced her to work out how to take him, service him as he desired, without any guidance other than his urgent lust. She struggled but worked through it, relaxing her throat. Her nails dug into his thighs, raked, and he snarled in lustful approval, his fingers pressing into her skull.

Suck me with that pretty mouth, sweet nurse. Give me what you give no other man.

She did. He held out a while, testing her until tears came to her eyes at the strain, but when at last he released, his guttural groan was so pleasurable to her, she unintentionally disobeyed her Master. He had made her stay off her heels, which increased the strain on her thigh muscles, her knees wide enough there was no contact to her dripping sex. But even so, as he came, her cunt contracted on itself and the orgasm swept through her, short, intense, making her shudder while he jetted to the back of her throat.

She finished him properly, though she had to exercise a tremendous amount of focus to do it, through the waves of her own intense reaction. When he finally tightened his hand on her, telling her to stop, she was making little noises of sensual distress, her breasts rising and falling with the exertion. He withdrew from her mouth slowly, and she cleaned him as he did, with reverent attention for every inch, sucking on the ridged head as gently as possible, since she knew it was sensitive after climax.

She was trembling. He'd not yet told her she could sit back. Her thigh muscles were screaming. He pressed a hand to her shoulder, and she sighed in relief, putting her buttocks to her heels. But then he pushed her all the way back, until her back was arched and the crown of her head was on the concrete, her knees still bent. It stretched out the thigh muscles, but it also...

"Oh..." The bolt of pain was excruciating, but she only had it for a second. In the time the leg cramp had seized her, Alistair had swiftly unfolded her legs and had them over his lap. He was massaging the knotted muscle with strong, capable hands, ensuring it did not become a full-blown spasm. She stared up at him. He could have insisted on doing whatever he wanted to do. Made her endure the pain.

He lifted his head, his eyes murky in the darkness, his mouth drawn. "Do you think I'm that kind of monster?"

"No." But sometimes, the way he was keeping her at arm's length from his heart, from his true thoughts about things, was almost as bad. "Alistair..."

He shook his head, silencing her. "There is pain I want you to endure, Nina. And other kinds I don't." He slid her ankle to his shoulder, and then stretched out on his stomach, slipping his hands under her buttocks and lifting her, her legs loose and open. "Leave them that way. You're not done with your climax."

He put his mouth between her legs, and the short, intensity of a moment ago suddenly returned to full, spasming life as he proved he knew her body even better than she herself did. The climax swept back in, this time long, drawn out, like a soft taffy, winding and winding and winding as her voice rose in pleading song to the night once more.

Tears ran from the corners of her eyes again, disappearing into her hair, but she knew the tracks were there. When her climax was finished, he cleaned her as she had him, and he allowed her to put her hand on his head, stroke his hair as she shuddered under his administrations. "Did I meet your expectations, my lord?" she asked shyly, but feeling a need to tease him a little. "Did I give you what I give no other man?"

"You did."

"And how do you know this?"

He was suddenly above her, shoulders blocking the night sky and making her heart jump in her throat at the look she saw in his eyes, so close to hers. "Because if another male tried to claim that gift from you, I would tear him to pieces in front of you, Nina. Do you wish to give another man what you give to me?"

The answer that leaped to her mind, straight from her heart, startled her. Feeling so vulnerable, she couldn't say it. "I don't have that choice, my lord," she said instead. "I am bound to serve you, and I will. Faithfully." She swallowed. "You don't have to doubt my loyalty."

His eyes pinned her. "Why won't you say what I can read so easily in your mind?"

"Thoughts like those come easily in moments like these," she said, and her voice broke a little. Like her heart. "But I promised you honesty."

Whereas he promised her nothing. Though she knew that wasn't entirely true. There were many promises that were not spoken, that the heart knew were true. But she was weak, and wanted to hear the words. Such moments, so strong and irrefutable, could perversely be the hardest to believe in the light of day. The heat of passion was something easy to rationalize into something else, and she wouldn't let herself be a fool.

Despite that, she couldn't deny that midnight had become a part of her day she anticipated. Even if it left her body satisfied, but a yearning in her heart and soul that could be unbearable. Those meetings emphasized something that always seemed just out of reach. A door to which it felt like she should have the key.

Alistair touched her brow, her mouth. He massaged the tears away with his fingers, kissed her, as she sobbed in his mouth and didn't put words to what couldn't be said.

Her lips parted, her heart thudding, at the tenderness with which he touched her, kissed her. He held her, and let himself be held. After a time, when she was calmer, he asked her more questions about her day. Not a test of her control this time, but to hear the stories she could bring him.

But she talked about more than that. Somehow, other things would spill out. The worries she had about patients, the things a nurse carried within her even when she left their bedsides, things that one usually could only talk about with other nurses. And he listened. He gave her that connection, holding her in his arms, stroking her hair as she curled in his lap in a chair. He laid his head against the chair back, his gaze on the ocean, then his eyes closed, and she knew he was listening to her fully, absorbing everything.

During those conversations, he also responded with thoughtful replies, insights that were genuinely helpful and intelligent. He drew on his own experiences and decisions, but didn't share many details about them, particularly the ones that related to his role as Region Master now.

She tried not to push for that, but it was difficult. When she pushed too much, as she invariably did, he lifted her to her feet. Retrieved her robe and slid it over her shoulders, belting it. He wrapped the ties around his hands for a brief moment, holding her securely to him. His gaze delved into hers, locking, holding, confirming what she already knew. That she was his.

"That's all I need for tonight, sweet nurse. Thank you."

CHAPTER TWENTY

*S*o it went. Their midnight meetings were a ritual. Structured within certain boundaries. But what happened within those boundaries until she stepped over the wrong one...it was limitless as the sky. By the time he was done, she felt like a soaring bird. It was only when she walked out of his presence she felt like she was in a cage. For he would not seek her out again until midnight the following day. His own structure and ritual, keeping their relationship contained to that handful of hours.

He wasn't even speaking in her head during the in-between times, like he had during those few days between their visit to the cottage and his decision to let her work at the hospital. When she tried to initiate those intimate, informal dialogues, she received either no response, or a brief, exceedingly courteous, 'I'm busy' kind of answer.

When he did speak in her mind, it was mostly functional things now, instructions. She wasn't even sure if he lingered in her mind at all when he didn't have immediate need for her. Why was he staying so removed from her, while unleashing such incredible intimacy during the feeding?

Oh, crikey. She was in love with him. She loved him. No reason to deny it, no matter how incomprehensible a lot of their relationship was. But he was making it clear that was something she could feel as much and as deeply as she wished, but he couldn't reciprocate. That was not what he could give her.

Bollocks. Absolute bollocks. She didn't care what they said about vampires not loving their servants. Something was going on here that wasn't a good thing. And not just because it made her an emotional mess. Alistair's detachment wasn't good for him, either. She was sure of it.

Nero was the most circumspect of employees, but at times she'd caught both him and Mr. Coleman watching Alistair with a look that said they were concerned about him, about whatever was happening on his overnight trips or even in the hours he spent working in his study. She wouldn't put them in the position of having to talk about their boss, but one morning, she decided she wasn't going to let things go on like this.

As a nurse, she looked for clues when a patient in need couldn't tell her what the problem was. And she didn't wait until he was on death's door to do it, either. She would approach this problem the same way.

Following her instincts, she went down to the small bedroom next to Alistair's. As always, the door between their rooms was closed, but she didn't let herself focus on that. She noticed things. Like how there were always fresh flowers in her room here, every morning. Flowers she liked.

She sat down on the bed, picked up the snow globe and weighed it in her hand. On her first day here, she'd thought of it as the room's one personal touch, something that had seemed like a welcome message to her. Reaching out to brush her fingers over the flowers, she wondered if they were another.

Her gaze slid to the small shelf of books in the room. Last night, she'd finished an Australian mystery novel she'd enjoyed. While there were an assortment of books on the shelf, she noticed now that there were a couple there that hadn't been there before. Another mystery, and a memoir written by a nurse who'd spent a decade in the Congo.

She retrieved that book and sat back on the bed, paging through it, then looked at the wall between their two rooms. Thinking, she stretched out on her hip, and put her hand against the wall. His bed was against it on the other side. If he put his hand up, the wall would be the only thing separating their palms.

She laid her head on the pillow and let her mind drift, her fingertips gliding along that connecting wall. He was here, so he'd be sleeping now. *Sleep well, my lord.*

No response, but that could be because he was sleeping. Of course. She chided herself. What was she doing? She could say she was looking for clues, but what if the only thing she was going to accomplish was making herself ache all the harder for something she couldn't have? That everyone from her parents to Sher to The Mistress to Alistair himself had told her wasn't possible?

She squeezed her eyes shut. She didn't care. She wished he'd leave his door open, so she could look in on him. She didn't really know if he went to sleep right at dawn, dropping like a stone when the sun rose, or if he pottered about his room like a normal kind of person at bedtime. Did he listen to some radio, read a book?

Back to clues. She needed more clues. He slept alone downstairs. Maintained his curious detachment after their otherwise passionate midnight encounters. But was he detached at all?

When he touched her at midnight, it was as if he never wanted to let her go. She thought of the day of their terrible fight in the driveway. He'd let her rant, scream at him, but he'd held on, hadn't been willing to let her go then, even as he had said very little until she calmed down.

She thought about his attitude toward her earning money. About his possessiveness when she'd teased him with a movie star character's name.

He hungered for her, reached out for her... Now her mind went back to his cryptic comment about taking her back to The Mistress.

I'm not sure either role is something to which you can only give half of yourself. Sometimes it's worse to have a taste of what you can never have your fill of, than to not have the temptation at all... Which is why there've been times I've thought about taking you back to The Mistress before those thirty days are up.

Slowly, she sat up in the bed, her heart thudding up into her throat. Just like with a patient, she knew when she was on the right track to figuring out the problem.

You make me feel.

The way he'd said that in her mind, a voice in the darkness, stuck in her head. Since she'd been here, she'd communicated in so many ways that this wasn't what she wanted. That she was simply accepting a path she couldn't escape. A male she hadn't chosen. That was the crux of it, wasn't it?

She couldn't prove to herself or him that she *would* have chosen him until she did, actually, choose him. He wouldn't let her go, but knowing she hadn't chosen him, thinking she wouldn't choose him if given that choice, wasn't likely to make a man fortressed to the gills come out of his shell. Not one who'd lost many of those he'd loved.

Hal had been with him eighty-six years. Nick, thirty-nine. Then there'd been the men he'd lost in this latest conflict, his mates. He had Stanley, but he'd mentioned no other friends...

God, could it be that simple? He was a vampire, but he was also a man. One who could love, lose, grieve. She thought of how she'd closed herself off from her own twin, not even willing to spend what likely would have been their last birthday together. The crushing guilt of knowing Sher had been coming to see her had become part of all the rest. The fear of feeling again was equally balanced with the fear of feeling too much.

She rose, setting the book aside, and decided to go to the second-best place in the house to build onto what she was thinking. The rest of the staff handled most of his needs, but what went on in his office was an exception.

Hurrying up the stairs, she took the quickest way there that wouldn't have her encountering any of the staff. She was on a mission now, and didn't want to be distracted with idle conversation.

His office, unlike his bedroom, was usually open. As she crossed the threshold, she drew in a breath. His scent lingered here. God, she really was a besotted ninny, but there it was. She took a second inhale and noticed he'd left a jacket carelessly tossed over a chair back. Moving to it, she slipped it on, rationalizing the morning air could be chilly in the house, and sank down in the desk chair. A ruled pad with a couple dozen to-do reminders on it was on the desk blotter. He had bold, clear handwriting. Picking it up, she started reading through it.

Within a very few minutes, she knew she needed help. Well, she wasn't going to be dissuaded now, and for once, found herself grateful it was close to the height of the day, when Alistair was most likely in his deepest sleep.

She took it as a good sign that Nero was here, having had to switch to a day shift today due to his daughter's nurse needing the night off. Winifred had been moved to the day shift some time ago, a boon since that was when Nina was most often off at the hospital, but in this instance she found them together, in the dining room.

Nero was admonishing the maid to do a better job on the silver, pointing out the blemishes on that, and the chandelier over the table. Winifred nodded stiffly and retreated, with a barely contained flounce. She gave Nina a cold stare but said nothing as she passed by.

"Finish it before you go home," Nero called after her sharply. "And I'll want to see it before you do."

As he turned to Nina, she could tell the adjustment back to his normal impassivity took monumental effort. "Would taking a strap to her help?" she queried.

His lips twitched. "There is no strap big enough to make that one into a decent servant. She has big dreams, but no patience for the work of achieving them."

"She's young," Nina said diplomatically.

"She is, I believe, two years older than yourself."

"Oh. Well." It wasn't the first time that had happened. Since the war, she'd felt more at home in the company of those like her, who had served, or people old enough to be her parents' age. She wondered if that was why she and Alistair had hit it off so well. Though if he was three hundred, that either meant the war had aged her far more than she knew, or he hadn't matured in accordance with his years.

He was male. That answered the maturity question.

At Nero's patient though pointed look, she returned to the matter at hand. "I need some insight into what Lord Alistair does as Region Master, to be a better help to him. Can you come to his office and walk me through some of this? I know you don't do that work for him, but I get the feeling you have the gist of it better than most."

Nero blinked at her. "I have helped him in the past. He's shouldered more of it since we moved here, because the household demands, and the comings and goings of his territory vampires, require more of my butler skills."

"Then my help might be useful, mightn't it? Will you help me?"

Nero studied her a moment. He was a shrewd man and surely knew she was up to more than that. As a result, she felt greatly encouraged when his face at last creased into a somber yet approving smile. "It would be my genuine pleasure. Lead the way."

~

An hour and a half later, she accepted the tea Nero poured for them both, feeling the need for it. "So...he has roughly a hundred vampires in his Region, and a good third of them are...like Stanley."

"Yes, miss. Pretty much good for nothing except needing his protection. Don't get me wrong." Nero shook his head. "Mr. Stanley's making a good go of his tailor shop, but that's been the story for a lot of them. They come here, broken strays from other places, ones that their territories are happy to be rid of, though they accept the payoff Lord Alistair gives them to compensate them for the misfits running off. Then Lord Alistair helps get them back on their feet."

Nero took a sip of his tea and crossed his legs in the chair across from the desk. "In the meantime, he's got Lord Ruskin in the Northwest Region to contend with. Lord Ruskin is a made vampire, but he lords it about like he was born. Lady Bertrice, one of Alistair's overlords, houses the former Region Master, Luigi, and both of them are fond of Alistair. But neither of them provides him much help or support, and likely would not be displeased if he ultimately failed and a born vampire takes his place. Like Donovan Schultz."

Nero tapped the pad where they'd listed out all Alistair's territory vampires under the names of the overlords beneath him.

"Donovan. Sharon Martin, Jerry Tims. Susan Tiers. Susan and Jerry, they're not bad sorts for their kind. But Lord Donovan clearly has his eye on Alistair's chair. Brutal ambition is a celebrated trait among vampires, and he takes it to the extreme. He keeps Alistair on his toes. He's a born vampire, like Lady Bertrice, so it sticks in his craw, Alistair getting the post instead of him. The vampires in Donovan's territory are pretty loyal to him, so they also cause Alistair headaches, passive things that disrespect him without being overt snubs."

"Hmm. Looks like Alistair has on his to-do list to call him about a one-on-one meeting about finances."

Nero made a noncommittal noise and she narrowed her gaze at him. "You keep doing that whenever I talk about Alistair doing something. You're evading."

"I am not evading," Nero said with stern dignity. "I am following my employer's orders, not to burden you with any additional tasks."

She sat back, studied him. "So whenever you've made that odd grunt, it's because whatever I just outlined Alistair doing is something his InhServ is supposed to do."

He took another sip of his tea. "Fine then," she said, as if he'd said the answer plain as day, which she expected he had. "So, I'm supposed to call Donovan's servant and set this up."

"Yes. The two of you compare the calendars and set up the meet. Alistair is good about keeping his up-to-date, so you needn't worry there's something not on it."

"Right then. Okay, let's backtrack to all the grunt moments..."

Another hour and she'd made a separate list of things she could do to reduce the pile, making phone calls and the like. The Mistress had given her a good sense of an InhServ's duties, and she'd put herself through nursing school by working in a secretarial pool, not wishing her parents to shoulder all the costs of it. But with this part of things well under way, she wondered if Nero was willing to answer something else for her. He was collecting the tea tray to depart and resume his duties, but at her regard, he lifted his head and raised a brow.

"Is there something else?"

He wasn't impatient with her, but he was a man who took his role very seriously when it came to discretion. So she wondered if he would understand why she was asking and make an exception, just once.

"Nero, why did he stop playing footy? He loved playing, didn't he?"

Nero set the tray back down and considered her. Nina waited him out, trying to keep her expression composed, calm, as if it was the most normal thing to ask. Even sensing just how personal it was. The longer the silence drew out, the more she was sure of it. And that Nero had the answers she sought.

With a sigh, the butler took a seat back in the chair across from her. "He said it was because he wanted to focus on his Region Master responsibilities. Before the war, he loved his footy matches. Was out at the fields a couple nights a week with his mates, or brought them back to the house to listen to the games on the radio. Or took them to professional matches. Always had the money for tickets. Think he would have sold some furniture if needed for those."

She would have smiled, but there was too much behind Nero's answer, too much pain she sensed. Nero met her gaze. "You know as well as any, as do I. Guess I wouldn't have thought about it affecting one of his kind the way it did my daughter, but there are times...he's far more removed from us now than he once was. He took it inside him, and I don't think he knows how to let it go." Nero paused. "He lost over half of them in the war, Miss Nina. His mates on the field."

"And his last two servants," she said quietly.

"It catches up to us all, even one who lives as long as him," Nero confirmed. "And the worse it affects us, the more we take it inside, and the less we talk about it."

She thought about that. Thought about nurses who'd only been on the periphery of what she'd seen and done. Who would make much of some near-brush they'd had with the violence, bursting to tell a story about it. Whereas those like her...they didn't want to talk about it at all.

"Did he love Hal, Nero?"

"Yes, he did," Nero said simply. "Not the same as he feels for you, but it was the bond of brothers-in-arms, a strong thing."

That took her by surprise, but she decided to leave it alone. She was all too aware that everything she could be thinking about why Alistair was holding her at arm's length could be true...and it still wouldn't change his position on it. Because at the end of the day, he was still a vampire, a Region Master, and the structure of the vampire-servant relationship could be dictated by that, more than any other factor.

And if that was the case, things were a little too raw in that part of her heart to handle a close examination of what might or might not be true in Nero's remarkable statement. "Thank you, Nero. For all your help. I...ah... I'm going to work in here most of today, I think."

Nero nodded, studied her. But when he rose, rather than picking up the tray, he gestured to her arm. "Have you ever thought about what that means?"

She glanced down at the InhServ mark. "I know what it means. The fleur-de-lis. It says I belong to another. It's a—"

"Not that. Your third mark. The one that appeared when Lord Alistair gave it to you."

She looked back down at her wrist, at the Y-shaped mark that flanked the InhServ mark, something she'd thought of as a flourish, merely emphasizing it. "What about it?"

"It's a forked road, Miss Nina. The universal symbol of a choice to be made. Also looking like the letter 'Y', which makes us think of the word 'why.' A one-word question we ask ourselves quite often during our lives."

She frowned down at it, her hand covering the symbol. She thought of how Alistair had described it. *It usually means something, but it's nothing that we control. It's some other magic that makes that decision.*

"That's a fanciful take on it, Nero," she said, though her mind was turning it over. "You aren't usually the fanciful sort."

"No. I am certainly not that. But you remember what I told you, that night on the stairs, about how Lord Alistair insisted upon you? A servant is the closest thing a vampire can have to a family, Miss Nina. The closest relationship to anyone he has. I think you've started to realize that, haven't you?"

She couldn't deny she'd thought of it, so she gave him a short nod, even as she continued to clasp the symbol, feel the imprint of it in her palm. Nero locked gazes with her, though.

"From what I've seen, Miss Nina, when a vampire gets lost? If he can't find his way home, his servant is the only one who can. Perhaps you're not the only one who feels lost and alone. Who needs help finding that path."

"You're his third mark," she pointed out.

"Yes and no." His lips tugged in a serious smile. "All the other servants he's had, they had something pop up like that, when he gave them the third mark. Me, not a blemish. Not even a new freckle. Because I'm not that for him. He gave me the third mark for me and my daughter, not for himself."

He picked up the tray, nodded one more time to her. "Let me know if you have any further questions. I'll help however I can."

She had a lot to think about. Worry about. Speculate about. So she avoided driving herself too mad by spending the rest of the day in Alistair's office, labeling things that needed his personal attention, making a stack of things she could do but which required some answers from him before she handled them. But there was one stack, that of things she was able to complete, that grew to a satisfying size as the day went on. When she'd put it off as long as she could, though she wasn't sure why she was delaying, she placed a call to the home of the passive aggressive overlord, Donovan Schultz.

A chap with a sharp voice answered. "Schultz residence."

"This is Nina Smithfield. I'm calling on behalf of Lord Alistair."

A pause, then the voice became less formal. "Ah, yeah. The new InhServ for his lordship. Welcome to the Region. This is Curtis, my Lord Donovan's third mark. Been in his employ since the Great War. Worked explosives and nearly blew his arse up crossing a bridge."

She blinked at the gregarious greeting. "So, after that, he decided you'd make the perfect servant for him?"

"Eh. Took a bit of time for that notion to grow. I pulled his body out of the wreckage, took him for dead, but then he revived enough to grab hold of me and damn near drink me dry. Too insensible to conceal what he was. We became mates for a short time, and then he offered me this gig. Said it'd be right up my alley, living on the edge. Kind of miss the excitement of it all, you know."

She couldn't imagine anything she missed less than seeing broken men being brought to her care, but she understood what he was saying. Living on the edge of life and death, things were crystal clear. Life was lived fully in the moment. It could make the mundane seem... grey. Or blissful, depending on your perspective.

"What was it..." He sounded as if he was searching his memory. "You were a nurse, weren't you?"

"I was. I didn't realize word had traveled."

"A henhouse of gossips got nothing on vampires and servants, love. Have to shout you a beer when we meet. Was that why you were calling? Got the monthly tango coming up?"

"The monthly tango?"

"Where Lord Alistair and Lord Donovan pretend to be cordial while matching dick size. I heard you're a pretty one. Can't wait to see what they come up with for us to do for dinner entertainment. Wouldn't mind sinking my wick into a sweet, wet InhServ. You'll enjoy me. I keep the ladies happy."

Had he really segued that simply into the high likelihood that their vampires would require them to have carnal knowledge of one another? Nina's grip tightened on the edge of the desk. "I'm sure you do," she said evenly. "Lord Alistair would like to meet on a Thursday next month…"

It took a few moments to align schedules, but then they had a date and time set. Which unfortunately would now be branded into her brain. She thought of the other night, with Lady Anahera and Tane. Alistair had made that work for her, had even helped her find enjoyment during it, if not acceptance in the aftermath. But in the unembellished light of reality, realizing her life might become a series of situations where she would be rogered by strangers, at the behest of her Master…she had a sudden desire to be on that train again, going far, far away.

"See you soon, love." Curtis cut the call before she could say anything, leaving her more than a little uneasy. The feeling continued even after she set aside the sex game side of it. The whole call… despite Curtis's apparent friendliness, bordering on instant camaraderie, it felt like a game of chess, where she was being measured. The dismissive way he'd ended the call said she'd been deemed a non-threat.

But why should she need to be a threat? What dangers did Donovan and Curtis pose that she could be a key piece in Alistair's defense? She needed to ask Alistair. She didn't want to be caught unprepared, but she also suspected getting past the learning curve as fast as possible was key to that preparation. God help her survive the lessons.

When she finished up the paperwork at dusk, she went down to the lower level. Expecting his door to be closed as usual, she was surprised to find it open, just a crack, and a heart-surging moment later, realized Alistair was still in his rooms. Which meant he was planning to be here this evening, or at least he was at the moment.

Right or wrong, she took that open door as an invitation, slipping in and following the sound of water to the bathroom.

His shower was so large, no curtain or doors to shield the surrounding room from water spray was needed. It had dual heads and a floor made up of tiny, smooth stones arranged like a spiral, the spiral in grey, the outlining stones in cream and light brown shades. There were benches on either side of it. She'd never seen anything so practical and decadent at once, but that wasn't what had her attention now.

She leaned in the doorway. He had his back to her. The soap was in one hand as he lathered himself, working the creamy suds over his shoulders so they ran down his back in rivulets, over the taut arse. He put his foot on one of the benches, to work on that leg, giving her a glimpse of heavy testicles, the dark seam of his buttocks. She found herself caught up in visually tracing all the angles of his body, the protrusions of bone from his spine, and shoulder, the curves of biceps, the flex of his thighs and arse as he shifted. Then he braced himself against the wall of the shower as he lifted his foot and wiggled his toes beneath the fall of water to rinse them.

It affected her unexpectedly, the whimsical, vulnerable movement, something he might have done ever since he was a child. He was Region Master now, her Master. But he was also so much more, wasn't he?

Sher had never even considered having any interests that didn't serve her Master's. While Nina couldn't be that, she could be other things.

As Alistair shut off the shower, she picked up a fresh towel from the bin and came to him. When he turned, she realized he'd been deep in his mind on other things, because he looked genuinely surprised to see her there. As well as somewhat unsettled that she'd come upon him unawares. She dipped her head and offered the towel.

While there were many things that lowering her gaze could mean, getting a full, sweeping view of her wet, muscular and virile vampire Master wasn't an unpleasant side effect of it.

But then she reached his toes and bit back a smile. As he took the towel from her, he gave her a bemused look. But when he started to flip the towel around to dry his back, she reached out again. "Even for vampires, I expect that's a hard place to reach," she said shyly.

"Yes. That's true."

He gave the towel back, but his hand closed over hers through the terry cloth an extra moment before he turned. As she ran the towel over his back, drying it, he tilted his head so she was in his peripheral vision. There were beads of water on his neck, sprinkled over his shoulders. She rubbed the towel over them, which brought her closer, her knee brushing his leg.

"Did you need something, Nina?" His tone was neutral, hard to read.

"I did some work in your office today," she said. "Took some things off your list. I can do more of that, so when it's convenient, there are some things I'd like to go over with you so I can help you more."

He turned, retrieving the towel, wrapping it around his hips and hooking it there. "Not keeping you busy enough at the hospital?"

"We're busy enough," she said. "But my primary job is as your InhServ, isn't it? I don't mind helping to take care of you, too."

He studied her, shifting to one hip. She sighed, tired of being diplomatic about it. "Wanting to have that as part of my life doesn't mean I don't want to share yours, you know. Help you."

He made a noncommittal noise. "But my day is paperwork and politics. Dreadful stuff. Whereas you get to take care of two blokes who jump off a building onto a seesaw to see if they can propel themselves through the air like circus folk."

So he did sometimes dip into her head to see what was going on with her day. The idea pleased her. She wouldn't mind glimpsing what was going on in his. Politics and paperwork might not be all that scintillating, but being in his head, hearing his dry commentary about it all, being caught up in how he made decisions, the variables he weighed. She might like that quite a bit.

He didn't react to that. He seemed more curious about her two foolish patients. "Did they learn their lesson?"

"Oh, of course." She rolled her eyes. "They were so traumatized by it their mates smuggled in some beer and they were toasting one another when I came in to check their dressings. At least in the hospital they're not at risk for further terminal stupidity."

"What happened to the beer?" Alistair's lips curved slightly.

"The Matron confiscated it, much to their chagrin."

"The Matron, hmm?" That curve became deeper. "How did she handle its disposal?"

"She divided it between the girls at the end of shift," Nina said without missing a beat. "They sat around the picnic tables in back and toasted the generosity of stupid men. Tracy said they did share with the orderlies, though."

"Very generous." He chuckled and moved to the counter.

It was impossible for her not to enjoy the play of muscle across his back and at his waist, the stretch of the towel over his firm arse. But she had another purpose here, if she could focus around the bloody beautiful male. Before he noticed and acted on it, and then the rest would be hopeless for tonight.

As an InhServ, she could never refuse him, but she had a feeling even without that designation she'd be helpless to tell him no.

"So you didn't share with them?" Alistair said, bringing her out of her head.

"It was close to dark then and I needed to head home. Nero was waiting."

"Ah. Sorry about that."

The casual apology startled her, and she shook her head. "No. You've been more than generous. I didn't mean to sound—"

"You didn't. Not in the slightest. I just know it's nice to spend time with mates."

But when was the last time you did? she thought. She cleared her throat. "I also...there's a park nearby. I was going to have Nero drive me, but I thought...you've been working so hard, perhaps you'd like to do it with me tonight. We could pack my dinner and a few things for you, and enjoy the evening. It's a pleasant night."

She realized she really wanted him to say yes. For him, for both of them. Why couldn't they find other moments like they had in the cottage? Couldn't there be room for more quiet intimacies, shared experiences?

His gaze was on her face, her mouth, making her cheeks warm. She moistened her lips and let her knees give, taking her down before him, as she laid her hand on his thigh. She bowed her head, aware that his cock had twitched, was beginning to swell.

"May I give you pleasure, my lord?"

He trailed his fingers over the top of her head, along her ear. "You do, Nina. I'm in your mind while you're working. I hear your laughter when you're talking to Nero. I feel your dreams when you sleep."

Most of the intimate things he said to her fell under the context and timing of when he took her body, fed from her. It had been a while since he'd said such a thing to her...like this.

She hadn't had any nightmares since she'd come here. Since he had third marked her. Which gave his words additional significance. She looked up at him, dipping her head into his touch, enjoying his caress there. "Do you...can you influence my dreams, my lord?"

"I don't know. Do I have that power?" The light smile on his face was tinged with something poignant.

"I meant in the literal sense," she said, attempting to smile back.

"Yes, sometimes," he said. "If your mind goes to dark places in your sleep, I can draw it back to better dreams."

"Who does that for you, my lord?" she asked softly.

He said nothing for a few moments, and she lowered her gaze to rub her cheek along his upper thigh, turning her head to drag her lips along the side of his turgid sex. He made a warning noise, but she had no intent of taking it in her mouth until he gave her leave. She was simply expressing...devotion. It made her wonder at herself.

"I have no bad dreams," he said at last. "Except for the ones where the paperwork in my office turns into a tentacled monster that devours me whole."

She chuckled. "I tried to help reduce the size of the monster today."

His gaze narrowed. "You could have worked at the hospital today."

"I did work. For you." Her fingers curled against his thigh. Saliva was gathering in the heated crevices of her mouth, she realized, an aching hunger. "Please, my lord. Let me please you."

She needed his permission. Her realization of it, and his acknowledgement of her awareness, was reflected in the sudden stillness of his face. It only made her desire grow.

His touch along her face became more deceptively casual, a deliberate tease. "Are you happy, working at the hospital?" he asked.

"I am. I'm grateful to you for allowing it. But..." She nestled her face into his touch again, gazed down at his feet. "I miss you. I asked you if I had to lose myself to gain...other things. You've allowed me to hold onto a vital part of myself, but it feels as if to do that, I've had to sacrifice another possibility. A possibility...I want to explore more."

"There are some paths that are one-way only, Nina. If you go down them, there's no turning back."

She closed her eyes as his thumb stroked over her lips then pressed between them, insistent. She sucked on the digit, teasing it with her tongue, and made a small noise in her throat as his cock jumped in reaction.

I am yours for three hundred years, my lord. That is the path Fate has given me, and I do not want to tread it alone. She lifted her eyes to his face. *Do you?*

In answer, he took her hand, drawing her to her feet. Before she could despair that he was going to rebuff her, he began to move backwards, drawing them into the shower. When they were both standing on that mosaic of smooth gray stones, he unhooked the towel, folded it over and dropped it at his feet, nodding to it as he braced a palm on the side of the shower wall. "I've a picnic to attend," he said roughly. "Service your Master so we can get to it."

The spear of pleasure his words shot between her legs, through her chest, was strong enough to have a quiver running through her thighs. But she knelt before him again, arousal spiking further at the sight of him from that perspective, all smooth, powerful muscle and an impressive erection, his blue eyes staring down at her with male hunger.

Gripping the base of his cock, she ran her thumb along the bottom of his shaft before she closed her mouth over his ridged head, savoring the musky taste of him, the teasing hint of salt as she played the tip of her tongue over his slit. His hand tightened in her hair, and she reveled in the demand.

She wanted to be a nurse. She also wanted a Master. One who would demand things of her, who would stretch her to her limits. He'd given her back herself, and won her trust. Which meant the things she thought she wanted had gained a far wider scope. Only he could help her explore that new terrain.

Damn right. The possessiveness was as welcome as his active presence in her mind. After his mention of her hapless seesaw patients, she wondered if he'd been there far more often than she'd realized, a part of the shadows. Standing amid her running mantra of whose vitals needed to be checked, what medications needed to be pulled, who needed her assistance most on the floor.

"How often do you think of me, sweet nurse?" There was a strain to his voice she treasured as she licked and sucked, teased. Nipped him deliberately with her teeth and flicked her gaze upward to meet his eyes in playful challenge.

Didn't he know? But she answered, teasing him. *Your head's swollen enough, my lord, without me adding to it.*

His teeth flashed, fangs lengthening, and he withdrew, sliding his hands under her arms in the same movement and putting her up against the shower wall.

"The size of my head is your doing. You and that double-edged tongue of yours." He reached between them, up under the skirt. She gasped as he tore the underwear away, jerking it from her body so she clung to his upper arms for balance. He kept a secure arm around her waist, though, and held the tatters up where she could see.

"When you're here, or with me, you don't wear these anymore unless I order it. So I can do this without any impediment."

Her fingers convulsed as he sheathed himself in once forceful, slick movement. Strewth, he'd become even bigger as she teased him, bigger than usual. The breath of effort she made as she worked her hips on him made his eyes flash with heat, his mouth tighten.

I like feeling you struggle to take me, Nina. Makes me harder. Makes me want to push you to the limits of your endurance and beyond, so you have to rely on me for strength. Except you're so fucking strong, I don't know if you have any limits I can test beyond bearing.

It was a peculiar thing for him to say, laced with some emotions her arousal made it too difficult to decipher, but then he was thrusting against her, and she could only hold on. He let her wrap her arms around his shoulders, tuck her face in against his, so she felt the hard planes of his jaw and cheek bone against her softer skin, the brush of his wet hair against her temple. She inhaled him, moaned at the strength of his invasion, her body already rippling with the response she wanted to give to him.

Gripping her arse with one powerful hand, he pushed her down on him. His knee braced on the bench gave him additional leverage. The wall vibrated behind them, and she realized he'd adjusted his other arm so his palm was cupping her skull, his forearm cushioning her between the shoulder blades as he hammered into her. Even with a third mark, she'd feel the results after this was over, between her legs. Enough to make her want to do it again, sooner rather than later.

He registered that, his blue eyes becoming fiercer, more vibrant, and she realized the power of it, of opening her mind fully to him, giving him everything there. Her inexplicable desire to be taken over. Owned. Cherished.

She faltered a little over that one, because it crossed into a realm she knew didn't exist in his world, but he wrapped her loose hair around his knuckles, turned her face to accept his kiss, a deep, soul-touching kiss, offering her feelings that helped drive away those shadows again.

He could chase away her nightmares while she was awake as well.

~

Earlier, she'd asked Mrs. C to prepare a sampling of foods that were Alistair's favorites. As Alistair handed her into the Buick Phaeton under a night sky, she peeked into the basket, curious. A seasoned chicken salad, a container of colorful fruit, and a bread so fresh she inhaled the scent of the heated yeast through the bread cloth. Cubes of various cheeses. The cook had packed Nina the makings for a chicken salad sandwich. There were also biscuits with chocolate chips and walnuts.

"Your cook spoils you, my lord."

"I think my servant does. She requested the meal, didn't she?"

"I told her to pack me a sandwich and throw in a few crusts of moldy bread for you that the dogs didn't want."

"Your impertinence will be rewarded," he said, hand flashing out to squeeze her knee. She squealed, for he knew how ticklish her knees were, and pulled out of his grasp. He tossed her a satisfied look and put the car in gear. Her handsome Master wore a pair of slacks, spotless linen shirt and a silk-backed brocade vest, his jacket tossed into the back. His hair had already dried in that artful way that could make her hate him. But he had his hand on her nape now and was playing with her hair, telling her he had no objections to her fluttering wayward feathers.

The park to which they were going was one that Nero had assured her would have what she was seeking. While Alistair had some familiarity with it, it had apparently been a while since he'd been there. As he pulled in and saw the bright lights over the footy field, the men playing, he slowed the car down. His eyes went to the field, lingered there. Stayed.

"Alistair," she said quietly. They had no cars behind them right now, fortunately, but she didn't want a blaring horn to pull him out of a place deep in his head. She touched his hand on the wheel and his head jerked, his gaze shooting toward her.

"Let's find a parking place and watch the games while we eat," she said. "I haven't watched a good footy match in a while."

He looked conflicted. For a second, she had a feeling what he most wanted was to turn the car around and leave. So she made much of looking eagerly toward the field and shooting him a bright smile. "Sher knew nothing about the game. Dad and I wanted to strangle her the few times we dragged her along to the local matches. Her questions came at the most inopportune times. I remember once, my father was answering one of them just as the most exciting point of the game was made. He never laid a hand on either of us, but I thought he might clout her, then and there."

"Well, there's family, and then there's footy." Alistair seemed to recover himself, enough to make the declaration with a hint of his normal humor.

"Exactly. I expect a judge would send him to prison for murdering his own daughter, but he'd likely be as lenient as possible in the sentencing."

Alistair's tense mouth relaxed even more. Nina curled her hand around his on the gear shift as he parked the car and switched off the ignition. He lifted his troubled gaze to hers, and she held it. "Do you know," she said steadily, "There are things I never want to forget, that I always want to honor, with a fierceness bordering on violence. But there are other, more personal things I want back, too. Things that are mine, and I'm going to have them back. But I might need some help with that."

"Yeah? Like what?"

"You read my mind. You should know."

"I know some things. Other things...I don't stay in your mind that much, sweet nurse. When I'm there, I don't want to leave. So I resist. And as a result, I can have the pleasure of hearing you explain things to me in that lovely, practical voice of yours."

She'd call it practiced charm if he didn't speak so seriously. *When I'm there, I don't want to leave.*

"I miss having you there, talking to me. I wish you would, during your days or nights. As much as you wish. I also miss being with you." She tightened her hand over his. "I watch you sometimes. I thought you knew but maybe you don't. I sat upstairs in my room the other night and watched you wading in the waves. I wanted to come down to the beach and be with you, but I was afraid...you'd make me come into the water with you. I'm doing well—I can walk in front of the dunes, on the ocean side now, but I don't know about going all the way to the edge, or getting in. It makes me remember, you see, and I lose everything else. Like I did at Hal's cottage. It bothers me. I used to love swimming, spending the day on the beach."

She lifted his clasped hand to her mouth, held her face there, as she ran her other arm up his forearm, curling her fingers into his shirt sleeve, holding on.

A weighted pause, and then his lips touched her temple, his head bent over hers. "We'll work on that. I'll take you wading, hold you in my arms. I'll give you experiences in the water that will take away your fear."

He didn't say memories, and she appreciated that he understood that couldn't be done. But the pain of them could be eased. Balanced with other memories.

"What else do you want, Nina?"

"I want to...I'd like to start sleeping in the room next to yours. And maybe sometimes...you'd let me come spend some time sleeping with you in yours. I mean...you do have a pretty big bed."

"I'm a terrible sprawler."

She smiled against his flesh, then closed her eyes as he laid his hand against her back, between her shoulder blades and dug in. Then abruptly, he straightened and drew away, but not before he gave her hand a reassuring squeeze. "C'mon. The smell of that bread's becoming too much to resist. Your stomach's growling."

"I thought that was yours," she teased. Her voice and her insides weren't entirely steady, a lot of dense emotions packed into that moment. He hadn't agreed, but he hadn't said no to any of it. She would let it all stay there, an idea, one he might find appealing, too.

He exited the car, waving at her to stay when she would have opened the door for herself. He handed her out and took the picnic basket, giving her a look.

You may be my servant, but you are also a lady, and I am a gentleman. You can expect manners from me. At least in public. His eyes twinkled.

Then a burst of shouting came from the field, snapping his attention away from her. She saw enough of it to guess it was a response to the other team spoiling the mark. A lot of good-natured insults were being tossed back and forth.

Alistair stared at the field for a blink, and then his gaze was back on her. As he closed the door and they proceeded to a picnic spot, she noticed he now kept his eyes averted from the play in an oddly deliberate way. "So, sweet nurse. Do you really know much about the game, or are you one of those girls who pretends to know about it to impress a boy?"

She snorted as he led her to a patch of grass on a slope that gave them a good view of the closest playing field, but still at a distance they could easily chat. It also put them somewhat beyond the brightest circle of the field lights. She'd noticed most vampires didn't care for intense brightness, even at night. She pulled the blanket out of the basket and spread it out. As she did, she noticed he'd turned his back to the field, continuing his strange avoidance of seeing it. Rather than address that, though, she went for the sideways angle to it.

"There are three classes of girls when it comes to footy, my lord. The ones who don't know a thing and could care even less about it, but flutter their eyelashes and pretend they care because they're mad about the boy passionately explaining it." Straightening after she spread out the blanket for them, she ticked off the next point on a second finger. "Then there are the ones who know as much as the boys and yet pretend not to, in order to give him the opportunity to impress her and feel more comfortable in her company."

She knelt to pull out the food and set it out. Crossing his arms, Alistair looked down at her. "And the third?"

She slanted a glance up at him. "The ones who know as much as the boys and aren't afraid to show it, because they aren't worried about whether he likes her or not, or if he thinks she likes him. She already knows the answer to those questions and would rather enjoy the game with him."

"Sounds like a mythical creature to me." He dropped down beside her. It put him in profile to the field, and she noticed his gaze sliding to it, then jerking away, like a child touching a hot stove. She prepared the food, idly chatting about this or that, making the occasional comment about the play. He responded in absent monosyllables, his attention staying out there more and more. She noted his fist was clenched in the blanket, though, his jaw tense as he watched.

She took a closer look at him, and realized his eyes were glassy, the way a person's gaze was when what they were seeing was an overlay of the past with the present. Did he see Jonathan out there? Mort?

She spoke quietly. "Do you remember that night, when you said paths to oblivion were far better than stagnant rituals we both know mean nothing?"

He lifted a shoulder, acknowledging her words, but the direction of his gaze didn't change. "I think some rituals do mean something," she said, gesturing to it. "And can help us stay out of the fields of blood."

She covered his hand then, and spoke simply. "I know you miss them very much. I'm sorry."

His gaze shifted to her, and his jaw, held so tight she thought it might crack, eased a fraction. "It's not expected for vampires to grieve. Especially not for humans. We're not even supposed to go on much about our servants, no matter how long we've had them."

"Sounds like vampires can be a hard lot. Thank God you come from Brit stock, with a lot of Aussie influence. We're a reticent bunch when it comes to sentiment ourselves."

"Yeah. We are." He looked at her. "You dream about it, and you think about it, even when you don't think you are. I see it in your mind. The evacuation, the bodies in the streets of Singapore, all the fires."

She began to shake her head, try to divert the topic, but he touched her face, her chin, making her lift her gaze to him again. "I see you on the *Vyner Brooke,* before the Japanese hit the boat." His jaw set. "The Matrons called you together soon as you set sail, set up a course of action. Laid out how you'd make sure that the civilians on the boat would be protected and given the life rafts first if you were attacked. I'd expect that, all that preparation. Nurses are an organized lot. But when the bombs hit, and it all became a reality, and the ship went down, that's what you all did."

"It was our charge. We had to take care of all of them." She looked down at the food, began to rearrange it, but his hand came into her field of vision, closed over her fingers, stilling her.

"You weren't just nurses. You were bloody well soldiers, every damn one of you."

She put her own hand over his, not looking up, but feeling his regard, the weight of his emotions, strong as hers, both caught in the past. The footy field was still there, the boys still calling. A breeze had kicked up, but here there was just that intent stillness between her and Alistair.

"No one expects it of women," he said bluntly. "The lot of you didn't even want to evacuate. You were prepared to stay with your patients until the end. You cried when you had to leave. The Matron had to choose who went on the first boat because no one volunteered. If you had, you would have made it home, Nina, because the first boat did. You never would have had to see what happened at Bangka Island."

She shook her head. "But someone other than me would have."

He touched her face. As he sat up, bent over her, her eyes closed, and his lips were against her temple. "Exactly my bloody point," he said roughly. "You were every bit of the soldier any man in the field was. Though I wished it could have been different for you."

She lifted her eyes, saw his own were brilliant and hard, a warrior who'd wanted to protect her.

"I wished it hadn't have happened to any of us," she said. "I wished Sher hadn't died. She was so full of life...so beautiful...and a part of my heart that will always be empty."

She swallowed, brushing back the tears with frustration. That wasn't why she was here. She'd come here for him. Not for her. He cupped her face, took them away.

"Maybe this is for us both. It brings it out, doesn't it?" He looked toward the footy field and squinted, as if the lights were too bright, but she knew it wasn't the light. The glare of other people's realities could be too harsh against one's own. "If she'd lived, you wouldn't have to be here with me." He said it low, and there was the weight of many things on it.

"True." She would have wished her alive, but not for that. After Nina had met Alistair, during the three years before Sher died, far too often she'd wished...

His head came back around. Her stomach jumped at his look.

Now, of all times, he'd chosen to be in her head. His gaze pinned her. "What did you wish, Nina? Tell me."

This was a precarious moment, she realized, where all that she thought might be going on with him could be proven. If she was brave enough to open herself to him. Heart and soul.

I wished that she'd had the vampire master she wanted, but that it didn't have to be you.

Now his stillness was different. It wasn't about the past. It was vitally here, in the present. Yet when he spoke, there was a deceptive mildness to his tone.

"Thought of me some during those years, did you?"

"On occasion. Not so much, really."

He knew how much she thought of him. He only had to look. It was too much; the memories, the loss, the yearning, all jumbled together in the same few moments. She couldn't think of a way to distract him from pursuing it further, but he picked up on her need. Or maybe it matched his.

"I can understand why you didn't want her to be with me," he said gravely. "After having met me, seeing how odious I am, you didn't want her to have to put up with me for three hundred years."

"That was it. For certain. And your looks..." She shuddered. "So repulsive."

"Well, we vampires are a repulsive lot."

He touched her chin and she lifted her face obediently, though meeting his gaze was hard. His smile was as painful as the tightening of her heart in response.

"We should probably head back," he said. "I've gone and ruined it."

"Nothing of the sort," she said staunchly. "We've barely started our meal, and it's a fine night." Suspecting he was about to overrule her, she added, "Please, my lord. I'd really like to stay for a little while."

As he appeared to waffle, she pressed the advantage. "We'll watch for a little while and then, if it's too unbearable, we'll go. If I can tolerate watching handsome men in shorts, so can you."

Amusement cut through the intensity of his gaze, relieving her. "Deal. For now."

Clasping her hand, he tugged her down on her side with him and pulled her flush to him, gripping the side of her throat as he put his mouth on hers and unleashed a demand she hadn't anticipated. The force of it pushed her to her back and had him leaning over her, his arm tight around her waist as her fingers curled into his shirt, her thumb slipping between two buttons to stroke hard flesh.

Where had this come from? She didn't know, but she wasn't objecting. She was always overwhelmed and amazed at what his kisses, ones like this, could do to her, sweeping her away from everything, from every worry.

When at last he raised his head, he framed her face with one of his strong hands, giving her an intent look. "I want to have more of this conversation at home. Sooner rather than later."

"Deal," she said faintly, echoing his words. His blue eyes flashed with humor, though it didn't dilute their heat one watt.

"Oi, mate! Are we boring you, then?"

Nina smiled as her Master grimaced. "Should have known. Footy players and their goddamned cheek." He sat up, and shot a derisive look at the two players on the sidelines at the bottom of the hill, grabbing some water.

"Those that have pretty girls, do this. Those that don't…" Alistair shrugged and spread out his hands. "I guess they play footy."

Nina laughed as the men tossed insults his way along with wide grins. "Big talk there." The tall redhead nudged his mate, a shorter dark-haired man. "I think it's his clothes. They're too pretty. He can't come and have a kick with us and get them dirty. One of ours just had to take off for work. Want to fill in and keep us even? Got a spare pair of shorts and shirt and we look a similar build. Except for me being more manly and all." He cocked a brow at Nina. "If you can spare him."

She managed a shrug and a flippant move with her not-so-steady hand. "I was hoping someone would relieve me of his unwanted attentions."

She laughed and shrieked as Alistair lunged at her. Rolling, she jumped to her feet and went down the hill, him chasing after her. The two men called encouragement and waved their arms to block Alistair as she used them as a buffer to help her dodge him.

For just a moment, she remembered the youthful girl she'd been, who'd laughed so much more easily, all the possibilities of the world still open. And in him, she saw a trace of the same, a young man who'd perhaps been headed for a different path, but had chosen this one, had embraced it, even as he still had that part inside him, ready to be called forth by someone who could pull him out of darkness.

I'd have had you down on the ground beneath me if we didn't have an audience. He was ten feet from her, had paused as one of the men shoved at him good-naturedly. Though he wasn't even looking at her now, the silky thought stroked across her skin as if he still had her in his embrace.

Easy to say when you can move like a vampire.

His gaze slid to her, held her with that piercing look he did so well, that weakened her knees, shortened her breath and accelerated her heart rate, all at once.

I'd have caught you even if I were no faster than these blokes. I have incentive. I know what you look like, wet and begging.

A strategic retreat seemed advisable before her whole face was the color of an apple. One of the men distracted him, bringing him the spare clothes. As they began to talk and get to know one another in the way men did, Nina made her way up the hill with her flushed cheeks.

Taking a seat on their blanket, she packed away his portion of the food and drink to keep them fresh, then picked up her own sandwich. Eating a bite or two was a good cover, helping her take furtive looks through her lashes at the male vampire stripping off his shirt, without looking too obvious about it.

Unless the vampire in question was in her head and could know everything she intended to do before she did it.

Alistair stripped socks, shoes and pants, the boxers beneath a dark color that weren't much different in coverage from the shorts being worn on the field, so he didn't have to worry that he was exposing himself more than was proper in the public park. After he pulled on the borrowed shorts, socks and shoes, he gathered his clothes, folded them over his arm.

She was already rising and moving down the hill before he turned. The heat in his gaze as he noticed her coming to tend to him could have melted ice into a puddle, and made her heart beat higher in her chest.

Her fingers closed over the shirt. When he continued to hold it, it created a tether between them.

You run from me again tonight, sweet nurse, you'll learn what really happens when you're caught.

She lowered her gaze. *I expect that depends if you really can catch me, my lord.*

His dark chuckle was as blatantly sexual as the bar of steel he'd had pressed against her leg moments ago.

The shorter dark-haired man approached, slapping Alistair on the back. "Can't imagine my girl moving that swift to be my personal valet, mate," he teased, shooting her a wink.

It took her aback some, thinking not only of how it looked, but how instinctively she'd done it. She hadn't even thought of it. Just that she needed to care for his needs.

She braced herself for Alistair to pass it off with some typical male retort that would likely hint how his sexual prowess made her eager as a puppy to please. And she'd poison his chicken salad. It wouldn't kill him, but it might give him some discomfort.

"I'm a lucky bastard," he said, surprising her. "And I don't deserve her."

CHAPTER TWENTY-ONE

*S*he'd wondered how Alistair played footy without it being obvious he had the advantage in speed and strength. He could have lapped the field five times in the time it took a man to get straight to the goal from center field. But after three hundred years, it was apparently second nature, altering his physical reactions to blend into a human world.

Beyond that, he was good. Really, incredibly good at the sport, and not because of the vampire advantage. He knew the game well, and had obviously played it as often as Nero had said. If his skills were rusty from disuse, she didn't see much evidence of it. He drop-kicked the ball with graceful ease and handballed to other players with frightful accuracy. That part might be helped along by the vampire side, she imagined, for his hand-to-eye coordination and reflexes would be formidable.

She found herself most surprised by how well he worked with his new teammates. He wasn't a showboat player, trying to steal all the good plays. He handed off quickly and let them get the lion's share of the payoff.

When he spoiled the mark of the opposing team, knocking the ball off track, he won cheers not just from his own side, but from her. As he walked back to the center, he glanced up at her, tossing his hair out of his eyes. The cocky smile he sent her made her chuckle at him, wrap her arms around herself at the silly surge of feeling. There was a bit of swagger to his step, no denying it. He liked that she was watching, that he could show off before her. Like any man before his girl.

Careful, her sense of self-preservation warned her. *He's not any man. He's a vampire, and you're his InhServ. Not his girl. Not that way. How many times do you have to hear it?*

Fine. That'll do, and bugger off, she told that part of her mind. She didn't need anyone to tell her what her reality was. She was more than aware. But if she could have a few moments of fantasy to make the reality easier to deal with, then so be it.

But that was the point of the warning, wasn't it? That sometimes fantasizing made reality harder to accept.

Bugger. Off.

The two teams were fairly evenly matched, so as the game progressed, the level of play became more competitive, attracting more spectators. Dog walkers, people who'd finished work shifts, families out for a late stroll after the dinner meal.

Nina surged to her feet with another cry as the redhead leaped into the air, high enough he shoved his knee against the back of the man trying to block him, using his body to give him the leverage to snatch the ball out of the air. He hit the ground hard and rolled, the ball securely in his arms, and was on his feet, running, the other team in hot pursuit.

He bounced the ball as was required, then feinted left as another man came in to his right, trying to keep him off course. A shout from Alistair and the red head handballed it with sizzling force. It popped off somewhat high, but Alistair tracked and caught it, when it was just within the right range that his leap to catch it didn't look otherworldly. He'd kneed up on the cluster of men around him and twisted in the air to come down with the ball tight in his arm. The others threw themselves on him with enthusiasm to keep him down.

Nina called out derision for them, and encouragement for her vampire and his team. Though logically she knew he couldn't be hurt, she still watched closely until they unpiled and he emerged. One of them gave him a hand up, slapping Alistair on the back. He smiled at what the man said, laughed.

He laughed.

She stopped in mid-clap, her heart in her throat, seeing the flash of teeth from his smile, the transformation of his face. He was handsome, yes. Not the least bit repulsive. But when he laughed...she expected every woman on the sidelines had felt the same jump in pulse she had.

He had loved this. He did love this. But uneasiness touched her as she remembered what sometimes happened in the moments when she recalled her love and enjoyment of something. Like simple daily living, having toast and tea in the morning, enjoying a sunrise... She could dwell there for a moment or two, but then that sunrise would be rising over the shore, and there were bodies scattered there, lying in the shadows, the crabs...

She snapped herself away from that fast, but saw a shadow cross Alistair's face as he watched the man walk away from him. A man who looked somewhat like Charlie. Half of them hadn't survived, but half had. Had Alistair gone to visit them? She knew Horace had died of complications. But Charlie and Rigby...

She pushed that away, cheered for him some more, drew his attention. He gave her a half-smile, shook his head at her. Maybe at both of them.

When the game was called, Alistair's team was the winning side. Beer was broken out and it looked as if the humans were planning to camp out on the grandstand for a time. She wondered if Alistair would let them stay for a while. She wouldn't mind.

She'd begun to fold up the blanket, pretty sure he would, when a man spoke near her.

"I'd heard he was a good footy player, even if he wasn't what he is. Though it certainly doesn't hurt, having that advantage, does it?"

Startled, she looked to see the male standing a few feet from her blanket, a spectator who'd ostensibly drifted closer to her. He had the thumb of his right hand caught in his pants pocket as he watched the game. Smoking a cigarette, he squinted down the field against the lights. He had a lined face, as if he smoked far too much, and his body, while so spare it could be called bony, had a sinewy quality to it. The eyes he turned to her were a pale grey, like water.

"Least he's not shifty enough to try to play pro. Though our lot might like seeing a footy star we know is from our kind, it's still kind of cheating. Not like seeing the real thing. Someone who's earned where they end up. Curtis," he said, giving her a nod. "Lord Donovan's servant."

"Oh." She glanced toward Alistair. He was involved in conversation with the other men, but she suspected from the sudden tightening sensation in her mind that he was fully cognizant of the new arrival. Which reassured her. She put on a polite expression and extended a hand. "Nina, though I expect you know that."

"I do." Curtis took her hand and squeezed it, his fingers a whispering caress rather than a formal shake. Before she could draw back, he did, took another drag on the cigarette. "I was a few blocks away, in the neighborhood, and Van told me Alistair was close by. They can sense that kind of thing, even through us. We can too, but not quite at the same range they do. You're probably not seasoned enough to know that. At the beginning, it's hard to sort out all the different input. Like a dog given her sense of smell long after being a puppy."

"Hmm." She didn't rise to the bait. "Did you come to watch, or did you have a message for my Lord Alistair about the upcoming meeting between him and Lord Donovan?"

"Yeah." Curtis lifted a shoulder. "Van wants to know if Alistair can come to his place next week for it. Got some territory business pressing in on him, regarding money stuff. Figuring Alistair knows how important that is, and his fancy house needing the blunt, he might be okay with that. Plus, Van has a new skeet shooting setup he wants Ali to try."

"Hmm." Nina bent and retrieved a bottle of beer from the cooler, extended it. "Would you like one?"

"Don't mind if I do." He gave her a wink, drawing closer to the blanket. As they transferred the bottle, his fingers brushed hers in blatant intimacy. "Though I'd much rather drink it off your pretty body."

"That's for our masters to decide," she said without inflection. "No."

"Excuse me?" Curtis lifted a brow.

Nina reached into the basket. Her eyes were on the contents, but her voice was firm, and after she found what she sought, she rose to her feet to face him. "No, Lord Alistair will not meet Lord Donovan at his house. He may accept the skeet shooting invitation another time, but not for a formal review. The date and time were provided. They were not suggestions, Curtis. Lord Donovan must present himself at that time and date, or answer to Lord Alistair as to why he was not in attendance."

"Oh, really? You making decisions for Alistair, now? Think you can do that?"

Nina's brow creased. "My Master can speak in my mind. I take my orders directly from him. Do you not do the same with your Master?"

Curtis's gaze flickered, a barely concealed flash of irritation. "Ah. So that's coming from him, then."

"The next time you call him familiar, he will segment your tongue so that you have time to think it through before you are that forward again. I expect your Master would prefer to have the use of your tongue."

Curtis blinked as she extended a package wrapped in foil. "There. A chicken salad sandwich and biscuits for you, and a sampling of the same for your Master. The bread is particularly fresh, from our cook. Is there anything else?"

Curtis shook his head. "You're a delicate-looking lass," he said, eyes running up and down her body. "You should—"

Her glance slid past Curtis's shoulder and he stiffened as Alistair placed a firm hand upon it. "She should what, Curtis?"

He'd come up on Curtis so suddenly, she wondered if he'd risked some of his preternatural speed to make it happen. Well, they could move faster than the human eye could follow. As long as his conversation with the others had been over, anyone who caught the quick movement would have thought they'd already drunk too much.

She gave Curtis credit, but then he was an experienced servant. Not by a flicker did he betray that Alistair's appearance had flustered him. "My lord."

"I will see your lord when scheduled," Alistair said. "Do you have other business here?"

"Just passing by. I enjoy a good footy match, and some of the blokes at the pub down the street said there was one happening up here in the park."

"Game's over. For now."

"Yeah. It is. My lord." Curtis dipped his head, shot Nina a glance with a half-smile, and then left their company. She noted he didn't turn his back on Alistair until he was a good twenty paces away, and Alistair made sure he observed the formality, his blue eyes tracking him. Then his attention came back to Nina, and his brow lifted, silent question.

"My apologies, my lord," she said. "I know you said none of that in my head. But it felt as if he were trying to seek an advantage in the relationship, and...it felt wrong. The Mistress gave me enough instruction to tell me where the lines are between overlords and Region Masters, and the vampires who report to them." She lifted a shoulder. "The AANS was an arm of the Army. I recognize the signs of someone bucking and testing chain of command."

"So you took it upon yourself to cut him back down to size."

"Well, servants take rank from their vampires. Which means I outrank him, and he was being an arse. Not trying to be too subtle about it, either, though I expect he thought he was being clever."

"He was testing your cleverness, seeing if you could cross blades with him and hold your own. You did. Unflappably. Well done."

Her gaze flicked up to his. He still wasn't smiling, though. "Have I done something to offend you, my lord?" she asked.

"No. Unless you gave him the rest of the chicken salad before giving me a bite."

She shook her head at him, but when she bent to open the basket, he waved a hand at her. "Let's head for home. I'll finish it in my room." His gaze slid over her. "And you."

On the way back to the house, when he wasn't shifting gears, he had his hand on her thigh. "Keep your knees open, Nina," he said, his eyes on the road.

He gave the order, but didn't touch her between them which just heightened her awareness there. She expected that was the point, and struggled to remember she had an important question for him.

"Why do Nero and the others protect me on the way to and from the hospital, my lord? Does it have to do with those like Lord Donovan and Curtis?"

"It does." His hand tightened on her leg and the look he cast upon her gave her a flutter in her chest. "There are a few vampires in my territory who test me on a regular basis. Giving you a hard time would be a way of poking the bear. I'd rather you not be caught in the middle of an absurd pissing match."

He sighed. "I should just rip Donovan's heart out of his chest at the next overlord meeting and say, 'Anyone else have a problem with me being Region Master?'"

"So, what's stopping you?"

He slanted her an appreciative glance. "Bloodthirsty woman. The carpet in that room took me a while to find, and blood wouldn't come out of it easily."

"Put down painter's cloth, then. I'm sure I can scare some up from the maintenance shed, or Nero can."

"You don't like Donovan either, then?"

"I've not met him, so you know I can't say that one way or another. But I don't like Curtis. He has a meanness to him, a watchfulness that...bears watching."

"So it does." He turned down the gravel-covered maintenance road, taking it toward the house instead of the main drive. She raised a brow.

"Are we looking for cloths now?"

"No." He smiled as he parked by the maintenance shed. "You just reminded me of something."

Coming around and opening the door for her, he drew her out of the car. He took her to the back of the shed. Once there, he moved aside a large wheelbarrow leaning against the wall and then dug his fingers into the grass. She blinked as he lifted what looked like a patch of weeds, to reveal a cleverly-covered trap door. A ladder descended into the earth.

"The opening is narrow, and left rough to blend, this first part of it, so you may get your clothes dirty. I'll precede you to guide you down," he said. "Pull it closed behind you. It's well tended to ensure it settles right into the ground, leaving no trace of its presence."

She already knew his Victorian home was on high enough ground that he could have an underground level for more comfortable daylight sleeping, so it made sense he had a tunnel that led from that level. An escape route.

As he fit himself in the hole and disappeared into the dark, she followed. His hands closed on her ankles, helping guide her down the steps, moving to her calves, her thighs, when she pulled the door closed. As he'd described, it settled right back in place, and they were in darkness. Since a third mark could see in the dark functionally well, she saw the walls were earthen in appearance, but when she put her hands on them, she felt the wood framing behind the facade, holding the walls up.

Then her hands dug into that surface as his fingers slid up her thighs to her buttocks, his thumbs teasing between her legs as he brought her down another couple ladder steps. He pushed up her skirt, and she gasped as he bit her buttock. Not an easy bite, either. His fangs sank into her, holding her in place as his hands wandered over her legs, her arse, then around to her front to play over her clit, her mound, her stomach. She leaned back into his touch, his hold, shifting her own to the ladder steps to hold on against the unsteadying assault.

Thought you needed a lesson in what happens when you run from a vampire.

"You didn't give me a fair lead," she said shakily, pressing her forehead hard against the slat of wood. "Oh. *Oh...*"

"My responsive servant. God, I love your cries." He brought her down another step, pushing his knee against hers so her foot left the step and she was kneeling on the thin slat instead. It wasn't comfortable, but he was a master at balancing discomfort with the exact opposite kind of stimulus.

He snaked an arm around her waist, through the ladder slats, and his body was full against hers, helping to take the pressure off her bones. He'd opened his slacks and she felt his cock at her opening. Her thighs loosened for him and he was pushing into her, a slow, slow glide, the broad head and thick shaft stretching her

"Didn't want to wait for a bed, did we?" she managed, and sucked in another gasp as he gripped her throat and pulled back her chin, her head pressed alongside his.

"I wanted to have you the moment I looked up the hill and saw you cheering for me. Fuck, you're like honey-flavored oil, all slick inside. Is that all for me?" As he made it to the root, he punctuated it with a hard push that had her groaning. "If you know what's good for you, the answer, inside and out, will be yes."

"Yes," she said, and meant it truthfully. "Yes, sir."

"And there's the other side of it," he said, in that near growl.

She wasn't sure what he meant, but she couldn't think anyway. Not when he did this to her. He held her as he thrust, retreated, thrust. Thrust harder, his grip near bruising. He was a passionate and considerate lover, always bringing her up with him, but he would take his time letting her release, always reminding her he was her Master.

He made her serve his pleasure, demanded from her, used her hard. She was panting, flushed, her sex swollen with need when he pulled from her. Her response made her thighs slippery. She almost whimpered when he pulled her skirt back down. He used the arm around her waist to take her off the ladder, bring her along with him on her unsteady legs. He hadn't released either this time, but she was sure he'd been close. It made her feel somewhat better and not, at the same time. She wanted him to find release.

"I will, sweet nurse. That's just a first sampling I couldn't deny myself. Pay attention now. This leads to my bathroom, a door that opens into the plumbing access area. Like the trap door, it's not obvious it's there. I'll show you how to get it open. If ever there's a need to get out of the house quickly, that's the way to do it."

"Why would I need to..."

"It's a precaution. If I tell you to go here, get away from the house, you'll do it, you understand me? I'll need to be sure you're safe. Best way for both of us to stay alive."

His voice had that tone that told her he wouldn't be disobeyed in this. She wanted to ask a lot more questions, but he quelled her by stopping her in the darkened hallway, which had widened out enough for them to stand side by side. He turned her toward him, though, and framed her face with his hands. "Close your eyes."

She obeyed, feeling a tremor at the sternness of his voice.

"Now, part your lips. Hold them that way."

She did, and let out a tiny sound as his lips and tongue played over them, teasing. Her body swayed, and he made an admonishing noise that stilled her.

You obey my every command, Nina. If I want you to stand like a statue for an hour while I do this, you will. You would eventually release from just that, more of your honey running down your sweet thighs, tempting me to lick it all off, and start again, this time between those lips instead of these. Equally sweet. Tell me why you would release that way. First thing in your mind.

Her mind stumbled over it, at a fork where one way was right there in front of her; the other down the path of reason, logic. Self-protection.

Fuck reason. Answer me. "Now."

He barked it, low and sharp, and she jerked, the words spilling out of her, against his mouth, since his lips were still on hers.

"Because I'm yours. Because I want...I want to do everything you tell me and I don't know why. I want to please you and it tears me apart inside."

"Not a tearing apart. Just an opening of a flower earlier than she expected," he murmured. "When we get to my room, go to my bed. Lay yourself down. Put your arms over your head, spread your legs, close your eyes. And stay that way as long as I wish, while I do things that will make you scream and ache for more."

"Do I get to do things that make you want...more?" she whispered to the darkness. To him.

"I never stop wanting more with you, Nina."

More was the correct word. More and more and more. When she begged him for mercy, he gave her only spare draughts of it, before demanding surrender from her again. She thought The Mistress's regimen had been brutal, the way it wrung every possible ounce of response from her body. Now she realized it was like basic training to a soldier, making sure she was prepared for actual battle.

If she was a flower, that flower was cut, limp and wilted on the bed. She was sprawled across his chest, her body damp and heated still. His fingertips trailed up and down her back while his heart thudded beneath her cheek. Her hand rested on his flat abdomen, her gaze able to wander over the intriguing terrain of his torso, his thighs, his cock, momentarily at rest in a curve against his pelvis.

"What did you mean?" she asked sleepily. "When you said, 'there's the other side of it?'"

His fingers paused, then resumed, more slowly. The tingling of her nerves was like a trail of starlight in her mind. His jaw shifted, and she thought he'd smiled.

"I like that. Starlight." He tapped one of those fingers on her lower back. "All those times you thought of me, before we came back together. The bits you've reflected upon, since I gave you the second and third marks. If they'd been dreams of me as a husband who went to work at the office, coming home to dinner and you, to a normal human life, I would have known that what we had was simply a moment. You had merely plugged me into your true dreams of a husband, part of a human world. But it wasn't."

She considered that, closing her eyes. "You could be both in my mind. They are my dreams. I don't have to limit them to one path. They can be a maze."

He chuckled, the rumble through his chest and deepness of his voice stirring her. She tilted her head up as he cupped the back of her skull, stroked her hair, wound his fingers in it and tightened the hold so she was held in that position. She curled her nails into his chest.

"I've enough of your nail marks on my back, sweet nurse," he said mildly.

"But they disappear far too soon."

Heat flared in his eyes, his mouth getting that taut, concentrated look she liked. The Mistress had taught her body to rouse to any sexual stimulation, as training. But it was Alistair himself, his proximity, coupled to her third mark, that made the wanting seem endless.

His gaze softened, and he eased his hold, letting her lay her cheek on his chest once more.

He ran his hand down her back again, to her arse, and laid a hand possessively over it, stroking. "You can say it started with the ideas Sher gave you when she described her service. And that those ideas progressed into detailed imaginings because you're a young woman with a healthy interest in sex. Yet, though you had never been part of my world at that point, what I saw in your mind were things that fit more into a vampire's life. You, content to sit at my feet while we shared a drink by a fire. You replayed in your mind, over and over, me taking your wrist, only you imagined what it would be like to feed me from your throat." His gaze slid down. "Or from your lovely thigh."

In a move like flowing water, he shifted her to her back, and he was between her legs, sliding down, his hands on her thighs, holding them open. His gaze moved between them, lingered on what he'd enjoyed so thoroughly these past couple hours, then shifted to her inner thigh. She could almost hear the pulse speeding up, beating harder. Drawing him.

"All sexual things," she managed. "Fantasies. Lust."

"Not sitting by the fire. But yes, a lot of them." He nodded. "Except now I have access to all the layers. The fascination, the physical reaction, they're on the surface. Beneath is a deeper need. You want to give me all I need, be cherished for it, as a servant well should be, no matter what others of my kind may feel about being that straight forward about it."

Now that thudding moved to her heart, and she swallowed as he pressed his lips to her inner thigh, keeping his eyes upon her face.

"When you came to retrieve my clothes before I even ordered it, I felt the wife in you, wanting to care for her husband by doing that, and packing away my meal for later. But I also saw the quick light in your eyes, because you knew I expected you to respond as my servant, and you were taking pleasure in serving your Master."

His tone became more serious. "That's closer to our reality, so I was pleased to see it take the lead in your mind. For a variety of reasons, practical and...not."

He knew how to draw them together, heart, mind, her soul. She could pretend it was only her body he claimed most thoroughly, but did he know how potent it was, when he touched upon this part of her?

"I do. And I do not do it to play with you, Nina. I hope you can trust me that much. I have always been honest with you, what I can and can't be, what I do and don't feel. Do you agree?"

She thought it through, nodded again. There were times he'd been cruel. When he could have been manipulative instead, he'd chosen honesty, no matter how it cut. It was why, she realized, she trusted him.

He brushed his lips over the femoral artery, then higher, all the way to her mons, teasing her clit with tongue and lips, holding her legs down with his body and arms as she shuddered. He shifted to the other leg, nuzzled her there, his hair brushing her sex, her thighs. She loved the feel of it, wanted to thread her fingers into the thickness of it, lift her body up and rub against it.

The light smile on his lips was eclipsed by the fierce heat in his eyes as he accommodated her briefly, turning his head to brush his hair against thighs and sex, several times, as she made a soft moan.

She reached down and stroked him, oddly touched when he laid his head down on her thigh, stayed that way. He curved his big hand around her other thigh, thumb rubbing in a back and forth motion over the tender skin.

"Your other servants," she ventured shyly. "Was it...like this?"

"Yes and no. Nick and Hal were good men. Our relationships had moments of true intensity, and I loved them well. They were bedsport, my closest friends, my brothers. My servants. It's a hard concept to entirely frame in a human way. But you..."

He shook his head against her, nuzzled her flesh. "Sometimes I get lost there a bit, watching through your eyes and mind at the hospital, hearing your thoughts, seeing what you're doing. You're subconsciously aware of me, because at times you use my energy, my mind, to center and steady yourself."

He glanced up at her, a smile touching his face. "When I was still human, my parents had the occasional banquet for guests. In England, of course. I came here with some of the first colonizations, so I've always thought of myself as Australian."

He sounded, looked and acted it, so she didn't disagree.

"There'd be different conversations going on at the table," he mused, "my mum chatting up the ladies while my dad did the same with the lords. Sometimes they'd have their faces turned away from one another, but I noticed my mother had her hand on my father's arm the whole time. Keeping that connection."

He lifted a shoulder. "That's the way it feels when I'm in your mind. Even when you've been working at the hospital and there's been distance between us, throughout my day, there's this moment where I'll suddenly think, 'She's there. We're connected. I can reach out and touch her mind.'"

He'd just described the elemental thing she would have wished to have from the man she'd chosen to share a life with, raise a family. Her fingers constricted in his hair. "Alistair," she whispered. Then she closed her eyes. She couldn't forget. Couldn't ever forget.

But why not? Why couldn't he be her vampire master and still be what her heart was seeking? It had taken a shape and form that she hadn't expected, but did that mean it wasn't what she wanted?

He pressed his lips to her thigh and said nothing. Not because he agreed or disagreed, she was sure. This was something she had to resolve in her own mind.

He cleared his throat, drawing her away from the problem for now. "Thank you for today. I'd forgotten...or made myself forget, about the footy."

She opened her eyes, looked at him. Her hand was still on his head, her touch drifting along the side of his strong face. "Did it help?"

She didn't have to clarify about what, and not just because he could be in her mind.

He didn't say anything for a while. He settled his cheek back against her thigh, his gaze where she couldn't see it, but she felt the tightening of his face, the set of his chin, when he finally spoke again. "They didn't make it. None of them."

Nero had said half. Had he not known? Had Alistair not even told him? She dropped her touch to his nape, massaged there. When he adjusted higher, to rest his head on her upper abdomen, his forehead brushing her breasts, she curved her arm around his shoulders, his broad back. Held him close. He was rigid, but he didn't tell her not to do it.

"What happened to Rigby and Charlie?" she asked softly. Rubbing her palm against him, hoping to soothe what couldn't be mended.

"Rigby should have given himself more time, but he went back to the front line," Alistair said after another weighted pause. "Tried to hold it with the others as long as they could. He was part of the thousands surrendered to the Japs. Died en route to a POW camp, bayoneted when he got sick, probably the unhealed head wound making him more susceptible to the malaria. He couldn't keep up. Charlie...well, it was what it was."

He was thinking of how his words might impact her. She could tell, as if she had as much access to his mind as he had to hers. She wouldn't let him shield her. Even though she dreaded the words, she'd suspected and feared the truth of it, ever since the day she'd had to leave the hospital and board the *Vyner Brooke*. So she said the words herself, rather than making him do it.

"He was in the hospital when it was overrun," she guessed. "And even if they'd had any thought to spare them, he wouldn't have been able to walk, keep up with the other prisoners."

She put her hand over her eyes and face, rubbing them hard. "We just left them," she said. "God damn it."

"You were ordered to evacuate."

"We shouldn't have listened. If we'd stayed..."

He shifted them, so they were sitting up, her in his arms, and up close to his intent expression. His hand closed on one of her wrists, pulling her hand from her face and gripping it tight between them. "You would have been bayoneted with him," he said roughly. "At best, you would have been separated from him, treated as an internee, not as an officer, and you would have died in the camps, from illness and starvation. Same as the nurses who survived the boat sinkings and had to surrender to the Japanese at Muntok."

"Some of that hasn't been made public yet. How did you know?"

"I have my sources, same as you." A shadow crossed his face, and he eased her to a sitting position next to him. "But like you, I found out after it was all over. I could have saved some more of them, maybe, but instead I came back here when my mates died, checked out like a goddamned corpse myself."

His voice went flat as he said it, but she detected the rage and helplessness behind it. They were feelings she knew so well that even someone as poker-faced as he was couldn't mask them from her.

She wouldn't let him get away with that, any more than he'd let her shoulder the guilt of leaving her patients. She lifted her hands to his face, held them there, stared hard into his eyes. "You saved me. I was nowhere near the best of them out there, and not a one of them deserved to die. But I am grateful for my life. To be here with you now. I promise."

"I'm the bastard who insisted on making you be here with me." His grip on her tightened, his voice roughening in a way that was both the command of a Master and something different, the need of the man who'd gazed with such loneliness at men playing a game on a field, as if he watched from behind a veil, like a ghost.

"I knew giving you up was likely the right choice, for so many reasons. My needs, your needs. But in the end, it wasn't any of that. I

VAMPIRE'S EMBRACE

wanted you. And I haven't regretted it," he said, touching her face. "Not for a single second."

She remembered what Nero had told her, Alistair's sudden adamant behavior when it came to the decision of taking a new servant or having her. A completely untrained woman for a Region Master who sorely needed every advantage he could get.

"Why? Why me?" She wasn't fishing for compliments. In such a painfully honest moment, she needed the answer to the question that had gnawed at her in so many ways. At first with pain, and now sometimes with a confusion laced with occasional wonder. What had she done, that could possibly have drawn his attention away from those so better suited, like beautiful Sher?

"The last thing a woman like you would ever do is fish for compliments." He gave her a light shake, but it was gentle. He didn't answer her right away, thinking it through. This time, she didn't think he was choosing words to protect her as much as figuring it out for himself.

"I appreciate all Lyssa does for me," he said at last, "but an InhServ isn't something I ever asked for."

He brought his attention fully back to her, and the look in his eyes, a Master's look, sharpened her awareness of him, of what he might want next from her. His gaze flickered. Keeping his attention on her face, he trailed his fingers along her throat. They both registered the increase in pulse, the leap when he clasped that slim column, tipped up her chin.

But he didn't stop there. He drew her away from the bed, drew her down to her knees, watching her every moment of the descent, until she was on her knees. Then she went lower, until she was curled around her feet and he was kneeling over her, holding her and sheltering her both. Without a word or command spoken, she'd known he'd wanted her in the position, the gift she could give him.

She closed her eyes, that calm stealing over her. He made a noise in his throat that was a combination of yearning and dangerous male possessiveness.

"This is what I want," he said. "A submissive's desire to both serve and be sheltered by her Master's love. And such a gift deserves his regard in return."

Another long silence, during which she opened her eyes. When she dared a look up at him, she saw a mix of emotions there. Shadows, but also something better.

"That night, when I drank from you for the first time," he said, "I realized what you said was true. I needed the comfort you were offering far more than the vengeance of making the enemy suffer. You bring me comfort, Nina. A center. You have since the first time I met you. If I'd had to feed myself on the blood of the enemy that night...it might have been more than my soul could handle."

She couldn't breathe, couldn't move. And he wasn't done.

"Over the past three years, being able to reach out and feel that mark I had on you, know you were somewhere in the world... It kept me from getting completely lost. Otherwise I might have just told Stanley and those like him that it's a wretched world and stayed out of all this Region Master business."

She wouldn't have expected him to say most of what he'd just said, and all of it echoed and ached inside her, stirring the things in her heart she wanted so damn much. The vampire world had taken those dreams from her. So had he, in a way. But his words made her feel as if he'd just been holding them in safekeeping for her.

She wet her lips. "So even vampires need to feel like they aren't alone in the world."

"Don't tell anyone. We put a lot of effort into our anti-social tendencies." But the smile didn't reach his eyes. She gripped the wrist of the hand he still had on her face.

She'd learned that they all felt alone. Everyone going through the same things, yet feeling all alone with it. Because there was something so damn uncertain about life that could make one believe that any connection could be broken, was temporary. Or that the person they needed was farther away than they seemed. Like her parents. Or Sher and her, when Sher would talk about being an InhServ.

And yet here Nina was, unable to deny she was more closely bound to this male than anyone she'd ever met in her life, no matter all the rest.

His jaw tightened at that and he scooped her up, holding her close. When he took them back to the bed and cradled her in his lap there, she spoke against his chest, shyly. "I did think about it. 'If Alistair weren't a vampire, and he'd come to you the way he did, just a bloke helping his mates, who helped and saved you, would you have wanted to see him after the war, be with him...maybe even married him?'"

Tears stung her eyes suddenly. "I have to be honest with you because I've no other choice, do I? It's painful. Because the answer to that was yes. You are what I want. The kind of man I want. And yet... your world, and you, are so different...they frighten me. As much because what you said is true, that I want to serve you, be this thing I don't understand, for you. But it has to be in a world I'm not sure I want at all."

"Well..." He brushed his forehead against hers, an oddly tender move. "You've just described every pair of souls who've fallen together in an uncertain world."

Fallen together. He didn't say love, but it wasn't like that, was it? Or not like what she'd call love. At least not a few weeks ago.

His arms slid around her back, bringing her in closer, and he tilted his head, using his nose and jaw to brush her hair away as his mouth found her throat. Her head tipped back, giving him access as her hand landed on his arm, fingers digging in. She drew in a shuddering breath as his fangs grazed her.

"You've told me you want me. Now show me, Nina. Lie back on the bed and lift your arms over your head. Give yourself to your Master. There's no holding your heart and soul back from me. There's nowhere they can go far enough. But I will have a care for them, Nina. I promise you that."

She floated back, held in his one arm, his mouth creating sensations along the column of her throat that had her lips parted and her chin lifting higher. As she slid her arms up over her head, the blue fire in his gaze made everything tighten, her body readying itself for him again.

He took his time, though, making his way down her with lips and tongue, the whisper of his fingertips. She drew in a shuddering breath as his fangs sank into her thigh. His tongue lazily traced the flesh, taking blood in slow draughts, his mouth pressed to the penetration to contain the initial spurt from the wild pump of her heart. He slid his hand up, his thumb pressing into her, his other fingers stroking her perineum as her thighs trembled, widened for him.

You make me want to fuck you endlessly, sweet nurse.

I'm beginning...to understand...why third marks need good healing proper-
ties. Fast recovery to overstretched...places."

Suggesting I'm well-endowed enough to make you sore and 'overstretched'
only ensures I'll be using you again. His voice was a sultry heated wind
through her mind. She felt a tickle of wry humor, even riding a wave
of helpless desire.

Men are so...simple.

But a vampire male...not so much. She gave herself to the
moment, with no energy to spare for the dilemma that was their relationship. She wasn't sure what problem she was trying to solve,
anyway.

It's less confusing not to question it.

It's less confusing not to question anything, my lord. That's hardly the point.

But she had to admit, the answers seemed less important when—
as he said—she chose not to think.

While feeling could be as problematic as thinking, perhaps more
so for a woman, these in-the-moment feelings were good. She let that
be enough.

Watching her get lost in her pleasure, Alistair had some of those same
mixed feelings. He'd wanted to tell her something else, but had
stopped short of it. It was something she'd either sort out for herself,
or she never would. Hal had. Nick hadn't. But then it had been a good
lark for Nick, being a vampire's servant. He'd enjoyed both men and
women, as many as there was time to have. He was a hard drinker, and
never met a party he wouldn't join and make all the better for his presence at it. He'd never truly had the desire or need for family, perma-
nence...love, in any kind of romantic, one-on-one form.

Both had been good servants, but it was Hal's loss that had
lingered the longest and hardest as a result.

It wasn't that vampires couldn't love their servants. It was that the
connection between them was different from how humans classified
love. The power differential, the vampire holding all of it and the
servant having none, made it a very sticky thing. Randoms, servants
who weren't born and groomed InhServs, did have one choice—

whether to become a vampire's servant or not. After that, all the choices belonged to the vampire. Nina hadn't even had that choice.

To give her the answer he'd wanted to say when she said, "A vampire can't love a human" would have only muddied those waters. But the simple fact was a vampire could do any damn thing he wanted with respect to his servant—including be in love with her.

He just couldn't tell her that. Or let anyone else in the whole bloody vampire world know it.

But he could use every skill he had to give her endless pleasure. He could do that so bloody well, maybe the rest would stop mattering. To both of them.

CHAPTER TWENTY-TWO

*T*he day at the hospital had started out slow, but in the way of it, things picked up suddenly. Before Nina knew it, the afternoon had flown by and it was getting close to dusk. Too close. Nero would already be waiting.

After the past few days she'd spent with Alistair, she was eager to be at the house. He had a meeting that would take him away from home the first part of the night, but he'd told her they'd get together when he returned. He was seeking out her company and help more frequently. He'd certainly been talking in her head more since the night of the footy field. And he enjoyed being playful with her, like when she'd been examining a child who'd put a wooden block inside an unmentionable part of his body.

How in the bloody hell did he do that?

Alistair's voice had come into her head when she was crouched by the examining table with the doctor, trying to determine the best manner to dislodge the foreign object. She'd managed, just barely, not to yelp.

Very creatively, I'd say. He better hope the block doesn't leave any splinters behind.

Ouch. Maybe you should talk to him about far more pleasurable things that can go up an arse.

Away with you now, vile man.

His sensual chuckle had danced sensation down her spine, all the way to her tailbone and flaring outward.

When the doctor had given her an odd look, she realized she might be smiling. She'd wiped away the look with a mental deprecation to her vampire Master that kept those chuckles coming in waves.

She returned to the present and Tracy, standing before her.

"Sly's having a particularly bad day, Nina. Can you check in on him?" Tracy lifted a hand. "I know you're pretty rigid about when you have to leave, but he responds better to you. I wouldn't ask except, truly, I think he's having a worse than usual time today. Too much in his head. I'm a little worried about him, if we can't pick up his spirits."

She couldn't stay even a minute longer. But she couldn't not, could she? Maybe just a moment. Hopefully Alistair would understand. She tried reaching out, a tentative question, but received no response. It was a little bit of a letdown, that he wasn't paying as close attention to what she was doing as earlier in the day, but she chided herself for foolishness. The male could hardly be expected to linger about in her head all day when he needed to sleep, or had a Region to run.

After all, she'd been so busy today she couldn't reach out to him much, either. But she had sent a few warm thoughts. Maybe he'd done so as well, and that was why she'd felt strengthened, more reassured during a couple of harrowing moments. He'd said he did that too, didn't he? It was a nice thought.

Surely he'd understand. She nodded resolutely to Tracy. "I'll go see him for a minute."

Tracy pressed her arm in thanks and moved away. Nina had taken a handful of steps toward Sly's room when she heard her name being called.

"Sister Nina."

She suppressed a curse at the smooth voice. It was Mr. Grant, one of the hospital administrators, who had far more interest in nurses than hospital management.

"I'm on my way to see a patient and then I must leave, Mr. Grant," she said, turning in his direction as he strode toward her. He wore a tie and a striped shirt, and had his hair neatly sleeked back to emphasize his strong cheekbones and chin. He was a handsome man...if that was all a woman knew about him. For Nina, a man's looks were sculpted and enhanced by what was inside his heart. Mr. Grant's heart was lacking, in her opinion.

"I've someone at home waiting on me," she added, reinforcing it.

He closed his hand over her left wrist, lifting her hand for his inspection. "That someone hasn't put a ring on your finger, though you're well past the age for it."

Like most women in service roles, nurses were wearily accustomed to men who somehow thought that gave them the right to touch without invitation, sometimes quite inappropriately. When it happened with patients, they learned to deal with it in firm ways that didn't reduce the care they provided for the misguided bloke. However, supervisors and doctors always presented a challenge. Nurse matrons ran interference when they could, but none were available at the moment. From the determined glint in Mr. Grant's eye, Nina wasn't sure if it would have deterred him regardless. Tracy had warned her to keep him from drawing her into a too-private place.

She knew the diplomatic ways to handle the situation. Act like she didn't understand the man's intent and courteously brush him off. Act apologetic, as if it were somehow her fault that she had patients at the moment and couldn't respond to him as he wished.

Yet when his grip tightened on her arm, the feel of his touch on her skin roused something not the least bit diplomatic in her.

"Mr. Grant, you will release me this instant."

His gaze snapped up and his mouth settled into an unpleasant line. "You are overreacting, Nina. Being dramatic and female."

"You are touching me in a way I do not welcome, Mr. Grant. I respect you for your position. Respect me for mine." She tapped the name plate pinned to her apron. "It says nurse, not whore. You may have been able to intimidate others into backrooms with you, where I expect you've done unforgiveable things they've allowed because they need a job. I do not need this job. But you need all your appendages, though I suspect you'd make smarter decisions without one in particular."

When his face reddened, and he looked as if he were about to sputter something unwise, she stepped closer. She was suddenly remembering Anahera and The Mistress, and she took the move from them. That sudden invasion into his personal space, their eyes inches apart, startled him into momentary silence. The move was not intimate but assertive, something she knew he didn't expect from a woman.

"If you decide to dismiss me," she said, "I will explain to the man who calls me his why you decided to do so. In detail. He is very particular about who lays hands upon me."

She stepped back, and fixed a professional smile on her face. "Mr. Grant, if there's nothing else, I'll return to my duties."

An orderly and nurse were passing with a patient. At their curious looks, she saw Grant regroup and clear his throat. She also noted he looked a shade paler than usual, his eyes darting away from hers nervously. "Ah...yes, Sister Nina. Thank you."

She headed back down the hall. Though she felt a surge of satisfaction from the exchange, it was short-lived, changing to something else when she reached the door of her patient's room.

Sly Whitaker had had both legs blown off, ironically on the day that the war had been declared over in the Pacific. Repeat infections kept him coming back to the hospital, and the doctors couldn't determine the underlying causes that made his immune system so susceptible. It was assumed the extreme trauma to his body was keeping his natural defense systems from rallying the way they once had. But unlike the ups and downs of his roller coaster health, his mood had been going in only one direction. Down.

The nurses and volunteers took turns trying to bring it back up, wheeling him out for some brief forays of fresh air, playing cards with him, reading to him. He'd been an active bloke, though, all about sports and drinking with his mates. Everything made him restless in spirit, even as his body was pinned down by a lethargy he loathed.

Entering his room, she saw his current roommate was absent, likely taken off for some tests. He was an older man in the final stages of cancer, not the best match for Sly, but there were no private beds and swapping didn't happen much in the busy hospital, since the administration got very growly about it.

She was about to say bugger it and do it anyway. She'd put him in the children's ward with Timmy Werther, who'd just had his appendix out and was milking it for all it was worth, yet in a very charming little boy way.

He'd be fascinated with Sly's condition, asking him those blunt questions no adult would. Not guarded and awkward, or laden with pity.

What happened to your legs? Will you walk on peg legs, like a pirate? Will you get a parrot?

Just imagining it, she knew she was definitely going to put him in a bed next to Timmy.

Sly was in his wheelchair, facing the windows. He stared at the curtains covering them. Even though it was getting past dark now, there was a good view of the street, things to see, if he'd chosen to open them. The cord was within his reach. Since he had his lamp off, anyone who passed by and gave him a glance would have thought he was asleep, his shoulders slumped and head dropped slightly forward, but she knew better.

"Do you think you'll get the advantage of me in cards by putting me in the dark there, Sly?"

He didn't respond, just stayed where he was, staring at the curtains as if they were the way to something far away from this. "Why didn't I die?" he said. "What God is this cruel?"

She sank down in the chair beside him. His voice was hoarse. Though she saw no evidence of the tears, his face was lined and tired, like after a hard cry that no man would admit to doing.

Sometimes people tried all manner of things to cheer someone like him up, but they didn't think to go to that dark place with him, see it through his eyes. Work out the path from it *with* him, rather than flinging open doors and windows in places where he couldn't yet bear the light.

Reaching out, she took his hand. Gripped it, hard. He turned his gaze to it. He stiffened as if he might pull away but then, unexpectedly, he shifted their grips to lace fingers, tighten on hers. He held up their tangled hands and stared at the way they looked, displayed between them. "No woman's touched me like that. Not since... Just a pat on the shoulder like you'd do a child. Or your grandfather."

Dealing with Mr. Grant in an assertive manner wasn't the only thing that had changed about her communication style. "Your cock works just fine, Sly," she said.

When his gaze snapped to her, she continued in a brisk manner. "Your arms, your chest...you've had some muscle wasting, but if you do your exercises and rehabilitation, they'll be as fine-looking as any man's. There are exercises you can do to give yourself a nice-looking bum, too. You're not paralyzed. You're just missing your legs below the knee, and that's far better than missing them above. Surgeons busted their arses to save that right one, knowing just that."

"How do you know my..." He glanced her way, colored. "That I'm able to be with a woman."

Lifting a brow, she stood up and leaned over him. His gaze slipped down automatically, stealing a look down her blouse. She was wearing one of those tiny bits of lace that Alistair favored.

"That's how I know," she said. "Where your eyes go, even when you're trying to be a gentleman."

"Do the underwear match?" he attempted the tease, and warmed her heart.

"If I was wearing any. Yes."

His gaze shot back to her, and then his mouth eased into a rueful smile. "Sure, taunt the guy who isn't a threat."

"No threat?" She took his hand, moved it to her arm, molded his palm over it, showing her the difference in their sizes. "You're a man, Sly. A strong man who can make a woman feel fragile and feminine. The reason you're not a threat isn't because of your legs. It's because you're a good man who takes care of a woman, who wouldn't harm her. Am I right?"

"Yes, ma'am," he said slowly, staring at that connection. A sliver of something that might be hope was trying to struggle to the surface, her words shaking things up enough to give it that chance, but the path wasn't wide enough yet.

"What you mean by a 'threat' is you think you can't give a woman that quick breath," she continued. "The weak knees that hint that you can overpower and overwhelm her with pleasure. But you can."

She touched his face, drawing his gaze to hers. "But not if you sit in the dark, caught up by the things you can't change. No woman wants that kind of bore. But the man who says bugger it, I'm going to find me a gorgeous girl to marry and shag the rest of my life, and talk her into bringing me coffee in the morning, playing up the whole wheelchair thing just to see her running about in cute slacks and skirts, her pretty hair swinging along her back, her smile just for me..."

Tears had filled his eyes, spilled out, and she leaned forward, catching them on her fingertips. "Oh, Sly. I know. I know it's so very difficult. But I'm not blowing smoke up your arse. I've seen men in your same shape and even worse, who put it all back together. Found love and family. And though no one ever wants to hear it when they're feeling like this, it's about strength of heart. You can build it up, a day at a time, same way you're building your muscle strength. Hard and vital, but not impossible. You're not what you were, but that doesn't make what you are now worse. Not by a long shot."

"You're different from any nurse I've ever met. You..." Overcome by it, he stopped. Swallowed. "I can do all that. I know I can. But I'm just so mad, and tired..."

"I know. I know, love." She stood and put her arms around him, let him bury his face in her bosom and sob, in a way he hadn't yet. The loss of his legs had to be mourned, in the same stages of grief she'd seen men experience when they lost a mate.

Just as she'd had to mourn the loss of the life she'd expected, in order to set it aside and see the possibilities in what she had now. Wondrous possibilities, as she thought of Alistair's eyes upon her, the touch of his hands. The way his mind worked. The complicated things their relationship had become, the simple way she felt around him.

She thought of that as she stroked Sly's back, as she held him. When he seemed to be pulling it back together and on the cusp of feeling embarrassed, she eased away and shifted to grip the handles of his wheelchair. "If you're up for it, I'm taking you for a spin to another room. Timmy Werther is in need of a playmate for a few hours. There's only so much back door basketball you can play by yourself. He wants everyone possible to see his appendix bandage. But what he really wants is to pry it off and show the wound to everyone. You can tell him why it's important to keep that on."

"Why's that?" Sly asked, teasing her. "I might take mine off to compare."

"You won't do that. Because you know the sooner they heal into scars, the sooner you can impress the ladies with them. Timmy's not old enough to appreciate the benefits of that, but I expect you can give him other reasons that make equal sense to an eleven-year-old."

Sly went quiet another moment. Sensing the direction of his thoughts, she put her hand on his shoulder as she wheeled him toward the door. "I'm glad it's over," he said. "The war. I don't want him to...I hope he never has to do what we did."

"Me too, Sly." If she'd had the chance to have children, what she'd seen in the war would have planted a seed of terror in her heart that her sons might have to don a uniform and lose their lives—or their souls—in battle.

"But I'm very glad you blokes were willing to do it," she said quietly, tightening her hand on him. "Timmy's future, a lot of people's futures, are brighter because of what you all did. Remember that."

Even as she knew he'd also remember, in the graveyard hours of the night, the ones that didn't have a bright future because of what they'd done, what had happened.

They all would.

As she took Sly down the hallway, she left her hand on his shoulder, using the heel of it and the grip on the other handle to push him along, because he hadn't let her go. Then she sensed something, a heat along her nape, and glanced left.

Alistair was standing at the end of the hall. It startled her to see him there, a tall, handsome man with extraordinarily vibrant eyes and an odd stillness to him. Her vampire, not in his normal milieu, but instead in hers. He still managed to overshadow everything around him, that dense energy of his pushing up against the hallway walls and reaching out to her.

The smile that crossed her face was warm and instantaneous. *What are you doing here? I thought you had a meeting.*

I did. I got your message.

She remembered sending the thought in her head, waiting for an answer and getting none.

I decided to deliver it in person. Protect you myself and give Nero the night off.

She'd expected him to smile back at her, but he didn't, so she sent him a quizzical expression. His own was shadowed. *Finish with him and then come to me.*

All right. She wanted to ask if he was irritated by her being late. She knew the rule he'd set, and he'd been adamant about it, but he could be in her head. She'd asked ahead of time, waited for an answer. Since he'd obviously gotten the message, he could have told her no. But his tone in her mind was hard to read. It gave her a little frisson of uneasiness, truthfully. But now wasn't the time to try and manage two conversations.

She took Sly into Timmy's room, aware that Alistair began to walk down the hall, trailing them. As she settled Sly in with Timmy, she suspected he was right outside, leaning against the hallway wall, listening to her talk to the two males, get them acquainted.

She'd made the right call. Timmy took right to Sly and, not having to deal with the awkwardness of his friends and family, their constant worry they might say the wrong thing, Sly relaxed and responded to the boy.

Nina slipped away when Timmy had talked Sly into a game of cards. As she stepped into the hallway, she was surprised not to see Alistair. Frowning, she moved to the stairway exit where he'd been standing. Nothing. Then she realized she might be able to find him another way.

She hadn't tried it before, but she closed her eyes, focused, looked for that line of awareness that existed between them. There. A smile crossed her face. She could feel him. It warmed her, because she knew he could block that connection if he wished. She pushed open the stairwell door and descended in quick steps.

"Playing hide and seek with me, are you, my lord?" she murmured, as she reached the basement level and came out at the boiler room. Her pulse was already tripping at a more rapid pace as she put her hand to the doorknob and slipped in. He'd never come to see her at work, and she realized now she wished he had. After the steps they'd made together recently, him coming to visit her here felt like an additional endorsement of who she was with him.

She was right, that he could block her awareness when he chose, for as she closed the door behind her, the sense of that connection vanished. She blinked, reaching for the main lights to supplement the dim auxiliaries.

She never found the switch. Instead her wrist was clasped in his strong grip as he pulled her back against his body. His other hand dipped, found its way between her legs and rubbed, a hard stroke. She was damp, because as she'd come down the stairs, thinking of him, her body reacted to the mere thought of his presence, what he might want from her. As a result, when he spoke, she expected sensual teasing.

Not menace.

"Would you have given him this, as well as a look at your breasts, if it helped lift his spirits? Perhaps he's not the one that needed the reminder that a nurse isn't a woman paid to have sex with him."

Anticipation was replaced by shock, quickly followed by anger. She wrested away from him, or tried, and was held in place.

"You're done working here," he said flatly. "It obviously detracts from your InhServ training, if you forgot yourself so decidedly."

Now he did let her go, and turned toward the door. With another spurt of astonishment, she realized he was planning to leave on that note. Though her senses were still reeling from the abruptness of the accusation, the coldness of it, the utter strangeness of his behavior, she found her voice.

"I forget nothing, my lord," she said. "But I wonder how far you have to have your head up your arse to be thinking what you're thinking."

He stopped and whipped his head around, those blue eyes frost. "Who do you think you're speaking to?"

"An idiot," she spat.

His gaze narrowed. "An idiot. Yes, I am. For thinking that allowing you to do this would work."

"Is there something you needed that I wasn't providing, my lord? You indicated you didn't need my attendance until later tonight. Has something changed?"

He took a step toward her. "I told you the rule."

"Which is why I reached out to you. Are you saying you decided to come all the way here to tell me no, rather than speaking in my head right then, when I could have made my excuses to Tracy and left before you got in a blue over me being late?"

It didn't make any sense, she realized. She was missing a piece. His jaw worked, showing he was struggling with something, whatever nonsense he was going to say. That was fine. She could say enough for both of them.

"You think because I treat a wounded soldier like a man, remind him he's a man, that it means I'm disloyal? I'd say unfaithful, but there's no value on that in your world, is it? You can be with whomever you wish. I am allowed no claim on you, while you have every claim on me, can follow every whim you wish to take with my life. I even have to ask bloody permission to sleep in the same room as you."

She mimicked him, deepening her voice. 'I'll *allow* you to work as a nurse.' Her lips curled in a snarl. My life's calling, as long as it pleases and doesn't discomfit you. And why does it discomfit you, my lord? I am meeting all the terms you gave me."

"You were late."

"We just covered that. I'd say you're acting like a jealous lover, but that doesn't make sense. There are servants who indulge with other humans as long as it doesn't interfere with what their Master or Mistress needs from them."

His expression hardened. "If their Master or Mistress gives them that permission. You don't have that permission."

"I didn't ask for it, did I? For all the bloody good it didn't do me, there was one thing the training I received from The Mistress did accomplish. Even the things I've learned from you. They've made me more comfortable talking to these men about something that matters deeply to them…how desirable they will be to a woman. Being a nurse has given me the experience to do that and still maintain the proper boundaries. Sly did nothing inappropriate and neither did I. I dare you to say otherwise."

She threw up her chin as his face darkened like thunderclouds. He'd gripped her upper arm, had hauled her up to her toes, but as she threw out the challenge, he said nothing, just stared down at her, his jaw tight.

She took a breath, even as her fists remained just as clenched. It seemed each time they took a step forward, they took two steps back, but she refused to let herself get mired down in that despair. Down that path lay tears, sadness, regrets, yearnings, things that could drain the strength of what she thought they'd shared these past few days. Anger could, too, but anger let her fight off the despair.

"If taking my hand or putting his head on my bosom lets him know that his whole world as he knows it wasn't lost, I will do that. If you had been fully in my mind, you would have known I used how *you* make me feel to give me the confidence to handle it the way I thought best. I didn't ask for this life, but I agreed to honor it, and I do so, every day. I don't bloody well deserve your disrespect."

∾

416

Christ, she really didn't know anything about being an InhServ, or even a vampire's servant. For any of them to stand fast as she was doing and demand respect, of all things...

But why shouldn't she? She could have bolted and run. Could have initially refused, never mind what would have happened to her family. She'd done her best to honor her sister's commitment, done her best to understand what Alistair needed. He had a well-ordered office and a schedule that had improved exponentially thanks to her involvement. They hadn't yet handled any social events together, but from their time with Anahera and Tane, he knew she'd handle those, giving it a sincere effort. And he'd liked being so deep in her mind, helping her get there.

He liked any moment where he felt like she was all his. She said she couldn't imagine her vampire master acting like a jealous lover. Well, she didn't have to imagine it.

He absolutely, fucking was.

I didn't ask for this life. She was right. They took a step forward and tried to pretend the root of it wasn't still there, but it was always ready to crawl in and plant the insidious thoughts that had him acting the way he was acting.

He hadn't focused on her thoughts, only her actions, seen through her eyes, and Sly's. What had set him off wasn't the bloke looking down her dress. She'd be surprised by that, he was sure. It was the peace in Sly's face when she touched his hand, his shoulder. The same kind of peace Alistair had felt when she touched him after the night on the footy field.

For a singular, insane moment, he'd thought of himself as the only recipient of that gift, but he'd just seen it wasn't custom tailored. It was something she gave freely to any who needed it. Evidence of her bone-deep service-oriented nature, yes, but grounded in a deep well of compassion that didn't flag, no matter her surroundings or circumstances.

She did deserve respect, whether it was stamped in the damn vampire-servant etiquette handbook or not. It didn't dissipate the violent aggression in his vampire blood in the slightest, but the logic helped him hammer it down, speak in what he hoped was a reasonable voice. And swallow his pride, another thing he wasn't all that used to doing.

"You're right," he said, and saw the surprise flicker over her face. With a sigh, he moved to a chair that had been left for the maintenance crew and sat down in it. "I tuned in for your moment with Dr. Grant first. It provoked my temper—toward him—and it perhaps made me interpret things incorrectly with your patient."

"I handled Dr. Grant," she told him, a cautious assurance, even as she remained in a defensive posture, her color high. She was still angry.

"Yes, you did. I was going to rip his head off," he said wryly. "But you did me one better. You cut him off at the knees and kicked him in the balls with nothing but your tongue and that steel core of yours. It was a thing of beauty to watch."

She cleared her throat, now looking uncertain. "Well, I didn't do it all myself. I did have to intimate I had a terrifying...boyfriend."

"The man who calls me his," Alistair corrected. "That's what you called me. I quite liked that one." He extended a hand to her. "Come to me, Nina."

She hesitated, which told him under the anger was hurt. An apology was in order, but vampires didn't apologize to their human servants. Strewth, it was just the bloody two of them, wasn't it? Yet he'd been a vampire for three centuries. He knew what was proper and fitting, but what was proper and fitting was not acting like an irrational arse. To find balance, he had to skirt the lines.

"I was jealous," he said. "I was being a jealous prick, and I said something so unbelievably untrue and hurtful, I'm ashamed of myself. I missed you," he said simply. "So when I heard your message in my mind, I decided I'd surprise you, answer you in person. Perhaps take you to dinner in town. I got here, found Nero still waiting on you, sent him home. Came to find you."

"Oh. I'm sorry about being late. I hope..."

"Nina, I told you to come to me. As my servant."

She swallowed, that delightfully nervous gesture that drew his attention to her lovely throat, her soft lips, and then she was moving. Once in motion, there was no hesitation at all, which tightened his heart in his chest.

But as she started to sink to her knees before him, he stopped her long enough to shrug out of his coat, and put it down so she wouldn't snag her stockings on the concrete floor. Or have discomfort in her knees. Then he pressed her down on it, though he noted her head remained up and chin set. He touched it.

"It's true," he said. "I do consider you mine. I liked, very much, knowing not only that you know it, too, but that you relied upon it to handle that arse."

She gazed up at him, and there was confusion and hurt still in her brown eyes. "I consider it true, too, Alistair. More every day, in ways that admittedly make me uncomfortable. I've no idea where three hundred years will take us, but the way you have made me feel, I consider myself loyal, and faithful, to you alone."

"In short, I've commanded your trust, so is it so much to ask for some modicum of the same in return?" he said, echoing her subconscious thought and caressing her flushing cheek. "You do deserve that respect, sweet nurse. I am new to having a female servant, so you might have to be patient with me. Though use your sharp tongue all you want, because it will be my pleasure to vigorously remind you of the consequences of using it on your Master."

The flush deepened. He could easily turn this into a sexual moment, but instead he felt a curious compulsion to keep doing just this. Stroke her cheek, her neck, tangle his fingers in her ponytail. Reaching up, she released the clip and let her hair spill over his hand, unimpeded. She knew he liked it loose like that. Turning her face into his touch, she rubbed, closed her eyes. Her hand fell on his, resting on his other knee. Her fingers curled in between his knuckles.

He brought her in closer between his spread knees, until he had his hand clasped in her hair, palming her skull. He liked doing that, too, something about the delicate shape of it, the way the curve of bone fit into his palm, emphasizing the differences in their strengths, at least physically. He'd been telling her the truth about how strong she was. It impressed him deeply, even as it concerned him, because when such a strong will broke, it was a deep, soul-wrenching thing that needed someone just as strong to hold her together. She wanted him to be that strength. Knew he could do it, had done it before, but she wasn't sure she could rely on it. He'd just underscored that, hadn't he? He was a daft prick for certain.

"You can continue to work here, Nina," he said. "And...I will stop dangling it above you like a carrot. I cannot guarantee that my world will make it possible for you to do it indefinitely, and if ever you are not safe, I may have to curtail it for short periods, but I will not arbitrarily take it away in a fit of temper or pique. All right? I don't want you to have to walk on eggshells about it, or fear it will be taken from you from moment to moment. I know how important this is to you."

He shook his head, corrected himself. "I know how important this is. You do good work and help these lads. You help all your patients. Though Sly might not be thanking you after putting him into interrogation with that young rascal."

A faint smile touched her lips. Her eyes softened, telling him he was somewhat forgiven, but there was a sadness there, too. "I know I'm not the InhServ you were expecting, Alistair. That you are having to make allowances very few vampires would."

You are the servant I want. The only one.

He didn't let her hear that thought, but he did speak. "Vampire relationships with our servants vary. Behind closed doors, it's very different than one might imagine. You might be surprised at what allowances occur." He managed a light smile, but then what grew inside him made that smile disappear. He knew that she'd registered it, as well as the hardness to his eyes and tightness around his mouth, the signs of sternness he intended, to put her full attention upon him.

"I have my own caveat to it. You may continue to work here, and offer men like Sly the comfort you did, but every hand you take, every face you stroke, you will keep a tally of it and tell me of the instances whenever I ask. Then I will punish you. You are right in what you do, but I will be right in what I do as well."

Her initial puzzlement gave way to understanding, and the heat that gathered inside her was a direct result of her mind's acknowledgement of it. She had freedom, but it was backed by the reminder she was his.

She'd stopped there, he realized. Hadn't added property or servant. It was how she'd described it to Mr. Grant, and not because the other words would have given the human world pause.

As the significance of it gripped them both, he murmured the next words. "Lower your gaze."

She did, her fingertips on his knee tightening. He slid away from her, only to lock the door and place a crowbar under the knob to slow down someone with a key coming to service the boiler. Not that he anticipated that, since it sounded like it was running as smoothly as one could wish. He unfastened his belt and slacks, opened them and sat down on the chair. Then he put his hand to her jaw, the side of her throat, and exercised a light upward pressure that told her what he wanted. She rose, graceful as always, and he lifted her to straddle his lap. Cupping his hands around her arse, her skirt gathered around her hips, he sheathed himself in that ready wetness, watching her lips part and her pulse thunder up high in her fragile throat, like a tiny bird's egg.

It was impossibly erotic, doing this to her in her nurse's uniform, with nothing beneath it to slow him down. She gripped his shoulder for balance, but he captured that hand, kissed it, even as he kept his other hand firmly cupped over her arse, pushing her down on him more deeply. She made a low moan in her throat he treasured.

"I do like how you don't wear any knickers, even when you're not around me," he said low. "Because you want me to know you're ready for whatever I desire. I think I shall have to let you work some night-time hours on occasion, so I can surprise you here, just like this."

He considered her fingers thoughtfully, playing with them. His cock was aching, the muscles in thigh and torso tight, wanting to drive into her, but he made himself wait. "If you're going to keep working around males like this bastard Grant, I think I shall have to put a more blatant sign of ownership upon you."

He was aware of how both their bodies vibrated, small movements to destroy concentration. She bit her lip, her pulse rabbiting. Her nipples were pressed against the bra. He wanted to open the dress, cup her breasts and suckle them. He liked watching her come unraveled, lose herself to him. Then he recalled her words.

Do I have to lose myself to have you...

No. She didn't. But by willingly losing herself in him, in what he could do to her, he knew he was dangerously willing to do anything for her. Which his next words proved.

"In human societies where intimacy between unmarried men and women is met with social condemnation, it is acceptable for vampires and servants to avoid difficulties with certain symbols. Like a wedding ring."

Her gaze snapped to his. "There is no wedding," he said quietly, to ensure he didn't raise her hopes. "Just the acquisition of the certificate. It is to maintain the ruse when needed."

"Of course," she said, and she did understand. But the emotions his words had stirred were there for him to feel. She didn't ask for more details. Instead, she slipped her arms around him, pressing her jaw to his temple. A small sound hitched in her throat. He closed his own arms around her, cursing his stupidity even as he exacerbated it.

"Lady Lyssa's mother married her servant years ago, to remove any questions. In her case, they did have a wedding ceremony, so there was no issue of disrespect toward her mother, like how Winifred or Mrs. Clyde treated you. Which, if she was anything like Lyssa herself, I suspect would have been highly inadvisable," he added. "Would you like a wedding ceremony, Nina? It would have to be quiet, something at the house, but if you'd like it, you can have it. Otherwise, it will simply be a matter of paperwork."

Her arms tightened around him. He could see the answer in her mind, a mixture of things, like her. Hopeful and pretty, quiet and dark, a mixture of joy and grief. He held her, moved inside her, and closed his own eyes, caught in the feel of her, the scent of her. She was his. The InhServ program, the unfortunate death of her sister, had made that an official thing, a feudal contract, as it were. She'd accepted that. But that still hadn't made her truly his.

She did trust him, though, trusted him with her heart. Which he understood with a depth of humility and terror he hadn't expected himself capable of anymore.

God help her. God help him to deserve it, and still be everything he had to be in a brutal vampire world.

CHAPTER TWENTY-THREE

"*N*ero, I want to stop at the market. Tessa, one of the girls who helps at the hospital, said they had fresh fruit that would be heavenly on that homemade vanilla ice cream Mrs. C made."

"You're assuming there's any left," Nero said dryly. "After Coleman and the yard boys had at it."

"She assured me she set some aside for Alistair. I'm thinking he'd like the tangy flavor of fruit on top."

"Long as he's good with it," the man said, giving her a look. "It's almost dark. The market is closing."

"Dan is usually there an hour or so after." When Nero merely shot her a look, she blew out a breath. "Fine." She put her fingers to either temple and closed her eyes, humming out a breath like a circus medium. "Oh lord and Master, hear me now. Are you out there? Can I stop and get fruit for your ice cream?"

She started a little at the push of response. It made her lips curve. "Of course Nero's not with me," she said aloud. She cracked open an eye. "Picking me up is just an excuse to shirk his household duties. He's off drinking at the pub as usual."

Nero only lifted a brow, making her chuckle. *It will only take a moment, my lord,* she added in her mind.

Another push, an approval of sorts. "He's good with it, as long as I make it quick, which I will. My feet are killing me."

"I can go in and get them," Nero offered.

"No, I want to pick them out."

She wanted to know when Alistair bit into the fruit tonight that it was one she'd chosen.

Nero pulled up to the curb in front of the market. As he exited the vehicle, scoped the area, she waited. Over the past few weeks, as they drew closer to the scheduled meeting with Donovan, with no signs of trouble from the overlord, she'd begun to feel it was an overabundance of caution. But it was Nero's job, and she wouldn't get him into trouble with Alistair by pushing him to relax some of his vigilance. Not that she expected Nero would.

He opened the door and she stepped out. As he followed her toward the maze of market stalls, she couldn't help teasing him, though. "Are you expecting me to be menaced by stalks of corn. An attack of potatoes?"

"These vendors can be pretty aggressive," he said, giving her a mock stern look. "Oi, watch it now."

She yelped as a fleet of children on bicycles descended upon them, shooting out of the alley around a blind corner. They hadn't seen her or Nero, hence his shout of alarm. She backed into a stall where the displays had been covered in canvas for the night. As Nero had said, most of the market vendors had already closed shop. Dan was further in the recesses, and she retreated a few more feet to get clear. Nero was still in the midst of them, tossing out a few admonishments that made her smile. "Watch where you're going, you little monsters," earned replies along the lines of a cheeky, "Watch yourself, old man."

Except for one little girl's apologetic wave as her legs pumped, her attempt to keep up with the others. "So sorry," she called. "He said to go now. So sorry..."

Nero's eyes narrowed, and his head suddenly snapped up and around, toward Nina. "Nina," he bellowed. "Run toward me."

Nina cried out as his words were lost in the roar of an engine. A truck swerved out and around a parked car, striking Nero and sending him flying. He landed hard against one of the covered displays, rolled and thudded down onto the curb, his head smacking against the drain gate.

Even as she shouted his name, she was already on her way to him to help. But she was stopped abruptly by hard hands that seized her by the waist. A cuff alongside her head had her seeing stars.

Her third mark didn't make her such an easy victim, though. Even through the dizziness, she kicked against the one holding her, wriggled and clawed at the face close behind her head. She was struck again, even as whoever was holding her moved more swiftly than her spinning mind could follow.

Vampire. Only a vampire moved that fast.

Nausea from the concussion of the blows and the rapid movement had her almost losing her lunch, but she managed to hold onto it as she fought. The world passed in a blur, and then she was in darkness. Christ, she was below ground, beneath the streets. She smelled dampness, and then she was tossed into foul, rank water and held there, held under.

She couldn't drown. She was a third mark. She knew that rationally, but she also knew she had to breathe for her own comfort, and when the heart was pumping so fast, oxygen left the body quickly. Plus, immersing her in water brought back too many things. She'd no time to indulge such nonsense, though. Before those traumatic memories could paralyze her, she grabbed for the image of Alistair, holding her gently in the water, kissing her, stroking her, giving her good memories so she could swim in the waves once more...

She went limp, but the vampire holding her was cleverer than that. He waited her out, waited, waited, until she gave it up and began to thrash, her lungs bursting, her mind screaming at the helplessness. Blood and gunfire, staring eyes, swept everything else away. When she was at the peak of that fear and panic, she was hauled up and thrown on the concrete. And kicked.

She rolled with it, tried to get up, and was punched in the face. Blood spurted from her nose and lip, and she dropped to her knees. Her hand landed on loose brick. She gripped it and, when her hair was seized, her body yanked up, probably to take another blow, she smashed that brick into the slightly bent knee before her.

She used all her third mark strength and her knowledge of anatomy, and got lucky. The howl of pain, the loosening of the hand on her head, let her bolt free.

But she was disoriented, and it was pitch dark. For all she knew, she was running deeper into the tunnels. The vampire could smell her but...

Nina, turn around, run the other way. Ladder to the street about fifteen feet away.

She pivoted and bolted, staggering drunkenly. She was vaguely aware of the vampire trying to get to his feet, a silhouette in the darkness. She banged against the ladder, grappled for the rungs and stumbled up them. She made it three steps and was grabbed around the waist, dragged back down.

She was yanked up against a body that was far bigger than hers. One hand nearly circled her throat and the other wrenched her arm up against her back.

"That...was...rude." He had a smooth voice, a drawing room aristocrat voice, but she detected some strain from the knee injury. Good. Her vicious satisfaction disappeared into agony as he drove her shoulder up and it dislocated, tearing a scream from her throat.

Then came a widening spiral of confusion as he slammed her forehead against the metal ladder. The edge bit into her face, terrifying her as she shut her eyes, hoping to protect them, but she couldn't fight with him holding her this way.

Alistair...

Hold on, Nina. Just hold on. I'm coming.

I'll be... Thoughts were swimming in her head, just swimming, first like darting fish, but they were slowing, drifting. *I'll be in the water.* Always in the water, looking for his hand to cut through it, pull her from the depths.

"This is how easy it is, Alistair," that silky voice said. "How easy it is for me to prove your incompetence. Come get your garbage out of my territory. If you dare."

The male vampire dropped Nina at the bottom of the ladder. A few hazy moments later, she realized she was alone. Alone with the drip of water off stone and the fetid smell of sewage and her own blood. Her fingers dug into the rock.

Peaches. I was getting you peaches. Alistair...don't come. No. He wants you to come. Something about what he said, what was it? It worried her. She couldn't get her mind to work. Hell, she probably had a skull fracture, something that would worry her if she didn't know that most everything could be healed with Alistair's blood. But not if he wasn't there, if he walked into a trap. That mattered more than her getting blood.

She had drifted. She was in the water again. Always in the water. Would she ever find joy in it?

Right now, sweet nurse. It's a sunny day on my private stretch of beach. You're floating in the surf, in a swimsuit that shows plenty of bare skin.

I am dying, and you are thinking about sex.

His chuckle in her mind was tight, grim. *If you're dying—which you're not—what would* you *be thinking about?*

Her lips peeled back from her bloodstained teeth. *Killing that bloody bastard.*

A flash of violent heat brought vicious satisfaction. She wasn't alone in that desire. *All in good time. First, I was promised peaches and ice cream.*

Dan...might not stay open late enough.

A hand clasped hers, a touch moved over her, and then she was being lifted. She cried out, and she was lowered. Hands gripped her shoulder, which made her want to bat them away as pain went from red embers back to lightning.

Tell me you love me.

It was a startling demand, and one that had a simple, puzzled answer. *Of course I love you. That's not the problem, you daft man. You can't love me back—*

She screamed as the bone popped back into place, the dislocation relocated. When her vision cleared, she was still fuzzy, aching, in pain, but Alistair had lifted her. He and someone else were taking her up the ladder. She saw Nero's face in the darkness and realized full night had fallen. She didn't know where they were, but it was quiet, just the three of them, so it must be an alley.

"Nero." She sought him with fluttering fingers and he gripped them gently. "You're all right."

"Isn't a truck big enough to knock me out of it, Miss Nina," he said grimly. "Not when some blighter goes after you." His face was worried, his mouth tight and angry as he gazed upon her face, and he spoke low. "Jesus and Mary."

"Put her in the back." Alistair's voice. "Fuck. Now, Nero. Get her out of here."

She could hear other voices, whistles and catcalls. Taunts. Danger was rife and sharp. "Alistair, no."

But Nero was putting her in the car and slamming the door. She tried to struggle up, tried to see where her vampire master was, but the car was in gear and plunging forward. "Alistair... *Alistair*."

Alistair watched the car make the turn around the corner and then pivoted. He said nothing. Merely kept his watchful eyes on the network of fire escape ladders lining the abandoned brick buildings that flanked the alley. Four were hiding in those shadows. He knew all the vampires in Donovan's territory. Donovan was not here with them, but he'd be somewhere, watching.

"Prime reason I'm Region Master and you're not," Alistair said clearly. "I do my own dirty work."

"He sullied his hands with your servant, sure enough," one of the hidden vampires drawled. "If you'd left him more time, could have done more. Fast, speedy car. We'll take that when we're done with you."

Alistair laughed, his fangs flashing. "Come and try, then."

They came out of the gloom. Three males, one female, varying ages, all younger than him. Donovan was testing. That was fine. Alistair had his own tests.

"I'm your Region Master, mates. You attack me, you earn a death sentence, whether you reap it in this alley, or I decide to take it later."

"We kill you, Donovan gets to be Region Master."

The sorry thing was, they were likely right about that. Donovan would have some smooth explanation for why Alistair was too weak to hold the Region, and had got himself killed, and it was best if the Region Master post went back to a born vampire, blah blah blah. The European-based Council would accept it, because who gave a shit about Australia? Even if Lyssa came to his defense, a posthumous defense wouldn't really change the outcome.

It was a good thing he didn't plan to die or relinquish his role as Region Master. The title he'd taken on reluctantly was a surprisingly good fit at the moment, with cold rage pumping through him. But he knew against whom it should all be directed.

"You decide not to do this, the repercussions won't be as serious against you. You do it, at least one of you won't leave this alley alive, and the other three will wish they'd done anything else tonight rather than serve their overlord's futile political agenda."

The one who leaped first was another big son-of-a-bitch, big like Donovan, but not as old and experienced. But he didn't come alone, two more coming with them. Fine then. If it was a fight they wanted, a fight they'd have. He pictured Nina's bleeding, ripped face, felt the pain she'd suffered as he popped the bone back in, and had all the fuel he needed.

He'd said one would die, because there really weren't enough vampires in Australia to carelessly sacrifice more than was needed for the lesson. But holding back was going to take some effort. He wanted to murder every one of them.

He'd throw Donovan's body on the top of the heap and watch them all burn.

Nina struggled up out of darkness with a cry, and then realized she was against Alistair. Lying in his bed, his arm around her. She breathed, evening out her heart rate, pressing her forehead against his bare chest. He wore loose lounge pants on his lower body and, as she settled back against him, she nestled her feet against his. Hers were cold and his weren't.

"Bad dream," she muttered. "And—"

She sat bolt upright and winced, her hands going to her face and finding bandages there. Alistair's touch was upon her fingers, drawing them gently away.

"The vampire...Nero..."

"It's all right," he told her firmly, drawing her back down. "It's sorted for now."

Her shoulder was sore, but not nearly as much as she would have expected it to be.

"Third mark healing abilities. Even without my blood, it kicks in faster than for a mortal. When you take some of my blood, the cuts on your face will heal up, leaving you as lovely as ever."

She was getting her wits about her, remembering. Which made her look closer at him. He was lying against his bent arm, his other hand stroking her lightly from shoulder to hip and back again. He looked like Alistair, only more tired. Paler. She noted then that, while he had no open wounds, there were marks upon him, like healing scars.

"The young ones Donovan sent after me got in a few good shots here and there. I'll be glad to train up the ones who survived as allies." At her expression, he added, "Here you thought putting up with me was the worst part of being a vampire's servant. I suppose no one mentioned to you the politics."

"I guess they assumed I had enough to handle, the whole sex slave deal, and how to set up a twelve-person dinner."

Alistair shuddered. "That last would make me prefer the politics. Maybe. The sex slave stuff doesn't sound bad."

"Oh really?" She tipped her head back. "You'd be okay being a sex slave?"

"I'm male. The only word I heard there was sex."

She managed a smile, and then the quiver in her belly made its way up to the corners of her mouth. Alistair's gaze shadowed and he stroked the side of her face. "It's all right," he murmured. "I'm sorry, Nina. So sorry."

"It's not that," she managed, pressing her face to his chest. Her fingers had curled around his biceps, holding on to his strength. He'd come for her. Kept her safe again. Though she knew there was some truth to it that the danger had come because she was part of his world, there were other things she knew. She remembered the hellfire in his eyes, the regret and fury. She saw the remnants of what had been serious wounds on his body, and felt far more emotions beneath the surface of his casual words than he was expressing. Maybe it was her third mark connection that allowed that perception. Maybe it was simply having a deeper understanding of what to look for after a man had been in battle. But she wouldn't be an additional burden to him.

"It's not that," she repeated, with a sniffle. "This is nothing. You should see the drama when nurses get in a blue with one another. It's the darn peaches making me cry. I really wanted those tonight."

"Well, women always fight dirtier. And no worries. Dan sent a delivery boy with the peaches." He wrapped both arms around her, held her close as she continued to cry quietly against him, getting it out. Even as she held him back and kept saying, "It's all right. We're all right."

"Yeah, we are."

At length, she lifted her head, looked up at him. She didn't want him to think she was falling apart. A good cry could give a woman strength. The strength to tease.

"The lengths I have to go to, in order to be in your bed," she said. "It's rather ridiculous."

"I expect I'll have to let you share it with me from here forward then," he said seriously. "Someone did mention it was a large bed."

He stroked a new fountain of tears away from her face, but his eyes were on the bandages. "I want you to take some of my blood now," he said quietly. "I can't bear to see you in pain."

"They don't hurt much at all. You need blood, too."

"You first," he said firmly. Reaching over her, he drew a knife from the nightstand drawer. It pressed her to her back, his chest against hers, and she reached up to caress his throat and shoulder. He dipped his head, kissed her wrist, and she feathered her fingers over his face. His blue eyes lifted, held hers.

"Can we take one another's blood at the same time?" she asked shyly. "I'd like...to feel that."

He nodded slowly, and then lifted his wrist, making the cut with clean precision before he brought it to her mouth. She curled her hands over his forearm as he shifted behind her, his other arm going around her waist and snugging her up against him, her backside in the cradle of his thighs. His firm cock pressed against her, and his breath teased the back of her shoulder as she turned her head toward the edge of the pillow, presenting her artery more conspicuously. All while she sealed her mouth over the cut he'd created and began to lick away the blood.

She arched, pressing her arse more firmly against him, as he sank his fangs into her throat and began to take strength from her as she was from him. His free hand moved over her abdomen, caressing. She wore nothing, his preference when she was in his bed, and her thighs loosened as his touch descended.

My beautiful servant...so willing to please...

The words made her tremble, the truth of them giving her pride in her Master's pleasure, not worrying her as they might have done in the very recent past. She moaned against his flesh, her tongue curling around the tangy richness of his blood, as his fingers eased into the wetness between her legs.

He was testing her readiness, she realized, for his hand withdrew, and then he was pushing the lounge pants down and out of the way so he could guide his cock into her from behind. His palm returned to flatten itself on her lower abdomen, holding her at the right angle for that penetration, one he punctuated with short, slow movements that rubbed her inside and sent sensation spiraling through her. She began to move with him, God bless third mark healing abilities.

She kept her mouth pressed against the cut, no longer drinking but helping the wound to close. She'd noted that the blood ran faster when she was drawing on it, and closed quickly when she didn't.

When a servant is feeding upon her Master, the flow increases, to provide what she needs.

Tears stung her eyes at that, the tightness in her stomach moving higher, to her heart, when he added, *A servant's blood does the same. Squeeze down on me. I love to feel the grip of your cunt, sweet nurse.*

She obeyed, and gasped at the result. She continued to grip his forearm in both hands, an anchor as they rose and fell together, building toward that pinnacle. When they reached it, she waited, holding, holding.

She was waiting for his permission. That brought tears as well, but they weren't painful tears. Tears of change and acceptance, that life might not be what she expected...but she couldn't say anymore that it wasn't what she wanted.

His arm constricted across her body, holding her closer, suggesting he'd heard the thought, and it mattered to him. A great deal.

"Come for me, precious servant," he whispered.

She released only seconds before him, and relished his hard groan, the way his body tightened to keep the movements controlled, as the position demanded from them both.

When they were done, he slid from her, but stayed pressed against her backside. She stroked his arm, back and forth, her eyes upon the wall before her, but her mind wholly in the grip of his.

"This wasn't really what you wanted for your life either, was it?" she said quietly.

"What? A gorgeous, willing sex slave in my bed?" He chuckled when she reached back and attempted to swat him, which he thwarted by gripping her wrist. He brought her arm further behind her, first kissing her palm and then lowering her hand, guiding it so it was behind her back. Molding his hand around her fingers, he made her cup his sated cock and testicles. He pressed into that grip with a hum of satisfaction, and bade her leave it there with a squeeze. His now free hand returned to fondle and stroke her breasts.

"You know what I meant," she said, trying to stay focused when he seemed determined to arouse her again.

I'll have you again before I sleep. But he spoke aloud to answer her question, and when he did, his hand upon her slowed, rested upon her breast, and his tone became thoughtful. "Yes, and no. Same reason I went to war, every time. I don't like it when others take more than their share. But I'd prefer everything be solved with a good footy match."

She couldn't disagree with either statement. "Who was that, who attacked us?"

"Donovan. It's always Donovan. Always testing, and tonight he went too far. He attacked you and Nero, and pulled four of his territory vampires into it. I've taken blood from the survivors, a sire's portion, so that I'll not only know where they are, but what they're bloody thinking, if they have a single disloyal thought. It's the primary way to determine what a vampire is doing, get into his head like that. And you can make inroads into his overlord or Region Master's head too, if..."

He broke off abruptly. Sensing the sudden tension in his body, Nina twisted her head around to look at him. He released her and sat up, raking his fingers through his disheveled hair. "Damn it," he swore.

His gaze held more than anger. It was a trace of the haunted grief he carried within him toward his fallen brethren, mixed with frustration and something that suggested he wasn't entirely sure what to feel. She put it together with his words and sat up next to him, dread gripping her.

"You think he's done that to someone you thought was loyal to you. Who, and why do you think that?"

"I have an inkling of who," he said grimly. "As to the why, it's the only way what Donovan did tonight makes sense. He's too aware of my movements, yours and Nero's schedule. My relationship with you.

The political insults he's throwing my way, about my weaknesses... they're drawing on knowledge he shouldn't have."

"What weaknesses?"

He glanced at her. She was beginning to read his cues, and knew he was a breath from pulling back from her. That detachment was sometimes about the things they couldn't quite work out with one another, but other times it was about protecting her. She could tell this was one of those times.

But she was his servant. She wasn't going to be shut out if she could help it. Her mind was working faster now that she had blood to rejuvenate her. "Me. I'm a weakness. Because you let me work at the hospital, and you're not taking me with you to the things where it's expected an InhServ would be at your back. You're showing a softness toward me that says you're maybe not the right one to be Region Master."

"It's only one more bogus thing he's using to prop up his position. He has plenty others."

When she opened her mouth to say more, he pressed her back into the bed, abruptly on top of her again, his body pressed insistently between her legs, his eyes sparking. When he spoke, his voice was low, even, and as dangerous as a snake about to strike.

"If you're truly mine, then what I say you can and can't do is my bloody business. Those who consider that a weakness will learn differently, quick enough. Understand me?"

She swallowed. Managed to whisper her fingers across his jaw, and got pricked by a fang. "Yes, Master."

He sucked the drop of blood away, then brushed his lips across her mouth. "Good."

Before she could rally from that, he left the bed and picked up his clothing. "Get dressed, sweet nurse. Raise Stanley on the phone and inform him his Region Master wants to see him. Right now."

CHAPTER TWENTY-FOUR

*T*hough Alistair didn't indicate he needed her in attendance, he didn't command her not to be. She wasn't sure if she would have obeyed him if he had.

When Stanley arrived, she was dressed in slacks and a blouse, hair and makeup done so she was put together exactly as an InhServ should be. She was also at the front door. As she stood in the foyer, watching for his arrival, she saw Nero in the opening to the kitchen. Alistair had disappeared soon after confirming Stanley was on his way, but she knew he was in his study and wanted time to himself. She wasn't sure what was happening in his mind, what plan of action he had, but she reluctantly gave him his space to determine it.

"Quiet in here," she noted to Nero.

"Alistair sent the rest of the staff home, except for me and Coleman. He's around the back."

She held Nero's gaze as they both listened to Stanley mount the veranda stairs. The butler was almost as still and calm as Alistair was before he did something deadly, but he unbent enough to reach out, pass a surprisingly gentle and paternal knuckle down her face. "That looks much better. Still hate seeing any evidence of it there."

"I am far tougher than I look. A little scrape is all it was."

"Mmm." Nero looked toward the door, but Nina put a hand on his arm.

"I'll get this one." Clearing her throat, pulling herself out of the harrowing possibilities that Nero's explanation for the staff's absence had conjured in her head, she moved to the entrance and opened it before Stanley had to knock. She offered a cordial nod. "Mr. Welch."

Stanley wore his usual jaunty hat, with a grey suit and a slim pink tie. His shoes were shined. For all that his tongue could run amok, he always came to Alistair properly dressed. She wondered if there was some extra polish to him this time, though. Was that because he was confident of Donovan's backing, or was he trying to make a better show of himself to Alistair?

As bad a start as she'd had with Stanley, she'd come to realize his rough and crude ways were as Alistair had said, a function of his raising and experience. He didn't have a bad heart. But he was a vampire. As she gazed upon him, she realized she didn't know whether to treat him as foe or misguided fool. Or an outright enemy who'd helped ambush her Master.

Her expression must have warned him, because rather than his jovial crudity, he stepped into the foyer and gave her a fairly sedate nod before he attempted his normal demeanor. "Nina. Where's his high and mightiness then?"

"In his office."

"I know the way."

She nodded, but fell in behind him. When they reached the doorway, she stayed at the threshold as Stanley entered. Alistair was sitting at his desk, looking out at the beach in darkness. Only one lamp was on. It threw shadows in the corner but highlighted the planes of his face, the deep set in his eyes, making them more severe as he turned them toward Stanley. He rose.

"What's up, then?" Stanley asked. He'd removed his hat, was turning it in his hands. Nina was going to step forward, ask if he wanted her to take it, offer him a drink, but she was waiting for Alistair's lead. She was aware of Nero, another shadow in the hallway, and suddenly recognized the tone of all of this. Violence. Impending, inevitable violence. Then, before she could act, Alistair had.

It was both terrifying and absurd, how quickly a vampire could do something. Almost no noise at all, just a flutter of wind, and Stanley was crumpled on the floor like a balled-up piece of paper. Back curled, head tucked in as Alistair kept his hand clamped on his neck, his forehead shoved at a painful angle to his knees.

"Who do you take me for, Stan?" Alistair said, his voice laden with menace. "Think I'm a fool because I had mercy on you? That makes two of us at the moment."

"What? I don't know what—"

Alistair twisted him around, seized his arm and wrenched it. The sound of the break was a sharp crack, drowned out by Stanley's raw scream. Nina gasped, feeling a sympathetic shard of pain through her recently dislocated arm, but in the time she'd experienced that, Alistair had already shoved him to the ground again. Stanley shrank into a fetal ball, but he didn't curl everything in fast enough. Alistair stepped on the arm, pinning it, and earned another shriek.

"Alistair." Nina had tried to lunge into the room, but Nero was holding her around the waist, pulling her back. He couldn't silence her, though. "Alistair, don't. Don't do this to him. He's not fighting you."

He wasn't. He could have tried, but Stanley was simply trembling, helpless. Submissive to a stronger animal who might just kill him where he lay. It twisted something in Nina's belly, something terrible, as much to see Alistair doing it as Stanley surrendering to it.

"What world do you think you live in, Stanley?" Alistair demanded. His expression was deadly cold and calm, his eyes twin shards of ice.

"Same one I always have. Do what I got to do to survive. Vampire, human, don't matter. Always the same. Always."

Stanley raised his head when he said the words, and the glassy-eyed glare he gave Alistair had some surprising defiance to it. With a heavy helping of despair. He cringed as Alistair pulled his foot away, but only to crouch over the hapless male in a swift, angry movement.

"Maybe what never changes is you. Not the world." Alistair shoved his knee into Stanley's side as he seized his hair. "When did it happen? How did you let him get into your head? And when did you agree to hide it from me?"

He punctuated each question with a hard jab to Stanley's face. Blood spurted. Nina was catapulted back to that underground drain, with Donovan slamming her head into the ladder, over and over. He hadn't wanted anything from her, had merely wanted to send a message to Alistair, but here was more of the same. Always more of the same, hurting and killing, hurting and killing some more.

"For the love of God, stop, Alistair. Please. *Stop.*"

She couldn't bear it. It was in the broken quality of her words, somewhere between a hoarse shout and a desolate scream. She didn't expect it to get through. Like Stanley, she'd given up on the world being a place where people could change, but perhaps just like his defiant taunt, her scream was for her. A voice in the wilderness thrown out to ears that might hear.

Alistair's head went up. The eyes he fastened upon her were still fierce with anger, but she felt the questing beneath it, him reaching out to her, to steady her. No words, just feelings, emotions. He could see in her mind, see the images of violence and death, and he had his own. Perhaps it was his reflection upon them both that pulled him back.

With a sound of disgust, he spat on the carpet next to Stanley, made him flinch again, but Alistair let him go and stood. Nero's grip loosened, but Nina stood in place, staring at her vampire master. He wasn't breathing or moving. He was a statue, his gaze fixed upon her.

She assumed and hoped looking at her, instead of the object of his displeasure, might calm him. Instead, gazing upon her recently damaged face seemed to be drawing the anger back to him, for the storm cloud of energy intensified once more.

If he went at Stanley again, she was certain Alistair would kill him. She could think of no other reason he'd sent the rest of the staff home and Nero had that executioner's watchful look on his face. The most unlikely butler ever.

It was about her, she realized with a shock. What had been done to her. Even now, Alistair wouldn't say that in front of another vampire, giving the whole lot more ammunition against him, but she saw it clearly in his eyes. And that was all that mattered, wasn't it?

May I go to him, Master? See what I can do to help?

Alistair gave her a barely perceptible nod and turned back toward the window.

She moved swiftly to the other vampire, knelt beside him. Medically she didn't know what needed to be done, if anything. She was certain Alistair wouldn't allow her to give him blood. But she checked the break on the arm.

Because she'd been curious about their anatomy and extraordinary healing abilities, during the in-between times at the InhServ school, few though they were, she'd asked questions. Vampire bones tended to knit correctly, even if a bone was sticking through the skin, which this one fortunately was not, but trying to set it in place accelerated the healing process, made it somewhat more comfortable.

She could also maybe save the younger vampire's life as she did it. After she sent Nero for her medical kit, she spoke in a calm voice. "Stanley, what happened?"

With a man's embarrassment, Stanley swiped impatiently at the tears that were leaking out of his eyes.

"I didn't think none of it. Nothing," he said, his feverish gaze flickering up to a stone-faced Alistair who still wasn't looking at him. "He just...he didn't say nothing bad about you. Just wanted to shag a bit, and then he bit me while we was...you know. I didn't realize he'd...that he'd marked me like a sire. I know it's hard to miss, but he was pretty good timing-wise, and I guess it was lost in that moment, when he had me bucking under him. And I..."

"And when he was digging into your brain to find out things about me, you didn't notice that?" Alistair spoke tightly.

"Well, once I knew...I couldn't keep him out. I tried. Once." His cheeks colored, and he looked away, his fists clenching and unclenching. "I tried," he said softly. "I know I don't deserve to live, Ali. My lord." He swallowed, as if realizing he'd lost the right to call her Master familiar. "I get it. Just know I'm sorry."

Nina lifted her gaze to Alistair. *Please, my lord. He's right. He's done what he needed to do to survive.*

So have you. And you didn't sell your soul to do it.

His gaze went back to the crumpled man on the floor, but she saw his expression flicker with something other than a killing rage and pressed her advantage.

Only because I haven't been backed into the corners he has been. I suffered a moment of hurt, Alistair. I'm fine now, thanks to your blood and your quick thinking. He may not have acted as your ally, but he's not your enemy. And he is your friend.

Vampires don't have friends.

Of course they do. You do. Three of us are in this house right now. It's nonsense for you to say otherwise.

He glanced at her. She couldn't have found a smile to save her life, not in this environment where death and vengeance hovered so close, but when she saw the easing of his jaw, she felt a tentative spurt of relief.

"Step back, Nina," Alistair said flatly.

She understood she needed to comply immediately and did so, but it took effort. Stanley's gaze stayed on Alistair's as her Master moved forward, dropped on his heels a few feet from him. Alistair tented his hand on the floor, tapped it, his moody attention on the connection before he lifted his head and pinned Stan with a hard look.

"If I kill you, I kill a symptom. I want to eradicate the disease. Will you never learn how to be more than a hustler, Stanley?"

"I'm not strong enough to—"

"You could have told me, soon as it happened. That mark he gave you can go both ways. I can get access to his mind. If he detects it, he'll resist me, and you'll have to stand fast, you understand? Even if he doesn't, this will be uncomfortable, invasive. Tracing vampire-to-vampire marks isn't easy on the go-between. I'm going to have to tunnel deep."

Stanley paled, if such a thing was possible for a vampire. A hard quiver ran through his taut body. Alistair had just broken his arm, and yet it was now that vulnerability gripped Stan's features. The fingers of his non-injured hand curled into a fist. Not to show aggression, but to contain fear.

From the flicker in Alistair's gaze, he understood the reaction. And so suddenly, did she. She rose when Alistair did, coming between the two men. "My lord," she said softly. "Can we speak?"

"Later." As he began to move around her, she shifted with him, put out a hand. Alistair's gaze snapped to her. What she was doing was against all the vampire-servant rules, especially doing it in front of Stanley. She was inviting Alistair's displeasure...and a requirement that he punish her for overstepping her place. But she had an oath that superseded all others.

"Please, my lord." *Has he not been violated enough in his life? At some point, his mind was broken, and he lost the ability, the strength, to resist, to fight. He learned there was no hope in it. That he could only go with the currents, and pray that he was never caught between Scylla and Charybdis. As I said, you are his friend.*

In this, I must be his Region Master first.

Truly? See him, my lord. He trembles. He'd rather you break all his limbs than do this to him. Isn't there a way to get what you wish and not harm him further? You did it with me. Please, I beg you. Do it with him.

Step back, Nina. Or I will have Nero remove you.

She closed her eyes at his impassive expression, but shifted away. Not far, though, her body tense. He gave her one more warning look before he dropped to one knee by Stanley.

Stanley kept his eyes down, his fists clenched. Alistair reached out, and when his hand settled on Stanley's shoulder, he flinched, then grimaced, as if he detested showing the weakness.

If he was like anyone else who'd kicked Stanley around in his life, Alistair suspected he would have masked the flinch, shown off more of that paper-thin layer of defiance. But Stan was more vulnerable to Alistair. Emotionally. Alistair ran his free hand over his face. Damn the woman. His grip tightened. "Stan, look at me."

Stanley slowly raised his gaze to Alistair's. "I need to be sure," Alistair explained. "Know for sure what he's done, what he might be planning. So I can justify how I'll need to handle it. I'll need to reach through you to get to him, to find it. I can do it without your permission. I can do it, even if you resist. But what I'd prefer, mate, is if you'd help me. If you'd trust me, let go. I'd rather not hurt you if I can help it. It's uncomfortable, but if we work together, it's not...it doesn't have to feel like it's against your will."

Alistair paused, his eyes locking with Stan's to make the point. "It can be your choice."

Stanley stared at him, and his lip quivered in a way that looked painful, if how he ducked his head to hide it were any indication. "Don't deserve that," he muttered. "I fucked up."

"Yeah, you did. You do it again, I will kill you." Alistair kept his tone mild, though Stanley would know he meant every word. "But maybe you'll trust me next time, enough to tell me when someone's taken advantage of you. You're mine, Stanley."

Stanley's head lifted again, his expression cautious. Alistair nodded at his look.

"Everyone in my Region is. If you fuck up, you're mine to rake over the coals or exact judgment upon. But if someone is taking advantage of you, it's also my job to fuck them up, teach them that I'm not a door mat. That if they mess with someone who's mine to protect, they'll pay the price for that. We have to correct Donovan's illusion he can step out of line just because he's a fucking born vampire. Don't we?"

Stan's jaw looked firmer now, though his eyes were glassy with more unshed tears. "Yeah," he managed. "Sounds good."

"Okay." Alistair shot Nina a look. "You can help me punish Miss Busybody for being a goddamn pain in my arse later."

"Take a braver man than me, mate, to lay a finger on that one."

Alistair lifted a brow. "Is that because she scares you, or I do?"

"Both." Stan shifted his gaze to her and Nina felt a moment of shock at what she saw in his face.

"My apologies, for what I said about you, that first day," the younger vampire said with an odd formality. "You're far more than just a willing bit of quim."

As apologies went, the wording could use some work, but since vampires never apologized to humans, she wasn't going to quibble over it. She accepted the offering, just as formal and gracious.

"Thank you, Mr. Welch. Stanley."

Stanley attempted a half smile, and drew a deep breath that quavered only a bit. He looked at Alistair again. "What do I need to do?"

"Nina, come here. Get him as comfortable as you can. I'll pour him a stout whisky."

"Don't mess with a glass. The bottle's enough," Stanley managed, though he muttered it to his knees, swiping at his eyes once more.

"It's expensive whisky. You're lucky I'm not making you drink ocean water," Alistair said.

"Here you go." Nina helped Stan to a sitting position. Nero had returned, and she spent a few moments setting the bone in the vampire's arm, best she could with the knowledge she had, and wrapping it. Stanley was far more stoic about it, despite the pain level she knew was no different for a vampire than a human. When she was done, she gave Stanley a damp cloth so he could wipe his face, and had Nero bring an ice pack for his nose and mouth, swollen from Alistair's fist.

Nero brought something else as well. A packet of blood. Alistair added a generous portion to the whisky, and handed it to Stanley.

"Blood from a local unmarked donor," Alistair said. "Randomly chosen to ensure it's clean. We keep a stock. It should heal everything up pretty fast. One of these days, you might find yourself a third mark, so I don't have to waste my liquor or blood reserves on you."

"Yeah, lesser miracles have happened." Stanley downed the drink in a few swallows. It helped in a matter of minutes. His shirt, as well as her slacks and blouse, were marked with blood, but that was okay.

Alistair next had her take a seat between Stanley's spread and bent knees, pressing her back up against his chest. Alistair directed Stan to curl his arms around her waist, drop his head to her shoulder. "Just hold onto her. Not too tight. Don't break her, and don't bite her, or I'll defang you. But breathe with her. Measure heartbeats. Relax. She has a steadiness, like a ticking clock. Don't worry about anything. Don't tighten up. Like the first time I buggered your arse, remember if you tighten up, it hurts worse."

"You wanted it to hurt, then."

Alistair gave him a feral, very male look. "Yeah, I did. And you did, too. Neither of us wants this to, though. Start breathing."

Stanley dropped his head to Nina's shoulder. Following instinct, she lifted her hand to his face, stroked his cheek, his hair, held his forearm across her midriff. Nina met Alistair's eyes, and then briefly lifted the hand across her stomach to cup his cheek. *Thank you.*

He pressed his mouth to her palm. *I mean it. I'm taking a strip out of your arse later for defying me. But thank you, too. I would have been pissed at myself later for roughing him up. Like kicking a damn psychotic puppy. How he's lived this long...*

His grumbling subsided into his usual mantra about Stanley, so she smiled and closed her own eyes, letting him work. Because Alistair kept his mind open to hers, letting her see how things unfolded, she felt the amazing structure of it, the way his mind reached into Stanley's.

Let me know if that nurse's radar of yours registers any distress from him that I might miss focusing on other things. I was telling the truth. It won't be comfortable, but if he relaxes, it should go okay.

He needn't be worried. Stan did trust Alistair, in a way that she saw moved her Master, even as it worried him, as Stanley's vulnerability always did. He truly did consider it a miracle the male had survived the brutality of their world this long. It gave her a harrowing glimpse of the realities he'd shielded her from until now. If Stanley hadn't ended up under Alistair's direct supervision, he might have ended up with someone far worse.

Like Donovan, who'd regularly rape his mind and body with no care for either. After all, Stanley had been a prostitute. To some, that meant Stanley had sold his heart and soul with his body.

She saw that in Stanley's mind, that Donovan had said that to him when he took him down the first time. Nina's hand tightened over his forearm as she saw the terrible things Donovan had done to his body and mind that night, until Stanley begged for mercy.

Easy, Nina. My mind is open, so your emotions are filtering to him. Don't take him to a bad place.

She redirected immediately. It was simple common sense, knowing a patient in the right state of mind accepted a treatment better than one in the wrong place. As she projected good images, Alistair at the footy game, he and Stanley sharing a cigar on the rooftop deck, Stanley relaxed further, gave himself to Alistair's penetration of his mind and deeper, deeper...

As a third mark, Alistair had direct access to all corners of her soul. She could no more resist it than a blade of grass the pressure of the wind, and the flow was as simple, easy. A vampire marked by another vampire had a whole arsenal of conscious and unconscious shields against a full soul invasion, and the alarms for them could be tripped by what Alistair was doing, looking for that link to another vampire's mind, multiple layers of shielding.

Stanley shuddered, and she tightened her grip, stroking his jaw once again, pressing her cheek to his. His body was quivering, and she murmured to him, incoherent, soothing sounds. And followed another instinct she had.

"Easy, man. Easy. He's your Master, too," she whispered. "You are not his servant, but you are his man. In his service. In his care. This honors that protection. He deserves your devotion. Your trust. Believe in him, and he will care for you. He's never failed me. Relax and let him in. You don't need to fight him. He won't hurt you."

Stanley's breath left him, another little shudder, and she felt Alistair sink deeper. Deep as he needed to go. She continued to murmur to and stroke the other vampire until, after what seemed like a long while, she felt Alistair begin to withdraw from him. It was only then she realized Alistair had shifted. He was sitting behind Stanley, arms around them both. He gazed at her over Stanley's bent head. Then he was rising to squat at Stanley's side, touching the male's arm.

"Stan, mate. Drifted off on me there, did you? Taking a nap?"

The male vampire lifted his head, looking at Alistair a bit blearily. "No, my lord. Just…thought it might be better if I let myself go a bit hazy. Used to do that for the harder clients, you know."

Alistair cupped the back of his head and pressed his forehead to Stanley's. "Don't do something like this again, mate. Don't make me kill you. Got enough bodies on my conscience. Hear?"

Stanley nodded, his eyes closing. Alistair cleared his throat, then ran brisk fingers through Stan's thick, tousled hair, tugging a little. When Stanley lifted his head, Alistair managed a smile. Stanley shoved at him, mates picking on one another.

"Show some respect. This hair is a full-time job."

"I've no doubt."

Stan paused, registering the tightness of Alistair's jaw. "Did you get what you needed? If you need to go in again…"

"I don't. I have what I need." Alistair's gaze shifted to Nina. "What happened at the market was a distraction. His next target is the hospital."

"What?" Alarm filled her. "What is he going to do?"

"His man Curtis did explosives during the war. It seems to have something to do with that."

She scrambled to her feet even as Stanley spoke, his brow furrowed. "If his intent was to kill your servant at the hospital, why'd he attack her first? He'd have to know that would keep her from going back, at least for a while."

"He doesn't care if Nina is there or not. The whole chain of events is intended to unbalance me, and prove to the Council I have no control of my Region, nor even of my servant, allowing her to work. An explosion, connected to her, to a human hospital with mass casualties, would lead back to me, attracting undue attention from the human world. I would be forced to pack us up and leave after a human tragedy of that magnitude. Leave the Region altogether."

He glanced down at Stanley, resting under his hand, his cheek lying on Alistair's biceps.

"So what do we do?" Nina asked, quelling her natural desire to race for the hospital, to do she knew not what. Tracy was on shift today.

Dr. Jones. All the faces of people she knew flashed through her mind, patients and nursing staff. God, the children's ward. "Does Donovan know you know?"

"I don't think so. Thanks to Stanley remaining so relaxed, I was barely a feather brush in his mind." Alistair's hand tightened on her. *I will go find the explosives, if he's put them in place, and take care of it. Stay here.*

It was still full dark. He might also run afoul of Donovan and more of his vampires. "Alistair, I know that hospital. I know people who can help us there."

"You are going nowhere near that hospital."

"Alistair—"

"You will not cross me on this, Nina. I won't lose you. I'm not standing over another destroyed body. Particularly yours."

He spoke baldly, in front of Stanley, and gripped her shoulder, his thumb against the base of her throat. "You promise me."

She would do no such thing. It didn't take an extremely clever person to know that Donovan would likely have traps ready just in case. Alistair shifted his attention to Stanley and Nero. "You keep her here. Even if you have to lay hands on her."

"Going to have to let your butler handle that, because you can't go there without some kind of backup, mate," Stanley said. He struggled to his feet, planted them with a determined look. And started to sway. Nina and Nero caught him before he crumpled.

"Damn it to fucking hell," the young male said.

"Yeah. It takes something out of you," Alistair said. He put a hand on Stanley's shoulder, a palm against Nina's face, looked hard at both of them, then at Nero. "Just stay here, the lot of you. We'll have tea when I get back and hash out what's left to be done."

His attention came back to Nina, and his blue eyes were suddenly deep enough to drown in, a storm that held her in its powerful turmoil. *I know your courage. But let me do this without the distraction of worrying about you. I can reach out to your mind if I need guidance at the hospital. It will be as good as you standing beside me.*

No, it wouldn't. But he was going to go without her, and there was nothing she could do about it. She understood the why, but it still frustrated her. She gripped his wrist, digging her nails into his skin. "You better succeed, or I'll be right angry with you, my lord."

He almost smiled, though it didn't reach his eyes. "Take care of Stanley," he said. He pulled her to him, a hard, rough kiss, over too soon, and then he was gone.

She ran down the hallway, and came out the front entranceway, in time to hear and then see his car start up and peel out of the drive, spitting gravel. She stood on the veranda, hands clenched as helplessly as Stan's had been. *Keep him safe*, she prayed. She knew how futile that could be if the Fates were already decided, but it was all she could do at the moment. *Please keep him safe, damn you.*

"Miss Nina." Nero had followed her, probably dropping Stan on the floor like a sack of potatoes to stay on her heels. She turned to him.

"Nero, can't you... I don't know. Oh, bloody hell."

"I can't leave you, Miss Nina. He's made it clear you're my charge. He's depending on me to let him know if this is a ruse by Donovan to draw him out and away from you. In case."

Though she didn't know why Donovan would bother with her again when he easily could have killed her, maybe it was as Alistair said. If he kept him off balance, chasing his tail, not sure what Donovan would do next, it would suit his ultimate purpose. Though she had a terrible fear Donovan's ultimate purpose was to be rid of Alistair altogether, not just deposed as Region Master.

She didn't give a damn about what made sense. But when it seemed there was nothing to be done, she'd do what she knew how to do.

Going back inside, she returned to Alistair's study. Stanley was still sitting on the floor, looking steadier but still not quite up to being on his feet by himself, so she and Nero helped get him onto the couch and she sent Nero for a fresh ice compress for his still swollen face. Stan sat upright there, obviously attempting to pull it together.

"Never had a mind probe done before," he grunted. He'd managed to secure the bottle Alistair had left on the side table and took a healthy swig from it now. "How do you servants manage it all the time like that?"

Nina extricated the whisky from his hand with a reproving look and poured more in his glass. "A vampire getting into a vampire's mind is a far craggier terrain than it is for a Master in the mind of his third mark. Alistair describes it like sinking into melted butter."

"A good thought. Never had a servant yet, but that sounds a lot like sinking into a willing arse. Might have to think harder on it."

She shook his head at his unconscious crudity, and he flushed a little. "Got to work on my manners some, don't I?"

"No more than I do on my InhServ etiquette," she said truthfully, and surprised a smile out of him. No sense pretending with someone else who could see the truth clear enough. "Maybe I'll get you a manners manual," she said. "And then—"

It was like being struck full in the chest and head with a bag of bricks. She stumbled back, hitting the table and knocking over the tea set, sending it crashing to the ground. The whisky bottle dropped out of her hand, the heavier glass thudding to the carpet, the contents sloshing out. She went down with all of it, broken glass cutting her. She barely felt it. Panic at the unknown grabbed her, but something far worse sliced through it. Alistair.

She struggled through a haze, registered Stanley yelling for Nero. Crunching glass, people lifting her free of it as she thrashed weakly, tried to orient herself.

She was...he was...alive. They were alive, but he'd... His mind was suddenly wide open, and she fell into it, still writhing in pain, and saw what had happened in the same moment he tried to make sense of it. Driving the car along the winding drive from the house. Crossing the bridge over the small creek that marked the end of his property and the intersection with the main road. The car gave a hitch and...

Fire, searing heat, an explosion so loud even recalling it had her flinching, covering her ears. Oh God, the burning...and the pain. The pain was...he couldn't make sense of anything.

Him, not her. She was not hurt, but he was. Very badly. She struggled through it all, swam upward like she was swimming through bodies, through blood, through hunger and fear, through a mass of faces, people she'd cared for and lost, patients she'd never seen again. Some of whom she'd been the last to see, pulling the sheet over their faces, a tender shroud so the departing soul didn't have to see the mangled condition of the body they'd had to escape.

"Alistair," she gasped. "*Alistair.*"

She was gripping someone, and realized it was Nero. She was on the couch where she'd told Stanley to sit, but he was kneeling next to her, holding her steady as Nero barked something at Coleman, who'd come at a run.

Get out of it, the Matron snapped. *A man needs you.*

The voice beyond the grave brought her back, even if she felt weak as dishwater. "Nero, my nurse's bag... Stanley, car. We must go. Alistair. At bridge. Blown up. He's hurt."

Nero and the vampire exchanged a look, and Nero's face hardened. Following the same thought herself, she acted on it even before Nero did. Vampire or no, she was on Stanley in a heartbeat, her fists curling into his shirt as she yanked him up close to her face. Adrenaline gave her the strength to hold him, snarl at him. "God help you, did you—"

"No," Stanley said hastily, and the paleness of his face, the wideness of his eyes, told her it was the truth. "Fuck, no. Donovan must have had a backup plan. Or maybe this was the plan. He knew I'd give it up about being marked. He planned for it, planted the wrong info. It wasn't the hospital." Stanley got even paler, and despair, hopeless guilt gripped his features. "Fucking hell, the blighter used me. Used my mind to kill Alistair."

"Don't," she snapped at him. "He's not dead. No time to wallow in it. We need to help Alistair."

As Nina struggled up, Stanley proved he was worth something by indeed shoving it aside enough to help her. Nero had her bag, and they were headed for the door out to the garage. Nero instructed Coleman to stay put, to ensure the house stayed secure until their return.

"He wanted to take Alistair out," Stanley said. "That was the plan. The rest of it was just distraction. He knew Alistair was too smart for a frontal attack."

Nina nodded. "Going after me was just a way to make sure Alistair would be home, in the proper place for them to plant the bomb. Why would Donovan waste time on a servant when killing the vampire would kill us both? He didn't care about savoring it, making Alistair suffer. He just wanted him gone."

"Or both," Stanley said, anger in his voice. Good. She wanted him angry. "If he could have his cake and eat it too, that's bloody Donovan to a T."

Nero and Stanley ushered her into the car that Nero usually used to pick her up from the hospital. Thank God Alistair was flush and had three or four of the damn things. Hurry, hurry, *hurry*.

Nero took the wheel and Stanley the back as she gripped her bag in both hands. Her head was reeling, so she did everything she could to hold onto consciousness. She had to help him. *You hold on. I can't bloody help you if you die.*

She'd tell him that if they ended up at the gates of the afterlife together. She'd give him a piece of her mind.

As the end of the driveway came into view, her hands tightened on the bag, her heart leaping in her throat. His car was a mangled mess, pieces of it everywhere. The main body of the vehicle was halfway into the creek below the destroyed bridge. A couple trees overhanging the bridge had branches on fire.

He was there and still in one piece. He had to be, because she was still alive, even if she did feel like a hive of bees were roaring in her head, and her limbs needed to be told what to do several times before they reacted.

Nero and Stanley were out of the car ahead of her, Nero splashing down into the creek and Stanley scouring the surrounding area.

But she knew where to look because she could feel him. She stumbled from the car, staggered toward the trees. He'd had the top off of the convertible, for that was how he liked to drive it. He'd been thrown free. He hadn't been trapped in the car and burned...

When she saw him, she wasn't sure for a moment what she was seeing, and then the horror of it nearly dragged her into the blackness. She fought it like a demon, screaming her rage, refusing to let it take her. Her Master needed her.

She fell to her knees next to him. If he'd been human, it would have been over. His head...his neck looked half severed by the blast, but a quick, terrified probe told her the cervical bones were still intact. There was a crater in his chest and he lay in enough blood to kill two people, if they'd lost that much. Thank God all his limbs were intact, but that wasn't saying much, since one arm seemed to be holding on only by scraps of veins and muscle. She had a brief, absurd flashback to his teasing her about a finger and the butcher knife.

She clung to the things she'd been told could kill a vampire. A wooden stake through the heart. Decapitation—hopefully only full decapitation, not just partial. Burning. Everything she was looking at could heal, as impossible as that seemed. It had to.

She couldn't feed him if he didn't have any ability to swallow. A direct transfusion then. She'd supplemented her field kit over time, adding in things that would allow her to perform procedures she'd learned from battlefield medics, the doctors at casualty clearance centers. Things a nurse didn't usually do, but she'd made it her business to learn. Anything that could help a patient.

"Nero, I need you here to hold his shoulders." As she showed him what she needed, she positioned herself so Alistair's head was between her knees. While a vampire might not need his neck and shoulders aligned properly for the protection of the spine, it would heal faster if they were, just like with Stanley's arm.

She dug into her bag and found a line, needles. Despite the fog in her brain, her hands were steadier than they'd ever been in her life. She refused to look again at Alistair's face. Not right now. She instead thought of him as a man depending on her for his life. Any man, any patient, still vitally important, but not as unbalancing as knowing it was the man she loved, sliding down the perilous slope toward his death.

Stanley knelt at their side. "I will need blood from you both after I give him as much of mine as I can without becoming useless," she said shortly. "And then—"

The shot caught her high in the shoulder, slamming her down over Alistair. The report echoed through the night, followed by a couple startled bird cries.

Her first reaction was pure, killing rage. "Bloody fucking hell," she spat. The burn of it only added to the fire in her blood. She was cursing some more as Nero dragged her away from Alistair, behind the cover of the car. She fought him like a she-lion, but even with her third mark strength, she couldn't throw him before he talked sense into her.

"Stop it now. You won't do him any good with a bullet in your head. Be still now. Let us find the blighter."

"He's over there," Stanley said, crouched next to them. His expression was hard, and she remembered the night he and Alistair had wrestled. She saw the predator in Stanley's face now, the lethal fury. In the next blink he was gone, like a bullet himself. Headed in the direction from which the shot had come.

"There, Stanley has him in hand," she said, struggling. "Let me..."

"When he finds him," Nero said, holding her fast. "And makes sure there's no more of them. Let's check and see that you're not hurt worse than you think."

Impatiently, she brushed aside his hands and ripped the shoulder of the blouse out of her way. A quick probe, and she shook her head. "It went through." She held out her arm, wiggled all the fingers. "No serious damage. Nero, he needs me."

At the sound of a heavy thud and a groan, Nero leaned cautiously out around the bumper. Nina scrambled after him, pressed against the arm he used to hold her back. The body that hit the pavement like a landed fish was still wriggling, but Stanley leaped onto the man like a mountain cat. "Damn sniper," he said. "Only one, far as I can detect. Didn't kill him yet, in case you need the blood."

"A sniper who's a bad shot," Nero said. "Though I think you turned your head at the last moment, Miss Nina. No predicting that. You're working your guardian angel overtime."

She barely acknowledged him, scrambling back over to Alistair. Nero, apparently determining she was safe for the moment, helped Stanley secure their prisoner, but they both came back to her quickly, Nero taking Alistair's shoulders as before.

Later, she would remember that Stanley positioned himself over them like a guardian angel, watching in all directions, a protective detail. For now, there was just her and her patient.

She set up the line, and didn't draw an easy breath until the blood started to flow from her body into Alistair's. Then she turned her attention to whatever else she could set to rights, to help the healing process. She put her hand on that terrible wound in his neck, needing to feel it when it started to come back together. His eyes were open, staring like a corpse's. She couldn't bear it. She closed them, told herself it was the vampire's version of being unconscious after a terrible, mortal wound. She wished she knew more about vampire anatomy, had asked a hundred more questions at the school. None of this would work for a human. They would already have pulled the sheet up over his face.

At least there wouldn't be any question in her mind if he died, because she'd fall right over him. If he died, she did, but it was the last thing on her mind right now.

To keep herself from thinking too much about the thing that *was* most important to her, she focused on what Stanley and Nero were discussing as they kept watch.

"Donovan sent one of his lackeys to blow the car," Stanley was hypothesizing to Nero. The sniper had been dragged close, flat on his stomach, hands tied behind his back and wrists bound. He'd been blindfolded with Stanley's tie. She had an impression of a lean, muscular male in dark clothing, with snarled brown hair.

"And hang around to take out anyone who tried to help him," Nero added.

Nina recalled Curtis mentioning how he'd blown Donovan up by accident and Curtis had happened by at the opportune time for Donovan to seize him, take his blood to regain strength. He remembered such opportunities, and had taken steps to ensure they didn't benefit Alistair.

"Makes sense. Alistair would have detected a vampire," Nero continued thoughtfully. "There are occupied houses close enough to us a human scent wouldn't have raised an alarm for him."

"But this one hasn't been marked by Donovan," Stanley gestured to the sniper. "The dumb bastard. He can't tell Donovan he's fucked."

"Just paid to do a job, mate," the man whined beneath him. "Don't know nothing. Just told me to blow the car, take out any who tried to help the driver. Odd blighter, too intense, but paid well."

"Glad you earned a payday worth your life," Stanley said shortly. He grabbed the man's hair, pulled off the blindfold, and wrenched his head around so he came eye to eye with Stanley. The vampire unsheathed his fangs to full, gleaming length. "If you're lucky, I won't eat you before I kill you."

The man's eyes widened, his mouth opening on a scream, but Stanley thumped his head soundly on the ground first, knocking him out.

"Hopefully we'll not need him. Don't like to think of Ali having to use that arse's blood."

Nero drew her attention. "How's he doing, Miss Nina? Stable enough to get him in the car, out of the open like this?"

"Yes," she said shortly. "Will Donovan come check when his man doesn't let him know it's done? Bring vampires to help finish the job, like when they came after Alistair in town?"

"Don't know," Stanley said unhappily. "I don't have Alistair's age or strength to ferret it out. Donovan would feel me there in a heartbeat and gut my head."

"We need to get Alistair back to the house, then." She met Nero's gaze, and received a confirming nod. "Let's move him."

As they helped her lift Alistair, she held his head carefully, easing him onto the car blanket they'd stretched out in the second seat. She climbed in with Alistair while Nero took the wheel and Stanley stayed in back with her, helping to keep Alistair as stabilized as possible. Though Nero put his foot down, wheeling the car around quickly to go back the way they came, she and Stanley kept her patient steady. Her mind was already reviewing the possibilities.

"Are there any other vampires nearby that can come to his aid, Stanley?" she asked. "Help protect him?"

"None as close as Donovan, and he's an overlord. Region Master's property is not part of no territory, but he sits smack on the edge of Donovan's. Might as well be in it, and ain't none of them going to go up against Donovan in his own territory."

"You did," she said, meeting his gaze. "I want a list, Stanley, of those who are most likely to help. There are those who will stand for Alistair, if for no other reason they know what happens if Donovan kills Alistair and he's in charge."

Stan clicked off names, and she logged every one of them, the same way she kept drugs straight in her mind.

When they reached the house, Mr. Coleman met them at the driveway. They took Alistair to the lower level, got him situated. There was a phone in his bedroom suite. She hooked up Nero to do the next blood donation and started calling the numbers of the vampires that Stanley had said might be sympathetic.

She had plowed through half, hooked up Stanley to Alistair next and was waiting for another servant to get his Mistress on the line with her, when she tuned in to a conversation going on between the butler and Stanley. It was Nero's chuckle that caught her attention, a rare sound.

"Never heard no woman respond like that to being shot. Did she really shout 'bloody fucking hell'?"

"Like someone had rudely interrupted her tea one too many times," Nero responded fondly.

"She might not be the kind of InhServ those Europeans go on about," Stanley observed, gazing down at the unconscious Alistair. "But I think she fits our style fine. And I won't hesitate to tell any vamp just that."

"Indeed."

Nina straightened in her chair and grasped the phone. Donovan had planted doubts that she was a proper InhServ.

He was about to find out just how wrong he was.

CHAPTER TWENTY-FIVE

*I*t was the longest hour of her life. After she did what she could, she had to give up worrying who was about to show up on their doorstep—friends or foes were equal concerns— and focus on the one thing that mattered.

They'd all donated blood, including Mr. Coleman, and drained the reserves. She'd given more of hers, until Nero firmly told her enough was enough, because he'd claimed she was turning the color of the bedsheets.

But Alistair was healing. She was sure of it. She was watching the mangled arm recreate itself, the harrowing notch taken out of his throat close and fill in. At a later time, when she wasn't dealing with so many other emotions, the healer in her would be marveling and wondering at it. A species blessed with inexplicable miracles the human body lacked. All that was needed was human blood. A servant's blood and a vampire's—Stanley—were particularly rich sources for the healing power.

When she was too antsy to sit at Alistair's side, she prowled his room. Looked in his dresser and walk-in wardrobe not to pry, but for what she was sure was there. Weapons. Wooden knives with thick shafts and lethal points. Stakes with handles, essentially. Firearms. A crossbow she gave to Nero when he said he knew how to use it. She also gave him the rest to hand out wherever appropriate. He left only a small handful of the wooden stakes behind. She didn't object, since she knew how to use a gun, but not as capably as one of them would.

When she went back into the depths of Alistair's dressing room to make sure she hadn't overlooked anything, she remembered the day she'd looked through here, found that trunk. She sat down on it now, and turned her face against the dress shirts hanging neatly above it. She inhaled Alistair's scent and something trembled hard and low in her belly. She'd almost lost him. Could still lose him.

No. Not on her watch.

"Bloody hell. Nina." It was Stanley, voice urgent.

She surged off the chest and was back into the bedroom in a heartbeat. Alistair was struggling between Stanley and Nero, snarling, fangs fully exposed, his eyes crimson. Fortunately, he wasn't quite strong enough to do them harm or throw them off, but it was a near thing, as the panic in Stanley's voice had indicated.

Heedless of any risk to herself, ignoring Nero's barked protest, she ducked under Stanley's grip and touched Alistair's face, his chest, filling his vision with her leaning over him.

"Alistair. I'm here. It's all right. We're all right."

Men who'd been wounded badly in battle sometimes came out fighting, particularly if they'd gone down the same way and it was the last thing they remembered. Seeing a woman usually derailed that train, told them something different was happening. She made her voice brisk, no-nonsense, firm, though she couldn't help the little tremor when his blue eyes focused on her at last, saw her, and the fangs started to retract.

"What? What happened—" His voice was raw, like he had a cracked eggshell planted in his throat.

"It was a trap. Donovan blew up your car with you in it. A man he hired. You're home. We got you back here."

Now he was still struggling, but it was to sit up, not to fight them. The one arm still wasn't working properly yet, no muscle strength, but it was no longer in shreds. She helped him. Nero and Stanley moved closer to join him again, but Alistair reflexively hissed, showed his teeth, the bloodred color still glinting in his gaze. She held up a hand, warding them off. Too soon.

He stared at her. Then slowly, his gaze went to Stanley. His mind was working, for certain. She shifted, blocking his view again. "No. He

wasn't part of it. Remember, you said it yourself. Donovan was anticipating what you might do. He planted the hospital idea."

"Which he could do because the bloody idiot let him mark him."

Nina could almost feel Stanley's cringe behind her, but she kept
her attention on Alistair. It was irritation in his voice, though, not
homicidal venom, so she knew the male was safe.

"Born vampires are too damn good at the mind fucks," Alistair
muttered. He flexed his hand, stared at it. "Why's it not working
right?"

She gave him the quick rundown on all of it. His gaze lifted to her
as she spoke. When she finished, she realized her voice was shaking.
She squeezed his wrist. "Sorry. Been a crazy time."

He reached up with his other hand, cupped her chin, used his
thumb to brush away the tear she hadn't noticed on her cheek. "Been
a bit of a bother to you today, haven't I?"

"More than usual. And the Phaeton is demolished."

"I've no chance of competing with Rick now at all, have I?"

"None," she said staunchly, as another tear pooled on his
knuckle.

He attempted a smile, though his gaze was still flickering with
those hellfire sparks. He shifted his gaze back to Stanley and Nero,
but to different purpose this time. "What's our status? Buggered
beyond all hope?"

"Not necessarily, thanks to Brigadier General InhServ here."
Stanley cleared his throat, nodded to Nina. "We've got about nine
vampires guarding the perimeter, watching for him and his lot to
show. He'll come, I'm pretty sure. He'll not have heard from his man,
the one who blew you up."

"Where's he at?"

"He gave us blood and information, and that was all the use he had
for us," Stanley said matter-of-factly. "Think your landscaping bloke
took the body off to grind it up for fertilizer. Expect it'll do wonders
for your spring plantings."

"Time?"

"It's about three hours until dawn, my lord." This from Nero.

"Yeah. He'll come," Alistair agreed. He'd gripped Nina's hand, was
thoughtfully rubbing his thumb over it. "He'll want to install himself
in my home, as acting Region Master, before dawn comes." His gaze

moved to the table, where the handful of stakes were left. "Raided my closet, I see. Ready for an invasion, are you?"

"Just wanted to have some things at hand," Stanley said. "Gave most of them to the blokes handling guard duty. Assumed you wouldn't mind. Told her to leave the pearl-handled pistols in their box in your wardrobe, though. Know those are your babies and you wouldn't want anyone else handling them without your say-so. Never thought you'd feel that way about anyone living."

His gaze shifted back to Nina. Nina realized then that Alistair's eyes had left her only for those brief movements between the two men, to check on the status of things. Each time, his attention came back to her. He didn't seem like he planned to let go of her hand anytime soon. The pressure of it was almost too strong, but she took the pain as reassurance that he was alive and regaining his strength. But it was also an indication of other things, the way he was staring at her face.

"Why did you call her Brigadier General?" her Master asked.

"Because she marshaled the troops. Called up half the local vampires I thought were pretty loyal to you, got their arses here in record time. Think she talked to most of them direct. Told their servants she didn't have time to dick around with the help."

Alistair lifted a brow as Nina flushed. "Did you now?"

"I think I put it far more diplomatically than that," she said.

"Actually, I was cleaning it up some," Stanley said. Nero hid a smile as Nina shot him a severe look.

"I'll have a moment with her, then. Let me know if anything changes up top."

He and Stanley met gazes once more, and this time Nina sensed more to it. A muscle flexed in Stanley's jaw. "You know any of us here will go to bat for you, Alistair. I'll make good on what I buggered up. Best I can."

"It reassures me to hear that."

Another prolonged moment, and then Stanley sighed and left the room. Nero followed, giving Nina a look that she had a feeling was trying to tell her more as well, so once they'd both departed, she brought her attention back to Alistair. "I do hate it when men do that," she said. "The whole silent male code thing."

"Women have a similar one, though it almost always translates to

'This bloody man doesn't have a clue, girls. We'll just get it done the way it needs to be and leave him out of it.'"

She wanted to smile at him, but the uneasiness in her stomach, quickly supplanting her relief that he was on the mend, wouldn't let her. "Whereas the male code is 'I have to do it this way, no matter how stupid it is.' You're going to fight him when he gets here."

"I must," he said simply.

"No, you mustn't," she snapped. "You have a near dozen vampires here, plus Coleman and Nero. Unless he brings his own army, he'll back down."

"Those vampires are to back down his army. But he and I must face each other. They will all expect it." His expression hardened. "I'm Region Master, Nina. He's attempted to kill me, has attacked my servant, my home, my property. I tried to work with him, far more than he deserves. He's done."

"Seems redundant to single me out, since I'm your property too, aren't I?" she said tartly. She didn't mean to be shrewish, not now, but all this had been hell on her nerves. First the attack on her, then the attack on Alistair, and now he was about to plunge into it again. She resisted him when he curved the hand up around her skull, her nape, and drew her in to him, but he wouldn't be resisted.

That arm was fully functional, more than capable of bodily overcoming her resistance. Once she was close to his upper chest, she couldn't resist her own needs, either. She pressed her face there, her hand resting on his bandaged abdomen. Beneath, she knew the tissue and muscle had mostly reknitted, because she could feel the smooth ridges she was used to feeling there.

"You do belong to me," he said quietly. "But not just because you are my property. You are also my heart. He attacked my heart, caused her harm. By attempting to kill me, he would have killed you. And that earns him a death sentence. I'm not cruel when I don't have to be, Nina. I didn't kill Stanley for his infraction. Thanks to you, admittedly. But this is one that can't be excused or worked out any other way. Not if I'm going to hold this Region, keep it safer for those like Stanley. For all of us."

She spread her hands out along the sides of his rib cage, her mouth against his pectoral, the smooth heat of it. His heart. He'd called her that. He was warmer now, so much warmer. He'd been cold before, terrifying her. "Does it never end, then?"

He paused, and she sensed something moving below the surface. Regret, pain, a shadow she hadn't meant to disturb. "Maybe it will, eventually," he said. "But not today."

"Fine then." She sat up, thrust her wrist at him. "Then you drink once more. Take as much strength as you need from me. If you insist on doing something this utterly stupid, I'm going to make sure you are as prepared as possible."

He closed his grip around her wrist, but only to hold her still as he framed her chin in his other large hand and leaned forward, holding her still as he tilted her head away from him, breathed a tendril of air along her throat.

"You're worried for me. But there's no need. When this is over, we're going to discuss your disrespect for your Master."

She closed her eyes as his fangs stroked her. She couldn't bear the thought of losing him. But for the first time she saw that third mark mortality link as a boon. If he fell, she wouldn't have to grieve him. She'd die with him. It was the most reassuring thing she'd ever heard.

"I expect you'll chastise me for my male foolishness on the other side of that veil," he said.

"Count on it," she said unsteadily.

"Sshh. Quiet now." He pressed his lips to her throat, held there. Her fingers tightened on his sides, and she realized she was crying quietly, her throat hitching on little sobs. He realized it too, curving his arms around her now to bring her in close, hold her tightly.

"You do love me," he said quietly.

"I don't want to." That was sort of a lie, but he had her at a disadvantage. Still, she saw shadows in his eyes as he lifted his head, looked at her.

"I know." *I don't need any more of your blood, Nina. Keeping you alive is the only incentive I need to vanquish my enemy. You're too pale. When this is done, you'll have some of my blood, so you can get those soft roses in your cheeks I enjoy so much.*

As her tears fell again, because she seemed to have a limitless amount when it came to him, he held her even tighter to him once more.

Sshh...I'm all right. Thanks to you, I'm all right.

~

She helped him dress, which did nothing to alleviate her worries, when she had to help him guide the right arm into the sleeve of his pressed shirt. Though he was expecting a fight, he chose clothing as if he were going to a dinner party. Dress shirt, slacks, vest, coat. He didn't wear a tie, though, and his shoes were not slick-soled Oxfords, but shoes with a heavier rubber tread that still looked gentlemanly stylish. He combed his hair, flexed the arm and kept flexing it, working it so the muscles would kick in, use the blood he'd been given to embrace full strength and flexibility. It was improving, but far too slowly, and she knew his torso was still sensitive, the abdomen and chest showing pink scarring. When she touched them, the epidermis was not yet smooth and firm. It felt more like paper, and as easy to tear, exposing the innards beneath.

"Don't worry," he told her. "I'm fine."

"Course you are," she said stoutly. "Fit as a bull. Twice as hard headed."

He caught her to him with a swift arm to the waist, pulling her full against his body with a decisiveness that took her breath. He brushed his lips against her mouth. "When you play the stern and cranky nurse matron, it makes me want to put you on your back and bury myself in the sweetness between your legs all the more. I'll be attending to that shortly." He eased her back and ran an appraising eye over her. "Especially in that outfit. What did you do with my practical Nina?"

Despite how much time she'd spent resisting InhServ training, the mind that was able to remember every detail about a ward full of patients had forgotten none of what she'd been taught. Though Alistair had bought the extensive selection in her wardrobe, she'd been certain it was The Mistress who had sent him the list of appropriate things to buy, in all the right sizes. As a result, she was dressed as an InhServ would be expected to dress. By embracing it, she felt much as she did when donning her nurse's uniform—properly prepared for what lay ahead.

It was a red shirtwaist tea dress with flared skirt, standing collar, V-neckline and short sleeves. The fit emphasized her breasts, the fabric flowing in curved lines to the nipped waist. Her hair and makeup were done, and she wore black heels. At her throat she wore a pendant she hadn't worn before. One he hadn't bought for her, at least not directly.

While taking a short break at the hospital, one of the other nurses, Rose, had talked her into walking down to the market with her. It hadn't been an expensive thing, but Nina had been so taken with it, she'd used some of the cash Alistair gave her for sundries to buy it.

The circular pendant showed a nighttime scene, a small plane flying under bright moonlight and over sparkling water, thanks to the working of the metal.

Alistair touched the necklace and lifted his gaze to hers. "It was one of the best and worst moments of my life, if that makes sense," she said.

"It does." He shifted his grip to the side of her throat, squeezed lightly, though from his expression, he wanted to hold her much more aggressively. "Let's go get this done, shall we? He's coming up the maintenance road."

Sooner we get it done, sooner we can shag.

The man was diabolical, because he had her laughing as they stepped out the front door. Just as Donovan was pulling up, with a harrowing three carloads of vampires and servants. She saw a flash of shock on Donovan's face as he registered her expression, the matching devilish grin on Alistair's. Only she saw the coolness in Alistair's eyes as he held her gaze one last moment before turning and moving to the top of the stairs, his face going expressionless.

She didn't know until Nero told her later that hers matched him, her smile disappearing into an impassive but wholly unconcerned look as she took her rightful place to Alistair's right, just a pace behind him. She had her hands folded demurely before her, head up and eyes leveled contemptuously on the show of force below. Their nine vampires, the landscapers, Coleman, Nero and Stanley had arrayed themselves on one side of the steps, and they were a tough-looking group, too.

She'd never gotten a good look at Donovan, but she instantly knew he was the male who'd dragged her below street level and beaten her. The look in his eyes made her skin crawl, a post-traumatic reaction she viciously kept inside herself. He was a big male, as she remembered, with long dark-blond hair tied back, unnaturally still brown eyes and a strong-boned face. He wore the clothes of a gentleman as Alistair did, only a brown suit and gold vest. Donovan carried a walking stick with an eagle's head gold handle.

Curtis stood at his back, a mirror of Nina's position. When their eyes met, the servant grinned at her, a baring of teeth. She was a healer, a nurse, but she indulged a momentary fantasy of driving a knife into his abdomen, taking away that smug expression and delivering him into the grip of agonizing, prolonged pain

"You're a bit tougher than I expected," Donovan said to Alistair. "For a made vampire."

She shoved down another reaction as he brought back the sound of his voice against her ear, his hated breath shivering along her throbbing neck and shoulder.

"Shame that can't be enough for you," Alistair replied. "I could have used an ally with your brains and strength in my Region. Guess I'll have to train up one of these others, unless they show your short-sightedness."

Donovan's gaze shifted briefly to Nina and then came back to Alistair. "Shame to lose her when I kill you. She ended up being more of an InhServ than anyone expected. The Council gifted you with more than you deserve."

Alistair lifted a brow. "And you tried to take more than your share. We'll see who the gods favor."

"What?" Donovan drawled. "No tea first?"

Alistair scoffed. "The Devil's waiting on you to share his."

Nina managed, barely, not to react with a startled shriek when Alistair leaped from the veranda and plowed into Donovan, driving the vampire back so they both hit the hood of his car with a loud thump and creak of protesting metal.

There'd be no fifteen paces and turn, no cordoned off fight zone. When Alistair erupted into motion, the mask of civility was ripped away. In a blink, she realized the rage that Alistair had shown when he'd first woken from the explosion had never left him. He'd locked it down, a river of fire flowing beneath everything between that moment and now. The torrential storm of fury triggered by the presence of his enemy had that river roaring forth.

The heat was as overwhelming as the chilling control it had taken to channel it until now. Those who doubted that made vampires could match the control of a born one could just go bugger themselves.

The others obviously hadn't expected such a show of fury, either. They thought because he'd tried to deal fair with Donovan, with her, it made him weak. Only violence and death would teach them different. God, she hated human nature. Or vampire nature. Hell, any species that God had made the mistake of imbuing with more brains than sense.

But she also remembered another side of that coin, the breathtakingly dangerous side of her vampire. *If you're truly mine, then what I say you can and can't do is my bloody business.*

She was as daft as the rest. She moved to the top step. Those on their side were watching tensely. Nero stood shoulder to shoulder with Stanley at the apex of that group, and she could tell just by observing them if things were going well or badly. But she could barely tear her eyes from Alistair.

It was hard to follow, because the two vampires were moving almost faster than a third mark could track. Over the car, beside it. Through the plantings. Kicks, punches, grunts, snarls. Blood spurted as Donovan landed a nasty face punch, but Alistair retaliated with a kick that sent the other vampire spinning and crashing headlong into the driver's side door of one of the parked cars. Both groups of onlookers shifted like water from the tide line as the two fighting males went this way and that. Then they hit the base of the stairs, making the boards vibrate and shake.

She couldn't tell who was getting the upper hand. Neither, she suspected, at least at the moment. The two of them were well matched and she suspected that, too, was a surprise to Donovan. He was a born vampire, but he was about fifty years younger than Alistair, and apparently the age difference made their strengths more equitable. Both were skilled fighters.

Apparently realizing it, they backed off from one another for a moment, circling, eyes locked, but minds evaluating. "Ready to give up?" Alistair said pleasantly. "You could just fall on a stake for me and be done with it."

"My sentiments exactly, mate."

"Not your mate. Your Region Master, and you either call me that and mean it, or you get to see your Maker."

"No made vampire is ever going to be my Master." Donovan leaped again.

This time, Alistair had switched from full out brute force to strategy. He ducked beneath the lunge, slammed into Donovan, and charged with a yell, crushing him against the car. His speed increased past a blur as he punched the male in the rib cage, again, again and again, not giving him time to recover, marshal defenses or retaliate. Nina came down the stairs, giving Nero a sharp head shake when he would have stopped her. "I know what I'm doing."

She sort of did. She knew she had to be close, but she was also aware she didn't have the speed of a vampire to stay out of the way. She glanced Stanley's way and he was at her elbow in an instant. "I have to be within a few feet of him," she said, "But I have to be out of the way, too, so they don't roll over me. And I'm not perceived as interfering."

"Got it. They're moving faster than me, but I can anticipate them well enough." And then, she did gasp, for as Alistair and Donovan came so close to her she felt the wind of their passing, Stanley had snatched her and moved her out of their violent path.

"Like that," he said, with a certain level of satisfaction, though his gaze, like hers, remained fixed on the other two.

Curtis was circling as well, and had copied her initiative, using the help of one of Donovan's vampires. Damn it. They had to move quickly to stay out of one another's way, and he bared his teeth at her once or twice, that humorless, mocking smile.

Alistair had done some damage, but it had also marshaled another level from Donovan. Nina fought back a scream as Donovan went for Alistair's upper torso, and she saw the area she knew to be far too tender get bludgeoned by the other vampire's fists. When Alistair was bent double, Donovan grabbed his arm and wrenched it. The right arm.

Alistair bit off the hoarse scream, but twisted with the motion, avoiding the break and taking them both down. Using legs locked around Donovan's body, he flipped them both and then kicked the other vampire squarely in the face, knocking his head back and breaking his nose with a sickening crunch.

Now. As Alistair rolled on top of the other vampire, Nina surged forward, yanking up her skirt and pulling the wooden stake from the garter. He glanced her way, hand lifted, and she slapped it into his palm. Just before she did it, Donovan's arm shot out and he grabbed her ankle, fingers biting into it like a bear trap. She discovered that a vampire could crush bone in his grip. Curtis grabbed her around the waist, but Stanley turned on him with an animal-like hiss. The other vampires on both sides were closing in.

She bit back the scream despite the mind-blanking agony, made sure Alistair's hand closed securely on the stake before she let go. She'd do nothing to distract Alistair from...

Donovan had made a strategic mistake, trying to stop her instead of shoving Alistair off him. He tried to block him, but Alistair wouldn't be denied. He slammed the stake down, with such a decisive, aimed and controlled movement it was clear he still had his wits well about him. He didn't even glance off a rib, despite Donovan's attempt to struggle. The stake went straight in.

Everything else in the tableau froze. Donovan arched, a bitter wheeze escaping his lips. His eyes, flashing with battle rage, dialed over to lingering hatred before everything just left him. Eerily, it reminded her of the sun's quick drop below the horizon when it touched firmament, its hold on the day released for night.

One brief moment of tense silence, and then Alistair shoved the body away from him. "Back off," he said, death in his voice, and Donovan's forces melted back, even as Alistair's took a step forward, reinforcing the point.

In the next blink, Alistair had moved over to Nina, who'd gone down on her arse. She could barely think through the pain, but it would be fine. She just needed a minute to struggle past it and then...

"Drink, my brave and clever InhServ," Alistair said quietly, and she realized he had a wrist before her mouth, had cut it open and was pushing the blood to her lips. She latched on before she could think to deny herself, so he could conserve his strength. She'd no idea what any of the rest of them were going to do, he might need to be on alert, handling...

Oh, blessed miracle, it only took a few swallows for the pain to ebb enough for her to think again, as good as morphine. The bones would take more time to assemble themselves from the puzzle pieces she knew they must be, but they would, because that too was part of the miracle of being a third mark. No surgery needed. Just the blood of her Master.

Look. There's nothing for you to manage.

She did look, and saw that Donovan's vampires were standing in a far less belligerent and certain-looking cluster, while Alistair's vampires, Nero and the male staff were nearby, their watchful attention an obvious warning. If any of them unwisely chose to break protocol and attack Alistair, they would be met by an immediate response.

She and Curtis had been allowed to serve as squires, so to speak, and Stanley could come to her defense and protection in that role. However, the fight between Donovan and Alistair had to be strictly vampire against vampire, or protocol was broken. Alistair had explained that when he handed her the stake from the weapons left on the table in his bedroom.

But you'll stay well out of the way, Nina. You take no risks. He'd given her a steady look as he put the stake in her hand, holding it an extra moment as if he was going to rethink her insistent offer of aid. But in the end, he'd let her help. Trusting her to be there when he needed her.

He might take her to task for coming within Donovan's reach, but that was all right. Alistair was alive.

She'd committed every one of their faces to memory, these vampires who'd stood for Alistair, and knew she owed their servants an apology for her brusqueness with them. Later.

No apologies. You conducted yourself as an InhServ would, and earned their respect by kicking their arses into gear.

Alistair sent her a quick look as he thought that. He was holding himself well, but as a healer and his servant, she could feel the pain vibrating from him. Donovan hadn't shattered the arm anew, but it had been a near thing, and she knew his upper torso and the assembly of organs beneath his ribs weren't up for that kind of pummeling so soon after the car explosion.

Donovan said I'm tougher than expected, Alistair reminded her.

I believe he said 'a bit' tougher. And not invincible. She slanted him a glance. *JD is going to give you a piece of his mind, the way the two of you ran roughshod over the landscaping he's worked on so hard.*

Alistair's lips twitched, and he brushed a hair away from her cheek. *When we get behind closed doors, I'm going to steep myself in you, sweet nurse. But for now...don't protest, because I have to look strong.*

She did bite back a protest as he slid his arms beneath her and hefted her up in his arms. She noticed the tightening of his body, the pain responses, but they were so subtle, she knew she would be the only one that would. To those watching, he appeared as well as he'd been before the match.

Tremendous, bloody control. Once again, she saw that Lady Lyssa hadn't endorsed him for Region Master out of favoritism. Or, if it had been, it had been balanced by the knowledge he could more than handle the job.

Well, at least one person thinks so.

I see at least a dozen others, including myself. She assumed it was all right to link her arm around his neck, but made herself not rest her cheek against his chest, though she really wanted to do so. He took her up onto the veranda and put her gently down on a bench. He'd jerked his head at Nero, so the butler came with them. Alistair put a hand on Nina's shoulder. "Make sure she stays here until I handle the rest of this lot. She's done enough."

"Right-o, sir."

Alistair went back down the steps, striding across the driveway to where his men and Donovan's stood. She remained tense, no matter that the battle seemed over. That was often when all hell would break loose. She noticed that Nero watched just as carefully as she did, and his hand was not far from the pistol at his hip.

"What butler school teaches you to carry a pistol?" she murmured.

"The smart kind. Especially in a household like this one. I'll be glad when this is handled. I'm tired of putting together my own meals. Mrs. C is far better at it."

Nina almost smiled, though her eyes didn't leave Alistair. With her third mark, she could hear parts of the conversation, but his body language gave her most of it. Stiff and formal, borderline menacing, with Donovan's vampires. He was waiting, and promptly getting, individual declarations of loyalty and determining not by the words, but by the manner, if he could accept it. She noticed his vampires had adjusted so they stood behind each declarant. From the slightly nervous glances over shoulders, he'd done a good job of convincing

Donovan's followers that if the answer was delivered wrong, they might not leave that spot alive.

When he said something she couldn't quite make out, Donovan's vampires looked toward her at nearly the same moment, then brought their eyes back to Alistair, a quick snap. They appeared more than a little uneasy, but their nods came quickly, their spoken "my lord" reaching her with particular emphasis.

He wasn't going to kill them. She hoped. What was it he'd said? He wasn't cruel when he didn't have to be. His mercy had to be earned, though. He wouldn't hesitate to cut any one of them down, right here in the driveway, if he thought that vampire would be a problem for him like Donovan. She didn't let out an easy breath until he stepped back, gestured. The vampires headed for the cars. One began to collect Donovan, but Alistair said something sharply, and he was left where he lay. Her gaze slid from that body to a second one.

Curtis had fallen near his Master, his hand outstretched, his staring, lifeless eyes focused on him.

She swallowed. "He won't let Donovan be buried?" she asked quietly.

"He will burn there with the morning sun, the ash becoming a mark upon the drive that will remain long enough to be a reminder," Nero said.

"And Curtis?"

"Probably the same fate as our sniper. More food for JD's plantings."

"My guess, Lord Alistair will be even more flush for a while." Stanley joined them on the veranda. "Donovan's lot have kept their lives, but the penalty for being on the losing side is going to be a hefty hike in their quarterly tithes." He tossed Nina a grimly amused look. "Maybe you can talk him into funding a new wing for the hospital. Not good for a man to make too much money off the misery of others without giving back. Long as he has enough left over to stock his liquor cabinet to the brim."

"Stanley." Alistair had turned toward the veranda. Stanley tipped his hat to her, nodded to Nero, and trotted down the stairs again. Nero closed his hand over Nina's.

"Steady, girl."

She nodded. Made herself look away from Curtis, even though the memory would be there, in her head, like so many others. Lived together, died together. And yes, whatever Donovan's feelings...the pose in which they lay told her the truth of it. Curtis had cared for his Master. Maybe even loved him.

Donovan's lot loaded up the cars, drove away. Alistair spoke to his vampires. He shook each one's hand, glanced toward the veranda, gestured at her, spoke. They nodded. A few vampires smiled, sending her a speculative, somewhat amused look, and then they, too, went to where they'd left their cars, along the drive and by the garage area.

It was just them, now. Them and the two lying in the driveway.

No. She was wrong about that. Alistair didn't come to her immediately. He waited, until Stanley and three other vampires returned, bearing drop cloths from the maintenance shed. They wrapped up the bodies and carried them back in that direction.

I'll let Donovan burn in the sun behind the shed, Nina. They'll bury Curtis next to him.

She let out a breath she didn't realize she'd been holding, close to a sob, and swallowed it down, her eyes closing.

You're right. There's violence and hate enough in our world without feeding the beast. Be easy, sweet nurse.

Alistair returned to the veranda, mounting the steps with decisive steps. He was upright, his arms swinging naturally, and she had a feeling the effort to do that was equal to him trying to lift the whole house on his shoulders. There was a paleness under his usual skin tone, suggesting she wasn't the only one who needed more blood. Again.

"Soon." He came and sat next to her on the veranda bench, putting his arm around her and lifting a casual hand as each car passed. Stanley was in one of them, and he gazed upon Alistair an extra somber minute before he, too, was gone.

Alistair let out a long breath. "Nero, I think there's still some lemonade in the refrigerator. We could use some. Get yourself a glass, too. We'll go sit on the back veranda, watch the ocean for a while."

He rubbed a hand over his face and looked at Nina. A searching, long gaze that had her wondering what was going through his mind. He slipped his arms around her again.

"Don't carry me, Alistair. They're all gone. I don't want to hurt you."

"You're mine to care for as I see fit. So be quiet, sweet nurse. And the pain of carrying you in this moment is only an additional pleasure."

She sighed at his stubbornness, but looped her arms around his neck. This time she did lay her cheek on his chest. He went through the house as Nero peeled off near the kitchen to get the beverages Alistair had mentioned. Alistair carried her out to the screened veranda, settled her on a long carved bench there, but this time he left her in his lap, her legs bent and stretched out beside him so he could rest his arm on her knees, fingers curved over her calf. His other arm held her close, his palm warm against her rib cage, his shoulder and chest supporting her head.

"You need..." she began.

"Nina, who is your Master?"

"You are."

"Then be still," he said absently. Just stroked her hair, gazed out at the ocean. She was curved against him, her face resting against his chest, so she wasn't looking at the ocean. Just hearing it, smelling the sea air and him, feeling his heat against her. None of it was disturbing her.

Nero came with the lemonade, but he didn't stay. He left the two of them there, cocooned in shadows, and went down the steps, headed toward the beach. As his silhouette disappeared among the dunes, Nina listened to the thud of Alistair's heart. She wondered what he was thinking. What he'd said to the other vampires that made them look toward her, made some of them smile. What had made Donovan's vampires look toward her the way they did.

"We are on the edge of Donovan's territory here."

She nodded. "Stanley told me."

"Then you know a Region Master's property is an independent wedge amidst the territories, like Australia's capital Canberra is, between Melbourne and Sydney. The hospital, where my staff goes to the market, that's in Donovan's territory. What used to be his territory," he amended, a dangerous satisfaction to his tone. "I'll be evaluating who's best suited to be head of that territory, but for now, I'll be doing double duty as Region Master here and overlord there, so I can get a full sense of who populates it."

He nudged her with his chin, rested it against her temple. "I indicated that my InhServ is a gifted nurse, and it suits me to have her work at the hospital to keep her skills sharp, both for human interaction and other requirements. And that if anything untoward happens to her as a result of that, I would hold every one of their lives forfeit."

She glanced up at him. His expression reflected the lethal surety of it. He would not hesitate to kill every one of them. It was the face he had shown them as he spoke to them, and now she understood that quick look toward her, the even quicker "my lord," acknowledging it. She shivered, and he held her closer, rubbing his hand up the goosebumps on her arm.

"I mean you no harm, sweet nurse," he said quietly. "You needn't fear my wrath."

"Violence chills me, my lord," she said, just as low. "I wish there was no need for it."

"Wishes mean little in my world. In either of our worlds. Didn't we cover that once, long ago?"

I hope we both see a day where wishes are more than a candle, sweet nurse. I'd like them to be a fucking bonfire in the night, and dance in the flames with you.

"Look," he whispered, and she did.

A fire had been started on the beach. A bonfire, Coleman apparently having collected enough wood to get it started. It was already starting to throw sparks to the sky, an erratic pattern carried by the sea breeze.

She turned her gaze back up to Alistair. The lights from inside the house threw shadows up against his cheekbones and forehead, glittered over his gaze that was mostly dark in the night.

"My lord...will we have children?"

He looked down at her. He didn't appear surprised by her question, and she suspected he might have caught it in her mind once or twice before now. When she was drafted into the InhServ role, she'd pretty much assumed children would not be part of her future, but at some point during the journey she'd taken with Alistair, she'd started thinking and wondering exactly how born vampires came about. She swept her gaze down, drawing small circles on his chest with her fingertips. His hands tightened on her.

"It's very rare," he said at last. "So rare that no one ever counts on them. But it happens. Also...once you're third marked, the only way you can get pregnant is by your vampire."

He brushed her hair from her cheek, and his touch was gentle as she lifted her attention to his expression. The sea breeze continued to lift and dance the strands across her parted lips. "I'm sorry, Nina," he said. "I can't even pretend to be sorry for keeping you, but I can be sorry that I can't give you everything you wanted in your life."

She didn't like the shadows that had come back into his gaze, a trace of that distance that sometimes came between them in moments like this. To counter it, she put both her hands on his face, tried to tell him in her eyes, in her voice, what she felt, which was so much truer than whatever confusion her thoughts were.

"I've been given a lot."

"And had a lot taken away."

"So have you," she said, and meant it.

"No," he said. "It doesn't feel that way right at this moment. We ask so much of life, when so much is already given. If only we notice. Someone very wise I know once had that thought."

"Oh, Alistair." She caressed his jaw, tried to lighten the weight she felt on both their hearts. "Getting everything we wish for in any life is too much. Far better to always have some wishes pending, right?"

His lips curved in a grim smile. But he cupped her head in that way he had, and pressed a hard kiss to her forehead. When he released her, he rose to his feet, taking her with him.

"Come dance with me by the bonfire, sweet nurse. We can't dance in the flames, but we can dance near them."

He didn't give her a chance to say or think anything else, simply scooped her up off her still tender ankle. He was moving even more stiffly now, but he still wouldn't let her give him any blood. He carried her through the dunes, along the sandy path, toward that bonfire.

When he put her on her feet by the fire, he slid his arm around her back, taking her hand to fold it in his, high on his chest. She sighed and put her cheek against him, lips brushing his biceps as they swayed and four-stepped at an easy pace through the sugar-soft sand. She could smell the ocean, the rush of it some yards away, but the fire was between them and it, masking it with the heat and crackle of the flames. The sky above sparkled with stars.

Behind them, the Victorian house was a picturesque silhouette dotted with welcoming lights in the windows. The flame warmed her back, and Alistair warmed her front. She tipped her head back to gaze at him. She didn't have to think. She just wanted to look at him.

When she'd thought of having a husband, she'd imagine a bloke who was nice-looking enough, but it wasn't as important as how big his heart was, and if he was kind. She'd seen men do kind things for one another in her wards, time and again, to bring a mate's spirits up. The plainest man in the world suddenly became Jimmy Stewart or Gregory Peck when he showed his character that way.

"I guess I'll have to settle for being a handsome shell," he murmured. "Because I'm not particularly kind."

"Kind isn't always what you expect it to be, either," she said. She slid her hand over his shoulder to tease the short dark hair on his neck. As she scraped his flesh with her nails, she earned sparks from his blue eyes, dark as night against the flames. It made her think of the many things he demanded from her, so ruthlessly. Until she craved that ruthlessness. "There's a type of cruelty that's a far cry from wanting to be cruel...just to be cruel."

Perhaps it was the proximity of the ocean that made those four simple words invite in a memory she decidedly hadn't intended. The Japanese soldiers lined up behind the machine gun, their expressionless eyes. She'd always thought of cruelty as an active thing, but what she remembered most was their apathy. Her life, Helen's life, all of the nurses and soldiers they'd executed...their lives had meant nothing. A logistical inconvenience to be eliminated, too many prisoners to manage in the wake of the fall of Singapore. She'd read that in some of the post-war reports.

"Nina. Come back to me, sweet nurse."

She put her head on his shoulder, closed her eyes when he began to stroke her hair.

"So sorry," she murmured. "Bollocks."

"No sorries to be said," he responded, giving her a squeeze of reproof. "But it does tell me what we're going to do next."

"What?" She spoke against his firm flesh, anticipating what her thoughts about his ruthlessness might have conjured. He dug fingers into her hair, a light scalp pull that had her drawing in a breath, but when he spoke, it wasn't at all what she'd expected him to say.

"We're going swimming," he said.

That brought her head up. "Oh, I... There's no need to do that right now."

"Hmm. I disagree." He eased back from her, squeezed her hands. Then he started unbuttoning his vest.

Since he necessarily had to let her go to do that, she started backpedaling toward the house. "We really shouldn't... You've just gotten over being injured, and I'm sure there are other things, far better things, to do. Wouldn't you prefer to do other things?"

She kept babbling on, quickly explaining why they needed to wait, and the things that needed doing in the house. He shrugged out of the vest, then went to work on his shirt. Normally that would distract her, the way his fingers flicked open the buttons, the shrug of his broad shoulders as he removed it. But this time, she couldn't take her gaze off his, which stayed locked on her, tracking her every retreating step.

Then came his socks and shoes. His trousers. When she was nearly at the boardwalk back to the house, he finished. He set his clothes to the side, straightened, and his gaze sharpened in an unmistakable way.

"Oh, crikey," she muttered. She turned, intending a straight bolt for the house, and he was standing in front of her, just a bit of breeze fluttering through his hair explaining how fast he'd moved. He put his hands at her waist.

"We've discussed you running from me," he mentioned. He began to peel the dress from her shoulders, remarkably efficient, though he took the time to stroke her skin as he exposed it to the night air. She shivered, but it wasn't from cold.

"I was running from the water, not you, my lord."

"Hmm." He unhooked and slipped off her bra, making her breath catch as he cradled and caressed flesh before setting it aside. Per his mandate, she wore nothing else. His gaze swept her, and she grasped a momentary hope that typical male priorities might derail his intent.

Her male was not so typical. Taking her hand, he put them in a waltz position. Then he started to sway as if they were dancing, no matter that they were doing it naked, standing on the sand.

"You're mad," she told him. "Short a full quid."

"I have an abundance of quid. Don't think about it," he admonished gently as she glanced nervously over her shoulder, gauging the distance between them and the surf line.

"Notice you didn't remove your boxers," she said.

"Neither man nor vampire fully exposes his dangly bits to the murky ocean depths," he informed her. When she tensed at the next turn, he made a soothing noise.

"Look at me. Let's imagine the life we would have had if we were just Joe and Jane Average. I think I would have been a banker. And a volunteer footy coach, for the kids."

"A banker?" The wholly unexpected subject managed to pull her attention away from the approaching water. Mostly.

"A banker," he confirmed. "I'm good with numbers. Put your hand all the way up on my shoulder. You're digging a hole into my arm. We're dancing. Just waltzing."

At his encouraging look, she made herself put her hand on his shoulder. Yet her fingers stayed tight on him as he moved her in the waltz step, circling closer to what terrified her. But she rallied. She would do this. She could do it. "And a footy coach?"

He shrugged. "I like watching kids learn how to play it."

She met his gaze, held onto that lock, and made herself go along with it. Told herself it would work. "You'd call me from the office," she said bravely. "Remind me that you were coaching a game that night and wanted me to pack you a dinner."

"Which you would already know, being my efficient wife. I'd just be calling for the excuse to hear your voice. And to tell you I expected you to go with me."

Her cheeks flushed, and she found herself stifling a chuckle, even as her stomach leaped with nerves. "Daftie. So you'd come home to our tidy house in a tidy neighborhood. You'd look so handsome in your business suit. I'd see you out the kitchen window when you pulled up, got out of your car." She remembered him getting out of the car with Stanley, that first night, but overlaid it with the fantasy they were crafting. "When I sent you off that morning to work, I'd straightened your tie for you. It's still straight, but a bit loose, because you like to loosen it on your way home."

"Because I want it to be ready for other uses," he said smoothly. "But tonight there's a game. So I need to go get changed. Which I do. After I roger my wife over the kitchen table, because when she wears that apron, she knows what it does to me. And I like bending her over, lifting up her skirt, pulling down her knickers and taking her like that, right when I come home."

While still wearing his suit, Nina imagined, and her body tightened at the thought. That thought helped the noise of the water die back better than the rest of their imaginings so far. "After that?" she said.

"We'd head off to the fields. My wife made us a picnic dinner, after all." He smiled down at her. "We'd wave to our neighbor Bill. Who I know fancies my wife because she's such a looker, but is proper with it, watches after her when I'm not home."

"And I watch after Bill, because he eats too much salt and fat in his diet and I'm always afraid he's going to keel over in a stroke when he's mowing his yard. We'd invite him to go with us to the footy field, but he'd say there was a radio program he wanted to hear that night."

She stopped. It was getting too close. Alistair got her started again, merely lifting her off her feet for the turn. Nina's gaze shifted down to their interlocked hands, folded on his chest, as his fingers tightened. "It would have been a nice life, wouldn't it?" she said.

"Yeah." He brought her hand to his lips as the poignant ache in her chest spread. She tried to dispel it with humor.

"Except when my husband, Mr. Banker, was being difficult or thickheaded."

His lips curved. "There's the pot calling the kettle black. Stubbornest sheila I know, right here. Even as Mr. Banker, I suspect I'd regularly have to turn her over my knee and spank some sense into her."

"Mr. Banker is a twisted bloke himself, one who'd be looking for the right excuse to do that far too often."

His vivid blue eyes smiled easily, but she saw a lot of other darker and more serious things behind them. The water was much closer, she realized. She could almost feel the mist from the crashing waves. Then her feet faltered, her hands tightening on him. Her feet were in the water. She made a noise, clutching him in panic, and he shifted a hand to her face.

"Alistair," she whispered. "I can't. I'm frightened."

All these images of a life she wasn't going to have vanished. What had happened to her, the terrible things that had brought her to now, were rushing into that void. She needed out of the water. Needed out now. Those memories, too close to be called something as harmless as memories, would swallow her whole.

"Nina, look at me."

She shook her head.

"It wasn't a request. I won't repeat myself."

Her head came back up. The sharpness of his gaze, the firm way he was holding her, his tone, it had all shifted. And suddenly the ocean's noise, its proximity, was competing with something else. Something that might be stronger than an element of nature itself.

He saw it, his blue eyes flickering with a burning light. He shifted his touch to the side of her face and throat, his grip on her waist tightening. "Joe Banker can't get you into this water, can he?"

She shook her head. "Who can?" he demanded.

"My Master...you can." Her voice shook.

Alistair dropped to one knee in the ankle-high surf, and held both her hands, looking up at her. He'd done that so many times, she realized, kneeling so she was gazing directly into his face, even with her eyes lowered, as a proper servant. And from the very first time he'd done it, she'd realized he lost not a whit of control over her in the pose, and so it was right now, as well.

"None of it has the same hold on you that I do. It's done, Nina. Even if I let you run, you would come back to me here, on this shoreline, because no memory is stronger than your will, your desire to obey your Master."

He'd teased her as a man would, but now she saw the vampire, felt it in his grip. Responded to it. When her fingernails dug into his flesh, it was because she hungered for him, for his commanding touch, for the bruises he might leave on her with that heavy-handed grip. For the total ownership that went far beyond what was acceptable for husband and wife. There were parts of their relationship that were in a far different territory than that.

Parts that she wanted.

His expression was fierce. "Then ask me, Nina. Ask me to care for you."

"Alistair," she whispered. "Tell me you love me. Please. Help me learn to swim again."

There were so many layers to that, and she believed he understood every one of them.

He didn't answer her with words. He rose, put his arms around her, lifted her. He walked her into the water, until it was up to his waist. Once there, he kissed her, drowned her in that feeling over and over until she was floating in the water, clinging to him, and the tears overflowed.

He held her in the waves as the sparks from the fire danced in the sky. And she trusted him, and learned to love the water again. Because in his arms, she could.

CHAPTER TWENTY-SIX

She thought about that. Thought about it a lot. Several weeks later, when an insidious rumor started circulating in town that she was an unmarried woman living with a wealthy member of Brisbane society, she could have cared less. Tracy told her to ignore the wowsers, and Nina could handle herself with any doctors or management staff who thought that meant she was fair game. More than usual.

But it got back to Alistair. She'd tried to squelch it in her own head, but even if he hadn't picked it up from there, she suspected he'd found out through Nero, who was more protective of her than her own father had ever been.

Two things immediately happened. Winifred was fired, since she ended up being the source of the malicious rumor. Nina learned that from Nero. Apparently, Alistair had the maid brought to his office after learning of the now-public gossip. According to accounts Nina learned from Mrs. W, the girl had emerged a scant twenty minutes later, looking as if she'd escaped with her life.

Knowing Alistair's temperament on certain issues, Nina thought that might be truer than the housekeeper knew. Shaking and white-faced, Winifred had departed without even a peep about the rest of her week's wages, though Nero had courteously sent those along with Mrs. C.

Mrs. C had come quite a ways in her feelings toward Nina, and had merely shook her head about it in discussions with Mrs. W. "I'm afraid our Winnie will never make a good domestic," she said. "But she's quite had the wind taken out of her sails since the meeting with Lord Alistair. Perhaps it will do her some good. I've a friend cooking for a restaurant in town. They'll put her on in their kitchens, keep her out of trouble. There are some nice young men who work there. Maybe she'll learn to be less sullen and discontent and catch one of their eyes, give her mother some grandchildren at last."

Alistair had not spoken of the incident to Nina when she asked, merely noting it was handled. When she would have pressed it, he distracted her quite ably with the second thing he'd decided upon. He told Nina they would be proceeding with getting the wedding certificate. What's more, they'd have a wedding reception with a few key guests from town; his business associates, her friends from the hospital, people sure to spread the right message about it.

A story was already being cleverly spread in the community that she was a distant cousin, one who'd been properly chaperoned in the house by the staff, staying in a guest bedroom until the wedding date had arrived.

Whether anyone questioned that or not, it had all the elements necessary to leave behind any stigma that she was not as Alistair presented her. A reputable woman, one who could be accepted by the community. And, as Alistair dryly pointed out, since he provided income to the community and generous donations to several popular society charities, money had a way of fixing all perceived social shortcomings.

So here they were, several weeks later, and tonight she would be "married." From this night forward, she'd be seen as his wife when traveling and interacting with the human world. Which would allow her to travel more with him on Region Master business as well.

All of the steps he'd taken fit with the official way he'd told her vampires handled such things with their servants, to blend in human society. What bemused her were other pieces of it. He said the two of them, with Nero as witness, would have a handfasting ceremony before the reception. The ceremony would happen in the highest parapet of the house, the glass-enclosed one adjacent to the rooftop deck where she'd had so many memorable midnight encounters with Alistair.

He'd also bought a ring for her. She hadn't seen it, but when she heard Mrs. W whispering about it with Mrs. C, she told herself it would be a serviceable and appropriate symbol. He could have given it to her in a matter-of-fact way, but he'd told her he'd do it at the ceremony.

She thought of the normal life fantasy game they'd played together. The humor of it, the gentle poignancy. He'd insisted she get herself a dress, one she'd want to be married in. She'd resisted. He'd insisted, and when her Master was in an insistent mood...there was only one response to that.

As a result, she couldn't completely avoid the thoughts and emotions that went along with all this, no matter if it was merely a façade. She stood in her room, wearing the dress she'd chosen, gazing at herself in the mirror. A little while ago, before she dressed, Nero had delivered two things. A little bouquet JD had thoughtfully put together for her. And a gift from Alistair.

The triple-stranded choker had pearls gleaming with a soft bronze light. The way it held her throat so snugly reminded her of Alistair's hand there. His claim upon her.

Mere formality or not, she wished she had a female friend who could stand as her maid of honor. If she'd lived, it would have been Sher. Or Helen. But she was good at visualizing, and it wasn't hard to see translucent aspects of the two women, dressed in lavender brides-maid gowns. People who had shaped her, guided her destiny to this moment, their spirits always close to her heart.

The past, the present and future. The real and the fantasy. They had the power to overwhelm her tonight. Make her feel almost... happy. Had her dreams changed? Or had fate opened up the path to her she was meant to walk all along?

All she could do was get through and follow her heart. Taking a breath and picking up the little bouquet, she left the room.

She found Nero at the bottom of the winding stairs to the rooftop. As he looked her over, a soft smile touched his face. It warmed her, she couldn't deny it.

She'd relented enough to pick out a dress she really loved. The bodice was simple, fitted points over the bosom and following her upper body closely. A wide scoop neck edged with lace, with short lacy cap sleeves. The satin skirt was sewn with a lace overlay that started around mid-thigh, a mix of wing patterns that reminded her of birds playing over the froth of the surf.

She grasped Nero's hand and, with a playful smile, she stepped out of the satin ivory pumps. As she took the first step up the spiral winding staircase barefoot, Nero was close behind. When they reached the tower, Nero took her hand again. He had obviously assumed the role of "giving away the bride," and she smiled at him, telling him she was pleased.

With Nero here, and those specters of Sher and Helen close, they had all the witnesses they needed for this. Then she saw Alistair, and a whole wealth of other needs rose inside her.

Alistair looked as fine and prepared as any groom she'd ever seen. He wore a double-breasted dark blue suit with a gleaming white dress shirt. His grey tie had blue stripes that picked up the color of his eyes. Silver links gleamed at his cuffs, and his black oxfords shone. His dark hair was brushed, thick and silky.

On his lapel was pinned a New Zealand tea tree rose, a tribute to Sher that stung her eyes. He also wore an Australian flag pin. She recalled what Rigby had said, what seemed like so long ago.

Bought his way out of a uniform...

Soldiers were usually married in their uniforms, a symbol of all the qualities they valued—honor, loyalty, dedication—brought to bear before their intended wives. So the pin was his uniform. She was sure he'd worn it for that reason. Alistair had fought in multiple wars, served as scout, spy and guerilla-style combatant. But because he was a vampire, he'd never been able to enlist. A soldier could not be available only after dark, could he? But because he'd fought with and for his mates, he was a soldier. It was at the heart of him. Which explained why he'd become Region Master. As he'd said, he didn't like a situation where someone took by force more power than was their right or share.

It also explained how he'd understood, and given her, the dream of being a nurse. He'd done his best to give her what he could in his limited world.

"Alistair," she whispered. "what are we doing?"

"Getting married," he informed her. "Didn't I explain that?"

She gave him a look. "For form's sake. This...feels..."

He took her hand, squeezed it, stilling her words with those piercing eyes of his, the set of his firm mouth. "You belong to me, Nina," he said. "You're my servant. I will ensure that whatever world we inhabit sees you as mine, under whatever customs they prefer. That's what this is about. But there is more I would say to you here, before a man I trust."

He glanced at Nero, emphasizing that his next words were a testament he wanted heard, witnessed, which increased that overwhelming feeling inside her. Nero's eyes flickered with surprise, then some deeper emotions. He gave Alistair a slight nod.

Alistair turned his attention back to her, taking both of her hands, so they were facing one another. Like a bride and groom. Her heart accelerated even more.

"I'm used to thinking these things to you," he said, a trace of somber amusement crossing his face. "So I'm going to sound just like an awkward schoolboy reciting his letters. Don't hold that against me. All right?"

She nodded, her throat thick.

"I've been at war or on the periphery of it, for a very a long time," he said quietly, as if it were just the two of them. "The world was always at a full roar. Once in a while, I'd think, 'Is there any quiet space, a still spot in a chaotic world?' And there she was. In the middle of hell and blood and death, in a converted school. A treasure. One I had to have, damn everything else." He paused. "Even her own dreams."

She swallowed, and his eyes darkened with those shadows that never seemed too far away from him. "But I'll do my best to make sure it's not the worst life you could have. And show you things you never imagined were possible, that might make up for those other dreams, even if they can't ever replace them."

He already had. But with his words, he told her something else. He was trying to give her what she'd lost. While those shadows told her he believed she would never truly stop grieving for it.

As he straightened and stepped back, framed against the waves crashing on the beach below, she knew the answer she wanted to give him.

"Nero." The butler stepped forward, took her hand again, a courtesy and affection. "Would you mind leaving us alone?" she asked.

He shook his head, after a glance at Alistair, and then he kissed her hand in an oddly formal way and offered it to her vampire. Alistair took it, and the butler nodded to him, a blessing of sorts.

"You take care of her, now. Or I'll come after you, young man."

Alistair smiled. "You'll help me with that, I expect. Let me know if she needs something and I'm being too much of a daft bastard to see it. Nothing gets past you, Nero. You'll give me your word," he added, more seriously.

Nero nodded, and offered his hand again, for a firmer shake. "You have it, sir."

Then he turned, met Nina's gaze briefly, and descended the stairs.

Nina faced her Master. His attention coursed over her with deep, heart-fluttering appreciation. "You look beautiful," he said. "But we have no witness now."

"So do you, and we don't need one."

He'd said his words. Now it was her turn, and they came easily, no matter the rough road they'd travelled to get here.

"I was thinking," she said slowly. "About that normal life we talked about. Having someone to share it with, who can sit in your heart and head." *In your soul.* "Who you get to spend your life figuring out, and even at the end, is still enough of a mystery to keep you guessing. In the right ways. But familiar enough to be a comfort through most all of it. That's the root of it."

He cocked his head. "Yeah. I think so. Sounds about right for a banker and his wife."

She shook her head. "No. For anyone who feels like I do, right now. For you."

She treasured all of this. Treasured it because *he'd* given it to her. She didn't need a world of possibilities. Just his heart, his trust, his confidence. That was the treasure she'd always wanted, needed. The still spot in the chaotic world.

He held her gaze, his own becoming so very still. "You did better than me," she whispered. "I couldn't say it aloud. The words were too close to my heart."

She squeezed his hands, then extricated hers. Slowly, holding his gaze as long as she could, she pivoted. "Would you unfasten the back, please?"

She hadn't known if he would be in her mind, see her intent, but truly, she hadn't been entirely sure what she would do until she was here. Now it was so very clear. Clear enough she almost felt light-headed with the import of it. When he touched her, holding her arms as if sensing she was dizzy, she pulled herself together. "Please?" she repeated.

"Nina." His voice had that steady authority she knew, but it was also touched with a thrilling kind of wonder. "What are you doing?"

"Something I'm finally ready to do. That I was supposed to do, a long time ago."

His fingers touched her nape. She'd swept her hair up, and shivered at his touch there. He unzipped the dress all the way, just past the top of her buttocks. Beneath the dress, she wore a confection of ivory lace, white satin, and gauzy stockings pinned with dainty garters, an outfit she knew would please him. She let the dress slither off her curves and stepped out of it. Then she turned, and knelt in the froth of it.

She did it in the best InhServ fashion. Not just the form, but with the correct intent infusing the movement, its true meaning, that she perhaps understood fully for the first time in her life.

She knew the shape of his darkness. And how to bring light into it.

"I am your servant," she said quietly. "You are my Master. I desire no husband, except as that certificate makes that part of who you are to me. You're the only husband I want. Now and always. The vow I take here...I will mean it and honor it, all the days of our lives."

Lifting her head so she met his gaze, she spoke the words. It was not just the InhServ oath. It was her oath to him, and so she modified it accordingly. Just as she would tailor being an InhServ to his needs and who she was, and therefore hold fast to the truth she knew here, so clearly in this moment.

"I will serve you with everything I am. Mind, heart, body and soul. No reservations, nothing withheld. My life belongs to you, my Master, the vampire who owns me, and I will never hesitate to give you what you desire, be it my last drop of blood or my last breath of life. I choose you, Alistair." She reached up, gripped his hand. "I choose you, Master."

Just as she'd hoped, the shadows lifted so she could see what was there, in the darkness. She had to lower her eyes because his had become too brilliant. It filled her with joy, such that she wanted to give him both sides of herself, the human and the human servant. "I will keep you in sickness and in health, love, honor and obey you, so long as we both shall live."

Husband and wife, Master and servant...it all went back to the connection between two unique hearts. What they were to one another, versus what they presented to the world, and it was the former that mattered. That at worst made everything else bearable, but ideally became an adventure to be explored, not feared.

As long as she knew she had his love. Something he couldn't tell anyone else, but she could make a life out of that, as long as his actions told her it was truth. And almost everything he'd done for or toward her told her it was.

"Nina." He dropped to his heels, his hand closing over her shoulder, then moving to the crown of her bowed head. She stayed that way and he did too, curved over her a long moment where she absorbed the import of it and more, how it affected him. She could feel it coming off him in waves, nothing hidden or held back from her.

"I may become even more intolerable now," he said, low. "Knowing you've given yourself fully to me. My demands when it comes to you are infinite, Nina."

"I'm yours, Master," she said, and went lower, until she could press her mouth to his knee. His grip had adjusted as she moved and now his fingers tightened on the base of her skull, over her neck. *And for every demand you have for me, I crave to give you that and more. My desire to serve is infinite.*

It was so easy, when she no longer had to doubt herself or him. She could just be and give whatever her heart and soul told her she was and should.

He muttered an oath. "You're going to destroy my intent to be a proper groom. I intended to behave as if there were a whole room of witnesses. You kneeling here like every man's fantasy is not helping. Sit up, sweet nurse, and let me do at least one thing the traditional way."

She obeyed, and trembled at the look in his eyes, the heat there. Then she realized he was gripping her left hand, and holding something else in the other, something he was slipping onto her finger. A ring with a cool weight to it.

"As one more acknowledgement that you belong to me, then," he said.

She lowered her gaze and started. He hadn't bought just a wedding band, but a full set. What would have been the engagement ring had a white gold band, curvy like ocean waves. The center European cut diamond was flanked by a set of three cut diamonds on either side, as well as a bezel set diamond accent. The center diamond flashed with fire. The wedding band had a similar six bead set of diamonds and was shaped to lock up against the engagement ring.

The detail on the ring itself was mesmerizing, tiny silver ridges flanking the diamonds, the setting for the center diamond giving it a rounded square shape. It wasn't gaudily big, but he'd obviously spent time picking it out. And he'd found the perfect one that she would have wanted for herself.

"It would have been far easier on my nerves if you could have been dreaming of the perfect ring. Had to make my best guess," he said roughly.

"You did...wonderfully," she said softly, closing her fingers over it and him, lowering her head to press her cheek to his hand.

Someone had started up music in the dining area. A soft, poignant instrumental of "You Made Me Love You" was wafting up to them, so appropriate it made her smile through her tears.

Alistair's other hand came to rest on the crown of her head again. When he spoke, he was closer, talking so his breath stirred the hair on her nape, and his voice stroked along her bare spine, a welcome vibration.

"You are my heart, Nina. I spoke that truly. I will care for you through good and bad. And yes, here together where I can speak aloud my mind as I wish, I love you, and will continue to love you, through this life and any other we're given. And I lied to you, because I could never have given you back to the InhServ program. Never. You're mine, and I'll tear through anyone who tries to take you from me."

She closed her eyes tightly, tight as her grip on his hand and that ring. While the violent declaration matched his world and his way, it was the declaration beneath that meant so much to her.

Only his. Even if his world required times where the body must be shared, her heart and soul would be his exclusively. Remarkably, she could accept that, especially as she remembered their times with both Anahera and Stanley, where he'd shown her, vividly, her body could still be wholly his, even when shared with others. It was not the way of the human world she'd once inhabited. It was the way of vampires and their servants, the world where she belonged now.

When she lifted her gaze, met his eyes, she felt what that truly meant. What was more, she accepted and embraced it. She was the InhServ of Lord Alistair, and she wanted to be that more than anything else in the world.

Because he loved her.

~

The End

AUTHOR'S NOTE

My humble thanks to Ian W. Shaw who put together the accounts that formed the memoir *On Radje Beach*. The book provided incomparable detail to bring to terrible life the tragic events that occurred on Bangka Island and afterward, while also painting a vivid picture of life for the nurses before, during and after. Whenever I write a story that includes a historical event, I try to honor the people who were part of that event and avoid giving them words or actions that were not their own. I hope I was mostly successful, but like most events of this nature, I am left in tears and awe, respectively, at what we are capable of doing to one another...and overcoming.

The only deliberate variance I made involved placing a handful of hospital patients on the *Vyner Brooke*. To my knowledge, that did not occur, but Nate showed up in the scene and I did not have the heart to take him out, especially when he showed such gallantry to Nina until the end.

Another acknowledgement and thanks to Reginald Rigby, who wrote the lullaby "The Night Nursery," included in his book, *The Little White House* (music by Claude Arundale). It's sometimes unnerving, how an author will stumble upon something that fits the emotional needs of a scene as well as this song did. But I learned a long time ago to have faith in the muse. She never lets me down, even if I'm not anywhere near as infallible.

VAMPIRE MASTER

Book XVI in the Vampire Queen Series

Read on for a sneak peek at Chapter One of the next book in the award-winning Vampire Queen series, the story of Wolf and Ella...

∾

Big and bad enough to be any girl's nightmare—or her best dream ever...

Beyond your grasp. Those are the three words that come to mind, every time Ella sees Wolf at Club Atlantis. He earns the term Master, in and out of scene, yet there is something deeper and darker about him. She wants to dive into that abyss.

Wolf sees the yearning. But the submissive he ultimately claims becomes his servant, soul-bound to him for all eternity. Ella is a natural submissive, with an endless desire to please. She's perfect for the role, really.

Except Ella is a gift he doesn't deserve.

However, vampires are wired one way—to take what they want, no matter what their conscience tells them. Even Wolf isn't strong enough to resist his nature...or the salvation Ella's love offers.

CHAPTER ONE

*S*he'd made herself a promise that she'd stop getting these obsessions. They were too painful, and sometimes embarrassing. But she kept coming back to this one. To him.

He scared her, like walking the narrow ledge collaring a tall building did. That thrilling fear of being so close to the line between the known and unknown.

She wanted to walk that ledge all the way around, see from every angle. Then, letting go of fear with two open hands, she'd stand at one corner, position her toes over the edge. She'd raise her arms above her head, and tip her face up to the wind and moonlight. Totally trusting, she'd feel joy when he at last laid his palm in the center of her back, giving her the heat of his touch before he gently pushed her into space.

He'd do it, knowing she could fly.

At that moment she would finally *know* what life was supposed to be, not simply long for the frustratingly nebulous sense of it. She was sure it was there, just past a boundary she needed to step across. That ledge, the point of no return.

She'd stepped across a lot of lines, looking for it. While that worried people who cared about her, it wasn't the jump she sought, but what lay beyond it. She didn't know how to explain that.

Any more than she knew how to explain her feelings about Wolf, since the sum total of their meaningful interactions was the length of a sitcom episode.

She grimaced. If she was at home in her bed, she might argue the whole "time is a relative construct" thing with herself, but fortunately she was at Club Atlantis. Too much good stuff was happening tonight. Time to lock the obsessive part of her mind in a closet and focus on the here and now.

"When the Lights Go Out" by Five was pummeling the air, heating it, giving it an edge and sparkle, for those with the eyes to see it. It was just before midnight, the best time to wander through the club. People were settling into their scenes, and those who couldn't lock into anything had left, so that swirling, heavy energy could permeate every corner of the club without disruption.

Entering the club from the outside world at this time of night was like stepping into a fairy circle. At least how Ella imagined it would be. Dancing until her heart was exploding, but not wanting to stop. Even if, when the night ended, she found a hundred years had passed, everything she once knew as her life left behind.

That would be okay, because the people she loved best in the whole world were here, in the place where she felt most at home.

Ella let the music take hold of her, twisting and rolling her body, her head dropping back and long hair brushing her backside. The blood red waist cincher she wore tightened its hold. The white gauze shirt beneath the laced garment had a scoop neck and flowing sleeves, looking like something a pirate woman would wear. The far thinner, finer fabric revealed and caressed the soft smudge of her nipples, and strained over her full breasts.

Her staff sub service collar and a pair of black latex shorts completed the look, the points of the shirt loose and fluttering over her hips and backside. A temporary ink tattoo of a flight of birds crossed her sternum, a few fluttering up the side of her throat.

As she danced, she threaded her way through the groups of people milling in the social areas, sometimes rubbing up against the ones she knew, rewarded with smiles, an affectionate touch in return.

Mistress Chantal was leaning against the divider between two booths, twirling a gleaming red carbon cane deftly over her scarlet painted fingernails. She wore a black form-fitting dress printed with a gold and red dragon. The whiskered creature wound its way over her breasts, waist and hips, enhancing those curves and making her even more enthralling than usual. Her hair was swept up and held with gold pins tipped with scarlet porcelain flowers. The look accentuated her delicate features and sharp eyes.

Chantal was a pure psychological Domme. Ella had seen physically powerful men stay at her feet in whatever position she demanded, for impossibly long stretches of time. Cocks stiff with agonizing levels of need, bulging muscles straining, but heads bowed as they waited on her command. As if they'd wait for her until hell froze over. When she finally let them come, the experience was so overwhelming that some of them blacked out.

It was hugely arousing to watch, but Ella's favorite part was the aftermath. Chantal might kneel, cradle the male in her arms, his head against her breast and her arm around his wide, rounded shoulders. She'd ground him with sips of water and soothing words, as gentle then as she'd been ruthless before.

The dress looked fabulous with her glossy black knee-high boots. When Ella reached her, the Mistress looped her toned arm around Ella's waist, the two of them moving into a playful bump and gyrate. The music had moved on to the primal drumbeat sounds of Gloria Estefan's "Don't Let This Moment End," the Hex Hector club mix.

Don't let this moment end...

Ella felt that way every night here. She never wanted the sun to rise. When she worked at Atlantis, morning was her least favorite time of day.

They had to dance fluidly while not stepping on the male sub Chantal had stretched out on the floor. His arms were out to his sides, his chin lifted and body frozen. Since he wore belted jeans and nothing else, a woman could appreciate the broad shoulders, the cut abs. He had a beard and a mane of coarse dark hair, a few strands scattered over the gleaming hair on his broad chest. His avid blue-grey eyes never left Chantal, though he didn't move his head even by a twitch.

Because Chantal hadn't commanded him to close his eyes, he had an intimate view of the two women dancing and grinding over him. Chantal must be in a mellow mood tonight.

As the music segued into "Dancing Machine" by the Jackson 5, the Mistress laughed, her white teeth flashing. On the horn section, she and Ella raised their arms above their heads and bumped hips, this way, that way, stepping left and right over the male, precise and graceful. As they kept it going, others joined in around them.

At length, Chantal stepped a foot out from her captive and cut a wider swathe around him using a teasing sweep of the cane, moving everyone back. With a provocative serpent-like roll of her upper body to her hips, she spun down to a seated position on her submissive's chest.

She arched, rubbing her ass in slow circles against that furred terrain. Ella watched his eyes course up her body, following the upward tilt of her breasts, before Chantal straightened, curved forward and pressed a kiss to his forehead. His mouth couldn't access anything unless he moved his head. His lips parted as if he had muttered a curse, while hers curved against his flesh in response.

Chantal stood again, one foot planted by his elbow, the other heeled boot propped on his chest. She reached under the stretched fabric of her dress, bringing a pair of black lace panties into view. With admirable balance, she worked them off, shifting her stance, then draped them over the edge of the carbon cane.

"Open your mouth," she said, gesturing to her own since she didn't care to shout over the noise. He read the command, his lips parting.

She brought the panties down, dropping them on the lower half of his face. His chest expanded as he inhaled deep. Chantal's eyes glowed at his response. Using the tip of the cane, she pushed the panties into his open mouth, balling them up.

Ella had seen her do the same maneuver with a violet wand, something Chantal would never activate while it was near her sub's mouth, but the threat of it was enough to amp up a sub's reaction. The cane was sufficient to have this one's cock straining against his jeans.

Chantal left the panties where they were and touched one of his arms, then the other. "My legs," she said, loudly enough to be heard by him this time. "No higher than my knees."

His large hands left the floor. Ella gave him credit for not grabbing Chantal like a sailor lunging for a mermaid. But this male was focused on giving her as much pleasure as she was giving him. He molded his palms over her calves, just above her ankles, slowly, each finger landing precisely, separately, pressing into her skin as he let her feel the strength in his hands.

Chantal's eyes glittered, her lips parting. An expression that said *Nicely done*. He was a worthy match for her skillset.

The spontaneous scene space the Mistress had created had drawn a watching crowd. Ella didn't think the male on the floor was aware of that, even if some subconscious part of him was feeding on the wave of voyeuristic energy.

When Chantal glanced at Ella, Ella fanned herself and did a little "go girl" spin with fist pump that had Chantal's lips curving. Then Ella leaned close enough to speak in her ear.

"You didn't tell me you'd caught Aquaman."

Chantal shot her a wicked look and tilted her head to nuzzle Ella's ear in return. She lifted her arm to comb her fingers through Ella's thick locks. Then she wrapped the strands up in her fist and gave them a firm tug. "Looks a lot like him, doesn't he? There's no fish I can't hook, little one. You know that."

After a few more pleasant moments, Ella left her to it, moving onward. Next stop was the largest public play area in the club. She stopped in the wide archway, hugging the right side to stay out of the flow of foot traffic.

Point Blank's rock and roll "Great White Line" had started up. *Never going home...* Ella's attention landed on the guest DJ stationed in the sound booth, an unassuming-looking guy, with curly brown hair, brown eyes, and a shy smile. This song had Ella imagining the golden age of metal bands and their groupies. Latex and body glitter, long hair and hungry eyes. The scene from Pink Floyd's *The Wall*, where the fan girls overran band security.

She should propose a Rock Star night to Anwyn, Club Atlantis's owner, and see how that played out in their world. While she expected most the Doms would go the rock star route and the subs would take a groupie or roadie role, she could imagine some who would flip it. A rock star who wanted to be under the command of a devoted Dominant fan. Or maybe a Dom roadie who wanted to exact some punishment for his rock star boss being too much of a diva.

She grinned at the thought. Anwyn called Ella her official Minion of Play. Gideon, who belonged to Anwyn and was part of the club's executive management staff, had nicknamed her "Julie," after *The Love Boat* cruise director. Ella wore both names with pride.

The first time she'd approached Anwyn with her ideas, she'd been so nervous. But Madelyn and Chantal, both Mistresses on the club staff, had encouraged her to do it. They'd told her to pitch it to Anwyn the same way she'd pitched it to them, as a free flow conversation, spoken straight out of her well of love for the club.

"New members or guests might want to play, but first they're not sure. They want to watch, get into the flow gradually. We also have a lot of people who come *just* to watch, because that's all they need or can do. We're already doing demos, which are great, but I think you need some fun, interactive stuff happening that shows the application, if that makes sense. Theme nights, performance nights, burlesque night, et cetera. Then the more self-conscious people start to feel more comfortable."

"Like getting people out on the dance floor, so the more bashful ones can join in," Anwyn had said.

"Exactly. And the bigger the voyeur crowd, the more energy it gives the public scenes."

Bringing in guest DJs had been another of Ella's ideas. She visited the clubs and raves where the DJs showed their stuff, listened to what they put together, and brought her recommendations back to Anwyn for vetting.

So far, this one was putting together some unusual and ambiance-creating pieces, perfect for the mood of the club. That was part of the fun of having the DJ; seeing how the moods he evoked altered whatever might happen, spontaneously or planned.

If he wasn't totally freaked out by what he was seeing inside the exclusive Club Atlantis, he'd hopefully become a regular. Since he was laughing in a relaxed kind of way at something a couple dressed in nothing but cuffs and chains were saying to him, while leaning into the sound booth, that was an encouraging sign.

He was back to Gloria Estefan, the hot fast Latin rhythm of *Oye*, by her and Pablo Cortez. Ella glanced back to see even more people crowding onto the dance floor, a mix of flesh tones, glinting metal and colorful fabrics, rippling and straining with writhing bodies.

Hey boy, I see you looking, I know you're watching...
But you won't make that move.

The line fit Chantal and her Aquaman. Except for the "boy" thing. That sub was a hundred percent knee-weakening grown man, head to toe. She bet Chantal had moved him to a private room, the preliminaries over. The overflow area around the dance floor perimeter was getting too crowded to safely keep him there.

While the DJ was piling them onto the dance floor, he was also boosting the energy feel in the public play area. Ella had seen every emotion happen here. Tears, laughter, revelations, from small epiphanies to life-changing ones. Sometimes a total breakdown of who someone thought they were. Or a new foundation laid for someone they'd never thought they could be. People could fall in love here or in lust, only for the moment or forever.

Usually when she wandered through this space, she would take her time, absorbing all those different possibilities. But now that she was here, her steps quickened, taking her toward the session happening in the back corner.

If she was being honest with herself, it had been her destination all along. Though when it came to Wolf, she didn't always believe in being honest. Comforting lies kept her from making a fool of herself.

Deep in her gut, she knew most of her short, intense crushes landed on people out of her reach. But in this case, "beyond her grasp" was the world's biggest understatement. Compared to those earlier obsessions, Wolf was another solar system.

Yet here she was.

People had sunk to the floor around him in a semi-circle, just outside the marked boundary of the session space. The marking was something the staff Doms had suggested a while ago. Now the more popular scenes didn't result in lookers-on pressing too close, disrupting the connection between the top and bottom, or causing safety issues if the Dom was throwing a whip or doing anything else that needed more elbow room. This corner was also set up with a dais two steps high, which helped reinforce that barrier.

She eased herself into a small opening close to the wall. It gave her an almost square front view of him, in the space open between him and the female submissive he had restrained on a black wood frame. The silver of the chains clipped to her cuffs gleamed like her perspiring henna-colored skin.

She was in her forties, and her stretch marks said she'd had children. She was wide-hipped, with a large, heart-shaped backside and full breasts. *Selena* and *Mario* were tattooed on one shoulder, surrounded by a spray of flowers. Her children, Ella deduced. Her long dark hair had been bound up in a strap and pinned to the cross, holding it out of the way and increasing her immobility.

It was rare to see Wolf with a woman. Initially, she'd thought men were his dedicated preference. However, the first time she'd seen him do a public scene with a female, his absorption and sexual interest had been no less intense, but there'd been a different tone to it. There'd been softer moments, more frequently.

The woman then had been blindfolded, and once or twice, he'd paced away, taken a seat to stare at her as he sipped from a bottle of water. Something about the straight set of his body, a tension in his shoulders, made Ella wonder if women were more difficult for him, more emotionally draining.

He did regular sessions, as well as BDSM therapy for issues like PTSD. Not just for their members, but also for guests from other clubs, since his reputation had gotten around. Those sessions were always private room scenes.

She would have dearly loved to watch one, and not merely because of the professional interest. He was so contained on the public floor, yet there was an energy behind his gaze that hinted of a storm of limitless magnitude. The kind that came with thunder and lightning which railed at the heavens, and brought torrential rains. Rains that could put out the fires that roared through the heart, leaving loss and never-ending pain in their wake. Was that his gift? Could he do that for others? Would she want him to do it for her?

She'd only have to ask. Like all the Doms and subs on staff, he pre-approved his session applicants, but she didn't anticipate any problems. She could book his time like anyone else, and received a hefty employee discount.

Yet she didn't ask. It wasn't what that obsessive side of her wanted, and she was smart enough to contain it, mostly. Taking only a bite of chocolate cake didn't do anything but increase the craving for something she likely couldn't have, or was imagining was there that wasn't.

In a futile attempt to prove she had some self-control, she'd made herself look at the female sub first. When she did glance his way, she made it a slow drift, rather than snapping her gaze to him like a rubber band fired from a pointed finger. Her reward was taking in all of him in a gradual way, a slow fill of her lower extremities with the sweetness of building desire.

So... No offense to the entity who had created him, but whoever had released Wolf to walk among mortals had been freaking insane to let him go.

Six foot five. Skin like charred bronze. Eyes like silver lightning. A stern mouth that went with the prominent sloped cheekbones and set jaw. His shoulders were broad. Tonight, Wolf wore metallic coated black denim jeans over laced boots, no shirt, exposing a lot of gleaming brown muscle. He was a giant, a sharply sculpted one, every muscle, bone and shape of him chiseled. One part ancient warrior king, one part sensual demon lord, comprised of black smoke and fire.

When she gazed at him, she saw the endless darkness surrounding that building ledge, far up in the clouds. She couldn't see what was in it, but it was waiting. Pulling at her to leap. When he pushed her, he would be pushing her into the abyss of himself.

Time to get a grip. Which she did with a mental reminder of their non-existent relationship. He never invited her to do a session with him, though he occasionally commandeered Ella's assistance to help him clean up after a scene, or provide backup aftercare. Whatever his thing was, she wasn't it. Which hurt, but that was okay. In their world, the only appropriate response to that was gracious acceptance. Temper tantrums or cathartic cries to handle rejection were handled alone and in private.

He was aware of everyone, demonstrating a grasp of details that made anyone in his sphere feel exceptionally noticed. Which meant his notice of her wasn't exceptional at all.

But what should be and what was, weren't always on the same page in her mind. When his gaze flickered in her direction now, marking her, her arms tightened against herself. She had them folded against her upper torso, her fingers wrapped over her hip bones as she leaned against the wall. A protective posture, or perhaps just a form of self-restraint so she didn't fling herself at his feet.

He turned his attention back to his submissive, putting his hand on the woman. Her spine was curved, every vulnerable vertebra visible. Her perspiring skin showed red marks where he'd flogged her. Her backside was stained red, handprints blotched beneath the sharp stripes of a switch. He'd worked her over hard.

He could be extreme, or he could handle a newbie. He evaluated what every sub needed and took them just far enough past what they thought their limit was to give them the experience they'd hoped for, with a thrilling glimpse of even deeper possibilities.

Or to give them an important reinforcement of where their limits were.

The woman let out a cry as he dropped his hand over her ass to dig his fingers into those switch marks. He pushed his knee between her legs, rubbed, a move that made his body flex from back to hip and buttock. "You going to come for me?"

"It hurts," she gasped. "So much..."

"Yeah, it does. You're still going to come for me. Pain doesn't exceed obedience. Does it?"

She shook her head, but her body was shaking, tears running down her face. "Lift your left foot," he said. As he slid his other arm around her waist, holding her securely, he kept moving her against his knee. Rubbing against the coated jeans would provide a wonderfully rough friction to aroused tissues.

She raised her left foot, trembling. At some point he'd put the switch away and now held a riding crop he'd drawn from his belt. He teased it across her sole, increasing the trepidation and anticipation. He rolled it in his hand, flick, flick, trail. Flick.

Whap!

He brought the crop down with a visual ferocity that wrenched a cry from her throat and had the crowd flinching, even as they remained wide-eyed, leaning forward.

"Work yourself against me as I tickle your feet, *mamacita*," he crooned. He had a deep voice with a rasping edge. Another erotic rough texture to tease the senses.

She shuddered, but twitched her hips on him. He moved the hand on her waist up to cup her breast, enjoy a squeezing massage of the curve. His grip showed flesh like rising bread dough between his fingers, and he tugged her nipple between his knuckles. He continued to move his leg back and forth, manipulating her on it as that crop kept falling, as he kept fondling her breasts. His coordination and rhythm were almost inhuman.

With every strike, her cries kept rising, short, clipped wails, pleas. "Please...no more...no más..." Then the words gave way to screams of pleasure, as the orgasm overtook the pain, his will demanding compliance from hers.

Ella's body was quivering, her wrapped arms and tight fingers still holding herself, as if she needed her own embrace to stay together and not shatter with the woman. Rapt attention held the crowd around Wolf and the woman, along with a smattering of critical study, from those learning from his technique. Ella glimpsed one or two people who looked a little uncertain, newbies unsure about the sub's pleas for no more. Ella knew the woman could safeword and end the scene whenever she wished, but even if she didn't, Wolf was closely monitoring her. If he thought she was too lost in subspace to protect herself, he would act upon that even faster than she could safeword.

His stern mouth curved as the woman lost herself to the orgasm. He took her all the way down that slide, until she was at the bottom, slowing down, hips jerking, body shuddering. Now she was talking again, mumbling. "Thank you, *Dios*, thank you..."

She was panting, her hands fisted around the chains, the fine hairs on her nape soaked.

Ella slipped across the session boundary. He hadn't asked for her help, but all staff members stayed alert to when a Dom needed more hands, particularly at the end of a strenuous session.

She knelt, reaching out and accepting the crop Wolf handed her without looking, as if he'd expected her to be there. "Water," he said.

She rose to put the crop in the open bag of tools he had left a few feet away. Then she withdrew a bottle of water from a small fridge concealed by a curtain.

He'd released the woman's hands, and eased her down to the floor, her legs too weak to hold her. Wolf dropped to one knee and braced her against it as he chafed her wrists. When Ella handed him the water, he fed it to the sub himself, one hand holding the bottle, the other cupping her face. His attention was on her and her alone. It was painful and glorious to watch. Glorious because that absolute attention was a drug to any submissive. Painful because Ella craved it like air.

"Small sips," Wolf told the woman. She nodded dazedly, her hands cupping his around the bottle. Then, without looking at her, he said, "Thank you, Ella. Stay here."

He didn't say why, but a Dom didn't need to do so. She'd knelt when he'd squatted, because she'd had two options—move back to a respectful distance, or assume a position where she wasn't standing over him, but could still remain close.

No brainer there.

She gazed at his wide back, the long valley of his spine that led to the rise of his taut buttocks covered by the jeans. The back center loop of the jeans stretched against his belt, and she could see the twin depressions marking his pelvic bones. Her eyes returned to the dip of his shaved head as he bent attentively over his charge. The dark bronze skin gleamed under the club lighting. He had no visible tattoos, which was strange for anyone these days, especially in their world. She'd never seen him fully naked, though when he was aroused, there was no doubt he was mouthwateringly equipped.

She imagined trailing her fingers along the curve of his smooth skull, down to his nape, following the track of his spine. Resting her fingers on his waistband, she'd hook them there to hold onto him as she knelt. She thought of putting her mouth all the places she imagined her fingers touching. What would he taste like? She knew his scent, a mix of spice and damp rain in the forest.

Wolf rose, lifting the woman as if she weighed nothing. He navigated the two steps of the dais with a sure stride, but he moved slowly, head bent over his charge, still talking to her. The pace gave the people clustered around the session area time to naturally ease out of their way.

Kevin was already sitting on a couch close by, waiting on him. The alpha submissive handled most of Wolf's aftercare for him. A fireman in his daily life, the male projected the steady confidence and calm that made him excel at both roles. He had red hair and freckles, and rich brown eyes that transformed ordinary features into exceptionally appealing ones.

Many staff Doms chose to delegate aftercare to a trusted sub or fellow Dom. If someone paying for a session confused the emotional intensity of a D/s scene with an invitation for a continued relationship, the incredible intimacy of aftercare could exacerbate that misunderstanding. Handing it over to someone else made a nice demarcation line and grounding step, helping the sub to pull her or himself together, and keep things in perspective.

Wolf put her in Kevin's arms, kissed the woman's hand, touched her face, and then pivoted, striding back toward the platform. His expression while looking upon her had been stern but caring. But when he turned away, Ella saw his expression return to its usual unreadable mien.

Everyone had their story for why they embraced a Dom or sub side, even those for whom it was the simplest natural evolution of their sexual interests. But he had never revealed his motivations or how he'd reached this level of expertise. He enjoyed his sessions, she had no doubt. But she'd not yet figured out the more complicated layers of them for him, except for her belief that men were easier for him.

After he'd left the platform, Ella had stood up and moved to the rack holding sanitary cloths, so she was wiping down the play area, getting it ready for who used it next. She expected clean-up help was why he'd asked her to remain. He withdrew another bottle of water from the fridge and took a swallow, watching her as he did so.

The audience viewing the session was dispersing. Sometimes he was approached afterwards with questions, but since he kept his attention fixed on Ella, he projected an unmistakable "not right now" vibe that the inquisitive respected.

He remained silent, though. She felt like her skin was tingling under his intent regard. When she finished and disposed of the wipes, he nodded.

"Follow me."

She was surprised when he took her hand, guiding her down the two steps off the dais. But she wasn't objecting. The few times he'd touched her, she'd noted a suppressed power to his grip. His fingers were warm and the right kind of smooth and strong.

Regrettably, he released her after the functional touch and proceeded, her trailing him, until he reached a quiet corner with an unoccupied deep easy chair. He took a seat in it, but sat on the edge, and pointed between his spread knees. It meant he was curved over her as she sank down between his feet. A tremor ran through her as she wondered what this was. She kept her gaze on the floor, though she had the pleasure of it traveling over some tempting terrain before it landed there.

"Lift your head. I want to see your face. What were you thinking when you were kneeling behind me, Ella?"

Well, shit. It was far easier for her to lie to herself than to a Dom.

And no way could she hold back while a Master like Wolf was staring right into her face.

She complied, but kept her gaze on the wall just beyond his right ear. He hadn't told her to look him in the eye. In her peripheral vision, she was aware of him studying her so intently, it was like a touch on her face. She had to remind herself of the question.

"I was thinking I'd like to be her," she said. "And I was thinking of touching you."

"Touching me how?"

"Touching your spine." She reached behind herself to run her finger up the mentioned area on her own body. The trail of her fingers on her lower back below the cincher tingled, as if it was his hand touching her instead. She blamed his stare for that transference effect.

It wasn't calculated, but the motion thrust her breasts out. His eyes rested there briefly, enjoyably, then went back to her face.

"And?"

How did he know there was more? He could be guessing, but the best Doms excelled at tormenting a sub this way, pulling way more out of them than they wanted to say.

"Um. Your head. I was thinking of touching your head, feeling the smoothness." She colored a little over that one. His expression remained unreadable. She fought not to squirm.

"What have you done to earn such a privilege?"

The answer to such a question was "Nothing," since a few minutes cleaning off his scene space hardly qualified for such a gift. However, other things surged forth, wanting her to supply a different answer. She boldly looked him in the eye for a split second. Perhaps less than that, so short a time it would have been undetectable by the human eye, but sometimes there were things about Wolf that seemed other than human.

"I could earn it, sir."

He leaned forward until there seemed to be less than a breath between them, though Ella couldn't test that theory since she'd stopped breathing. Wolf curled his fingers around her wrist. He tugged on it, so she stood up on her knees and inched closer between his, until her breasts brushed his bare chest. The thin fabric did nothing to lessen the jolt of sensation that sparked through her body and arrowed downward.

She had to tip her head back to keep her face in his view, as ordered. Those piercing eyes and stern mouth, his scent and heat, were so close, overwhelming her. It was almost a bittersweet relief when his gaze shifted downward.

His free hand lifted. She strangled on a soft sound as he brushed a curved knuckle over one now taut peak.

"These beautiful, beautiful tits," he said quietly. "Just out there, begging to be touched."

He moved his hand like a bird wing, fingers fanning out to caress the full mound of her breast. Then he curled those long, strong digits, and two of his knuckles closed over the nipple, a firm clamp like a hawk's beak. She swallowed, noisily.

With his other hand, he guided her captive one past his waist, to his back. The heat in the small space between their bodies intensified. "You can touch me as you imagined," he said, that deep, rough voice tagged with a growl. "As long as you can bear the pain. If you ask me to stop, then you have to stop."

"Yes, sir."

He let her wrist go. As soon as she started to slide her liberated hand toward his spine, his knuckles began to tighten.

She knew how to take a fair bit of pain, but she didn't usually have to balance it with the distraction of an enticement like this. She thought of how he'd brought a woman to climax while beating the soles of her feet. It wasn't the first time he'd demonstrated his mastery at keeping a sub poised right on the threshold where pain and pleasure had to go their separate ways. When he brought a sub to that moment, like now, she saw the sadist in him. One who would push a sub a little further past that threshold, feeding on how much she would be willing to take for him.

She wanted to give him that, almost as much as she wanted to touch him. So she was doubly motivated. But hellfire, he was taking her at her word. He *was* going to make her earn it. The pressure of that clamp continued to grow, the pain lancing through her breast as she reached the middle of his back.

It was just a man's back. She'd touched plenty, for plenty of reasons. Her middle and index fingers settled in the valley, the other three settling around it. His skin was warm, with an amazing solidity, as if the skin was merely thin gift wrap over muscle. She started low, just above the tempting dip between his buttocks. The hard bones of his pelvis were briefly under the heel of her hand as she trailed upward.

A gasp escaped her as he added a slow twist to the pincer grip. She'd dampened when he took her hand at the dais, so it was no surprise that she was fully wet between her legs. She was incapable of concealing her strong reaction to honoring a Master's will, earning his approval, all while enjoying the pleasures he gave her as a reward.

She reached the base of his neck and cried out softly as he twisted harder. Her fingers jerked, dug into his flesh. Hell, it hurt so much. Her body was contorted in a rigid curve around that central pain point, trying to ease what couldn't be eased.

"You just have to stop to get this to stop," he reminded her in a throaty rumble.

She shook her head, a quick snap, and pressed into his punishing touch so she could slide her fingertips along the slope of his ear, headed to his skull. She tipped her face up, gazing at the strong line of his cheek and jaw, his ear, the movement of her arm. She didn't look at him, eye to eye, but she could feel his attention, a Dom's total focus on her reactions.

He was tall, even sitting. He slid his other arm around her waist, hand over her hip and buttock to give her the extra lift needed to touch the crown of his head. She had a nicely rounded ass, but his hand spanned the whole cheek. He scattered her mind when he tightened his grip, kneading. Supporting her needs while he took what he desired. It was a powerful combination, one that could break open dangerous yearnings in her.

He increased the compression on her nipple, the torque of the twist. She was beyond true agony, but if she wanted to touch him the way she'd described, this was the price.

How badly do you want it? The question that had to be answered, because it always stood guard between a person and any goal worth having.

But there was more to this, and that, as much as her own desires, kept her enduring. What was she doing to him? What pleasures were her pain, her willingness to bear it simply for the right to touch him, giving to him?

She passed her fingertips lightly over his crown. Her hand was shaking, but she fought through the pain rocketing through her to make it a caress, to convey through her touch how much she liked the feel of him.

Abruptly, the compression stopped, which yanked a moan of relief from her. She sagged against his shoulder and upper arm, but he was still holding her up, letting her touch him. She blinked through the tears. Slowly, he tipped his head down, making her heart beat faster and giving her more access.

She breathed out a soft sigh as she trailed her fingers over the smooth terrain in a slow, skimming way. A man who shaved his head had to care for it, to keep it gleaming and smooth like this. She wouldn't mind helping with that, rubbing in whatever aftershave products he used to keep it pleasurable to the touch.

She imagined how this felt to him, the tiny tracks each of her fingertips were making over his bare skin, a slow, easy caress. Down to the nape, behind the ear, back up. The head, nape and occipital bone were all erogenous zones. His breath heated the base of her throat, and she realized his head had dropped further, giving her more access.

He closed his hand fully over her breast, massaging her throbbing nipple in the nest of his palm, soothing while he explored the fullness of the curve with his fingers. Her breath caught as he put his mouth on the top of her breast.

Now she had both hands on him, one stroking his nape, measuring the width of his shoulders, the other continuing to caress and explore his skull, the shape of ears, the creases at the base of his neck, then around to the temple and back up that crest again, to his crown.

He moved his touch up her back, wound his fingers into her hair, and drew her head back farther, way farther. He arched her over his arm as he nuzzled her collar bones, teased his tongue over her temporary tattoo, the delicate line of birds fluttering up her throat. She could hear the artery pounding harder beneath his mouth and he paused, his fingers tightening on her. When his teeth scraped her, she moaned and he muttered something that reminded her of Aquaman, the way he'd cursed against the demand for self-restraint. But she was the sub. Wolf could do as he liked. She wanted him to do whatever he wished.

After a charged moment, he moved downward, lips playing over the birds on her sternum. Then he changed direction, and placed his mouth fully over her nipple. An even more needy sound escaped her throat as he suckled her through the cloth, teased the folds of it against her. She swayed in his hold, her hands dropping to hold on to his shoulders. They felt wide enough to carry the world.

Most of the things she did at Club Atlantis had a very defined structure. Beginning of session, end of session. Wolf hadn't set any parameters. Just drew her over here, asked her a question, made clear his price for the answer. She didn't have any context or meaning for what he was doing. She was adrift on a heavy tide of feeling. Her sex was throbbing, making her want to rub herself against him.

He lifted his head, and cupped hers in one hand. She was bent back over his arm, still on her knees but almost parallel to the floor as he leaned over her. He'd left the chair and dropped onto one knee to hold her like this, suckle her nipple. Her hair was brushing the floor while his fingers remained buried in it, his palm supporting her skull.

He looked down at her breasts, straining against the gauzy cloth. "Show me the one I hurt," he said.

She fumbled her way to her chest, found the loose elastic of the scoop neckline and lifted it up and over the nipple, exposing the breast to him. Her whole body quivered at his look, the silver-touched-with-fire irises getting more iridescent.

"You've pleased me, Ella," he said.

"Thank you, sir." Her voice was barely a breath.

"There will be bruising around it. If you do a session, you'll tell the Dom to avoid that area." He lifted his gaze to her, and if he'd driven a spike through a collar around her throat, locking it permanently, he couldn't have her attention more completely. "No one touches that nipple but me, until I say so. The rest of you is fine, but that one belongs to my mouth and my hand. You understand?"

She found her voice again, somewhere, somehow. "Yes, sir."

He lifted her hand from his shoulder and examined it, his fingers spreading hers, his thumb running over her palm. Tingles shot through her arm, to her upper torso, flushing her neck and making her exposed nipple harder.

"Curious," he murmured. Then he brought her hand back up to his bare scalp and placed it against the broadest part of his skull. He pressed her palm against the heat of flesh and resilience of bone. His gaze pinned hers. "That is a place only you have touched, like this, in a very long time."

He straightened and brought her up out of the arched position, lifting her to her feet as if she weighed nothing, even though he stayed on one knee. Once she was upright, he adjusted the neckline of her shirt. She wasn't much taller than him, even while he was kneeling.

For a minute, she felt like a girl, her daddy straightening her clothes. The impression was enhanced by the stern way he was looking at her. Because of what he said next, she wondered if he'd intended that.

"I'm doing a short explanation of the Daddy Dom/little girl dynamic at Friday's early evening orientation session. I need an assistant. You'll be there at seven."

Though it wasn't the primary form of BDSM expression for either of them, they'd both had plenty of experience with guests and members who did enjoy Daddy Dom play. She had the experience, so he'd asked for her assistance. She told herself there was nothing out of bounds about that.

Except he'd never asked her to assist him before, no matter how much expertise she had.

Sorting quickly through her complicated schedule, she was relieved to find she could make that work. Saying that she couldn't would have been a far worse pain than what he'd done to her nipple. Now that he'd taken his soothing hand and mouth away, the throbbing was back. She wondered if the thumping pulse of blood she felt in the abused area had more to do with the awareness he'd planted in her mind than the physical trauma.

No one would touch that part of her but him. It was his, until he said otherwise. What was happening here? This wasn't a session. What was he doing?

One thing she knew well were the boundaries and negotiations that went into healthy Dominant and submissive relationships. She could ask for permission to ask questions, to ask him for definitions, structure, to whatever this was. She wasn't weak-minded or desperate, unwilling to ask things, or say no, for fear of rejection. That kind of mindset was born of insecurity, a poor self-image. Anwyn and the other Dominants were quick to detect it when it came through the doors. They either educated the sub to a safer mindset, or regretfully denied them membership until they could get to a healthier place.

So it wasn't that which kept her silent. Something about him had always been...more, when it came to the Dom thing. As if his Dominance went beyond a sexual orientation, which was an odd thought, since an orientation was part of a person's core identity. Regardless, she couldn't find it in herself to question him. Instead, she was drifting in a haze of instant recall, remembering the way he'd bent his head to let her touch his neck and head. Her mouth had been so close she could have pressed it to his skull, as she wound her arms around his head and shoulders, shoulders that looked as if they could carry the world, right along with her.

She realized that the music had changed radically. The DJ had dialed it down with "Danny Boy," sung by a female vocalist.

I will sleep in peace until you come to me...

She didn't know about that, but peace wasn't always peaceful. Sometimes it rode the current of something overflowing with possibilities, right over a waterfall and down beneath it, the pounding strength driving her to her knees, keeping her exactly where she wanted to be. In over her head.

"Yes, sir," she said again. *I'll be there.*

She didn't say that part, because there was no need. His expression said no other answer was possible.

AFTERWORD

Did you enjoy spending time with Joey's characters? If you did, then she asks that you do one simple thing in support of her future work. Please share that experience with at least one other book-reading friend who hasn't read her. Or mention her on a Facebook page, at a book club meeting or online forum, on Twitter, in an Amazon or GoodReads review, or wherever you feel comfortable. You, the pleased reader, are the best marketing strategy an author can have. If you do just one of those things to spread the word about her work, she will be very grateful!

READY FOR MORE?

Check out Joey's website at storywitch.com where you'll find additional information, free excerpts, buy links and news about current and upcoming releases for all of her books and series.

Love her series and want more? Revisit your favorite characters through FREE novellas and short stories, available on her website. Just choose the Cantrips (Vignettes) menu item on her website and find them in all the popular download formats. You can also go under her Books menu to choose Cantrips (Compilation) and buy the compendium volumes of these stories.

Want to know all the places you can talk to Joey, Joey's fans, and find more free content? Visit storywitch.com/community or click the Community link on the website menu. You can also review current and past editions of her monthly newsletter for information on upcoming releases, book signing events, contests, and more.

ABOUT THE AUTHOR

Joey W. Hill writes about vampires, mermaids, boardroom executives, cops, witches, angels, housemaids...pretty much wherever her inspiration takes her. She's penned over forty acclaimed titles and six award-winning series, and been awarded the RT Book Reviews Career Achievement Award for Erotica. But she's especially proud and humbled to have the support and enthusiasm of a wonderful, widely diverse readership.

So why erotic romance? "Writing great erotic romance is all about exploring the true face of who we are – the best and worst - which typically comes out in the most vulnerable moments of sexual intimacy." She has earned a reputation for writing BDSM romance that not only wins her fans of that genre, but readers who would "never" read BDSM romance. She believes that's because strong, compelling characters are the most important part of her books.

"Whatever genre you're writing, if the characters are captivating and sympathetic, the readers are going to want to see what happens to them. That was the defining element of the romances I loved most and which shaped my own writing. Bringing characters together who have numerous emotional obstacles standing in their way, watching them reach a soul-deep understanding of one another through the expression of their darkest sexual needs, and then growing from that understanding into love - that's the kind of story I love to write."

Take the plunge with her, and don't hesitate to let her know what you think of her work, good or bad. She thrives on feedback!

WHERE TO FIND JOEY W. HILL

- Website: storywitch.com

- Twitter: @JoeyWHill
- Facebook: JoeyWHillAuthor
- GoodReads: JoeyWHill
- Pinterest: jwhill23
- E-Mail: storywitch@storywitch.com

ALSO BY JOEY W. HILL

Truly Helpless

Naughty Bits Series

The Lingerie Shop

Training Session

Bound To Please

The Highest Bid

Naughty Wishes Series

Part 1: Body

Part 2: Heart

Part 3: Mind

Part 4: Soul

Vampire Queen Series

Vampire Queen's Servant

Mark of the Vampire Queen

Vampire's Claim

Beloved Vampire

Vampire Mistress *(VQS: Club Atlantis)*

Vampire Trinity *(VQS: Club Atlantis)*

Vampire Instinct

Bound by the Vampire Queen

Taken by a Vampire

The Scientific Method

Nightfall

Elusive Hero

Night's Templar

Vampire's Soul

Vampire's Embrace

Vampire Master *(VQS: Club Atlantis)*

Non-Series Titles

If Wishes Were Horses

Virtual Reality

Unrestrained

Medusa's Heart

Novellas

Chance of a Lifetime

Choice of Masters

Make Her Dreams Come True

Threads of Faith

Submissive Angel

Short

Snow Angel

CPSIA information can be obtained
at www.ICGtesting.com
Printed in the USA
LVHW011004030420
652122LV00020B/2487

9 781942 122807